ALEXANDER KENT

SUCCESS TO THE BRAVE

and

CROSS OF ST GEORGE

D0715673

The stirring story of the life and times of Richard Bolitho is told in Alexander Kent's bestselling novels.

Alexander Kent is the author of twenty-four books featuring Richard and Adam Bolitho. Under his own name, Douglas Reeman, he has written thirty novels and two non-fiction books.

Success to
the Brave

Alexander Kent

ARROW

Published by Arrow Books in 1984

Reprinted 14 times

Copyright © High Seas Authors Ltd 1993

The right of Alexander Kent to be identified as the author of this
work has been asserted by him in accordance with the Copyright
Designs and Patents Act, 1988

First published in the United Kingdom in 1983 by Hutchinson

Arrow Books
The Random House Group Limited
20 Vauxhall Bridge Road, London SW1V 2SA

Random House Australia (Pty) Limited
20 Alfred Street, Milsons Point, Sydney
New South Wales 2061, Australia

Random House New Zealand Limited
18 Poland Road, Glenfield
Auckland 10, New Zealand

Random House (Pty) Limited
Endulini, 5a Jubilee Road, Parktown 2193, South Africa

The Random House Group Limited Reg. No. 954009

www.randomhouse.co.uk

A CIP catalogue record for this book
is available from the British Library

Papers used by Random House are natural,
recyclable products made from wood grown in
sustainable forests. The manufacturing processes conform to
the environmental regulations of the country of origin

ISBN 0 09 936370 4

Printed and bound in Germany by
Elsnerdruck, Berlin

For Winifred with my love.
Until we meet again

Contents

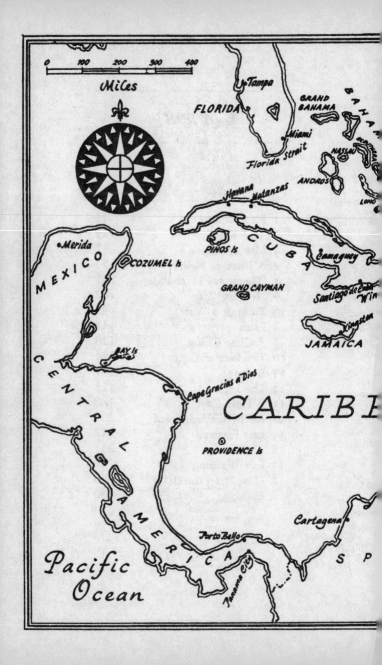

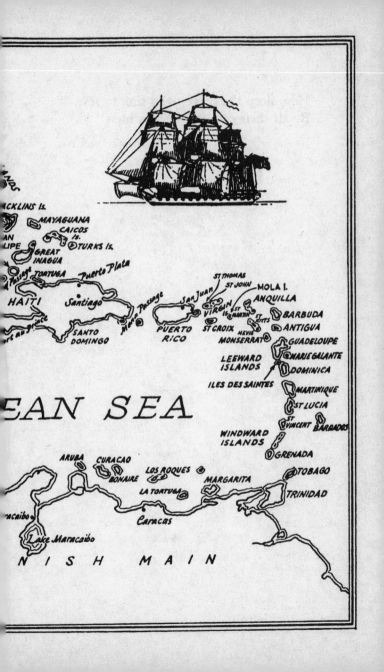

How sleep the brave, who sink to rest,
By all their country's wishes blest!

WILLIAM COLLINS, 1746

Flag at the Fore

Richard Bolitho leaned his palms on the sill of an open window and stared across the courtyard to the far wall and the sea beyond.

It should have been a perfect May day, and even the squat silhouette of Pendennis Castle which guarded the Falmouth approaches and the entrance to Carrick Roads seemed less formidable. After nine years of war with France and her allies England was at peace. It was still hard to accept. When a strange sail appeared off the coast the young men of Falmouth no longer stood to arms in case it was an enemy raider, or hurried inland with less enthusiasm if the newcomer proved to be a King's ship. The latter always meant the arrival of the hated press-gangs and men snatched from their homes to serve at sea, perhaps never to return. No wonder it was hard to believe it was all over.

He watched the carriage resting in the shadows near the stables. *It was nearly time*. Soon the horses would be led out and harnessed. It was no longer next week or even tomorrow. It was now.

Bolitho turned and waited for his eyes to grow accustomed to the room after the reflected sunlight. The big grey house which had served the Bolitho family for generations was very still, as if it too was holding its breath, trying to hold back the inevitable.

It had been seven months since he had returned here after the battle which had destroyed the enemy's hopes of an invasion and had equally crippled the French bargaining power at the peace negotiations. Seven months since he had married Belinda and had known a sublime happiness which he had never expected.

He walked to the foot of the great staircase and glanced at the shadowy family portraits. They must all have stood here at such a moment, he thought. Wondering when or if they would ever see the house again. His great, great grandfather, Captain Daniel Bolitho, on the deck of his blazing ship. He had died in the War of the Protestant Alliance. The Bolitho features were very clear in the portrait. Like Bolitho's father and his brother Hugh, also dead, and all the others.

Now he was off to sea again and the past few months seemed to have gone in the turning of an hour-glass. When he had been summoned to the Admiralty in London he had not known what to expect. With the Peace of Amiens signed and apparently holding, it seemed as if all the bitterly won lessons had been thrown aside. Most of the fleet had been laid up and thousands of officers and men discharged to fend as best they could.

Posts for junior flag-officers would be few and handed out as favours by the lords of admiralty. Bolitho had been astonished when he had been told of his orders to sail with a minimum of delay for America and then the Caribbean. Not in command of another squadron, but in a small two-decker with a mere frigate for communications and general escort.

He had been courteously if formally received by Admiral Sir Hayward Sheaffe who had succeeded old Admiral Beauchamp. He had seemed to stamp the difference between war and peace, Bolitho thought. Beauchamp, worn out by illness, had died in harness without knowing his last strategy had succeeded with the French invasion fleet's destruction. Sheaffe was cool, practical, the perfect administrator. It had been hard to imagine his ever being through the mill from midshipman to his present lofty appointment.

In this quiet room Bolitho could recall Sheaffe's words as if they had just been uttered.

'I know this must seem a hard decision, Bolitho. After

your escape from an enemy prison and your subsequent victory over the French admiral, Remond, you will have been expecting, and many would say rightly so, a more stable appointment. However . . . ' His voice had lingered on the word. 'War does not end with the last ball fired. Their lordships require a man of tact as well as action for this task. It is not without reward, I think. You are to be promoted to Vice-Admiral of the Red.' His eyes had studied Bolitho's features to seek his reaction. 'The youngest and most junior on the Navy List.' He had added dryly, 'Apart from Nelson, that is, the nation's darling.'

So that was it. Sheaffe was jealous of those who had become known and admired by friend and enemy alike. In spite of his status and power, Sheaffe still envied them.

Perhaps that was why he had failed to mention that the real reason for Bolitho's concern was that Belinda would be having their first child in just a matter of weeks. Sheaffe knew about it, it had even reached the London newspapers that the church here in Falmouth had been packed to the doors with officers and men of Bolitho's squadron on that special October day in 1801, last year. Perhaps he was jealous of that fact also?

Bolitho had said nothing. If Sheaffe wanted him to explain, to plead for a delay in the sailing date, he had not understood him at all.

He heard her steps on the flagged floor beyond the entrance and straightened his back.

Even with the sunlight behind her, and her face part hidden in shadow, she was beautiful. He never got tired of watching her, of the longing she roused in him. The sunlight touched her chestnut-coloured hair and the soft curve of her throat.

She said, 'It's time.'

Her voice was low and level, and Bolitho knew what the effort was costing her.

As if to mock their emotions he heard the hoofs of the two horses on the cobbles, the untroubled voices of the grooms.

She moved towards him and placed her hands on his shoulders. 'I am so *proud* of you, dearest. My husband, a vice-admiral – ' Her lip quivered and a new brightness in her eyes betrayed her distress.

He held her gently, her once slender body pressing against his as if the child was already with them.

'You must take every care while I am away, Belinda.'

She leaned back in his arms and looked at him searchingly as if she needed to remember every detail.

'You are the one who must take care. You have seen to all my wants. Everyone is so kind, wanting to help, to be near, when all I need is you.' She shook her head as he made to speak. 'Don't worry, I will not break down. In spite of your leaving, I am *happy*, can you understand that? Each day in the past months has been like the first time. When you hold me it seems a new experience. When you enter me and we are one, I am filled with love for you. But I am not a fool and would never wish to stand between you and your other world. I see your eyes as you watch a ship sail into Carrick Roads, your expression when Thomas or Allday mentions some place or experience I can never share. When you return I shall be waiting, but wherever you are, we shall remain as one.'

There was a tap at the door and Allday stood watching them, his homely face grave and uncertain.

'All ready, sir.'

Allday, like an oak, who represented so much of that other world which Belinda had described. Now in his best blue coat and nankeen breeches he looked every inch a sailor, the coxswain of a vice-admiral. He had stayed at Bolitho's side since he had been a junior captain. Together they had seen fine and terrible sights, had suffered and rejoiced in equal proportions.

When he had been told of the unexpected and advanced promotion, Allday had remarked cheerfully, 'Flag at the fore at last, eh, sir? Quite right too, in my opinion. Don't know what took 'em so long.'

'Thank you.'

He saw Allday open the new coat for him to slip his arms into the sleeves. Once the impossible dream when he had paced the deck as a harassed lieutenant, or even when he had taken command of his first ship.

She was watching him, her chin raised, her fingers clasped as if to contain her thoughts and words.

'You look so handsome, Richard.'

'That 'e does, ma'am.' Allday patted the lapels into place and made certain that each bright epaulette with the twin silver stars was exactly right.

At sea it would be different, Allday thought. But here in the big house they had given him a real home. He looked away, unable to watch their faces. He was one of the family. Almost.

She said quietly, 'I could come as far as Hampshire with you.'

Bolitho held her again. 'No. The ride to the Beaulieu River would take a lot out of you. Then there is the return journey. I'd be sick with worry.'

This time she did not argue. Although neither mentioned it, each knew that a wrecked coach had once destroyed his happiness, another such accident had given both of them this new life.

Bolitho was grateful that he had to join his ship where it was too far for her to follow and risk an accident with their first child. It was bad enough to be leaving her when she most needed him, without that. Ferguson, his trusted steward, would be here in the house, and the doctor was within easy call. Bolitho's sister Nancy had been more at the house than in her own palatial residence with her husband the squire, who was known throughout the county as the King of Cornwall.

And next week Thomas Herrick's wife Dulcie would be coming all the way from Kent to keep Belinda company at the time of the birth.

Herrick, almost embarrassed by his promotion to rear-admiral, had been given command of a small squadron and had already sailed to Gibraltar for orders.

There would not be many familiar faces this time, Bolitho thought. Maybe it was just as well. No reminders. The doubts, like the successes, were best left in the past.

She said, 'Take good care of yourself, Richard. I hate your leaving, but at the same time I understand why you must go.'

Bolitho held her against him. Why were there never the right words until it was too late?

Ever since his return from the Admiralty with his secret orders she had somehow contained her disappointment, her dismay. Only once during the night had she exclaimed, 'Why you? *Must* you go?' Then, like part of a bad dream, she had lapsed into an uneasy sleep, her question still unanswered.

He heard Allday's voice beyond the door, supervising the loading of some final piece of luggage aboard the carriage. Poor Allday, he thought. Off again after all he had endured with him as a prisoner of war in France. He was always there when he was needed, the relationship stronger than ever, and when Bolitho needed someone to confide in outside of his officers and the chain of command, Allday would be ready to speak out.

Often Bolitho had felt badly about Allday's loyalty. Beyond his service as his coxswain and friend he had nothing. No wife to keep house for him and await his return from the sea, no home beyond these walls. It did not seem fair to drag him off yet again when he had more than earned the right to put his feet firmly ashore for all time. But Bolitho understood that Allday would be resentful and hurt by the suggestion he should not accompany him.

I must leave now.

They walked together to the big double doors, quietly determined, dreading the actual moment.

The sunlight engulfed them like an enemy, and Bolitho looked at the carriage with something like hatred. He had already said his farewells to his sister, to Ferguson, his one-armed steward, to the many familiar faces who worked in and around the big grey house below Pendennis Castle.

He said, 'I shall send word by the first available courier brig. When I reach America I shall probably be required to return home immediately.'

He felt her arm stiffen against his and despised himself for giving her hope.

Admiral Sheaffe had left him in doubt that the mission was important. To sail for Boston, 'neutral ground', as he had called it, and there meet French and American officials to formalize the handing over of an island as part of the agreement made under the Peace of Amiens.

It all seemed wrong to Bolitho. To hand back an island to the old enemy which had been won with British blood. He had blurted out as much to Admiral Sheaffe. 'We gained a peace, Sir Hayward, we did not lose the war!'

Perhaps in that cool Admiralty room it had sounded childish.

Sheaffe had replied calmly, 'And we do not wish you to *provoke* a war either, sir!'

As if to finalize the moment of departure, one of the horses stamped its hoof on the cobbles.

Bolitho kissed her hard on the mouth and tasted the salt of her tears.

'I shall return, Belinda.'

Very gently they prised themselves apart and Bolitho walked down the worn steps to the waiting carriage.

Allday was standing with a groom, but Bolitho gestured to the open door.

'Ride with me, Allday.'

He turned and glanced back at her. Against the grey stone she looked strangely vulnerable and he wanted to hold her just once more.

The next instant he was in the carriage and the wheels were clattering over the cobbles and through the gates.

It was done.

Allday sat with his fingers clasped and watched Bolitho's grave features and tried to measure the depth of his mood.

Seven months ashore seemed a lifetime to Allday,

although he knew better than to suggest as much to Bolitho. It was probably the longest he had been away from a King's ship since that first time when he had made his living here in Cornwall as a shepherd, when a man-of-war, one commanded by Bolitho, had dropped anchor and landed her press-gang to scavenge for hands. There had been several local men caught that day. Allday had been one, the steward Ferguson another. Poor Ferguson had lost an arm at the Saintes but, like Allday, had stayed with Bolitho ever since.

The warm air, the heavy scent of the countryside were making him drowsy, and he knew that although Bolitho wanted companionship for the long haul to the Beaulieu River in Hampshire where their next ship was lying, he did not want to gossip. There would be time enough for that in the weeks and months ahead.

Another ship. What would she be like? Allday was surprised that he could still be curious. In his strong position as the vice-admiral's personal coxswain he had nothing to fear from anyone. But he was too much of a seaman not to be interested.

Not a great first rate of a hundred guns or more, not even a new seventy-four like *Benbow*, Bolitho's last flagship, but the smallest ship of the line still in commission.

His Britannic Majesty's Ship *Achates* of sixty-four guns was one of a dying breed. More like an oversized frigate than a massive line of battleship which could withstand the pounding and destruction of close action.

She was twenty-one years old, a true veteran, and had seen every kind of combat in her time. She had spent most of her recent years in the Caribbean and had sailed countless leagues from her base in Antigua to the far south along the Spanish Main.

Allday wondered uneasily why she had been allotted to Bolitho as his flagship. To his simple reasoning it seemed like one more slur. He should have been given a knighthood for what he had done and endured for England. But always there seemed to be someone in authority who nursed some dislike or hatred of the man for whom Allday would willingly die if need be.

He thought of the parting he had just witnessed. What a fine pair they made. The lovely lady with the long chestnut hair and the youthful vice-admiral whose hair was as jet-black as the day Allday had joined his ship as a pressed hand.

From the opposite seat Bolitho saw Allday's head loll into a doze and felt the strength of the man, was grateful for his presence here.

Allday had thickened out and looked as if nothing could ever break him. *The oak.* He smiled to himself in spite of his sense of loss at leaving Belinda when she most needed him.

He had known Allday like a raging lion on the reddened deck of one ship or another. And he had seen him in tears as he had carried Bolitho below when he had been badly wounded in battle. It was impossible to imagine any place without Allday.

Bolitho also thought about his new flagship for this special commission which would take him to America and the Caribbean.

There was comfort in knowing that her new captain was also a good friend. Valentine Keen, who had once been one of Bolitho's midshipmen, who had shared excitement and sorrow in very different circumstances. *Achates'* previous captain had died of a fever even as his ship had sailed home from Antigua to the yard where she had been built to undergo a much needed overhaul and refit.

It would be good to have Keen as his flag-captain, he thought. He watched Allday's head fall to his chest and remembered it had been he who had once saved Keen's life, had personally cut a jagged splinter from his groin because he had not trusted the ship's drunken surgeon.

Bolitho watched a group of farm workers by a field gate as they paused to drink rough cider from great earthenware jugs.

A few glanced at the carriage, one even raised his arm in salute. The word would soon be around Falmouth. A Bolitho was leaving again. Would he return?

He thought of Belinda in that big, quiet house. If only . . .

Bolitho looked at the new gold lace on his coat and tried to settle his thoughts on the months ahead. He was not the first sea officer to leave home when a wife or family most needed him.

Nor would he be the last.

The peace could not endure, no matter what the politicians and experts proclaimed. Too many had already died, too many scores were still unsettled.

With sixty of England's one hundred ships of the line laid up and out of commission, and some forty thousand seamen and marines discharged, the French would be stupid to ignore such complacency.

He tried to concentrate on *Achates'* eventual destination, the island of San Felipe which lay across the Windward Passage between Cuba and Haiti like a rugged sentinel. The island's history was as wild and bloody as some others in the Caribbean. Originally Spanish, it had been occupied and held by France until the American Rebellion when it had been seized by Britain after a series of attacks at great cost to both sides.

Now, as part of the agreement with France, the island was to be handed back as a sign of good faith. But when Admiral Rodney's ships had taken the island in 1782, just a year after *Achates'* keel had first slipped into salt water, it had been a barren, hostile place. Now, according to all the information Bolitho had obtained from the Admiralty, it was both prosperous and thriving.

The present governor was a retired vice-admiral, Sir Humphrey Rivers, Knight of the Bath. He had made his life on San Felipe, had even named the port Georgetown to mark the island's permanent place under the British flag.

There was an excellent harbour, and the island's trade thrived on sugar, coffee and molasses, the growing prosperity owing much to a secondary population of slaves which had been brought originally from Africa.

Admiral Sheaffe had explained that whereas in war San Felipe had provided an excellent outpost to command the routes to Jamaica and a strategic base for hunting down enemy privateers, in peace it was a liability, unnecessary to the British Crown.

It had made no sense at the time, and as the carriage gathered speed down a steep incline and the sea reappeared on Bolitho's right, it made even less now.

Surely if the island was worth dying for it was worth keeping?

It seemed like a betrayal, more callous than Bolitho would have believed possible. Why then had he been chosen for the task instead of a skilled politician?

A man of tact as well as a man of action, Sheaffe had said.

Bolitho smiled grimly. He had heard that kind of explanation many times. If you were proved right others received the praise. If you made the wrong move you took all the blame.

He shut his orders from his mind. It was useless to plan beyond the written word. Everything might have changed by the time his ship next dropped anchor.

It would be strange not to have Browne as his flag-lieutenant. Intelligent, skilled with the ways of admiralty and government, Browne had been a tower of strength since he had been appointed as his aide. Now Browne was the lord and master of estates and property Bolitho could only guess at, his father having died in the last few months.

Browne had come to Cornwall to say his farewell. It had been a wrench for both of them. Bolitho had decided then and there he would ask his nephew, Adam Pascoe, to take his place. With so many young officers being put ashore it seemed right to offer him the post, even though it went against Bolitho's instinct to use his authority to grant a favour. But he loved his nephew as if he had been his own son, and they had come through many hazards together. The experience would do him good.

Browne had raised a doubtful eyebrow at the idea. Perhaps he had been trying to warn him against having one so close as an aide, one who is supposed to stand aside and remain impartial when required.

But to be without a ship at the age of twenty-one, when he most needed a chance to further his career, had seemed a more weighty argument.

Bolitho rested his head on the warm leather seat.

Valentine Keen, Adam and Allday. They would sustain each other. There would be no other familiar faces this time, or would there?

Achates had originally commissioned at the Nore, whereas Bolitho was more used to West Country ships or those from Spithead.

Belinda had been so pleased at his sudden and advanced promotion, when all he had wanted was to be with her when their first child was born.

Vice-Admiral of the Red. It barely seemed to matter. Some had even compared him with Nelson! Curiously enough, this made Bolitho uneasy, as if he were merely playing a part. It was indeed odd to realize that *Achates* was almost a twin of Nelson's favourite and his last command before his own promotion to flag-rank. His famous *Agamemnon* had been laid down and built in the same yard, that of Henry Adams of Bucklers Hard on the Beaulieu River.

The dwindling number of sixty-fours had one sure advantage. Bigger than anything faster. Faster than anything bigger. No wonder captains of heavier vessels looked on them with begrudging admiration.

Nelson had once said of his little *Agamemnon* that she was an excellent sailer and even when running close to the wind under storm-staysails could match many a frigate.

Bolitho wondered if Keen was equally agreeable with *Achates*. After his recent command of a powerful seventy-four he might already be regretting his decision to accept the role of Bolitho's flag-captain.

The horses slowed to a gentle trot while some sheep crossed the narrow road and bustled their way into an adjoining field.

A young woman with a child on her hip, her husband's midday meal carried in a red handkerchief, stared at the carriage as it moved past. She bobbed her head to Bolitho and flashed him a white smile.

Bolitho thought of Belinda, how she would manage when their child was born. A son to follow the tradition, to walk the deck of a new generation of King's ships. A daughter perhaps, to grow up and win the heart of a young man in a world he might never know.

Bolitho had confided little of his mission to Belinda. He wanted to keep her free of worry. Also she might resent the reason for his leaving her when she had time to think about it.

He tried to think about San Felipe's governor, the man who would have to hand over his tiny kingdom to their old foe.

He glanced at Allday, now rolling gently to the carriage's motion and fast asleep. He had known all about Sir Humphrey Rivers, Knight of the Bath.

Bolitho smiled. Allday gathered information about the comings and goings in the fleet and hoarded it as a magpie guards its treasure trove of coloured glass and beads.

Rivers had captained a frigate named *Crusader* during the American Revolution at about the same time when Bolitho had been given his first command, the little sloop-of-war *Sparrow*.

He had made quite a name for himself hunting French privateers and taking prizes of every shape and size. One day near the Chesapeake he had misjudged the danger in his eagerness to run down an American brig. His *Crusader* had ploughed into some shallows and had become a total wreck. Rivers had been taken prisoner but had been returned to Britain after the war.

He was said to have made influential friends during his captivity, and afterwards when he had been promoted to command a squadron in the West Indies. He had money in the City of London, property too in Jamaica. He did not sound like the kind of man who would fit easily into the plans of the government in Whitehall.

Bolitho grimaced at his reflection in the dusty glass. Not even if the plan was to be offered by someone of equal rank.

The carriage wheels dipped and shuddered through some deep ruts in the road and Bolitho winced as the pain of his wound dragged at his left thigh like a hot claw.

Belinda had even helped to dispel his self-consciousness about that. Occasionally when the pain was re-awakened he found himself limping and he had felt humiliated because of her.

He stirred on his seat as he recalled her touch in the night, her soft body against his, the secret words which had been lost in their passion for one another. She had kissed the wound where a musket-ball and the surgeon's probe had left an ugly scar and had made the injury more a mark of pride than a cruel reminder.

All this and more he was leaving behind with each turn of the wheels. Tonight it would be worse when the carriage stopped for the first change of horses in Torbay. It was better to join a ship and sail with the first possible tide and leave no room for regrets and longing.

He looked at Allday and wondered what he really thought about quitting the land yet again with his future as uncertain as the next horizon.

Flag at the fore. Allday was genuinely proud of it. That was something which the Admiral Sheaffes of this world could never understand.

2

'Old Katie'

Captain Valentine Keen walked from beneath the poop and crossed to the larboard nettings. Around him and along the upper gun-deck, and high overhead on the yards and rigging, the hands were hard at work.

The officer of the watch touched his hat to Keen and then moved to the opposite side of the deck. Like everyone else, he was careful to appear busy but unconcerned at his captain's presence.

Keen glanced along his new command. He had already been pulled around *Achates* in his gig to study her lines and her trim as she rocked gently above her black and buff reflection.

Ready for sea. It was every captain's personal decision as to when that possibility was a fact. There was no room for second thoughts once the anchor was catted and the ship standing out from the land.

It was warm and humid even for May, and the protective folds of the land were misty with haze. He hoped that some kind of wind would soon get up nonetheless. Bolitho would be impatient to get away, to cut his ties with the shore, although Keen knew his reasons were different from his own.

He shaded his eyes and looked up at the foremast truck. *Achates* had never worn an admiral's flag before. It would be interesting to see if it changed her.

He moved into a patch of shade by the poop ladder and watched the activity along the upper deck. The ship had a good feel to her, he thought. Something permanent and hard-won over the years. Several of her lieutenants had once served aboard as midshipmen, and most of her hard core of warrant officers, the backbone of any man-of-war, had been on the books for years.

There was an air of confidence about her, a lively eagerness to get away from the land before she too suffered the fate of so many others. Keen's own ship, *Nicator*, a seventy-four, which had distinguished herself at Copenhagen and later in the Bay of Biscay, was already laid up in ordinary. Unwanted, like her people who had fought so hard when the drums had beaten to quarters.

The previous captain had served in *Achates* for seven years. It was strange that he had commanded the ship for so long a period and had left no trace of his own personality in his quarters. Maybe he had invested it in his ship's company. They certainly seemed contented enough, although there had been the usual desertions during the overhaul here. Wives, sweethearts, children grown out of all recognition; Keen could hardly blame them for giving in to the temptation to run.

Keen ran his finger round his neckcloth and watched one of the ship's boats being swayed up and over the gangway and then lowered on to its tier. Every boat would have to be filled with water if this heat held to stop it from opening up.

Keen examined his feelings. He was glad to be leaving, especially with Bolitho. He had served under him twice before in other ships. First as midshipman, then as third lieutenant. They had shared the pain of losing loved ones, and now that Bolitho had married, Keen was still alone.

His thoughts wandered to his orders which Bolitho had sent to him.

A strange mission. Unique in his experience.

He glanced at the starboard line of black eighteen-pounders, run out as if for battle to allow the sailmaker and his crew maximum space on deck for stitching some canvas.

Peace or war, a King's ship must always be ready. Twice

Keen had served under Bolitho between the wars and had known the folly of over-confidence where a signed peace was concerned.

He heard feet on the companion ladder and saw Lieutenant Adam Pascoe climbing on deck.

It never failed to surprise Keen. Pascoe could have been Bolitho's young brother. The same black hair, although Pascoe's was cut short at the nape of the neck in the new naval fashion, the same restlessness. Grave and withdrawn one moment, full of boyish excitement the other.

Twenty-one years old, Keen thought. Without a war and its demands on lives and ships Pascoe would be lucky to gain advancement or a ship of his own.

'Good-day, Mr Pascoe. Is everything in the admiral's quarters to the flag-lieutenant's liking?'

Pascoe smiled. 'Aye, sir. With four of the after eighteen-pounders removed to the hold and replaced by Quakers, the admiral will have plenty of space.'

Keen looked at the quarterdeck and said, 'I have seen him content with ten paces of a deck. Back and forth, up and down, his daily stroll to arrange his ideas, to exercise his mind as well as his limbs.'

Pascoe said suddenly, 'I see no sense in this mission, sir. We fought the enemy to a standstill so that he *needed* a peace to lick his wounds. And yet our government has seen fit to give up almost all of our possessions which we won from the French. Everything but Ceylon and Trinidad we have let go and cannot even decide definitely to keep Malta. And now San Felipe is to go the same way, and the admiral's lot is to have the dirty task of doing it.'

Keen regarded him gravely. 'A word of advice, Mr Pascoe.'

He saw Pascoe's chin lift stubbornly. That wary glance Keen had grown to know in the past.

He said, 'In the wardroom the lieutenants and others can speak as they please provided their private views do not spread among the people. As captain I stand apart, so too does the flag-lieutenant. Despite your wish to serve your uncle, I suspect you accepted the post more to please him than yourself?'

Keen knew he had guessed correctly and saw the shot go home.

He added, 'Being a sea officer is totally different from being an admiral's aide. You have to be discreet, cautious even, for there will be others who might wish to win a confidence.'

He wondered if he should go further and decided it was too important to avoid.

'Some may want to harm your uncle. So stay clear of the rights and wrongs of something you cannot alter. Otherwise, hurtful or not, it were better for you to go ashore right now and beg a replacement from the port admiral at Spithead.'

Pascoe smiled. 'Thank you, sir. I deserved that. But I'd not leave my uncle. Not now. Not ever. He is everything to me.'

Keen watched the young lieutenant's unusual display of emotion. He knew most of the story anyway. How Pascoe had been born out of wedlock, the son of Bolitho's dead brother. Bolitho's brother had been a renegade, a traitor during the American War, and had commanded an enemy privateer with no less audacity than John Paul Jones. It must have been hard on Bolitho. And on this youthful officer who had been sent to seek out Bolitho by his dying mother as his only hope of a future.

Keen said quietly, 'I understand.' He clapped him on the shoulder. 'Better than you realize.'

The midshipman of the watch hurried across the deck and touched his hat nervously.

Keen looked at him. He was new to the ship as well.

The boy stammered, 'Sir, there is a boat putting off from the yard.'

Keen shaded his eyes again and stared across the nettings. One of the shipyard's own boats was already pulling towards the anchored two-decker. Keen saw the sunlight glint on the gold epaulettes and cocked hat and felt something like panic.

Trust Bolitho not to wait for his barge to be sent across. So he was that eager to get on with the mission, right or wrong.

He kept his face impassive as he said, 'My compliments to the officer of the watch, Mr er . . . er . . .'

'Puxley, sir.'

'Well, Mr Puxley, pipe for the side-party and guard.'

He stopped the boy as he made to run for the ladder. '*Walk*, Mr Puxley!'

Pascoe turned aside to hide a smile. Bolitho had probably said as much to Keen when he had been a grubby midshipman. *He certainly did to me.*

As the boatswain's mates ran between decks and their calls shrilled like trapped birds, the marines stamped to the entry port, their scarlet coats and white cross-belts in stark contrast to the bustling seamen.

Keen beckoned to the officer of the watch and said curtly, '*And* Mr Mountsteven, I would trouble *you* to keep a weather-eye open for your betters in future.'

Pascoe straightened his hat and tucked some of his rebellious hair beneath it. Bolitho had probably said that too.

Keen walked to the entry port and looked towards the boat. He could see Bolitho sitting in the stern-sheets, that old sword clasped firmly between his knees. To see him join any ship without the family sword would be like sacrilege, he thought.

There was Allday too, massive and watchful as he eyed the boat's crew with obvious displeasure. What had Pascoe's predecessor, the Hon. Oliver Browne, called the squadron? *We Happy Few*. There were *very* few of them now. Keen glanced at the big red ensign which flapped only occasionally from the poop. But there were enough.

Achates' first lieutenant, Matthew Quantock, a tall, heavy-jowled Manxman, watched the boat and then said, 'All ready, sir.'

'Thank you, Mr Quantock.'

In his few weeks aboard while the overhaul was completed and he had gone through every list, log and book which concerned the ship, Keen had felt his way with care. It was not as if he was new to command. But to this ship's company he was different. A stranger. Until he had won their respect he would take nothing and nobody for granted.

The first lieutenant glanced at the signals midshipman by the foremast and said almost to himself, 'I'll lay odds *Old Katie* never expected to be a flagship, sir.'

Keen smiled. He had learned something new. *Old Katie*. A ship with a nickname was usually a happy one.

The boat hooked on to the main chains and Captain Dewar of the Royal Marines drew his sword. The thin rasp of steel never failed to touch Keen. Like a memory. A chord of battle.

Keen looked at his command. All the idlers had drawn away from the entry port, and even the hands working on the yards high above the deck were motionless as they peered at the little scene below.

The small marine fifers raised their instruments, the boatswain's mates moistened their silver calls on their tongues.

Keen stepped forward, proud, nervous, apprehensive; it was all and none of these things.

Bolitho's cocked hat appeared above the scrubbed grating and as the calls shrilled and twittered Captain Dewar roared, 'Royal Marines! Present *arms!*'

On the last command, as the pipe-clay hovered in a pale cloud above the slapped musket-slings, the fifers broke into *Heart of Oak*.

Bolitho removed his hat to the quarterdeck and then smiled at Keen.

Together they turned to watch as the Union Flag broke smartly from the foremast.

Bolitho gripped Keen's hand. 'They do you credit.'

Keen answered, 'And you us, sir.'

Bolitho looked at the stiff faces of the marine guard, the nervous watchfulness of some midshipmen. In time he would know most of them, and they him. He was back, and the green swathe of coastline was only part of a memory.

*

Bolitho tugged his shirt away from his skin and then put his signature to yet another letter which Yovell, his plump clerk, had prepared for him.

He glanced around the spacious stern cabin. It was larger than he had expected in a ship of some thirteen hundred tons.

Ozzard, his little servant, poured some fresh coffee and bustled away to the adjoining pantry. If he was sorry to be leaving the security of the Bolitho house in Falmouth he did not show it. He was an odd bird, who had once been a lawyer's clerk before he had chosen the uncertain life in a King's ship. Some said he had done so to avoid the gallows, but he was worth his weight in gold to Bolitho.

He looked at Keen who was standing by the open stern windows. His good looks and elegant manner revealed nothing of the competent sea officer he really was.

'Well, Val, what do you make of it?'

Keen turned towards him, his face in shadow from the hard sunlight.

'I have studied the chart and appreciate the value of San Felipe in time of war. Whoever commands there is in a strong position.' He shrugged. 'A great lagoon, a fortress on high ground which can control the approaches, the town too if need be. I can see no sense in giving it to the French.'

He thought Pascoe was smiling at his words and added, 'But I assume their lordships know more than I do.'

Bolitho chuckled. 'Do not rely on it, Val.'

The coffee was good. Bolitho felt surprisingly fresh and rested after his first night aboard. The journey had been tiring, the many pauses along the way to take refreshment, to sleep or to change horses had been even more so as he had thought of Belinda and what she had come to mean to him.

But the feel of a ship around him had awakened him also.

The smells of tar and fresh paint, cordage and the packed world of *Achates'* five hundred officers, seamen and marines was something he could not ignore, nor did he wish to.

Achates was a well-found ship, and from what he had already discovered held a record second to none. Perhaps

Admiral Sheaffe's choice had been the right one after all. A small sixty-four instead of a proud squadron which might intimidate the Americans and the French alike.

He said, 'I have already sent word to Captain Duncan at Plymouth. He will sail direct to San Felipe in his *Sparrowhawk* without delay.'

It was easy to picture Duncan's bluff red face as he read his orders. He too would be glad to get away before his frigate was paid off into oblivion. Duncan had also been with Bolitho's squadron. It was like knowing Keen in some ways, he thought. They were extensions of his own mind and ideas.

That was something which he still found hard to accept. No longer did he have to wait for the written word from his flag-officer. No more did he need to fret over the uncertainty or unfairness of his place in affairs. Now the decision as to when and how to act was his. So too the final responsibility.

He added, 'Duncan's presence at San Felipe may lessen the shock for the inhabitants there. I doubt if the governor will see it in the same way as Parliament.'

Ozzard tiptoed across the cabin and waited for Bolitho to notice his mole-like figure. Even his hands dangled at his waist like paws.

He said, 'Beg pardon, Captain, but the first lieutenant has sent his respects and requires me to tell you that the wind has shifted, though very slight.'

Keen looked at Bolitho and grinned. 'I told him to inform me, sir. It's still not much of a wind, but enough to break out the anchor. With your permission, sir?'

Bolitho nodded. It was infectious. It had not changed after all.

'Yovell, put my despatches in the yard-boat alongside.'

He saw his clerk hold the letter he had written to Belinda with special care. She would be reading it as *Achates* passed the Lizard on her way to the Atlantic rollers, he thought.

He heard Keen's voice through the open skylight, the trill of calls and the slap of bare feet over the dried planks as the seamen ran to their stations.

Bolitho made himself sit in his chair and sip the coffee. Keen would have enough to deal with as he sailed his ship clear of the land for the first time without having him there as well.

How many times had he stood at the quarterdeck rail, his heart bounding with hope and excitement, searching his soul in case he had forgotten something when it was already too late?

Tackles squeaked and cordage squealed through countless blocks, and very faintly, far away it sounded, Bolitho heard the plaintive notes of a violin while the shantyman added his weight to the men on the capstan bars.

Yovell came back breathing hard.

'All despatches ashore, zur.' His round Devonian dialect seemed to match his handwriting on the many copies of signals and despatches he had penned for Bolitho in the past two years.

Keen returned, his hat tucked beneath one arm.

'The anchor is hove short, sir. I wonder if you would care to join me on deck? It would do well for the people to see you are with them.'

Bolitho smiled. 'Thank you, Val.'

Keen hesitated and glanced at Pascoe.

'There is one thing I do not understand, sir. The courier delivered a letter for the flag-lieutenant. He only just reached the ship in time.'

Bolitho looked at his nephew. It was the moment, and it had almost been postponed because of the need to get under way while the feeble wind lasted.

He saw Yovell beaming at him and was suddenly fearful that he had done the wrong thing.

He said, 'I shall come on deck directly, Captain Keen.'

Bolitho took the sealed letter and glanced quickly at it to make certain it was the right one. Then he snatched his hat from Ozzard and walked with Keen to the door.

Keen was saying, 'I expect it was a careless mistake, sir.'

Bolitho pressed the letter into his nephew's hand.

'I shall be on deck if you need me.'

Entirely mystified, Keen accompanied him beneath the shadows of the poop deck and past the great double wheel where the helmsmen and quartermaster waited, tensed, for the anchor to break loose from the ground.

The ship was alive with seamen and marines. The topmen were already high aloft on the upper yards, spread out like monkeys as they handled the loosely brailed sails. The braces were manned, and as the pawls of the capstan clanked round to the tune of the fiddle, petty officers and master's mates watched their divisions like hawks, very aware of the flag at the fore.

Allday was on deck by one of the quarterdeck twelve-pounders when he realized that Ozzard had neglected to clip on Bolitho's sword for him. With a silent curse he darted aft and bustled past the marine sentry into the great cabin.

With a start he saw Pascoe was still there, an open document hanging from one hand.

Like Yovell, who had written most of the letters, Allday knew what the document contained. He had been deeply moved that he was one of the very few who did.

'All right, sir?'

When the youthful lieutenant turned to face him, Allday was shocked to see there were tears on his cheeks.

'Easy, sir! He wanted you to be pleased!'

'*Pleased?*'

Pascoe took a few paces towards the side and back again. As if he did not understand what was happening.

'And *you* knew about it, Allday?'

'Aye, sir. After a fashion.'

Allday had seen and done many things, and Bolitho had said more than once that with education he might have achieved a lot more than a sailor's life. But he did not need to be able to read what was written on the envelope. No wonder Captain Keen had been all aback, he thought.

The letter was addressed to *Adam Bolitho, Esq., Flag-Lieutenant on board His Britannic Majesty's Ship* Achates.

Adam stared at the writing, his eyes too blurred with emotion to read much further. The lawyer's impressive wax seals, the rights to the Bolitho property in Falmouth. He could not go on.

Allday took his elbow and guided him to the bench seat below the stern windows.

'I'll fetch you a wet, sir. After that we'll take the old sword on deck together.' He saw him nod and added quietly, 'After all, sir, you're a *real* Bolitho now. Like *him*.'

From another world a voice yelled, '*Anchor's aweigh*, sir!'

The stamp of feet and the harsh cries of the petty officers seemed to be held at bay.

Allday poured a glass of brandy and carried it to the lieutenant he had known since he had come aboard Bolitho's *Hyperion* as a fourteen-year-old midshipman.

'Here, sir.'

Adam said quietly, 'You asked me if I was pleased. There are no words for the way I feel. He didn't have to . . .'

Allday wished he could have a drink too. 'It's what he wanted. What he's always wanted.'

The deck tilted as the ship continued to pay off to the wind's thrust in her topsails and jib.

Allday took down the worn old sword from the rack and turned it over in his hands. They had nearly lost it for good last time. He looked at the young lieutenant, the image of the man on deck. It would be his one day.

Lieutenant Adam Bolitho wiped his face with his cuff and said, 'Let's be about it then, eh, Allday?' But the bravado would not hold. He gripped the coxswain's massive arm and exclaimed, 'I'm glad you were here just now.'

Allday grinned as he followed him from the cabin.

Pleased? He was pleased right enough. Otherwise, lieutenant or not, he'd have put the young rascal across his knee and beaten some sense into him.

Adam walked out into the sunlight. He did not see the curious stares, nor did he hear a muttered curse as a hurry-ing seaman almost fell to the deck as he tripped on the flag-lieutenant's foot. He took the sword from Allday and held it against Bolitho's side as he made to clip it into place.

Bolitho watched him and was glad. 'Thank you, Adam.'

The lieutenant nodded and tried to speak.

Bolitho took his arm and turned him towards the rolling shoreline as it glided abeam, moving away as the ship headed into deeper water.

'Later, Adam. There'll be plenty of time.'

The first lieutenant raised his speaking-trumpet and squinted up through the black rigging.

'Loose t'gan's'ls!'

He glanced at the group by the windward side. The youthful vice-admiral with his flag-lieutenant on deck to see if the ship was good enough, more than likely.

Allday saw the glance and hid a grin.

You've got a lot to learn, matey, an' that's no error.

3

Man of Action

For a full week after weighing anchor *Achates* was the victim of feeble and perverse winds. There was barely an hour when all hands were spared the tasks of trimming the sails in order to avoid losing steerage-way or being forced back over their previous course.

The deadly monotony was having its effect on the ship's company. After all the haste and excitement of getting away from the land, the sudden torpor had resulted in more than one flogging at the gratings because of frayed tempers and bursts of insubordination.

Bolitho had watched Keen's face after one of the floggings. Some captains would have cared nothing for the routine of punishment, but Keen was different. It was typical of Bolitho that it never occurred to him that Keen had gained his experience under his command.

Keen had remarked, 'The worst part of it is I can understand their feelings. Some have not set foot ashore since returning from the Indies. Now they're off again. Grateful to be spared the poverty of being without work, but resentful at what is little better than pressed service.'

The start of the second week brought a freshening wind from the north-east, and with spray bursting beneath her weathered figurehead it had brought life to the ship once more.

The masthead lookouts had sighted only a few sails on the blurred horizon, and these had changed tack and headed away immediately. Home-bound ships, out of touch for many months with the events in Europe, would take no chances when sighting a man-of-war. War might have broken out again for all they knew. Some masters might still not know that an armistice had even been signed.

It was as if the ship had the ocean to herself. Keen took the opportunity to get to know his command and for his men to recognize his standards. Sail and gun drill, musket practice for the marines, experienced lieutenants and warrant officers replaced by new and often barely trained counterparts. Keen may have gained their respect, but was roundly cursed at the start of each testing exercise.

Bolitho knew from hard experience there was nothing more likely to breed discontent in a ship's close confines than too much leisure.

He was having a breakfast of thinly sliced fat pork when Keen asked to see him.

Bolitho gestured to a chair, 'Coffee, Val?'

Keen sat down and said, 'I believe we are being stalked by another vessel, sir.'

Bolitho put down his knife. Keen had never been one to exaggerate or imagine things.

'How so?'

'Two days ago my best lookout sighted a sail. Well up to wind'rd. I thought little of it at the time. She might have been a merchantman on the same tack as *Achates*.'

He sensed Bolitho's curiosity and added simply, 'I did not wish to alarm anyone. But yesterday you will recall I was hove to while we exercised the starboard twelve-pounders on some driftwood. That sail was still there, and the moment I came about the stranger followed suit and stood clear.' He waited for Bolitho's reaction and said grimly, 'She's there now.'

The door opened and Adam entered the cabin with a chart beneath his arm.

Bolitho smiled at him. They had said little of his gesture towards his nephew since the day the ship had weighed anchor in the Beaulieu River. Yet there was a new closeness between them. Something which went beyond words.

He remembered Belinda's encouragement and insistence that he acted as he had. She had known from the beginning how Bolitho felt about his nephew, what they had been through.

He could almost hear her saying, 'When our child is born I do not want Adam to feel shut out, excluded. Do it for *me*, as well as for Adam.'

'Have *you* seen the ship, Adam?'

'Aye, sir. I went aloft at first light today. I believe she's a frigate. I took the signals telescope with me. There was a lot of haze, but I judge her rig to be that of a big fifth-rater. She's too agile for an Indiaman or some westbound trader.'

Keen said glumly, 'And if that vessel holds to wind'rd I'll never be able to beat up to him.'

Bolitho shook his head. 'It would lose valuable time too.'

But the news was unsettling all the same. If she was a ship-of-war she represented a menace no matter what his orders dictated. But whose and for what purpose?

His mission was supposed to be secret, but Bolitho knew ships as well as he understood the men who served them. Keen had been surprised at Adam's official change of name, but it had gone through the ship in seconds. A piece of really important information could spread through a shipyard, a town, even across the English Channel in no time at all.

'Keep me informed. If the wind changes in our favour we shall investigate. If not . . . ' He shrugged. 'We'll have to wait for him to show his intentions.'

Later, as Bolitho took his regular stroll up and down the weather-side of the quarterdeck, he found himself wondering about his mission and how the people of San Felipe would accept their new position. He thought too of the ship which was obviously stalking *Achates* with the persistence of a hunter after deer.

French most likely. Ready to support their own view-point if required, even at the point of a gun.

Up and down, his feet avoiding ring-bolts and tackles without conscious effort.

Some of the faces among the watchkeepers and the after-guard had become as familiar as those in previous ships. Bolitho hated the invisible wall which cut him off from closer contact. Even Keen as captain was free to talk with his men if the mood took him. More than once Bolitho stared up at his flag and tried to accept the enforced loneliness it had brought him.

He paused by the compass and glanced at it even though it had barely altered for days. He could feel the helmsmen avoiding his eye, and Knocker, the sailing-master, becoming suddenly absorbed in the midshipman of the watch's report.

Hallowes, the fourth lieutenant, had the watch, and even he was bent over the quarterdeck rail with exaggerated attention as he watched the eighteen-pounders at drill.

A boatswain's mate strode along the lee gangway and something about him made Bolitho look at him more closely.

The man hesitated, swallowed hard, and then came towards him.

Bolitho asked, 'Do I know you?' Then the man's name seemed to paint itself in his mind. 'Christy, isn't it?'

The man nodded and beamed hugely. 'Aye, 'tis that, sir. Maintopman in the old *Lysander*, I was. With you at the Nile, sir.'

'I remember. You were nearly lost that day when they shot the t'gallant mast away.' He nodded as the memory closed round them shutting out all else.

The boatswain's mate said, 'Were a sore hard fight, sir. The worst I seen, ever.'

Bolitho smiled and continued with his walk.

The man named Christy hurried away shaking his head. *He remembered him*. Out of all these men.

Quantock, the first lieutenant, who was doing his morning rounds with Rooke, the boatswain, and Grace, the carpenter, paused and beckoned to him.

'Knew your name, did he?'

Christy knuckled his forehead. 'Aye, sir. He did that.'

Quantock snapped, 'Well, don't stand there like a moon-struck farm boy, there's work to be done!'

Christy made his way aft. Why was the first lieutenant in a temper? He thought of that awful day at the Nile, the thunder of the broadsides, and of Bolitho walking amidst the smoke and carnage with that old sword gripped in his hand. And his face as they had cheered him when the enemy had finally struck their colours.

Quantock checked his list, the unending task of every good first lieutenant. The ship had had a refit but the work was always piling up. Sails to be renewed and patched, boats repaired, pumps and tackles overhauled.

He was angry with himself for his sudden hostility towards the boatswain's mate. Christy was a good seaman, and a volunteer as well.

Quantock stole a glance to the weather-side where the vice-admiral was walking up and down. What was so special about him anyway?

The boatswain, a great crag of a man with a lined and battered face, waited patiently for his superior to continue with the morning rounds. He had been irritated by the lieutenant's unwarranted attack on one of *his* assistants.

Rooke, Big Harry as he was respectfully known, guessed the reason for Quantock's temper. He was a good first lieutenant, if you happened to be the captain, that was. But he was hard with the people, unrelenting in matters of discipline.

Captain Glazebrook, who had died after a long bout of fever, had been too ill to see what was happening. Quantock probably thought *he* should be promoted, even be given command of *Old Katie*. Rooke did not like the first lieutenant, and the thought of him being in command of this ship was like blasphemy.

Quantock said sharply, '*Standards*, we must maintain them. I'll not allow anything to interfere with the efficient running of this ship!'

Rooke saw the new captain crossing the deck from the companion. He might have warned another lieutenant but Quantock's outburst was still annoying him.

'And further – '

'Mr Quantock.' Keen waited for the lieutenant to join him where he could not be heard by the men on watch. 'I admire your high standards. I would, however, prefer that you voiced your views to me in future, not the ship's company en masse.'

Bolitho had seen most of it and guessed the rest.

Did his flag at the masthead really make that much difference? Even Keen seemed on edge, regretting perhaps this appointment which was leading nowhere.

No, it was not that. It was uncertainty. An emptiness which the coming of peace had brought. They were used to action, expected it even.

'Deck there! Sail on th' weather-bow!'

Keen looked up and then turned questioningly to Bolitho. Their companion was still there, lurking just below the horizon like an assassin.

Perhaps they would get all the action they wanted even though the ink was barely dry on the peace agreement.

Bolitho continued his pacing with renewed energy, as if he wanted to tire himself out.

He was imagining things, he decided angrily. *He* was the one who craved excitement, if only to take his mind off the relentless passing of time.

Achates would still be making for Boston when Belinda gave birth. It was like being trapped. Helpless.

Bolitho saw Adam at the forward end of the gun-deck talking with Hawtayne, the young marine lieutenant.

I am as bad as Admiral Sheaffe.

I am envious. Not of success but of youth.

He was so lucky to have Belinda. He was after all ten years older than she. And now that she needed him he was marooned out here like a castaway on a rock.

Why you? He could still hear her voice when she had spoken out in the darkness. Why him indeed?

He stopped and allowed his body to sway with the ship as she rode contemptuously across a long Atlantic trough.

Perhaps it was a kind of madness which had never left him. Being taken prisoner by the French, the escape, the lives it had cost in that final battle with Remond's Flying Squadron had been too much and too soon after being badly wounded.

The pain stabbed through his wound again as if to taunt him. He tried to remember her soft touch in the night, when she had soothed the pain of the scar with her love.

But the picture would not form.

He called, 'Captain Keen, we shall douse all lights and change tack tonight. As soon as it is dark alter course to the nor'-west. By dawn I want to see that strange sail where we can run down on it.'

Keen opened his mouth as if to protest but instead touched his hat. Then he said, 'I'll get every stitch on her, sir.'

Bolitho strode into the poop's shadow and made his way aft to his quarters.

He had acted hastily, even childishly, some would say.

Achates was a solitary ship, and yet his responsibility was as great as if he commanded a squadron or even a fleet.

Those around him had not asked to be here. Keen, Quantock, the embittered first lieutenant, even the boatswain's mate named Christy who had been so grateful that he had remembered him, they all deserved better from the man who commanded them.

But there was a difference. To Keen the ship and her company came before all else, and the mission was secondary.

To Bolitho *Achates* had to remain a symbol and, if necessary, a weapon to enforce his wishes.

It was probably the first time he had considered what his new responsibility entailed, and the realization steadied him.

Allday padded into the cabin and replaced the old sword on its rack. Cleaning it made little difference but it gave him an excuse to come and go as he pleased.

He glanced at Bolitho as he sat on the bench seat by the stern windows, his black hair ruffling in the wind across the quarter.

Bolitho looked calm enough. The sudden squall had passed.

'I was wondering, sir . . . '

Bolitho turned, only half aware he was no longer alone. 'What about?'

'Well, I mean, sir, if *you* was the governor of this island we're about to toss away to the mounseers, what would you do?'

Bolitho got to his feet and strode to the wine cabinet where he poured two glasses of brandy.

He handed one to the astonished Allday and replied, 'Thank you. You have put your finger on it.' The brandy burned his lips. '*Do*, Allday? I'd stand and fight. And so probably will he.'

Allday breathed out slowly. He did not quite understand what he had done, but it was good to see the frown gone from Bolitho's features.

Bolitho eyed him warmly, 'You should have been in Parliament, Allday.'

Allday put down his empty glass. He had never seen him in quite this mood before.

'I'm too honest, sir.'

Bolitho laughed and turned to watch the patterns and colours twisting in the ship's wake.

There would be no easy solution for San Felipe.

Maybe that was why Sheaffe needed his 'man of action'.

And it had taken Allday to discover it.

'Hands at quarters, sir, ship cleared for action.'

Keen's voice came out of the gloom and Bolitho could barely distinguish him from the other dark figures at the quarterdeck rail.

The *Achates'* previous captain and Keen's regular drills had made their mark, he thought. All hands had been roused early and had a hot meal before the galley fire had been doused and the ship prepared for battle.

There was little impression of danger or anxiety, however. It was peacetime, so why should they worry?

Bolitho said, 'That was quietly done.'

He shivered as the cold, damp wind whipped over the

deck. In an hour or so the sunlight would raise steam from the planks and melt the tarred seams like toffee.

'Steady on west by north, sir.'

Bolitho nodded. That was Knocker's voice, the sailing-master. At the helm and compass he was king. He was a man who rarely smiled. Thin and gaunt with a priest's face, Bolitho thought. But his chartwork and his grip over the ship's daily progress was as good as any master he had ever known.

Some of the gun crews around the quarterdeck were whispering and nudging each other. Anything which broke the regular routine was welcome. What did it matter if their admiral was mad enough to clear for action because of some stupid stranger?

Another voice said, 'Dawn coming up, sir.'

The lieutenant who had spoken sounded awed by the occasion.

Bolitho turned to look astern and saw the horizon begin to betray the division between sea and sky. How many hundreds of dawns must he have watched, he wondered? And how many had he thought might be his last?

Someone remarked, 'The bugger might have slipped us during the night.'

The sergeant of marines tapped his hand-pike on the damp planking and muttered, 'Easy, lads. Stow the chat!'

The cross-belts of the marines who lined the poop nettings were already brighter, and when Bolitho looked up to the mainmast truck he saw it was touched with pale gold, like the tip of a lance.

The lookouts in the cross-trees or crouched in the swaying tops would see the other ship first. If she was still there.

All night long Keen had worked his ship upwind, a slow, wearying task with the yards so often close-hauled that they seemed to reach above the deck in a single barrier of spars and canvas.

All they had said of *Achates* was true. She handled well, and responded to sail and rudder like a thoroughbred.

Bolitho listened to the sluice of water below the lee side, the occasional creak of gun tackles as they took the strain.

The light seemed to spill down from the horizon like a separate layer, as if it was in pursuit of the ship which lay over to the wind just out of reach.

'*There she is!* Fine on the lee bow!'

Everyone was talking at once, and Bolitho saw Keen's teeth, very white in a grin, as he nodded to the sailing-master.

They had done even better than expected. Had taken, and could now hold the wind-gage if it came to a chase.

Bolitho stared at the distant shadow as the other vessel took on shape and substance against the dark water.

Keen closed his telescope with a snap. 'Bigger than a fifth-rate, Mr Pas—, er Bolitho.'

Several of those nearby chuckled, and Bolitho was glad Adam was here with him.

He heard his nephew say, 'I agree, sir. A cut down two-decker seems more likely.'

Keen crossed to Bolitho's side. 'What orders, sir?'

'Wait a while longer. He has not sighted us yet. But when he does, tell him to identify himself.'

It seemed incredible that *Achates* had got so near and yet remained unseen. The other ship lay less than a cable now across the larboard bow, and they could see the white tail of her wash beneath the counter. Even the din of *Achates'* canvas and drumming stays and shrouds seemed loud enough to wake the dead, but Bolitho knew from experience it was an illusion.

Suddenly above the noise of sea and wind Bolitho heard a shrill whistle. He could picture it exactly. A sleepy lookout, who had most likely been ordered to seek out *Achates* as soon as it was daylight, the watch on deck thinking of little but being relieved and getting something warm to eat and drink. It was all normal enough.

Quantock said sharply, 'She's setting her t'gan's'ls!'

Keen said, 'They're making a run for it, sir. So they *are* up to something.'

Bolitho felt a chill run through his body as if it was the first time. Elation, excitement or madness, who could say?

'As soon as it is light enough, make your signal. Until then hold him on the larboard bow.'

Keen nodded. The excitement was infectious. With him it had always been the same even as a midshipman a million years ago in another ocean.

'Hands aloft, Mr Quantock, if you please. We must make more sail.'

Calls trilled and the seamen swarmed up the ratlines on either side, their bodies and limbs glowing suddenly as they climbed higher and the pale sunlight discovered them.

'Bring her up a point. Hands to the braces there!'

Spray burst over the beak-head and bowsprit and spattered across the forecastle like tropical rain.

The other ship had also set more canvas and appeared to be drawing away.

Bolitho felt the deck quiver as *Achates* lifted and smashed down into a shallow trough. He could sense the rising power of the extra sails, and watched the huge main-course spread and thunder out to the wind as the seamen freed it from its yard.

Bolitho climbed on to a gun-truck and steadied his glass on the leading ship. The light was strengthening rapidly and already he could see the gilded gingerbread around the other vessel's poop and quarter gallery, the pale sunlight reflecting in her stern windows as if she had taken fire.

Keen said, 'Not a Frenchie.'

Someone else suggested, 'Dutch maybe.'

They were all wrong. Bolitho had seen ships very similar to this one and could be pretty certain which yard had laid down her keel.

He said, 'Spanish. I've crossed swords with her like before.'

Nobody spoke and Bolitho hid a smile. Right or wrong, you never argued with an admiral, no matter how junior.

Keen nodded. 'I agree with the flag-lieutenant, sir. She's

too large for a frigate. She's well armed by the look of her, fifty guns at least, by my reckoning.'

'Signal her to shorten sail.'

Bolitho sensed the sudden indifference of the men near him. The game was over before it had begun.

Flags soared up the yards and broke to the wind. Above the other ship's deck nothing appeared, not even an acknowledgement.

'She's falling off a mite, sir.'

Bolitho trained his glass again. He thought he saw the sun glint on a telescope near one of her poop lanterns. *Achates'* change of station during the night must have surprised them if nothing else.

Keen called, 'Follow her round. Alter course to west by south.' He glanced at Bolitho's impassive features.

Bolitho said, 'Keep the signal hoisted.'

Both vessels were in line now, as if the other one was towing *Achates* on an invisible cable.

Keen strode this way and that as he tried to estimate the stranger's next move. If he fell off to leeward *Achates* would hold the advantage. If she tried to claw upwind with so close a chase she would lose ground and precious time and *Achates* could drive alongside if so ordered.

The lieutenant of the after-guard lowered his glass.

'She does not acknowledge, sir. Even the Dons should know our signals by now!'

Quantock shouted, 'Take those men's names, Master-at-Arms!' He gestured angrily with his speaking-trumpet towards an eighteen-pounder's crew who had left their positions to peer at the other ship. 'God damn it, what are they thinking of!'

Keen was saying, 'If the wind holds I'll get the stuns'ls on her . . .'

Bolitho wiped his eye and raised the glass yet again. *Achates* was keeping pace with the other ship, even though the stranger had set her royals in an effort to draw away. But the wind might drop or go altogether. If they could not catch up before nightfall they might never know what she was doing.

It was very strange. He concentrated on the small, silent world within the telescope's lens. She was well painted, as if freshly out of a dockyard like *Achates*. But the broad red band across her counter had no name upon it. She had either put to sea with great haste or wished her identity to remain a secret.

He heard *Achates'* wheel begin to creak as the other ship's rudder moved further to leeward.

He blinked and peered through the glass again. For an instant he thought the light or his eye was playing tricks. On either side of the ship's rudder a gun-port had opened, and even as he watched he saw the daylight play across a pair of long stern-chasers.

Quantock exploded, 'Hell's teeth, he'd never dare fire on a King's ship!'

The air cringed from a double crash of cannon fire, and as the smoke rolled downwind in a thick cloud Bolitho felt iron smash hard into *Achates'* bows like a giant's fist.

Voices yelled to restore the sudden pandemonium, and faces peered aft to the quarterdeck as if each man was too astonished to move.

Bolitho snapped, 'Load and run out, Captain Keen.'

It was sheer stupidity for the other captain to try and mark down a sixty-four. In a moment Keen would stand away and loose off a full broadside. Men would be killed, and for what purpose?

Along *Achates'* side the port lids opened as one, and to the blast of a whistle the eighteen-pounders rolled squeaking down the tilting deck until they showed their muzzles to the sea and sky. On the deck below the main armament of twenty-four-pounders would be just a few feet above the water as it curled along the rounded hull. *Achates* was carrying such a pyramid of sails it was a wonder the sea was not already lapping through the lower ports.

'Bow-chasers!'

Keen had his hands clasped behind his back, and Bolitho could see the force of his grip betrayed by the pale knuckles. What did he see? An unexpected prize, or his own ruin?

Bolitho could hear Allday's heavy breathing behind his shoulder and sensed Adam on his other side. Extensions of himself. Each needing the other in a different way.

The other ship fired again, and Bolitho tried not to flinch as a ball ripped through the main-course and the wind tore it into a great flapping slash.

Achates' gunner had been caught napping. The bow-chasers would probably not even bear on the enemy, Bolitho thought.

Every gun-captain along the upper deck had his hand in the air.

Keen said tersely, 'Be ready to come about, Mr Knocker! We'll cross his stern and rake him. That'll give him something to ponder on.'

He sounded angry. Hurt that this should happen.

'Lee braces there! Stand by on the quarterdeck!' Quantock's magnified voice seemed to be everywhere.

At that moment the other ship fired again. Bolitho thought he saw the blur of falling shot before one heavy ball crashed through the forward gangway and the other hissed above the forecastle at extreme elevation.

A last desperate attempt to break off the chase, and it worked.

There was a single, terrible crack, and seconds later the whole of the fore-topgallant mast, the spars and wildly thrashing canvas plunged down to the deck. With torn canvas and rigging trailing after it like serpents, the broken mast thundered across the lee gangway and into the water with a tremendous splash.

Bolitho heard one of the midshipmen stifle a cry of terror as some seamen were plucked bodily over the side with the broken rigging, their voices lost in the din.

Like a great sea-anchor the trailing spars and cordage were already having effect as they pulled the ship's head round, further and further, until all the sails, so carefully set for the chase, were in wild confusion.

Rooke, the boatswain, was already among the chaos with his men, axes flashing as they hacked the debris clear.

The gun crews were working feverishly with tackles and handspikes, but as the ship was dragged still further down wind their muzzles pointed blindly at the sea, their target already standing well away.

Bolitho tried to relax his limbs but his whole body felt like a taut lashing which was about to snap.

In the blink of an eye, *Achates* had been rendered helpless.

Had this been a fight in earnest, their attacker would already be tacking about to rake them from stem to stern.

High above the deck the topmen yelled to one another as they tried to shorten sail before the ship was completely dismasted.

Keen exclaimed despairingly, 'I'll never forget this. *Never!*' He looked at Bolitho as if for an answer. 'They fired on us without cause.'

Bolitho saw order being restored, the motion becoming easier as *Achates* responded to the helm, her shorn topgallant mast poking above the confusion like a broken tusk.

He said, 'They had a cause right enough, and I intend to discover what it was. When that happens we shall be ready.'

Keen saw some of his lieutenants hurrying aft for orders. The older hands would be comparing him with the previous captain. Whatever they thought, it was not a good beginning.

Bolitho said, 'Stand down the people and get the ship under way.'

It was all he could do to keep his voice level. They had been hit, and men had been lost, unless the quarter-boat had found any survivors among the flotsam astern.

But for some instinct, a sense of warning, he might never have ordered Keen to close with the stranger.

It was pointless to pursue the chase, the other ship was already drawing away under every sail she could carry.

He felt sorry for Keen. After all his work to obey his admiral's wishes, his success at surprising the other captain, when the trap had been sprung the enemy had been ready, Keen had not.

Tuson, the ship's surgeon, his white hair ruffling in the wind, was gesturing towards the piles of tangled rigging. Some other men must have been caught there too.

Keen listened to his lieutenants, his face pale and grim.

It was a lesson he would not forget, Bolitho thought.

He saw Adam watching him anxiously. Thinking perhaps of his father. When he had flown false colours and fired on Bolitho's ship.

Bolitho walked to the poop and ducked his head as he strode into the shadows between decks.

I too had forgotten the lesson. It could have been the last dawn after all.

4

A Place to Meet

'Nor'-west by north, sir. Steady as she goes!' Even the helmsman sounded hushed as under topsails and jib *Achates* glided very slowly towards her anchorage.

It was noon, with the sun high overhead and burning the bare-shouldered seamen who waited at the braces or were spread out on the topsail yards for the last cable or so of their journey.

Bolitho stood apart from Keen and his officers as he watched the shoreline spread and strengthen through a shimmering haze.

They had passed abeam of Cape Cod at dawn, but with the wind dropping to a mere breath of a breeze it had taken them this long to close with the land.

Bolitho raised a glass to his eye and studied the foreshore, the mass of masts and furled sails, the living evidence of a port's prosperity. Ships and flags of every nation, with lighters alongside and harbour craft plying back and forth to the jetties like water-beetles.

There were several men-of-war, he noticed. Two American frigates, and three Frenchmen, one a big third-rate with a rear-admiral's flag flapping listlessly at the mizzen.

Bolitho shifted his glass to the spit of land which was reaching out slowly towards the larboard bow. There was a tell-tale line of grey fortifications with a flag high overhead.

He examined his feelings, aware of the sudden dryness in his throat. It was about nineteen years since he had sailed along and landed on these shores. Another war, and different ships. He wondered how it might have changed, how he would react.

He heard Keen say sharply, 'Begin the salute, Mr Braxton!'

The crash of the first gun echoed and re-echoed across Massachusetts Bay like a thunder-clap while the smoke billowed over the quiet water as if unable to rise. Gulls and other sea-birds rose screaming from their perches and from the sea itself, as gun by gun the ship and the shore battery exchanged salutes.

Bolitho thought of the days which had followed their mauling by the unknown ship. The anger and humiliation had given way to a feverish determination to 'put the score right', as Allday had described it. There had been more damage to rigging than to the hull, and everyone from Keen to the ship's boys had seemed unflagging in their efforts to complete the repairs before the ship anchored at Boston.

A new topgallant mast had been set up, fresh rigging and sails hauled aloft even in the teeth of a strong north-easterly wind. Paint, tar and sweat had achieved wonders.

The mood had been infectious, and Bolitho had even ordered the four wooden Quakers to be removed from his quarters and replaced by the eighteen-pounders. It might mean less room, but it marked a new determination that he would never lower his guard again.

He saw an American guard-boat riding above her own reflection, the oars motionless as she waited to guide the British man-of-war to the allotted place.

Bolitho shaded his eyes to watch the shore. White houses, several churches, the glitter of sunlight on carriages and windows along the waterfront. Perhaps there were many there who were watching the slow-moving ship and remembering the bitter times of revolution and war, brother against brother, hate against hate.

'Ready, sir!'

Keen replied, 'Hands wear ship!'

Quantock responded like a pistol-spring. 'Lee braces there! Wear ship!'

Bolitho glanced at the main-topsail. It had barely enough air to move its belly. Another minute or so and they would have lost the wind altogether.

'Tops'l sheets!' Quantock was leaning over the quarterdeck rail, his speaking-trumpet weaving from side to side as he watched his men high above. 'Tops'l clew-lines!'

Keen said, 'Helm alee.'

Achates turned gently into the dying breeze, the white ripple beneath her stem almost gone as the way went off her.

'*Let go!*'

Keen crossed to the opposite side of the deck before the great anchor had hit the sea-bed.

'Awnings and winds'ls, Mr Quantock. Lively now. There are a thousand glasses on us today.'

Bolitho bit his lip. Keen was on edge. He more than anyone aboard was still brooding over the short encounter with the mystery ship.

Two men had died that day. One drowned, the other crushed under an avalanche of broken rigging and canvas. But it went deeper than that with Keen. A sailor's life was full of hazards. More men died of falls from rigging and yards, or were permanently injured in their fight against sea and wind, than under an enemy's broadside.

Keen felt it badly. In spite of his experience and undoubted skill in battle, he felt himself to be lacking in judgement. Or perhaps it was because he was Bolitho's flag-captain which made it seem so much worse.

Bolitho had been a flag-captain more than once himself and could guess what Keen must be enduring. Once he had been grateful when his admiral had left him alone to consider his mistakes and to put them to rights. He would certainly allow Keen the same opportunity.

Achates swung easily to her cable, while on deck and gangways the hands worked like demons to sway out the boats and spread awnings in an attempt to hold the glare at bay.

Bolitho saw Knocker, the master, dismiss the helmsmen

and rub his long chin as he examined some calculations on the midshipman of the watch's slate by the compass.

He should feel pleased with himself, Bolitho thought. In spite of everything *Achates* had sailed from Hampshire to Massachusetts Bay in the record time of sixteen days. For a two-decker, repairing her wounds under way, that was no small achievement. He thought of voicing his congratulations to the unsmiling sailing-master but when he looked again he had vanished into the chart room.

Bolitho walked to the nettings and watched the boats which were already pulling slowly around the new arrival. Tanned faces, bright gowns, curious stares. Boston had seen every kind of vessel drop anchor, but not many King's ships since 'the troubles'.

He heard a step on deck and saw his nephew with a great wad of papers under one arm.

'I see you are taking your duties seriously, Adam.'

The black-haired lieutenant smiled. 'Aye, sir. I would never wish to rise higher than my present station if *this* is the reward!'

Bolitho matched his mood. They had still barely mentioned the one gesture which had drawn them even closer together. But it was there. Like a bond, something unbreakable.

In the evenings, as the ship had continued on her passage to Boston, Adam had made a point of visiting him in his quarters when Bolitho had known that the conviviality of the wardroom would have been far more in keeping for any young officer. But as day followed day Bolitho had thought of Belinda, had wondered how she was faring as her time approached. Adam had sensed his anxiety and had wanted to share it or, better still, dispel it altogether.

Bolitho knew that had he been in Keen's position the work and demands of the ship would have kept him from his private worries, but alone for long periods of time, or with only Allday or his clerk to talk to, he had too much leisure to brood on his concern for Belinda.

Now, with the ship at anchor, her work done for the present, it was at last his turn to act, to repay the confidence Sheaffe had allowed him.

Lieutenant Mountsteven, who was the officer of the watch, touched his hat and said, 'Boat approaching, sir.'

Keen nodded and looked at Bolitho. 'Visitors, sir.'

Bolitho knew it was his polite way of asking him to leave. 'I'll be in my cabin if you require me.'

Bolitho turned aft and heard the marines hurrying to the entry port, the bark of commands as *Achates* prepared to receive a greeting from the land.

Ozzard was tidying up the great cabin, although it always appeared perfect to Bolitho. He glanced at the tethered shape of one of the eighteen-pounders and was glad he had ordered its replacement. It would act as a reminder. The task he had been given was not going to be easy. He tried to stifle the bitterness. If it was a routine task, a more important officer would have been sent in his place. But if anything went wrong, they would, as always, require a scapegoat in the halls of admiralty.

He heard the calls trilling at the entry port and pictured the visitors being received with customary formality.

He walked to the open stern windows and saw a boat idling beneath *Achates'* great shadow, the passengers pointing and peering at the ship's gilded stern and counter.

It was unnerving to realize his brother had once sailed from here, had walked the streets among people like these. He had known nothing of Adam's existence then. Now Adam was here in his place. He felt a twinge of uneasiness. Perhaps he had been wrong after all to bring him, career or not.

The door opened and Adam stood watching him, a heavily sealed envelope in his hand.

He said, 'We are invited to a reception this evening, Uncle.' He held out the envelope. 'I have just been told that the President of the United States has sent one of his own senior advisers to meet you.'

Bolitho smiled wryly. 'In that case the whole world will

know what we are about, Adam. If they were expecting us it
was hardly surprising we suffered that encounter just eight
days out from England.'

Adam nodded. 'We seemed to have caused quite a stir.'
His face broke into a grin. 'Perhaps they want to pay their
taxes to King George after all!'

Bolitho shook his head. 'If you talk like that ashore,
Adam, we are far more likely to start another war!'

Later, as he lay back in a chair and Allday shaved him with
extra care, he tried to measure the extent of his responsibility.

The frigate *Sparrowhawk* would be on her way here shortly.
Captain Duncan was less of a diplomat than he was. He
would make his report to San Felipe's governor before con-
tinuing his way to Boston for orders, but would leave little
doubt as to what the eventual outcome would be.

It seemed inhuman and senseless to hand the island back to
the French, no matter what Sheaffe had said. It was not a
question of strategy or diplomacy, it was a matter of people.
The island had defended itself more than once against enemy
assaults, and had sent its own vessels to seek out prizes and
harass ships and islands alike in the King's name.

In London and Paris it would seem different. Now, as
Allday's razor moved steadily around his throat, it took on
the complexity of a Chinese puzzle.

The evening air was mercifully cooler after the oven-heat in
an anchored ship, and as Bolitho climbed down into the
barge he felt strangely excited. Like someone stepping into
the unknown.

Allday growled, 'Give way, all.' Then with measured
strokes the green-hulled boat pulled away from the main-
chains and turned in a shallow arc towards the shore.

The first lieutenant had been left in charge of the ship, a
bitter pill in such a pleasant looking town, Bolitho thought.
He glanced at Keen who was joining him at the reception and
wondered if he was feeling less strained. He had been kept

busier than anyone since the anchor had been dropped, for quite apart from the ship's affairs there had been a steady stream of visitors, each of whom had been received as befitted his station. The captains of the American frigates and some of their subordinates, the officer of the guard, and an extremely pleasant young man who was the son of their host this evening.

The barge pulled strongly beneath the tapering jib-boom and Bolitho could not resist the temptation to look for some sign of the damage sustained in their short encounter. He saw nothing, a compliment to the carpenter and his crew.

He glanced at the handsome figurehead. It was pure white, with one arm outstretched, the other holding a short sword. Achates, faithful friend and armour-bearer of Aeneas.

Beneath the paint the carved wood was smooth and well-worn. It had seen more horizons than any of the ship's company and had weathered every kind of storm.

The barge swept past a lordly Indiaman which was busily loading cargo, despite the lateness of the hour. An officer hurried to her taffrail and doffed his hat as the vice-admiral's boat swept past the stern.

It was ironic that it had been a Company dispute over tea which had fanned the fires of revolution, Bolitho thought. Now, whereas men-of-war were restricted to the necessary areas of their respective flags, the powerful traders came and went as they pleased.

Allday rapped out another order and the bowman rose from his thwart, boat-hook ready to snap down on to a mooring chain.

There were plenty of townspeople thronging the jetty, and many of them had seemingly been here all day to watch the anchored *Achates*. The watermen of Boston must be making a fortune from their curious passengers.

Keen, Captain Dewar of the Royal Marines, two lieutenants and Adam Bolitho were to be the guests of an influential Boston merchant named Jonathan Chase, while some of the ship's other officers had been invited elsewhere. Keen had warned them to guard their tongues and to listen for any mention of their encounter with the strange ship which would show that the news had preceded their arrival.

Bolitho glanced at some of the young women on the jetty. A few of the trusted seamen and marines would also be allowed ashore, and from the look of these smiling girls the British sailors would be hard put to hold their tongues.

But everything must appear normal and relaxed, with all the old animosities put aside if not actually forgotten.

The bargemen tossed their oars, and Allday removed his hat and watched to make sure Bolitho did not slip on the stone stairs.

Bolitho smiled at him. 'Good crew, Allday.'

Even Allday had admitted that the new barge was a credit to the ship. In their checkered shirts and tarred hats, each man with a pigtail exactly the same length, they could not have been better chosen.

Their host's son, Timothy, was waiting beside two elegant carriages.

As Bolitho approached and some of the onlookers pressed forward for a glimpse of the newcomers, Timothy Chase extended his hand.

'You are *welcome* here, Admiral. My mother says it is a sign for the future.'

Captain Dewar climbed swiftly from the barge and the sight of his bright tunic brought a cry from the crowd.

'Watch out, boys, the redcoats are comin' back!'

But there was no hostility and more than a few guffaws from the onlookers.

The journey to the Chase residence passed all too quickly for Bolitho, with his host's son pointing out landmarks and fine houses as the carriage rattled along the road from the harbour.

He was obviously very proud of the town where he had been born and brought up. At a guess he was about the same age as Adam, although less reserved as he described each important house and its occupants.

'Boston houses, taken collectively, make a better appearance than those of any other town in New England, sir.'

Most of them were built of wood, Bolitho noticed, but some had façades which had been cut and shaped to represent stone.

Bolitho smiled to himself. His host had done well. But he knew from his secret instructions that Chase had made his original wealth from privateering against the British during the revolution.

Boston had been a privateering lair, as had many smaller harbours as far north as Portland.

The two carriages left the road and rolled up a long driveway towards a beautifully proportioned house of three storeys. Like many of the others it was white with tall green shutters by each window, some of which were already brightly lit and welcoming.

Bolitho said quietly, 'Well, Adam, what d'you think?'

Keeping his features equally composed, his nephew answered, 'I could very easily get used to luxury, sir.'

It was not hard to picture their host as he had once been on the deck of a privateer. He had a loud, thick voice which must have found its edge when shouting orders in a storm or above the crash of cannon fire. Jonathan Chase was square and heavily built, with iron-grey hair and skin like tooled leather.

'Well, Admiral, this is indeed a pleasure.' He grasped Bolitho's hand and eyed him curiously. 'An honour too, to have such a gallant sailor in my home.'

Bolitho warmed to him. 'It was good of you to offer your house for this meeting.'

Chase grinned. 'When Thomas Jefferson *suggests* a thing you don't argue too much, my friend! He may have been president for only a year, but he's learned already that power is heady medicine!' It seemed to amuse him.

Negro footmen whisked away the hats of the guests and Bolitho followed Chase into a great hall filled with people. Chase nodded towards a tray which was loaded with glasses.

'I hope the wine is to your taste, Admiral. It's French.'

Bolitho smiled gravely. 'Is it, indeed.'

Faces swam round him, and as Chase introduced his friends and associates Bolitho became very aware of the man's presence and authority.

Keen had been immediately partnered by two very attractive ladies, and Captain Dewar was being led out on to a terrace by another who was clinging to his arm as if she intended to share him with nobody.

Chase lowered his glass and studied Adam for several seconds.

'Your aide, Admiral, what is he, son, or little brother?'

'Nephew.'

Chase beamed. 'You and I will creep away presently and split a bottle of excellent brandy.' He tapped the side of his nose. 'We can have a talk before our government man arrives.'

He gestured suddenly. 'Nephew, eh. Should have guessed.' He raised his voice. 'Over here, Robina. Someone I'd like you to meet.'

The girl named Robina was a beautiful creature. Slim, graceful, and with a sparkle in her eyes which would turn any man's head.

Chase boomed, 'My niece, Admiral.'

She slipped her arm through Adam's and said, 'I'll show you the gardens, Lieutenant.' She tossed her head at her uncle. '*They'll* want to yarn about old times!'

Bolitho smiled. Adam was obviously entranced and allowed himself to be led away without a word.

Chase chuckled. 'Look good together, eh?'

Then he glanced around at his chattering guests.

'I think we can go to my study now. They've forgotten we exist.'

The great study was panelled and like a part of America's young history. Chase had collected many relics of the sea and ships, symbols perhaps of his own stormy beginnings.

Whales' teeth and a harpoon were just a small part. 'To

remind me of the old days here.' Paintings of battles, with a British ship on fire in the process of surrendering.

Chase said cheerfully, 'You didn't win all the fights at sea, y'know, Admiral.' He became suddenly serious. 'Samuel Fane, the President's emissary, is a hard bargainer. I like him well enough, for a government man that is, but he hates the British.' He grinned hugely. 'Thought you should know, though from all I've read and heard about you, you're more than able to take care of yourself.'

Bolitho smiled. 'I appreciate your frankness.'

Chase slopped some brandy into two enormous glasses.

'Think nothing of it. I fought against King George and I was good at the trade. But peace, like war, makes strange bedfellows. You accept that or capsize in the world *we* live in.'

In the gardens at the rear of the big house the trees and shrubs were already deep in purple shadow. Adam walked arm in arm with the girl, barely daring to speak in case he said something clumsy and spoiled the moment forever. She was without doubt the most beautiful being he had ever laid eyes on.

She stopped and, seizing his hands in hers, swung him round to face her.

'Now, *come along*, Lieutenant, I have done too much talking. They say I chatter so. I want to know all about you. Your name is Adam and you are the admiral's aide. Tell me more.'

Surprisingly, Adam found it easy to speak with her. As they strolled through the shadows he told her of his life as a sea officer, of his home in Cornwall, and all the while he was very conscious of her hand through his arm.

She said suddenly, 'You are the admiral's nephew, Adam?' Even the way she spoke his name was like pure music. 'Yes.'

She said, 'I do not live in Boston. My family is in Newburyport, some thirty miles north from here. It's strange, I hadn't thought of it before. My father sometimes speaks of a man who used to live in our town. His name was Bolitho too.'

Adam tried to think clearly. 'In Newburyport?'

'Yes.' She squeezed his arm. 'You sound as if you have remembered something.'

He looked at her and wanted to hold her.

'I think it must have been my father.'

She was about to laugh when she realized the seriousness of his tone, the importance of this discovery.

'My uncle says that your ship will be in Boston for weeks. You shall come to Newburyport and meet my family.' She reached up and touched his cheek with her gloved fingers. 'Do not be sad, Adam. If you have a secret, I can share it with you. But tell me only when you want to.'

'I want to.' He found that he meant it with all his heart.

From the study window Bolitho saw them cross the terrace and was moved.

It was time Adam found some enjoyment, even for a fleeting moment. He had known nothing but war and the hard life in King's ships since he had walked all that way from Penzance to find his place in the Bolitho family. Bolitho could picture him exactly. A thin, frightened boy, and yet with the defiant restlessness of a young colt. He thought he heard the girl named Robina laugh. Yes, he was glad for Adam's sake.

A footman opened the double doors of the library and a tall figure in a bottle-green coat and white stockings strode into the study.

Chase said quickly, 'This here is Samuel Fane from the capital.'

Fane had a narrower face with all the animation contained in a pair of deepset eyes which crowded against a strong, beak-like nose.

'Vice-Admiral Bolitho.' He nodded a greeting. 'Well, let's get down to business.'

Bolitho let his arm fall to his side. Maybe Fane did not like shaking hands with an old enemy. But it was a snub, intended or not.

Curiously, it made him feel calmer in some strange way.

Like fighting a duel. When you accept there is no easy way out after all.

Fane said in the same flat voice, 'San Felipe. Now, could you please explain to me, Admiral, how it is that your government thinks it has the right to take or give away people and territory as if they were of no consequence? By what *right*?'

Chase said uneasily, 'Calm down, Sam. You know it is not like that.'

'Do I?' The deepset eyes had not moved from Bolitho.

Bolitho said, 'It was agreed at the peace conference.' He smiled gently. 'As I am sure you are aware. May I assume that the French government has already spoken to yours about it?'

Chase interrupted angrily. 'Course they did. Tell him, Sam, and get down off your high horse. The war's over, remember?'

Fane regarded him coldly. 'I am constantly reminded of it when I see how some have grown rich on the blood of others.'

Bolitho saw the sparks in Chase's eyes and said, 'I thought the French were still your friends?'

Fane shrugged. 'Once, and in the future mebbee. But on San Felipe, across the southern approaches, that's different.'

Bolitho said, 'The people on San Felipe are British subjects.'

Chase grinned. 'So were most of us. Once.'

Fane did not hear him. 'Some while ago I received a despatch from the governor of San Felipe. He was worried, naturally, at the British government's intransigence. He has no desire to accept the choice given him, that is to leave a prospering island to the French or to remain there under a foreign flag.'

'I can understand that.'

'Can you, Admiral? That encourages me a little. However, the United States government is not prepared to stand by and allow human beings to be used for barter like cattle in an African slave village.'

Bolitho found that he was on his feet, his voice angry as he retorted, 'Then there is no point in my wasting your time, Mr Fane, or mine!'

Chase said quickly, 'Easy, you two! Blazes, Sam, the admiral is my guest. I'll not have you brawling like a pair of hell-cats!'

Fane relented slightly. 'It will have to be a compromise.'

Bolitho sat down again. 'In what fashion?'

'Our government would be prepared to accept San Felipe's request to come under the United States' protection.'

'That's impossible.'

'If the French agree, Admiral, would *you*?'

Bolitho glanced at Chase but he was staring at the whales' teeth.

He knew too. They all did. It was not a compromise at all. It was blackmail.

He tried to keep his voice calm. 'The governor had no authority to make such a request, from you or anyone else. We are caught in the tragedy of history. There is nothing we can do about it.'

Fane regarded him bleakly. 'We shall see.'

He added, 'Your flagship has the extended courtesy of my government. This matter cannot be settled in minutes. We must think on it further.'

Bolitho nodded. Fane had been testing him, goading him, for reasons he could still only guess at.

He could not resist saying, 'Your government has also extended a welcome to another of my ships, Mr Fane. The *Sparrowhawk*. She will be joining me shortly.'

Fane grunted. 'Yes. I know.' He thrust his hands beneath his coat tails and added, 'I must leave now.' He gave a curt nod. 'Admiral.'

Chase left the room with him and Bolitho walked to the window again. But where the young lieutenant and the fair-haired girl had been walking was all in darkness.

Bolitho turned to face the doors as he heard Chase's heavy footsteps returning.

In many ways it was harder than fighting a battle, he thought. And far less rewarding.

5

'There may be thunder . . .'

The weeks which followed the reception at Chase's fine house taxed Bolitho to the limit. Jonathan Chase and several other wealthy Bostonians took it upon themselves to make them welcome, and nightly entertainment of one kind or another had become a regular feature for *Achates'* wardroom.

And yet Bolitho was plagued by the idea that the lack of news and assistance by the President's representative, Samuel Fane, were linked in some way.

Perhaps he should have ignored the outline of his orders and proceeded first to San Felipe without entrusting the opening move to Captain Duncan in the *Sparrowhawk*. But had he done so his action might have been construed as arrogance or worse.

And where was *Sparrowhawk*? What had Duncan found so important that he had delayed joining him here at Boston?

On this particular day Bolitho had been unable to touch his midday meal at all. The meat and bread were fresh, brought off shore by one of Chase's own boats, yet he could not face it.

Around and above him the ship was resting in the swelter-ing heat, and there was the usual heady smell of rum as each mess issued its ration for the day.

Maybe Sheaffe had known it would all be a waste of time which might end in disagreement with the Americans.

He tugged the shirt away from his skin. It felt like a wet rag. He made himself remain in his chair, knowing he would only begin to pace about the cabin like a caged lion if he did not.

Belinda. He twisted round in the chair and stared through the stern windows until his eyes watered. It would be over by now. They would have a child, unless . . .

Suppose something had gone wrong? It was her first time. Anything might happen.

He saw the distant houses move into view as *Achates* swung indifferently to her cable. It would be better to get to sea again. To *do* something.

There was a light tap at the screen door and Keen entered, his eyes moving quickly to the untouched plate on Bolitho's table.

'The American frigates are shortening their cables, sir.'

Bolitho nodded. 'Yes. Only the French will be here now.'

Keen said, 'In my opinion, sir, we should have another vessel attached to us for communications.'

'You've been thinking about Duncan's *Sparrowhawk* too?'

Keen shrugged. 'Well, yes, as a matter of fact. Without even a brig in company we are deaf and dumb to everything beyond the harbour limits.'

Yovell, the clerk, hovered in the doorway. 'Beg pardon, zur, there are some papers for yew to sign.'

Bolitho thought suddenly of his nephew. Adam had asked permission to escort Chase's niece to her home in Newburyport. He could envy him his freedom from the endless waiting and the uncertainty. Bolitho knew he had been poor company and he had even exploded over one of Allday's comments. He had immediately relented. It was not Allday's fault. It was not anybody's.

Bolitho read swiftly through Yovell's handwriting and then put his signature at the bottom. No wonder they said the Admiralty was crammed with written reports. Did anyone ever read them? he wondered.

He said abruptly, 'I shall try once more to discuss the matter of San Felipe with the Americans, after that I shall be pleased to sail for the island, *Sparrowhawk* or not. You might send word privately to Antigua if you can discover a ship's master for the task. The admiral at English Harbour should be told what we are about. If I add a line to your despatch we *might* even worm a brig out of his command, eh?'

Ozzard entered and removed the tray with nothing but a reproachful glance to reveal what he thought about it.

Keen said, 'You don't think the Americans would interfere with our affairs, sir?'

'Those frigates, you mean?' Bolitho shook his head. 'It would be unwise. They may voice their displeasure, but they're more likely to remain on the fence as spectators.'

The first lieutenant appeared at the screen door, his head stooped beneath the deckhead beams.

'Your pardon, sir, but Mr Chase's launch is approaching. He has the *other* gentleman with him.'

Bolitho and Keen exchanged glances.

Bolitho said quietly, 'Fane, the President's emissary, at long last. Now perhaps we can settle the matter.'

Keen picked up his hat and grinned. 'Full guard of honour, Mr Quantock. If there is to be a squall, it will not be of our making!'

Allday padded from the adjoining cabin and glanced at the sword rack, then with a slight hesitation he took down the brightly gilded presentation blade which had been given to Bolitho after the Battle of the Nile.

He gave the old sword a pat and murmured, 'You rest easy.'

Bolitho allowed him to clip the glittering presentation sword to his belt.

The old family sword was for fighting. This was a time for diplomacy.

Some twelve hundred miles south of where Bolitho contained his impatience and waited to receive Mr Samuel Fane, His Britannic Majesty's frigate *Sparrowhawk* of twenty-six guns was becalmed in blinding sunlight. Two of her boats moved sluggishly on tow-lines ahead of their parent ship, more to give her steerage-way than with any hope of finding a wind.

It had been like this for three whole days since the frigate had weighed anchor in San Felipe, her mission there only partially completed.

In his cabin Captain James Duncan sat at a table, his face set in a frown, as he added another paragraph to an already lengthy letter. It was to his wife and, like most married sea officers, Duncan continued each letter with the same regularity as a personal log. He did not know when the letter would be completed, even less when he would be able to pass it to some home-bound vessel so that his wife would eventually read it in their Dorset home.

Duncan, for all his bluff ways, was very soft where his wife was concerned. They had been married for only two years, and he had been with her in that time for less than a month. He had no regrets, it was part of the sacrifice you had to make if you intended the Navy as a career. Duncan was a post-captain and had only just passed his twenty-seventh birthday. If he held this command under Bolitho there would be no stopping him, even in a time of uneasy peace.

Like many of his contemporaries, Duncan had little faith in a lasting peace. He had distinguished himself in three major battles and had been extremely successful in other ship-to-ship engagements where the cut and thrust of every good frigate captain showed its worth.

He admired Bolitho tremendously, not merely for his courage and skill – that Duncan could take for granted – but for his true interest in those who served him. Although he would never admit it, Duncan tried to model himself on Bolitho.

That was the main reason for his frown. His visit to San Felipe had not been a success. The governor, Sir Humphrey Rivers, had treated him more as a stupid subordinate than the captain of a King's ship and Bolitho's own representative.

Duncan knew all about ships and the sea, but he had no knowledge at all of men like Rivers.

Rivers had lost his temper at their first meeting. In his

impressive house which nestled comfortably amidst a great plantation, Rivers had shouted, 'There's a graveyard by the harbour, Captain! Full of good men who have fought for this island. I'll not betray their trust by handing over everything to the French. Damn your eyes if I shall!'

Duncan secretly agreed with him, but he was used to obeying orders. In any case, he did not like the man, and thought him an arrogant pig.

Bolitho would not thank him for bringing him such empty news. If Rivers refused to comply with the agreed terms he might find himself charged with treason, or an act of mutiny, or whatever governors were disciplined by. Duncan frowned more deeply and put his pen to paper again.

The deck gave a shudder and a pair of brass dividers clattered from another table.

Duncan lurched to his feet as the ship slowly came to life beneath him.

He hurried on deck and found his first lieutenant and sailing-master staring up at the limp canvas as very gently a breeze pushed against the rigging.

Duncan dashed the sweat from his eyes. It was not much, but . . .

'Mr Palmer! Recall those boats and hoist 'em inboard. Pipe all hands.' He clapped the lieutenant on the shoulder and added, 'God damn it, Mr Palmer, maybe we've seen the last of this place, eh?'

He crossed to the side and grasped the sun-heated rail with his powerful hands. He saw the first boat cast off the tow and . pull gratefully towards the ship, its sunburned oarsmen almost too weary to make the effort.

Duncan wondered how the other ship was faring. They had sighted her just before both vessels had been becalmed in the stifling heat.

The first lieutenant returned as the hands swarmed up to man halliards and braces.

He said, 'The masthead reported that our shy companion was still with us at eight bells, sir.'

To confirm it the lookout's voice made several of the seamen look up at his lofty perch.

'Deck thar! Ship on th' weather-bow! She's settin' 'er t'gan's'ls!'

Duncan grunted and turned to watch his own ship lean slightly to the mounting pressure. The second boat was being swayed up and over the gangway. His *Sparrowhawk* was moving again.

The sailing-master said, 'She'll be on a converging tack with us, sir.'

'Put a good man to watch her.'

Duncan pushed the sudden anxiety from his thoughts. For a small moment he had thought it might be *Achates*, Bolitho coming to look for him, to discover the meaning of the delay.

Blocks clattered and lines snaked through the sheaves as slowly, and then more confidently, *Sparrowhawk* responded to the pressure in her sails.

'North by west, sir! Full an' bye!'

Duncan rubbed his reddened face and waited for the sails to fill again. It was not much, but enough to make her thrust through the water. Even the tiny island which had shown itself on the horizon had dipped over the sea's rim before the master had identified it. Probably one of the islets of the Bahama chain, Duncan thought.

There were some little ones off San Felipe too. One even had a strange mission church on it, and he had been told that some monks existed there, entirely cut off from everything.

San Felipe had originally been Spanish, so it seemed likely that the monks were the last survivors of that occupation.

Duncan felt in better spirits. He had, after all, done what he had been ordered to do. Bolitho would know how to interpret what he had seen and heard.

'I'm going below, Mr Palmer. I've a letter to finish. Who knows, I may be able to send it off sooner than I thought!'

Palmer smiled. When the captain was in good humour the ship was always a better place.

As the wind continued to fill the sails, and froth gurgled

around the bows, the other ship grew larger while she continued purposefully on a converging tack.

Too large for a frigate, Palmer thought, as he clung to the weather shrouds and trained his telescope on her. She was shining in the bright glare, her chequered gun-ports almost awash as she found the wind which had not yet reached *Sparrowhawk*.

West Indiaman probably, he decided. They were as smart as paint these days. It was said that a grocery captain could earn as much on one passage as would take ten years in the Navy.

'She's hoisted a signal, sir!'

'I can see that, dammit!' Palmer was tired from standing so long in the heat, praying for a wind. It put an edge to his voice which was unusual for him.

The signals midshipman swallowed hard and levelled his big glass on the other vessel, his face screwed up with concentration as he held the lens on the brightly coloured flags at her yard.

'She wishes to speak with us, sir!'

The first lieutenant swore under his breath. It was probably of no importance at all, and to heave to while they exchanged useless information might mean losing the wind again.

He snapped, 'Acknowledge the signal, Mr Clements.' He beckoned to the midshipman of the watch. 'My respects to the captain, Mr Evans. Tell him we shall have to heave to.'

Palmer swung away. The captain's good mood would vanish now.

Duncan, his shirt open to his waist, strode from the companion-way and eyed the other vessel without comment. She could have important news which had a bearing on their mission. Her master might just as easily be eager to exchange gossip. Two ships meeting far from home were all that was required.

'Shorten sail, Mr Palmer. Stand by to come about.'

He clasped his hands behind him and watched his men scamper to their stations.

'Put the helm down!'

Duncan beckoned to the midshipman. 'Glass, Mr Evans.'

He took the telescope from the boy's hand and glanced at him as he did so. Midshipman Evans was thirteen, the youngest in *Sparrowhawk*'s gun-room. A likeable youth, who had been mastheaded more than once since leaving England for his practical jokes.

Duncan levelled the glass and braced his legs as the ship heeled violently in a trough and the men up forward loosed the head-sail sheets to allow *Sparrowhawk* to swing through the eye of the wind. To a landsman the ship would appear in confusion, with rippling sails and clattering rigging, but in a moment or so she would come round on the opposite tack and reduce sail even more.

Duncan smiled grimly. He liked his ship to be handled firmly, like a strong-willed horse.

He stiffened as the other ship swam hugely into the lens. Her yards were swinging, her sails filling like metal breast-plates as she changed tack, not into the wind, but to starboard, and as her fore-course thundered out from its yard she seemed to lean forward as she swept down across the frigate's stern.

Duncan yelled, '*Belay that order*, Mr Palmer! Bring her about again!'

Men tumbled in confusion and braces and halliards squealed through the blocks and more hands threw themselves among their companions to try and haul the yards round.

Duncan reeled as his ship tried to respond, but she was nearly aback, the sails billowing and cracking against the masts and shrouds.

'*Beat to quarters!*'

Duncan stared wildly at the other ship, his skin like ice despite the sun's heat. *He should have seen it*. Now it was already too late, and even as he stared he saw the other vessel's gun-ports open, the black muzzles poking out into the sunlight, while his own startled marine drummers started the staccato beat which brought more men pouring up from between decks, some still unaware of the danger.

Duncan made himself face the regular flashes along the other vessel's side, the darting orange tongues and rolling bank of smoke. Then in seconds a torrent of iron smashed into the frigate's hull and above the deck, tearing down rigging and spars, punching holes in the flapping canvas, and worse, ploughing through the stern to turn the crowded gun-deck into a bloody shambles.

Duncan clung to the nettings, bellowing like a wounded bull as a ball slammed into one of the quarterdeck guns and flung splinters across the planking, cutting down men and daubing scarlet patterns to mark where they fell.

He felt a blow in his side like the blade of an axe, and when he looked he saw blood pumping down his leg, and when the pain came he could hear himself moaning with agony.

A great shadow swept over him, and with a thundering roar the mizzen-mast and rigging crashed over the side carrying seamen and marines with them.

More violent shocks battered at the hull like iron rams, and Duncan had to hold on to the nettings to prevent himself from falling. Their attacker was following them round, her sails rising above the smoke like the wings of hell itself. She was firing without a break, and still not one of *Sparrowhawk*'s guns had been loaded. Men lay dead and dying everywhere, and when he peered at the helm Duncan saw that the wheel was in fragments, the master and his helmsmen scattered by the fury of the bombardment.

'Mr Palmer!'

His cry was less than a croak. But the first lieutenant was on his knees by the rail, his mouth like a black hole as he screamed silently at his hands which lay before him like torn gloves.

Duncan fell down as more great crashes rocked the hull. He could hear the balls slamming through the deck below and saw smoke rising from an open hatch. *She was on fire*.

He tried to stand, his rage and his despair making him

terrible to see. He had fallen in his own blood, and he could feel the strength running away to match the terrible patterns on the deck around him.

'Let me help, sir!'

Duncan thrust his arm around the boy's shoulders. It was little Evans, and the realization helped to steady him.

He gasped, 'Done for, boy. See to the others.' He felt the midshipman shudder and saw the fear bright in his eyes. He gripped him more tightly with his bloody arm. 'Stand to, boy, you're a King's officer today. Get them — ' Then he fell and this time he did not rise.

A few seamen and marines ran aft and would have flung themselves into the sea astern but for the thirteen-year-old midshipman.

He shouted, 'Quarter-boat! Bosun's mate, take charge there!'

When one tried to knock him aside he snatched a pistol and fired it above their heads. For a moment longer they stared at each other like madmen, then, obedient to their training, they tossed their weapons aside and ran to haul the quarter-boat alongside.

A few shots were still hitting the hull, but *Sparrowhawk* had no fight left in her. She was settling down, the sea exploring the orlop and reaching up further still so that there was a glint of water below the companion.

Evans ran to aid his friend, the signals midshipman, but he was already dead, a hole in his chest big enough for a man's fist.

Evans stood up very carefully, his feet sliding in blood as the stern began to go under.

He thought he heard one of the other boats nearby, the third lieutenant trying to restore order and rally the survivors.

He looked at his dead captain, a man he had feared and admired. Now he was nothing, and Evans felt unnerved by it, cheated.

A burly marine, one of his comrades over his shoulder like

a sack, paused and gasped, 'Come along, sir. Nothin' 'ere now.'

The wounded man groaned and the one who was carrying him peered round, looking for a boat. But something in Evans' face held him there like a shouted command on the square. The marine had been at St Vincent and the Nile, and had seen many of his friends die like this.

He said roughly, 'You've done yer best, so come along er me, eh?'

The hull gave a great shiver. She was going.

The midshipman walked with the marine and did not even blink as the foremast thundered down like a falling cliff.

'I'm ready, thank you.' It seemed little enough comment for such a terrible moment.

As guns tore themselves loose from their lashings and crashed along the deck among the corpses and whimpering wounded, *Sparrowhawk* lifted her bows and dived steeply. The whirlpool of swirling wreckage, men and pieces of men remained for a long time, long enough for their attacker to make more sail and alter course to the westward.

There were two boats and a roughly lashed raft left as evidence of what had happened, with survivors floundering in search of a handhold or a place in one of them.

A week later, the American brig *Baltimore Lady*, on passage from Guadeloupe to New York, sighted one drifting boat and hove to to investigate. The boat was filled with sun-blackened men, some dead, apparently from wounds or burns, others barely able to speak. Deep score marks on the boat's planking showed where sharks had torn others from their handholds alongside. There was an officer of sorts in charge of the boat. The brig's mate later described him as 'less'n a boy'.

Midshipman Evans had obeyed Duncan's order, *'See to the others.'*

It was something he would remember for the rest of his life.

*

Samuel Fane regarded Bolitho without emotion as he said, 'I have spoken with the President and have also discussed the matter of San Felipe with the French admiral.'

Bolitho watched him calmly. There was no point in attacking Fane for going behind his back and speaking with the French flag-officer. He had every right to, if Boston was to be a neutral ground for the discussions.

Also, being aboard his own flagship made more of a difference than he would have expected. Ashore in Chase's fine house he was the stranger. Here in *Achates*, with familiar faces and sounds all around him, he felt assured and confident.

He said, 'No steps can be taken until I receive the report from my frigate captain. A compromise may be worked out, but only under the present conditions. Sir Humphrey Rivers is the British Governor of San Felipe, but nothing more than that.'

Jonathan Chase, who had swallowed two glasses of claret in his anxiety that it should be a better meeting than the previous one, exclaimed, 'No harm in that, eh, Sam?'

Fane's deepset eyes settled on him only briefly.

'Our government will not tolerate a war, large or small, where it might endanger United States' trade and progress. It makes more sense to me that the island should come under *our* protection, if that is the will of the people there.'

He gave a deep sigh. 'But if the admiral wishes to show his authority *first*, then I suppose we must indulge him.'

Chase held out his glass for Ozzard to refill.

'God damn it, Sam, do you never relax?'

Fane smiled wryly. 'Hardly at all.'

Feet moved on the deck overhead, and Bolitho heard a voice calling an order. It was his world. This sort of double-tongue was alien to him.

He stood up and walked to the stern windows. There was a slow, hot wind across Massachusetts Bay and the sky was slashed by thin, pink clouds. How inviting the sea looked.

Fane was saying, 'It might take a few months to settle, but

what of that? The French will not insist on immediate
occupation of the island. It will give all of us time.'

Bolitho suddenly saw a naval brig turning into the wind,
her anchor splashing down even as her sails were smartly
furled at their yards. The ensign which licked out from her
gaff was the same as the one at *Achates'* taffrail.

He replied, 'His Majesty's Government has entrusted me
with the task of handing over the island, sir. None of us
wants an uprising, especially now that the West Indies are
recovering from the war.'

A boat had been dropped from the brig and was already
speeding across the water towards the flagship.

Bolitho felt a nerve jump in his throat. What was it? News
from home already, could it be . . . ?'

He forced himself to face the others, his eyes almost blind
in the cabin's shady interior.

'I shall send a letter to your President. I appreciate very
much what he is trying to do – ' He broke off and turned
sharply as Ozzard murmured, 'It's the captain, sir.'

Keen stood in the doorway, his hat jammed beneath his
arm.

'Please forgive this interruption, sir.' He glanced at the
others. 'The commander of the brig *Electra* is come aboard.
He has news for you, sir.' His eyes were pleading. 'Very
serious news.'

Bolitho nodded. 'I'll not be long, gentlemen.'

He followed Keen from the cabin and saw a young officer
waiting by the chart room.

Keen said tightly, 'This is Commander Napier, sir.'

Bolitho looked at him impassively. 'Tell me.'

Napier swallowed hard. *Electra* was his first command, and
he had never spoken with a vice-admiral before.

'I was on passage to the south'rd when I sighted an Ameri-
can brig. She signalled for assistance, and when I boarded her
I found her to be carrying British seamen.' He flinched under
Bolitho's gaze. 'They were survivors.'

Bolitho saw Keen's face, he looked pale in spite of the sun.

The commander added quietly, 'From *Sparrowhawk*, sir.'

Bolitho clenched his hands together behind him to control his sense of shock. In his heart he had nursed a dread that something had happened to the little frigate. A storm, a reef, or one of a dozen disasters which can befall a ship sailing alone.

Napier continued, 'She was attacked, sir. A two-decker to all accounts, although – '

Bolitho could see it as if he had been there himself. Just as their attacker had fired on *Achates*. Without warning, except that this time her victim had been hopelessly outgunned even if Duncan had been expecting trouble.

'How many?'

Again the young commander could barely speak above a murmur.

'Twenty-five, sir, and some of those are in a poor way.'

Bolitho felt his skin go cold. Twenty-five, out of a company which had numbered two hundred souls.

'Any officers?' He barely recognized his own voice.

'None, sir. Just a midshipman. First commission too.'

Bolitho eyed him bitterly. Duncan had perished with his ship. He could picture him without effort. Duncan had even been to his wedding at Falmouth. A good man, strong and reliable.

It was impossible. A nightmare.

The commander took his silence for displeasure and hurried on, 'The midshipman said that the third lieutenant was in another boat but was badly wounded in the face and neck by splinters. During the night the boats drifted apart, and then the sharks came.' He looked at the deck.

'Bring the midshipman to me.' He saw his hesitation. 'Is he wounded?'

'No, sir.'

Keen said shortly, 'See to it.'

As the commander hurried away Bolitho said, 'Send word to my flag-lieutenant. He must return at once. Fast horse, anything.'

Keen stared at him. 'It *was* the same ship, wasn't it, sir?'

'I'm certain of it.' He eyed him steadily. 'Ask the surgeon to help with the wounded. The rest of *Sparrowhawk*'s people can be signed on to your books. I want them to be with us when we run that butcher to earth!'

Bolitho strode aft to the cabin. He knew he must look different in some way. Chase had a glass poised in the air, Ozzard was frozen in the act of refilling it. Fane's eyes followed him to the stern windows before he asked, 'Bad news, Admiral?'

Bolitho looked at him and tried to fight the sudden all-consuming anger which coursed through him like fire.

'I am leaving harbour as soon as all my people are aboard.'

Chase shifted in his chair as if to see him better.

'Not waiting for your frigate after all?'

Bolitho shook his head.

'I'm heartily sick of waiting.'

He saw the brig's boat going alongside again. It was cruel to send for the young midshipman after what he had endured. But he had to know everything the boy could tell him.

He said quietly, '*Sparrowhawk*'s been sunk.'

He heard Chase's quick intake of breath.

Bolitho added, 'So you see, gentlemen, there may be thunder before we can settle things to *everyone*'s satisfaction.'

6

No Easy Way

Captain Valentine Keen sat with legs crossed on one of Bolitho's chairs and watched his superior as he read through a despatch for the Admiralty. It would be put aboard the brig *Electra* and eventually be transferred to a fleet-courier so that it would be completely out-of-date by the time Admiral Sheaffe was able to examine it.

Keen glanced through the open stern windows and silently cursed the oppressive heat. It seemed to pin the whole ship down so that even the smallest movement was uncomfortable.

Bolitho signed the last page where Yovell had indicated and looked questioningly at his flag-captain.

'Well, Val, are we ready for sea?'

Keen nodded and instantly felt a trickle of sweat run down his spine.

'The water-lighters have cast off, sir. There's just your — '

Bolitho stood up as if pricked by a thorn and strode to the windows.

'My nephew. He should be back on board by now.'

He was thinking aloud. The ship was waiting to weigh anchor. Boats were hoisted, and all hands accounted for. He stared hard at the little brig which had brought the news of *Sparrowhawk*'s loss. Napier, her young commander, would be glad to rid himself of his responsibility to an admiral other than his own. His tiny command would soon be free of Bolitho and hurrying to Antigua to pass the news of the mysterious assassin, the ship which bore no name and showed no colours. Bolitho would have given a lot to hold on to the *Electra*, but the need to spread the word of the unknown attacker was paramount. Other ships might be lost in the same fashion.

Keen watched the emotions as they chased each other across Bolitho's features. They had seen and done so much together in every kind of action. Now, supposedly in peacetime, they were faced with something which was both baffling and terrible.

Feet thudded overhead, and calls trilled as the watch on deck was ordered to some new task under the first lieutenant's eye.

Bolitho did not see Keen's sympathetic scrutiny. His mind kept swinging from tack to tack, as if he was imprisoned by his own thoughts. Wait in Boston or set sail for San Felipe? It was his decision alone, just as his decision had cost Duncan his life. Keen had spoken with the one surviving midshipman, Evans, but had got little out of him. Bolitho had asked Allday to speak with the boy in his own way and the result had been startling. Allday had that casual, effortless way of talking to people, especially youngsters like Evans, and as he had described what Evans had told him Bolitho had been able to relive that brief, savage encounter which had ended with *Sparrowhawk*'s total destruction.

It was a wonder a boy like Evans had not collapsed completely, Bolitho thought. It was not like going to war with the fear of death a constant companion. It was Evans' very first commission, his only voyage in a man-of-war. He did not even come from a naval family but was the son of a tailor in Cardiff.

To see his best friend, a fellow midshipman, smashed down like a slaughtered animal, to be the last one to speak with the mortally wounded Duncan while the ship exploded around him was more than most could have withstood. Perhaps later, months later, the shock would show itself.

Allday had explained how Evans had sensed an explosion even as his boat had pulled away from the sinking frigate.

The gallery fire had not been doused. Flames had probably spread to the magazine or powder-room, so that for many of the ship's company the end had been quick and the horror of the sharks held back for the others.

Another of the survivors, an experienced gunner's mate, had told Allday that the cannon fire had sounded flatter and louder than he would have expected. She was carrying far heavier weapons, he thought, even though the numbers had been reduced.

Bolitho glanced at the eighteen-pounder near his desk. Probably thirty-two-pounders. But *why?*

The door opened cautiously and the clerk, Yovell, peered in at them.

Bolitho said, 'Despatches are ready to go.'

What did they matter anyway? He knew it, and so did Keen. Words, words, words. The facts were plain as they were brutal. He had lost a fine ship with most of her people. And there was Duncan and his pretty widow. He had been a good friend. A brave officer.

Yovell remained hovering in the screen doorway.

'There is a mail-packet coming to anchor, sir.' He hesitated. 'From England.'

Bolitho stared at him and was shocked to see the anxiety on Yovell's round features.

My God, he's afraid of me. The shock hit him like a fist. He's terrified because there may be no word from Belinda.

The realization did more to steady his apprehension and doubts than anything. He recalled how only yesterday, as he had waited for Adam to return on board, Yovell had said something to put him at ease. Bolitho had exploded and had cursed him roundly for his interfering. Yet Bolitho had always hated martinets who used their rank and authority to terrorize their subordinates. And it was all too easy. A captain was like a god, so an admiral could do no wrong at all in his own eyes.

He said, 'Thank you, Yovell. Take the quarter-boat and pass my despatches to the *Electra*. Also any letters from our people.' He watched the man's uncertainty and added, 'Then go over to the mail-packet, will you? There may be something, eh?'

As the clerk made to leave he said quietly, 'I treated you badly. There was no cause for that. Loyalty deserves a whole lot better.'

Keen watched the clerk's wariness change to gratitude, and as the door closed he said, 'That was good of you, sir.'

Bolitho made himself sit down and tugged his shirt free from his moist skin.

'I have been hard on you too, Val. I apologize.'

Keen gauged the moment and said, 'As your flag-captain, I have the freedom to suggest and warn if the occasion arises.'

'You do.' Bolitho smiled grimly. 'Thomas Herrick was quick to use that freedom, so speak your mind.'

Keen shrugged. 'You are beset from every side, sir. The French will not discuss San Felipe with you, nor do they need to as our two governments have signed an agreement on its future. The Americans do not wish to have the French on their doorstep as it could make their own strategy difficult in any future conflict. The governor of the island will fight you all the way, and I suspect that Admiral Sheaffe knew that from the beginning. So why should *we* worry? If the governor refuses to submit we can arrest him and put him in irons.' His tone hardened. 'Too many men have died to make his position count. Better we take command of the island than to leave its future with him. He probably craves independence from the Crown and will play one faction against the other if we allow it.'

Bolitho smiled. 'I have thought of that. But *Sparrowhawk*'s loss and the unwarranted attack on this ship do not fit the pattern. That ship was Spanish-built, if I'm any judge, and yet His Most Catholic Majesty has voiced no protest about San Felipe. So we either have an attempted coup in the offing or piracy on the grand scale. Hell's teeth, Val, after all these years of war there would be plenty with the experience and the desperation to play for such high odds.'

Keen placed his fingertips together. 'And I know you are deeply concerned for your wife, sir.' He watched, waiting to see Bolitho's grey eyes give a flash of danger. 'The waiting has been hard on you, especially after your experiences as a prisoner of war.'

A boat pulled below the counter and Bolitho strode to the windows to examine her passengers. But they were only a few sight-seers, a local trader or two still trying to bargain with the sailors on the upper deck.

Adam was not here.

Keen read his thoughts and said, 'He is young, sir. Maybe it was a wrong choice to appoint him flag-lieutenant.'

Bolitho swung on him hotly. 'Did Browne say as much?'

Keen shook his head. 'I formed my own opinion. Your nephew is a fine young man, and I have nothing but affection for him. You have watched over him from the beginning, treated him like a son.'

Bolitho faced him again. He had no fight left. 'Was that wrong too?'

Keen smiled sadly. 'Certainly not, sir.'

Bolitho walked past his chair and rested his hand momentarily on the young captain's shoulder.

'But you are so right. I did not accept it because I did not wish to.' He waved down Keen's protest. 'I never saw Adam's mother, nobody did. The one good thing she ever did was to send him across the country to Falmouth, to me. But you were correct about me. I love him like a son, but he is *not* my son. His father was Hugh, my brother. Maybe there is too much of Hugh in him – '

Keen stood up quickly. 'Let it stop there, sir. You are tiring yourself to no good purpose. We all look to you. I believe we are in for trouble. I do not think we would have been sent otherwise.'

Bolitho poured two glasses of claret and handed one to Keen.

'You are a good flag-captain, Val. It took courage to say that. And it is true. Personal feelings do not come into it.

Later maybe, but now the slightest anxiety may transmit itself through this ship.' He held the glass to the sunlight. 'And *Old Katie* will have enough to contend with. She can manage without an admiral who is so wrapped up in his own troubles he can think of nothing else.'

There was a nervous tap at the door and Yovell entered, his eyes fixed on Bolitho.

Keen looked away, unable to watch as Bolitho took the single letter from his clerk's hand.

He wanted to leave but, like the clerk, was unwilling to snap the spell.

Bolitho read the short letter and then folded it with great care.

'Get the ship under way, if you please. The wind will suffice to clear the harbour.'

He met Keen's even stare.

'The letter is from my sister in Falmouth. My wife . . .' His lips hesitated on her name as if they were afraid. 'Belinda is not well. The letter was written some time ago for the packet made another landfall before Boston. But she knew that the packet was sailing. And she wanted to let me know she was thinking of me.' He turned away, his eyes suddenly stinging. 'Even though she was too ill to write.'

Keen looked at Yovell's stricken face and gave a quick jerk of the head.

When the clerk had gone he said gently, 'It was what I would expect her to do, sir. And that is how you must see it.'

Bolitho looked at him and then nodded. 'Thank you, Val. Please leave me now. I shall come up directly.'

Keen walked through the adjoining cabin space and past the motionless marine sentry at the outer screen door.

Herrick would have known what to do. He felt helpless and yet deeply moved that Bolitho had shared his despair with him.

He saw Allday beside an eighteen-pounder and gestured to him.

Allday listened to him and then gave a great sigh. It seemed to come from the soles of his shoes, Keen thought.

Then Allday said, 'I'll go aft, sir. He needs a friend just now.' His face tried to grin. 'He'll no doubt take me to task for my impertinence, but what the hell? He'll crack like a faulty musket barrel if we allows it, an' that's no error.'

Keen strode out into the noon sunlight, adjusting his hat as his lieutenants and the master turned to face him.

'Stand by to get under way, Mr Quantock. I want to see your best today with half the port watching us.'

As the officers hurried to their stations and the boatswain's mates sent their shrill calls below decks, Keen ran lightly up a poop ladder and looked briefly at the anchored shipping, at the angle of the masthead pendant.

Then he glanced at the open skylight on the poop deck and thought of the man beneath it.

He cupped his hands. 'Mr Mountsteven, your men are like cripples today.'

He saw the lieutenant touch his hat and bob anxiously. Keen made himself breathe out very slowly.

That was better. He was the captain again.

The negro groom wiped his hands on a piece of rag and announced, 'Wheel all fixed, sah.'

Adam helped the girl to her feet and together they walked reluctantly from the shade of some trees and down to the dusty road.

The carriage had shed a wheel as it had rounded a bend in the road and had dipped into a deep rut.

There had been momentary confusion, the carriage lurching over and a door opening to reveal the road rising to meet them. Then in the sudden silence Adam had realized his unexpected good fortune. What might have ended in injury and disaster had become a perfect conclusion to the visit.

As the carriage had bounced to a halt Adam had acted instantly and without conscious thought other than to save his companion from hurt. Then as the dust settled, and the coachman and groom had hurried fearfully to look inside, Adam had found the girl held tightly in his arms, her fair hair pressed against his mouth, her heart pounding to match his own.

It had taken longer than expected to repair the damage, but Adam had barely noticed. Together they had walked through the green woodland, had held hands while they had watched a stream and spoken of anything but their true feelings.

The whole visit to Newburyport had been an adventure, and Adam had been taken to visit a small, comfortable house by Robina and her father, and they had watched him, fascinated, while he had walked through every room with the owner, a friend of the family, and had touched the walls, the fireplaces, and one old chair which had always been in the house.

Robina had tried not to weep as he had sat in the big chair, his hands grasping the well-worn arms as if he would never let go.

Then he had said quietly, 'My father once sat here, Robina. *My father.*'

He still could not believe it.

She slipped her hand through his arm and nestled her cheek against his coat.

'You must go, Adam. I have made you late enough as it is.'

Together they moved back to the coach and climbed inside.

As the horses came alive again in their harness, the girl said softly, 'We shall be in Boston very soon.' She turned and looked directly into his eyes. 'You may kiss me now if you wish, Adam.' She tried to make light of it by adding, 'No one can see us here. It would not do for local folk to think that Robina Chase was a fizgig!'

Her mouth was very soft and she had a perfume like fresh flowers.

Then she gently pushed him away and dropped her eyes.

'Well, really, Lieutenant . . . ' But the jest eluded her. She said breathlessly, 'It's love, isn't it?'

Adam smiled, his mind in a daze. 'It must be.'

The coach rolled across cobbles and on to a stretch of old ships' timbers.

Several people paused to glance at the fair-haired girl and the young sea officer who helped her protectively from the coach.

Adam stared in astonishment and then looked at the girl on his arm.

'What shall I do now, Robina?'

It was like a douche of cold water. *Achates* had gone.

'So here you are.' Jonathan Chase nodded to his niece and then said grimly, 'Sailed yesterday. Your admiral was hell-bent for San Felipe.'

He toyed with the idea of telling the young lieutenant about the *Sparrowhawk*'s end, but as he looked from him to his niece he decided against it.

Instead he said, 'You'd better come home with me, young fella. Tomorrow I'll see what I can do about arranging passage for you. You'd not want to miss your ship, eh?'

He saw their hands touch and knew they had not heard a word.

Chase led the way to his own carriage, his face frowning in thought. His niece was the apple of his eye, but you had to face the facts squarely as you did a problem at sea.

They made a striking pair, but the family would never allow it to go further. He could not imagine what he had been thinking of when he had first introduced them.

A young sea officer, an English one at that, with few prospects other than the Navy, was not the right match for Robina Chase. So the sooner he found his ship again the better.

Bolitho left the shadow of the poop and walked forward to the quarterdeck rail. He noticed the curious glances darted in his direction by the bare-backed seamen who were working on the endless tasks of a fighting ship. Even now they were not used to having a flag-officer in their midst, and could not accept that he did not dress in the style suited to his rank. Like the other officers, Bolitho wore only an open-necked shirt and breeches, and would willingly have stripped naked to gain relief from the heat had that not violated every rule in the book.

He looked up at the canvas, sail by sail. Filling tightly for the present, but at any moment they could fall limp and useless as they had for much of the time since leaving Boston.

Bolitho tried not to allow his mind to dwell on it. Why had his sister Nancy written? Was it really as Keen had suggested, or was she trying to prepare him for bad news? Belinda had been ill. It might be something from her earlier life in India when she had nursed her sick husband until he had died.

He paced across the pale planking, worn smooth by a million bare feet in *Old Katie*'s twenty-one years at sea.

He tried to shift his thoughts away from Falmouth but they lingered instead on his nephew.

Bolitho had wanted, *needed* to remain in Boston more than anything in his heart and soul. To wait for one more word from Belinda, and to have his nephew rejoin the ship. He should not have allowed him to go to Newburyport. Maybe Keen, like Browne, had been right about that too. He ought not to have chosen one so close as his aide.

Keen crossed the deck and said, 'Wind's holding steady, sir.'

He watched Bolitho's reaction. For eight of the longest days he could remember Keen had worked his ship to the southward, spreading every stitch of canvas to coax another knot out of her. It had been a poor average all the same, and he guessed that Quantock was comparing him with the last captain. He did not care about his dour first lieutenant, but was more conscious of the fact that Bolitho had never levelled a single criticism or complaint. He knew better than most that in these waters the wind was never reliable, rarely an ally when you most needed it.

Bolitho looked at the flapping masthead pendant.

'Tomorrow then, Val.'

'Aye, sir. Mr Knocker assures me that we shall be off San Felipe by noon, if the wind holds.' He sounded relieved.

Bolitho looked abeam, at the regular swell and occasional feather of spray as a fish broke the surface. Like Keen, he had studied the charts and sketches of San Felipe until he could see them in his sleep. Fifty miles long but less than twenty miles wide at its broadest parts, it was dominated by an extinct volcano and a huge natural harbour on the southern side. The northern approaches were fiercely guarded by reefs, and there was a further barrier of coral adjoining the little islet on the opposite side. It was a formidable place, even without the old fortress which commanded the approaches to Rodney's Harbour, as the anchorage was named. There was fresh water in plenty, while rich crops of sugar and coffee made a tempting prize. Bolitho found himself inwardly agreeing with the island's governor, Sir Humphrey Rivers, that it was a madness to hand the place back to the French.

Keen was saying, 'I shall use the prevailing wind to approach the harbour from the south-east, sir. I'd not care to run in under cover of darkness.'

He was making light of it, but Bolitho could guess at his concern for his ship. The waters around San Felipe were used to brigs and trading-schooners, but a ship of the line, even a small sixty-four, needed room to breathe.

Bolitho said, 'I shall go ashore and meet the governor as soon as possible. We know that Captain Duncan had an audience with him.'

He glanced forward as Midshipman Evans walked past some of the sailmaker's crew who were speaking with Foord, the fifth lieutenant. The midshipman turned and stared at the little group and then hurried, almost ran, to the nearest hatchway.

Keen explained, 'Another of *Sparrowhawk*'s wounded has died, sir.'

Bolitho nodded. One more dead. The sailmaker's mates would sew him up in an old hammock and drop him overboard at sunset.

'Tell Midshipman Evans to report to my clerk for duties in the cabin. Keep his mind off things.'

He strode away and began to pace up and down until his shirt was plastered to his skin.

Keen shook his head. *Take his mind off things*. Bolitho had enough worries and responsibilities for ten men, yet he could still spare a thought for the stricken midshipman.

'Deck there!'

Keen looked up and shaded his eyes against the fierce glare.

The masthead lookout on his perch in the cross-trees yelled, 'Land on th' lee bow!'

Keen looked at the master and grinned. 'Well done, Mr Knocker. We shall remain on the present tack until we can gauge the final approach.'

Knocker grunted. His priest's face gave away neither pleasure nor resentment.

Keen glanced at Bolitho. He had heard the cry but gave no sign either.

'I'll drop the corpse outboard during the last dog watch, sir.' Quantock was tall and ungainly but could move like a cat.

Keen faced him and tried not to feel dislike for his senior lieutenant.

'We shall *bury* him with due honour, Mr Quantock. Have the watch below piped aft at dusk.'

The lieutenant shrugged. 'If you say so, sir. It's just that he was not one of ours – '

Keen saw the little midshipman being led away by Yovell, the clerk, and said sharply, 'He was *somebody's*, Mr Quantock!'

And as shadows crept down from the horizon and enfolded the slow-moving ship, *Achates* paid her respects to the dead.

Bolitho donned his uniform and stood beside Keen as he read a few words from his prayer-book, a boatswain's mate holding a lantern so that he could see the page, although Bolitho suspected he knew the words by heart. He noticed too that the man with the lantern was the one he had spoken to who had served in his *Lysander* at the Nile.

He looked at the darkening horizon but the island had already disappeared. All that day it had risen slowly above the dark blue line, taking shape, spreading out as if growing in size.

Keen said, 'Carry on, Mr Rooke.'

Bolitho heard the slithering sound on a grating, then a splash alongside as the sailor made his journey to the sea-bed.

Bolitho felt himself shiver, and then a sudden stab in his wounded thigh, like a taunt, a reminder.

A Royal Marine was already folding up the burial flag, the hands were moving away to their messes. The officer of the watch was eager to hand over to his successor and join his companions in the wardroom. The ship's routine took over again, as it always did.

But Bolitho pictured the pathetic bundle sinking in *Achates'* wake. He had heard the first lieutenant's comment and Keen's angry retort.

Not one of ours.

Next time, he thought bitterly, it would be.

The sky above Massachusetts Bay looked angrier than it had since *Achates* had first come to her anchor.

As Adam stood with a small group on the quay he noticed that several of the ships in harbour had men working on deck, as if they expected a storm.

Jonathan Chase rubbed his chin and squinted at the fast-moving clouds.

'Sorry to hurry you, Lieutenant, but it's best you use the tide before the weather closes in. Won't last much longer than a few hours.'

Adam turned to the girl whose hair looked like silver in the dying light.

He said, 'It was good of you to find me a vessel, sir.' But his heart and eyes told another story.

She took his arm and they looked at the little brigantine which was already pitching heavily, her loosely brailed sails puffing and drumming in the hot wind. She was named *Vivid*, and Adam guessed it was just luck that Chase had been able to find a master willing to make the passage of some fourteen hundred miles to San Felipe.

The girl said in a fierce whisper, 'Don't go, Adam. There's no need. You can stay with us until . . . ' She looked at him, part pleading, part defiant. 'My uncle will find you employment.' She squeezed his arm more tightly. 'You'll be like your father then.'

Chase said gruffly, 'Here comes a boat. I've had your gear sent over, and a few luxuries to carry back to your ship. Give your uncle my best wishes.' He was speaking quickly as if to hasten the moment of departure.

Adam bent his head and kissed her. He felt moisture on her skin. Spray or tears, he did not know. He knew that he loved her more than any living thing. That he was just as surely going to lose her. He felt as if he was being torn apart. In hell.

The small boat scraped alongside and a voice called roughly, 'Jump in, Lieutenant! No time to dawdle!'

Adam tugged his hat firmly on to his head and did as he was told. The boat was old and scarred, but the oarsmen smart enough.

He peered astern as the boat butted away from the piles and saw her watching him, her face and raised hand very pale against the land.

I shall be back.

He gritted his teeth as spray swept over the gunwale and the boat's coxswain said curtly, 'Here, get ready!'

The brigantine was pitching right above the boat, her two masts spiralling as she tore at her anchor cable.

Adam was almost glad of the sailor's abruptness. He did not want courtesy. They were doing it for Chase's money, not out of respect for a foreign officer.

He clambered up the side and would have fallen headlong but a big man loomed from the shadows and gripped his arm to steady him.

Adam noticed that the man walked with a bad limp, and as he made to thank him saw to his astonishment that he had only one leg. But there was no mistaking his authority as he shouted at his men to work on the capstan.

'Get below, if you please.'

He had a powerful voice with an easy colonial drawl, quite unlike the Bostonians. He was already limping away to supervise his small crew but hesitated and came back again.

'Would you mind takin' off your hat?'

As Adam removed it, and his hair ruffled in the wind, the *Vivid*'s master nodded, well satisfied.

'Thought so. Soon as I laid eyes on you.' He rubbed his hand down his jerkin and thrust it at him. 'My name's Jethro Tyrrell. Welcome aboard my humble command.'

Adam stared at him. 'You knew my father?'

The man called Tyrrell threw back his head and laughed.

'Hell no! But I *knew* Richard Bolitho.' He limped away and added over his shoulder, 'Useter be his first lieutenant, would you believe?'

Adam groped his way aft to a tiny companion-way, completely mystified.

It did not really matter who commanded the *Vivid*'s destiny, he thought. He was taking him away from Robina. The first love of his life.

7

To Start a War

'The entrance to Rodney's Harbour is narrow, sir. A mile wide at the most.' Keen lowered his telescope and pursed his lips. 'A well-sited battery could hold a fleet at bay.'

Bolitho walked to the opposite side of the quarterdeck so that his view of the island would not be obscured by shrouds and rigging.

They had made better progress during the night, and now with the morning sunlight outlining the massive pyramid of the extinct volcano he could gauge its size and the rugged shoreline of the island.

The helmsman called, 'Nor'-west by west, sir.' And Knocker grunted an acknowledgement.

Keen glanced at the masthead pendant. It pointed towards the larboard bow with barely a shiver. The wind was still holding.

Bolitho could feel Keen's mind at work as his ship headed warily towards the pointing spur of headland.

The wind would take them directly into the shelter of the harbour. But they were on a lee shore, so every care was necessary. Keen had sent two good leadsmen forward to the chains at first light and their regular cry of 'No bottom, sir!' warned of the dangers.

The sea-bed shelved very steeply, but once they drew level with the small islet off the southern tip of the headland there would be reefs ready to rip out the keel if the ship lost steerage-way.

'Take in the fore-course, Mr Quantock.' Keen sounded

calm but his eyes were everywhere as he watched the topsails hardening to the wind.

'Deck there!'

Bolitho grasped his hands behind his back as the lookout yelled down, 'There's a boom across the entrance, sir!'

Keen stared at him. 'What the *hell* are they thinking of?'

Bolitho said sharply, 'Send an officer aloft. Then prepare to anchor.'

'But . . . ' Keen's protest stopped with the one word. He knew that Bolitho understood well enough. To anchor on a lee shore in deep water was tempting disaster. If the wind got up *Achates* might drag her anchor and run helplessly on to the hidden coral.

Bolitho took a few paces while he considered it, determined not to watch a lieutenant's frantic scramble to the masthead.

The governor could reasonably do what he liked to protect the island. Maybe he had already been attacked, and would withdraw the boom when *Achates* was identified. He dismissed the idea instantly. The ship had served in these waters for most of her life. She would be easily recognized before any other vessel.

The lieutenant who had climbed up to join the lookout called, 'The boom is a line of moored craft, sir!'

He was one of the junior officers who had recently been promoted from midshipman and had a shrill, almost girlish voice, so that several of the seamen on the quarterdeck grinned and nudged each other until silenced by a roar from Quantock.

Keen shut his telescope with a snap. 'Stand by to come about. Man the braces. Anchor party up forrard at the double!'

The young lieutenant shouted again, 'There's a yawl approaching, sir!'

Keen looked at Bolitho, anxiety in his eyes.

Bolitho said shortly, 'Anchor then.'

'Helm alee! Stand by, Mr Quantock!'

The yards swung noisily when they turned into the wind, the canvas banging and clattering as the way was taken off the ship.

'*Let go!*'

The anchor hit the sea violently and threw spray high over the beak-head, while Rooke, the boatswain, and a lieutenant of the forecastle peered over the side. At the same time the topmen worked above the deck to take in the sails and ease any strain on the cable as it continued to run out into deep water.

'All secure, sir!'

Keen nodded but murmured, 'Bloody bastards!'

The yawl thrust slowly away from the land, tacking this way and that as it clawed towards the anchored two-decker.

The midshipman of the watch said, 'There's an officer of sorts on board, sir.'

Captain Dewar of the marines asked, 'Man the side, sir?'

Keen glared at him. 'After refusing my ship an entrance? I'll see him in hell first!'

The yawl's tanned sails were furled, and as she glided against the *Achates'* tumblehome Bolitho said, 'I'll receive him in the cabin.' He strode aft, unable to watch Keen's anger and humiliation.

It seemed an age before the visitor was brought to the cabin, and Bolitho found himself wondering what Nelson might do under this set of circumstances.

He could not blame the islanders, nor could he condone this behaviour.

The door was opened by Yovell and Bolitho looked at his visitor as he strode to the centre of the cabin. He was certainly dressed in uniform, a blue tunic and white trousers, and wearing both sword and pistol on a highly polished belt. He was aged about thirty, Bolitho thought, and when he spoke he had a faint West Country accent. A Devonian, he decided, like his clerk.

'I bring word from the governor.'

Keen, who had followed him aft, snapped, 'Say *sir* when you speak to the vice-admiral!'

Bolitho said, 'And what is your name, may I ask?'

The man glanced angrily at Keen. 'Captain Masters of the San Felipe Militia.' He swallowed hard. 'Sir.'

'Well, *Captain* Masters, before either of us says something which cannot be retracted, let me explain *my* intentions.'

The man was recovering his confidence and interrupted, 'The governor has instructed me to tell you that the boom will remain in place until all negotiations are completed. After that . . . '

Bolitho said quietly, 'After that, as you put it, you are not concerned. But how am I expected to see the governor if my ship is prevented from entering?'

'I shall take you in the yawl.' He saw Keen take a pace forward and added quickly, 'Sir.'

'I see. Now I will tell *you*, Captain Masters of the San Felipe Militia. I am going ashore in my barge and will pass the written decision of His Majesty's Government to the governor.'

Masters said, 'He will not accept it!'

Bolitho looked at Keen. 'Have my barge dropped alongside.'

He saw a protest forming on Keen's face. Just like Thomas Herrick.

Masters persisted, 'I shall lead the way then.'

'No. You are under arrest. Any act of rebellion will be treated harshly, and you shall hang for it, do I make myself clear?'

Bolitho saw his calm words smash home like pistol shots. Masters was probably used to bullying slaves on the plantations and the sudden change of fortune left him speechless.

Keen snapped, 'Remove those weapons.' He raised his voice, 'Sergeant Saxton, take charge of this man!'

Masters gasped as the Royal Marine removed his sword and pistol, and exclaimed, 'Your threats do not frighten me, Admiral!'

Bolitho stood up and walked to the stern windows. Many eyes would be watching the ship from the fortress, waiting to see what would happen. The governor might fire on his barge, even hold him as hostage until . . .

He stopped his racing thoughts and said coldly, 'Then they should.'

When he turned round Masters had been led away, and he heard shouted commands as armed marines took charge of the yawl.

Keen asked anxiously, 'Let me ram the boom, sir? Then we'll enter harbour as planned and rake the mutinous scum for good measure!'

Bolitho eyed him fondly. 'It would take a full day, maybe much longer. Even if you succeeded it would cost many lives, and if the wind rose unexpectedly you would have to disengage and beat clear of the land, past that battery again.'

Keen seemed resigned. 'Which officer will act as your aide, sir? I think I should come with you.'

Bolitho smiled, suddenly relieved that the waiting was over, no matter what the outcome might be.

'What, leave your command? With both of us at Rivers' mercy there's no saying what might happen!' He relented at Keen's crest-fallen expression. 'A junior lieutenant and, er . . . the midshipman, Mr Evans. They will suffice.'

Ozzard took down the old sword from its rack but Bolitho said, 'No. The other one.'

If anything went wrong today the sword would be here for Adam. He knew from their glances that they had both guessed the reason.

On deck the sun had risen above the volcano and the decks were already as hot as bricks in a kiln. Tinder-dry, with tarred rigging and sails which would flare like torches if the island's battery used heated shot. Even with ordinary balls a well-sited battery was more than a match for a slow-moving vessel within the confines of a harbour.

He saw Allday watching him grimly, the curious stares of the seamen and marines on the gangways.

He hesitated at the entry port and looked at Keen.

'If I am *wrong*.' He saw the captain's jaw tighten. 'Or

should I fall today, promise me you will write to Belinda. Try to explain.'

Keen nodded and blurted out, 'If they lay one hand on you sir . . . '

'You will do as I ordered, Val. Nothing more or less.'

He touched his hat to the quarterdeck and climbed down into the waiting barge.

He found Trevenen, the sixth lieutenant, and Midshipman Evans already seated in the stern-sheets and said, 'A fine day for it, gentlemen.'

Trevenen was beaming at the unexpected honour of being the admiral's temporary aide, but by contrast Evans looked around him, his eyes dark and empty.

Allday murmured, 'This is no good, sir.'

Bolitho settled down and glanced at the waiting bargemen.

'It won't help by talking about it.'

Allday sighed. He recognized all the signs by now.

'Bear off forrard! Give way, all!'

Bolitho glanced quickly astern and saw the ship drawing away, the faces at the entry port merging and losing individuality.

He looked at his companions. The ship's most junior lieutenant and a thirteen-year-old midshipman might hardly be what the governor would be expecting. But, as in leaving the family sword aboard, he was taking no chances. If things went badly wrong, Keen would need every experienced officer and sailor he could lay hands on.

As the barge dipped into the inshore swell Bolitho heard a clink of metal and realized that cutlasses and pistols were stacked beneath each thwart within easy reach.

He looked up at Allday's impassive features and for a moment their eyes met.

It did not need words, he thought. Allday had made plans all of his own.

The lieutenant said nervously, 'There is the other island, sir.'

Bolitho shaded his eyes and studied the humpbacked islet. It was treeless but with plenty of vegetation around the stone-built mission and outhouses. There was a strip of white beach, and he saw some boats pulled up clear of the surf. Monks, priests or whatever they were, they had to fish and cultivate their land as well as pray, he thought.

He turned his attention to the boom. Lighters and old hulks had been moored in the middle of the entrance, the channel which *Achates* and any ship of her size would have to use. He looked up at the fortress. Bigger than he had expected, with a sheer drop on the seaward side, impossible to scale, and impervious to twenty-four-pounders.

He could see pale houses on the far side of the harbour. He smiled wryly. Georgetown, Rivers' little kingdom. There were several craft at anchor, mostly traders and fishing boats.

Allday said between his teeth, 'Armed men on the boom, sir.'

Bolitho nodded. 'Steer for the starboard side of the entrance.'

He turned briefly to look for the ship but she had been shut off by the spur of headland. Only *Achates'* mastheads and topgallant yards showed above the land as if they had been planted there.

Beside him Evans shifted on his thwart and his fingers locked suddenly around his dirk. Like taking a needle to stop a charging bull, Bolitho thought.

He said, 'I brought you with me in case you should remember something.'

The boy looked at him and replied quietly, 'I know, sir.' His gaze shifted beyond the makeshift boom to the centre of the harbour but he said nothing further.

Bolitho guessed that Evans was seeing his ship *Sparrowhawk* lying there under the guns of the fortress. A King's ship, his home, the start of a career, friends like the other midshipman who had been shot down. But something, anything, might jar his memory. They did not have much else to go on.

Allday tensed at the sharp bang of a musket, and Bolitho saw a ball skip across the water like a fish before dropping abeam.

He said, 'Hold the stroke. Keep pulling.'

His calm tone steadied the bargemen who, with their backs towards the boom, must be expecting the next shot to hit them.

Bolitho squared his shoulders. His cocked hat and bright epaulettes would make a fine marker for any sharpshooter, he thought.

But there were no more shots, and as the barge thrust past the end of the boom he saw groups of men peering at them. All were armed, and one shook his musket threateningly at the grim-faced sailors.

There was no turning back now. No escape.

Bolitho watched a cluster of figures on a jetty below the fortress. It suddenly seemed a long, long way from Sir Hayward Sheaffe's quiet office in the Admiralty where this precise moment had been predicted.

Bolitho was not sure what he had been expecting in San Felipe's governor, but Sir Humphrey Rivers was not it. He was tall, heavily built to a point of grossness, his face very red from both climate and drink, Bolitho thought. But he greeted Bolitho with a jovial, expansive grin and ushered him straight into the cool shadows of the fortress.

As he led the way through a studded door and into a corridor which had been transformed by rugs and several paintings, Rivers said over his shoulder, 'Later I hope you will visit my house. But I guessed you would be eager to settle matters, eh?'

Bolitho saw another door open, a bewigged negro footman giving a bow as they passed him.

Rivers mopped his face with a silk handkerchief and eyed Lieutenant Trevenen and the small midshipman with some amusement.

'By God, Bolitho, do you have a company of boys to do the Admiralty's bidding?'

He snapped his fingers and another footman stepped noiselessly forward with a tray of goblets.

Rivers gave a dry smile. 'Maybe your young companions would care to withdraw?'

'I agree.' There was no point in involving the others.

Then Bolitho said, 'You know why I am here, Sir Humphrey?'

Rivers settled his bulk on a chair and examined his goblet critically.

'Of course. Everyone does. Equally, you know what I think about it?' He chuckled and drank deeply. 'I apologize for the inconvenience of the boom but it *is* necessary.' He seemed to remember that Masters had not returned with Bolitho and asked abruptly, 'Where's my captain of militia?'

'On board *Achates*, Sir Humphrey.'

'I see.' He lowered the goblet to be refilled. 'The signs are that the wind is getting up. You will know from your own experience in these waters that it can be savage even at this time of year. It would not do to let your, er, flagship remain so close inshore under such circumstances.'

Bolitho sipped the wine. It was strange he could feel so calm. Rivers had thought of everything. Where a ship would have to stand off if the harbour remained closed.

Rivers was watching him intently. 'Let's face facts. Your ship cannot stay there indefinitely. Soon you will have to weigh. You can ration water until the people are ripe for mutiny, you can even wait for assistance which may never arrive. *Or* you can draw up a fresh agreement here and now. I will remain as governor with total responsibility for the island's betterment and defence.'

And profit, Bolitho thought.

Rivers stood up with some difficulty and walked to a window.

'This place is impregnable. You must know that. The Americans will help me if need be. I'll not have the Frogs hoisting their colours here. I told your impertinent frigate captain as much.'

'The *Sparrowhawk* was sunk soon after she left here.'

He watched Rivers' florid face and knew it was a complete surprise to him.

'*Sunk?* What are you saying?'

'She was attacked by a larger man-of-war, blown to hell without a challenge or chance to defend herself. So you see, Sir Humphrey, there are those other than the French who are interested in the island's future.'

Rivers tossed back the wine and turned away to hide his confusion.

'I don't believe it. Probably a pirate, the waters are full of them. With the King's Navy cut to the bone, it's hardly surprising.'

'I want to show you something.' Rivers almost threw down the empty goblet and strode panting to another door at the far end of the chamber. A footman darted ahead of him like a pilot-fish to open it.

Beyond the door the rugs and comfortable chairs were gone. A long embrasured stone wall and a line of heavy artillery looked across the water. Rivers' authority.

Rivers strode to the end cannon and laid one hand on its rounded cascabel with something like affection.

'Here, take a look, Bolitho.'

He stood aside and Bolitho could feel his sense of power. He was filled suddenly with loathing for this man who cared nothing for Duncan or anyone else.

He stooped and peered along the black barrel and saw that the gun was laid on a line of mooring buoys. Tied to one of them was his barge. He could even see Allday standing to shade his eyes and peer at the fortress.

Rivers added smoothly, '*Sparrowhawk* was there. I could have sunk her just as easily as I can that boat of yours.'

Bolitho stood up and eyed him calmly. 'You were a flag-officer yourself, Sir Humphrey. You know the Navy would never rest — '

Rivers snorted. 'There would be no choice. To suffer great losses to aid the French? Even Parliament would not be that stupid!'

Bolitho glanced across the anchorage again. The water was ruffled like beaten pewter. The wind was rising steadily and he could see the flags whipping out from the moored craft. But they were in shelter. *Achates* was not.

He said, 'I shall return to my ship.' He did not hide his contempt. 'Unless you wish to detain me also?'

'No agreement, Bolitho?'

'Do not try to deceive me, Sir Humphrey. You knew I would not condone treason.'

Rivers smiled. 'Not like some in your family, eh?'

Bolitho took his hat from a footman. He did it slowly to give himself time to control his anger. It was just as well Adam was elsewhere. Such a crude slur on his father would have brought out his sword, and Rivers' guards would have ended it here and now.

He said, 'That was cheap, but not totally unexpected.'

Rivers sat down and mopped his face again. He could not hide his excitement, the pleasure which his victory was giving him.

Bolitho walked to the door and saw Midshipman Evans standing alone beside an open window.

Rivers said, 'I have taken the liberty of detaining the young lieutenant until my boat and men are returned.'

Bolitho nodded gravely. 'As you wish.'

Rivers seemed disappointed. 'There is still time for you to reconsider.'

Bolitho gestured to Evans and replied, 'You said yourself, Sir Humphrey, that these waters abound with pirates. I think I have just been speaking to one of them.'

He turned abruptly on his heel and strode through the door, half expecting a shot or a sudden challenge.

Evans almost had to run to keep up with him.

Bolitho snapped, 'Signal the barge.'

He felt the hot wind on his cheek, saw the air of menace in

the sky. It would have to be smartly done, he thought. There was no choice. Not for him anyway.

Allday watched gratefully as Bolitho and the midshipman climbed into the boat and murmured, 'That's that then, sir.'

Bolitho watched the oar blades dig into the water and said, 'An *easy* stroke, if you please.' His mind was reeling with the urgency of what must be done, but under no circumstances must Rivers suspect his intentions.

Once in the great cabin Bolitho tossed his gold-laced coat to Ozzard and watched Keen, Quantock and the two Royal Marine officers as they were ushered in by Yovell.

'I intend to attack, Captain Keen.' Bolitho was surprised that the glass of wine which Ozzard had just given him did not splinter in his grasp.

Keen said, 'Mr Knocker has doubts about our safety here, sir. The wind – '

'Is it steady?'

Quantock said in his hard voice, 'Rising by the hour, sir.'

'That is not what I asked. Is it steady?'

Keen looked anxious. 'Aye, sir.'

'Very well. So make ready for sea.' He saw Keen's sudden relief vanish as he added, 'Then Rivers' lookouts will imagine we are leaving.'

'With respect, sir, no sane man would believe otherwise. We will surely drag our anchor if we remain.'

Bolitho smiled at him. 'Remember Copenhagen, Val?'

Keen nodded, his face pale. 'I do, sir. So you intend to attack in the dark?' He sounded incredulous.

'I do. I know how the battery is laid on the entrance and the main anchorage. Rivers was good enough to show me, although I think he had different reasons.'

What was happening to him? It could and would probably end in complete disaster. *Remember Copenhagen?* he had asked Keen. This was nothing like it. There they had had a whole fleet, and they had had Nelson.

There was a world of difference here. If he lost the ship

there was nothing, a costly failure which if he survived would end in a court martial, and would break Belinda's heart.

Yet, in spite of the terrible risks he was actually elated, a madness coursing through him like ice-water.

Keen cleared his throat and glanced at the other officers. 'Right then, sir.'

Bolitho looked away. Keen had accepted. Right or wrong he would follow his orders to hell.

Bolitho made himself smile but his lips felt stiff and unreal.

'At dusk we shall send Masters and his yawl into harbour to exchange with Mr Trevenen.'

Keen shook his head. 'I had forgotten all about *him*!'

Bolitho looked at the two marines. 'And that will be when you come into things.'

It was a matter of perfect timing, and Lady Luck, as Herrick had always proclaimed. Keen thought it was an act of madness, or vanity to cover his defeat by Sir Humphrey Rivers.

That was their only chance. That Rivers would imagine himself to be safe with such odds.

He was probably on the fortress wall at this very moment. Picturing the argument and despair he had flung in their midst.

He briefly outlined his plan of action and saw their varying expressions, their doubts and their uncertainty. But there was the same excitement too. Even Quantock, who said very little, seemed fascinated.

Bolitho said quietly, 'It is hard to fight a war, gentlemen, as you all know. But it seems a great deal easier to start one.'

They filed out to speak with their subordinates and Bolitho sat at his table, a pen poised above some paper.

There might be no time later on, and he wanted her to know his thoughts, just as she had tried to send him her best wishes.

Feet thudded overhead and tackles creaked as his barge was hoisted on to the tier.

Suppose he was mistaken? That Rivers was right about the island being impregnable.

He tried to force the new uncertainty from his mind and wrote, *My dearest Belinda* . . .

Then he deliberately folded the paper and put it in a drawer. If he was killed she would soon know. There was no point in reopening the wound with a letter which might reach her months later.

Allday entered the cabin and stood watching him, his body angled to the screen door as the ship swayed restlessly in the wind.

Allday said bluntly, 'Attack, sir.'

Bolitho nodded. 'Yes. Did you do as I asked?'

Allday had to grin despite the gravity of the moment.

'Aye, sir, we trailed a boat'd lead an' line all the way to those mooring buoys. It only touched bottom once, and there's room a-plenty for *Old Katie*, once she's snug inside.' He shook his head with admiration. 'With all those other things to bother you, I don't know how you thought of it, and that's no error!'

Bolitho said, 'Pour us each a glass of brandy, Allday.'

He watched the man's powerful fist as he filled two goblets and waited for the deck to settle.

Allday added as an afterthought, 'Mebbee that's how you becomes an admiral, knowing them things, sir?'

The officer of the watch paused in his prowling on the poop deck as their laughter came through the skylight.

It would be his first action as a lieutenant. He had felt the iron fingers of fear dig into his stomach as Quantock had explained what must be done.

But hearing their vice-admiral laugh like that with his coxswain gave him new strength and he continued with his pacing.

8

Faith

Bolitho took a last glance through the stern windows before
Ozzard fastened them tightly and closed the protective shutters. *Achates* was pitching heavily at her cable, and Bolitho
guessed that Keen had doubled the anchor watch for a first
sign of its dragging.

It should still have been daylight, but low, angry clouds
and drifting spume had closed around the ship like an early
dusk.

He could not wait much longer. *He dare not.*

With the cabin sealed Bolitho felt the air tormenting him
like steam and he was running with sweat in seconds.

There was a tap at the outer door and Keen's voice murmuring to someone. He was exactly on time. Had probably
been aching for the moment to arrive.

Bolitho nodded to him. 'Let's be about it then.'

He saw the unwilling hostage in the background flanked
by the ship's corporal and Black Joe Langtry, *Achates'* fearsome master-at-arms. The latter had a pair of grotesque black
brows and, despite years at sea, an ashen countenance. More
like an executioner, Bolitho thought.

'Well, Captain Masters, you will be leaving us directly.'
He watched the gleam return to the man's eyes. He had
strong faith in his master and might be quick to throw
Bolitho's words back in his face. But there was no time to
waste.

'The yawl is waiting to cast off and take you back to
harbour.' Bolitho lifted his arms and saw Masters' eyes shift

to the curved fighting hanger which Allday deftly clipped to his belt. 'I am afraid it will be carrying a different crew this time, but *you* will take us past the boom.'

He watched his words touch a cord in Masters' mind.

'But, but . . .'

'The governor has acted unlawfully. I intend to take control of the island, and to do that with a minimum loss of life you will steer us through the entrance.' He counted seconds before adding quietly, 'What happens to Rivers will depend on others. But if you attempt to raise an alarm you will be killed. If you betray us in any other way I will treat such action as treason against the Crown. You know what that will mean.'

He adjusted the hanger on his belt, sickened by the man's stunned features, by his own brutal remedy.

Then he thought of Duncan and the others and said, 'Put him aboard the yawl. I shall follow.'

He looked at Keen. 'This is the only way. *You* must command the ship.'

They both glanced up as the wind moaned through the shrouds and ratlines like a taunt.

'Your first lieutenant is an excellent seaman, but ashore with men he sometimes abuses too much, who can tell? And we have *no margin at all for error.*'

He looked from Keen to Allday. Friends. Comrades. So few of us left.

'You, Allday, have the most dangerous part. You will lower the barge at the seaward side. It cannot be seen now from the fortress.'

Allday eyed him stubbornly. 'I know what to do, sir. Take the boat past them moorings and light a beacon.'

'It is a hard thing to ask. If we fail you will be cut off.'

Allday grunted. 'I'd rather stay with you, sir. It's my right, my place.'

Bolitho gripped his arm and tried to hide his emotion.

'Without that beacon *Achates* has no chance of entering harbour. No chance to avoid running aground in this wind.

And you *shall* be with me, old friend. Make no mistake about it.'

Keen said, 'I still believe . . . ' Then he shut his mouth and gave a rueful grin. 'But it's done.' He loosened his shirt and touched his sword. 'Rivers may be surprised, but that compares little with my own feelings!'

He nodded to Allday and strode from the cabin, his voice going ahead as he rapped out his orders.

Bolitho took a pistol and thrust it into his belt. Did it really matter if Quantock led the attack? In his heart he knew it did. Men being asked to face death while fighting for a cause they did not understand, or if they did probably had a greater sympathy for the foe, needed to see him there too. To watch him die or share whatever fate he had flung them into.

Allday followed him from the cabin, breathing hard as he ducked beneath the deckhead beams. Around them in the gloom half-naked seamen were already standing to the guns, while on the deck below the hands had cleared for action with barely a sound or an order being shouted by the lieutenants and warrant officers.

On the quarterdeck more figures stood in dark clusters or tottered about in the hot wind. It felt like burning sand, the spray hard enough to blind a man.

Bolitho tilted his head to peer at the thrashing canvas as it rippled and boomed against the spars. Once set free the ship would be like a wild thing. A good sailer, they said. She would need to be all that and more.

Tackles squeaked and he heard the barge being lowered down the side. Even though he was hidden in the menacing gloom he could almost feel Allday's resentment, his anxiety, as once more he was parted from him, from his special place in things.

Keen shouted, 'Good luck, sir!'

They made a quick handclasp, their fingers running with warm spray. Then Bolitho was out and swinging down to the pitching yawl, where hands reached out to help him aboard.

A voice growled, 'Who's this, Ted? Gawd, let's get on with it!'

Another gave a hoarse cheer. ''Tis th' admiral, lads!'

They pushed round him as if they did not believe he was joining them. In his sodden, grubby shirt he could have been anyone, but they knew, and from the darkness a voice called, 'Welcome, Equality Dick!'

Bolitho groped his way aft, moved and, as usual, ashamed that he had not even considered that these unknown seamen might trust him.

He heard Mountsteven, the second lieutenant, say cheerfully, 'Smells like a Portland whore-house, sir.' His total lack of respect showed that he too was caught in the madness like the rest.

'It's powerful.'

Bolitho reached the tiller and peered at the men nearest him. He saw Christy, the boatswain's mate who had been in the *Lysander*, and the vague shape of Masters, who was easily recognizable in his militia uniform.

The boat certainly stank. It was crammed with inflammable materials. Old canvas, cordage soaked in grease and pitch, oil and various oddments from the gunner's store. One careless spark and the whole boat would ignite like a grenade.

Once they had seized the boom and cut its moorings, Allday's barge, followed by *Achates'* two cutters with the marines, would spread the attack. He had noticed that the yawl's original crew, like the guards he had seen around the fortress, were mostly of slave stock, left-overs and half-breeds from the island's various occupations.

It was unlikely that officers like Masters would live in quarters within the fortress. It would take time for them to be called from their comfortable homes. He shivered slightly. Unless of course Rivers had already seen through his scheme and every gun was loaded and ready for the first sign of an attack.

He said, 'Cast off, Mr Mountsteven. Show a lantern forrard

as planned.' He glanced at Masters. 'You have your instructions. If you value your life and the chance to rejoin your family, I would advise you to be prudent.'

He heard Christy rattle his cutlass in its scabbard as an unspoken warning.

With the mooring lines released and the sails spreading over the deck like giant wings, the big yawl reeled away from *Achates'* protection.

Rivers' men on the boom would be wary, but they had no cause to expect such a rash course of action. He had a sudden stark picture of *Achates* in the first dawn light, wrecked across the entrance and a ready target for the great guns.

A voice whispered, 'Land ahead, sir!'

Bolitho felt a murmur run through the crowded space between decks where the mass of seamen crouched and waited for the onslaught. Blades scraped each other, and men groped for pistols and muskets in total darkness to make certain they were dry and ready. One foolhardy move, a musket being fired by accident, and all would be lost. Bolitho was grateful that *Achates'* people were mostly experienced hands. Well trained, part of a family.

He clung to a backstay and peered through the spray towards the darker wedge of land on the larboard bow. To starboard the fortress and the fifteen-hundred foot high volcano were a vague blur in this eerie light.

A lantern bobbed across the water, seemingly from the sea itself, and Bolitho thought he heard a shout.

Masters said harshly, 'Dip the forrard lantern!' He sounded as if he could barely breathe. *'Twice!'*

The lantern dipped and rose twice as directed, and Bolitho found that he was holding his breath. It was Masters' chance to betray him, to prove his last loyalty to Rivers. But nothing happened, and the light on the boom remained steady and flickering above the tossing wavecrests.

The tiller-bar creaked as Masters guided the helmsman's hand. He had committed himself and had no intention of drowning because of faulty steering.

Bolitho saw the end of the boom and a few hunched figures around the guide light. Someone was shouting at the yawl, and Masters waved, his lordly gesture made pathetic by his treachery.

'*Now!* Helm hard to starboard! Take in the sails!'

The seamen, used to working in all weathers in daylight or darkness, brought the yawl hard against the moored craft and heavy timbers. As their grapnels soared across the startled guards the first concealed sailor leapt on to the boom, his cutlass silencing a challenge and changing it to a terrible cry.

The boom was suddenly swarming with men, and while some took care of the wretched guards, others dragged out the yawl's dangerous cargo and wedged it into position.

'Light the fuses! Slow-match there! *Lively!*' Mountsteven barked out his orders while the prisoners were flung unceremoniously into the yawl.

Bolitho peered up at the fortress's blurred shape. No sound or sign. Maybe Rivers had really expected him to ignore his honour and his future and sign some illegal document. It would not have been unique in naval history.

'Moorings cut, sir!'

One slow-match sparked briefly like a glow-worm and then another as the last sailor jumped into the tossing boat.

'*Cast off!*'

Barely glancing at the cowering survivors from their swift attack the seamen thrust with long sweeps, boat-hooks and anything else they could find to carry the yawl away from the boom.

Lieutenant Mountsteven in his excitement seized Bolitho's arm and pointed with his hanger.

'There goes your man, sir!'

With only the oar blades visible like trailing white snakes the barge swept through the gap and was into the harbour before the yawl had staggered clear.

'Steer for the shore!'

Bolitho strode to the opposite side where Masters was leaning over the gunwale to peer towards the fortress.

It was like being in a mill-race, with the deck swaying from side to side, sometimes awash as the sweeps fought to hold steerage-way.

'That was well done, Masters.' Bolitho ignored the man's astonished glance and shouted, 'Stand by, lads!'

There was a muffled explosion and suddenly the yawl and their upturned faces were bathed in a vivid orange glare as the drifting boom burst into flames. In seconds it had moved well past the headland and was breaking up into smaller fiery shapes as the lashings parted.

Bolitho tightened the hanger's thong around his wrist and tested his wounded leg. If it failed him now . . .

The yawl hit the land, rebounded with the sea boiling over the gunwale and sweeping men aside like untidy sacks, and then drove ashore yet again. Bolitho heard wood splintering, the inrushing water surging and dragging at his legs as the boat continued to batter its way along a line of rocks.

But grapnels were already finding a grip, and as the first men clambered cursing and spluttering on to firm ground Bolitho heard the far-off blare of a trumpet.

He tried to fix the picture of the hillside in his mind, then turned to watch as another part of the drifting boom exploded in a great plume of sparks and flames.

The whole of Georgetown must surely be on the alert by now.

Crack . . . crack . . . crack . . . Musket shots whined impotently through the spray as some sentries fired from the fortress walls.

'Rally the men, Mr Mountsteven.'

The lieutenant was regarding the remains of the yawl. There was no way out by that method.

Someone gave a hoarse cheer which was instantly silenced by an unseen petty officer.

But Bolitho felt like cheering too. The *Achates'* cutters were pulling like demons as they swept through some last remnants of the boom, the marines' white cross-belts stark and clear despite the gloom.

From the bows of one came the sharp crack of a musket and a yell of command, magnified through a speaking-trumpet to add unreality to the moment.

A cutter was pulling directly for one of Rivers' own boats. Doubtless one which was bringing the unfortunate Lieutenant Trevenen to be exchanged. If they had harmed him . . .

He did not let his mind dwell on it as Mountsteven shouted, 'All accounted for, sir!'

'Carry on! Fast as you can! Across the track from the town. Scatter the men among the rocks, anywhere so that they can slow an attack until the marines support us!'

In spite of his racing thoughts he almost smiled at the absurdity of his orders. More like a general than a naval officer with a boatload of seamen and a company of marines, if they ever managed to reach here.

He ran with the seamen through dark rocks and great bushes which loomed and shook like monsters in the fierce wind as if to frighten them from their purpose.

'Here, sir!'

That was Christy, and Bolitho dropped beside him but gasped as the pain stabbed from his wounded thigh.

Christy was peering at his pistols and had a cutlass bared and lying beside him.

Bolitho saw others running and stooping as they sought out cover, while more musket shots whimpered overhead. Where was Rivers, he wondered? In his fine house, or up there on the fortress wondering if they were all going mad?

He pounded the wet ground with his fist. Everything depended on Allday. He might have run into a guard-boat like the one confronted by *Achates'* cutter. Even now Keen would be weighing anchor, watching the flames on the severed boom, all he had to divide sea from rock.

Soon those flames would have died too.

A voice yelled a command and a loose volley of shots cracked up the slope towards the fortress.

Scott, *Achates'* third lieutenant and Keen's next most

experienced officer, yelled, 'Reload! *Steady*, lads!' He must have seen some movement at the fortress gates.

Bolitho tried not to think of Keen's helplessness as his ship tore free from the ground and began to claw her way round and into solid darkness. Short-handed because of the landing party, and with at least three of his officers out of the ship, it must be a living nightmare.

He saw Christy's eyes glow like twin matches and turned as a column of fire gushed from the end of the moorings.

Allday, in spite of all his doubts and arguments, had done it. The fire was burning brightly where the bargemen had lashed it to one of the buoys, and another would be ready when it died.

Then a cannon roared out like a thunder-clap. Where the ball went nobody saw. It had probably ripped over the very buoy which Rivers had indicated when he had made his casual threat.

Masters was crawling on the ground and when he saw Bolitho flopped down beside him. Now that he had done it he was unable to stop shaking with fear.

Bolitho looked at him and asked, 'What is the date, Mr Masters?'

Masters gulped and managed to reply, 'J-July the ninth, I believe, sir!'

He would have jumped to his feet if Christy had not dragged him down for his own safety.

Masters' voice cracked as he asked, 'I heard something! What's happening?'

Bolitho had heard it too. The faint rattle of drums and the frail sound of fifes.

He could see it as if he were there with them. His marines, marching along a rough road in this howling wind, the little drummer boys keeping an even distance behind their officers as if they were on parade. A road none of them had even seen, and some would never see it when daylight came.

Bolitho managed to say, 'The date is important. One we shall remember.'

He twisted his head to see another of Allday's blazing flares, but this time his eyes seemed blurred.

He drove the knuckle-bow of his hanger into the ground near his face and whispered, 'We shall win. *We shall win!*' It sounded like a prayer.

Keen ran up the poop ladder and clung to a rail as the wind drove along the full length of his ship, the sound rising and strengthening like some obscene chorus.

His mind reeled as he tried to calculate the time and distance he had left to bring *Achates* about once the anchor broke free. He could dimly hear the creak of the capstan, the hoarse shouts of petty officers as they waited for the moment.

Keen returned to the quarterdeck, his face stinging as if the flesh were raw. He saw the dark outline of the wheel and a handful of helmsmen, the master with a midshipman standing nearby. Seamen of the after-guard at the braces, their half-naked bodies shining in the gloom like wet marble.

Soon . . . soon. Now or never. Keen had read it often enough in the Gazette or some Admiralty report. One of His Majesty's ships driven ashore and lost. *A court martial later pronounced* . . . He stopped his racing thoughts and shouted above the din, 'Ready, Mr Quantock?'

The tall figure of the first lieutenant, angled like a cripple's against the sloping deck, staggered towards him.

'It's no use, sir!'

Keen faced him angrily. 'Keep your voice down, man!'

Quantock leaned forward as if to see him better.

'The master agrees with me. It's madness. We'll never manage it.' He was encouraged by Keen's silence. 'There's no shame in standing away, sir. There may still be time.'

'Anchor's hove short, sir!' The cry came like a dirge.

'*Time?* What has that to do with it, damn your eyes!'

Keen strode to the nettings and saw some seamen watching him anxiously.

Quantock persisted, 'Captain Glazebrook would never – '

Keen retorted, 'He is dead. We are not. Do you suggest that we abandon our admiral and all his party because *we* are at some risk? Is that what you are advising, Mr Quantock?' The release of his bitterness and anger seemed to help him. 'I'll see you, the master and all else in hell before *I* turn and run!'

He walked to the quarterdeck rail and peered aloft at the wildly thrashing canvas. They might lose a sail or a spar, perhaps the whole lot. But Bolitho was out there beyond the swaying poop. Pictures flashed through his thoughts. The Great South Sea. The girl he had loved, who had died of the fever which had almost done for Bolitho. In spite of his own despair Bolitho had tried to comfort him. Leave him now after what they had endured together? Never in ten thousand bloody years.

'Pass the word to the topmen, Mr Fraser. It will be close. Clear lower deck and put every available man on braces and halliards.' He grappled for the name of the lieutenant nearby. 'Mr Foord, prepare to drop the larboard anchor if the worst should happen.' It might hold her long enough to get some of the hands ashore.

He heard himself say calmly, 'Well, Mr Quantock?'

Quantock was glaring through the drifting spray.

'Aye, *aye*, sir.'

He snatched up his speaking-trumpet and strode to the side.

Keen gripped the smooth rail. How many captains had stood here? In storm or becalmed, entering harbour after a long and successful passage, or concealing fear as the deck had quivered and rocked to the roar of cannon fire.

Was he to be the last captain? He listened to the clank of pawls around the capstan, the crack of a starter across someone's back as a boatswain's mate drove the men on the bars to greater efforts. Their weight and muscle to shift *Achates'* bulk against wind and sea.

He glanced once more at the crossed yards, the great rippling shapes of loosened sails where the topmen clung and waited to free them to the wind.

There was no sign of a light. The burning boom had vanished. Perhaps Allday had been prevented from reaching his objective. He would have given his life if so. One more picture rose in his mind. Of himself gasping and sobbing in agony. A mere midshipman with a great wooden splinter thrust into his groin like a spear. Of Allday, suddenly gentle, carrying him below and cutting the splinter away rather than trust his life to the ship's drunken surgeon.

'*Anchor's awei* . . . ' The rest was lost as the ship toppled to one side with waves rearing above the gangways and nettings like breakers on a reef.

'*Loose tops'ls!*'

The helmsmen slithered and fell but clung stubbornly to the big double wheel as the ship swung madly with the wind, the freed topsails crashing out from their yards, the sound of the gusts through canvas and shrouds drowning the cries of officers and seamen alike.

Keen forced his eyes to remain open as the sea dashed over the nettings and drenched him from head to toe. The water felt warm, jubilant in its efforts to throw the ship out of control.

He saw the *Sparrowhawk*'s midshipman, little Evans, clinging to a stay, his feet kicking at air as the deck plunged and yawed beneath him.

A dark object fell from the mizzen, hit the gangway with a sickening crack and vanished into the waves alongside. The man must have been torn from his precarious perch by the straining canvas. He had not even time to cry out.

Voices ebbed and died through the terrible chorus like souls already lost.

'More hands to the weather fore-brace there!'

'Mr Rooke, send two men aloft . . . '

'Take this man to the surgeon!'

'Lively there! The gig's breaking adrift!'

Suddenly the master shouted hoarsely, '*Answering*, sir!'

Keen turned and peered towards him. He could feel the wind flaying his mouth so that his lips were forced apart in a wild grin. But she *was* answering. With her main-yard braced hard round, the sails forcing her over so that the sea boiled through the sealed gun-ports in fierce jets, *Achates* was beginning to turn her full length into the teeth of the storm.

Broken rigging streamed down-wind like dead creeper, and Keen had already heard the rip of tearing canvas from overhead and knew that men were there to fight the damage with their bare hands.

'Nor'-east by north!' The man sounded breathless. 'Nor' by east!'

Keen gripped the rail until his fists ached. She was trying. Doing the impossible as with every second the wind drove her towards the blacker shadows of the land.

The yards creaked again and Keen watched the seamen straining wildly at the braces, some with their pale bodies almost touching the deck as they hauled with all their strength. Quantock's harsh voice was everywhere, harrying, threatening, demanding.

The deck seemed to lean forward and down in a great single thrust, and the sea roared through the beak-head and over the forecastle in a solid flood. Men tumbled and were washed aside like puppets, and it was a marvel that none of the guns was torn from its lashings. Keen had seen that too. A great gun thundering about the deck like an insane beast, crushing men who tried to snare it, smashing anything which stood in its path.

He watched with chilled fascination as the bows rose very slowly, the sea cascading away with a subdued roar. The ship was pointing towards the land. At the solid, unmoving barrier.

To confirm his disbelief he heard Knocker yell, 'Nor'-west it is, sir!'

There was still no signal. Nor would there be, he thought.

He should have felt despair for what he had done. Quantock had been right. There would have been no blame. Officially. He had been ordered to force the entrance rather than face the carefully sited battery in broad daylight. *Achates* was the only King's ship, Bolitho the only flag-officer here to act and decide. Nobody could have laid the blame on Keen's shoulder.

Now he might lose the ship and every man-jack aboard, and the island's defiance would remain as if they had never come to this damned place.

Yet in spite of the realization he was glad. He had tried. Bolitho would know it. And other ships would come to avenge them, British or French, it would make no difference in the end.

The lieutenant named Foord yelled wildly, 'The signal! Hell's teeth, the *signal*!' He was almost weeping with disbelief.

Keen said sharply, 'Control yourself, man! Mr Knocker! Bring her up a point to starboard!'

He tried to relax his limbs one at a time as he watched the hissing glow against the swift-moving clouds. Men ran to the braces again, and he heard the fore-topgallant sail boom out from its yard and knew that the topsail had been the one torn apart by the wind.

There it was. No mistake. Allday had done it.

'Nor'-west by north, sir! Steady as she goes!'

They seemed to be tearing through the water at a tremendous pace, like a runaway coach, its horses gone mad.

But Keen had heard something different in the gaunt sailing-master's voice. Not merely surprise or relief. Respect perhaps?

'Leadsmen in the chains!'

Keen pushed himself from the rail and walked to the opposite side to watch a leaping hurdle of breakers. The reefs looked close enough to touch with a pike.

He heard the cry of a leadsman but had no idea what the depth would be.

He saw the land suddenly close alongside, more spray, and felt the deck shiver as the keel ploughed into dangerous shallows.

Knocker was passing more helm orders, his voice suddenly

loud as the ship ran past the headland where the boom had once been.

There were vague explosions. Musket fire and the occasional boom of artillery. But it was unreal. Nothing to do with the plunging two-decker and her men.

Keen heard shouts from forward and then caught his breath as the ship gave a violent lurch. Then down the side he saw the dark outline of a small vessel, battered from her moorings by *Achates*, and capsizing slowly as they continued up the harbour.

The flare was still burning fiercely and Keen could see the flames reflecting on a paler shape nearby, Allday's barge. He snatched a telescope from a midshipman and trained it across the larboard bow.

In the reflected glow he could see the bargemen standing and waving their tarred hats as they saw the ship heading towards them. *Achates* must make quite a sight, Keen thought. Sails shining in the flare, while her hull remained locked in darkness.

'Prepare to shorten sail, Mr Quantock!'

Keen found that his whole being was shaking uncontrollably, like a man on the verge of death.

Then he saw the lights of the town for the first time, glittering through the spray like tiny jewels. They were almost there. It was incredible. Impossible, some would say.

Somewhere another cannon banged out, but Keen had no idea where the ball fell.

'Stand by to wear ship, Mr Quantock.'

There was still plenty of real danger. If the ship failed to respond this time they could drive on to the beach or become entangled with anchored shipping like a porpoise in a net.

Perhaps they had created their own trap? Keen found he could consider it without emotion. It would not matter now. If they could not leave, neither would anyone else. He pictured Bolitho's grave features and hoped he had seen *Achates* drive into the harbour like a phantom ship.

If it could only be settled in a battle of wills, he knew who would emerge the victor.

'Man the lee braces!' Quantock loomed towards him. 'I've ordered both anchors to be ready, sir, and put a lieutenant in charge of the compressor. In this gale the cable might part if . . .' He left the rest unsaid.

Keen regarded him calmly. 'Carry on, if you please.'

There was no change in Quantock and Keen felt strangely glad. It seemed wrong that he should change in any way because of a single reckless act. When you considered it, Keen thought, there was no other description for it.

'Tops'l clew-lines!'

Keen watched the flurry of activity above the deck. Those men had done well, he thought. To preserve their lives, their ship and their pride as only sailors could.

'Helm alee!'

Once again the deck tilted over, Allday's barge swinging away from the jib-boom as if it had taken flight. But the wind and sea had lost their punch. Momentarily. They would bide their time. There was always another battle.

'Let go!'

Keen heard a splash and felt the planking quiver slightly as the second anchor banged against the hull as it swung from its cat-head in readiness to drop if the other failed.

Blocks squealed, and slowly but surely the unseen topmen kicked and fisted the rebellious canvas to each yard and secured it.

The motion eased immediately, and Keen said as calmly as he could, 'Lower the remaining boats. I want a warp run out from aft. Tell Mr Rooke to report to me.' He turned away from Quantock's bitter silence. 'I also want a muster of all hands immediately. Casualties and serious injuries too, if you please.'

A tiny figure appeared at his elbow. It was Ozzard, Bolitho's molelike servant.

'Here, sir.'

He held out a silver tankard, one of Bolitho's own.

Keen held it to his lips and almost choked on rum.

But it did what Ozzard intended and he handed him the tankard.

'That was thoughtful. Thank you.'

They both watched as the gig and then the jolly-boat were hoisted from the tier and swayed out above the gangway. More men were bustling aft while boatswain's mates bawled instructions for laying out a massive warp. Against the pale planking the huge rope looked like an endless serpent.

Ozzard asked timidly, 'Will he be safe, sir?'

Keen saw a lieutenant and Harry Rooke, the boatswain, hurrying towards him for orders, but there was something in Ozzard's voice which held him.

Safe? It was a word rarely considered in the King's service.

Faith had more meaning. Faith to enter a strange harbour despite the hazards and possible consequences. Faith of men like Allday who would risk anything because of Bolitho's word and reputation.

He smiled before turning towards his waiting sub-ordinates.

'He will be expecting a lot from us tomorrow, Ozzard, *that* I do know.'

Ozzard bobbed and nodded. It was good enough for him.

9

A Close Thing

Bolitho felt a hand touch his arm and tried not to groan as the stiffness plucked at his wound. Had he really been asleep? The realization shocked him into immediate alertness.

'What is it, man?'

Lieutenant Mountsteven watched him curiously, as if he did not really believe he was sharing a small rough gully with his vice-admiral.

'Dawn soon, sir. I've roused all hands.'

Bolitho sat up and rubbed his eyes. They felt raw and tired, and he noticed for the first time that the wind had almost died.

Looking back, it still seemed unreal, an impossible hallucination. He peered over the edge of the ground and saw the vague glint of water, as if he expected to see *Achates* forcing the entrance, her sails bulging like metal breastplates, burnished gold by the spluttering flares. *Achates* was only a small sixty-four, but in the eerie glare she had seemingly filled the harbour and had brought wild cheers and not a few tears from Bolitho's seamen.

Around him he heard men gathering up their weapons and recalled the Royal Marine corporal who had been sent by Captain Dewar to report that all his men were ashore and in position.

That too seemed like part of a dream, the corporal apparently unmoved and immaculate in his scarlet uniform.

He grinned, despite his anxieties. By comparison he felt like a vagrant in his stained shirt and his hair full of grit and blown sand.

The fortress was still lost in darkness, but the old volcano had a fine rim of grey light around its summit.

Mountsteven handed him a flask and said, 'I've put a good lookout to watch for the ship, sir. The marines will prevent any attempt to move a cannon from the town to fire on her.'

Bolitho held the flask to his lips and felt his eyes water as the raw brandy burned his tongue. So much depended on Rivers. Given time he could move his heavy battery to another wall where with ordinary shot he could pound *Achates* to fragments. With heated shot he could achieve it in minutes.

It was as if the whole island was unwilling to wake, to enter the new day. He doubted if Rivers had had much sleep, wherever he was.

He looked round as somewhere a cock crowed defiantly in the damp air.

The third lieutenant scrambled down the slope and said breathlessly, 'They're moving artillery in the fortress, sir. I put a picket as close as I could.' He too took the flask from the other lieutenant and raised it to his lips. He grimaced and added, 'But the gates are still shut.'

Bolitho nodded, his mind grappling with such frugal intelligence. Rivers must be regaining confidence, whereas the first excitement of the landing and breaking the boom was already fading with the dawn.

Bolitho stood up carefully and wiped his face with his sleeve. What a wretched situation it was. People in England would question the need for men to die for such a cause when the French would gather all the spoils anyway. He cursed angrily and knew he was thinking only of himself, of his hopes for a future with Belinda. No wonder youthful lieutenants like Mountsteven and Scott eyed him with some curiosity. He should have known, have remembered his own service as a lieutenant. Then he had never considered the personal problems of *his* superiors, their wives, or that they might be as apprehensive as their subordinates when the time came to fight.

He shook the mood aside like an old cloak. To live without Belinda would be unbearable. But to live without honour would be beyond him.

There was a startled challenge from the waterside and Bolitho heard Allday's voice, hushed but fierce as he retorted, 'It's me, you blind fool! Hold your noise or I'll spit you, so I will!' He stumbled down the slope and peered uncertainly at the three officers.

Bolitho smiled. 'You performed a miracle. It was well done!'

Allday seemed to realize that one of the dishevelled shapes was Bolitho and bared his teeth in the gloom.

'Thankee, sir.'

Scott said, 'Thought you might have run into a guard-boat, Allday.'

Allday looked at him as if to consider if a mere lieutenant was worth his attention, then said, 'We did, sir.' He drew his hand across his throat. 'No bother at all.'

The violent crash of a single cannon made several of the men gasp with surprise. Birds rose screaming and squawking in pale clouds from land and water alike, and as the sailors watched the smoke drift from the ramparts they all heard the unmistakable thud of a direct hit.

Bolitho fastened his sword-belt and snapped, 'They've found *Achates*.'

As if in answer to his words there was a swift response from the direction of the town. Musket fire for the most part, and then the sounds of horses clattering along a road.

Rivers' militia intended to attack them before they had found their proper bearings on the island, while a re-sited battery would concentrate on the anchored ship.

Bolitho said, 'Captain Keen will have to be quick. We must win him some more time.'

He peered round and noticed that already the landscape and the nearest huddle of seamen had grown sharper in the feeble light.

Mountsteven asked quietly, 'What do you intend, sir?'

'Flag of truce.' Bolitho saw his look of amazement and added sharply, 'Two volunteers, if you please.'

He tried not to flinch as the gun fired again. He did not hear the ball strike, but in a few moments the gunner would have his target in full view.

Allday said bluntly, '*One* volunteer. I'm comin', sir.'

Bolitho walked from his patch of cover and faced the track which wound its way up to the fortress. A bluff? He had nothing else to offer.

With Allday breathing hard at his side, and the boat-swain's mate, Christy, a step or so in the rear, Bolitho strode along the rough ground. Christy was carrying a shirt on a boat-hook as a flag of truce and was quietly whistling to himself as he followed his admiral. He had even managed to make a joke of the fact that the shirt belonged to one of the two midshipmen who were with the landing party. 'The only young gentlemen with one clean enough for the occasion,' as he had put it.

Bolitho was astonished that he could still raise a grin or two with his remark.

'*Halt!* That's far enough!'

Bolitho stood quite still, the fortress looming over him like a grey cliff. He thought he heard a scrape of metal and imagined a marksman taking careful aim at him, white flag or not. Again he felt the same bitterness welling up inside him. Who would care? Hundreds, thousands of sailors and soldiers had died all over the world for one cause or another, but who ever remembered why?

He cupped his hands. 'I want to speak with Sir Humphrey Rivers!'

There was a derisive chuckle. 'Don't you mean *parley*, sir?'

Bolitho pressed his hands tightly to his sides. He had been right. Rivers was inside. Otherwise the unknown men above the gates would have said so, to mock him for his mistake.

Allday muttered, 'I'll give that bugger *parley*!'

'Oh, it's you, Bolitho! I thought we had some beggars at the gates, what?'

Bolitho found he could relax now that he knew Rivers was really here.

'And pray, what can I do for you before I take you and your ruffians into custody?'

Bolitho felt his heart pumping against his ribs as if it was the only part of his body still able to respond. Surely the light was brighter? But for the storm the whole fortress would already be visible.

Somewhere beyond the wall he heard a man yell, 'Ready to fire, sir!'

But Rivers was enjoying himself. 'A moment longer, Tate! I must hear the gallant admiral's request.'

Bolitho said in a whisper, 'They cannot shoot while Rivers is there. The ship is in direct line with him.' He raised his voice again, 'I ask you to hold your fire and stand down your men. You have no chance of defeating us, and your people must know full well of the consequences for their actions against a King's ship.'

He tried to picture his words being passed from man to man behind that wall. But they were all islanders, and probably little better than pirates in times of war, although the more sensitive term 'privateer' had made their trade almost legal.

Rivers shouted angrily, 'God damn you, Bolitho! You had your chance, now you shall pay dearly for your bloody arrogance!'

Bolitho blinked as a shaft of bright sunlight pierced the ramparts of the fortress's central tower and laid bare the hillside behind him.

Bolitho heard some of the seamen calling from their hiding places and guessed the sun had also uncovered the anchored two-decker.

Rivers' voice rose higher still as he shouted, 'There's your target, lads! Make every ball tell. That captain is a bigger fool than his admiral!'

Bolitho turned very slowly and looked across the water to the white houses and the cluster of moored vessels. He found that he could ignore the chorus of jeers from Rivers' men as he saw what Keen and his depleted company had achieved in complete darkness. The long cable which had been run out to a mooring buoy from *Achates'* stern held the ship motionless, so that her whole broadside was exposed to the fortress battery. Keen had converted the ship from a living creature to a moored double battery. One side faced the town, the other commanded the anchorage and anything which tried to enter or leave. No wonder Rivers had mistaken their intentions.

Rivers yelled, 'I have a force of mounted men coming to deal with *you*, Bolitho. Your disgrace and ignominy after this reckless escapade will put paid to any future assaults on *my island*!'

Bolitho could see him framed against the washed-out blue sky, could feel the loathing in the man like something solid. He saw smoke rising lazily above the grey stones and knew they were heating shot to destroy *Achates*. There was no more time to spare.

He called, 'I shall return to my men, Sir Humphrey . . .' He felt a nerve jump in his throat as he heard the far-off but familiar rumble. This time he dared not turn, dared not take his eyes from Rivers' silhouette as the muffled sound suddenly ceased.

Rivers exclaimed, 'What good can that do? Not one of her guns can even scratch these walls!' But he sounded less forceful, as if, like Bolitho, the sound of *Achates* running out her guns on both broadsides had released a memory.

'Do you have a telescope, Sir Humphrey?'

It was difficult to stay calm when every fibre made him want to charge at the gates and smash them down with his bare fists.

Rivers was already peering through a glass towards the motionless ship. *Achates'* total stillness made it somehow unnerving. Each sail neatly furled, not a soul moving above the black and buff hull.

Bolitho said, 'You will see a man in the mainmast crosstrees, a lieutenant to be exact. He too will have a telescope this morning, Sir Humphrey. Trained inland towards *your* house and estate.'

Rivers said, 'Don't play for time!'

'And after *that*, the town, Sir Humphrey, until not even a stone stands on end.'

The roar when it came was tremendous, thrown back from *Achates'* hidden side by the land, so that it echoed and re-echoed around the fortress as if the battery there had already opened fire.

Bolitho twisted round to watch the dense smoke moving away from the ship towards the shore, where moments earlier many people had been waiting to see the uneven battle.

Aboard ship Keen's officers would be passing instructions to the capstans, another turn on the massive warp to swing the ship further still towards the target.

He saw the scar on *Achates'* tumblehome where the first ball had found a mark. It was nothing to what heated shot would do.

A small pendant rose smartly to *Achates'* main-yard and flapped in the breeze.

Bolitho said flatly, 'The next broadside is laid and ready. It is your decision.'

Behind him he heard Christy murmur, 'Gawd.'

Allday said, 'The cavalry are comin', sir.'

Bolitho saw the cluster of horsemen cantering along the track which led from the town. They looked unruly, startled probably by the sudden blast of cannon fire. Mercenaries, local planters, militiamen, it did not matter. If they took control of the road and captured Bolitho's party it would mean another change of fortunes.

A bugle blared briefly and Bolitho saw the files of scarlet-coated marines emerge from the brush where they had lain in hiding and prepared for this final moment.

He saw the glitter of sunlight on the fixed bayonets, and could imagine Dewar and his lieutenant receiving the reports of the seasoned professionals like Sergeant Saxton.

The horses had gathered speed, the dust spewing away from the hoofs in a solid bank.

There was a ragged volley of shots, and Bolitho felt a cold grip in his stomach as three of the tiny scarlet figures fell across the track.

The marines seemed to take an eternity, the front rank kneeling beside their dead comrades while the rear rank took aim above their heads. More shots. This time it was a small drummer who fell.

Allday gasped, 'Jesus, why don't they shoot, damn them!'

Dewar's blade flashed down and the crash of muskets seemed as if a single shot had been fired.

Horses and men tumbled in confusion, but when the smoke cleared from the hillside the scarlet lines were unchanged. The horsemen were returning to the town, their dead and wounded left to their own resources.

Christy said fiercely, 'The gates are openin', sir!'

It was over. In twos and threes, and then in a flood, the fortress's garrison hurried into the sunlight, dropping their weapons as they ran.

Last of all came Rivers, swaying from side to side as if he were drunk.

But there was no slur in his voice as he faced Bolitho and said, 'I'll see you in *hell* for this!' He stared wildly at the lush green slope beyond the town. 'My house, my family, you fired on them without caring – '

Bolitho said sharply, 'By your orders some of my men have died today.' He tried to hold his anger under control. 'And for what? Because of your greed and ambition.' He turned away, afraid he would finally lose control. 'And have no fear, Sir Humphrey. While you were prepared to burn a King's ship to her water-line and murder every man-jack aboard if need be, Captain Keen took care to keep his guns *unshotted*. You were defeated by smoke, nothing more.'

It should have been a proud moment but Bolitho was sickened by it.

To Allday he said, 'We shall return to the ship. Dewar's men will take charge here.'

Allday gestured towards the stricken Rivers. 'What about 'im?'

'See that he is well guarded for his own safety.'

Allday glared as two seamen seized Rivers and hustled him back towards the fortress.

Almost to himself Bolitho added, 'It is always easy for the victor to exact revenge.' Then he clapped the burly coxswain on the arm and said, 'The sea is where I belong.'

Allday breathed out very slowly. It had been a close thing that time. He shivered despite the growing warmth. Getting past it. Leave it to the youngsters after this.

The delusion cheered him slightly and he quickened his pace.

The seamen stood on either side of the track and grinned as Bolitho walked amongst them.

Bolitho knew or could guess what they were thinking. *One of us.* Because he was as dirty and dishevelled as they were. Because he had been with them when the bluff could so easily have gone the wrong way.

There was so much to be done. The fortress to be occupied by Dewar's marines, the islanders to be sorted and placated. Despatches to be written. Explanations to be made.

Somewhere a wounded horse screamed in agony. Like a woman in terror. Mercifully it was silenced by a pistol shot.

Bolitho paused by the place where Dewar had made his stand. The drummer-boy lay on his back, his blue eyes and pinched features frozen at the moment of impact.

Allday thought he heard Bolitho murmur, 'Too young for this game.' Then he pulled out his handkerchief and laid it on the boy's face.

One of us. It seemed to mock him as he walked through the grinning, nodding sailors who had all expected to die on this fine morning.

I lead. They follow.

He stared across at the *Achates* and his flag which flapped occasionally from the foremast truck.

He saw the barge idling by some rocks ready to carry him

to the ship. He straightened his back and looked neither right nor left.

A lieutenant was standing in the stern-sheets, his hat in his hand. In a moment they would start to cheer. They were the victors, and that was enough for them. It had to be.

He hesitated and looked at Allday's homely face.

'Well, old friend, what are you thinking?'

Allday frowned, off-balance at this mood which he did not recognize.

Bolitho said quietly, 'I think I know anyway.' He faced the bargemen and forced a smile. 'Now let us find that other damned pirate!'

The lieutenant raised his cocked hat and the men began to cheer.

Bolitho sat down and looked at his torn breeches.

One of us.

Bolitho sat in his day-cabin and sighed as Yovell placed yet another copied letter before him for signature.

The fear and thrill of their attack seemed far behind them, even though it was still less than a week since he had faced Rivers outside the fortress. Their casualties had been mercifully few and had been buried on the hillside in the island's own graveyard.

Bolitho stood up and crossed restlessly to the stern windows and leaned over the passive water of the anchorage. The sill was hot beneath his palms, the sun high above the extinct volcano.

He saw *Achates'* guard-boat pulling slowly and with little enthusiasm in the blinding glare and could guess what they, like most of the ship's company, were thinking.

With their governor under arrest the islanders had settled down to await events. All resistance and hostility had ceased, and some of the local militia had been resworn to assist the Royal Marines mount guard on the fortress and battery. But it went deeper. It was a passive resistance, the townspeople taking pains to look away whenever a naval working party or sea officer walked past.

The sailors were at first hurt then resentful. Some had died, few really understood why, but they deserved better, they thought.

It was noon and the smell of boiling tar mingled with the headier aroma of rum as the daily ration was served to each mess throughout the ship. Fewer hammers broke the stillness now, and there was little to show of the damage made by the fortress's cannon, although one seaman had lost an eye because of a flying splinter.

There was a tap at the outer screen door and Keen entered, his hat beneath his arm. He looked less strained, Bolitho thought. He guessed that Keen had been dealing with his own procession of demands and reports. The surgeon and the first lieutenant, the purser and the master, they all paid their respects to the captain, if only to shift their own loads on to his shoulders.

'You sent for me, sir?'

'Sit down, Val.' Bolitho loosened his shirt for the hundredth time. 'How is the work progressing?'

'I turn the hands to work if only to keep their minds busy, sir. *Achates* is ready for anything. Bandbox neat, she is.'

Bolitho nodded. He had already noticed the new pride Keen had shown for his ship. Maybe her previous captain's example had haunted him and dominated the other officers from the grave.

Bolitho had heard of Keen's clash with Quantock before the headlong charge into harbour. It was hard to believe any of it had happened. But the Union Flag flew above the fortress, and to all outward appearances the island was as before.

Soon he would have to send a despatch to the French admiral whose ships lay waiting at Boston. If they were indeed still there.

Then the peace would shatter here and the pain begin all over again.

Keen watched Bolitho's grave features and said, 'The admiral at Antigua will send aid if you request it, sir.' He saw the line of Bolitho's jaw harden and added, 'But doubtless you have already considered that.'

'I was given this task, Val. Perhaps it is pride which stands in my way. Some might say conceit.' He waved down Keen's protest. 'We all have some. But I need eyes and ears, not another flag-officer to breathe down my neck. But for *Sparrowhawk*'s loss . . .'

They looked at each other. It still seemed as if Duncan was alive.

Keen said, 'Once we weigh and go in search of that damned ship the island could erupt. These people could starve out the garrison, but not the other way round. I think we should order a summary court martial and run Sir Humphrey up to the main-yard on a halter.' He spoke with unusual bitterness. 'Alive he is still a menace.'

They stood up as a single musket shot echoed across the water.

'Guard-boat. Must have sighted something.'

Keen snatched up his hat. 'I'll find out, sir.'

Bolitho took a telescope from its rack and waited for *Achates* to swing gently to her anchor. He watched the fortress swim into view, the upper ramparts half hidden in heat-haze so that the Union Flag seemed to be pinned to the sky itself. There was the headland and the tiny island and its Spanish mission beyond. Then he saw a solitary tanned topsail rounding the point before settling down on a final approach towards the anchorage.

The guard-boat, one of *Achates*' cutters, rocked on the swell, her oars protruding along either side like bleached bones.

A small brigantine. Probably some local trader. Her master would get a surprise when he saw *Achates*' bulk in the harbour.

Keen came back, his face moist with sweat.

'I've ordered the guard-boat to lead the brigantine to a buoy.' He waited for Bolitho to turn. 'She's been fired on to all acounts, sir. I'm sending the surgeon over immediately.'

'Fired on?'

Keen shrugged. 'That's all I know.'

'I see. Well, signal any local craft to stand away. I have an uneasy feeling about this.'

He raised his glass and steadied it on the brigantine as her flapping jib was taken in and she rounded smartly on to a mooring buoy.

He moved the glass carefully along the vessel's side. Black pock-marks marred her paintwork. Grape or cannister. Anything heavier would have sunk such a frail craft. The glass settled on two figures aft by the tiller. A big man in a blue coat with untidy grey hair. The other . . .

Bolitho exclaimed, 'God damn it, Val, it's young Adam! If he's taken any unnecessary risks, I'll . . . '

They faced each other and laughed.

'I'm a *fine* example for him, eh?'

It seemed an eternity for a boat to make the passage between *Achates* and the newcomer.

Bolitho replaced the glass on its rack. It would not do for Adam to think he was worried and over-protective. All the same . . .

Keen said, 'I'll go on deck and er, welcome them, sir.' He hid a smile as he shut the door behind him.

Adam entered the cabin, his features anxious and apprehensive.

'I'm sorry, sir – '

Bolitho strode to him and gripped his shoulders. 'You're *here*. That's all that matters.'

Adam looked round the cabin as if afraid of what he might see.

'The guard-boat, Uncle. They told me about the battle. How you had to fight your way into this place.' He lowered his eyes so that a lock of black hair fell across his forehead. 'I heard about *Sparrowhawk* too. I'm so sorry.'

Bolitho led him to a chair and said quietly, 'Never mind about that. Tell me about your troubles.'

It was an amazing story which the young lieutenant

blurted out. Just a few days ago, after riding out a fierce storm near the Great Bahama Bank, they had been confronted by a frigate. She had been Spanish and had ordered them to heave to and to await a boarding party. The brigantine's master had apparently been suspicious and when the frigate's boat had been almost alongside he had clapped on all sail and had headed away, a favourable wind taking him into some shallows too dangerous for the frigate to follow. But not before the Spanish boarding party had opened fire with swivels and a bow gun which had peppered the side and killed the brigantine's mate.

Bolitho listened without interruption. You were never safe. Not *really* safe. While he had been fretting over San Felipe's future, Adam had faced an unexplained attack and possible death.

He said, 'The vessel's master must be an audacious fellow. Courageous too. I should like to meet him.'

Adam looked at him, his eyes shining. He wanted, no *needed* to tell Bolitho about Robina, but after what he had seen and heard on his passage from Boston he would not spoil the moment for a fortune.

'He came over with me! He's here!'

Bolitho eyed him questioningly. 'Well, let's have him in.'

The sentry opened the screen door and stood aside to allow the visitor to enter. Only the marine's eyes moved beneath his glazed leather hat as he said, 'Master of the *Vivid*, sir!' The 'sir' was accompanied by a sharp tap on the deck with his musket.

Bolitho opened his mouth to speak and then stared with astonishment. The patched blue coat with old navy buttons sewn on the cuffs, the wooden stump which protruded from one of his trouser legs, none of these things could destroy the man's identity.

Bolitho hurried to greet him and held out both hands.

'Jethro Tyrrell. Twenty years, man. And here you are!'

He watched as Tyrrell put his head on one side and regarded him with mock amusement.

'A vice-admiral, they tell me.' He nodded slowly, his

untidy grey hair falling over his collar. 'Never knew the Admiralty had that kind'a sense!'

He released his grip and limped around the great cabin, his hand touching things, his eyes everywhere.

Bolitho watched him, the memories flashing through his thoughts like fiery pictures.

The little sloop-of-war *Sparrow*, his first command, and with Jethro Tyrrell, a Colonist officer, as his lieutenant.

It was painful to see his dragging stump, his worn clothing.

Tyrrell paused by Bolitho's coat which was tossed carelessly on a chair.

He touched one gold epaulette with his forefinger and said softly, 'As you say. Twenty years. You've done well, Dick. Real proud o' you.'

Even the soft Virginian drawl brought back a hundred more memories.

Tyrrell sat down carefully and adjusted his coat. 'I'd best be off. Just wanted to see you. Don't want to – '

Bolitho exclaimed, 'I was your commanding officer once, remember? You'll *stay here* and tell me everything. I tried to discover your whereabouts after the war.'

Tyrrell watched Ozzard bustling round him with goblets and bottles.

He said, 'When I was sent young Adam there as a passenger I knew I had to see you.' His eyes shone in the reflected sunlight.

'They were great days, eh?' He glanced at the spell-bound lieutenant. 'Real young terror he was. Younger than me too. Fought a duel for a girl who wanted him dead, and almost took on the Frogs single-handed.' He was smiling broadly but his eyes were incredibly sad.

Bolitho asked gently, 'What are you doing these days?'

'This an' that. I command the *Vivid*, but she's not mine, worse luck. Do a lot o' trading between the islands. The Dons and the King's ships are always after me as they think I'm a smuggler too. That's a joke. Look at me!'

The door opened and Keen entered warily.

Bolitho said, 'This is Jethro Tyrrell.' He looked at the grey-haired man in the chair. 'My first lieutenant in the *Sparrow*.' He smiled at Keen's surprise. 'Another war, Val, but a fine little ship.'

Tyrrell shifted in his chair, uncomfortable under their stares.

'Anyways, I hear you're having a spot of trouble here. Goin' to hand back San Felipe to the Frogs, right?'

Bolitho nodded gravely. 'News travels a long way.'

Tyrrell grimaced. 'Not fast enough, it seems. It's the bloody Dons you want to worry about. They intend to take this island.' He regarded their faces with quiet satisfaction. 'They will too if you're not damn careful. They've got eyes everywhere. They even tried to stop my *Vivid* to search her and see if I was carrying despatches or letters.' He glanced at Adam. 'My God, if they'd found him aboard they'd have murdered the lot of us, I shouldn't wonder.'

Bolitho leaned towards him. 'Is that really true? About the Spaniards?'

Tyrrell looked at him grimly. 'I need money to buy the *Vivid*. She's not much, but it would be a new start for me.' He turned his face away. 'Just as you want the ship which put down your frigate.'

He sounded hurt. Ashamed. But there was no doubting his sincerity.

Bolitho said, 'I'll help you, Jethro. I would have done anyway if I'd only known.'

'I had some pride, Dick. *Then* I did. Now I'm desperate. Lost my family, all gone. All I've got left is the sea, and I *need* a ship.'

Bolitho walked past him and then stopped with his hand on the big man's shoulder.

'You shall have it. Trust me.'

Tyrrell gave a great sigh. 'Then I'll take you to that bloody Spaniard.'

Bolitho looked at Keen. He seemed too stunned to speak.

Twenty years. It could be yesterday.

10

The Face of Loyalty

'For God's sake close the skylight, Allday!'

Bolitho leaned over his chart again, his hands around neat calculations and soundings, San Felipe and the neighbouring shores of Cuba and Haiti.

With the stern windows shut and now the cabin skylight, the place was like a kiln. It was to no avail anyway, and Bolitho heard Black Joe Langtry's voice quite easily as the master-at-arms counted out the stroke of the cat-o'-nine-tails.

It was strange Bolitho had never accepted or grown used to it. A captain's last resort at maintaining discipline.

A roll of drums, a pause and then that awful crack of the lash across a man's naked back.

He stared hard at the chart until his eyes watered.

'Ten!' Langtry's harsh voice intruded again.

Keen would be up there with his officers, watching it. Hating it. But any King's ship sailing alone and without resort to other support was always in danger of exploding into chaos.

Three trusted seamen had deserted while working ashore for the purser, but had been hunted down and brought back by some of the local militia. They had apparently met some half-caste girls at one of the plantations. The rest needed little imagination.

Crack. 'Eleven!'

Now they were paying the price for their momentary pleasures. Keen had awarded the minimum punishment of twenty-four lashes apiece. But it was enough to turn a man's back into a tangle of raw flesh.

Bolitho thought of Tyrrell again. He was aboard his brigantine *Vivid* attending to storm damage and putting right the other scars left by the Spaniard's swivels.

It was unnerving that Tyrrell should appear like this. Memories of those far-off days together, of the little *Sparrow* and what she had meant to both of them.

Am I to be ever plagued by memory?

Just as the frigate *Phalarope*, which had been Bolitho's second command, had sailed in his squadron last year like a spectre from the past, now came *Sparrow*'s reminder to haunt him.

Was it really so? Was I happier then with less responsibility? Prepared to risk life, even lose it, rather than chance reputation as he was doing now.

The drums ceased and he realized the floggings had ended.

He knew Tyrrell, *really* knew him. Had been with him when he had been smashed to the deck and had lost his leg.

Now he was a shabby reflection of that other man. Outwardly he was no danger to anyone. He was just the sort of ship's master who would hear rumours about the movements and activities of men-of-war. Their nationality and colours mattered little to the master of a small trader. All were potentially dangerous. Seeking prime seamen, even through press-gangs, was no longer in use. Who would know or care until it was too late for the luckless sailor anyway?

Tyrrell had been unshakeable about the powerful two-decker. She wore no colours and carried no name, but Spanish frigates from Santo Domingo, even those from La Guaira hundreds of miles to the south'rd, knew her and kept their distance.

This mysterious ship, which had not hesitated to fire on *Achates* when Keen had outwitted her in the darkness and had butchered *Sparrowhawk*'s people without mercy, was in the Caribbean and its approaches for a purpose. A task in which she would risk anything if required.

He heard Allday open the skylight and knew that he, like Ozzard and everyone who came near, was being especially careful.

Bolitho looked at his big coxswain and shrugged helplessly. 'I do not know what is happening to me.'

Allday nodded his head and smiled. 'Waitin', that's what's wrong, sir.'

'I suppose so.'

Bolitho looked down at the chart again. It was a week since *Vivid* had sailed into the harbour and Tyrrell had re-entered his life. Without another ship Bolitho dared not leave San Felipe. An attack might be launched by Rivers' supporters, there were plenty of them in evidence. Bolitho could not blame them. They would have to quit their homes and their plantations when the French came. Perhaps Keen had been right. If they hanged Rivers it might end there.

But Rivers had powerful friends in America and the City of London. In Bolitho's eyes he was no better than a pirate. But a proper trial in London would be required by their lordships to prove it.

If Tyrrell was right and the unknown two-decker was preparing to mount an attack on San Felipe, it was folly to leave the harbour unguarded. *Achates* had proved what could be done when it seemed worth the risk.

The door opened and Adam walked into the cabin.

A full week since they had been reunited and yet they had said very little. Adam was keeping something from him. Or maybe he had been too busy and preoccupied to share the young lieutenant's confidences.

He said, 'Signal from the battery, sir. The brig *Electra* is standing into the bay. She should anchor within the hour.'

'Thank you, Adam.'

Bolitho's eyes moved back to the chart. He could picture the brig's commander clearly when he had described his discovery of the *Sparrowhawk*'s few survivors in an American trader. Napier, that was his name. He must have sailed under every inch of canvas to make such a fast passage to Antigua and then westwards to San Felipe. Dare he hope that *Electra* would be able to wait in the harbour as a show of authority? She was only a small brig, but she flew the same flag as *Achates*.

Bolitho suspected that many of the islanders would be happier if a King's ship was always here, rather than leave the door open for the French or, as Tyrrell had said, the Spaniards.

Bolitho walked to the windows and shaded his eyes with his forearm.

'Signal *Electra*'s captain to repair on board immediately he anchors.'

Adam smiled gravely. 'I have requested the battery to relay that signal already, Uncle.'

Bolitho turned and spread his hands. 'You'll make a fine commander one of these days, my lad.'

Keen entered the cabin and dropped into a chair at Bolitho's bidding.

'I wonder what news she brings us, sir?'

He took a glass of hock gratefully and held it to his lips. Ozzard had been keeping a special store of it in the bilges ever since the ship had left the Beaulieu River in Hampshire.

'Any news will be welcome. I sometimes feel like a man who has gone deaf.'

Keen said, 'Maybe their lordships will recall us.'

Bolitho said, 'Adam, make a signal to *Vivid*, better still, go across and speak with Mr Tyrrell. I'd like him aboard with me when we sail.'

Keen waited for the door to close and then put his glass down very carefully.

'May I say something, sir?'

'You disagree with my proposed strategy, is that it?'

Keen smiled briefly. 'You are taking a terrible chance. Two chances to be exact.' When Bolitho remained silent he continued, 'This man Tyrrell. How much do you know about him?'

'He was my first lieutenant . . .' Keen nodded. 'You mean that's not enough after twenty years?'

Keen shrugged. 'Hard to say, sir. He said himself he's desperate. He's lost his wife and family, even his reputation, because he fought for the King rather than Washington.'

'Go on.' Bolitho could sense Allday holding his breath.

'Suppose you meet with the Spaniard and bring her to action, what would we do if she hoists her true colours? Would you spark off a war?'

'Tell me about the second risk.'

Keen was perfectly right to point it out to him. But it made Bolitho feel more isolated than ever.

'The second one is that the Spanish ship, *if* she is still in these waters, might be waiting for you to leave harbour so that she can snatch *Achates*' place. You would have to fight your way back in. Not against a few stupid planters and the local militia, but a real ship, and the men to back up her authority. In my opinion, the risk outweighs the profit.' He dropped his eyes. 'I – I am sorry, sir. But it had to be said.'

Bolitho smiled sadly. 'I understand what it cost you. In truth, I do not know if a risk can ever be measured. I don't wish our people to die for no purpose. Nor do I want my own body divided between the wings and limbs tubs around the surgeon's table. I have everything to live for. Now. But . . .'

Keen grinned and took a refilled glass from Ozzard.

'Aye, sir, *but*. What a powerful argument that small word can raise against reason!'

Bolitho tapped the chart with his brass dividers.

'I believe that ship to be here, just as Jethro Tyrrell described. She has a sizeable company, so will require a good haven to shelter in while her captain seeks information about us. Beset as we are by enemies, that part will not be too difficult for him.'

Keen stood up and joined him by the table.

'*If* Tyrrell is right, it would make things very difficult in a war.' He ran his fingers along the islands. Puerto Rico, Santo Domingo, Haiti, even Cuba. 'The Spaniards would command all the approaches to the Caribbean and to Jamaica.' He nodded slowly, understanding spreading on his handsome features. 'And San Felipe stands astride the Windward Passage like a drawbridge. No wonder the French want the island for themselves. They need an ally, but they are not required to trust him!'

They were both studying the chart when a midshipman announced the arrival of *Electra* at the anchorage.

Keen buttoned his coat.

'I'll receive Commander Napier, sir.' He glanced at the table. 'I'm still not sure that I am convinced, sir.'

Bolitho smiled. 'You will be.'

He allowed Ozzard to assist him into his sea-going coat out of respect for *Electra*'s captain.

His body ran with sweat, and through the stern windows he saw the gentle rise and fall of the clear water and imagined himself swimming naked there. His thoughts turned instantly to Belinda. It only took a split second. Like dropping your guard through fatigue or over-confidence. The enemy's blade darting forward like a steel tongue. He had tried to occupy every moment of his time with his work and the puzzle which he must solve. But every so often he saw only Belinda and the distance which divided them like an eternal barrier.

He vaguely heard footsteps and lowered voices. He had to recover himself for their sakes as well as his own.

Soon now, probably very soon, they would have to fight. This was no haphazard scheme or piratical aspiration. The unknown ship had already proved that to be in the right was no protection. Too many had died already to support such an argument.

He faced the door. In any war the cannon was impartial. Its roar swept away saint and sinner with the same indifference.

Commander Napier, with a shining new epaulette fixed to his left shoulder for the occasion, entered and clicked his shoes together.

Bolitho took the heavy envelope from his hand and passed it to Yovell.

'You made a speedy passage, Commander Napier.'

Bolitho tried to contain his impatience as Napier was put in a chair and a glass of wine brought for him.

Napier said, 'English Harbour is almost empty of ships but for a third-rate which is refitting and two frigates. The admiral has taken the squadron to the Leeward Islands, sir. Commodore Chater is in temporary command.' He swallowed under Bolitho's grey stare. 'He sends you his respects and best wishes, sir.'

Bolitho heard Yovell breaking the seals on the canvas envelope and wanted to run and tear out the despatches from Antigua. But without the admiral there he was helpless. He knew a little of Commodore Chater. He was not one to risk the displeasure of his superior with some brave gesture.

Napier added huskily, 'I am commanded to place myself and *Electra* at your wishes, sir.' He screwed up his eyes as he tried to recall exactly what Chater had told him. 'When he learned of *Sparrowhawk*'s loss he wished to send some marines to enlarge your force.'

Bolitho nodded. 'But the marines have also sailed with the squadron, am I right?'

Napier replied miserably, 'Aye, sir.' Then he brightened and added, 'But I was ordered to embark a platoon of the Sixtieth Foot in their stead, sir.'

Keen, who had followed him aft, said quietly, 'That's something.'

Bolitho turned towards the windows while he tried to fit the pieces together.

Napier said brightly, 'But I expect you knew about the soldiers, sir. The commodore sent word with the courier-brig which sailed two days ahead of me.'

Bolitho swung round. '*What* did you say?'

Napier paled. 'The courier, sir. Despatches for the admiral at Antigua, others for you, sir.' He looked to Keen for comfort. 'From England, sir.'

Keen exclaimed, 'You were right, sir. They must have caught and sunk the courier-brig too.'

Bolitho grasped his hands behind his back and squeezed them until the pain controlled his dismay.

From England. With despatches. And letters. News of Belinda. And now . . .

He looked at Keen. 'So you are convinced?' He did not hear his answer.

To Napier he said, 'Have you a capable first lieutenant?'

Napier was completely lost. For hours he had rehearsed what he would say to Bolitho. He had had time to put on his best uniform. Now it had all shattered. Like opening a door to greet a friend and finding oneself confronted by a madman.

He managed to nod. 'Aye, sir. He is a good officer.'

'Just as well.' Bolitho looked at Keen. 'First opportunity tomorrow we will weigh and put to sea. In the meantime I shall endeavour to glean what I can from the gallant commodore's despatches. But before *that* . . . ' He crossed to the table and poured Napier another glass of hock. 'We shall all drink a toast. You too, Allday.'

Allday took a glass from Ozzard and watched the transformation in looks and tone.

Bolitho felt his mouth lift to a grin.

'A toast.' He raised his glass. 'To Mr Napier, the new acting-governor of San Felipe!'

'Sou'-west by south, sir! Steady she goes!'

Bolitho half listened to the helmsman's report but concentrated on the sprawling purple blur on the larboard horizon. It was afternoon and the sun still beat down on the slow-moving ship with relentless ferocity. But after the oppressive hostility in San Felipe it was like a tonic.

Bolitho could feel it in the ship around and beneath him, the cheerful banter of the seamen on deck. Mountsteven, who was officer of the watch, barely raised his voice as he supervised the final resetting of the fore-course.

Bolitho steadied his telescope and watched the vague suggestion of land, Haiti, which lay some fifteen miles to larboard. Despite the distance it had an air of menace. Whenever possible sailors avoided its shores with their tales of witchcraft and horrifying rites.

Achates had been delayed a further day in San Felipe for want of wind, but now with the prevailing north-easterly filling her topsails and courses she was standing down the Windward Passage as if she was enjoying it. Here the Passage between Cuba and Haiti was barely seventy miles wide, its narrowest part. In time of war it would be hard to force a convoy through, with San Felipe in enemy hands. The more he considered it, the less Bolitho could understand the reason for his orders.

He handed the glass to one of the midshipmen and began to pace slowly up and down the quarterdeck. He hoped he had not been too hard on Commander Napier. The latter appeared to be relishing his new, if brief, appointment as temporary governor. With his fourteen-gun brig anchored below the powerful battery, and a smart platoon of the Sixtieth Foot, or the Royal Americans as they were still known, in the fortress, he was able to present a show of strength.

He saw some marines having their muskets and equipment inspected by Lieutenant Hawtayne. He was glad they were back on board where they belonged. It seemed very likely they would soon be needed again.

He hid a smile as the marine lieutenant said in his piping voice, 'Smarten yourself up, Jones! You've *had* your rest ashore!'

Bolitho knew that the picture of the dead drummer-boy would last a long time in his memory.

He heard Adam's light step nearby and saw him waiting to speak.

'How is my flag-lieutenant today?'

Adam smiled. It was the moment.

'Miss Robina is a fine girl, Uncle. I've never met anyone like her . . .'

Bolitho let it pour out without interruption. So that was

the trouble. But for his own worries he would have realized that the ride to Newburyport would be a beginning rather than an ending.

'Have you asked her father for her hand in marriage?'

Adam blushed. 'It's far too soon, Uncle, that is, I hinted perhaps sometime in the future, that is, not the *too* distant future . . . ' His voice trailed away and he stared at the dark water abeam. Then he said, 'I know she won't have me, of course. Her uncle knows. He was glad to get rid of me aboard one of his vessels.'

Bolitho looked at him. *Vivid* was owned by Chase. It was strange that Tyrrell had not mentioned it.

'Let us walk awhile, Adam.'

They paced back and forth for several minutes while the ship moved and worked around them.

Bolitho said, 'You have a future in the Navy, Adam. A good one, if I have any say in the matter. You come of fine sea-going stock, but so have many others. Whatever gain you make, and whatever achievements you have won, you will have done so without the use of privilege, remember that. Yours will be a better Navy, or should be when young officers like you have positions of authority. We're an island race. We shall always need ships and those brave enough to fight them.'

Adam glanced at him. 'It is what I want. Have wanted since I joined your *Hyperion* as midshipman.'

Bolitho looked down at the gun-deck and saw the seaman who had lost an eye being greeted by some of his messmates as he swayed uncertainly past an eighteen-pounder. He was still unused to it. But with his black eye-patch to conceal the oakum which filled the empty socket he looked every inch a hero, and they were treating him as such.

Adam tried to find the words. 'Men like that one, Uncle. They mean a lot to you. They're not just ignorant hands, they *matter*, don't they?'

Bolitho faced him. 'They most certainly do. We must never take them for granted, Adam. There are plenty of others who do that!'

Adam nodded. 'When I sat in my father's old chair . . . '

Bolitho asked quietly, 'At Newburyport? Where his ship was once sheltered?'

Adam looked away. He had not meant it to slip out quite like that, or so soon.

'They showed me, Uncle. It was the family name, you see. Not common in New England.'

'I'm glad. You've seen more than I.'

He heard Keen approaching and was suddenly thankful. It was not just Hugh's memory, what he had done to their father when he had deserted to fight for the American rebels, not because of that or the shame which even Rivers had been quick to mention. Bolitho tried to face it. He was jealous. Hurt, even though it was ridiculous.

Keen touched his hat. 'Mr Tyrrell is in the chartroom with the master, sir. I think we should examine the next chart.' He glanced professionally at the clear sky. 'Should be able to maintain a fair speed all night at this rate.' He seemed oblivious to the awkward silence.

'Good, I'll come directly.' He nodded to his nephew. 'You too. It's all experience for whatever you intend.'

He hesitated outside the chartroom and said abruptly, 'Take charge, Val. I'm going aft. You can explain it all later.'

Adam asked anxiously, 'Are you feeling unwell, sir?'

Bolitho said, 'Just tired.'

He strode away and was soon lost in the shadows below the poop deck.

He was unable to face all of them crammed together in the small space of the chartroom. Knocker, the master, Quantock, Captain Dewar of the Royal Marines, and their assistants as well.

Bolitho had left another letter with Napier at San Felipe, and a copy to be sent by any other vessel which might happen to call at the harbour for supplies or water.

Not knowing about Belinda was tearing at him like claws. He had not realized how brittle his reserves had become. Not until Adam had reminded him of Hugh. *My father's old chair.*

Before, Hugh had remained misty and obscure. Now he was here amongst them. Fighting for his place.

Bolitho slumped down on the stern seat and stared at the glistening froth left by *Achates'* rudder.

Allday padded in from the dining space. 'Can I fetch you a glass, sir?' He was careful to keep his voice level.

'No, but thank you.' Bolitho twisted round to look at him. 'You are the only one who really knows me, do you understand that?'

'Sometime I do, an' then again sometime I don't, sir. By an' large I think I sees the *man* more'n others do.'

Bolitho lay back and breathed in the damp air. 'God, Allday, I am in hell.' But when he looked again Allday had vanished.

He watched a fish jumping astern. Who could blame Allday? He was probably ashamed of seeing his secret despair.

But Allday, as was his wont, had gone to his tiny, screened-off mess which he shared with his two friends, Jewell, the *Achates'* sailmaker, and the boatswain's mate Christy whom he had known in the *Lysander* at the Nile.

Three great tots of rum later he presented himself at Keen's cabin door.

The captain's clerk regarded him warily. 'What do 'ee want, Allday?'

The clerk winced as Allday breathed out the heavy fumes. 'Request to see the cap'n.'

It was unorthodox, and Keen was feeling weary after the discussion in the chartroom. But he knew Allday, and owed him his very life.

'Come in and close the door.' He dismissed his clerk and asked, 'What is it, man? You look like someone intent on a fight?'

Allday took another long breath. 'It's the admiral, sir. He's carryin' more'n his share. It's not fair . . .'

Keen smiled. So that was all. He had imagined something terrible had occurred.

Allday continued, 'I just wanted to say my piece, sir, seein' you're a decent man an' a real friend to 'im down aft. It's somethin' the flag-lieutenant said to 'im. I feel it in me bones. Somethin' which wounded 'im deeply.'

Keen was tired but he was intelligent and quick-witted. He knew he should have seen it. The unusual strangeness between the vice-admiral and his nephew.

He said, 'Leave it with me, Allday. I understand.'

Allday studied his face and then nodded. 'Had to speak, sir. Otherwise, officer or not, I'll put the flag-lieutenant across my knee and beat the hell out of 'im!'

Keen stood up. 'I didn't hear that, Allday.' He smiled gravely. 'Now be off with you.'

For a long while Keen sat at his table and watched the sun dying on the gently heaving sea.

He had a million things to do, for somehow he knew they would be called to fight very soon now. Like Allday, he thought, *in me bones*. The memory did not amuse him but he found that he was able to forget the conference, Quantock's silent disapproval and the man Tyrrell's brash promises to lead them to a place where they could hold an advantage against the other ship.

And all because of Allday. He had known Bolitho's coxswain on and off for eighteen turbulent years. Years of hardship and war, of momentary distractions and the incredible joy of staying alive when that seemed an impossibility.

One word stood out where Allday was concerned. *Loyalty*.

Keen reached wearily for the bell to summon his clerk.

He doubted if many people could describe what loyalty was, but he had been privileged to see what it looked like.

11

Revenge

'All hands, all hands! Hands aloft an' loose topsails!'

Bolitho stood at the quarterdeck rail and watched the dripping cutters being secured yet again on their tier. *Achates* had anchored for several hours while the boats had been lowered to examine an inlet where a ship might be concealed. As on all the other occasions, they had returned with nothing to report.

Bolitho shaded his eyes from the intense glare to look at the land. Santo Domingo was just a few miles to the north-west, then the Mona Passage, back to the northern approaches where they had started.

Two weeks wasted. Making use of winds which would barely move a leaf on an inland stream.

He watched the big topsails flapping and filling as the ship heeled slightly on her new tack.

Keen crossed the quarterdeck and waited for Bolitho to face him.

'With respect, sir, I think we should return to San Felipe.'

Bolitho replied, 'I know these waters well, Val. You can hide a fleet if need be. You think I'm mistaken, don't you?' He touched his crumpled shirt and smiled. 'I don't blame you. These past weeks have been hard on all of us.'

Keen said, 'I'm worried for you, sir. The longer we wait . . .'

Bolitho nodded. 'I know. My head on the block. I've always understood that.'

The shrouds creaked as the wind increased a little to fill the sails. High above the decks the extra lookouts strained their eyes and silently cursed their officers for their discomfort.

Bolitho heard the heavy tap of Tyrrell's wooden stump and turned to greet him. Keen made his excuses and moved to another part of the quarterdeck. His mistrust and growing suspicion were obvious.

Tyrrell glanced at Keen and said, 'Don't like me much, that one.' He sounded worried, less confident.

Bolitho asked, 'Are you still certain, Jethro?'

'She could have gone elsewhere.' He pounded his fist on the rail. 'But several friends told me she'd been usin' one of the inlets as a restin' place. She's nothin' to fear from the Dons. They *know* what she's about, I'm certain of that too.'

Bolitho looked at him thoughtfully. 'We're inside their waters now. I've no authority even to be here unless that damned ship is sheltering behind the Spanish flag.'

Keen returned, his face expressionless. 'We shall have to change tack again shortly, sir.' He purposely ignored Tyrrell. 'After that it will be a hard beat up to the Mona Passage. The wind is poor enough, but it seems intent on holding us back.'

Even as he spoke the fore-topsail flapped and banged against the shrouds and men scurried to the braces to retrim the yards yet again.

Tyrrell said suddenly, 'I know of a place. Give me a boat.' He was speaking quickly as if to stifle his own arguments against his suggestion. 'You don't believe me. I'm not even sure myself.'

They looked up as a lookout yelled, 'Deck there! Sail to the nor'-west!'

Keen murmured, 'Bloody hell! It'll be a patrol boat out of Santo Domingo!'

Tyrrell regarded him bleakly. 'They'll have been watchin' your fine ship for days, Captain, I'll wager a bounty on it!'

Keen looked away and retorted, 'You'd know about bounties right enough!'

Bolitho said sharply, 'Enough.'

He looked up at the masthead. A fine, clear day, the lookout would see better than anyone.

He cupped his hands and shouted, 'What ship?'

Bolitho was aware that several of the seamen nearby had stopped work to stare. An admiral, even a junior one, shouting? It must seem like heresy.

The lookout shouted down, 'Frigate, sir, by the cut of her!'

Bolitho nodded. A frigate. Keen was probably right. There was not much time. Two hours at the most.

He said, 'Heave to, if you please, and lower a cutter. Lieutenant in charge, and have the boat armed.'

Voices yelled around him and feet pounded across the sun-dried planking as *Achates* came reluctantly into the wind even as the boat was hoisted jerkily above the starboard gangway.

Knocker hovered at Keen's elbow and muttered, 'The inlet is a mere scratch, sir. Never get a ship in there!'

Tyrrell replied heavily, 'Your chart says that. I say different!'

Bolitho watched Scott, the third lieutenant, hastily buckling on his hanger while the wardroom servant followed him with his pistol and cocked hat. From fretting torpor to urgent activity, how often Bolitho had known and shared that.

'Cutter alongside, sir!'

There was a thud as a swivel-gun was mounted in the boat's bows, and two seamen began to ram a charge down its muzzle.

Bolitho said quietly, 'Did you always know about this inlet, Jethro? These past two weeks and before, you knew this was the place? Yet in a moment or two we would have changed tack and the opportunity would have been lost.'

Tyrrell said, 'You wanted that ship. I kept a bargain.'

Then he was gone, swinging his wooden leg in great strides as he made for the entry port.

Bolitho knew the truth at that moment, but something made him hurry to the nettings and call, 'Take care, Jethro! And good luck!'

Tyrrell paused, his big hands grasping the lines of the stairs down the tumblehome as he stared aft at the quarterdeck, his eyes watering in the sunlight. For just a few moments the years fell away and they were back in *Sparrow*. Then Tyrrell swung himself out and down into the cutter, his wooden stump jutting out like a tusk.

Keen murmured, 'I wonder.'

The cutter pulled quickly away from the side, the oars rising and dipping to a fast stroke, her coxswain standing upright behind the lieutenant as he headed for the shore.

Bolitho bit his lip. 'I trusted him. Perhaps it was too strong for him in the end.'

Keen shook his head. 'I don't understand, sir.'

Bolitho watched the boat swinging round in a tight arc as Tyrrell's arm pointed to larboard in a new direction. He could see the swirl of an inshore current, the way the trees and thick scrub ran down to the water's edge. It was hard to believe that the inlet was other than the chart had described.

There was a far-off bang and then the lookout called, 'Frigate's fired a shot, sir!'

Knocker remarked dourly, 'Couldn't hit Gibraltar from there!'

Bolitho glanced at Keen. Was it a warning to *Achates* to quit Spanish waters or a signal to someone else?

He said, 'I suggest you beat to quarters. Clear for action without delay.' He turned to watch the cutter's progress. 'We'll not be caught a second time.'

Around him men stood stiffly like crude statues, unable to believe what they had heard.

Then, as the drums rattled and voices barked hoarsely between decks, the truth became clear to everyone.

Keen folded his arms and looked down the length of his command. Men hurried along either gangway, tamping down the tightly packed hammocks in the nettings, while ship's boys dashed among the guns and spread sand which might prevent a man from slipping if the blood started to flow. Big Harry Rooke, the boatswain, was yelling at some of his own party as they scrambled along the yards to rig chain-slings to prevent the spars from falling on the men below. Others tore down screens between decks to transform the great space from small, individual messes and cabins into one open battery from bow to stern.

Quantock looked up from the gun-deck and touched his hat.

'Cleared for action, sir!' He had learned Keen's ways by now. Just as Keen had once learned them under Bolitho's command. 'Nine minutes, sir!'

Keen nodded. 'That was well done, Mr Quantock.'

But there was nothing between them, and neither smiled because of the small compliment.

Bolitho raised a telescope and watched the distant cutter. What Lieutenant Scott and the others must be thinking he could only guess. The roll of drums as *Achates* beat to quarters, the bang of a cannon, and all the time they were pulling further and further from their ship, their home.

He heard Allday give a discreet cough and saw him holding out his coat for him while Ozzard fussed around behind with his sword. Adam was here too, clear-eyed and looking incredibly young and anxious.

'Orders, sir?'

Bolitho allowed Allday to clip on the old sword and was saddened by Adam's formality.

He said, 'I am sorry, Adam. I should have known. You have every right to be proud. In your place I would have felt the same.'

The youthful lieutenant took half a pace towards him.

'I would cut off a hand rather than hurt you, sir. It was just that . . .'

'It was just that you wanted to share it with me and I was too busy to listen.'

Keen said, 'Ready, sir.'

He glanced from one to the other and felt strangely relieved. He looked directly at Allday but the coxswain did not even blink. Keen smiled. Allday was a fox.

'Very well.' Bolitho looked at his flag at the foremast truck. 'Run up the colours, if you please. And then, Mr Bolitho, make a signal. *Enemy in sight.*' He saw Adam's expression change from surprise to understanding as he added for the quarterdeck's benefit, 'We might as well give them the idea we are not totally alone, eh, lads?'

He looked at Keen. 'Let's be about it.'

Suppose there was nothing? That he had been wrong about Tyrrell, about everything else? He would be a laughing-stock.

He saw the signals midshipman, Ferrier, with his assistants, and little Evans from the *Sparrowhawk* busy at the halliards, and then as the bright balls of bunting dashed up the yard and broke to the breeze there was an excited cheer from the men at the upper-deck eighteen-pounders.

Most of them could not distinguish one flag from another. But to them it meant more than words. It was a symbol. A part of *them*.

Keen watched Bolitho's face and sighed. *I should have known.*

There was a sharp whiplash crack and several voices yelled, 'They've fired on the cutter, the buggers!'

Cheers one instant, fury the next.

Bolitho snatched a glass and watched the cutter coming about, the oars in momentary confusion as the water around it leapt with vicious feathers of spray. He saw a corpse pushed roughly over the gunwale to give more space to the oarsmen, and heard a loud bang as the cutter's swivel raked the trees nearest to the beach.

Keen was shouting, 'We may have to leave the cutter, Mr Quantock! But signal Mr Scott to return with all haste!'

He glanced at Bolitho but saw that he was standing by the nettings, his eyes fixed on the partly hidden inlet as if he was expecting something to happen.

The cutter was moving slowly now, and Bolitho knew that more than one of the seamen had been hit, probably by musket fire. He shifted his gaze from the lively current which betrayed the inlet and saw Tyrrell standing at the boat's tiller, waving a fist to drive the oarsmen to greater efforts.

The main-topsail lifted and cracked with sudden impatience.

Bolitho said, 'Be ready to get the ship under way again, Mr Knocker. We have a few minutes yet.'

Quantock said, 'The frigate's holding on the same course, sir.'

Bolitho felt his mouth run dry as something moved beyond and through a long bank of trees. Like a serpent's tail, yellow and red in the sunlight. The masthead pendant of a large ship, the remainder of her still hidden as she edged slowly through the concealed channel towards open water.

Then her tapering jib-boom and figurehead, blazing gold, and her forecastle and a tightly reefed topsail, her jib barely flapping as she moved sedately into the glare.

Another few moments and they would have lost her. They must have been holding their breaths as *Achates* had sailed past, laughed at their pathetic efforts to find them. Bolitho clenched his fists behind his coat tails. They would not laugh much longer.

The cutter was less than a cable away, and Keen said, 'Grapnel ready. No time to hoist the boat now!'

He tore his eyes from the other vessel as it moved from cover until she seemed to fill the shoreline.

'Hell's teeth, she's the one right enough!'

Bolitho lifted the old sword two inches from its scabbard and then snapped it down again.

'*Finally*, Captain Keen, you are convinced.'

He heard shouts as the boat's crew were hauled bodily up the side while the wounded were hoisted on bowlines, their anguished cries ignored in the haste to get them to safety.

Achates heeled more firmly in the wind, her hull brushing away the cutter like a piece of flotsam. Tyrrell remained standing at the tiller, his sole companion a dead seaman who crouched over an oar as if temporarily exhausted.

Bolitho exclaimed, 'Throw him a line! I'll not leave him!'

In his heart he knew Tyrrell intended to remain in the boat, to be carried away by the current. He had purposefully guided *Achates* from one false scent to another, and had even suggested that the boats should examine a cove directly alongside the other ship's real hiding-place. Nobody would ever have known. But something at the very last moment had persuaded him to act as he had.

Now the truth would come out. He would be lucky to escape with his life for what he had done.

Bolitho saw a heaving-line snake over the drifting boat, watched Tyrrell's uncertainty and anguish before he caught the line and took two turns around the abandoned swivel-gun.

Keen waited only long enough for Tyrrell to be seized by the waiting hands at the entry port before he yelled his orders and sent his men rushing aloft again to set the topgallant sails in what seemed like a rising wind.

Bolitho felt the ship shudder, the urgent clatter of blocks and rigging as *Achates* responded to the pressure.

Keen stared at him and said, 'What was the damn fool trying to do anyway? What chance will — ' But the rest of his words were lost in the jarring roar of gunfire.

Along the other ship's side the heavy muzzles were jerking back into their ports and suddenly the air above *Achates'* decks was filled with deadly iron. Several holes appeared in the tightly braced sails, and Bolitho felt the familiar jerk through his shoes as other balls struck hard into the hull.

He watched as Knocker's helmsmen took control and very slowly at first, and then more confidently, the ship pointed her bowsprit towards the land, the wind pushing her over with an invisible hand. The other ship was following suit to take the maximum advantage of the wind.

Had Bolitho ordered Keen to beat up the Mona Passage to take advantage of this same wind on the other side of the islands, it would have taken days to reach San Felipe. The ship which was now almost bows on as she clawed away from the shallows would have beaten them with time to spare. The little *Electra* would have fought to the finish, but nothing could have stopped the inevitable.

Keen held out his arm. '*Easy*, Mr Knocker! Easy now!'

Achates continued to turn, her sails bulging hard on the opposite tack as the seamen on braces and halliards threw their weight against the swing of the yards.

The master grunted over his shoulder and the helmsmen slowed the great spinning spokes of the wheel.

'Steady, sir! West by north!'

Bolitho licked his lips. The enemy's ports were at too extreme an angle to fire. She had made her challenge prematurely. But she was a well-handled ship and was already responding to the wind as she came about.

'Starboard battery!' Keen's sword came out of its scabbard with a hiss. 'On the uproll!'

Down the *Achates'* side and on the deck below the gun captains would be peering through their ports, trigger lines taut, as they watched their target swim into view.

The bright blade flashed down in the sunlight, and with a drawn-out roll of thunder the eighteen- and twenty-four-pounders of both decks hurled themselves inboard on their tackles.

The smoke billowed towards the bows and Bolitho watched as the enemy's rigging and canvas danced wildly under the onslaught. Tall waterspouts lined the enemy's bilge as other balls slammed hard down alongside, but she returned the fire even as she completed her manoeuvre.

Bolitho felt the deck shake and heard a terrible shriek from one of the hatchways.

Every gun crew was working like madmen, sponges, charges and rammers moving like parts of the men themselves. Finally those shining black balls from the shot-garlands, rammed home with a last tap for good measure. Each crew was racing its neighbour, and as every captain held up his hand Keen shouted hoarsely, 'Broadside! *Fire!*'

This time there was no mistake, and at a range of barely two cables it was possible to see *Achates'* weight of iron smashing into the other ship's hull, splintering a gangway and bringing down a tangled heap of rigging from the mizzen.

But the enemy's heavier thirty-two-pounders were already reloaded and poking through their ports like angry snouts. Again the stabbing line of orange tongues, the terrible commotion and crash between decks as many of the balls found their mark.

Bolitho saw a man hurled from his gun, his face a mask of blood. He also saw Midshipman Evans standing stiff and unmoving as he stared at the other ship. If he was afraid of the din of battle he did not show it, but in his pale features Bolitho saw the enemy through the boy's own eyes. He was remembering her as he had last seen her, when his ship had been smashed and set ablaze, when Duncan had died beside him.

Bolitho called, 'Walk about, Mr Evans!' He saw the boy look at him without understanding and added, 'You are small but still a prime target.'

Evans gave what might have been a smile and then went to aid the fallen seaman.

The guns rolled inboard again on their tackles, the air cringed to their explosions and men gasped in the dense smoke and charred fragments which surrounded them.

Hallowes, the fourth lieutenant, strode behind the forward division of guns, his hanger across his shoulder as he peered at his crews.

'Stop your vents!'

'Sponge out!'

Several men ducked as hammocks burst from the nettings and metal screamed against one of the guns on the opposite side. Two men fell, another limped away and crouched below the gangway like a frightened animal.

'Load!'

Hallowes pointed at the crouching seaman and shouted, 'Back to your station, *now*!'

'Run out!'

Again the squeaking rumble of trucks as gun by gun the

ship presented her full broadside to the enemy. The latter had changed tack slightly and was converging on *Achates*, her guns firing again and again.

Bolitho watched Keen moving from one side of the quarterdeck to the other. More shots hammered the side, and there was a great chorus from the lower gun-deck and Bolitho knew that a twenty-four-pounder had been upended or, worse still, had broken away from its tackles.

Both ships were evenly matched. *Achates* mounted more guns, but the enemy's heavier broadside was taking a terrible toll. One lucky shot was all it would take. He stared at Keen's shoulders, as if to will him to act. *Close the range*, Val. Get to grips before he dismasts you.

More cries and screams echoed through the crash and recoil of cannon, and a marine staggered away from the poop nettings, his hands to his face, his chest punctured by flying wood splinters.

'Jesus, what a mess!' Tyrrell limped between the trailing tackles and pieces of torn rigging which had found their way through the nets overhead.

Bolitho said, 'Get below. You're a civilian.'

Tyrrell winced as a ball shattered on the breech of a quarterdeck nine-pounder and splinters cracked around them and flung two more seamen into a puddle of their own blood.

Keen turned round and glared at Tyrrell. 'What the hell are you doing here?'

Tyrrell showed his teeth. 'Get that bugger alongside, Captain, your people can't keep up this pace!'

Keen looked at Bolitho. 'They'll know it's your flagship, sir!'

So that was it. Bolitho pulled out his old sword. 'Put the helm over. We'll give them a fight,' he raised his voice, *'eh, lads?'*

He turned away as they cheered him. Half-naked, blackened by powder smoke, their sweat cutting channels through the grime, they were hardly the romantic heroes portrayed in the fine paintings he had seen in London.

He felt the madness welling up inside him. 'Lively there!'

The yards swung slightly as the helm went over, and within minutes the range had fallen to a cable, then half as much; then as the other ship's sails rose high above the nettings and muskets joined in the deafening onslaught, it was down to fifty yards and still closing.

The other captain had no choice. He could not turn and run. The land which had hidden him was now a deadly enemy, with breakers in plenty to show the lie of the reefs. If he tried to come about he would be all aback for those vital moments when Keen's gun crews would rake him from end to end.

There was a loud, splintering crack and voices yelled, 'Heads below there!' Part of the mizzen cross-jack yard ploughed through the nets, rebounded and crashed down in a welter of rigging, blocks and trailing canvas.

Bolitho felt a blow on the shoulder like an iron fist, then he was face down on the deck. His first thought was near to terror. Another wound. Fatal. Then he cursed into the smoke which had almost blinded him when his presence would be most missed.

He felt Adam holding his arm, his grimy face set in a grim stare, then Allday dragging something away from his back and easing him over on to his knees, then to his feet. A huge block, cut down by a shot through the mizzen rigging but swinging on its cordage like a bludgeon, had laid him low. He was not even cut, and he managed to force a grin as someone gave him his hat and another yelled, 'You'll show them buggers, sir!'

Bolitho faced the enemy, his eyes smarting, his shoulder throbbing from the blow. If it had struck his skull he would be dead at this very instant.

Musket shots punched into and through the packed hammocks, and wooden splinters flew from the quarterdeck or stood motionless like quill pens.

Axes flashed in the smoky sunlight, and more wreckage was hacked free and levered over the side with handspikes.

All the relentless gun and sail drill was showing its worth. When a man fell wounded, or was dragged away to await the surgeon's mates, another was instantly in his place from one of the opposite guns.

Now the marines could join in with their muskets, Sergeant Saxton counting out the time and tapping the deck with his boot as the ramrods rose and fell like one, and then as the muskets rose once more to the nettings he would shout, 'Take aim! Every shot a Don!' The crackle of musketry from the fighting tops showed that more marines were up there trying to mark down the enemy's officers.

Bolitho paced this way and that, his shoe catching a jagged splinter as the other ship's marksmen tried to hit him.

Closer, closer still, and the guns were thundering at almost point-blank range, their crews blinded and deafened as their feet and hands fought to keep control over their massive weapons.

'*Cease firing!*'

Quantock had to repeat the order before the last gun on the lower deck fell silent. As the enemy did likewise the other sounds broke through the stunned stillness. Men crying out in pain, voices calling for help, orders shouting for men to clear away the wreckage, to release the trapped wounded.

'*Hard over!*'

As the wheel went down *Achates'* jib-boom swept through the other ship's foremast shrouds like a battering ram. There was a terrible splintering sound and both hulls rocked together in a deadly embrace.

Men were running forward, leaving the guns to snatch up cutlasses and boarding pikes, axes and anything they favoured for hand-to-hand fighting.

Lieutenant Hallowes, his hat knocked awry, his hanger waving above his head, yelled, 'At 'em, lads!'

With a wild cheer the seamen raced to the point of collision to hack and slash their way across a glistening sliver of water.

Some were impaled by pikes as they clung to the boarding

nets, others were shot down by marksmen even before they had left their own ship. But others were through, and as more followed Bolitho saw the fourth lieutenant dashing on to the enemy's larboard gangway, hacking down a shrieking figure with his hanger and slashing aside another before he was overtaken by his whooping, battle-crazed men, their cutlasses already reddened from the first challenge on the forecastle.

The marines were bustling to the side, their faces grim beneath their hats as they fired into the men along the enemy's quarterdeck, reloaded with less precision than usual and fired again.

Captain Dewar drew his sword. 'Forward, Marines!'

The scarlet coats and white cross-belts vanished into the smoke, the boots slipping on blood, the bayonets thrusting away any resistance as they joined the others on the enemy's deck.

Keen had gone forward to encourage his men, and Bolitho heard the seamen cheering, 'Huzza, huzza!' and even though some were falling to the enemy's fire others were already fighting their way on to the quarterdeck.

There was a great cry from *Achates'* boatswain. 'Fire! She's afire!'

Bolitho said, 'I can see the smoke!'

Tyrrell gripped the rail as he stared at the enemy who were suddenly throwing away their weapons and screaming for quarter as the wild-eyed sailors tore among them.

Bolitho called, 'Mr Hawtayne! Have your bugler sound the retreat! Stand by to cast off!'

A sullen explosion shook both ships and more black smoke gushed from the forecastle. If the ship burst into flames *Achates* would suffer the same fate.

Keen came back mopping his face, his eyes seeking out his lieutenants and master's mates as the truth made itself felt in another deep explosion.

Dragging their wounded, and fighting off any of the enemy who tried to follow, *Achates'* boarding party returned to their own ship.

With her wheel either shot away or abandoned, the enemy two-decker began to drift down-wind as soon as the last line was hacked free. Corpses bobbed in the sea between them, and others hung from the rigging where friend and foe alike had been shot down.

'Get the fore-course on her! Reset the flying jib! Hands aloft and loose t'gan's'ls!' Quantock's harsh voice echoed through the confusion like a steadying force.

A great tongue of flame licked through the enemy's gun-deck and started an explosion among some broken charges. Men were running through the corpses and destruction and nobody appeared to be trying to save them or their ship.

As the wheel went over *Achates* turned slowly aside from her stricken enemy, laying bare the damage, the bloody streaks on the planking, the discarded weapons, and the guns which still smoked as if under their own command.

Another explosion boomed across the water and fragments of burning wood and rigging splashed dangerously close to *Achates* as she continued to gather way, her punctured and smoke-grimed sails filling to the wind.

More explosions, and this time a gout of fire and sparks spouted from the midships section and began to spread to masts and canvas, until everything was burning fiercely. Rigging and canvas became ashes in seconds, men, some on fire, were leaping into the sea, others splashed about looking for something to keep them afloat as the ship continued to blaze above them.

Bolitho watched the other ship die, but in spite of *Sparrowhawk* could find little satisfaction. His men were cheering, embracing each other. They had lived through it. One more time, and for some it had been the first battle.

The Spanish frigate, which had remained a silent spectator to the fight, was moving cautiously towards the burning ship. She was going to stand between *Achates* and her victim, an act which made her just as guilty. Dead men tell no tales.

There was a vivid flash and a boom which stopped all the cheers like an iron door.

The other ship was turning on to her side, her gun-ports alight like a line of angry red eyes.

She was breaking up, her heavy artillery tearing loose to add to the horror and agony of those still trapped below.

Bolitho saw Midshipman Evans watching the other ship's last moment. But there was no joy on his face, just tears, and Bolitho knew why.

He was not seeing the rightful destruction of a callous enemy. It was his *Sparrowhawk* he was watching.

Bolitho said quietly, 'Attend to Mr Evans, Adam. His storm is about to break.'

Keen joined him and touched his hat.

Bolitho said, 'What is the butcher's bill for all this?'

They both turned as the air shook to a final explosion, and like a gutted whale the enemy rolled on to her side and dipped beneath the surface.

Keen replied quietly, 'That might so easily have been us, sir.'

Bolitho handed his sword to Allday. 'I get your point, Val. Then our bill is not yet fully paid?'

12

The Letter

Napier, *Electra*'s youthful commander, stood exactly in the centre of Bolitho's day cabin while he completed his report.

Contrary to his orders, Napier had brought his brig to escort the battered two-decker for the last two miles of her passage into San Felipe.

Even as he had been piped aboard from his gig, Napier had seemed unable to prevent his eyes from probing around him. The sewn-up corpses awaiting burial, the tired, dirty sailors who barely glanced up from their countless tasks of splicing, stitching and hauling fresh rigging to the topmen on the yards.

Bolitho thought of those last moments. He still did not know the enemy ship's name. But soon he would, just as he would learn who had commanded her. The Spanish frigate had been careful to stand between the victor and defeated, to prevent, it seemed, any attempt to pick up survivors.

Napier said, 'Two Spanish men-of-war did stand inshore for a while. They were going to land a party at the island mission.'

He sounded surprised that Bolitho had not already questioned him about it. In fact, Bolitho was so fatigued he had barely skimmed over the commander's neatly written report.

Bolitho made himself stand and walk towards the open stern windows as *Achates* continued towards the island. He could still smell the heat and sweat of battle. The scent of death.

'What did you do?'

Napier relived his proudest moment as acting-governor.

'I warned them off, sir. Fired a shot from the battery to liven things along.'

Liven things along. Bolitho wanted to laugh, but knew if he did he might not be able to stop.

When and where would it end? Tyrrell had betrayed him, or had been about to. Now, not only the French were intent on San Felipe but the Spaniards also.

Keen entered the cabin and said, 'We are about to enter harbour, sir. The wind is steady from the sou'-east.'

He looked strained and extremely tired. He was feeling the ship's pain as if it were his own.

The pumps had barely stopped since the battle. *Achates* had taken two bad hits in her bilge. And a 'long nine', as a thirty-two-pounder was nicknamed, could do terrible damage. *Achates* was, after all, twenty-two years old. That represented a lot of miles under her keel.

'I'll come up.' Bolitho added bitterly, 'There may be some watching from the shore who will be disappointed to see us still afloat.'

He thought of the two Spanish men-of-war and their apparent intention to land men on what they still claimed as Spanish territory. But for Tyrrell's change of heart, the two ships would have been joined by the ship which now lay below a Caribbean reef.

Napier suddenly went pale. 'I— I do beg your pardon, sir. I had almost forgotten. There was a packet-ship from England.'

Bolitho stared at him and said sharply, 'Continue.'

Napier fumbled inside his coat and then produced a letter. 'For you, sir.'

He seemed to shrink under Bolitho's gaze.

Keen snapped, 'Come on deck, Commander Napier, I wish to discuss certain matters about docking my ship . . . ' But he paused at the door and glanced back at Bolitho. He was holding the letter with both hands, afraid to open it, afraid to move.

He turned and almost bumped into the flag-lieutenant. 'Not yet, Adam. There's a letter.'

In the gloom between decks Allday leaned on a blistered eighteen-pounder and peered through the gun-port to watch a green finger of land slide abeam. There were people there to watch the stained and battered ship sail past, but nobody waved or cheered.

To Allday it was just another landfall. He had been in so many harbours they had become merged and mixed in memory. He sighed. That letter was all that mattered for now. He could remember as if it was yesterday when together they had clambered into the overturned coach and found a beautiful woman more dead than alive. The resemblance to Bolitho's previous wife had been too much to believe.

He cocked his head as a gun boomed out from the old fortress. Better than any mock tears, he thought. A proper welcome, though there were too many jacks who would not hear the guns now or ever again.

He straightened his back as the door opened in the cabin screen and the scarlet-coated sentry snapped to attention.

Bolitho ducked beneath the deckhead beams and then saw Allday waiting for him.

He looked at Allday's anxious features and felt his own strength begin to ebb away. The careful composure he had tried to build up as he had read carefully through her letter, the moments of despair when his gaze had become misty, each was taking a toll now on his reserves.

He paused and listened to the guns, the jarring response from *Achates'* upper deck as she returned the salute.

Then he reached out and grasped Allday's hard hand.

Allday asked thickly, 'Is all well, sir?'

Bolitho squeezed his hand. It was somehow right that he should be here. The first to know.

'We have a *fine* daughter, Allday.'

How long they stood like this it was hard to tell. *Achates* changed tack around the point, and on the poop the marine fifers and drummers struck up a lively march, *Come cheer up my lads 'tis to glory we steer* . . . To Bolitho it could have been anything.

Allday nodded slowly, savouring the moment as he would retell it when he eventually put his feet ashore for the last time.

'And Ma'am, sir?'

'Very well.' Bolitho walked towards the sunlight. 'She asked to be remembered to you.' He quickened his pace on to the quarterdeck. Now he could face anything. *Do* anything. He looked at Allday's great beaming grin. 'She hopes we are not too bored by being employed in peacetime!'

Allday glanced up at the splintered cross-jack yard, the stains and marks of battle which were everywhere.

Then, despite the solemnity of the moment, a King's ship entering harbour, the salutes and the flag which dipped to *Old Katie* above the battery walls, he threw back his head and laughed.

Keen looked at him and then at Bolitho.

The reward for the victor was plain to see.

Captain Valentine Keen watched his superior with unconcealed surprise and admiration. Since *Achates'* return to San Felipe the work of repairs, the replacement of timbers and spars, had continued without a break. The facilities in Georgetown were poor, and they had been confronted by non-cooperation and hostility at every turn.

English Harbour at Antigua was the only suitable place for a proper refit, but Keen was resigned to seeing his ship put to rights in what amounted to primitive conditions. If *Achates* quit the island he had little doubt that an invasion of some kind would soon follow.

He knew that Bolitho had not spared himself. He had been ashore many times, had visited the ex-governor, Rivers, had even allowed him to return to his own home under open arrest, although Keen had voiced his disagreement on that score.

It was late August and the heat unbearable. But any day, at any hour, the fortress lookouts might report the approach of Spanish ships, French too for that matter, and *Achates* had to be ready for sea and prepared if need be to fight.

Electra had sailed that forenoon for Antigua. Despatches for the admiral, if he had returned, and others to be sent with all haste to the Admiralty in London. All this and a lot more had kept Bolitho working in his cabin until the middle watches, and yet he never seemed to tire or show his irritation at the delays and lack of help from the islanders.

The letter from his wife in Falmouth had done more for Bolitho than a hundred victories, or so it seemed.

Bolitho looked up from the litter of papers on his table. It had been something of a relief to send Napier to Antigua with his ideas and intentions which Sheaffe would eventually read at the Admiralty. He had committed himself. Right or wrong, he had made a decision. It was what he had veered away from previously. Now he was glad, even eager, to act with a freedom he had once found hard to express.

'Rivers has agreed not to interfere. Others can decide later what will become of him.' He saw the deep lines around Keen's mouth and was moved to add, 'It has been a difficult time for you, Val. I understand that.'

Keen shrugged. 'Mr Quantock, the master, Mr Grace, the carpenter, all are in rare agreement, sir. If this ship is called on to fight without proper attention in a dockyard she may suffer severe consequences.'

Bolitho nodded. 'I know that. You are also short-handed because of our losses and with no chance of replacements.'

Keen said, 'If we do not get support from other ships, sir, we will be hard put to defend ourselves, let alone this island.'

'I have sent a full report, Val.'

Bolitho leaned over the stern sill and took some deep breaths. The air was scalding hot and without movement. Better to be at sea, becalmed even. Anything rather than stay here and wait. He thought of Belinda's letter which he had read at the end of each demanding day. A daughter. He could not visualize what she would be like. Belinda had written of her love, of her hopes, but he could read between the lines too. The birth had not been easy for her. It was just as well that she still believed his mission to be one of diplomacy and not one of danger.

Keen asked abruptly, 'What about Mr Tyrrell, sir?'

Bolitho bit his lip. He had sent Tyrrell over to his brigantine as soon as *Achates* had moored. They had spoken very little. Guilt or defiance, it was hard to tell. Yet.

He said, 'I shall see him directly, Val. I need his *Vivid*. She is all I can find at present.' He smiled at Keen's surprise. 'I intend to purchase her anyway, so she might as well sail under our flag for the present.'

'If you think that's wise, sir.'

'Wise? I am not certain of anything. But what I do know is that it will take several months to complete repairs on my flagship. In the meantime we may be attacked by the Dons. I cannot in all sensibility agree to hand over the island to the French until we have settled this matter once and for all. If there was any last minute conflict the French would be quick to blame us, accuse us of provoking a war so that they could not take over what is rightfully theirs.'

He watched Keen's face. He was unconvinced.

'I have this feeling, Val. That I was sent here to perform an impossible task. But if I am to be a scapegoat then I want to rest on my own decisions, not on those made by people who have never heard a shot or seen a man die.'

Keen nodded. 'Well, sir, I shall back you to the limit and beyond, but that you already know.'

Bolitho sat on the stern seat and plucked at his shirt to gain an illusion of coolness.

'When you attain flag-rank, Val, I hope you will remember all this. It is far better to sail in the line of battle with every enemy muzzle trained on the flagship than to sort through the dung of diplomacy. In a moment I shall speak with Jethro Tyrrell. He is a man who lost everything, but who once gave so much for the flag he honoured. He was a true patriot, but was branded a traitor by his own people. He has lived with bitter memories, as a wolf will live off scraps. But he still cares, and at that moment when he was about to betray us he stood firm and led us to the enemy. In his eyes it was madness. What is honour to him? It has done precious little to repay his sacrifices. He thought instead of saving us from harm, so that when we returned here the island would be under Spanish colours and it would be too late for me to do anything but report failure.'

Keen shook his head. 'Will you trust him again?'

'I hope to.'

Bolitho looked at the glittering water, the small vessels pinned down on their reflections by the glare.

'Rivers is a rogue. He became rich by offering favours to the scum of the Caribbean. Slavers, soldiers of fortune, pirates, all have paid him his dues. He has property in the South Americas, but needed his power as governor to take full advantage of the profits. I found some evidence in the fortress, but that is but the tip of an iceberg. I loathe him for his greed, but I *need* him if only to give some credibility to our being here.'

Keen listened to the renewed thud of hammers and the squeak of tackles as more cordage was hoisted aloft. He had had his own doubts from the beginning about sending a small two-decker to perform the work of a squadron. What was the matter with England? Instead of showing pride for past victories she seemed to cringe for fear of upsetting old enemies.

Keen would have hanged Rivers and anyone else who had shared in the deaths of his sailors and marines. The consequences could wait.

Bolitho had risen to his feet and was shading his eyes to watch the distant fortress. When he spoke he sounded untroubled, although his words held the impact of iron shot.

'You see, Val, I believe the United States are more concerned with improving their relations with the South Americas, the Spaniards and Portuguese. So Rivers' appeal for their protection rather than French reoccupation must have received a warm reception. I also believe that Samuel Fane, and certainly Jonathan Chase, have no illusions about the French, should there be another war in Europe.'

Keen stared at him, his tiredness forgotten. 'You mean that the United States' government connived with the Dons!'

'Not directly. But when you put your hand in a fox's hole you must expect to be bitten. The Spanish government could not afford to become openly involved so they employed a powerful privateer for the purpose. With *Sparrowhawk* destroyed and local shipping too frightened to move, there was only *Achates* to prevent the seizure of San Felipe. Chase must have known about Tyrrell's past connections with me, just as he was well aware of his desperate need of a ship. The rest we can guess, but nobody had allowed for Tyrrell's old loyalty.'

Keen looked astounded. 'If you say so, sir. It is precious flimsy evidence to support your reputation at any future enquiry.'

'I agree. So we shall have to manufacture some.' Bolitho looked at him calmly. 'I'll see Tyrrell now. Please ask my flag-lieutenant to join me.'

Later, as Tyrrell limped into the cabin and lanterns were being lit for an early dusk, Bolitho faced his old lieutenant with a sense of sadness as well as determination.

Tyrrell took a proffered chair and laced his powerful fingers together.

'Well, Jethro.'

Tyrrell smiled. 'Well, Dick.'

Bolitho sat on the edge of the table and regarded him gravely.

'As these are British waters for the present I am using my authority to commandeer your vessel and place her under our colours.'

He saw a momentary start but nothing more. Tyrrell was too tough to be budged by one shock.

'Also, I am placing her under the temporary command of

my nephew, who in his capacity of flag-lieutenant will carry a despatch with him to Boston.'

Tyrrell stirred and showed a first hint of uneasiness.

He exclaimed harshly, 'An' me? You intend to string me on the main-yard, eh?'

Bolitho pushed a letter across the table. 'Here is my authority to purchase the *Vivid* once you have returned to San Felipe. You see I kept my word. She'll be yours.'

He was barely able to watch Tyrrell's anguish, but continued, 'I have spoken with Sir Humphrey Rivers. To spare his own shame, and possibly his life, he will give me all the information I need about that Spaniard. If he changes his mind he has a choice of charges. Treason or murder. He will hang for either.'

Tyrrell stared at him then rubbed his chin. 'Chase will never agree to part with the *Vivid*.'

'I think he will.'

Bolitho looked away. It was all Tyrrell could think of. A ship of his own. A last chance.

Tyrrell stood up and looked around like a man already lost. 'I'll be on my way then.'

'Yes.' Bolitho sat and leafed through some papers. 'I doubt we shall meet again.'

Tyrrell turned almost blindly and started for the door. But Bolitho got to his feet, unable to play it out to the end.

'*Jethro!*' He walked round the table and held out his hand. 'You saved my life once.'

Tyrrell looked at him searchingly. 'An' you mine, more'n that.'

'I just want to wish you good luck, and I hope you find whatever it is you're looking for.'

Tyrrell returned the grasp and said gruffly, 'There's none like you, Dick, nor never will be.' There was emotion in his voice now. 'I lived all those years again when I met your nephew. I knew then I couldn't go through with it, though God knows this island is not worth the dyin' for. But I know you, Dick, and I know your values. You'll not change.'

He gave a wide grin and for a brief moment he was the same man. The one in the little sloop-of-war in these very waters.

Then he limped away, and Bolitho heard the midshipman of the watch calling for a boat alongside.

Bolitho leaned against the bulkhead and looked at his hands. They felt as if they were trembling.

Allday emerged from the adjoining cabin as if he had been lurking there to protect him from attack.

'That was *hard*, Allday.' He tried to hear the dragging thump of Tyrrell's stump leg. 'I fear it may be harder on young Adam.'

Allday did not understand what he was talking about. The man called Tyrrell had been an old friend of Bolitho's, so everyone said. But to Allday he had seemed like a threat, and for that reason he was glad to be rid of him.

Bolitho said, 'I feel different, knowing that I have a daughter.'

Allday relaxed. The mood was past.

'One thing's for certain, sir. She'll be a welcome change. Two Bolithos on the high seas are enough for anyone, an' that's no error.'

For a brief moment he thought he had gone too far, but Bolitho looked at him and smiled.

'Well, then, let's broach a bottle and drink the young lady's health, eh?'

On the poop Adam heard Allday's laugh through a skylight and gripped the netting with sudden excitement. Across the darkening water he could see the *Vivid*'s riding light, the faint glitter of a lantern from her tiny cabin.

Soon, far sooner than he had dared to hope, he would see and hold Robina in his arms. He could feel her kiss as if it had just been placed on his mouth, smell her perfume as if it was here on deck.

He was glad that Bolitho had seen fit to trust his old friend. It would be interesting to listen to his stories again once they had set sail from San Felipe.

The first lieutenant was doing his evening rounds of the upper deck and saw Adam's silhouette against the sky.

Quantock clenched his fists. It was unfair. He should have been given charge of the *Vivid*, no matter how brief it was to be. Damn them all to hell. If *Achates* returned to England in her present state she would likely be paid off like most of the fleet. Quantock knew he would be thrown on the beach to join the ranks of unwanted lieutenants without any chance of employment.

He swore at the evening sky. *Damn peace!* In war there was risk, but at the same time there was always a chance of promotion and honour.

The Bolithos and those like them had always had it. He peered around the deserted deck. My turn will come.

Achates swung quietly to her cable and, like the men who lay on the orlop within the surgeon's call, nursed her own wounds of battle.

In her crowded mess between the great guns below deck the seamen and marines sat by their glimmering lights and yarned with each other, or consumed their carefully hoarded rum. Some with tarred hands surprisingly gentle carved small and intricate models or scrimshaw work. One seaman who had the gift of being able to write sat beneath a lantern while one of his messmates stumbled through a letter for his wife in England. In the Royal Marines' quarters, or the barracks as they were known, the men worked on their kit, or thought of that last battle, and the next which, although nobody mentioned it, they knew was inevitable.

Down on the orlop where the air was thick as fog, James Tuson, the surgeon, wiped his hands and watched as one of the badly wounded had his face covered and was carried away by the loblolly boys. He had died just a minute or so ago. With both feet amputated it was better so, Tuson thought.

He looked along his small, pain-wracked command. Why? What was it all for?

These sailors did not fight for flag or King as so many landsmen fondly believed. The surgeon had been at sea for twenty years and knew this better than most. They fought for each other, the ship, and sometimes for their leader. He thought of Bolitho standing on deck, his stricken expression as these same men had cheered him for taking them into hell. Oh yes, they would fight for *him*.

As he ducked beneath the massive deck beams he felt a hand touch his leg.

Tuson stooped down. 'What is it, Cummings?'

A surgeon's mate raised a lantern so that he could see the wounded man better. He had been hit in the chest by an iron splinter. It was a marvel he had survived.

The man called Cummings whispered, 'Thankee for takin' care of me, sir.' Then he fainted.

Tuson had seen too many men crippled and killed to feel much emotion, but this sailor's simple gesture broke through his guard like a fist.

When he was working he was too busy to care for the crash and rumble of guns on the decks above. The procession of wounded men always seemed as if it would never end. He rarely even looked up at his sweating assistants with their wild eyes and bloodied aprons. No wonder they call us butchers. A leg off here, an arm there, the naked bodies held on the table while he worked with blade and saw, his ears deaf to their screams.

But *afterwards*, at moments like these, he felt differently. Ashamed for the little he could do for them. Ashamed too for their gratitude.

The surgeon's mate lowered the lantern and waited patiently.

Tuson continued along the deck and tried to shut from his mind the tempting picture of a brandy bottle. If he gave in now, he would be finished. It was what had driven him to sea in the first place.

Somewhere in the gloom a man cried out sharply.

Tuson snapped, 'Who was that?'

'Larsen, sir, the big Swede.'

Tuson nodded. He had taken off the man's arm. It sounded

as if it had grown worse, maybe even gangrene. In which case . . .

He said briskly. 'Have him brought to the table.'

Tuson was calm again. In charge. He watched the figure being carried to the sick-bay. A Swede. But in a King's ship nationality did not count.

'Now then, Larsen . . .'

Bolitho was with Keen on deck when the brigantine *Vivid* slipped her mooring and tacked slowly towards the harbour entrance.

He raised a telescope and scanned the little vessel from bow to stern and saw Adam standing beside Tyrrell's powerful figure near the tiller, his uniform making a smart contrast with the men around him.

Whatever he found in Boston might hurt him, but would not break his heart. Bolitho knew he must not interfere, must face the risk of turning Adam against him when he would have offered anything to prevent it.

Keen was reading his thoughts. 'He may not even see the lass, sir.'

Bolitho lowered the glass and allowed the brigantine to become a small model again.

'He will. I know exactly how he feels. Exactly.'

The headland slid out to shield *Vivid* from view. Only her topsail and driver showed above the land, and then as she changed tack again they too were gone.

Keen respected Bolitho in everything, but he could not understand why he had bothered to pay good money to give Tyrrell the *Vivid*. He should have felt lucky to be spared the hangman's halter. Then he looked at Bolitho's profile and saw the sadness there. Whatever there had once been between him and Tyrrell would not be shared with anyone, he thought.

Bolitho turned his back to the sea.

'Now we must prepare the defences of this island, Val.' He

pounded his fist into his other hand. 'If only I had some more ships I'd stand out to sea and meet them gun to gun.'

Keen said nothing. Bolitho was certain of an attack. The Peace of Amiens meant nothing out here, especially to the Spaniards. He looked at the glistening horizon and wondered. But for Tyrrell's change of heart they might be out there now, and San Felipe under another flag. Rivers had played a dangerous game by setting one against the other, but it seemed to Keen that only *Achates* would pay for the consequences.

Bolitho clapped him on the arm. 'Why so grim, Val? Never turn your face away from what is inevitable.'

He seemed in such high spirits Keen was shaken from his apprehension immediately.

He said, 'Where would you like to begin, sir?'

It was infectious. Keen had watched it happen before so many times. When he himself had been nearly killed in battle, that too had been described as a time of peace.

'We will obtain some horses and ride around the island. Check each vantage point against Mr Knocker's chart and any local map we can discover.' Bolitho pointed at the haze around the old volcano. 'The island is like a great juicy bone, Val. And now the hounds of war are taking up their positions around us.'

He had seen the anxiety on Keen's face, and if he was dismayed at the prospect of fighting an undeclared war over San Felipe, so too would be most of his ship's company.

Bolitho did not really need to ride round the island, he could picture its strength and its weakness as he had gauged it on the charts. But he needed Keen and the others to know he was determined to stand firm. To hold the island until he was certain in his mind of the right course to take.

The wound in his thigh throbbed and itched in the humid air and he wanted to rub it.

Why was he troubled by the prospect of a siege or an open attack? Was it because of Belinda, or was it the chance of action which drove him on?

He thought suddenly of Sir Hayward Sheaffe's quiet room at the Admiralty. It seemed like another world now, with the fortress and the spent volcano shimmering across the placid water. But Sheaffe's words were quite clear, as if he had just uttered them. 'Their lordships require a man of tact as well as action for this task.'

Bolitho thought of Midshipman Evans' expression when the nameless two-decker had burst into flames. Of the shocked surprise on the dead marine drummer's face. He thought too of Duncan and others he had not even known.

The man of tact would have to step down for a while.

13

A Holy Day

Adam Bolitho stood by a window in Jonathan Chase's study and stared at the unending ranks of white horses across Massachusetts Bay. Just an hour ago he had been brought ashore in *Vivid*'s boat and had been met by Chase's astonished agent. In fact, *Vivid*'s return to Boston under British colours had caused quite a stir along the waterfront.

It was like part of a dream. Chase had made him welcome at his house, but had seemed restrained, cautious even, as Adam had given him the big sealed envelope from his uncle.

He shivered, conscious of the New England weather, the restless change in the September Atlantic. He thought of San Felipe and felt strangely guilty. The worst part was that it did not seem real, any of it. He was here, and Chase had mentioned before he had left in some haste to read Bolitho's letter that Robina and her mother were also in Boston and might be expected shortly.

Adam turned and looked at the fine room with its paintings and nautical relics. The right place for a man like Chase, he thought, an ex-sailor, ex-enemy too, who now had his roots here.

He thought of the ten days' passage from San Felipe to Boston. How different from that other occasion when he had yarned away the hours with Jethro Tyrrell. This time, despite the cramped conditions of the brigantine, he had barely spoken to Tyrrell, and then only on vague matters of navigation and weather.

And why had his uncle made the offer to purchase *Vivid* for him, and why should Chase be prepared to sell? None of it made much sense, but then none of it seemed to matter now that he was back here with the prospect of meeting Robina again.

'I am sorry for keeping you waiting.'

Chase was a powerfully built man and yet he had re-entered the study as noiselessly as a cat.

He seated himself carefully in a chair and said, 'I have read your uncle's letter and have ordered that the other one which he enclosed be carried immediately to Sam Fane at the capital.' He regarded the lieutenant thoughtfully. 'Strange he should send you.'

Adam shrugged. He had not really considered it before. 'I was available, sir. Captain Keen needs all his own officers aboard the flagship.'

'Hmmm. Your uncle once told me he hates politics, but he seems to understand them well enough.' He did not explain but continued, 'As you will have observed when you entered Boston Harbour, the French men-of-war have gone. News travels on the wind. The French admiral will have no wish to insist on receiving San Felipe from the British until the position is made clear.'

'But the French and Spanish governments have been allies more often than not, sir.'

Chase smiled for the first time. 'The French would need Spain as an ally if there was another war. If there is to be any conflict over San Felipe the French intend it shall not be of their making. It would suit them very well if your ships withdraw under a cloud after they have repulsed any Spanish claims to the island. *Then*, and only then, the French admiral will see fit to assume control and install a governor.'

Adam said, 'I think it wrong to gamble with people's lives in this fashion.'

Chase nodded. 'Possibly, but San Felipe is a *fact*. In war or peace it commands an important sea route. The government of my country would prefer to see it in friendly hands, better still, under our own protection. That was what Sir

Humphrey Rivers suggested. As Vice-Admiral Bolitho's aide, you will of course know all about it. I can see that you are as sharp as your uncle in such matters, and you will have realized that Rivers, despite all his claims of loyalty to King George, is hell-bent on being his own man. He played a dangerous hand by discussing the island's future with Spain or, to be precise, with the Spanish captain-general at La Guaira. A secret shared is no longer a secret.' He gave a heavy sigh. 'Anyway, it is impossible to share anything with a tiger.'

He watched Adam's reactions and saw that he had his full attention.

'I can speak freely to you because neither of us has any control over the affair. I was aware of the Spanish interest because I trade with both the captain-general at La Guaira and his neighbour in Caracas. They have always thought their own government to be out of touch with their expanding empire in the South Americas. Every week the slave ships bring more labour for the mines and the plantations, and they probably pass the great galleons of Spain on passage home loaded to their deck beams with gold. San Felipe's position has threatened their freedom of movement in the past. They intend it shall not happen again.'

Adam had a sudden picture of *Achates* at San Felipe with some of her yards sent down for repair work being carried out by the ship's company which really needed the proper skills of a dockyard.

He exclaimed, 'That two-decker . . . '

Chase smiled gravely. 'The one you sunk? Oh yes, Lieutenant, I heard all about that from my own sources. *Like the wind*, remember? She was the *Intrepido*, and was refitted at Cadiz and armed to be a match for anyone foolhardy enough to interfere with her intentions. A privateer, a hired adventurer, call him what you will, but her captain was ordered to sweep aside all opposition and take command of the island. Later a proper governor would be installed and the Spanish flag would be raised, to, I suspect, small interference from either the British or the French. Your government would be too embarrassed to waste more time and lives on a lost cause, and the French would raise no objection as it would put Spain under obligation for any future strategy on their part.' He leaned back in his chair and added, 'Does that explain?'

Adam nodded, confused and sickened by the apparent simplicity of such cruel logic.

Chase said, 'But things are never what they seem. The Dons thought like the Dons. Quick, clever, ruthless, but they had failed to take your uncle's stubbornness into their scheme of things. Nevertheless, he is the one I pity. He is the one man who stands between the Spaniards and their claim to San Felipe. I believe all this was known when he was sent here in the first place. I mean no disrespect, but the British can be devious in their negotiations. What does honour matter to some when it concerns events on the other side of the world, eh?'

'I cannot *believe* it, sir. My uncle will stand firm.'

Chase looked concerned. 'Of course, I'm sure of that if nothing else. But without the islanders to back him, what can he do? Stand and fight?'

Adam clenched his hands so tightly that the pain made his eyes smart.

'He will!'

Chase looked away, as if unable to watch his despair.

'Then God help him.'

The door swung open and Adam heard the girl ask excitedly, 'Where have you hidden him, Uncle? And what is all this *stuff* about you selling the *Vivid*, she's a favourite of yours!'

She turned and saw him by the window and gasped with surprise.

'You really are here!' She ran to him and kissed him lightly on the cheek. 'Now everything is wonderful!'

Adam did not dare to touch or hold her, and could see the anguish on Chase's grim features across her shoulder.

Chase said heavily, '*Vivid* has always been on the small side for my fleet. Tyrrell has earned her twice over.'

He kept his eyes on Adam's and said nothing about Bolitho's money.

He moved towards the door, his face still on the young couple by the window.

There was no easy way, and his tone was almost brutal as he said, '*Vivid* must weigh before nightfall. Lieutenant Bolitho here will have important news for his uncle, isn't that so?'

Adam nodded slowly, hating him, yet admiring him at the same time.

For how long they stood together he did not know. He held her to him, murmuring lost words into her hair, while she clasped his shoulders as if still unable to realize what was happening.

Then she leaned back in his arms and stared at him as she asked, '*Why?* What does anything matter now? We shall have each other! Everything we've ever wanted! So *why?*'

Adam brushed a strand of fair hair from her eyes, all his hopes and happiness spilling away like sand in a glass.

'I have to go back, Robina. Your uncle knows why. He can explain better than I.'

Her eyes flashed with sudden anger. 'How can it concern you? You are only a lieutenant, why should he discuss such things?'

Adam held her firmly as she tried to force herself away.

'There has been a lot of fighting. Our ship sank an enemy but we were badly damaged too.' He felt her arms go limp as his words struck home. 'My uncle discovered what dangers threatened the island, and who was behind them. He sent me here to give his despatches to your uncle, so that this information could be sent to your president.'

She watched his eyes and his mouth as he spoke. 'But why should it involve my uncle or any of my family?'

Adam shrugged wretchedly. 'Because they were involved. They knew the Spanish intentions long ago, your uncle as good as told me just now. Apparently it would not suit your government to have either the French flag or ours flying above San Felipe. But now that my uncle has brought it into the open, nobody else will dare to interfere.' He could not hide the bitterness even from her. 'So my uncle stands alone to act as he must.'

She stepped away, her eyes towards the floor as she said in a small voice, 'Then you do not intend to make your life here among us?'

'It is not like that! I love you with all my heart.'

'And yet you deny me this?'

Adam moved towards her but she took two paces away.

'It's my duty – '

She looked at him again, her eyes hot with tears. 'Duty! What do I care about that! We are both young, like this country, so why should you throw your heart away for a meaningless word like *duty*!'

Adam heard Chase in the passage-way, and other, lighter footsteps, Robina's mother.

They both appeared in the doorway, Chase's face stern and determined, the woman's pale with anxiety.

Chase asked bluntly, 'You told her then?'

Adam met his gaze evenly. 'Some of it, sir.'

'I see.' He sounded relieved. 'Your Mr Tyrrell seems eager to leave. The wind's backing . . . ' His voice trailed away.

'Thank you.' Adam turned and looked at the girl, the others unimportant and misty as he said, 'I meant every word. One day I'll come back and then . . . '

She dropped her eyes. 'It will be too late.'

Chase took his arm and accompanied him through the beautifully panelled entrance hall. A black footman opened the outer door and Adam saw the cold blue squares of sea and sky beyond it, mocking him.

Chase said quietly, 'I'm sorry, I really am. But it's all for the best, you'll see that one day.'

Adam walked down the steps and saw Tyrrell waiting by the gates. He watched the lieutenant's face every foot of the way and then with his swinging, limping gait fell in step beside him.

'You decided then?'

'It was decided for me.' Adam could barely see where he was walking in his despair and pain.

'I ain't so sure about that, Lieutenant.' Tyrrell shot him a glance. 'I can guess how you feel.'

Adam looked at him, his voice angry. 'Why the difference? On passage here you barely said a word?'

Tyrrell grinned. 'Just wanted to be sure about you. You could'a stayed put right here.'

He quickened his pace as his eyes found the moored brigantine.

'But, like me, Lieutenant, you couldn't bargain away your loyalty.'

They stood together on the jetty and waited as a boat cast off to collect them.

Once Tyrrell looked at Adam's face and then across to his new possession. Tyrrell knew all about having a broken heart. He had learned it in a dozen ways. But a ship of your own was something else.

He clapped the lieutenant roughly on the shoulder.

'Come along, young fella, we'll catch wind *and* tide for once.'

Adam hesitated and looked back but the house was completely hidden from view.

He repeated what he had told her just moments earlier. 'I love you with all my heart.'

He had not realized he had spoken aloud, and Tyrrell was moved to say, 'You'll soon forget. Only dreams last forever.'

Bolitho climbed the last of the stone stairs to the fortress's battery parapet and discovered that he was not even breathless. It must be the change from shipboard life.

It was early morning, the air cool and damp from a heavy overnight downpour. It was so typical of all the islands hereabouts, he thought. Drenching rain at night and yet within an hour or two of sunrise the place would be bone-dry again.

Lieutenant George Lemoine, who commanded the platoon of the Sixtieth Regiment of Foot, touched his hat and smiled.

'I heard you were up and about early, sir.'

Bolitho leaned on the parapet and stared down at the shining harbour. A lot of the anchorage was still in shadow, but soon the sun would appear around the old volcano and the ships, like the town beyond, would quiver in another morning haze. He could see the black and buff lines of *Achates'* gun-decks, and wondered if Keen was still fretting about mounting lists of needs for his command.

They were running short of fresh stores. Even drinking-water had to be man-handled in casks by the seamen. There was still no sign of cooperation from the islanders, who showed their resentment by pleading poverty even when it came to fresh fruit or juices for the sailors.

Bolitho had done all he could to get to know the islanders. As admiral in command, governor and in charge of the island's defences he had seen the hopelessness of the situation. The planters and traders resented the fact that they could not move their vessels in or out of harbour, while ships which called at San Felipe to collect cargoes had to be checked before they could be allowed to anchor. It needed a full garrison and several ships to perform what Lemoine's soldiers and the marines had to carry out unaided.

Bolitho breathed in deeply. He saw his barge tied to the fortress's jetty where he had first met Rivers over three months ago. Down there too was the point where Rivers' men had fixed their boom, where *Achates* had burst through in pitch-darkness. Battles fought, men dead and wounded, probably a trifle to the planners in government and Admiralty.

Now it was late September, and Adam should be back at any moment. He thought of his purchase of *Vivid*. Reward or bribe? He still could not be sure of his own motives.

He thought too of Falmouth. Autumn. Red and brown leaves, the smell of wood smoke in the evenings. Resolute, cheerful people, now at peace because of ships like *Achates*.

He had received no more letters from Belinda, but then there had been no news from any direction. The island seemed as if it were totally isolated, even though the lookouts had sighted the topsails of unidentified men-of-war on the horizon on several occasions.

Perhaps it was all over before it had begun? *Achates'* unexpected discovery of the hidden two-decker and putting her to the bottom within the hour might have killed all the ardour for an attack.

But uncertainty had made him restless and often unable to sleep. He had taken to riding around the island while it was still cool, or visiting the fortress if only to show the soldiers he had not forgotten them.

He wondered if the news of what had happened had reached the streets of London and the countryside. Would Belinda understand what was really happening? There would be those ready enough to describe his efforts as a reckless adventure to cover up the loss of Duncan's *Sparrowhawk*.

A sentry shouted, 'Gunfire, sir! To th' east'rd!'

Lemoine tensed. 'By God, he's right.' He cupped his hands. 'Corporal of the guard! Sound the alarm!'

Bolitho watched the red-coated soldiers running from their cave-like quarters below the battery walls.

It was probably nothing, or a show of impudence by some passing Spanish vessel. But they could not take chances.

He looked round and saw Midshipman Evans' shadowy figure below the watch-tower, already removing a telescope from its case.

It was uncanny how the boy followed him and seemed able to guess what he was going to need next.

But it was still too dark around the point to see anything. Or was it? There it was. A flash reflected on the belly of a low cloud. Then another. Not enough for a sea-fight. More likely a chase.

He said, 'Mr Evans, pass word to the guard-boat. Warn the ship. And my compliments to Captain Keen, and tell him we may have company before the day's out.'

He saw Crocker, *Achates'* most senior gunner's mate, hurrying along the upper battery, some soldiers panting behind him.

Crocker was probably the oldest man in the ship, and with his white hair in a spiky pigtail, and strange, loping gait, he was quite a character. His left eye was almost sightless, he had been part-blinded by a splinter when he had been not much older than Adam. But his right one was as keen as steel, and he could manage, lay and train any gun better than a full crew. He also knew how to heat shot, and Bolitho thought he could already smell the acrid fumes from one of the ovens behind the parapet.

Crocker seemed surprised to see his vice-admiral on the wall. He knuckled his forehead and twisted his head round to get a better view. It made him look even more villainous, and Bolitho was able to appreciate why all the gun captains feared his wrath.

'Good mornin' fer a shoot, sir!'

Bolitho smiled. 'Be ready.'

Lemoine watched the man lope away with his helpers.

'He's certainly kept my men on the bustle, sir!'

Somewhere in the town a church bell chimed. It sounded strangely sad on the damp air.

Bolitho trained his telescope towards the ship once more.

'What was that, Mr Lemoine?'

The lieutenant hid a yawn. He had been awake until the early hours playing cards unsuccessfully with his second in command.

'A lot of the islanders are Catholics, sir. The bell is for early mass.' When Bolitho remained silent he added helpfully, 'An important celebration for them, sir. St Damiano's Day.'

Lemoine had not wasted his time in the regiment, Bolitho thought. Some would never bother their heads with matters outside their own ordered world.

There was another thud of gunfire. They must be trying to prevent a ship from entering harbour. He thought of Adam.

No, not him. Tyrrell was too old a hand to be caught at this early hour.

He moved his glass again and saw the opposite headland shaking itself from the shadows. He could see the leap of surf around the reefs, and the further necklace of rocks by the point named Cape Despair, probably with some justification.

Feet clattered on the stairs and a runner barked out his report to Lemoine who in turn said, 'Message from your flagship, sir. All boats lowered and patrols alerted.'

Bolitho could see them in his mind. Small pickets of marines, backed up by volunteers from the local militia. A puny enough force, but properly used it could prevent any attempt at landing men through the reefs. There was only one safe way, and that was the one which Keen had used. And old Crocker with his heated shot would do his best if the enemy tried to force the entrance.

Sunlight ran down the slopes and laid bare the water at the harbour mouth. Bolitho trained his glass again and saw the guard-boat moving slowly below the land, a midshipman in the stern-sheets, probably enjoying his own freedom of command.

Lemoine said, 'There she is, sir!'

The ship appeared around the headland, sails emptying and then refilling instantly as she changed tack. She was a large vessel, and Lemoine said, 'Indiaman, sir, I know her, she's the *Royal James* and was in Antigua several months back.'

Men were leaning through the gun embrasures, and others ran along the jetty below to see what was happening.

Bolitho made up his mind. 'I'm returning to the flagship, Mr Lemoine. You know what to do here.' He was halfway down the stairs before the lieutenant had time to reply.

The bargemen came to life, and Allday jumped to his feet as Bolitho appeared half-running through the gate.

'To the ship, Allday.'

He ignored their startled glances and tried to discover what was troubling him. The Indiaman should be able to reach safety unless her pursuers gained a lucky hit and brought down a vital spar or two. But with this powerful south-east wind the other ships would soon have to stand away from a lee shore or face the havoc of the guns. In broad daylight Crocker could not miss.

The oars rose and fell, and with each powerful stroke the barge seemed to fly across the water as if eager to lift over it.

Bolitho seized Allday's arm. 'Alter course! Steer for the headland!' When Allday hesitated he shook it and shouted, 'I must be blind! Lemoine told me without knowing it. This is a very holy day!'

Allday swung the tiller so that the barge heeled over, but not a man aboard missed his stroke.

'Aye, if you says so, sir.'

He thinks I'm mad. Bolitho said urgently, 'And yet on this St Damiano's Day there was not a single movement from the mission!'

Allday stared at him blankly.

Bolitho looked around for the guard-boat but it was too close inshore, near the entrance, and every eye would be watching and waiting for the *Royal James* to burst into view round the point.

Bolitho banged his hands together. *I should have seen it.*

'Are the men armed?'

Allday nodded, his eyes slitted against the early sunlight.

'Aye, sir, cutlasses and three pistols.'

He darted a glance at Bolitho's face, knowing something was about to happen, yet held back from asking in front of the bargemen.

'It will have to suffice.' Bolitho pointed at a tiny patch of sand. 'Beach her there.'

As the bargemen tossed their oars and the boat glided into the protection of a high slope of land it seemed suddenly peaceful.

'Clear the boat.' Bolitho climbed over the side and felt the sea tugging at his legs as he waded ashore. Cutlasses and three pistols against what? He said, 'Send a man to fetch the patrol from the point. Tell him to stay out of sight.'

Allday watched him anxiously. 'Is it an attack, sir?'

Bolitho took one of the pistols and then picked up a heavy cutlass from the pile of weapons on the beach. Now, of all times, he had come ashore unarmed.

'The mission. I feel there is something wrong.'

The men gathered up their weapons and followed him obediently up the steep slope and across the long piece of headland.

The wind was quite strong, and Bolitho felt the sand whipping from the tough gorse and scrub which always looked so inviting from seaward.

He saw the huddled buildings of the mission on the little islet, the deserted beach, the air of utter desolation. Not even any smoke to betray a fire or sign of life.

He heard far-off cheering, the voices thinned by the wind, like children at play. He paused and looked across the harbour entrance and the old fortress with the flag curling above it. The shouts were most likely from the guard-boat as the big Indiaman suddenly loomed above the headland and headed towards safety.

There was a large boat towing astern, but other than that few hands on deck to shorten sail once the ship had reached the anchorage. At that moment he saw the guard-boat sweep into view, the midshipman raising a speaking-trumpet to his lips as he shouted at the incoming ship.

Bolitho tore his eyes away and looked at his handful of seamen. Keen and the others could take care of the *Royal James* now. He had seen the raked sails of a frigate rounding-to as she stood away from the land as her quarry slipped beneath the fortress battery.

Allday said, 'The boats have gone, sir.'

Bolitho stared at the little islet. It was true. The fishing boats had vanished. Perhaps that was the simple explanation for it. The monks or missionaries had gone fishing. Food must often come before prayer.

'*Look*, sir!'

Allday's cry made him turn towards the nearest line of

rocks. They were no longer deserted but alive with scrambling, running figures, the sunlight glittering on swords and bayonets.

'Soldiers!' Allday raised a pistol, his chest heaving with alarm. 'A hundred o' the buggers at least!'

There were a few shots, distant and without menace until the balls whined overhead or smacked into the hard sand.

'Take cover!'

Bolitho saw the bargeman with two marines from a patrol running along the edge of the land. One fell instantly, and the others vanished from sight.

Then there was a muffled explosion. It was more of a feeling than a sound. As if all the air had been sucked from your lungs.

As Bolitho rolled on to his side and looked back to where they had left the barge he saw the *Royal James* give a great convulsion. Then every gun-port along her side burst open, but instead of muzzles he saw searing tongues of flame shooting out, then leaping above to lick and consume sails and spars with terrifying speed. The boat which had been towing astern had cast off and was being rowed back towards the entrance.

Allday whispered, 'A fire-ship!'

Bolitho saw his eyes gleam in the growing wall of fire, could even feel the heat across the water like an open furnace as the wind fanned the towering flames and drove the abandoned ship unerringly up the harbour. Straight for the moored *Achates*.

More shots ripped above the headland, and Bolitho heard the yells of the oncoming soldiers.

Without *Achates* there was no hope, no protection, and the fortress battery had guarded her killer from destruction.

Allday peered at him, his eyes wild. 'Fight, sir?'

Bolitho hung back. Was that all there was to it? To die here on this desolate place for nothing? Then he recalled the drummer-boy as he had covered his face.

He stood up and balanced the heavy blade in his hand.

'Aye, fight!'

On either side of him the bargemen stood up and shook their cutlasses.

Bolitho tried to shut out the terrible roar of flames and fired his pistol at the line of soldiers. There was no time to reload. There was no time for anything.

He bounded across some loose stones and hacked aside a man's sword with such force that he fell headlong down the slope.

The clash of steel on steel and a few haphazard shots, it was less then enough. Bolitho felt figures pressing around him, staring eyes, teeth bared in hate or desperation, as the overwhelming number of soldiers drove them back towards the water. He slashed out with all his strength and saw a man's face open from ear to chin, felt his cutlass jar on ribs as he knocked down another's guard and drove the blade into him.

He heard a gasp and with horror saw Allday fall among the struggling, stabbing figures.

'*Allday!*'

He knocked a soldier aside and tried to reach him. It was no use. Not for a gesture. His own pride.

Bolitho dropped his blade. '*Enough!*'

Then ignoring the levelled weapons he fell on his knees and tried to turn Allday on to his back. At any second he expected to feel the hot agony of steel enter his body, but he no longer cared.

The soldiers stood motionless, either too stunned by the ferocity of the brief action or too impressed by Bolitho's rank, it was impossible to tell.

Bolitho bent over him to shield his eyes from the glare. There was blood on his chest, a lot of it.

Bolitho said desperately, 'You're safe now, old friend. Rest easy until . . .'

Allday opened his eyes and looked up at him for several seconds.

Then he whispered, 'Hurts, sir. Real bad. Th' buggers have done for poor John this time . . .'

A seaman dropped beside him. 'Sir! Th' Dons are runnin' away!'

Bolitho glanced up and saw the soldiers running and limping towards the rocks where they had left their boats.

It was not difficult to find the reason. A line of horsemen, with Captain Masters of the San Felipe Militia, were cantering over the sky-line, sabres drawn, their approach all the more menacing because of the silence.

Masters wheeled his horse and dismounted, his face shocked beyond belief.

'We saw what you tried to do.' The words fell out of him. 'Some of us decided to head them off.'

Bolitho looked at him, his eyes seeing nothing but the man's shadow and the great pall of smoke from the chaos in the harbour.

'Well, you're too late!'

He prised the cutlass from Allday's hand and flung it after the disappearing soldiers.

He felt Allday grip his wrist, and saw him looking at him again, his eyes tight with pain.

Allday muttered, 'Don't take on, sir. We beat th' buggers, an' that's no error.'

Boots pounded over the sand and more red coats appeared on every side.

Bolitho said, 'Take him *carefully*, lads.'

He watched four soldiers carry Allday down towards the barge. There were explosions in the distance and voices were calling from every direction. They needed him. There was no time for grief. He had heard that often enough.

But he hurried after the soldiers and gripped Allday's arm. 'Don't leave me, Allday. *I need you*.'

Allday did not open his eyes but seemed to be trying to smile as they lowered him into the boat.

When Bolitho reappeared above the beach the sunlight glanced off his bright epaulettes and a few militiamen gave a cheer.

One of the bargemen, his wounded arm tucked inside his shirt, paused to glare at them.

'Cheer, yew buggers, will yew? 'Cause yew'm safe fer a bit?' He spat contemptuously at their feet. He jerked his head towards Bolitho's shoulders. ''E's worth more'n yew an' the whole bloody island!'

Bolitho strode through the scrub, some of which had been set alight by drifting sparks from the fire-ship.

Another attack might come at any moment. Keen would be needing help. But nothing seemed to have any substance.

Allday could not die. Not like this. His was the strength of an oak. *He must not die.*

14

No Better Sentiment

There were cries of horror and dismay as the harbour entrance was suddenly filled with flames and billowing black smoke. To any sailor fire was one of the greatest enemies. In storm or shipwreck there was always a chance. But when fire rampaged between decks, where everything was tarred, painted or tinder-dry, there was no hope at all.

Lieutenant Quantock dragged his eyes from the blazing Indiaman and shouted, 'What shall we do, sir?' Hatless, and with his hair blowing in the wind, he looked wild and totally unlike *Achates'* normally grim-faced second in command.

Keen gripped the rail and made himself face the oncoming inferno. *Sparrowhawk*, the Spanish privateer and now his own *Achates*. There was no time to kedge the ship along the harbour. Anyway, most of the boats were away on picket duty.

He could feel Quantock staring at him, sailors nearby frozen in various attitudes of alarm and disbelief. One moment they had been jubilant as the Indiaman had passed beneath the battery's defences. The next, and the enemy was right here among them and intent on burning them alive.

Keen knew the signs well enough. Hesitation, then panic. Nobody could be asked or commanded to stand and await death like a beast at slaughter.

Thank God he had had the ship cleared for action after Midshipman Evans had brought the message from Bolitho.

'Mr Quantock! Load and run out the larboard battery, both decks!' He punched the lieutenant's arm. *'Move yourself!'*

Calls trilled and men jerked from their various stances to

obey the order. With trucks squeaking on both decks of *Achates'* larboard side, the one which lay helpless to the fire-ship, the guns were run out.

Keen felt the smoke stinging his eyes as he tried to gauge the progress of the other vessel. Her sails were charred remnants and her foremast was burned to a stump. But the wind was all she needed to carry her to her victim. Even as he watched he saw the Indiaman brush almost gently against a moored topsail schooner. Just a mere touch and in seconds the vessel was fiercely ablaze, her anchor-watch splashing in the water alongside.

'Ready, sir!' Quantock sounded desperate.

Keen found himself thinking of Bolitho. Where was he? Had he gone with some of the patrols to repel an attack from one of the beaches? He tightened his stomach muscles. Maybe Bolitho was dead.

'As you bear!'

He walked to the quarterdeck rail and looked at his gun crews, as he would if they were engaging a living enemy.

'*Fire!*'

In the confined harbour the roar of the broadside was like a giant thunder-clap. Keen watched the mass of iron show its passage across the water like an opposing wind, felt the deck sway over as if the ship was trying to free herself and escape.

He saw the fire-ship stagger, spars and burning fragments fall around her in tall columns of steam.

'*Reload!* Steady, men!' That was Mountsteven with his guns.

Keen shouted, 'Mr Rooke! Send some hands aloft to douse the sails. Put some others along the gangway.'

The boatswain nodded and hurried away bawling orders. He knew that buckets of water hauled to the upper yards, or flung down over the exposed tumblehome would be next to useless. Like trying to put out a forest fire with a mouthful of spit. But it kept them busy and occupied. No time to feel terror, no time to abandon ship until the last, disciplined moment.

'*Fire!*'

Keen saw the broadside smash into the Indiaman's fore-castle and felt sick with despair as great gouts of flame burst through the holes made by the iron shot.

The master said in a whisper, 'We'll not stand her off, sir.'

Keen did not look at him. Knocker was a careful man and had probably unshipped his chronometer so that it would not go down with the ship.

Keen looked at the grim-faced gun crews with their rammers and sponges, the menacing way that the smoke was curling between the ratlines and shrouds as if the rigging was already ablaze.

He could do nothing to save her. This fine ship which had seen and done so much. *Old Katie*, they called her. And now . . .

Quantock raised his speaking-trumpet. '*Fire!*'

Tuson, the surgeon, hovered by the ladder, and Keen said, 'You wish to get your wounded on deck?'

That, if anything, might snap the last strand of order. There were not any of Dewar's marines aboard to prevent the stampede once it began. He saw the grateful look in Tuson's eyes and was glad of what he had done.

Goddard, the quartermaster, yelled, 'Look yonder, lads!'

The Indiaman had bumped against another moored craft and that too was well alight, sparks shooting from her hold and adding to the horror.

But it was not that which Goddard had seen.

Keen stared until his eyes throbbed with pain as the little brigantine *Vivid* nosed through the smoke and falling fragments, her yards braced as she overreached the other vessel.

Quantock said hoarsely, 'Christ Almighty, she must have followed her through the entrance! It'll be her turn to burn in a moment!'

Keen tore the telescope from a midshipman's fingers and trained it on the advancing wall of flames. In the lens it looked even worse, terrifying, and Keen could feel his mouth and throat going dry as he watched.

He saw Tyrrell's big frame by the tiller as he steered his *Vivid* closer and closer to the other vessel's starboard bow. Through the haze of smoke and whirling smuts he looked as if he would never budge. Even now the sails were swinging and snapping in the wind, although how Tyrrell's men could find the strength to work at halliards and braces against that heat was a miracle.

Keen heard shouts from the gun-deck as the first of the wounded were brought from the orlop but did not turn away from the awesome sight in the harbour. He imagined he could feel the heat and knew he could not delay the order to abandon much longer.

'Secure the guns, Mr Quantock.'

He expected a chorus of insults at the absurdity of his order, but instead he heard the squeak of trucks and hand-spikes as the eighteen-pounders were secured at their ports.

There was a mingled groan as the *Vivid*'s masthead pendant vanished in a puff of smoke. Any second now and all the care in the world would not prevent her taking fire.

Keen saw the two vessels lurch together, the impetus of *Vivid*'s full set of sails swinging the fire-ship slightly to larboard.

Lieutenant Trevenen murmured thickly, '*Vivid*'s afire, sir.'

Keen watched the flames jumping like terrible demons from rigging to rigging, multiplying and spreading until the fore-course was reduced to ashes.

But *Vivid* was holding her way against the other, heavier hull, pushing her round. There were men too at the point where both vessels were locked together, and moments later Keen saw a splash as one of the Indiaman's anchors was released from the cat-head. Given time the anchor cable would burn through too, but as the flukes dragged along the harbour bed the fire-ship's shape began to lengthen as she took the strain of the cable.

Her smouldering mizzen and yards cracked and fell in

charred fragments alongside and Knocker gasped, 'She's *aground*, by God!'

Keen nodded, unable to speak. Tyrrell probably knew the harbours hereabouts better than most, and had gauged his action to the second, so that the blazing Indiaman was already pushing herself firmly into the shallows.

Keen heard himself say, 'Send every boat you can, Mr Quantock.'

Vivid was blazing fiercely. It was almost impossible to see which vessel was which. There was still danger, the ship might refloat herself, or a fragment might drift down on *Achates*.

Keen turned and looked at his command. But whatever happened they had stood firm. Like Bolitho had told them. Together.

They were staring up from the gun-deck and watching him. Because of the smoke, and the carefully rationed water aboard ship, they looked more like a mob of filthy buccaneers than jack-tars.

They were cheering now, waving their fists and capering as if they had won a great battle. He saw Quantock looking at him, his eyes bitter. The sailors had at last discarded their dead captain and had adopted Keen.

Keen grinned at them and felt like weeping. Then he made up his mind.

'Call away the gig. I'll fetch Tyrrell myself.'

They found Tyrrell and most of his small crew clinging to a spar and half an upturned boat.

And there too was Adam Bolitho, half-naked and with a livid burn on one shoulder.

Tyrrell allowed himself to be hauled into the stern-sheets where he slumped and looked across at the remains of his brigantine.

She was already burned to the water-line. Unrecognizable.

Keen said, 'I'm sorry for what happened and the way I treated you. It was a close thing. You lost your ship but you saved mine.'

Tyrrell barely heard him. He put his arm around Adam's shoulders and said roughly, 'Seems to me, you an' me both lost somethin', eh?'

As the gig approached *Achates'* side the seamen ran along the gangway and swarmed into the shrouds to cheer as Tyrrell looked up at them.

Keen said, 'They're grateful to you.'

'Quite right too.'

Tyrrell looked at his wooden leg; even that had been charred by the blaze. What was the point of going over it again? If *Achates* had not been here when the attack had started, none of this would have happened. He looked at his beloved *Vivid* as she broke in halves and slipped into the shallows in a rising cloud of steam. And *Vivid* would still be his.

He felt the young lieutenant's hand on his arm as he said quietly, 'We'll both get another chance one day, Jethro.'

Tyrrell bared his teeth. 'Sure as hell hope so. Can't spend the rest of my days lookin' after you!'

Keen stood by Bolitho's table and watched him with concern. He had noticed that Bolitho had been studying the day's log of events but that his eyes rarely moved.

Keen said, 'Mr Mansel, the purser, reports that fresh fruit and vegetables have been coming on board from the town, sir. It is still arriving. They don't seem to be able to do enough for us now.'

Bolitho smoothed out the papers on his table. *Now.* That word said so much. He heard Ozzard tiptoeing behind him to close the stern windows as dusk filled the harbour with shadows once more. But there were still a few sparks and glowing embers to mark where the fire-ship lay in the shallows. It was only this morning when he had passed the time with Lieutenant Lemoine at the fortress.

Keen knew Bolitho needed to be alone but was unwilling to leave him. He recalled his own shock when the barge had hooked on to the chains and he had seen Allday carried aboard as if already dead.

All his other feelings had been scattered like the ashes of the fire-ship.

Pride in his men, of what they had done in spite of the terrible danger. A deep, inner satisfaction that he had not broken under the strain. Neither seemed to count any more. Allday had become part of his life too. In fact, when he thought about it, most of the people he knew and cared for had been helped and influenced by Bolitho's coxswain.

At times like this Allday would have been the one to enter the cabin and gently hustle away unwanted visitors, like his dog had once done when he had been a shepherd in Cornwall.

Now he lay in Bolitho's own sleeping quarters, a sword-thrust in his chest which had even shocked the taciturn surgeon.

Keen tried again. 'We took several prisoners, sir. The crew of the fire-ship, some soldiers from the mission too. You were right. They are all Spaniards from La Guaira. After this the Dons will never dare to attack San Felipe. The whole world will know what they did. I would give little hope for their heads when their King is told of their bungling.'

Bolitho leaned back in his chair and rubbed his eyes. He could still smell smoke. Could see Allday's attempt to smile just for his benefit.

He said, 'Tomorrow I will draft a report for Sir Hayward Sheaffe.' London would be grey and wet in September, he thought vaguely. 'After that it will be up to Parliament.'

His words seemed to mock him. What did any of it matter?

'But for the moment it can wait.'

He looked up sharply but it was only one of the duty watch pacing the poop overhead.

Tuson was a good surgeon in spite of his early record. He had already proved that several times over. But if only . . . He cut his thoughts short.

He said, 'I was sorry to hear about Jethro Tyrrell's loss.'

'He took it well, sir.' Keen hesitated. 'He was asking if he might visit you.'

The adjoining door opened and Adam stepped noiselessly into the cabin.

Bolitho asked, 'How is he?'

Adam wanted to comfort him but said, 'He remains unconscious, and Mr Tuson says his breathing is poor.' He looked away. 'I spoke to him but . . . '

Bolitho got to his feet, his limbs heavy. There were lights in Georgetown, and he wondered if the people were still standing quietly on the waterfront as they had since the action. Sharing the pain or the guilt he did not know, or care.

Adam was saying, 'Allday and I were once taken prisoner together, sir.' He was speaking to Keen but his gaze was on Bolitho. 'Afterwards he said to me it was the only time he had ever been flogged. He seemed to think it was a bit of a joke.'

Keen nodded. 'He would.'

Bolitho clenched his fists. They wanted to help but they were ripping him apart.

He said abruptly, 'I'll go to him. You both get some rest. Take care of that burn, Adam. In this climate . . . ' He did not go on.

Keen led the way from the cabin and said softly, 'Hear the silence? And they say that ships are only wood and copper!'

Adam nodded, glad of the darkness below the poop. Bolitho had told him to take care of his burned shoulder. He was incredible.

Bolitho opened the small door and stepped into the sleeping-cabin. The ship was so still at her moorings that the cot barely moved.

Tuson was holding a small bottle up to a shuttered lantern but turned as Bolitho entered.

'No change, sir.' It sounded like a rebuke.

Bolitho looked into the cot where he had fretted over the months since hoisting his flag above *Achates*.

Allday was heavily bandaged and had his head on one side as if to breathe better. Bolitho touched his forehead and tried not to show his anguish. The skin felt like ice. As if he was already gone.

Tuson said quietly, 'Narrowly missed the lung, sir. Thank God it was a clean blade.'

He watched Bolitho's shadow rear across the massive timbers and added, 'Would you like me to stay, sir?'

'No.' He knew Tuson had plenty of people awaiting his care. 'But thank you.'

Tuson sighed. 'I'll come when you need me.'

Bolitho followed him into the cabin. 'Tell me.'

Tuson slipped into his plain blue coat. 'I don't know him as well as you, sir. He seems strong enough, but it is a bad wound. Most would have died there and then. I am deeply sorry.'

When Bolitho looked again Tuson had gone. Down to the bowels of the ship, to his sick-bay and solitude.

Ozzard hovered nearby. 'Anythin', sir?'

Bolitho looked at him. So small and frail. He too was feeling it badly.

'What was Allday's favourite drink?'

Ozzard's watery eyes lit up. 'Well, rum, sir. Always liked a wet.' He fumbled with his hands. 'I – I mean, *likes* a wet, sir.'

Bolitho nodded. Even that was typical. In moments of crisis and danger, disappointment or celebration, he had often offered Allday a glass or two of cabin brandy. And all this time he had preferred rum.

He said gently, 'Then fetch some, please. Tell the purser I want the very best.'

He was sitting beside the cot, the cabin door half open to catch some air, when Ozzard returned with a copper jug. In the cabin's heat the rum made his head swim.

Bolitho tried to concentrate on what he must do tomorrow, on the ship's affairs, on Tyrrell's future. But he kept seeing Belinda's lovely face when they had made their last farewell. How she had told Allday to look after him and Adam.

He heard the muffled trill of a call, the distant patter of bare feet as the duty watch was turned to for some task or other.

The voyages they had done together. And just last year when they had both been prisoners of war in France when Allday had carried the dying John Neale in his arms, it had been his strength and confidence which had held them and had given them courage.

He remembered his own early days as a midshipman and lieutenant when he had fondly believed that the admiral in his quarters was beyond pain and protected from personal doubts.

Bolitho heard the squeak of a fiddle from the forecastle and pictured the off-watch hands enjoying the cool evening air.

He saw himself in the mirror above the little desk and looked away. What price your vice-admiral now?

He took a clean handkerchief and dabbed it in a glass of rum, then with great care he wiped a little of it on Allday's mouth.

'Here, old friend . . . ' He bit his lip as the rum trickled unheeded down Allday's chin. There was a bright scarlet stain in the centre of the bandages. Bolitho restrained the urge to yell for the sentry to summon the surgeon again. Allday was fighting his own battle. It would be cruel to make him suffer further.

Bolitho stared at Allday's homely face. It looked older, and the realization made him get to his feet, too stunned to accept what was happening, yet unwilling to share it with others.

He clenched his fists and peered around the small cabin like a trapped animal. There was nothing he could do. Barely seeing what he was doing he held the glass to his lips and swallowed the rum, the fire on his tongue and throat making him gasp and retch.

Then he waited until his breathing had returned almost to normal. He saw Ozzard's small shadow through the open door and said in a voice he barely recognized, 'My compliments to the surgeon . . . '

Ozzard seemed to shrink even smaller as Bolitho's words reached him.

'Quick as I can, sir!'

Bolitho swung round as one of Allday's hands groped over the side of the cot.

'Yes, I'm *here*!'

He held it between his own hands and stared fixedly at Allday's face. It was set in a frown, as if he was attempting to remember something. His hand had no more strength than a child's.

Bolitho whispered, 'Easy now. Don't let go.' He tightened his grip but there was no response.

Then Allday opened his eyes and stared at him for what seemed like minutes without any sign of recognition. When he spoke his voice was so small Bolitho had to bend over him until they touched.

Allday murmured, 'But you don't like rum, sir, you never have!'

Bolitho nodded. 'I know.' He wanted to talk, to help him, but the words would not come out.

Doors banged open and feet pounded on companion-ladders, then Tuson, with Keen and Adam behind him, burst into the cabin.

The surgeon pressed his hand on to Allday's chest, oblivious to the blood on his cuff. Then he said, 'Breathing's a whole lot better.' He sniffed. 'Rum, was it?'

Allday was unable to focus properly but he needed to speak, to reassure Bolitho in some way.

'Could do with a wet, sir.'

Tuson stood aside and watched gravely as the vice-admiral put one hand under the coxswain's head and held a glass to his lips. He knew that if he lived until he was a thousand he would never forget this moment.

He said, 'Leave him now.'

He watched as Bolitho dashed some water from a bowl on to his face, the way he was trying to prepare himself to confront the others in the cabin.

Tuson said quietly, 'Never mind about them, sir.' Afterwards he was surprised he had dared to address his admiral in such a fashion. 'It'll do no harm for them to see you have feelings too. Just a man like the rest of us.'

Bolitho took another glance at Allday. He looked at rest.

He said, 'Thank you. You will never know . . . ' He left the sleeping-cabin to face the others.

Tuson looked at the rum on the desk and grimaced. Allday should be dead. All his experience pointed to just that. He began to snip at the bloodied bandages.

Then even Tuson's severe features broke into a smile. *Could do with a wet indeed*.

In the great cabin they sat or stood in total silence as Ozzard brought some wine.

Then Keen raised his glass. 'This happy few, sir.'

Bolitho looked away. There was no better sentiment.

15

Last Farewell

The weeks and then months which followed the attack on the
harbour seemed to Bolitho like a slow record of Allday's fight
against death. Any progress was often marked by an immediate set-back, and Bolitho guessed that he was fretting about
his inability to move, his 'uselessness', as he put it.

A few vessels visited the island, and slowly but surely
things returned to normal. There were no more attacks, and
traders reported that they had not sighted any Spanish men-
of-war or suffered further interference.

In October that year two hurricanes struck San Felipe with
a ferocity which made a military attack puny by comparison.
Great tidal waves had threatened *Achates* and destroyed smaller
vessels, and torn the roofs off many of the houses. Plantations
were laid to waste, and several people had been killed or badly
injured, their livelihoods destroyed.

But it was the turning point between the islanders and the
Achates' company. Without the disciplined efforts of the
seamen and marines it seemed unlikely that anything of value
would have been saved. The ship, once a symbol of law and
oppression, had taken on a new guise, that of protector, so
that for the officers and men alike the daily routine was less
demanding.

Three months to the day after being cut down by a Spanish
sword Allday walked across the *Achates'* quarterdeck for the
first time. Ozzard went with him, but Allday, true to his
fashion, would not lean on him for support.

Bolitho made a point of being on the poop and watched

while Allday moved into the sunlight, his feet unsure and dragging, as if he had never walked a ship's deck before. Bolitho noticed too that several of Allday's friends were much in evidence, as they had been throughout his struggle to survive. But they understood and were careful to keep their distance, outwardly engrossed in their various trades.

Bolitho heard Adam's light step beside him and said, 'I never thought I would see this day, Adam.' He shook his head. 'Never.'

Adam smiled. 'He's doing well.'

Bolitho saw Allday reach the quarterdeck rail and grasp it with both hands as he took several breaths and looked down at the gun-deck.

Scott, the third lieutenant, who was in charge of the watch, took elaborate care not to see him, even walked to the compass and peered at it as though the ship was at sea and not alongside.

Bolitho turned and looked at his nephew. All these weeks and they had barely discussed Boston and what had happened there, although Tyrrell had told him the bones of the matter.

He said quietly, 'What we have done here is important, Adam. I put my views to the Admiralty, my beliefs as to what should happen here after we have gone.' He shrugged. 'I have to believe they will act upon them. Too many have suffered and died to throw it all away. I used to hear my father say we in England are so often like that. We do not take proper care of what we have won with blood and sweat.' He gestured towards the anchorage. 'Just a pair of frigates here and the Dons would never have attempted to seize the place. Likewise the French would have looked elsewhere to make a bargain.'

'Suppose their lordships still insist on handing over the island, Uncle?'

'The Spanish attack should have shown them the importance of San Felipe. If not, then I have failed here.' He touched his arm impetuously. 'But it was wrong to use you the way I did. I knew that Chase would trust you, would tell you what I needed to know. But as a result you lost a chance to win his niece. I cannot forgive myself for that.'

Adam moved his shoulder and felt the burn beneath his shirt. He gave a rueful smile. 'We were nearly too late anyway, Uncle.'

They both looked at the charred fragments in the shallows. Sea-birds were perched in rows on the blackened ribs of the fire-ship, and weeds grew where Tyrrell had driven his brigantine to her destruction to save them all.

Adam hesitated. 'At least I saw my father's house.'

Bolitho glanced at him and was glad that the jealousy had gone.

Adam sounded far away. 'I told her I would return some day.'

'Perhaps we shall go together. When that happens you can take *me* to see Hugh's old house.'

They looked at each other, sensing the bond between them. It was as if Hugh was very much here with them. Like this island, Bolitho thought, without threat or hostility.

He tensed as Allday swayed after releasing his grip on the rail.

Then Allday looked up to the poop and grinned. He had known they were there all the while, Bolitho thought.

He said, 'Without Allday . . . ' He did not need to go on.

The midshipman of the watch clattered up the poop ladder and touched his hat.

Bolitho looked at him. 'Well, Mr Ferrier, are you going to tell me about the sail?'

The midshipman flushed, his carefully worded speech scattered.

'I, er, the captain sends his respects, sir, and a courier-brig has been sighted to the east'rd.'

Bolitho nodded. 'Thank you. It is a while since I "enjoyed" the midshipman's berth, Mr Ferrier, but I have not yet forgotten how to read a signal.'

Adam exclaimed. 'You knew? And yet you carried on talking to me as if the brig and her news are of no importance!'

Bolitho watched the midshipman pausing to speak with two of his friends. The story would be enlarged somewhat by tonight, he thought.

Ferrier was the senior midshipman, and the brig's arrival would affect him too. Homeward bound and a lieutenant's examination, the young could always find room for optimism.

He said simply, 'It was important that we should talk. As to the rest, I shall have to fall back on Thomas Herrick's Lady Luck.'

Bolitho moved to the rail and looked along the upper decks. Men were on the gangways or working high overhead on the yards. But their eyes were towards the harbour entrance, and Bolitho could guess what many of them were thinking. They had been glad to leave England and the humiliation of being thrown on the beach like so much unwanted top-hamper. Now, after what they had seen and done together, they would be eager to return to their homes.

Bolitho thought of Falmouth, what they would say when they met again, whenever that might be? Of his very own daughter. What name had she chosen for her?

He said, 'I'm going below. My compliments to the officer of the watch and please tell him to keep the people working. I don't want any long faces if the news is bad.'

Adam stood back and touched his hat. It was difficult to know which tack his uncle would take next.

Bolitho hurried into his cabin and saw to his astonishment that Allday was hard at work putting a shine on the old sword.

'You should be resting, man! Will you never do as you are told, dammit?'

But for once his mock anger failed to have the right effect.

Allday ran the cloth once more along the blade and then looked at him squarely.

'The surgeon says I'll not be the same again, sir.'

Bolitho walked to the open stern windows. So that was it. He should have guessed. He had seen that Allday was unable to straighten his back properly. As if the deepness and pain of his chest wound prevented it.

Allday added quietly, 'Not much of an admiral's coxswain I'll be an' I wanted . . .'

Bolitho looked at him and said, 'You've earned your time ashore in comfort more than anyone I know. There's a place for you at Falmouth, but you know it.'

'I know, an' I'm grateful. It's not just that.' He looked at the sword. 'You won't need me any more. Not like this.'

Bolitho took the sword from him and laid it on the table.

'Like what? A bit knocked about, is that all? You'll be your old mutinous self in no time, you see.' He rested his hand on his shoulder. 'I'll never sail without you. Not unless you wish it. You have my word.'

Allday stood up and tried not to grimace as the pain probed through him.

'That's settled then, sir.'

He moved from the cabin, his feet dragging on the painted canvas.

His determination, his pride were as unbeatable as ever, Bolitho thought sadly. And he was *alive*.

Later that day, as the sun dipped towards a placid sea, Bolitho stepped into *Achates'* wardroom. After his own and Keen's cabins it seemed small and overcrowded, he thought.

Quantock said stiffly, 'All officers and senior warrant officers present as ordered, sir.'

Bolitho nodded. Quantock was a cold fish, even the action had not changed him. Nor would it now, he decided.

He heard his nephew close the door behind him and said, 'Please be seated, gentlemen, and thank you for inviting me here.'

It had always amused him. Any senior officer, even Keen, was a guest in his ship's wardroom. But had anyone ever denied one an entrance, he wondered?

He glanced around at their expectant faces. Sunburned, and competent. Even the midshipmen who were crammed right aft by the tiller-head looked more like men than boys now. The lieutenants and the two Royal Marines, Knocker, the priest-like sailing-master, and Tuson, the surgeon, he had grown to know and understand them in the time they had carried his flag at the fore.

Bolitho said, 'You will know that the courier-brig brought despatches from England. Their lordships have given full consideration to the reports on San Felipe, and to the large part your efforts played in an otherwise difficult mission.'

He saw Mountsteven nudge his friend the sixth lieutenant.

'Furthermore, I have been advised that French interference in the Mediterranean, and their pressures on His Majesty's Government to evacuate Malta in accordance with the *same* treaty which obliged us to hand this island to them, makes further negotiations impossible. As a direct result, gentlemen, all French and Dutch colonies which we had agreed to restore will now be retained. That, of course, will apply to San Felipe.'

It seemed impossible. In the neatly phrased despatches it was still hard to compare the complex negotiations which had swayed back and forth across Europe while *Achates* had been fighting for her very survival.

Bonaparte, now named Consul for life, had annexed Piedmont and Elba and showed every intention of retaking Malta once the British flag came down in the name of independence.

Bolitho saw the excitement transmit itself around the wardroom. So much for the Peace of Amiens. The signatures were barely dry on it.

He said, 'I am ordered to remain here until sufficient forces are despatched from Antigua and Jamaica to reinforce the garrison.'

He saw Keen drop his eyes. He knew what was coming next.

'The recent governor will be replaced as soon as possible. Sir Humphrey Rivers will be returning to England to stand trial for treason.'

He could find no satisfaction in that. After the luxury and

wealth of his little kingdom he would be taken home in a King's ship, the first of any size which could be made available. And after that, with this totally unexpected shift of events, he would very likely hang.

He looked from face to face and added, 'You have performed very well, and I should wish you to carry my thanks to the people also.'

Keen watched as Bolitho smiled for the first time since he had begun to speak. Whatever anyone else might think, Keen could see plainly enough where the strain and responsibility had made their mark.

Bolitho said quietly, 'And after *that*, we are going home.'

Then they were all on their feet shouting and laughing like boys.

Keen opened the door and Bolitho slipped away. He had two letters from Belinda, and now there was time he would re-read them from the beginning.

Keen and Adam followed him up the companion and then Keen asked, 'Will it be war, sir?'

Bolitho thought of the young and jubilant faces he had just left behind, of Quantock's sour disapproval.

'There is little doubt in my mind, Val.'

Keen stared around in the gloom, as if already preparing his ship for another battle.

'God, we've hardly recovered from the last one, sir!'

Bolitho heard Allday's unfamiliar dragging footsteps and turned towards his cabin with its motionless scarlet sentry.

'Some never will, my friend. It's too late.'

Keen sighed and said, 'Join me, Mr Bolitho, and share a glass. Doubtless you'll be getting a command of your own if war does come about.' He gave a smile. 'Then you'll discover what hardship really means!'

Aft in his cabin Bolitho made himself comfortable in a chair and opened the first letter.

Going home. They would have been surprised had they known just how much it meant to their vice-admiral.

Then he listened to her voice again as it lifted from the page.

My darling Richard . . .

'See that these letters are put aboard the packet with the others, Yovell.'

Bolitho listened to the squeak of tackles through the cabin skylight, the stamp of feet on deck as another net of fresh food supplies was hoisted above the gangway.

After all the waiting it was difficult to accept that the moment had arrived. Not that time had been allowed to drag on their hands, he considered.

A smart frigate and two bomb-vessels were now anchored below the battery, and a big armed transport had brought more soldiers as promised to reinforce the garrison. He smiled at Lemoine's reaction when a full colonel had taken charge.

'I was just getting a taste for power, sir,' the lieutenant had said.

He heard Allday coming through the dining space and looked up to greet him. Allday had made great strides where his health was concerned and the colour had returned to his face. But he still could not straighten his shoulders, and his smart blue coat with the gilt buttons seemed loose on his big frame.

It must be close on six months since he had been struck down, three since the brig had arrived here with the Admiralty's final instructions on the island's future.

Bolitho said, 'It will be spring in England when we reach there. A year since we left.'

He watched Allday's expression but he merely shrugged and replied, 'Probably all have blown over by that time, sir.'

'Maybe.'

He was still brooding. More afraid of the land than the hazards at sea. Allday had once told him that an old sailor was like a ship. Once tied up and unwanted, and with nothing useful to do, both were doomed.

And Allday had been a lot younger when he had said it.

Calls shrilled along the upper deck and voices barked commands as some marines marched to the entry port.

Bolitho stood up and waited for Ozzard to bring his dress-coat. The new governor had arrived in San Felipe aboard the frigate. A small, birdlike man, he seemed dull by comparison with Rivers.

His warrant made it clear that Rivers was to take passage in *Achates*. A cruel twist of fate for both of us, Bolitho thought.

As Keen had remarked, 'Why this ship, damn his eyes? A plague on the man!'

Ozzard patted the gold-laced coat into place and eyed the epaulettes with professional interest. He reached for the fine presentation sword on its rack but dropped his hands as Bolitho gave a quick shake of the head.

He waited for Allday to take the sword and clip it to his belt. As he had always done.

Bolitho had written to Belinda about Allday's courage and the price he had paid for it. She, better than anyone, would know what to do. In a fast packet his letters would reach home long before *Achates*.

'Thank you. I shall go and meet our, er, guest.'

He glanced quickly round the cabin but Ozzard had already gone.

'Ready, Allday?'

Allday made to straighten his back but Bolitho said, 'Not yet. It takes time.' He watched his despair. 'As it did when I nearly died, remember? When you cared for me every hour of the day?'

He saw something of the old sparkle in Allday's eyes.

'I'll not forget that, sir.'

Bolitho nodded, moved by Allday's pleasure at the memory.

'Flag at the fore, remember that too? I'll see you an admiral's coxswain yet, you scoundrel!'

They went on deck together and Bolitho saw Rivers waiting by the entry port flanked by an escort of soldiers. He wore manacles on his wrists, and Lieutenant Lemoine, who was in charge, said hastily, 'My colonel's orders, sir.'

Bolitho nodded impassively. 'Sir Humphrey is under my protection, Mr Lemoine. There will be no irons here.'

He saw Rivers' look of extraordinary gratitude and shock. Then he watched as his eyes moved up the foremast truck where the flag lifted in a fresh breeze. As a vice-admiral himself he was probably hanging on to this moment as his other world fell in ruins.

'Thank you for that, Bolitho.'

Bolitho saw Keen frowning in the background and said, 'It is all and also the least I can do.'

Rivers looked across at the waterfront. People had flocked there to watch him leave. No cheers, no rebukes either. San Felipe was that sort of place, Bolitho thought. With a stormy past and a future just as uncertain.

Why should I care? Even feel sorry for the man, he wondered? A traitor, a respectable pirate who had caused too many deaths because of his own selfish greed. Rivers had two sons in London, so it was likely he would be well defended at his trial. He might even talk his way out of it. After all, if war came, the island's security owed much to him, whatever the true reasons had been.

In his heart Bolitho knew that the real blame lay with powerful men in London. Who had allowed Rivers to extend his role here for his own advantage.

Keen watched Rivers being escorted below and said, 'I'd have put him in the cells.'

Bolitho smiled. 'When you've been a prisoner, Val, and I hope that never happens to you, you'll understand.'

Keen grinned, unabashed. 'But *until* then, sir, I don't have to like him!'

Ferrier, the senior midshipman, touched his hat to Keen.

'Mr Tyrrell's come aboard, sir.'

Bolitho turned. He had imagined that Tyrrell had stayed ashore for most of the time since *Vivid*'s loss because he did not want to talk about it. Or, independent to the end, he had been seeking a berth in some other vessel.

He had heard *Achates* was sailing very soon. The whole island seemed to know. There would likely be a few more babies on the plantations, black and white, after *Achates* had crossed the ocean. It was good to hear the seamen calling out to the people in the boats in the harbour and along the waterfront. The yards of the ships were festooned with coloured streamers, and every inch of space had been filled with fresh fruit and gifts from the islanders who had once hated and feared them.

He saw Tyrrell's shaggy head appear above the ladder to the quarterdeck and walked to meet him.

'Thought I'd make a quick farewell, Dick. To you an' the youngster. Next time he an' I meet he'll be a post-cap'n.'

Like Allday, he was finding it hard, and at any second he would blunder away on the wooden pin which he hated so much.

Bolitho tried to gauge the moment, knowing that any careful speech would be taken as charity, even condescension.

'Will you go back home now, Jethro?'

'Got no home. All gone, dammit, I told you!' He relented immediately. 'Sorry about that. Bein' with you again has unsettled me quite a bit.'

'Me too.'

'Really?' Tyrrell stared at him, wary of a lie.

'I was thinking . . . ' Bolitho saw Knocker from the corner of his eye hurry to the first lieutenant, who in turn looked at the captain. Bolitho knew why. He had felt the shift of wind on his cheek even as he had been speaking with Rivers. It was not much, but with the winds here so perverse it must not be wasted. But just as when Ferrier had come to tell him about the brig's arrival, so now he would not break the spell by looking up at the masthead pendant. He continued, 'There's England, you know.'

Tyrrell threw back his head and laughed. 'Hell, man what are you sayin'? What would I do over there?'

Bolitho looked past him at the shore. 'Your father came from Bristol. I recall you telling me. It's not all that far from Cornwall, from us.'

Tyrrell watched the sudden activity as the relaxation on deck changed to purpose and movement. He knew all the signs. A ship leaving was nothing new. But homeward bound . . .

He said desperately 'I'm a *cripple*, Dick, what th' hell use am I?'

'There are plenty of ships in the West Country.' He dropped his voice. 'Like *Vivid*.'

He saw Keen moving nearer. It could not wait.

Bolitho said, 'Anyway, I want you to come.'

Tyrrell gazed around as if he could not trust his own judgement.

'I'd work my passage, I'd insist on that!'

Bolitho smiled gravely. 'It's settled then.'

They shook hands and Tyrrell said, 'By God, I'll do it!'

Bolitho turned to his flag-captain.

'You may get the ship under way when it suits.'

Keen yelled, 'Hoist all boats inboard! Both watches of the hands, Mr Quantock!'

He looked at Bolitho and the one-legged man by the quarterdeck rail and shook his head.

Men were dashing aloft and out along the yards, and with her capstan manned *Achates* shed her ties with the land and moved slowly out to her anchor.

Adam said excitedly, 'Hear them, Jethro? They're cheering us!'

Along the waterfront the handkerchiefs waved and voices echoed across the water as the great capstan continued to clink round.

Tyrrell nodded. 'Aye, lad, this time they are.'

Captain Dewar marched across the deck and touched his hat with a flourish.

Keen caught the mood too. 'Very well, Major, you may play us out if that was what you were about to suggest?'

Bolitho found that he was gripping the worn rail with unusual force. He had seen it all before countless times, but somehow this was quite different.

'Anchor's hove short, sir!'

'Loose the heads'ls!'

Bolitho turned and saw Allday beside him. *His right arm*.

'Man the braces there!' Quantock strode about, his head jutting forward, immersed for the moment in the complexities of his trade.

'Anchor's aweigh, sir!'

It was not a blustery departure, with the ship heeling over under a pyramid of canvas. With all the dignity of her years *Achates* swung slowly across the wind, the sunlight glancing off her figurehead, the armour-bearer, and along her sealed gun-ports and freshly painted tumblehome.

'Get the t'gan's'ls on her, Mr Scott! Your division are like old women today!'

The sails hardened and shivered at their yards, and with barely a ripple below her dolphin-striker *Achates* glided towards the harbour mouth.

Bolitho watched the narrow strip of water. It looked no wider than a farm gate. A glance at Keen's tense features told him that he was remembering that wild charge through it in total darkness.

'Steady as you go!' That was Knocker. Even he seemed different as he called, 'Mr Tyrrell, you may be able to offer some local knowledge. If so, I'd be obliged.'

Here was the fortress. The sloping track where the marine drummer had died, where Rivers had made his greatest mistake.

The flag above the old battery dipped in salute and Bolitho saw a line of redcoats on the jetty, bayonets fixed, colours lowered, as *Achates'* topgallant sails made little patches of shadow on the fortress wall.

Allday murmured, 'They'll not forget *Old Katie* in a hurry.'

He turned his head to listen as the small cluster of fifers and drummers broke into *The Sailor and His Lass*.

Once Bolitho saw him thrust one hand to his wound, and then he removed it from his fine blue jacket and laid it on the rail beside his.

As if, like the island, he was leaving the pain astern.

16

The Secret

Bolitho walked up the slippery planking and gripped the nettings at the weather-side of the quarterdeck.

The ship was plunging and shuddering as rank after rank of waves surged against her quarter in an unbroken attack.

Bolitho watched as the bows dropped yet again and the sea thundered over the forecastle and cascaded along the upper gun-deck like a flood, breaking over the guns before surging away through the scuppers until the next onslaught.

In spite of the savage movement and damp discomfort Bolitho felt a sense of exhilaration, the nearest thing he could remember since his last command as post-captain.

How different was the Atlantic's grey face to the waters around San Felipe. Lines of angry, rearing waves, their crests like broken yellow teeth.

Achates was making the best of this unexpected storm under jib and close-reefed topsails and was as steady as could be expected. Nevertheless, during the time he had been on deck Bolitho had seen the boatswain and his men floundering amongst the surging water to secure lashings on boats and guns, or to fight their way aloft to repair broken cordage.

Keen was here too, his tarpaulin coat flying in the wind as he bent over the compass and had a shouted conversation with the master.

How perverse the weather had been since the day they had set sail from San Felipe. The breeze had dropped almost as soon as the island had vanished below the horizon. They had been becalmed for days before they had been able to spread

more sails again. It had taken more time then to recover what
they had lost on the lazy currents and tides.

Now, deep into the Atlantic, they were seeing its other
face. The ship was standing up well in spite of her repairs,
many of which had been makeshift because of the lack of a
dockyard. It was just as well, he thought grimly. The nearest
land was Bermuda some two hundred miles to the north-
west.

Here was another. He held his breath as the sea boiled over
the weather-gangway and swept some seamen aside like
twigs on a flooded stream. He looked up at the tightly
braced yards, the reefed canvas like grey metal in the dim
light.

Stooping shadows waited for the right moment before
dashing from one handhold to the next. A few noticed him at
the weather-side and probably thought him crazy for leaving
his fine quarters.

Keen staggered towards him, his face shining with spray.

'Mr Knocker says it cannot last more than another day,
sir.' He ducked as a solid sheet of water deluged over the
quarterdeck and ran down the ladders on either side.

'How is Sir Humphrey taking to all this?'

Keen watched two of his men as they dragged some fresh
cordage towards the mainmast in readiness to haul it aloft to
the topsail yard. He relaxed slightly as they scampered into
the ratlines before the next incoming sea could sweep them
away or smash them senseless into one of the guns.

He shouted, 'Well enough, sir! He spends much of his
time writing.'

Bolitho tucked his chin into his cloak as the spray and
spindrift dashed down from the poop. Preparing his defence. Making a last will and testament. Probably just to
keep his mind away from the miles as they dragged beneath
Achates' scarred keel.

The officer of the watch moved hand over hand along the
quarterdeck rail and yelled, 'Time to call the first dog-watch,
sir!'

Keen grinned into the storm. 'God, it looks more like midnight!'

Bolitho left him and groped his way aft beneath the poop, where by contrast it seemed almost quiet, the sounds of sea and wind muffled and held at bay by the ship's massive oak timbers.

But in the cabin it was just as lively, with water spurting through the sealed gun-ports and the gallery on the weather-quarter. Every lantern swung in a wild dance, and the cabin furniture did all it could to tear itself from Ozzard's storm-lashings.

Ozzard appeared from his pantry and clung to the screen for support. His face was pale green, and Bolitho did not have the heart to ask him for something hot to drink.

'How is Allday?'

Ozzard gulped. 'Resting, sir. In his hammock. He had a large tot of — ' But even the memory of the neat rum was too much and he fled, retching, for the door.

Bolitho went into his sleeping-cabin and grasped the side of his swaying cot. Where Allday had almost died.

He waited for the deck to rise again and then hoisted himself, fully clothed, into the cot.

He hated being out of things, it was the part of his flag-rank which he found least acceptable. Strategy was one thing, but at times like these, as the ship fought her natural enemy without respite, he felt little better than a passenger.

Bolitho kicked off his shoes and grimaced at the shadows which loomed and died around him like macabre dancers.

But if the ship foundered, passenger or not, it would be better if the people saw their vice-admiral fully dressed.

During that night the storm blew itself out and the wind, although still strong, veered to the south and enabled Keen to set more sails and his men to carry on with their repairs. Between decks the trapped water and scattered possessions were cleared away, and when breakfast was piped the galley funnel was pumping out its usual plume of thick, greasy smoke.

Bolitho sat at his table, drinking scalding coffee and munching thin strips of pork fried pale in biscuit crumbs. It was one of his favourite meals at sea, and none could serve it better than Ozzard.

Despite the foul weather and unavoidable delays they should sight the Lizard, the southernmost tip of Cornwall, in fourteen days.

He was surprised that it should make him feel so nervous, unsure of himself. All he had longed and hoped for and yet he was as unsettled as a callow midshipman.

He got up and walked to the mirror above his desk. He was a year older. The lock of hair which hid the cruel scar above his right eye was still black, and yet he was sure there were some grey strands too. He tried to shrug it off. The youngest vice-admiral on the List, apart from Our Nel, that is. But he found no consolation. He was forty-six and Belinda ten years his junior. Suppose . . .

Bolitho turned almost gratefully as Keen entered the cabin, his hat beneath his arm.

'Have some coffee, Val, what — ' He saw the grim expression on Keen's face and asked, 'Trouble?'

Keen nodded. 'The masthead has reported drifting wreckage to the nor'-east. Victim of the storm, I expect, sir.'

'Yes.' He pulled on his faded sea-going coat. 'Not the packet which set sail before us?'

'No, sir. It would mean too much drift.' He watched Bolitho curiously. 'If we change tack to examine the remains we will lose valuable time, sir.'

Bolitho bit his lip. He had once seen a drifting boat with only one man alive in it. All the rest were corpses. He thought of little Evans, how he must have felt in his drifting boat, his ship gone, his companions wounded and dying around him. What must it be like? The last one alive, like the man he had seen all those years ago?

He said, 'There's always a chance, Val. Alter course and send a boat away when you consider it near enough.'

An hour later, as *Achates* shortened sail and tacked uncomfortably close to the wind, the quarter-boat pulled swiftly towards the great spread of bobbing flotsam and broken timbers.

It had seemed an eternity before they had got near enough to examine the storm's success. In such Atlantic weather it seemed likely that several ships had shared this one's fate.

Bolitho had stood on the poop with a telescope and had watched the remains spreading out across *Achates'* bows, tragic and pathetic.

She had not been very large, he thought. She had probably been struck by one gigantic wave across her unprotected poop, driven over before she could recover.

Keen lowered his glass. 'There's a boat, sir!'

Bolitho moved his own glass and stared at the swamped, listing thing which had once been a long-boat.

Keen exclaimed, 'They're alive! Two of them anyway!'

Lieutenant Scott, who was in charge of the quarter-boat, was already urging his oarsmen to greater efforts as he sighted the survivors.

Bolitho heard Tyrrell's wooden stump on the wet planking and asked, 'What do you make of it, Jethro?'

Tyrrell did not even hesitate. 'She's a Frenchie. Or was.'

Keen steadied his glass and said excitedly, 'You're right! They're no merchant sailors either!'

Bolitho saw Tuson and his mates waiting by the entry port, a tackle being rigged to haul the survivors aboard.

Bolitho asked, 'Who speaks the best French in *Achates*?'

Keen did not falter. 'Mr Mansel, the purser. Used to be in the wine trade before the war.'

Bolitho smiled. He had heard slightly differently, and that Mansel had in fact been a smuggler.

'Well, tell him to be ready. We may be able to discover what happened.'

There were ten survivors in all. Knocked, dazed and half-blinded by the mountainous seas, they had lost hope of rescue so far from land. Their vessel had been the brig *La Prudente*, outward-bound from Lorient to Martinique. Their

commander had been swept overboard, and their senior
lieutenant had managed to clear away one boat before he too
had died from a blow on the head from some falling wreckage. The dead lieutenant was still in the boat, his face very
white beneath the water which filled it almost to the gun-
wales.

The coxswain of the quarter-boat yelled, 'Shall I cast 'er
off, sir?'

But Lieutenant Scott snatched a boat-hook and dragged
the dead lieutenant towards him.

The survivors must have been too shocked and weak to
push their officer over the side, Bolitho thought. He watched
them being carried and helped to a companion-way. They
still did not seem to know what was happening.

Keen said, 'Mr Scott has found something, sir.'

He could not hide his eagerness to get under way again, to
fight back to their original track.

The dead officer rose above the gangway, water running
from his mouth and his uniform as he swung above the
gun-deck like a felon on the gallows.

Scott hurried aft and touched his hat. 'He had this tied to
his waist, sir. I saw it when the boat tilted over.'

Bolitho looked at Keen. It was like robbing the dead.
The French lieutenant lay on the deck, his arms and legs
stretched out, one eye part open as if the light was too strong
for him.

Black Joe Langtry, the master-at-arms, covered the corpse
with a piece of canvas, but not before he had removed a pistol
from the man's belt. It had probably been his only means of
maintaining some order on that terrible night when his ship
had been overwhelmed.

Keen said, 'All the same, sir. Lorient to Martinique.'

Bolitho nodded. 'My thoughts entirely.'

It took a few moments to open the thick canvas envelope
and break the imposing scarlet seals.

Bolitho watched the purser's lips move as he scanned the
carefully worded despatch which was addressed to the

admiral in command of the West Indies Fleet at Fort de France.

No wonder the dead lieutenant had tried to save the package.

The purser looked up from the table, uncomfortable under their combined gaze.

He said, 'As near as I can tell, sir, it says that upon receipt of these orders hostilities against England and her possessions will be resumed immediately.'

Keen stared at Bolitho. 'That's near enough for me!'

Bolitho walked to the stern windows and watched the quarter-boat being warped round in readiness for hoisting. It gave him time to think, to weigh chance and coincidence against a small act of humanity.

He said, 'For once a storm was a friend to us, Val.'

Keen watched as Bolitho tipped a handful of pistol balls from the envelope, to carry it to the sea-bed rather than let it fall into the wrong hands. But the lieutenant had been killed before he could act, and his men had been too ignorant or too frightened to care.

Keen said, 'So it's no longer just a threat. It's war.'

Bolitho smiled gravely. 'At least we know something which others do not. That is always an advantage.'

With her yards retrimmed and her helm hard over *Achates* turned her jib-boom away from the drifting pattern of flotsam and the waterlogged boat which would sink in the next storm.

That evening at dusk the dead lieutenant was buried with full honours.

Bolitho watched with Adam and Allday close by as Keen said a few prayers before the corpse was dropped alongside.

The next Frenchman they met would not be so peaceful, Bolitho thought.

'Well, Sir Humphrey, I believe you wish to speak with me.'

Bolitho kept his tone level but was shocked to see the

change in Rivers' appearance and demeanour. He looked ten years older, and his shoulders were bowed as if he was carrying a great burden.

Rivers seemed surprised when Bolitho indicated a chair for him and sank into it, his eyes wandering around the cabin without recognition.

He said, 'I have written down all I know of the plot to seize my — ' He faltered. 'To seize San Felipe. Rear-Admiral Burgas, who commanded the squadron at La Guaira, was to govern it until Spanish ownership was recognized.'

'Did you know about the Spanish mission, that it might be used to shelter an invading force?'

'No. I trusted the captain-general. He promised me more trade along the Spanish Main. I could see nothing but improvement.'

Bolitho took the papers from him and scanned them thoughtfully.

He said, 'These might help with your defence in London, although . . . '

Rivers shrugged. '*Although*. Yes, I understand.'

He looked at Bolitho and asked, 'If you are in England during my trial, would you be prepared to speak for my defence?'

Bolitho stared at him. 'That is an extraordinary thing to request. After your action against my ship and my men . . . '

Rivers persisted, 'You are a fighting officer. I want no defence for what I did, but understanding of what I had been trying to do. To keep the island under the British flag. As it is now, thanks to you.'

When Bolitho remained silent he continued, 'After all, had the Dons made their move before you came, my actions might have succeeded, and I would have been seen in a very different light.'

Bolitho eyed him sadly. 'But they did *not*. You must know from past experience, Sir Humphrey, that if a captain fires upon or seizes an enemy ship, or what he believes to be a foe, only to discover when he reaches port that their two countries are at peace, what then? That captain could have had no way of knowing the facts, and yet . . . '

Rivers nodded. 'He would be blamed nevertheless.' He stood up. 'I should like to return to my quarters now.'

Bolitho rose too. 'I have to tell you that we shall be in sight of land within the week. After that your affairs will be taken out of my hands.'

'I understand. Thank you.'

Rivers walked to the door and Bolitho saw two Royal Marines waiting for him.

Adam, who had been present throughout the brief interview, said, 'I feel no sorrow for him, Uncle.'

Bolitho touched his scar beneath the rebellious lock of hair.

'It's too easy to judge.'

Adam grinned. 'If you had been appointed governor, Uncle, would you have behaved as he did?' He saw Bolitho's confusion and nodded. 'There you are then.'

Bolitho sat down. 'Young devil. Allday was quite right about you.'

Adam watched him, his features suddenly serious.

'I was glad to join you as your flag-lieutenant, Uncle. Being with you for such a long period has taught me a lot. About you, about myself.' He looked wistfully around the cabin. 'I shall miss the freedom more than I can say.'

Bolitho was moved. 'The same applies to me. I was warned against bringing you. Too close, Oliver Browne said. Perhaps he was right in some ways, but when we reach Falmouth things will – '

They both looked up at the skylight as a lookout's voice pealed down, 'Deck there! Sail to the sou'-east!'

Bolitho stared at the square of blue above the skylight. He felt his heart quicken, an unexpected dryness in his throat. Like the hunter caught off guard when he needed his vigilance the most.

He crossed to his chart on the table and examined it,

following the neat calculations, the unerring line which led all the way to the Cornish coast. It was unlikely that a merchantman would be outward-bound from either England or France if war had just been declared. It would take time for the rules to be accepted or broken.

'I'm going on deck.'

He strode to the door and out into the sunlight. The sea was lively with white-caps, and the wind still steady from the south so that *Achates* had her yards tightly braced to hold her on a starboard tack.

Men stood about in small groups or stared up at the seaman in the mizzen cross-trees.

Keen cupped his hands. 'Mizzen topmast-head there!'

'Sir?' The man peered down at his captain far below.

'What does she look like?'

'Man-o'-war, sir!'

Keen beckoned impatiently. 'Get aloft with a glass, Mr Mountsteven, that fellow is a madman!'

He saw Bolitho and touched his hat. 'I beg your pardon, sir.'

Bolitho looked at the empty sea, suddenly apprehensive. Did going home mean so much? Was it that different now?

Keen said, 'From the sou'-east, it seems, sir. Too far out for the Bay.'

Mountsteven had reached his precarious perch beside the lookout.

He yelled, 'She looks, sir, like a whacking frigate!' A pause. 'A Frenchie, I'd suggest!'

Bolitho made himself walk calmly to the quarterdeck rail as the conjecture buzzed around him like a swarm of hornets.

A French frigate standing well out to sea, probably steering north for the Channel or the tip of the Bay, Brest perhaps?

He thought of the dead lieutenant, the envelope, the little brig on passage from Lorient to Martinique.

'Deck there! There's another sail astern of her, sir!'

Knocker, who had silently appeared by the wheel,

muttered, 'Pork and molasses! More bloody trouble, I'll be bound!'

Keen said, 'She's on a converging tack, sir. She'll have the wind-gage, by God.'

Bolitho did not turn but stared along the full length of the deck. So near and yet so far. Another two days, maybe less, and they would have met with ships of the Channel Fleet as they endured the weary task of blockade duty.

He said, 'The Frenchman is taking a chance, Val.' He turned and saw understanding on Keen's face. 'Maybe they do not know the news, as *we* would not but for loss of *La Prudente*.'

Midshipman Ferrier, who had swarmed into the weather-shrouds at the first sighting report, yelled, 'I can see the first one, sir! A big frigate! I can't make out the other but — '

Mountsteven's voice cut him dead. 'Second one is a ship of the line, sir! A seventy-four!'

One of the helmsmen sucked his teeth. 'The bastards!'

Bolitho took a telescope and climbed up beside the midshipman.

'Where away, Mr Ferrier?'

Then he saw the leading Frenchman, her topgallant sails like gold in the sunlight. Even as he watched her outline changed slightly. He remarked half to himself, 'She's setting her royals.'

Bolitho climbed down to the deck and looked at his nephew.

'As *you* will know, a frigate's job is to sniff out danger and identify strangers.'

Adam nodded. 'Then they cannot know about the war.'

Bolitho tried to clear his mind. The pattern was all wrong. The French ships were closing rapidly with the southerly wind well in their favour.

He snapped, 'Ship's head, Mr Knocker?'

'East-nor'-east, sir! Full an' bye!'

Keen murmured, 'If I let her fall off two points or so they'll suspect something, that we're trying to keep clear of them.

On the other hand, sir, a change of tack would give us a few extra knots.'

A change of course away from the enemy, setting more sail, either of those would arouse the interest of any frigate captain, let alone one with a seventy-four in close company.

'Continue as we are, Val. They'll be watching us too, remember.'

Keen glanced up at the masthead pendant. 'But for the damned weather we'd have been at anchor by now.'

Six bells chimed out from the forecastle and Bolitho saw the purser emerge with his clerk in readiness to issue the rum to each mess. He thought of Allday, how the rum had touched him like a memory.

'I suggest you send the people to their messes, Val. The galley can serve a hot meal a little earlier today.'

Keen hurried away and spoke to Quantock by the rail, and seconds later the calls shrilled between decks and the sailors grinned at each other because of the unexpected break in routine.

Bolitho took the telescope again and sought out the other vessel. One of the newer French frigates, he decided. Forty-four guns. He could just discern her hull now as it lifted on a long roller before dropping again in a great welter of spray. She was flying.

Bolitho listened to the subdued chatter of the men on watch. The prospect of a sea-fight did not seem to be troubling them. They had already dispatched a Spanish two-decker and had captured an island. A French frigate would be simple compared with that.

Keen joined him again. 'They might stand away when they know our flag, sir.'

'Very well. Run up the colours.'

But when the scarlet ensign broke from the gaff nothing changed other than Mountsteven reporting that the frigate had hoisted her tricolour.

Tyrrell appeared on deck, his jaw working on a piece of salt beef.

He squinted up at the mizzen truck and asked, 'D'you reckon you could get me up yonder, Cap'n?'

Keen stared at him, his mind grappling with other problems.

'Bosun's chair, d'you mean?'

Tyrrell glanced at Bolitho and grinned. 'Just had a thought. You recall that seventy-four in Boston, the one which was supposed to be doin' the parley. Could be her. If so, she'll likely not know about the war yet.' He grinned more widely. 'Now, that'd be a terrible shame, eh?'

They had forgotten about Mountsteven but his voice made them all remember as he called, '*Third* ship, sir! 'Nother frigate, I think!'

Keen said softly, 'Jesus!' Then to the boatswain he said, 'Assist Mr Tyrrell aloft, if you please.'

Many of the watch on deck turned to stare and to follow Tyrrell's jerking progress up the mizzen-mast, his wooden stump clicking against halliards and spars.

Keen dropped his voice. 'Three to one, sir. The odds are formidable.'

Bolitho handed his glass to a boatswain's-mate. 'Do you suggest we run?'

Keen said, 'I'll run from nothing, sir. But I cannot answer for the ship's state if we are called on to fight.'

Bolitho watched the frigate's outline alter again as she changed tack until she was pointing directly towards him.

He said quietly, 'It's another war, Val, not some petty quarrel. With half the fleet still laid up, England has never been less prepared. If our people are expected to endure a long, bitter conflict they will need victories, not leaders who turn and run away because the odds are *formidable*!'

He turned and studied Keen's concern. 'We've no choice, Val. The frigates will be round us like hounds after a stag. That would give the seventy-four time to close the range and finish the fight. If we are to be beaten, I'd prefer it to be facing the enemy, not being chased until the wind has gone out of us.'

Bolitho faced Tyrrell as he was lowered carefully to the deck.

'Damn near cut myself in half.' Tyrrell glanced at them questioningly, then added, 'She's the same one right enough. Must have gone south when she quit Boston. Rear-admiral's flag at the mizzen.'

Bolitho said, 'Then she's the *Argonaute*, a new third-rate. I know her admiral from times past. Contre-Amiral Jobert. One of the few of the old Royalist navy to escape the Terror. A good officer.'

He knew that the others nearby were listening to him despite their efforts to conceal the fact. Trying to discover what was about to happen. What would become of them.

He said lightly, 'I shall go aft and have a bite to eat, *then* we can clear for action.'

Bolitho strode beneath the poop and knew his casual comment about food would spread through the messes like wildfire. He could almost hear it. Nothing to worry about, lads. The admiral's having his grub.

He barely saw the sentry who flung open the screen door for him and he did not stop until he reached the stern windows. When he leaned over the sill he could just discern the frigate's topsails. An hour or more yet to wait. Maybe nothing would happen. Why must they fight if only to die? Who would blame him for standing away from the odds which were bearing down on him?

He felt his chest and the urgent hammering of his heart. Was it fear? Is this what it is like? That one action too many. God alone knew it had happened often enough to far better men.

Bolitho wiped his face with his shirt cuff and turned blindly into the cabin again.

Fear of losing something so precious he could think of nothing else beyond it.

He had been hoping too hard and too much. A weakness when so many were depending on him.

What were hopes anyway? In the roar of a broadside they counted for very little.

Ozzard entered the cabin with a tray.

He said, 'Fresh chicken, sir.'

Bolitho watched him as he laid the tray carefully on the table. So the ship's purser had had hopes too. He would not have sacrificed one of the ship's own stock of chickens otherwise.

Ozzard watched him patiently. 'A glass of something, sir?'

Bolitho smiled. Poor little Ozzard. Trusting and loyal. It never seemed to occur to him that before evening he might be dead.

He said, 'Yes, Ozzard. Some of your special hock.'

As he hurried away Bolitho buried his face in his hands.

The French admiral had obviously not heard about the outbreak of war. Otherwise he would certainly have changed his formation, ready to attack from three bearings at once. *Achates* could fire on and possibly cripple the leading frigate before her captain realized what was happening, and then thrust on to attack the seventy-four. Still bad odds, but some improvement.

He recalled his own fury and disbelief when the Spanish two-decker had attacked *Achates* and destroyed *Sparrowhawk*, how they had all cursed her for her cowardice and deception.

Could he now bring himself to act in the same fashion? *Honour*. The word seemed to echo around the cabin like a taunt.

He looked at the old family sword on its rack and remembered how his father had handed it to him instead of to Hugh. Hugh was the elder son and should have had it. But his disgrace, the shame which had followed Bolitho like an evil spirit even as far as San Felipe, which had broken their father's heart, had put the sword into his trust.

Bolitho said, 'Then so be it!' The choice had never been his, and his mistake had been to believe otherwise.

When Ozzard returned with a bottle from his cool store in the bilges he found Bolitho as he would have expected, calm and outwardly untroubled.

Things could not be so bad after all.

17

Fair Warning

Bolitho stepped over some trailing lines and walked to the weather-side of the quarterdeck. The French frigate was much nearer but had shortened sail as if uncertain what to do next. He estimated that she was about half a mile from *Achates'* starboard quarter.

He heard men crawling about the deck behind him, as if the best part of the ship's company had suddenly become cripples.

It was essential that the ship should be cleared for action without all the obvious bustle and movement which the French lookouts would immediately recognize.

Keen was saying to the boatswain, 'You shall send your people aloft to rig chain-slings only when we begin to engage.'

Big Harry Rooke rumbled something in reply and Keen rapped, 'They've no choice, man. One stupid move now and we'll be feeding the fish before dusk!'

He turned and saw Bolitho watching him.

'Mr Quantock is sorely ashamed of his record, sir. Twenty minutes to clear for action!' His attempt to joke seemed to steady him and he added, 'What are your orders for this memorable day, sir?'

Bolitho pointed. 'In a moment we will alter course three points to lee'rd. It is my guess that the frigate will close the range to take station on our quarter again. But he'll be much nearer.'

If only his heart would settle. The tension might so easily reveal itself in his voice.

Keen looked past him at the frigate's shortened pyramid of canvas. 'She's new, like the third-rate. Probably to impress the Americans.' He did not conceal the bitterness. 'Whereas our masters thought fit to send the oldest sixty-four still in service!'

Bolitho walked to the rail and glanced along the gun-deck and the black eighteen-pounders. Their crews were stripped for battle and were concealed beneath the gangways or huddled against their guns with their tools and weapons.

'It will have to be quickly done, Val. The French seventy-four is well astern of us now. But it will take time. They'll be ready for us after we show our intentions.'

Keen nodded, his mind working on the next manoeuvre and the one after it. 'The third French vessel is smaller. Mr Mountsteven thinks she is a twenty-six-gun frigate. As I recall, she will be the *Diane*, a real veteran by comparison.'

Knocker turned the half-hour glass by the binnacle and said, 'Ready, sir.'

'Pass the word to the lower gun-deck.'

Keen looked round as Allday appeared from the poop. He was carrying Bolitho's old sword and his features were stiff as if to conceal the pain of his wound.

Bolitho held up his arms so that he could clip the sword into place.

Allday muttered, 'You should not be wearin' them epaulettes today, sir.' He shrugged and gave a brief grin. 'But I've sailed with you often enough to know better'n to argue, I suppose.'

Bolitho looked at the Frenchman's sails. He saw sunlight lance from a levelled telescope in her foretop. At any second they might see something suspicious and beat to quarters.

But he said, 'Take care of yourself, Allday. No risks today.'

He touched his arm, and two of the quarterdeck powder-monkeys nudged each other, the enemy forgotten as they shared something private.

Allday eyed him bleakly. 'Don't insult me, sir. If them

buggers come at us, they'll find me ready enough, an' that's no error!'

Bolitho smiled. 'I also know better than to argue, old friend.'

He swung away as Keen said, 'They've made a signal to the *Argonaute*, sir!'

Midshipman Ferrier lowered his big signals telescope and said, 'It's code, sir.'

Bolitho said, 'Alter course.'

Ready and waiting, the helmsmen put the wheel over, and while others ran to trim the yards, Knocker reported, 'Three points it is, sir! Nor'-east by north!'

Bolitho could feel the difference as the wind thrust more forcefully into *Achates*' canvas.

Keen said, 'Recall Mr Mountsteven from aloft. I had all but forgotten him again.'

'The Frenchie's changin' tack, sir.'

Bolitho held his breath as the powerful frigate turned a point or so towards *Achates* and at the same time spread her main-course and driver.

Keen slammed a fist into his palm and exclaimed, 'He's overhauling us, sir.'

A marine dropped something on the poop as he crawled closer to the hammocks and Sergeant Saxton snarled, 'I'll skin you alive if you make another move!'

Bolitho watched the frigate and saw the clear spray bursting over her beak-head and bowsprit. If she continued to overhaul them she would pass down the starboard side at less than half a cable's distance.

He raised the telescope and saw intent faces staring across the lively water, strangely alien after the familiar ones he met every day.

'Stand by on the gun-deck!'

Keen folded his arms and stared at the enemy. As soon as *Achates* changed tack again she would be laid hard over to leeward by the wind. But her sudden manoeuvre would carry her across the frigate's bows. It was now or never, for in a matter of minutes both vessels would collide once *Achates* began to turn.

'Man the braces!'

Bolitho gripped the old sword and pressed it against his leg.

'Now!'

The big wheel squeaked violently as the helmsmen threw their weight on the spokes, and as the yards began to shift with the wind two more ensigns were run up to the main and mizzen trucks.

'Open the ports! Lively there! *Run out!'*

Bolitho watched the frigate and could not take his eyes from the towering mass of sails and rigging as she swept towards *Achates'* side.

He heard a trumpet and pictured the wild confusion aboard as the vessel they had been stalking suddenly turned like a lion at bay, her guns bared, each one double-shotted, every captain seeking his own target.

Keen yelled, *'As you bear!'* His arm flashed down. *'Fire!'*

For an instant Bolitho thought he had left it too long. That he should not have wasted valuable time by hoisting his battle ensigns. If their roles had been reversed . . .

His mind cringed as the eighteen-pounders of the upper battery hurled themselves inboard, while from the lower gun-deck the heavier roar of the twenty-four-pounders shook the ship from truck to keel.

Men stumbled about in the choking smoke as it was swept through the open ports and above the gangway while *Achates* exposed her broadside to the wind.

At such a close range the effect was immediate and terrible.

The frigate's foremast and main-topmast staggered under the onslaught of the double-shotted guns. Then spars, sails and rigging joined together in one great avalanche of destruction which thundered over the bows and sides, hurling spray into the air and dragging the hull round.

'Sponge out! *Reload!'*

Keen shouted, 'Stand by to come about, Mr Quantock.' He did not need telling the need for haste.

As the helm went down again and *Achates* surged round into the wind, Bolitho was grateful that they had not made more sail. In such a stiff wind the ship might have been in irons, or worse, dismasted.

Gun by gun along the starboard side the captains were holding up their hands as each barrel poked its muzzle through a port.

The frigate was still floundering down-wind under the dragging weight of fallen spars and sails, but Bolitho was not deceived and knew what could happen once that wreckage was hacked away.

'Main-tops'l braces there! Heave! Put your backs into it!'

Achates continued to turn, the frigate suddenly appeared above her starboard bow as if she and not the little two-decker was moving.

To any inexperienced eye it would look like chaos. The boatswain and his party swarming out on the topsail yards to rig the chain-slings, while below them their ship pirouetted around her masts to cross the enemy's stern.

'Starboard battery! *Ready!*'

Keen had his hand in the air and did not even blink as here and there along the enemy's side a gun fired in defiance. But for her it was already too late, and as *Achates* crossed the frigate's starboard quarter even those guns fell silent, unable to traverse enough to find a target.

Bolitho saw a ripple of musket fire from the poop and mizzen-top and instant response from Dewar's sharp-shooters.

He felt something like sickness in his stomach as *Achates'* jib-boom passed the frigate's stern. He saw her glittering cabin windows, her name, *La Capricieuse*, in gold letters across her counter.

Then *Achates'* starboard carronade belched fire from the forecastle and the enemy's stern and poop appeared to open like an obscene cave. When the carronade's massive ball burst within the crowded hull its packed charge of grape would transform the gun-deck into a slaughter-house.

Men, weapons, the rudder, everything would be blasted aside and incapable of movement for many hours.

Keen cupped his hands. 'Get the royals on her, Mr Quantock!'

He had no time to wait and worry about the carronade's harvest. The frigate was out of the fight.

Once again *Achates* clawed her way round to hold the wind on her quarter. It was as if nothing had changed. Not a man lost, not a scratch on wood or canvas.

Bolitho climbed the poop ladder and levelled his glass to seek the French seventy-four. Even in distance she looked fierce and enraged, he thought. She was spreading more sails, and had hoisted a signal to her yards for the benefit of her remaining companion.

He heard Knocker shout, 'East-nor'-east, sir!'

The Frenchman was steering north-east. Again they were on a converging tack. But the *Argonaute* held the wind-gage and would probably try to cripple her enemy by dismasting or by tearing down her rigging with chain-shot while keeping at a safe distance.

Bolitho trained the glass on the dismasted frigate. It must have been a terrible shock. Bolitho remembered his time as a prisoner of war in France. Never again, he had vowed then.

Keen touched his hat. 'All guns loaded and ready, sir.' He glanced aloft. 'Mr Rooke has even managed to rig his nets and slings.'

Bolitho smiled. 'I *know* it was a risk, Val.'

Keen looked away. 'You gave them fair warning. They'll not need it this time.'

He stared hard at the French seventy-four. Just over a mile distant, while the little frigate was standing away from her heavy consort and tacking down-wind to be ready to dash down and harry *Achates* from another angle. After seeing the fate of *La Capricieuse* it was unlikely she would force home an attack yet.

Bolitho also watched the French flagship and felt the nearness of their contest like claws in his loins. She was new, big and better armed. But *Achates* was more agile, and had proved her worth a hundred times over.

Keen was thinking aloud. 'If he holds the wind we cannot reach him, sir. Whereas he can move in when he pleases or chance some long shots which might score a serious hit.'

'I agree.' Bolitho climbed up to the nettings and peered over them. 'The other frigate, the *Diane*, she's steering for the west'rd, next she'll come about after us.' He shot him a grim smile. 'To snap at our heels!'

Keen nodded. 'She could do some damage if we were already engaged with the *Argonaute*, sir.'

Bolitho stepped down. 'Tell me what you think. Shall we use the *Diane* as bait?'

Keen's eyes lit up. 'Go for the frigate, sir?'

Bolitho nodded. 'Contre-Amiral Jobert is, I believe, an honourable sailor. I cannot see him standing by while his remaining frigate is attacked by a ship of the line!'

Bolitho looked at the sun. Only an hour since the carronade, the Smasher as it was termed, had blasted away the other frigate's resistance.

He said, 'You have a gun captain named Crocker. I met him at the fortress. A fearsome fellow but, I understand, the finest of his trade.'

Keen said, 'Lower gun-deck, sir. I'll send for him.'

Crocker came aft, his good eye shielded from the sun. After the cool gloom of the lower gun-deck he was finding it irksome. He knuckled his forehead and gazed at Bolitho, his deformed figure at odds with the scarlet-coated marines nearby.

Bolitho said, 'I want you to take charge of the two stern-chasers. We shall have company there directly, and when I give the word I want you to damage her badly enough to cause concern to her admiral.'

Crocker twisted his head further as if to fix his good eye on him.

'*Sir?*'

Keen said wearily, 'Just do it, Crocker. The French seventy-four will close the range when her admiral sees what is happening.'

'Oh, I *see*, sir!'

'Pick all the men you want, but I need that frigate winged.'

Crocker showed his uneven teeth. 'Bless you, sir, I thought you was makin' do with the little 'un!'

He loped away with his strange swinging gait, and Keen said, 'If we let the Frogs get alongside, old Crocker will frighten them to death!'

Bolitho loosened his neckcloth and looked at the sky. Sea-birds floated high above the embattled ships, indifferent, and coldly watching for the gruesome scraps which would soon be theirs.

He thought of Belinda, the green slope below Pendennis Castle where she could watch and wait for the ships to pass.

He heard Adam say, 'It won't be long.'

Bolitho looked at him. Was he afraid? Resentful that he might die so young?

But the lieutenant saw his glance and said, 'I'm *all right*, sir. I shall be ready.'

Bolitho smiled. 'I never doubted that. Come, Adam, let us take a walk together. It will pass the time.'

The swivel-gun crews and marine marksmen in the tops peered down as the vice-admiral and his youthful aide walked up and down the quarterdeck, their shadows passing over the naked backs of the seamen at their tackles with their rammers and charges.

Midshipman Ferrier lowered his glass for the hundredth time, his eye sore from staring at the oncoming seventy-four. It seemed such a short while ago that he had been thinking of home, of the chance to take his lieutenant's examination. In that towering pyramid of sails and the double line of guns which glinted in the sunlight like black teeth, he saw his hopes already gone. Now the thing which worried him most was whether or not he could stand up to what lay ahead.

He saw Bolitho pass by, speaking with his nephew, the way the flag-lieutenant was smiling at something he said. When he raised his telescope again his fear had gone.

On the lower gun-deck Midshipman Owen Evans peered through the gloom until he found Lieutenant Hallowes who was in charge of the twenty-six cannons here and ran to pass a message from the captain.

Hallowes listened to what the midshipman reported and remarked laconically, "Pon my soul, Walter, we're goin' for the frigate first!'

His assistant, the fifth lieutenant, laughed as if it was the greatest joke he had ever heard.

Evans paused at the foot of a ladder, his eyes taking in the red-painted sides, the shining skins of the men by the open ports, the air of watchful tension. Every man had his ears covered by his neckerchief. In this confined space the roar of the twenty-four pounders could deafen anyone in minutes.

Evans stared at his hand on the scrubbed woodwork. It was shaking uncontrollably, as if it had a will all of its own.

The shock made him look round at the gun-deck again. It was unlike the other times when he had been on deck near the vice-admiral when the Spanish ship had burst into flames after that fierce battle. Or even when he had taken command of *Sparrowhawk*'s boat. It was nothing like it at all.

Scenes flashed before his eyes. His pride and excitement at being accepted as midshipman in a fine frigate like *Sparrowhawk*. His first uniform made with loving care by his own father. Evans came of a large family, but he was the only one who had chosen the sea rather than tailoring.

Foord, the fifth lieutenant, saw the boy hesitating by the ladder and snapped, 'Move your feet, lad. There'll be messages aplenty in a moment or two!' Foord had once been a midshipman in this very ship and was only nineteen himself. He added in a gentler tone, 'What is it, Mr Evans?'

Evans stared up at him. 'Nothing, sir.' But his mind was screaming instead, *I'm going to be killed. I'm going to die.*

Foord watched him run up the ladder and sighed. Probably still thinking about Captain Duncan's death, he thought.

On the orlop deck beneath Foord's feet, Tuson, the surgeon, walked slowly round his makeshift table, his eyes taking in the array of glittering saws and probes, the empty 'wings and limbs' tubs, the leather strap to wedge between a man's teeth. The great jar of rum to ease the agony. Away from the slowly spiralling lanterns his mates and loblolly boys stood like ghouls, their hands tucked in their clean aprons while they too waited.

Tuson entered his small sick-bay and stared unseeingly at the cots, at the cupboard which contained more rum and brandy. He found that he was clenching his fists, his mouth like parchment as he imagined what that first drink would be like.

He heard footsteps outside and saw Corporal Dobbs with his musket and fixed bayonet peering at him uncertainly. Dobbs had the additional duty of ship's corporal in which he assisted the master-at-arms. But now he was a proper Royal Marine again and was needed at his station on deck.

Tuson saw that Sir Humphrey Rivers was also standing by the door, his head bowed between the great deckhead beams.

Dobbs said uncomfortably, 'Couldn't very well put a gentleman like 'im in the cells, sir.'

Tuson nodded. In case the ship went down under them, he thought.

Dobbs continued, 'An' it didn't seem proper to leave 'im with the Froggies we picked up from the wreck.'

Tuson looked at Rivers. 'If you stay here, Sir Humphrey, it may not be pleasant either.'

Rivers looked at the swaying shadows, the sense of doom which seemed to lurk here.

'It will be better than being alone.' He nodded curtly. 'I appreciate it.'

His face filled with relief that he had rid himself of his burden, the corporal all but ran to the ladder.

Bottles and jars clinked on the shelves as a gun banged out from aft.

Tuson exclaimed, 'What are they doing?'

Rivers smiled coldly. 'Stern-chaser.'

Tuson massaged his fingers. 'You've not forgotten then?'

Rivers hung his richly embroidered coat on a hook. 'That's one thing you never forget.'

Deep in the ship's fat hull, in his own private store-room, Tom Ozzard, the vice-admiral's servant, folded his arms and rocked back and forth as if he was in pain.

By the light of a single lantern he could see all of Bolitho's possessions stacked around him. It seemed wrong to leave them in such careless disarray, Ozzard thought. The fine table and chairs, the splendid wine-cooler, the desk and the cot, like everything else above the orlop deck which had been removed and torn down when the ship had been cleared for action. Now on both gun-decks *Achates* lay open from bow to stern, the crews unimpeded, the way clear for the young powder-monkeys to run with fresh charges and shot.

Ozzard had heard the boats being swung out and lowered for towing astern. Once action was joined the boats would be cut free, to be recovered by the victor, whoever it was. But tiered boats on deck were an additional source of deadly, crippling splinters when an enemy's iron crashed inboard.

Ozzard looked at the bolted door and shivered. It was cold down here where he kept his wine, and in times like these took refuge.

Like Allday, he was privileged to come and go as he pleased, and was grateful for the profession Bolitho had given him. Now in his store, in the lowest portion of *Achates'* hull, he was afraid. But it did not trouble him. He had accepted it long ago.

When he had carried the fresh chicken to the cabin for Bolitho, he had found time to glance at the master's chart below the poop.

Ozzard held his arms across his narrow chest even more

tightly. Below where he sat was the keel, and beyond it there was nothing but a bottomless ocean.

He winced as another gun made the deck quiver. But it seemed far away and without danger. Later he might venture up on deck. There was another muffled bang and he decided to wait.

Isolated from the enclosed world between decks, Bolitho climbed to the poop and looked at the French seventy-four. She had spread more canvas, but although she had closed the distance between them she had not yet fired a shot. He estimated that she had changed tack slightly and was now steering along an almost parallel course. By contrast, the little frigate had run with the wind before coming about to take station on *Achates'* lee quarter.

He said, 'Open fire.' He heard his order being passed to the quarterdeck, felt the response as the helm went over and the ship came reluctantly as close to the wind as she could manage.

He watched as the frigate appeared to move over until she lay directly astern. Then, as the word reached him far below, old Crocker jerked his trigger-line and the starboard stern-chaser recoiled with a sharp bang. Bolitho did not blink, and thought he saw the dark blur of the ball as it reached the apex of its flight before it splashed down almost alongside, the tall waterspout falling and scattering in the wind.

Bolitho heard the marines at the netting whispering and probably making bets on the next shot.

Old Crocker was good all right. He had almost winged the frigate with his first ball.

Now he had the range, and the 'feel' of it, as every gun captain should. Furthermore, the *Diane's* captain would know it.

The frigate fired one of her bow-chasers, and its thin spout of water well astern of *Achates* brought a roar of derision from the marines.

Their lieutenant snapped, 'Sar'nt Saxton, you will oblige me by keeping those ruffians quiet and in good order!' But he was grinning as he spoke and the reprimand was more for Bolitho's benefit than anything.

Adam climbed to the poop with a telescope and looked astern as another gun fired from below the counter.

This time there was no splash to betray the fall of shot. Instead a great streamer of torn topsail broke free and curled from its yard like a pale banner.

Bolitho heard the muffled cheers from below. They had hit her. If one of Crocker's eighteen-pound balls struck the *Diane*'s slender hull it could be serious.

Adam exclaimed, 'Look, sir! *Argonaute*'s setting her main-course!'

The seventy-four seemed to puff herself up as with sail upon sail she leaned over to the wind, her lower gun-ports almost awash as she changed tack towards *Achates*.

Bolitho heard Keen shout, 'Let her fall off three points again, Mr Knocker! Steer nor'-east by north!'

Even as the hands hauled at the braces and Knocker stood over the binnacle like a watchful hawk, Crocker fired yet again, and this time one of the frigate's jib sails was cut away to join its ragged companion.

Quantock was yelling, 'Mr Mountsteven! Another pull at the weather-forebrace there! Now *belay*, dammit, sir!'

Men bustled about at the braces and halliards, while only the crews of the starboard guns, which pointed towards the enemy, remained at their stations.

Bolitho gripped the nettings as the deck tilted to the thrust of the canvas overhead.

The French captain would have to close the range whether he wanted to or not. Unless he ordered his frigate to stand away, in which case *Achates* would be able to meet his challenge gun to gun. Bolitho smiled. Well . . . almost.

One of the marines who was leaning against the hammocks, his musket already cradled against his cheek, saw Bolitho's smile and dared to say, 'Us'll teach them Frogs a lesson, sir!'

He seemed to realize he had spoken to a vice-admiral uninvited and lapsed into confused silence.

Bolitho glanced at him. He did not even know his name.

In a while they would be fighting for their very lives. The heaviest casualties were usually aft on the unprotected poop and quarterdeck. This marine might be one of them.

He said, 'I am relying on it.' He looked at their expectant faces, hating his own words. 'So give your best, lads.'

There was a jarring crash as Crocker laid and fired another gun. The frigate had changed tack very slightly, but it had not passed unnoticed by the grotesque gun captain. As her shape lengthened momentarily Crocker pulled his trigger-line and the ball smashed through the enemy's larboard gangway, hurling planks and splintered wood high into the air.

There were more cheers, and Bolitho held his breath as the frigate paid off down-wind, her torn canvas still whipping above the deck as she opened the range between them.

Then he ran down the poop ladder and strode to the rail above the gun-deck.

It would be very soon. He glanced quickly abeam and saw the seventy-four's bows edging into view, her canvas bulging to the wind as she changed tack still further towards the *Achates*.

'Stand by!'

The cheering ceased instantly and gun crews crouched beside their eighteen-pounders, staring through the ports.

'As you bear!'

The French ship had the wind-gauge, but so strong was the pressure in *Achates'* sails that her gun muzzles were elevated to maximum advantage by the slanting decks.

'Fire!'

Deck by deck, gun by gun, the carefully aimed broadside flashed along *Achates'* side from stern to forecastle. Some of the forward guns were traversed to full extent, their crews leaning on their handspikes until they too could train on the enemy.

Bolitho watched intently as the *Argonaute*'s topsails danced wildly, the wind ready and eager to explore the holes punched by the double-shotted guns.

Along and beyond her hull he saw the sea alive with flung spray as more balls slammed down with terrible impact.

It was impossible to determine if they had hit anything vital. But the range was still closing, the French captain just as aware as Keen of the danger of a lucky shot. One ship knocked out of the fight, another driven off by Crocker's two stern-chasers, the French captain would feel the humiliation too with his admiral breathing down his neck.

Bolitho saw the flashing line of bright tongues from the seventy-four's side, tensed for the sickening shriek of iron, the crash of shots slamming into timber. Instead he heard the insane whine of chain-shot and saw long streamers of broken rigging floating from the upper yards, the forward topgallant sail ripped apart like a handkerchief in the invisible onslaught.

'Ready!' Keen had his hand up high. '*Fire!*'

Again the guns recoiled madly on their tackles, their crews leaping forward to sponge out and ram in fresh charges while the muzzles were still spewing smoke.

'Ready!' Keen wiped his streaming face with his forearm. '*Fire!*'

The gunnery was superb. All the drills, the demanding discipline, were paying off now. Two broadsides to *Argonaute*'s one.

They were hitting her too. Her mizzen-topmast was dangling like a fallen bridge, and her sails were pock-marked by shot and flying splinters.

Bolitho held his breath again as the guns flashed along the enemy's side.

He felt the jarring thud of balls hitting the hull, and saw the fore-course punctured in several places at once. The wind did the rest, and soon the fore-course was little more than rags.

'*Fire!*'

The pace was slower, the response more irregular, as the gun captains jerked their lines and jumped clear as each great breech charged inboard again.

There was a great crack and then amidst a writhing tangle of stays and rigging *Achates'* main-topgallant mast thundered down. It ploughed into the larboard gangway like a battering ram, tearing aside the protective nets as if they were cobwebs before toppling overboard.

Rooke and his men were there in an instant, axes flashing as they cut the wreckage away. Two seamen were down too. Dead or knocked unconscious by falling rigging, Bolitho did not know.

The guns roared out once more, the din scraping at his mind, as fallen cordage and great strips of canvas fell over the sweating gun crews while they reloaded and then fired again.

Keen shouted, '*Argonaute*'s coming at us, sir!'

He looked wild-eyed, his hat knocked from his head in the turmoil which surged around him.

Bolitho wiped his eyes and looked at the enemy. The trick had worked. The *Argonaute* was charging down-wind with every available sail set, her forward guns firing haphazardly, some hitting, but others, because of the fine angle of approach, ripping through wave-crests far astern.

The little frigate had made no attempt to press home her attack, and was probably grateful to be a mere spectator. She was too far away now to be of any use. It was already too late for last-minute strategy.

Bolitho heard himself shout above the crash and recoil of the guns, 'It's *men* not ships, Val! They're what count in the end!'

Smoke belched over the gangway and a marine fell from the main-top, his scream lost in the bombard nent. One of the forward eighteen-pounders was on its side, two men down and bleeding badly beside it, another writhing and screaming, pinned to the deck by its overheated muzzle.

Men from the disengaged side ran to replace the dead and injured, others obeyed Quantock's speaking-trumpet and hurried to splice hasty repairs and set the big main-course. It was too close to the fighting, too great a risk if fire should spread from sparks or a burning wad from a gun.

Bolitho gauged the distance. The French ship was a cable away, her guns firing intermittently, but at this range she was hitting *Achates* again and again.

Keen was right to set the bigger sails. If *Achates* lost steerage-way now through lack of canvas, she would fall down-wind and present her unprotected stern to the Frenchman's heavy guns and suffer the same fate as the frigate. If the enemy got the chance to fire through *Achates* full length, both decks would suffer crushing losses.

Bolitho raised his smarting eyes to the foremast and saw his flag flying above the smoke and destruction. As the French admiral would see it. The additional spur to drive him on, to bring both ships together regardless of consequences.

'*Fire!*' Keen paused only until the guns roared out towards the enemy. 'Mr Trevenen! Take charge there!'

Bolitho saw that Mountsteven was lying near one of his guns. He had lost an arm, and part of his face had been scorched like burned canvas.

The lower gun-deck was firing without respite, and Bolitho could picture it as if he were there. It had once been his station as a midshipman, a thousand years ago. The red-painted sides to hide the blood of battle, the leaping, grotesque shadows of the gun crews as they pranced and struggled around their weapons, and all the while the low confines of the deck filled with smoke, like a scene from Dante's inferno.

A ball came through an open gun-port, and Bolitho could follow its progress as men were hurled aside, some painted in blood as one of their companions was almost cut in halves before it eventually crashed into the opposite side. Men fell and rolled in torment, and Bolitho saw Tyrrell striding among the debris and patterns of blood, his wooden stump adding to his fierce and wild appearance.

Another ball slammed through the quarterdeck nettings

and flung hammocks across the deck like torn dolls. Two helmsmen dropped, and one of the master's mates fell screaming, a foot-long wood splinter in his stomach like a barbed arrow.

Bolitho looked round frantically but saw Adam pulling himself to his feet. Through the smoke, his voice lost in noise and deafness of battle, he smiled before turning away to assist the after-guard.

'By God, sir, this is too damn hot for my taste!'

Bolitho looked at Allday. He was obviously in pain, but was gripping his cutlass with both hands like a broadsword.

Bolitho felt his hat plucked from his head and knew that they were close enough for the marksmen to test their skills.

'Walk about, Allday, or go below.' He tried to grin but his face felt stiff, like leather.

A midshipman darted forward and retrieved his hat. There was a neat hole just below the binding.

Bolitho made himself smile. 'Why, thank you, Mr — '

But the youth merely stared at him, the life dying in his eyes, like a candle being snuffed out. Then he fell, blood flooding from his mouth.

Bolitho replaced his hat and stared at the enemy. He had not even remembered the boy's name.

A great shadow swept across the deck, followed by a chorus of shouts and screams. The fore-topmast, complete with topgallant mast and spars, had been shot away as cleanly as a carrot. It thundered over the side, taking rigging, men and pieces of men in its wake.

He heard Allday gasp, 'Th' flag, sir! They've shot your flag away!'

Even in the midst of disaster and death Bolitho could feel his outrage and bewilderment.

Bolitho drew the old sword and carefully laid the scabbard on the deck without really knowing what he had done.

The enemy was almost alongside, the guns still firing, the air filled with flying, whining fragments.

So this was where it was to be. Destiny had always known. Men merely deluded themselves.

He saw some sailors below the quarterdeck cringing as more falling wreckage bounced on the nets or splashed into the sea alongside.

They had given everything. Far more than should be expected of them.

He flung his hat down on the nearest gun and yelled, 'Come on, my lads! One last broadside!'

A gold epaulette was cut from his shoulder by a musket ball and a marine scooped it up and hid it in his tunic.

Dazed, bloody and filthy with powder smoke, the seamen returned to their guns, their rammers moving like extensions of themselves, their eyes blind to everything but the bright tricolour above the smoke.

Bolitho shouted, 'One more broadside, then she'll be into us, Val!'

Then he realized that Keen was clutching his side and there was blood on his fingers and white breeches. He saw Bolitho's concern and shook his head.

Between his teeth he gasped, 'Not yet, the people must not see me fall!'

Quantock saw what had happened and waved his hat. '*Fire!*'

The guns roared out at point-blank range, the balls passing through a return of fire from the enemy. Splinters burst from the deck, men reeled about gasping, others yelled orders to those who had already fallen.

Quantock was aware mainly of a feeling of triumph. At the very moment when they were to engage at close quarters, when hard discipline and not softness would win through, he and not Keen had been the one to take command.

But something was wrong. He was slipping and then falling. But it was all right. Someone would help him. By the time he realized that the blood was his own, his eyes, like the midshipman who had retrieved Bolitho's hat, were dead.

18

How Sleep the Brave?

Here and there along both ships guns continued to fire right until the moment of collision. It was as if the men on the lower deck were out of control, or were so dazed by the continuous thunder of their guns they no longer associated with anything outside their private hell.

On the upper deck the air was filled with death as musket and pistol-fire was directed towards officers and seamen alike.

Bolitho watched the gap narrowing between the hulls, the trapped water leaping over the tumblehome and changing to steam on the blistered gun muzzles.

Shots hammered the deck or smacked into the hammock-nettings, while from the fighting tops a murderous hail of canister ripped above the smoke and painted the decks of friend and foe alike with glittering rivulets of blood.

Keen clung to the quarterdeck rail with one hand while he pressed the other to his side, so that his coat helped to slow the loss of blood from his wound. But his face was deathly pale, and he made no effort to move as musket balls ploughed into the deck by his feet or cracked among the men around him.

Adam drew his curved hanger and yelled, *'Here they come!'*

His eyes were very bright as the two hulls crashed together and more broken spars fell from aloft to hold them fast.

Allday thrust his shoulder against Bolitho, the cutlass weaving about as if to reach the enemy as he shouted, 'They'll make for you, sir!'

Indeed, some French boarders had already clambered

across from the *Argonaute*'s beak-head as it ground over the forecastle, the rigging and nets becoming further entwined as the sea lifted and rolled both ships together.

But a crackle of musket-fire brought some of them down before they could cut the nets, and several were run through with boarding pikes even as they tried to retreat.

Captain Dewar waved his sword. 'At 'em, Marines!'

They were his last words on earth as a ball took away his jaw and flung him down a poop ladder to the deck below. His lieutenant, Hawtayne, stared aghast at his superior, unable to accept that he was dead.

Then he yelled, 'Follow me!'

Bolitho watched the scarlet coats dashing into the smoke towards the bows, some falling, others firing their last shots before using their bayonets as more boarders dropped seemingly from the sky itself on to the decks.

It was too much and the enemy too many. Bolitho heard them cheering, the sound changing to screams and curses as another swivel cut through their ranks like a bloody scythe.

He saw Midshipman Evans cowering by the companion hatch.

'Get below! Tell them to *keep firing*! Tell them it's my order!'

It might set both ships ablaze but it was their only chance.

From the corner of his eye he saw more French seamen climbing their mizzen shrouds, the smoky sunlight glinting on steel as they waited for the sea and wind to push the two hulls into a closer embrace. Soon there would be more men to support them from the lower deck.

Bolitho winced as some of the *Achates'* twenty-four-pounders roared out against the Frenchman's side. Smoke, sparks and splinters flew above the gangway and several of the enemy boarders vanished to be trapped or ground between the ships.

There were Frenchmen running along the gangway, although he had not seen them fight their way aboard. One, a lieutenant, cut down a seaman as he tried to jump clear, and several shots cracked over the quarterdeck where Knocker and his men stood around the wheel like survivors on a raft.

The French officer saw Keen by the rail and lunged forward with his sword. Bolitho realized that Keen had his eyes tightly closed against the pain and stood no chance of saving himself.

Bolitho shouted, and when the lieutenant's eyes turned towards him he struck him across the neck with the old blade, and as he tumbled over, his scream choking on blood, Allday brought his cutlass down on his ribs like a woodsman with a rebellious tree.

Steel clashed on steel as *Achates*' seamen rallied on the quarterdeck, their eyes and minds empty of everything but the need to fight and not to fall under those stamping feet and cruel blades.

Bolitho saw Adam lock swords with another French lieutenant and wanted to reach him, to help in any way he could. But even in the noise and horror of the hand-to-hand fighting Bolitho was able to see his nephew's skill as a swordsman, the way he took the weight of a heavier opponent and used it against him. Then he began to advance, stamping down with his right foot as with each thrust and parry he forced his adversary back towards the forecastle.

Allday yelled, 'Watch out!'

Bolitho swung round and saw a petty officer aiming a pistol at him. A blade flashed past his eyes and the pistol dropped to the deck and exploded. The Frenchman's hand was still gripped around it.

With a cut across his forehead, a cutlass in one hand and a belaying-pin in the other, Tyrrell managed to gasp, 'Near thing!' Then like an unsteadying giant he forced his way amongst the struggling men, his weapons swinging and hacking while he bellowed encouragement to anyone who could still understand him.

On the lower gun-deck it was frightening because of the clatter and slap of feet overhead. It was as if a mob had gone completely mad and out of control.

Midshipman Evans groped through the smoke as he tried

to find his way back to the upper deck. He slipped on some blood and almost fell across the body of a dead gun captain, then as he regained his feet he saw figures clambering through an open port where a gun had recoiled and had been abandoned for lack of powder.

They were the enemy.

The shock held him motionless, unable to breathe, as he realized that the other ship was pressed tightly alongside.

He wanted to run, to hide from the fighting and terrible sights around him. But a wounded seaman staggered away from one of the guns, his fingers clutching a deep wound in his stomach, his eyes white and rolling with agony as he tried to escape.

Two French sailors saw him and charged beneath the deck beams. The seaman fell and tried to grasp Evans' foot with his fingers.

He gasped, 'Help me! Please, in the name o' God!'

Evans was only thirteen years old, but even in his pain and despair the seaman had recognized authority and perhaps safety in the blue coat and white breeches.

Evans dragged out his short midshipman's dirk and pointed it at the two Frenchmen.

They both slithered to a halt, their madness checked by the sight of their small opponent.

In the half-darkness old Crocker's white hair moved through the smoke like a patch of light.

He swung a rammer with both hands and knocked the men to their knees. Another seaman joined him, his cutlass just a blur as he finished it.

Crocker twisted his head to stare at the midshipman and then wheezed, 'Proper little fire-eater, ain't 'e?'

Evans stared up the ladder as someone clattered down towards him. His mind could not accept what had happened, other than that he was alive.

Adam Bolitho wiped his eyes as the smoke funnelled up around him. It was hard to breathe, let alone see what was happening.

'Where's the fourth lieutenant?'

He saw the long rammer in Crocker's hands, the reddened cutlass held by one of the seamen.

Lieutenant Hallowes lurched through the smoke, his hanger held at the ready.

'Who the hell wants me?' He saw Adam and grinned. 'Why, our dashing flag-lieutenant!'

Adam asked urgently, 'How are you managing?'

Hallowes waved his blade carelessly. 'I've got my people at the starboard ports, as you can see.' He gestured angrily. '*Simms!* Cut that Frog down!'

It was like a macabre dance. A French seaman dashed from the smoke, his hands over his head as if to protect himself. He must have flung himself bodily through a gun-port expecting to find the gun-deck filled with his companions. He dropped to his knees, his eyes very white in the smoky gloom.

A marine sentry from the main companion lunged forward with his bayonet, the force so great that he pinned the luckless Frenchman to the deck.

Adam tore his eyes away. 'I've an idea. We'll go aft, through the wardroom.' He wondered if Hallowes understood or cared. He looked half-mad. 'The *Argonaute* has a big stern gallery . . . '

Hallowes exclaimed, '*Board* her?' He looked up as a violent crash shook the deck timbers. 'How is it up there?'

Adam thought of the exposed quarterdeck and terrible splinters, the combined chorus of yells and screams as men fought each other to win mastery of the ship.

'Bad. But many of the French boarders came from below decks.'

He ducked as a ball slammed through a port and ricocheted from a gun on the larboard side.

He looked at Crocker. 'Could you blow down her mainmast?'

Crocker stared at him and then said hoarsely, 'Course, sir. I'm with you.' He rattled off several names and men ran from the guns to join him.

Hallowes glared at him, the wildness momentarily held at bay.

'Why? What's the point? We'll never get out alive.'

Adam tossed down his scabbard as he had seen Bolitho do and shrugged. How could he explain? Even if he wanted to. In his mind he saw Bolitho up there on the torn and splintered deck. He was the obvious target. Without him there would be no resistance now that Keen was wounded and Quantock killed. In seconds it would too late.

He said simply, 'I owe him everything. *Everything*, d'you understand?' He did not wait for an answer but shouted as he ran aft, 'Come on, boy, if you care to!'

Hallowes wiped his mouth with his hand and gave a wild laugh.

'Don't you *boy* me, Mister Bolitho!'

Then he was running after him, others snatching up loaded pistols to follow even though they knew not where.

Evans stared aft to the wardroom, his mind reeling. Then he saw an officer lying propped against one of the guards and knew it was Foord, the fifth lieutenant, who moments earlier had been trying to reassure him.

He knelt beside him and saw the blood which soaked the lieutenant's waistcoat and breeches. He was dying even as he watched, and did not even flinch as another ball slammed into the upper hull and made the ship tremble as if she had hit a reef.

Foord saw the young midshipman and attempted to speak. Evans held his hand, not knowing what to say.

'Tell the captain . . . ' His eyes rolled up in agony. 'Tell him . . . '

Evans felt his hand stiffen and then go limp. He wondered vaguely why he was no longer afraid. With great care he prised the hanger from Foord's fingers. He could feel the lieutenant's empty stare on him as he stood up and walked deliberately aft towards the wardroom.

'Ready, lads?' Adam looked at their strained faces.

Crocker slung his leather bag over one shoulder and eyed

the Frenchman's ornate stern right alongside. The gallery was a few feet higher than the wardroom, but it would provide some cover when they attempted to board her.

Crocker nodded. 'Give the word.'

Adam pulled himself through the shattered stern windows and after a small hesitation leapt out on to the other ship's quarter. For a moment he thought he would lose his grip and fall into the sea. There were several corpses already bobbing between the two sterns. Unconcerned and untroubled by the savage battle overhead.

At any moment he expected a face to loom over the gilded rail, to feel the thrust of steel or the blast of a pistol.

He slipped his arm around a life-sized carved figure of a mermaid which adorned the end of the gallery. Her twin on the opposite side had been beheaded by a ball earlier in the battle.

Adam eased himself warily around the mermaid, very conscious of her unmoving stare, the touch of her gold breast under his fingers. All at once he wanted to laugh like Hallowes had done. The complete insanity of it all was beyond his grasp.

He looked again at the mermaid's placid features and thought suddenly of Robina. Just a dream. He ought to have realized it.

Hallowes shouted, 'Move yourself, *boy*, make way for a King's officer!'

They both laughed like madmen and then Adam was up and over the rail, his feet sliding in broken glass as he kicked open a window and vaulted into the big cabin beyond. As in *Achates*, the ship had been completely cleared for action. But the place seemed empty except for corpses and moaning wounded, while some other figures were leaning out through the ports to lock blades with the men on *Achates'* lower gun-deck.

A French petty officer, wounded in one arm, saw the figures burst through the smoke and opened his mouth to yell a warning.

Hallowes hacked him across the face with his hanger and ran on towards the great trunk of the ship's mainmast. It was huge, like a smooth pillar, and when Adam leaned on it to regain his breath he felt it trembling under all its weight of topmast, rigging and spars as if it were alive.

Crocker bent down without hesitation and with a gunner's mate made a quick lashing around the mast with bags of powder arranged at intervals like a necklace.

Figures swayed through the haze and a pistol ball smacked into one of the British seamen like a metal fist. He dropped without making a sound.

Crocker swivelled his good eye. 'Slow-match, matey!'

He pressed it to the short fuse and made to back away.

Hallowes aimed his pistol and fired into the nearest group of shadows. 'We'll hold 'em off! The buggers'll cut the fuse otherwise!'

Adam bounded forward to touch blades with a French officer. He felt the man's breath on his face as they reeled against one of the guns, the hatred giving way to fear as he pushed him clear with the hanger's stirrup-hilt and then cut him down with a blow across the shoulder.

Hallowes darted past him and hurled his empty pistol into a man's face, and when he staggered hacked him down with two quick slashes across arm and neck.

But more men were clambering down a ladder from the deck above, their legs pale against the trapped smoke and dark paintwork. One of Hallowes' seamen stabbed through the ladder with a pike and sent one of them screaming on top of his companions, but a pistol shot killed him before he could recover his balance.

Adam strained his eyes through the choking smoke. But he could see none of the others. Crocker had probably run aft before his charges exploded, and of Hallowes there was no sign.

Two French seamen loomed around an abandoned gun. One raised a pistol but Adam knocked it upwards so that the ball cracked into a deckhead beam. The second man hurled himself the last few feet and smashed Adam on to his back.

The lanyard around his wrist snapped and he heard his hanger fly clattering across the deck.

The seaman was big and extremely powerful. He held Adam's wrists, his tarred fingers like steel as he forced them out on to the planking, as if he were being crucified.

Adam could feel his knee smashing up between his legs to find his groin and cripple him before he could struggle free.

He tried again but it was hopeless, and knew that despite the battle which raged over both ships this man was enjoying the moment.

Adam heard himself cry out in agony as the man's knee jammed into his groin. He tried not to show his pain and despair, but lights flashed before his eyes as he hit him again.

A small shadow rose above the man's shoulders and then all the pain ceased as the French seaman rolled sideways on to the deck.

Midshipman Evans stared at the man with disbelief. Then, as Adam tried to get to his feet, he lowered the hanger with which he had hit his attacker and said urgently, 'This way, sir! I've found a place — '

The rest of his words were drowned by one terrible bang.

Adam got to his knees, the pain searing through his loins like a hot iron. He was blinded by smoke and flying dust and his ears had lost all sense of hearing.

He grasped the boy's shoulder and lurched through the choking fog, only partly aware of what was happening.

He felt Evans pull at his torn coat and wanted to protest as he lost his balance and fell headlong between two of the guns. Through his dazed and confused thoughts he knew he could see sunlight where there should be none.

Then as Evans crouched down beside him he saw a great jagged spar which had crashed through the deck above and then the planking within a yard of where he had been standing.

It was made worse by the complete silence. He saw Hallowes staggering through the dust and pausing to stare up at the seemingly endless length of mast and broken shrouds which poked through the hole like a battering-ram.

Hallowes saw him and yelled something, his face set in a crazy grin as he waved his blade at Crocker's handiwork.

Adam dragged himself to his feet and leaned on the midshipman's shoulder. His hearing was returning and he realized that the din, if possible, was worse than before.

Hallowes shouted, 'That'll give them something to ponder about!'

Now that he had completely given up the idea of staying alive he seemed beyond fear.

Evans thrust the fifth lieutenant's hanger into Adam's hand and they stared at each other like confused strangers.

Like his hearing, his memory came back with brutal urgency.

He heard himself say sharply, 'Come on then, let's be about it!'

Even that reminded him of his uncle so that he knew instantly what he must do.

Tyrrell yelled, 'Can't hold 'em back any longer!'

He brought his belaying-pin down on the head of a man trying to wriggle over the torn hammock-nettings and struck out at another with his cutlass.

Bolitho did not waste his breath to reply. His lungs were on fire and his sword-arm felt like lead as he drove off another boarder and saw him fall on to the mizzen-chains.

It was hopeless. Had been from the beginning. The whole of the upper gun-deck seemed full of the enemy, while *Achates'* men rallied again on poop and quarterdeck, their eyes blazing, their chests heaving from their efforts.

He saw Allday raise his cutlass as a French seaman clambered up through the quarterdeck rail, the terror on the man's face giving way to triumph as he realized that for some reason the English coxswain was unable to move.

Bolitho jumped over a wounded marine and drove his blade blindly beneath the rail. He felt the point jar into the man's shoulder-blade and then slide easily into his body before he fell screaming out of sight.

Bolitho thrust his arm around Allday and dragged him away from the rail.

'Easy, man!' He waited for Midshipman Ferrier to run to his aid as he added, 'You've done enough!'

Allday twisted his head to stare at him, his eyes blurred and wretched.

'It's my right to . . .'

A ball ripped through Bolitho's coat and he vaguely saw Langtry, the master-at-arms, cut down the marksman with a boarding axe.

They were all dying. And for what?

A new explosion made both ships roll and groan together, and for an instant Bolitho imagined that a magazine had caught fire, that both ships would be joined in one terrible pyre.

Swords and cutlasses hovered in mid air, marines paused in their desperate efforts to reload their muskets, as like a towering forest giant the Frenchman's mainmast began to topple. It seemed to take an eternity, so that even some of the wounded tried to prop themselves up to watch, or called to their friends to discover what was happening.

Bolitho let his arm fall to his side, the pain tearing at his muscles as if they were exposed.

Knocker yelled hoarsely, 'There it goes, by Jesus!'

Slowly, and then with greater haste, the mast began to drop. Topmast and topgallant, spars and loosely brailed canvas tore apart as shrouds and stays snapped like threads, unable to hold the tremendous weight or restrain its fall. The fighting-top, complete with swivel-guns, barricades and men, split in halves, hurling its occupants to the deck below, or carrying them down with the topmast as it crashed through timber, rigging and guns into the hull beneath.

Even in *Achates* Bolitho could feel the weight and power of the fallen mast, the way the deck beneath his feet tilted steeply to the new pressure.

A trumpet blared through the rising smoke and some of the boarders retreated into a larger group near the forecastle.

It was the usual sailor's instinct to save his own ship no matter what.

Bolitho cleared his raw throat and shouted, 'To me, *Achates*!'

It was their only chance, if a precious frail one.

But from forward came a sharp command and then a sparkling line of musket-fire. Bolitho stared, unable to believe it. It was like the moment at San Felipe when Dewar had chosen his moment on the track to the fortress. The neat lines of scarlet, the muskets ready and waiting. But now Dewar lay dead, his face shot away, his body trampled on a dozen times as they had fought back and forth across him. And the marines had not been waiting, gauging the moment. They had been in action since the first shots.

And yet they were doing it. He could see Hawtayne's hat above the smoke, hear his shrill voice as he shouted, 'Rear rank, advance! Present! *Fire!*'

The shots raked through the packed mass of French boarders.

There would be no time to reload.

Bolitho dashed down one of the quarterdeck ladders, the pain of his wound forgotten as he ran through the litter of bodies and fallen rigging, his eyes fixed on the enemy.

Hawtayne was calling, '*Advance!*' The bayonets glittered in the hazy light as the marines moved into the attack.

Bolitho saw a young officer running to meet his challenge. He was about the same age as Adam, with similar dark good looks. The steel clanged against steel and Bolitho was almost blinded by the realization that his nephew was very likely dead.

The young French officer lost his stance as Bolitho parried his blade away. Just for the merest split-second he saw the officer's eyes widen with understanding or acceptance. Then he was down. Bolitho pulled the sword free and felt his men surge past him, their voices strengthened by the sudden change of roles.

Lieutenant Scott waved his sword. '*Boarders away!*'

Cheering, cursing, and sometimes dying, a tide of seamen and marines fought their way across to the other ship.

Bolitho hacked another officer to one side but could barely raise his sword now. How long could they hold out?

He was on the gangway, carried part of the way along by his men as they rushed aft to seize the poop.

Small pictures flashed across Bolitho's mind. Adam's face when he had tried to tell him about the girl in Boston. Tyrrell's old pride returning as he had stepped aboard the ship for passage to a country he had never seen. Little Evans, watching the burning Spanish ship, or following him like a small shadow. And Allday, trying to protect him when his own terrible wound was tearing him apart. Pulling him down like a fallen oak.

Shouts and screams exploded across the broad quarterdeck and bodies were flung about in bloody bundles from a murderous blast of canister.

Bolitho wiped the sweat from his eyes with his forearm and stared up at the poop.

He must really be mad. But surely it was Adam and another lieutenant up there with some of *Achates'* men? The smoking swivel, depressed on to the mass of defending seamen and their officers, had had the same effect as the sight of the marines charging from the smoke with their levelled bayonets.

Lieutenant Scott forgot all his usual self-control and clapped Bolitho hard across the shoulder.

'By God, it's the flag-lieutenant, sir! The young devil's blown the heart out of 'em!'

He ran after his men but paused to look back at his vice-admiral. It was just a glance, but it spoke more than a thousand words.

The enemy still outnumbered *Achates'* men and at any moment a leader would emerge, one for them to follow, to renew the fight.

Bolitho looked at his gasping, gashed and bruised seamen, the way they leaned on their cutlasses and pikes. They could not take another battle.

Lieutenant Trevenen marched across the deck and touched his hat with the hilt of his sword.

Achates' junior lieutenant, who had been a hostage in Rivers' fortress.

Seconds ago he had been fighting with his men and working the guns in his division.

Now, filthy but bright-eyed, he was a boy again, and his eyes shone with emotion as he reported, 'They have hauled down their colours, sir.' He fell silent as the seamen and marines crowded closer to hear. Then he tried again, 'Mr Knocker has sent a messenger across . . . ' He looked down, the tears running unheeded on his grimy cheeks.

Bolitho said quietly, 'You've done *well*, Mr Trevenen. Please continue.'

The lieutenant looked at him. 'A ship has been sighted to the south'rd, sir. One of *our* seventy-fours!'

Bolitho moved through his men, hearing them cheering and slapping each other. It was as if it was all somewhere else and he was a mere spectator.

He found the French rear-admiral by the wheel. He had been slightly wounded in the arm and was supported by two of his officers.

They stood and faced each other.

Then Jobert said simply, 'I should have known when I saw it was *your* ship.' He tried to shrug but the pain made him wince. He added, 'You were to give me an island.' He struggled with his sword. 'Now I must give you this.'

Bolitho shook his head. 'No, *M'sieu*. You've earned the right to it.'

He turned and walked back towards the side, his ears ringing to the shouts and wild huzzas.

Hands reached out to assist him across to the *Achates'* torn and littered deck, and he saw Midshipman Ferrier and Rooke, the boatswain, watching him, grinning and waving their hats.

If only they would stop.

He glanced at the figures on the gun-deck, ones who

would never cheer now. *How sleep the brave?* And he thought of the others on the orlop who were paying the price of his victory.

He turned as he heard Allday's painful, dragging steps and saw that he was carrying Jobert's flag over his shoulder.

Bolitho gripped his arm. 'You old dog! Will you never do as I say?'

Allday shook his head, his breath wheezing. But he managed to grin as he replied, 'Doubt it, sir. Too long in th' tooth now.'

Bolitho walked blindly to the rail where Keen was sitting propped in a chipped and blood-stained chair while Tuson examined his wound.

Keen said huskily, 'We did it, sir. I'm told the ship which is heading this way is a seventy-four.' He tried to smile. 'You'll be able to shift your flag to her and be home long before us.'

Bolitho heard the cheering again and again. *Three to one.* Yes, they had won, and all England would soon know about it.

He said, 'No, Val. My flag stays here. We'll sail home together.' He smiled sadly. 'With *Old Katie*.'

Epilogue

Bolitho's home-coming was more than he had dared to hope for during the long months he had been away. In other ways it was sad, as he knew it would be. The farewells at Plymouth were as moving as the welcome when the scarred and battered *Achates* had dropped her anchor, her prize, the *Argonaute*, given immediately into the hands of the dockyard.

It must have been *Old Katie*'s finest hour, Bolitho thought, with her pumps going as they had every hour of the day since that terrible battle. Even her ill-matched jury-rig had somehow managed to look rakish with his flag fluttering at half its proper height. She had brought crowds to the Hoe which few could remember.

Adam had watched Bolitho's grave features as he had walked from beneath the splintered poop to say good-bye to those who had become so familiar to him since they had sailed from the Beaulieu River a year ago.

Scott and Trevenen, Hawtayne and young Ferrier. And Tuson, the surgeon, who had removed a metal splinter from Keen's side the size of a man's thumb. And little Evans, who in his own way had become a man.

Bolitho had been thinking of those he would not see again, who could not share in the home-coming.

The captured seventy-four would be under the British ensign in a matter of months, a very valuable addition to the depleted fleet. But *Achates* had taken the battle badly. It was unlikely she would ever feel the blue waters of the Caribbean again, and would probably end her days as a hulk.

It had been a slow and painful passage up the Channel, and they had sailed so near to the Cornish coast that Adam had shinned aloft to the mizzen cross-trees with a glass to see it for himself.

When he had returned to the deck he had said simply, 'I saw part of the house, Uncle.' It had seemed to bring to him then and there how near he had been to not seeing it again. 'There are crowds on the headland, all the way to St Anthony.'

So slow had been their progress in the warm spring airs that a carriage had been sent to Plymouth in time to meet him.

He was thankful Belinda had not come herself. He had made her promise because of Allday, and if she had seen the ship, listing and blackened, she would have been deeply distressed.

Keen had accompanied him in the barge for the last time. The crowds on the waterfront had cheered and thrown their hats in the air, and women had held up their babies to see Bolitho. The news of his victory had preceded him like a rainbow. He had noticed there were few young men in the crowds.

Once again England was at war with the old enemy, and the press-gangs would be quick to snatch any suitable hands left over by the recruiting parties.

He had also said good-bye to Tyrrell. That had been harder than he had expected. But Tyrrell's dogged independence forced them apart.

Tyrrell had grasped his hands in both of his own and had said, 'I'll be lookin' around for a while, Dick. Just to discover if I like what I see.'

Bolitho had persisted. 'Come to Falmouth soon. Don't forget us.'

Tyrrell had slung his bag over his shoulder and had said, 'I never forgot you, Dick. Nor will I. Ever.'

That had been a week ago. Now, as Bolitho stood by a window and looked out across the flowers and shady trees, he could still scarcely believe it.

Their first meeting had been one of joy and tears.

Belinda had pressed her face into his coat and had whispered, 'I made Ferguson take me to the headland. I saw you sail past. That poor little ship. I was so afraid, and yet *so proud*.' She had looked up at him, searching out the strain on his face. 'There were people everywhere. They began to cheer. You couldn't hear them of course, but they seemed to want you to know they were there.'

Bolitho saw Allday speaking with the groom, making the man laugh with one of his yarns. That was another memory fixed in his mind.

When Allday had walked from the coach, worried and trying not to drag his feet up the stone steps.

She had gone to him and had put her arms round his neck and had said quietly, 'Thank you for bringing my men home, Allday. I knew you would.'

She had given him life, as she had this old house, he thought. Her very presence here had made its mark.

How quickly the week had flashed past and yet they had not left the grounds. Her gentle understanding after what he had endured, her passion which she gave without restraint, had brought them closer than ever.

He thought too of his first meeting with their child. He smiled as he recalled the exact moment.

The way Belinda had laughed at him and had cried at the same time when she had said, 'She won't break, Richard! Pick her up!'

Elizabeth. A new person. Belinda had chosen the name herself, like she had managed everything else during his absence.

Nothing seemed to matter now beyond here and his family. Rivers had gone to London in the same coach as Jobert. The French admiral would be exchanged eventually, but Rivers' fate was less certain.

He looked from the window again but Allday had gone. It was hard to think there was a war again. What had happened to the peace?

The door opened and she entered carrying Elizabeth. Bolitho took her and carried her to the window while the child's hands tugged at his gilt buttons.

It was all perfect, and he felt he should be ashamed when so many had nothing, and so many had died.

Adam entered the room and looked at them. He belonged here. They had made it possible.

Allday hurried towards the outer doors and Bolitho heard him say to one of the maids, 'Quick, girl, here's a courier!'

Belinda's hands went to her breast. In a mere whisper she said, 'Oh no, not now, not so soon!'

Bolitho heard her despair and held the child more tightly to his body.

In this very room his father had once said to him, 'England needs all her sons now.' That had been another war, but the same was just as true today. It was here that his father had given him the old sword, and the last time he had seen him alive.

Adam strode from the room and returned a few minutes later with a heavy, sealed envelope.

He said, 'The courier's not from the Admiralty. He is from St James's in London.'

Belinda nodded without understanding. 'Please read it, Adam, I am too afraid . . .'

Adam opened the envelope and read it in silence.

Then he said, 'Thank God.'

Allday hovered by the door with Ferguson at his side as the young lieutenant handed the imposing letter to her. As he watched her surprise and happiness he said, 'Well, Allday, you must have influence in the right places. It's what you wanted.'

Allday stared as Belinda moved to the window and kissed her husband on the cheek, her arms round him and their child.

Adam smiled and said softly, 'I think my uncle is content with the reward he is holding!'

But Allday did not hear him, and his eyes were far-away as he said, '*Sir* Richard Bolitho.' He nodded firmly, the old gleam back in his eyes once more. 'Not before time, an' that's no error neither.'

Cross of
St George

Alexander Kent

ARROW

Published by Arrow Books in 1997

Reprinted 9 times

Copyright © Bolitho Maritime Productions 1996

The right of Alexander Kent to be identified as the author of this
work has been asserted by him in accordance with the Copyright,
Designs and Patents Act, 1988

First published in the United Kingdom in 1996
by William Heinemann

Arrow Books
The Random House Group Limited
20 Vauxhall Bridge Road, London SW1V 2SA

Random House Australia (Pty) Limited
20 Alfred Street, Milsons Point, Sydney
New South Wales 2061, Australia

Random House New Zealand Limited
18 Poland Road, Glenfield
Auckland 10, New Zealand

Random House (Pty) Limited
Endulini, 5a Jubilee Road, Parktown 2193, South Africa

The Random House Group Limited Reg. No. 954009

www.randomhouse.co.uk

A CIP catalogue record for this book
is available from the British Library

Papers used by Random House are natural,
recyclable products made from wood grown in
sustainable forests. The manufacturing processes conform to
the environmental regulations of the country of origin

ISBN 0 09 942166 6

Printed and bound in Germany by
Elsnerdruck, Berlin

For Kim with love,
and with thanks for sharing
your Canada with me

CONTENTS

Wherever wood can swim,
there I am sure to find this flag of England.

Napoleon Bonaparte

Sword of Honour

The Royal Dockyard at Portsmouth, usually a place of noise and constant movement, was as quiet as the grave. It had been snowing steadily for two days, and the buildings, workshops, piles of timber and ships' stores which made up the clutter in every big yard had become only meaningless shapes. And it was still snowing. Even the familiar smells had been overwhelmed by the white blanket: the sharp tang of paint and tar, hemp and new sawdust, like the sounds, seemed smothered and distorted. And, muffled by the snow, the echoing report of the court-martial gun had gone almost unnoticed.

Set apart from the other buildings, the port admiral's house and offices were even more isolated than usual. From one of the tall windows, which overlooked a nearby dock, it was not even possible to see the water in the harbour.

Captain Adam Bolitho wiped the damp glass and stared down at a solitary Royal Marine, whose scarlet tunic was a stark contrast to the blinding whiteness of the backdrop. It was early afternoon; it could have been sunset. He saw his reflection in the window, and the light of the blazing log fire on the other side of the room, where his companion, a nervous lieutenant, sat perched on the edge of his chair with his hands held out to the flames. At any other time Adam Bolitho could have felt sorry for him. It was never an easy or a welcome duty to be the companion ... his mouth tightened. The *escort*, for some one awaiting the convenience of a court-martial. Even though everyone had assured him that the verdict would be unquestionably in his favour.

They had convened this morning in the spacious hall adjoining the admiral's house, a place more usually the venue of receptions than a courtroom where a man's future, even his life, could be decided. Grotesquely, there had even been a few traces of the Christmas ball which had been held there recently. Adam stared at the snow. Now it was another year: January third, 1813. After what he had endured, he might have imagined that he would have grasped at a new beginning like a drowning man seizing a lifeline. But he could not. All he loved and cared for lay in 1812, with so many broken memories. He sensed the lieutenant shifting in his chair, and was aware of movement elsewhere. The court was reassembling. After a damned good meal, he thought: obviously one of the reasons for holding the proceedings here, rather than force the court to endure the discomfort of a long pull in an open boat to the flagship, somewhere out there in the snow at Spithead.

He touched his side, where the iron splinter had smashed him down. He had believed he was dying: at times, he had even wanted to die. Weeks and months had passed, and yet it was hard to accept that it was less than seven months since he had been wounded, and his beloved *Anemone* had been surrendered to the enemy, overwhelmed by the massive artillery of the U.S.S. *Unity*. Even now, the memories were blurred. The agony of the wound, the suffering of his spirit, unable to accept that he was a prisoner of war. Without a ship, without hope, someone who would soon be forgotten.

He felt little pain now; even one of the fleet surgeons had praised the skill of *Unity*'s French surgeon, and other doctors who had done what they could for him during his captivity.

He had escaped. Men he had barely known had risked everything to hasten his freedom, and some had died for it. And there were others, who could never be repaid for what they had done for him.

The lieutenant said hoarsely, 'I think they've returned, sir.'

Adam acknowledged it. The man was afraid. *Of me? Of having become too intimate, if it goes against me?*

His frigate, *Anemone*, had turned to face a vastly superior enemy, out-gunned and out-manned, with many of his company sent away as prize crews. He had not acted out of arrogance, or reckless pride, but to save the convoy of three heavily laden merchantmen he had been escorting to the Bermudas. *Anemone*'s challenge had given the convoy time to escape, to find safety when darkness came. He remembered *Unity*'s impressive commander, Nathan Beer, who had had him moved to his own quarters, and had come to visit him as he was treated by the surgeon. Even through the mists of agony and delirium, Adam had sensed the big American's presence and concern. Beer had spoken to him more like a father to his son than like a fellow captain, and an enemy.

And now Beer was dead. Adam's uncle, Sir Richard Bolitho, had met and engaged the Americans in a brief and bloody encounter, and it had been Bolitho's turn to give comfort to his dying adversary. Bolitho believed they had been fated to meet: neither had been surprised by the conflict or its ferocity.

Adam had been given another frigate, *Zest*, whose captain had been killed while engaging an unknown vessel. He had been the only casualty, just as Adam had been the only survivor from *Anemone* apart from a twelve-year-old ship's boy. The others had been killed, drowned, or taken prisoner.

3

The only verbal evidence submitted this morning had been his own. There had been one other source of information. When *Unity* had been captured and taken into Halifax, they had found the log which Nathan Beer had been keeping at the time of *Anemone*'s attack. The court had been as silent as the falling snow as the senior clerk read aloud Beer's comments concerning the fierce engagement, and the explosion aboard *Anemone* which had ended any hope of taking her as a prize. Beer had also written that he was abandoning his pursuit of the convoy due to the damage his enemy had inflicted. At the end of the report he had written, *Like father, like son.*

A few quick glances were exchanged in the court, nothing more. Most of those present were either unaware of Beer's meaning, or unwilling to remark on anything that might prejudice the outcome.

But to Adam, it had been like hearing the big American's voice in that hushed room. As if Beer was there, offering his testimony to an adversary's courage and honour.

But for Beer's log, there was little else to confirm what had truly happened. *And if I were still a prisoner? Who would be able to help? I should be remembered only as the captain who struck his colours to the enemy.* Badly wounded or not, the Articles of War left little room for leniency. You were guilty, unless proven without doubt to the contrary.

He was gripping his fingers together behind his back, so hard that the pain helped to steady him. *I did not strike my colours. Then, or at any time.*

Curiously enough, he knew that two of the captains who were sitting on the board had also been court-martialled. Perhaps they had been remembering, comparing. Thinking of how it might have been, if the point of the sword had been towards them. . . .

4

He moved away from the window and paused by a tall mirror. Perhaps this was where officers examined their appearance, to ensure it would meet with the admiral's approval. Or women.... He stared coldly at his reflection, holding back the memory. But she was always there. Out of reach, as she had been when she was alive, but always there. He glanced at the bright gold epaulettes. *The post-captain.* How proud his uncle had been. Like everything else, his uniform was new; all his other possessions lay now in his chests on the sea-bed. Even the sword on the court-martial table was a borrowed one. He thought of the beautiful blade the City merchants had presented to him: they had owned the three ships he had saved, and were showing their gratitude. He looked away from his reflection, his eyes angry. They could afford to be grateful. So many who had fought that day would never know about it.

He said quietly, 'Your duty is all but done. I have been bad company, I fear.'

The lieutenant swallowed hard. 'I am proud to have been with you, sir. My father served under your uncle, Sir Richard Bolitho. Because of what he told me, I always wanted to enter the navy.'

Despite the tension and unreality of the moment, Adam was strangely moved.

'Never lose it. Love, loyalty, call it what you will. It will sustain you.' He hesitated. 'It must.'

They both looked at the door as it opened carefully, and the Royal Marine captain in charge of the guard peered in at them.

He said, 'They are waiting, Captain Bolitho.' He seemed about to add something, encouragement, hope, who could tell. But the moment passed. He banged his heels together smartly and marched out into the corridor.

When he glanced back, Adam saw the lieutenant staring after him. Trying to fix the moment in his mind, perhaps to tell his father.

He almost smiled. He had forgotten to ask him his name.

The great room was full to capacity, although who they were and what they sought here was beyond understanding. But then, he thought, there was always a good crowd for a public hanging, too.

Adam was very aware of the distance, the click of the marine captain's heels behind him. Once he slipped. There was still powdered chalk on the polished floor, another reminder of the Christmas ball.

As he came around the last line of seated spectators to face the officers of the board, he saw his borrowed sword on the table; its hilt was toward him. He was shocked, not because he knew the verdict was a just one, but because he felt nothing. *Nothing.* As if he, like all these others, was a mere onlooker.

The president of the court, a rear-admiral, regarded him gravely.

'Captain Adam Bolitho, the verdict of this Court is that you are honourably acquitted.' He smiled briefly. 'You may be seated.'

Adam shook his head. 'No, sir. I prefer not.'

'Very well.' The rear-admiral opened his brief. 'The Court holds that Captain Adam Bolitho not only acquitted himself of his duty in the best tradition of the Royal Navy, but in the execution of such duty has done infinite credit to himself by a very obstinate defence against a most superior force. By placing his ship between the enemy and the vessels charged to his protection, he showed both courage and initiative of the highest order.' He raised his eyes. 'But for those qualities, it would seem unlikely that you would have succeeded, particularly in view of the fact that you had no knowledge of the declaration of war. Otherwise. . . .' The word hung in the air.

6

He did not need to explain further what the outcome of the court-martial would have been.

All the members of the court stood up. Some were smiling broadly, obviously relieved that it was all over.

The rear-admiral said, 'Retrieve your sword, Captain Bolitho.' He attempted to lighten it. 'I would have thought you might be wearing that fine sword of honour I have been hearing about, eh?'

Adam slid the borrowed sword into its scabbard. *Leave now. Say nothing.* But he looked at the rear-admiral and the eight captains who were his court and said, 'George Starr was my coxswain, sir. With his own hand he lit charges which speeded the end of my ship. But for him, *Anemone* would be serving in the United States navy.'

The rear-admiral nodded, his smile fading. 'I know that. I read it in your report.'

'He was a good and honest man who served me, and his country, well.' He was aware of the sudden silence, broken only by the creak of chairs as those at the back of the great room leaned forward to hear his quiet, unemotional voice. 'But they hanged him for his loyalty, as if he were a common felon.'

He looked at the faces across the table, without seeing them. His outward composure was a lie, and he knew he would break down if he persisted. 'I sold the sword of honour to a collector who values such things.' He heard the murmurs of surprise behind his back. 'As for the money, I gave it to George Starr's widow. It is all she *will* receive, I imagine.'

He bowed stiffly and turned away from the table, walking between the ranks of chairs with his hand to his side as if he expected to feel the old torment. He did not even see the expressions, sympathy, understanding, and perhaps shame: he saw only the door, which was already being opened by a white-gloved marine. His own marines and seamen had died that day, a debt no sword of honour could ever repay.

There were a few people in the outer lobby. Beyond them, he saw the falling snow, so clean after what he had attempted to describe.

One, a civilian, stepped forward and held out his hand. His face seemed vaguely familiar, yet Adam knew they had never met.

The man hesitated. 'I am so sorry, Captain Bolitho. I should not detain you further after what you have just experienced.' He glanced across the room where a woman sat, gazing at them intently. 'My wife, sir.'

Adam wanted to leave. Very soon the others would be milling around him, congratulating him, praising him for what he had done, when earlier they would have watched him facing the point of the sword with equal interest. But something held him. As if some one had spoken aloud.

'If I can be of service, sir?'

The man was well over sixty years old, but there was an erectness, a pride in his bearing as he explained, 'My name is Hudson, Charles Hudson. You see. . . .' He fell silent as Adam stared at him, his composure gone.

He said, 'Richard Hudson, my first lieutenant in *Anemone*.' He tried to clear his mind. Hudson, who had slashed down the ensign with his hanger while he himself lay wounded and unable to move. Again, it was like being an onlooker, hearing others speak. *I ordered you to fight the ship!* Each despairing gasp wrenching at his wound like a branding iron. And all the while *Anemone* was dying beneath them, even as the enemy surged alongside. And Hudson's last words before Adam was lowered into a boat. *If we ever meet again. . . .*

Adam could still hear his own answer. *As God is my witness, I will kill you, damn your eyes!*

'We had only one letter from him.' Hudson glanced

again at his wife and Adam saw her nod, helping him. She looked frail, unwell. It had cost them dearly to come here.

He said, 'How is he?'

Charles Hudson did not seem to hear. 'My brother was a vice-admiral. He used his influence to have Richard appointed to your ship. When he wrote, he always spoke of you so warmly . . . he was so proud to be serving with you. When I heard about your court-martial, as they dare to call it, we had to come. To see you, to thank you for what you did for Richard. He was our only son.'

Adam tensed. *Was.* 'What happened?'

'In his letter he said he wanted to find you. To explain . . . something.' He dropped his head. 'He was shot, attempting to escape. He was killed.'

Adam felt the room sway, like the deck of a ship. All that time, the pain and the despair, the hatred because of what had happened; and he had thought only of himself.

He said, 'I shall tell my uncle when I see him. He was known to your son.' Then he took the man's arm and led him towards his wife. 'There was nothing for Richard to explain. Now he is at peace, he will know that.'

Hudson's mother was on her feet, holding out her hand to him. Adam stooped, and kissed her cheek. It was like ice.

'Thank you.' He looked at each of them. 'Your loss is my loss also.'

He glanced round as a lieutenant coughed politely, and murmured, 'The port admiral wishes to see you, sir.'

'Can't it wait?'

The lieutenant licked his lips. 'I was told that it was important, sir. To you.'

Adam turned to say goodbye, but they had gone, as quietly and patiently as they had waited.

He felt his cheek. Her tears, or were they his own?

Then he followed the lieutenant, past people who

smiled and reached out to touch his arm as he passed. He saw none of them.

He heard nothing but his own anger. *I ordered you to fight the ship*. It was something he would never forget.

Lady Catherine Somervell walked softly toward the window, her bare feet soundless as she glanced back at the bed. She listened to his breathing. Quiet now: he was asleep, after the restlessness he had tried to conceal from her.

She realized that the night was quite still, and there was a hint of moonlight for the first time. She groped for a heavy silk shawl but paused again as he stirred on the bed, one arm resting on the sheet where she had been lying.

She looked out at the ragged clouds, moving more slowly, allowing the moon to touch the street, which shone still from the night's downpour. Across the road, which was all that separated this row of houses from the Thames, she could just discern the restless water. Like black glass in the moonlight. Even the river seemed quiet, but this was London: within hours this same road would be busy with traders on their way to market, and people setting up their stalls, rain or no rain.

She shivered, despite the thick shawl, and wondered what daylight would bring.

Little more than a month had passed since Richard Bolitho had returned home, and the guns of St Mawes battery had thundered out their salute to Falmouth's most famous son. An admiral of England, a hero and an inspiration to the men who followed his flag.

She wanted to go to him now. Not to the public figure, but to the man, *her* man, whom she loved more than life itself.

This time she could not help him. His nephew had been ordered to face a court-martial, the direct consequence of losing *Anemone* to the enemy. Richard had told her that the verdict would vindicate Adam, but she knew him so well that he could not conceal his anxiety and his doubt. His business at the Admiralty had prevented him from being at Portsmouth where the court was convened; she also knew that Adam had insisted upon facing the court alone, and unaided. He knew too well how Bolitho hated favouritism, and the manipulative use of outside influence. She smiled sadly. They were so alike, more like brothers than anything else.

Vice-Admiral Graham Bethune had assured Richard that he would inform him immediately he heard anything: the fast telegraph from Portsmouth to London could bring a dispatch to the Admiralty in less than half an hour. The court had been convened yesterday morning, and as yet there had been no word. Nothing.

Had they been in Falmouth she might have distracted him, involved him in the estate's affairs, in which she had taken such an interest during his long absences at sea. But their presence had been required in London. The war with the United States, which had erupted last year, was believed to be at a turning point, and Bolitho had been summoned to the Admiralty to settle doubts, or perhaps inspire confidence. She felt the old bitterness. Was there nobody else they could send? Her man had done enough, and had too often paid the price.

She must confront it: they would soon be parted again. If only they could get back to Cornwall. . . . It might take all of a week, with the roads in their present state. She thought of their room at the old grey house below Pendennis Castle, the windows that faced the sea. The rides, and the walks they enjoyed so much. . . . She shivered again, but not from cold. What ghosts would wait for them when they took that particular walk, where the despairing Zenoria had flung herself to her death?

So many memories. And the other side of the coin:

11

the envy and the gossip, even the hatred, which was more subtly revealed. Scandal, which they had both endured and surmounted. She looked at the dark hair on the pillow. *No wonder they love you. Dearest of men.*

She heard the sound of iron wheels, the first sign of life in the street. Going to fetch fish from the market, no doubt. Peace or war, the fish were always there on time.

She slipped her hand inside her gown, her fingers cold around her breast. As he had held her, and would hold her again. But not this night. They had lain without passion in one another's arms, and she had shared his anxiety.

She had felt the cruel scar on his shoulder, where a musket ball had cut him down. So many years ago, when her husband, Luis, had been killed by Barbary pirates aboard the *Navarra*. She had cursed Richard on that day, blaming him for what had happened. And then, after he had been wounded, he had been plagued by the return of an old fever, which had almost claimed his life. She had climbed into the cot with him, naked, to comfort him and hold the icy grip of the fever at bay. She could smile at the memory now. He had known nothing about it. So many years, and yet it could have been yesterday. . . .

He had changed her life, and she knew she had changed his. Something that went far beyond his demanding world of duty and danger, something only they shared, which made people turn and look at them when they were together. So many unspoken questions; something others could never understand.

She touched her skin again. *Will he always find me beautiful when he returns from another campaign, another country? I would die for him.*

She reached out to close the curtains, and then stood quite still, as if she were held by something. She shook her head, angry with herself. It was nothing. She wiped

12

the window pane with her shawl and stared at the street below, The Walk, as it was called locally. A few patches of moonlight revealed the trees, black and bare of leaves, like charred bones. Then she heard it: the rattle of wheels on the cobbles, the gentle step of a solitary horse. Moving slowly, as if uncertain of the way. A senior officer returning to his quarters at the barracks nearby after a night of cards, or, more likely, with his mistress.

She watched, and eventually a small carriage moved across a bar of moonlight: even the horse looked silver in the cold glow. Two carriage lamps were burning like bright little eyes, as if they and not the horse were finding the way.

She sighed. Probably some one who had taken too much to drink, and would be overcharged by the driver for his folly.

Her hand was still beneath her breast, and she could feel her heart beating with sudden disbelief. The carriage was veering across the road towards this house.

She stared down, barely able to breathe as the door opened and a white leg paused uncertainly on the step. The coachman was gesturing with his whip. It was like a mime. The passenger stepped down soundlessly onto the pavement. Even the gold buttons on his coat looked like pieces of silver.

And then Richard was beside her, gripping her waist, and she imagined she must have called out, although she knew she had not.

He looked down at the road. The sea-officer was peering at the houses, while the coachman waited.

'From the Admiralty?' She turned toward him.

'Not at this hour, Kate.' He seemed to come to a decision. 'I'll go down. It must be a mistake.'

Catherine looked down again, but the figure by the carriage had vanished. The bang on the front door shattered the stillness like a pistol shot. She did not care. She had to be with him, now, of all times.

She waited on the stairs, the chill air exploring her legs, as Bolitho opened the door, staring at the familiar uniform, and then at the face.

Then he exclaimed, 'Catherine, it's George Avery.'

The housekeeper was here now, muttering to herself and bringing fresh candles, obviously disapproving of such goings-on.

Catherine said, 'Fetch something hot, Mrs Tate. Some cognac, too.'

George Avery, Bolitho's flag lieutenant, was sitting down as if gathering himself. Then he said, 'Honourably acquitted, Sir Richard.' He saw Catherine for the first time, and made to rise. 'My lady.'

She came down, and put her hand on his shoulder. 'Tell us. I can hardly believe it.'

Avery gazed at his filthy boots. 'I was there, Sir Richard. I thought it only right. I know what it is to face the possibility of disgrace and ruin at a court-martial.' He repeated, 'I thought it was only right. There was heavy snow on the south coast. The telegraph towers were hidden from one another. It might have taken another day for the news to reach you.'

'But you came?' Catherine saw Bolitho grip his arm.

Surprisingly, Avery grinned. 'I rode most of the way. I forget how many times I changed horses. Eventually I fell in with the fellow outside, otherwise I doubt I'd have found the place.' He took the glass of cognac, and his hand shook uncontrollably. 'Probably cost me a year's pay, and I don't think I'll be able to sit down comfortably for a month!'

Bolitho walked to a window. *Honourably acquitted.* As it should be. But things did not always end as they should.

Avery finished the cognac and did not protest when Catherine refilled his glass. 'Forced a few coaches and carts off the road – ' He saw Bolitho's expression and added gently, 'I was not in court, Sir Richard, but he knew I was there. Your nephew was going to see the port admiral. Someone said that he has an extended leave of absence. That is all the information I have.'

Bolitho looked at Catherine, and smiled. 'Seventy miles on dark and treacherous roads. What sort of man would do that?'

She removed the glass from Avery's nerveless fingers as he lolled against the cushions, and was asleep.

She replied quietly, 'Your sort of man, Richard. Are you at peace now?'

When they reached the bedroom they could see the river quite clearly, and there were indeed people already moving along the road. It was unlikely that anyone had noticed the sudden arrival of the carriage, or the tall sea-officer banging on the door. If they had, they would think little of it. This was Chelsea, a place that minded its own business more than most.

Together they looked at the sky. It would soon be daylight, another grey January morning. But this time, with such a difference.

She held his arm around her waist and said, 'Perhaps your next visit to the Admiralty will be the last for a while.'

He felt her hair against his face. Her warmth. How they belonged.

'And then, Kate?'

'Take me home, Richard. No matter how long we must travel.'

He guided her to the bed, and she laughed as the first dogs began to bark outside.

'*Then* you can love me. In our home.'

Vice-Admiral Graham Bethune was already on his feet

when Bolitho was ushered into his spacious rooms at the Admiralty, and his smile was warm and genuine.

'We are both abroad early today, Sir Richard.' His face fell slightly. 'Although I fear I have not yet had news of your nephew, Captain Bolitho. The telegraph, excellent though it may be in many ways, is no match for our English weather!'

Bolitho sat down as a servant removed his hat and cloak. He had walked only a few paces from the carriage, but the cloak was soaked with rain.

He smiled. 'Adam was honourably acquitted.' Bethune's astonishment was a pleasure to see. They had met several times since Bolitho's arrival in London, but he was still surprised that Bethune's new authority had not changed him in some way. In appearance, he had matured a good deal since his days as a midshipman in Bolitho's first command, the little sloop of war *Sparrow.* Gone was the round-faced youth, his complexion a mass of dark freckles; here was a keen-eyed, confident flag-officer who would turn any woman's head at Court, or at the many elegant functions it was now his duty to attend. Bolitho recalled Catherine's initial resentment when he had told her that Bethune was not only a younger man, but also his junior in rank. She was not the only one who was baffled by the ways of Admiralty.

He said, 'My flag lieutenant, Avery, rode all the way from Portsmouth this morning to tell me.'

Bethune nodded, his mind busy on another course. 'George Avery, yes. Sir Paul Sillitoe's nephew.' Again the boyish smile. 'I am sorry. Baron Sillitoe of Chiswick, as he is now. But I am glad to know it. It must have been hard for your nephew, losing ship and liberty at one blow. And yet you appointed him to command *Zest* at the final encounter with Commodore Beer's ships. Remarkable.' He walked to a table. 'I sent my own report, needless to

16

say. One has little confidence in courts-martial, as we have seen many times for ourselves.'

Bolitho relaxed slightly. So Bethune had found the time to put pen to paper on Adam's behalf. He could not imagine either of his predecessors, Godschale, or particularly Hamett-Parker, even raising a finger.

Bethune glanced at the ornate clock beside a painting of a frigate in action. Bolitho knew it was his own command, when Bethune had confronted two large Spanish frigates and, despite the odds, had run one ashore and captured the other. A good beginning, which had done his career no harm at all.

'We shall take refreshment shortly.' He coughed. 'Lord Sillitoe is coming today, and I am hoping we shall learn more of the Prince Regent's views on the American conflict.' He hesitated, momentarily unsure of himself. 'One thing is almost certain. You will be required to return to that campaign. What is it now, a bare four months since you engaged and defeated Commodore Beer's ships? But your opinions and your experience have been invaluable. I know it is asking too much of you.'

Bolitho realized that he was touching his left eye. Perhaps Bethune had noticed, or maybe word of the injury and the impossibility of recovery had finally reached this illustrious office.

He answered, 'I had expected it.'

Bethune observed him thoughtfully. 'I had the great pleasure of meeting Lady Somervell, Sir Richard. I know what this parting will mean to you.'

Bolitho said, 'I know you met her. She told me. There are no secrets between us, and never will be.' Catherine had also met Bethune's wife, at a reception at Sillitoe's house by the river. She had said nothing about her, but she would, when she judged that the moment was right. Perhaps Bethune had an eye for the ladies? A mistress, maybe

17

He said, 'You and I are friends, is that not so?'

Bethune nodded, not understanding. 'A small word, for what it truly means.'

'I agree.' He smiled. 'Call me Richard. I feel that rank, and the past, stand in the way.'

Bethune strode to his chair, and they shook hands. 'This is a far better day than I dared hope.' He grinned, and looked very young. 'Richard.' Another glance at the clock. 'There is another matter, which I would like to discuss with you before Lord Sillitoe arrives.' He watched him for a few seconds. 'You will soon know. Rear-Admiral Valentine Keen is being appointed to a new command, which will be based in Halifax, Nova Scotia.'

'I had heard as much.' Full circle, he thought. Halifax, where he had left his flagship, *Indomitable*, upon his recall to England. Was it really so short a time ago? With her had been their two equally powerful prizes, Beer's U.S.S. *Unity* and the *Baltimore*, which together carried as much artillery as a ship of the line. Fate had decided the final meeting; determination and a bloody need to win had decided the outcome. After all the years he had been at sea, pictures could still stand out as starkly as ever. Allday's grief, alone among all the gasping survivors as he had carried his dead son, and had lowered him into the sea. And the dying Nathan Beer, their formidable adversary, with Bolitho's hand in his, each understanding that the meeting and its consequences had been inevitable. They had covered Beer with the American flag, and Bolitho had sent his sword to his widow in Newburyport. A place well known to men-of-war and privateers; where his own brother Hugh had once found refuge, if not peace.

Bethune said, 'Rear-Admiral Keen will hoist his flag in the frigate *Valkyrie*. Her captain, Peter Dawes, who was your second-in-command, stands to accept promotion and is eager to take another appointment.' He paused discreetly. 'His father, the admiral, suggested that the present was as good a time as any.'

So Keen was going back to war, still in mourning for Zenoria. It was what he needed, or imagined he needed. Bolitho himself had known the haunting demands of grief, until he had found Catherine again.

'A new flag captain, then?' Even as he spoke, he knew who it would be. 'Adam?'

Bethune did not answer directly. 'You gave *Zest* to him out of necessity.'

'He was the best frigate captain I had.'

Bethune continued, 'When *Zest* returned to Portsmouth she was found to be in a sorry state of repair. Over four years in commission, and after two captains – three, if you count your nephew – and several sea fights, which left her with deep and lasting damage, and without proper facilities for complete repair ... the last battle with *Unity* was the final blow. The port admiral was instructed to explain all this to your nephew after the court's verdict was delivered. It will take months before *Zest* is ready for service again. Even then. . . .'

After the court's verdict. Bolitho wondered if Bethune shared the true meaning. Had the sword been pointing at Adam, he would have been fortunate to have remained in the navy, even with a ship as worn and weakened as *Zest.*

Bethune was not unaware of it. 'By which time, this war will probably be over, and your nephew, like so many others, could be rejected by the one calling he loves.' He unfolded a map without appearing to see it. 'Rear-Admiral Keen and Captain Bolitho have always been on good terms, both under your command and elsewhere. It would seem a satisfactory solution.'

Bolitho tried not to remember Adam's face as he had seen it that day in *Indomitable*, when he had given him the news of Zenoria's death. It had been like watching

19

his heart break into pieces. How could Adam agree? Knowing that each day he would be serving alongside and under the orders of the man who had been Zenoria's husband. *The girl with moonlit eyes.* She had married Keen out of gratitude. Adam had loved her . . . loved her. But Adam, too, might be grateful for an escape provided by Keen. A ship at sea, not an undermanned hulk suffering all the indignities of a naval dockyard. How could it work? How might it end?

He loved Adam like a son, always had loved him, ever since the youth had walked from Penzance to present himself to him after his mother's death. Adam had confessed his affair with Zenoria: he felt that he should have known. Catherine had seen it much earlier in Adam's face, on the day Zenoria had married Keen in the mermaid's church at Zennor.

Madness even to think about it. Keen was going to his first truly responsible command as a flag-officer. Nothing in the past could change that.

He asked, 'You really believe that the war will soon end?'

Bethune showed no surprise at this change of tack. 'Napoleon's armies are in retreat on every front. The Americans know this. Without France as an ally, they will lose their last chance of dominating North America. We shall be able to release more and more ships to harass their convoys and forestall large troop movements by sea. Last September you proved, if proof were needed, that a well-placed force of powerful frigates was far more use than sixty ships of the line.' He smiled. 'I can still recall their faces in the other room when you told their lordships that the line of battle was finished. Blasphemy, some thought, and unfortunately there are still many you have yet to convince.'

Bolitho saw him look at the clock yet again. Sillitoe was late. He knew the extent of his own influence and accepted it, knew too that people feared him. Bolitho suspected it pleased him.

Bethune was saying, 'All these years, Richard, a lifetime for some. Twenty years of almost unbroken war with the French, and even before that, when we were in *Sparrow* during the American rebellion, we were fighting France as well.'

'We were all very young then, Graham. But I can understand why ordinary men and women have lost faith in victory, even now, when it is within our grasp.'

'But you never doubted it.'

Bolitho heard voices in the corridor. 'I never doubted we would win, eventually. Victory? That is something else.'

A servant opened the fine double doors and Sillitoe came unhurriedly into the room.

Catherine had described the portrait of Sillitoe's father, which she had seen at the reception in his house. Valentine Keen had been her escort on that occasion: that would have set a few tongues wagging. But as he stood there now, in slate-grey broadcloth and gleaming white silk stock, Bolitho could compare the faces as if he had been there with her. Sillitoe's father had been a slaver, 'a black ivory captain', he had called him. Baron Sillitoe of Chiswick had come far, and since the King had been declared insane his position as personal adviser to the Prince Regent had strengthened until there was very little in the political affairs of the nation he could not manipulate or direct.

He gave a curt bow. 'You look very well and refreshed, Sir Richard. I was pleased to hear of your nephew's exoneration.'

Obviously, news travelled faster among Sillitoe's spies than in the corridors of Admiralty.

Sillitoe smiled, his hooded eyes, as always, concealing his thoughts.

'He is too good a captain to waste. I trust he will accept Rear-Admiral Keen's invitation. I think he should. I believe he will.'

Bethune rang for the servant. 'You may bring refreshments, Tolan.' It gave him time to recover from his shock that Sillitoe's network was more efficient than his own.

Sillitoe turned smoothly to Bolitho.

'And how is Lady Catherine? Well, I trust, and no doubt pleased to be back in town?'

Pointless to explain that Catherine wanted only to return to a quieter life in Falmouth. But one could not be certain of this man. He who seemed to know everything probably knew that, too.

'She is happy, my lord.' He thought of her in the early hours of the morning when Avery had arrived. Happy? Yes, but concealing at the same time, and not always successfully, the deeper pain of their inevitable separation. Before Catherine, life had been very different. He had always accepted that his duty lay where his orders directed. It had to be. But his love he would leave behind, wherever she was.

Sillitoe leaned over the map. 'Crucial times, gentlemen. You will have to return to Halifax, Sir Richard – you are the only one familiar with all the pieces of the puzzle. The Prince Regent was most impressed with your report and the vessels you require.' He smiled dryly. 'Even the expense did not deter him. For more than a moment, that is.'

Bethune said, 'The First Lord has agreed that orders will be presented within the week.' He glanced meaningly at Bolitho. 'After that, Rear-Admiral Keen can take passage in the first available frigate, no matter who he selects as flag captain.'

Sillitoe walked to a window. 'Halifax. A cheerless place at this time of the year, I'm told. Arrangements can be made for you to follow, Sir Richard.' He did not turn from the window. 'Perhaps the end of next month – will that suit?'

Bolitho knew that Sillitoe never made idle remarks. Was he considering Catherine at last? How she would come to terms with it. Cruel; unfair; too demanding. He could almost hear her saying it. Separation and loneliness. Less than two months, then, allowing for the uncomfortable journey to Cornwall. They must not waste a minute. Together.

He replied, 'You will find me ready, my lord.'

Sillitoe took a glass from the servant. 'Good.' His hooded eyes gave nothing away. 'Excellent.' He could have been describing the wine. 'A sentiment, Sir Richard. To your Happy Few!' So he even knew about that.

Bolitho scarcely noticed. In his mind, he saw only her, the dark eyes defiant, but protective.

Don't leave me.

2

For the Love of a Lady

Bryan Ferguson, the one-armed steward of the Bolitho estate, opened his tobacco jar and paused before filling his pipe. He had once believed that even the simplest task would be beyond him forever: fastening a button, shaving, eating a meal, let alone filling a pipe.

If he stopped to consider it, he was a contented man, grateful even, despite his disability. He was steward to Sir Richard Bolitho and had this, his own house near the stables. One of the smaller rooms at the rear of the house was used as his estate office, not that there was much to do at this time of the year. But the rain had stopped, and they had been spared the snow that one of the postboys had mentioned.

He glanced around the kitchen, the very centre of things in the world he shared with Grace, his wife, who was the Bolitho housekeeper. On every hand were signs of her skills, preserves, all carefully labelled and sealed with wax, dried fruit, and at the other end of the room hanging flitches of smoked bacon. The smell could still make his mouth water. But it was no use. His mind was distracted from these gentle pleasures. He was too anxious on behalf of his closest and oldest friend, John Allday.

He looked now at the tankard of rum on the scrubbed table. Untouched.

He said, 'Come along, John, have your wet. It's just what you need on a cold January day.'

Allday remained by the window, his troubled thoughts like a yoke on his broad shoulders.

He said at length, 'I should have gone to London with him. Where I belong, see?'

So that was it. 'My God, John, you've not been home a dog-watch and you're fretting about Sir Richard going to London without you! You've got Unis now, a baby girl too, and the snuggest little inn this side of the Helford River. You should be enjoying it.'

Allday turned and looked at him. 'I knows it, Bryan. Course I do.'

Ferguson tamped home the tobacco, deeply troubled. It was even worse with Allday than the last time. He looked over at his friend, seeing the harsh lines at the corners of his mouth, caused, he thought, by the pain in his chest where a Spanish sword had struck him down. The thick, shaggy hair was patched with grey. But his eyes were as clear as ever.

Ferguson waited for him to sit down and put his big hands around the particular pewter tankard they kept for him. Strong, scarred hands; the ignorant might think them awkward and clumsy. But Ferguson had seen them working with razor-edged knives and tools to fashion some of the most intricate ship models he had ever known. The same hands had held his child, Kate, with the gentleness of a nursemaid.

Allday asked, 'When do you reckon they'll be back, Bryan?'

Ferguson passed him the lighted taper and watched him hold it to his long clay; the smoke floated toward the chimney, and the cat lying on the hearth asleep.

'One of the squire's keepers came by and he said the roads are better than last week. Slow going for a coach and four, let alone the mail.' It was not doing any good.

He said, 'I was thinking, John. It'll be thirty-one years this April since the Battle of the Saintes. It hardly seems possible, does it?'

Allday shrugged. 'I'm surprised you can remember it.'

Ferguson glanced down at his empty sleeve. 'Not a thing I could easily forget.'

Allday reached across the table and touched his arm. 'Sorry, Bryan. That was not intended.'

Ferguson smiled, and Allday took a swallow of rum. It means that I'll be fifty-three this year.' He saw Allday's sudden discomfort. 'Well, I've a piece of paper to prove it.' Then he asked quietly, 'How old does that make you? About the same, eh?' He knew Allday was older; he had already served at sea when they had been taken together by the press gang on Pendower Beach.

Allday eyed him warily. 'Aye, something like that.' He looked at the fire, his weathered features suddenly despairing. 'I'm his cox'n, y'see. I *belongs* with him.'

Ferguson took the stone jug and poured another generous measure. 'I know you do, John. Everyone does.' He was reminded suddenly of his cramped estate office, which he had left only an hour ago when Allday had arrived unexpectedly in a carrier's cart. Despite the fusty ledgers, and the dampness of winter, it was as if she had been there just ahead of him. Lady Catherine had not been in his office since before Christmas, when she had left for London with the admiral, and yet her perfume was still there. Like jasmine. The old house was used to the comings and goings of Bolithos down over the years, he thought, and sooner or later one of them failed to return. The house accepted it: it waited, with all its dark portraits of dead Bolithos. Waited.... But when Lady Catherine was away, it was different. An empty place.

He said, 'Lady Catherine perhaps most of all.'

Something in his voice made Allday turn to look at him.

'You too, eh, Bryan?'

Ferguson said, 'I've never known such a woman. I was with her when they found that girl.' He stared at his pipe. 'All broken up, she was, but her ladyship held her like a child. I shall never forget. . . . I know you're all aback at the thought that maybe you're getting old, John, too old for the hard life of a fighting Jack. It's my guess that Sir Richard fears it, too. But why am I telling you this? You know him better than anybody, man!'

Allday smiled, for the first time. 'I was that glad about Cap'n Adam keeping out of trouble at the court-martial. That'll be one thing off Sir Richard's mind.'

Ferguson grunted, smoking. A revenue cutter had slipped into Falmouth, and had brought the news with some despatches.

Allday said bluntly, 'You knew about him and that girl, Zenoria?'

'Guessed. It goes no further. Even Grace doesn't suspect.'

Allday blew out the taper. Grace was a wonderful wife to Bryan, and had saved him after he had returned home with an arm missing. But she did enjoy a good gossip. Lucky that Bryan understood her so well.

He said, 'I love my Unis more than I can say. But I'd not leave Sir Richard. Not now that it's nearly all over.'

The door opened and Grace Ferguson came into the kitchen. 'Just like two old women, you are! What about my soup?' But she looked at them fondly. 'I've just done something about they fires. That new girl Mary's willing enough, but she's got the memory of a squirrel!'

Ferguson exclaimed, 'Fires, Grace? Aren't you being a bit hasty?' But his mind was not on what he was saying. He was still turning over Allday's words. *I'd not leave Sir Richard. Not now that it's nearly all over.* He tried to brush it aside, but it would not go. What had he meant? When the war finally ended, and men paused to count the cost? Or did he fear for Sir Richard? That was nothing new. Ferguson had even heard Bolitho liken them both to a faithful dog and its master. Each fearful of leaving the other behind.

Grace looked keenly at him. 'What is it, my dear?'

He shook his head. 'Nothing.'

Allday darted a glance between them. Although separated for long periods when he was at sea, he had no closer friends.

He said, 'He thinks I'm getting old, ready to be broken up like some rotten hulk!'

She laid one hand on his thick wrist. 'That's foolish talk, you with a fine wife and a bonny baby. Old indeed!' But the smile did not touch her eyes. She knew both of them too well, and could guess what had happened.

The door opened again, and this time it was Matthew, the coachman. Like Allday, he had protested against remaining in Falmouth and entrusting Bolitho and Catherine to a common mail coach.

Ferguson was glad of the interruption. 'What's amiss, Matthew?'

Matthew grinned.

'Just heard the coach horn. Sounded it, like that other time when he was coming home!'

Ferguson said briskly, 'Drive down and fetch them from the square,' but Matthew had already gone. He had been the first to know, just as he had been the first to recognize the St Mawes salute when Bolitho had returned to Falmouth a little over a month ago.

He paused to kiss his wife on the cheek.

'What was that for?'

Ferguson glanced at Allday. *They were coming home.* He smiled. 'For making up the fires for them.' But he could not repress it. 'For so many things, Grace.' He reached for his coat. 'You can stop for a meal, John?'

But Allday was preparing to leave. 'They'll not want a

crowd when they gets here.' He was suddenly serious. 'But when he wants me, I'll be ready. That's it an' all about it.'

The door closed, and they looked at one another.

She said, 'Taking it badly.'

Ferguson thought of the smell of jasmine. 'So will she.'

The smart carriage with the Bolitho crest on the door clattered away across the stableyard, the wheels striking sparks from the cobbles. For several days Matthew had been anticipating this, backing the horses into position at the time when the coach from Truro could be expected to arrive outside the King's Head in Falmouth. Ferguson paused by the door. 'Fetch some of that wine they favour, Grace.'

She watched him, remembering, as if it were yesterday, when they had snatched him away in the King's ship. Bolitho's ship. And the crippled man who had returned to her. She had never put it into words before. *The man I love.*

She smiled. 'Champagne. I don't know what they see in it!'

Now that it's all nearly over. He might have told her what Allday had said, but she had gone, and he was glad that it would remain a secret between them.

Then he walked out into the cold, damp air and could smell the sea. Coming home. It was suddenly important that there should be no fuss: Allday had understood, even though he was bursting to know what was going to happen. It must be as if they had only been from Falmouth for a single day.

He looked over at the end stall and saw the big mare Tamara throwing her head up and down, the white flash on her forehead very clear in the dull light.

There could be no more doubt. Ferguson walked over and rubbed her muzzle.

'She's back, my lass. And none too soon.'

Half an hour later the carriage rattled into the drive. The hero and his mistress who had scandalized the country, defying both hypocrisy and convention, were home.

Lieutenant George Avery regarded himself critically in the tailor's mirror, as he might examine a stranger. He knew very little of London, and on previous visits he had usually been on some mission to the Admiralty. The tailor's establishment was in Jermyn Street, a bustling place of shops and elegant houses, and the air, which seemed unclean after the sea, was alive with the din of carriages and hooves.

He must have walked for miles, something he always enjoyed after the restrictions of a crowded man-of-war. He smiled at his reflection; he was quite tired, unaccustomed to so much exercise.

It was strange to have money to spend, something new to him. This was prize money, earned over ten years ago when he had been second-in-command of the schooner *Jolie*, herself a French prize. He had all but forgotten about it; it had seemed unimportant in the light of his subsequent misfortunes. He had been wounded when *Jolie* was overwhelmed by a French corvette, then held as a prisoner of war in France; he had been exchanged during the brief Peace of Amiens only to face a court-martial, and to receive a reprimand for losing his ship, even though he had been too badly injured to prevent others from hauling down her colours. At Adam Bolitho's court-martial he had relived every moment of his own disgrace.

He thought of the house in Chelsea, where he was still staying, and wondered if Bolitho and Catherine had reached Cornwall yet. It was difficult to accept, let alone take for granted, that they had left him to use the house as he chose. But he would have to go to Falmouth soon himself, to be with the others when Sir Richard received his final instructions. His *little crew*, as he called them. Avery thought it was dangerously close to being a family.

Arthur Crowe, the tailor, peered up to him. 'Is everything satisfactory, sir? I shall have the other garments sent to you immediately they are ready.' Polite, almost humble. Rather different from their first meeting. Crowe had seemed about to offer some critical comment on Avery's uniform, which had been made by the Falmouth tailor, Joshua Miller. *Just another impoverished luff, at thirty-five old for his rank, and therefore probably under a cloud of some sort, doomed to remain a lieutenant until dismissal or death settled the matter.* Avery had silenced the unspoken criticism by a casual mention of his admiral's name, and the fact that the Millers had been making uniforms for the Bolithos for generations.

He nodded. 'Very satisfactory.' His gaze shifted to the bright epaulette on his right shoulder. It would take some getting used to. A solitary epaulette on the right shoulder had formerly been the mark of rank for a captain, not posted, but a captain for all that. Their lordships, apparently at the insistence of the Prince Regent, had changed it. The solitary epaulette now signified the rank of lieutenant, at least until some new fashion was approved.

The room darkened, and he imagined that the sky was clouding over again. But it was a carriage, which had stopped in the street directly opposite the window: a very elegant vehicle in deep blue, with some sort of crest on the panels. A footman had climbed down and was lowering the step. It had not been lost on the tailor: he was hurrying to his door and opening it, admitting the bitter air from the street.

Curious, Avery thought, that in all the shops he had seen there appeared to be no shortages, as if war with France and the new hostilities with America were on another planet.

He watched absently as a woman emerged from the carriage. She wore a heavy, high-waisted coat almost the same colour as the paintwork, and her face was partly hidden by the deep brim of her bonnet as she looked down for the edge of the pavement.

Arthur Crowe bowed stiffly, his tape measure hanging around his neck like a badge of office.

'What a pleasure to see you again, my lady, on this fine brisk morning!'

Avery smiled privately. Crowe obviously made a point of knowing those who mattered, and those who did not.

He thought of Catherine Somervell, wondering if she had persuaded Bolitho to patronize this prosperous street.

Then he swung away, his mind reeling, the new epaulette, the shop, everything fading like fragments of a dream.

The door closed, and he barely dared to turn round.

Crowe said, 'If you are certain I can provide nothing more, Mr Avery?'

Avery faced the door. The tailor was alone. Crowe asked, 'Is something wrong, sir?'

'That lady.' He made himself look, but even the carriage had gone. Another fragment. 'I thought I knew her.'

Crowe watched his assistant parcelling up the new boatcloak Avery had purchased. 'Her husband was a good customer. We were sorry to lose him, although not always an easy man to satisfy.' He seemed to realize that it was not the answer Avery had wanted. 'Lady Mildmay. The wife, or should I say, the widow, of Vice-Admiral Sir Robert Mildmay.'

It was she. Except that when he had last seen her, she had been only the wife of his captain in the old *Canopus*.

Crowe prompted, 'Was that the lady of your acquaintance?'

'I think I was mistaken.' He picked up his hat. 'Please have the other purchases delivered to the address I gave you.'

No arguments, no hesitation. Sir Richard Bolitho's name opened many doors.

He walked out into the street, glad to be moving again. Why should he care? Why did it matter so much? She had been unreachable then, when he had been stupid enough to believe it was more than just an amusing game to her, a passing flirtation.

Had she changed? He had caught a glimpse of her hair, honey-coloured; how many days, how many sleepless nights he had tried to forget it. Perhaps she had been part of the reason he had not resisted when his uncle, then Sir Paul Sillitoe, had suggested that he offer himself for the position of flag lieutenant to Sir Richard Bolitho. He had expected his application to be refused as soon as Bolitho had learned more about him. Instead, he had never forgotten that day in Falmouth, in the old house he had come to know so well, their kindness to him, the trust, and eventually the friendship which had done so much to heal the doubts and the injuries of the past. He had thought little more beyond the next voyage, the next challenge, even though it took him to the cannon's mouth yet again.

And now, this. It had been a shock. He had deluded himself. What chance would he have had? A married woman, and the wife of his own captain? It would have been like putting a pistol to his head.

Was she still as beautiful? She was two years older than himself, maybe more. She had been so alive, so vivacious. After the slur of the court-martial, and then being marooned on the old *Canopus*, he thought until the end of his service, she had been like a bright star: he had not been the only officer who had been captivated.

He quickened his pace, and halted as someone said, 'Thank you, sir!'

There were two of them. Once they had been soldiers; they even wore the tattered remnants of their red coats. One was blind, and held his head at an angle as though he were trying to picture what was happening. The other had only one arm, and was clutching a hunk of bread which had obviously been handed to him by a potboy from the nearby coffee-house. It had probably been left on some one's plate.

The blind man asked, 'What is it, Ted?'

The other said, 'Bit o' bread. Don't worry. We might get lucky.'

Avery could not control his disgust. He should have been used to it, but he was not. He had once come to blows with another lieutenant who had taunted him about his sensitivity.

He said sharply, 'You there!' and realized that his anger and dismay had put an uncharacteristic edge to his voice. The one-armed man even cowered, but stood protectively between the officer and his blind companion.

Avery said, 'I am sorry.' He was reminded suddenly of Adam Bolitho, and the presentation sword he had sold. 'Take this.' He thrust some money into the grimy hand. 'Have something hot to eat.'

He turned away, annoyed that such things could still move and trouble him.

He heard the blind man ask, 'Who was that, Ted?'

The reply was barely audible above the clatter of wheels and harness.

'A gentleman. A true gentleman.'

How many were there like that? How many more would there be? Probably soldiers from a line regiment, maybe two of Wellington's men: shoulder to shoulder, facing French cavalry and artillery. Living from battle to battle, until luck changed sides and turned on them.

Those around him did not realize what it was like, and would never believe that either he or his admiral could still be moved by such pitiful reminders of the cost of war. Like that moment in *Indomitable*'s cabin after Adam's ship had been lost, and a single survivor had been dragged from the sea by the brig *Woodpecker*, which, against orders, had returned to the scene. That survivor had been the ship's boy. Avery had watched Bolitho bring the child back to life with his compassion, even as he had endeavoured to discover what had happened to Adam.

Avery had once believed that his own suffering had left him indifferent to the fate of others. Bolitho had convinced him otherwise.

Somewhere a clock chimed: St James's, Piccadilly, he thought. He had passed it without noticing it. He looked back, but the two redcoats had gone. Like ghosts, momentarily released from some forgotten field of battle.

'Why, *Mister* Avery! It *is* you.'

He stared at her, vaguely aware that she was standing in the doorway of a perfumery, with a prettily wrapped box in her arms.

It was as if the street had emptied, and, like the two ghosts, had lost all identity.

He hesitated, and removed his hat, saw her eyes move over his face, and, no doubt, he thought bitterly, the dark hair which was so thickly streaked with grey. This was the moment he had lived in his dreams, when he would sting her with sarcasm and contempt, and punish her in a way she could never forget.

She wore a fur muff on one hand, and the parcel was in danger of falling. He said abruptly, 'Let me assist you,' and took it from her; it was heavy, but he scarcely noticed. 'Is there some one who will carry this for you?'

She was gazing at him. 'I saw what you did for those

35

poor beggars. It was kind of you.' Her eyes rested briefly on the new epaulette. 'Promotion too, I see.'

'I fear not.' She had not changed at all. Beneath the smart bonnet her hair was probably shorter, as the new fashions dictated. But her eyes were as he remembered them. Blue. Very blue.

She seemed to recall his question. 'My carriage will return for me in a moment.' Her face was full of caution now, almost uncertainty.

Avery said, 'I imagined that I saw you earlier. A trick of the light, I daresay. I heard that you had lost your husband.' A moment of triumph. But it was empty.

'Last year. . . .'

'I read nothing of it in the *Gazette*, but then, I have been away from England.' He knew he sounded curt, discourteous, but he could not help it.

She said, 'It was not in battle. He had been in poor health for some time. And what of you? Are you married?'

'No,' he said.

She bit her lip. Even that little habit was painful to see. 'I believe I read somewhere that you are aide to Sir Richard Bolitho.' When he remained silent she added, 'That must be vastly exciting. I have never met him.' The slightest hesitation. 'Nor have I met the famous Lady Somervell. I feel the poorer for it.'

Avery heard the sound of wheels. So many others, but somehow he knew it was the carriage that matched her coat.

She asked suddenly, 'Are you lodging in town?'

'I have been staying in Chelsea, my lady. I shall be leaving for the West Country when I have arranged my affairs in London.'

There were two vivid spots of colour in her cheeks, which were not artificial. 'You did not always address me so formally. Had you forgotten?'

He heard the carriage slowing down. It would soon be over: the impossible dream could not harm him any more. 'I was in love with you then. You must have known that.'

Boots clattered on the pavement. 'Just the one, m' lady?'

She nodded, and watched with interest as the footman took the box from Avery, noting his expression, the tawny eyes she had always remembered.

She said, 'I have reopened the house in London. We had been living at Bath. It is not the same any more.'

The footman lowered the step for her. He did not spare Avery even a glance.

She rested one hand on the carriage door. Small, well-shaped, strong.

She said, 'It is not far from here. I like to be near the centre of things.' She looked up at him, searching his face, as though considering something. 'Will you take tea with me? Tomorrow? After all this time. . . .'

He watched her, thinking of when he had held her. Kissed her. The only delusions had been his own.

'I think it would be unwise, my lady. There is enough gossip and slander in this town. I'll not trouble you again.'

She was inside the carriage but had lowered the window, while the footman waited, wooden-faced, to climb up beside the coachman.

For a moment she rested her hand on his, and he found himself surprised by her apparent agitation.

'Do come.' She slipped a small card into his hand. Then she glanced quickly at the footman and whispered, 'What you said to me just now. Were you really?'

He did not smile. 'I would have died for you.'

She was still staring back at him as the dark blue carriage pulled away.

He jammed on his hat and said aloud, 'Hell's teeth, I still would!'

But the anger eluded him, and he added softly, 'Susanna.'

Yovell, Bolitho's portly secretary, waited patiently near the library desk, his ample buttocks turned toward the fire. Sharing Bolitho's life at sea as he did, Yovell knew, more than any one, the full extent of the planning and detail through which the admiral had to sift before eventually translating this paper war into written orders for his captains.

Like Bolitho's other loyal, if difficult, servant Ozzard, Yovell had a small cottage on the estate, even as Allday had lived there when home from the sea. Yovell gave a small, amused smile. That was, until Allday had suddenly become a respectable married man. Through one of the windows he saw a cat waiting expectantly for somebody to open the door. That was Allday to a letter, he thought, on the wrong side of every door. When he was at sea he worried about his wife and the inn at Fallowfield, and now there was the baby to add to his responsibilities. And when he was home, he fretted about being left on the beach when Bolitho returned to his flagship. Yovell had no such domestic problems. When he wanted to give up his present work he knew Bolitho would release him, just as he knew that many people thought him quite mad to risk his life in a man-of-war.

He watched Bolitho's strong hand leafing through the pile of papers, which he had been examining for most of the morning. He had only returned from London a week ago and had been occupied with Admiralty business for much of the time. Catherine Somervell had waved to him as she had left the house to call on Lewis Roxby, their near neighbour and 'the King of Cornwall', as he was dubbed behind his back. Roxby was married to Bolitho's sister Nancy, and Yovell thought it a good thing that

Catherine had family of sorts to visit while they were all away at sea.

He admired her greatly, although he knew that many men called her a whore. When the transport *Golden Plover* had been wrecked off the coast of Africa, Bolitho's woman had been with them, and had not only survived the hardships of their voyage in an open boat, but had somehow held them all together, given them heart and hope when they had no reason to expect that they would live. It had made his own suffering seem almost incidental.

Bolitho looked up at him, his face remarkably calm and rested. Two weeks on the road from London, changing coaches and horses, being diverted by floods and fallen trees: their account of it had sounded like a nightmare.

Bolitho said, 'If you would arrange for copies of these, I should like them dispatched to their lordships as soon as possible.' He stretched his arms, and thought of the letter which had been awaiting his return. From Belinda, even though there was a lawyer's hand at the helm. She needed more money, a sizeable increase in her allowance, for herself and their daughter Elizabeth. He rubbed the damaged eye. It had not troubled him very much since his return; perhaps the grey stillness of a Cornish winter was kinder than blazing sun and the sea's mirrored reflections.

Elizabeth. She would be eleven years old in a few months' time. A child he did not know, nor would he ever know her. Belinda would make certain of that. He sometimes wondered what her friends in high society would think of the elegant Lady Bolitho if they knew she had connived with Catherine's husband to have her falsely charged and transported like a common thief. Catherine never spoke of it now, but she could never forget it. And like himself, she would never forgive.

Every day since their return they had tried to enjoy to the full, knowing that time did not favour them. The roads and lanes were firmer after days of a steady south-westerly, and they had ridden for miles around the estate and had visited Roxby, who remained in poor health after suffering a stroke. Poor humour, too: Roxby adored his style of living, hunting and drinking, and entertaining lavishly at his house on the adjoining estate, balancing the pleasures of a gentleman with his obligations as farmer and magistrate. He was even on intimate terms with the Prince Regent, and perhaps had been given his knighthood on the strength of that acquaintance. The advice of his doctors to rest and take things more quietly was like a sentence of death.

He thought of the long journey home on those appalling roads. Catherine had even managed to create happiness then, despite her discomfort. At one point they had been turned back by flooding, and set down at a small, shabby inn which had clearly shocked their fellow passengers, two well-dressed churchmen and their wives who were on their way to meet their bishop.

One of the women had said angrily, 'No lady should be expected to remain in such a dreadful place!' To Bolitho she had added, 'What does your wife have to say about it, I should like to know?'

Catherine had answered, 'We are not married, ma'am.' She had held his arm more tightly. 'This officer is running away with me!'

They had not seen their fellow passengers again. Either they had waited for another coach, or they had slipped away in the night.

The room had been damp and slightly musty from lack of use, but the landlord, a jovial dwarf of a man, had soon got a fire going, and the supper he had presented would have satisfied even the greediest midshipman.

And with the rain on the window, and the fire's dancing

shadows around them, they had sunk into the feather bed and made love with such abandon that they might well have been eloping.

There had been a short letter from Adam, saying only that he was leaving with Valentine Keen for Halifax, and asking their forgiveness for not having visited them in Falmouth.

Whenever he considered their situation his mind seemed to flinch from it. Adam and Keen. The two of them together, flag captain and admiral. *Like me and James Tyacke*. But so different. Two men who had loved the same woman, and Keen knew nothing about it. To share a secret was to share the guilt, Bolitho thought.

That same night at the inn, while they had lain exhausted by their love, Catherine had told him something else. She had taken Keen to Zennor, to the churchyard where Zenoria was buried. It was a good thirty miles from Falmouth, and they had stayed with friends of Roxby's in Redruth overnight.

She had said, 'Had we stayed anywhere else there would have been talk, more cruel gossip. I couldn't risk that – there are still too many who wish us ill.'

Then she had told him that while Keen had been alone at the grave she had spoken with the verger. He was also the gardener, and, with his brother, the local carpenter, and had confided that he made all the coffins for the village and surrounding farms.

She said, 'I thought I would ask him to see that fresh flowers were put on her grave throughout the year.'

Bolitho had held her in the firelight, feeling her sadness at the memory, and what had gone before.

Then she had said, 'He would take no payment, Richard. He told me that "a young sea captain" had already arranged it with him. After that, I went into the church, and I could see Adam's face as I saw it that day, when Val and Zenoria were married.'

What strange and perverse fate had brought Adam and Keen together? It could restore, or just as easily destroy them.

Yovell was polishing his small gold-rimmed spectacles. 'When will Mr Avery be joining us, Sir Richard?'

Bolitho eyed him thoughtfully. A man of many parts: it was rumoured that Yovell had been a schoolmaster at one time. He could well believe it. It was hard to imagine him as he had been in the boat after *Golden Plover* had gone down, his hands, unused to seamen's work, torn and bleeding on the oars, his face burned raw by the sun. But he could remember not a single word of complaint. A scholar, a man who enjoyed his Bible as another might relish a game of dice: even his casual question about the flag lieutenant held genuine interest. Perhaps they were two of a kind, both enigmatic in their fashion. George Avery was a quiet, often withdrawn man; even Sillitoe appeared not to know much about his nephew. Or care, possibly. Sillitoe's sister had been Avery's mother: of Sillitoe's brother, who had so inspired Avery that he had seemed to look upon him as a father whenever they had met, Bolitho knew nothing. Sillitoe's brother had been a naval officer, and very likely had sponsored Avery for his first appointment as midshipman. Avery's own father, and austere upbringing in a religious family, had never dampened his eagerness to follow the sea. Sillitoe's brother, in the *Ganges*, had fallen at the Battle of Copenhagen, like so many on that bloody day.

There was little to do in London for a lieutenant without connections, he thought, although Catherine had hinted that there had once been a woman in Avery's life. *Only a woman could scar him so deeply.*

She was probably right.

He said, 'Mr Avery will be coming down in a week or so. Or whenever he likes.' Or perhaps Avery would leave it until the last minute. Maybe he could not bear to see others who did not hide their love from one another, when he himself had no one.

He listened to the muffled thud of hooves. 'Her ladyship is home early.'

Yovell was at the window, and shook his head. 'No, Sir Richard, it's a messenger.' He did not turn. 'Dispatches, no doubt.'

Bolitho stood, trying to prepare himself as his secretary went out to deal with it. So soon. So soon. A month more, and already they were warning him of his departure. It would have been better if they had allowed him to remain in *Indomitable;* and in the same second he knew that was a lie. To be with her, only for an hour, would have made all this worthwhile.

Yovell came back, holding the familiar canvas envelope with its Admiralty fouled anchor, to dispel any lingering hope he might have had.

Yovell returned to the window and peered out at the trees. The cat, he noticed, had disappeared. He thought of Allday again. It was going to be difficult.

He listened to the knife slitting the envelope. The messenger was in the kitchen being given something hot to drink, no doubt full of envy for those who lived in great houses such as these. He heard Bolitho say quietly, 'It is brought forward by a week. We take passage for Halifax on February eighteenth.' When he turned from the window he thought his admiral seemed very composed: the man every one expected to see. Beyond the reach of any personal emotion.

He said, 'It is not the first time, Sir Richard.'

Bolitho seized a pen and bent over the papers on the desk. 'Give the fellow this receipt.' He stood up and held his cuff over his eye as he faced the light. 'I shall ride out to meet Lady Catherine. Tell Matthew, will you?'

Yovell hurried away, not wanting to leave, but understanding that he had to confront the prospect of separation alone. Three weeks, then an ocean, a world apart.

He closed the door quietly behind him. Perhaps cats had the right ideas about life, he thought.

They met by the slate wall that marked the boundary of Roxby's estate. She did not dismount until he got down and walked to her, and then she slid from the saddle and waited for him to hold her, her hair blowing out freely in the salt breeze.

'You've heard. How long?'

'Three weeks.'

She pressed her face to his so that he would not see her eyes. 'We will make it a lifetime, dearest of men. Always, always, I will be with you.' She said it without anger or bitterness. Time was too precious to waste.

He said, 'I don't want to go. I hate the thought of it.'

Through his cloak she could feel him shivering, as if he were cold or ill. She knew he was neither.

He said, 'Why must you suffer because of me, because of what I am?'

'Because I *understand*. Like your mother and all those before her. I will wait, as they did, and I will miss you more than any words can describe.' Then she did look at him, her dark eyes very steady. 'Above all, I am so very proud of you. When this is over, we shall be together, and nothing will ever force us apart again.'

He touched her face and her throat. 'It is all I want.'

He kissed her very gently, so gently that she wanted to cry.

But she was strong, too strong to allow the tears to come. She knew how much he needed her and it gave her the courage that was necessary, perhaps more now than at any other time.

'Take me home, Richard. A lifetime, remember?'

They walked in silence, the horses following companionably behind them. At the top of the rise they saw the sea, and she felt him grip her arm more tightly. As if he had come face to face with the enemy.

3

Morning Departure

Captain Adam Bolitho tightened his boatcloak around his neck as the jolly-boat pulled out strongly into the Solent. A strange departure from Portsmouth, he thought: without the snow, everything was normal again. Noise, bustle, marching men, and many boats milling around the stairs, waiting to carry their officers out to the ships at anchor.

Except that this was not his ship. He had paused only briefly to step aboard the frigate *Zest*, to sign some papers, to take his leave as quickly as possible. The ship had fought well; without her, even *Indomitable*'s formidable artillery might not have been able to beat the Yankees into submission. But that was as far as it went. He never felt that *Zest* was really his ship, nor had he attempted to make her so. His ship lay on the sea-bed, her beautiful figurehead staring into the deeper darkness, so many of her company still with her.

The midshipman in charge of the jolly-boat was very aware of his passenger's rank and reputation: even the name of Bolitho had sent a flood of rumours through the ship.

Adam looked at the chests at his feet. All new, everything, even the fighting sword he had purchased with such care. The rest lay with *Anemone*.

He glanced at his small companion. John Whitmarsh,

who had been the only one saved from the sea, had
served in *Anemone* for almost two years before she
foundered. A mere child. He had been 'volunteered' by
an uncle, if uncle he was, after the boy's father, a deep-
water fisherman, had drowned off the Goodwins. John
was to be his servant. Adam had never seen such pride
or such gratitude when he had asked him. The boy still
did not understand the lifeline had been for his captain,
and not the other way round.

The midshipman said stiffly, 'There she lies, sir.'

Adam tugged down his hat. She was the *Wakeful*, a
thirty-eight gun frigate, hard-worked and in constant
demand like most of her breed. Now she was completing
the last tasks before sailing, taking on fresh water, fruit
if there was any available, and, of course, men. Even the
most dedicated press gang would be hard put to find any
suitable hands in a naval port.

He looked at the boy again. Not much different in
spite of his smart new jacket and white trousers. Ozzard
had taught him some of it; the rest he would learn quickly
enough. He was bright, and if he was nervous or still
suffering from his experiences and the memory of seeing
his best friend, another ship's boy of the same age, drift
away beyond help, he did not show it.

Adam had sent a letter to the boy's mother. Had she
asked for his return, he would have put him ashore and
made certain that he reached her safely. She had not
acknowledged the letter. Perhaps she had moved from
the area, or taken up with another 'uncle'. Either way,
Adam thought his young charge had been quietly pleased
about it.

He ran his eye critically over the frigate. Rigging well
set up, sails neatly furled. She was smart enough. He
could see the scarlet and blue of the receiving party by
the entry port. He knew nothing of her captain, other
than that this was his first command. He found he could

shut it from his mind. It was not his concern. He, like Rear-Admiral Valentine Keen, who was arriving tomorrow, was a passenger. He smiled briefly. An inconvenience.

He thought with affection of his uncle, and how close they had been after his escape from the Americans. They would all meet again in Halifax. He still did not know why he had accepted Keen's offer. Because of guilt? To allay suspicion? He knew it was neither. It was simply a feeling, like some one or something leading the way. He recalled Zennor, the quietness of the place, the hiss of the sea on the rocks beneath the cliff. Her grave. He had touched it, and had felt her spirit watching him. The little mermaid.

'Bows!' The midshipman's voice was loud. Perhaps he had taken Adam's silence for disapproval.

The bowman was on his feet, boathook poised as rudder and oars brought the boat hard round toward the main chains. The oars were tossed, showering the seamen with salt water as the boat swayed and bounced alongside.

He looked at the midshipman. 'Thank you, Mr Price. That was well done.'

The youth gaped at him, as if surprised that his name was known. He thought once more of Bolitho, all the lessons learned. *They have names.* He could almost hear his voice. *In this life we share, it is often all they do have.*

He stood up, ensuring that the new sword was safely in position on his hip. He had never forgotten Bolitho's cautionary tale of the senior officer who had fallen headlong over his sword, in full view of the side party.

He glanced down at the boy. 'Ready, young John?' He knew that above his head they were all waiting: the ritual of receiving a captain on board. But this, too, was important.

Whitmarsh picked up his bag, his brown eyes unblinking as he stared at the tapering masts, the ensign curling out from the taffrail.

'Ready, sir.' He nodded firmly. 'Aye, ready.'

Adam smiled, and climbed swiftly up the side. He still wore a dressing on the jagged wound, but it was only to protect the tender scar from the pressure of his clothing.

He stepped onto the deck and removed his hat as the Royal Marines presented arms in salute. *And to remind me, so that I never forget.*

'Welcome aboard, Captain Bolitho! It is an honour!'

Adam shook his hand. Very young, and in the gleaming new epaulettes, he was like a youth playing the role of captain. He thought, *as I once did.*

The captain, whose name was Martin Hyde, led the way aft, and said almost apologetically, 'A bit crowded, I'm afraid. Rear-Admiral Keen will have my quarters, and there is an extra berth for you. I've arranged for your section to be screened off. I see you have a servant with you, so you should be comfortable enough.' He hesitated. 'I must ask this. What is the rear-admiral like? It is three thousand miles to Halifax, and he will be used to rather more luxury than I can offer, I imagine.'

Adam said, 'He is very agreeable, and a good man in every way.'

The other captain seemed relieved. 'I understand that his wife died recently. It can change one.'

Adam heard himself answer levelly, 'He will leave you free to direct your ship as you will.' He would have to become accustomed to it. People would always want to know.

He saw a corporal of marines pointing out something to Whitmarsh, and the boy nodding in agreement. He belonged. But just once Adam saw him glance uncertainly along the busy deck, where the guard was falling out and the hands were returning to their work.

Hyde said. 'He looks a likely lad. Young, but I'm often

49

so desperate for bodies I'd take them from their mothers' arms if I could!'

An officer hovered nearby, obviously the first lieutenant. Hyde said, 'I am needed, Captain Bolitho. We will talk later.' He smiled, and looked even younger. 'It is a privilege to have you aboard, although after three thousand miles you may feel differently.' Then he was gone.

Overhead, the familiar sounds resumed, the twitter of bosun's calls, the 'Spithead Nightingales', the thud of bare feet, and the squeal of tackles through their blocks. *His world, but not mine.* Adam sat on a chest and stared around at the great cabin, where he would live, and attempt to accept a future with Keen.

He heard Whitmarsh walking behind him, still very careful of his shining new shoes with their bright buckles.

Adam said, 'In that chest.' He tossed him the keys. 'There's some cognac.' He watched the boy opening it. Like the others, it could have belonged to a stranger. All new. He sighed.

John Whitmarsh asked quietly, 'Be you sad, sir?'

He looked sharply at the boy. 'Remember what I told you aboard *Indomitable*, when I asked you to come with me?'

He saw him screw up his eyes. 'Aye, sir. You said that when we were sad we should remember our old ship, an' our lost friends.'

Adam took the cup of cognac from his hand. 'That is so.'

The boy watched him anxiously. 'But we *will* get another ship, sir!'

The very simplicity of it moved him. 'Yes. We will, John Whitmarsh.'

He looked toward the stern windows, streaked now with salt spray like ice rime.

'But there will always be thoughts.'

The boy had not heard him, or perhaps he had spoken

50

only to himself: he was unpacking one of the chests in an orderly fashion, as Ozzard had taught him. He was content.

Adam stood up. *And so must I be. Others depend on me. It has to be enough.*

But when he had knelt by her grave, he had known then that it was not.

George Avery paused to get his bearings, and reconsider what he was doing. When he had watched her drive away in the smart blue carriage, he should have left it right there, put it back into the past with all the other memories and bitter experiences. He had returned to Jermyn Street and prowled up and down, simply to reawaken the breathtaking sensations of that chance meeting. He had almost expected to see the same two tattered veterans begging for food, but they had receded into the day's unreality. He frowned. There had been plenty of others, though.

She had been right about one thing. Her house was close by; he was not even breathless from the walk. It was cold, with watery sunlight, but he had not needed the new boatcloak which he carried loosely over his arm. The house, though, was enough to chill his blood. He did not quite know what he had expected, but it was large and elegant, with a presence to match. He stopped again. He should turn and go, now. And there were several carriages outside: she was not alone. Perhaps he should have gone to the house when she had asked him, to take tea. But that invitation had been two days ago. He had looked at her little card several times since then, unable to decide what to do.

And then an Admiralty messenger had brought him the letter, and the sailing date. They would leave from Plymouth, so it was time he began the long journey to

51

Falmouth, where Sir Richard Bolitho would be requiring his presence.

Instead, he was here.

What would she say? She might not even consent to see him. He stared at the house again, trying to remember his captain, her husband. He had assumed that Mildmay had been given the old *Canopus* as an insult, because of some past misdemeanour. Perhaps he had offended someone in high places: it was not uncommon. *That was why I was sent to her.* Taken originally as a prize from the French at the Nile, she had received such a battering and had subsequently been worked so hard that her greatest enemy was rot.

But Mildmay had left the ship while she had been in dock, and had been promoted to flag rank, with further promotion two years later. Now he was dead.

He felt his confidence, never very great, wavering. He would make an even bigger fool of himself this time.

The double doors of the house were before him, although he did not recall having mounted the steps. As though he had been secretly observed, one of them swung inward, opened by a tall, rather severe-looking woman dressed from neck to toe in grey, with a bunch of keys hanging from the chatelaine at her waist.

'Yes?' Her eyes moved over him swiftly. She was probably more used to senior officers and the quality, he thought, and, surprisingly, it made him smile. It was the same assessment and dismissal that the Jermyn Street tailor had given him.

He said, 'I wish to speak to Lady Mildmay.'

The eyes moved on, looking for a carriage or some other evidence of respectability. 'She is not expecting your visit?' It was not really a question.

Avery heard music, a pianoforte, and in the sudden stillness applause, like a scattering of dry leaves.

'No, not exactly. I – '

'What is it, Mrs Pepyat? I thought I – '

Avery removed his hat. 'I am sorry, my lady.' She was standing by the great, curving staircase, one hand to the bosom of her gown, as if she had been surprised or annoyed by the intrusion.

She said, '*Mister* Avery, you keep a poor diary!' But she smiled, and walked to meet him. 'Is something amiss?'

He took the cool hand she offered and kissed the back of it. 'I am recalled, my lady. I must leave for Cornwall shortly.' The pianoforte had started to play again, and Avery said, 'I will leave. You are entertaining.'

She watched him, her blue eyes questioning. 'No, no. That is a Mr Blount – he comes from Highgate to play for us, to raise money for the sailors' hospital at Greenwich.' She shrugged. 'It is an amiable way to meet old friends, or acquaintances, if you prefer . . .' She smiled. 'You like music, Mr Avery? It is Mozart, very fashionable, it seems.'

Avery was listening. 'Yes. His Fantasy in C Minor.' He did not see her raised brows. 'I sang in the choir, and my father's organist used to entertain us with that music afterwards.'

He must go. The formidable Mrs Pepyat obviously thought so.

'Take this gentleman's hat and cloak.' A footman darted out from nowhere, and took them from him. His line of retreat was severed.

She slipped her arm through his and guided him toward a tall doorway.

'We will sit by this pillar. See? No one has noticed a thing.'

He sat beside her. Although she had released his arm he could still feel her touch. The room was full, the women, some young, some not so young, sitting attentively, with here and there an expensively shod foot tapping in time to the music. The men were mostly older, and there were several red uniforms: senior officers putting on a brave face for society's sake, but, for the most part, obviously bored. The pianist named Blount was very small, with the frame of a youth, but his face could have been that of an old portrait, and Avery knew simply by watching him that he had completely dismissed his audience from his mind.

She leaned toward him, and Avery saw two other women turn instantly to observe them. 'There will be refreshments later. I shall have to entertain then, a little.'

She was very close, so close that he could smell her hair, her perfume, and see the rise and fall of her breasts.

'Am I as you remember, *Mister* Avery?'

She was teasing him again. Or was she.

He lowered his voice. 'Exactly as I remember.'

She turned away. The music ceased and people stood to applaud, some, he thought, out of pleasure, others with relief that it was over.

An act of charity. Avery glanced around at the rich gowns, the stylish hair arrangements, the men, smiling now as the first trays of wine appeared. How much of the collection would find its way to the sailors' hospital, he wondered, and was shocked by his own cynicism.

He remained by the pillar and took a goblet of wine from a passing footman. She was moving amongst her guests without hesitation or uncertainty. He heard her laugh, and saw two of the soldiers beaming at her.

He stepped back as a solitary naval uniform, a lady on one arm, paused to speak with Lady Mildmay before heading for the door. Escaping.

She was with him again, her eyes moving across the room. 'Are you enjoying yourself, Mr Avery?'

'That officer. I know him.'

'Vice-Admiral Bethune. Yes, he has risen like a bright star.' It seemed to amuse her.

54

'And that was his wife.' She was not as he had expected. Perhaps he had been misinformed.

She was looking at him steadily. '*Not* his wife. From what we hear, one can hardly blame him. He is very attractive, if I may say so as a woman.'

Some of the others were leaving now, their duty done. She asked suddenly, 'Recalled, you said? When do you return?' She turned to smile and curtsey to a big, florid-faced man and his lady. 'So good of you to come, Your Grace!' And as quickly, the smile was gone. 'Tell me.'

He shrugged. 'I am joining Sir Richard Bolitho's squadron.'

She put her hand to her breast again. Off guard, no longer so composed. 'The Americas? The war?'

He smiled. 'It is the way of sailors, madam.'

She turned again as two more women rose to leave. They smiled like old friends, but one looked directly at Avery, her eyes full of a hard curiosity.

Avery asked abruptly, 'And who was *that*?'

She closed her fingers on his arm, either ignoring or not caring for the consequences.

'That was your admiral's wife, Lady Bolitho. Did you not know?'

Avery shook his head. 'This is not my world.' He glanced at the door. 'I have things to attend to, my lady. I did not mean to disturb you. That was not my intention.' He saw the sudden doubt in her eyes.

'Do you have a carriage?'

'I can easily obtain one. I am going to Chelsea.'

Somebody called out to her but she did not appear to hear. She said, 'My carriage can take you there, and in more comfort.' She gripped his arm more tightly. 'Please.' No further pretence. 'Please stay.'

'I think we own Lady Mildmay a debt of gratitude for her charming hospitality, and the dedication with which she has always carried out her work on behalf of those less fortunate.'

She bowed low, her smile confident. The shadow between her breasts made a lie of her composure.

As she straightened again, she looked directly into his eyes. 'George . . . please, go tomorrow.'

It was madness. But there was the other madness, which they had all shared, the thunder of the great guns, the screams and the horror of battle. How could he explain, how extricate himself from this? But she had already vanished among the remaining guests.

Avery made his way through the house until he found the garden, which was already in twilight.

Madness, then. So be it.

The carriage had stopped at the crest of a slight rise, the horses stamping on the rough road, untroubled by the keen morning air.

Bolitho turned toward her, holding her hand beneath her heavy cloak, wondering how time could pass so swiftly and without mercy.

'We are almost there, Kate.'

'I know. I remember.'

They could have driven all the way from Falmouth without stopping, but had stayed the night at an inn outside Liskeard. Bolitho had been very aware of the danger of missing his ship because of a late arrival, or some accident on the road: that the tide waited for no man had been impressed upon him since he had first gone to sea at the age of twelve, or perhaps even earlier, as a child listening to his father and the local men who lived on and from the sea. Nor would he have Catherine travelling so far without some brief respite.

They had left the Turk's Head early; neither of them wanted breakfast. Even in such a small place there had been no escape from his own notoriety. People had been waiting outside the inn, and had waved and called to them, wishing them luck and happiness. Catherine had responded as she always did, although their kindness must have broken her heart. It was not next week or the week after. It was today.

The other members of his 'little crew' would already be aboard: Avery, more withdrawn than usual after his sojourn in London; Yovell with his books and his Bible, untroubled as always; Ozzard, who gave nothing away; and, of course, Allday. Allday was genuinely sorry to be leaving his wife and child, but there was something more to it, pride, or a certain satisfaction because he was still needed, and had returned to what he considered his proper role in life.

He had talked with Catherine throughout the night. The ship, *Royal Enterprise*, was a fleet transport, faster than most merchant vessels, and used to carrying important passengers to any destination so ordered by their lordships. The voyage should take three weeks to a month, weather permitting: the masters of such transports were highly experienced, making the best use of prevailing winds for an untroubled passage. So there might be a hint of early spring in Cornwall by the time he rehoisted his flag above *Indomitable* in Halifax.

At least he would have James Tyacke, as well as Adam and Keen to sustain him. What would she have?

He had told her about Belinda and her need for more money. Catherine had known, or guessed.

She had exclaimed, 'Need? Self-indulgence, more likely! I'll not have that woman troubling you, Richard.'

When the inn had fallen quiet for the night they had held one another and talked, until desperate passion had brought them together for the last time.

They heard Matthew speaking softly with Ferguson. Ferguson had insisted on accompanying them, and would escort Catherine back to Falmouth rather than entrust

57

her to the protection of a paid guard. He and Matthew had remained in the inn parlour yarning and drinking until they had eventually retired, Ferguson to one of the rooms, Matthew to sleep with his horses as he always did on the road.

Catherine twisted round to look at him again. 'Remember, I am always with you. I shall write often, to let you know how it looks in Falmouth, at our house.' She touched the lock of hair above his right eye; it was almost white now, and she knew he hated it. She thought the savage scar beneath it must be the cause; the rest of his hair was as black as it had been on the day she had first seen him.

She murmured, '*So proud*, Richard.' She lowered her head and her fist struck the seat. 'I will not weep. We have gone through so much, and we are so lucky. I will *not* weep.'

They had decided that they should part before he joined the ship: so different from that other time when she had climbed *Indomitable*'s side and been cheered by Tyacke's sailors, many of whom had since died in that last fight with Beer's *Unity*.

But now that the time had come, it was hard to contemplate leaving her.

Reading his thoughts, she said suddenly, 'May we get out, Richard, just for a few minutes?'

They climbed down and he took her arm as her cloak billowed out in the wind. Bolitho did not need any gauge: he knew the feel of it. A sailor's wind. The *Royal Enterprise* would be tugging at her cable, eager to go. He had known it all his life, though rarely as a passenger.

And there, like a dark, twisting snake, was the Hamoaze, and beyond it, misty in the damp air, Plymouth and the Sound.

She said quietly, 'The hills of Devon, Richard. How well I know these places, because of you.'

'We have done and shared so much.'

She put her fingers on his mouth. 'Just love me, Richard. Say that you will always love me.'

They walked back to the carriage where Matthew stood by the horses, and Ferguson, shapeless in a big coachman's caped coat, sat in silence, sharing it, as he had so many times.

The door closed and they were moving again. Downhill now, with more people about, some of whom pointed at the crest on the coach, and cheered without knowing if it was occupied or empty.

Houses next, a stableyard he remembered from his time as a junior lieutenant. He held her and looked at her, knowing what it was costing, for both of them. She was beautiful, despite the shadows beneath her eyes, as he always saw her when they were separated by the ocean.

She was saying, 'I shall keep very busy, Richard. I shall help Bryan, and I will visit Nancy more often. I know she frets over Lewis. He will heed nothing the doctors tell him.'

Matthew called, 'We're here, Sir Richard.'

She clung to his arm. 'I shall walk with you to the jetty. They may not have sent a boat yet. I can keep you company.'

He touched her face, her hair. 'The boat will be there. I am an admiral. Remember?'

She laughed. 'And you once forgot to tell me!'

He embraced her. Neither moved. There was no baggage: it had been sent ahead. All he had to do was get out, and walk through the gate and to the jetty. It was so simple. That was probably what they had told themselves on the way to the guillotine. . . .

He opened the door. 'Please stay here, Kate.' He held her again, and she leaned over and kissed him. Then he stepped back and stared at the others. 'Take good care of her.' He could barely see them. 'For me.'

Matthew grinned. 'None better, sir!' But there was no smile in his eyes.

Ferguson was down on the road. He said, 'God speed, Sir Richard.'

Bolitho stood quite still; afterwards, he thought it had been as if their spirits had joined.

Then he turned on his heel and walked through the gates.

She watched, her eyes smarting, afraid to miss the moment when he would look back. He had been right: they were waiting. Uniforms blue and scarlet; formal, austere voices. Respect for her man, an admiral of England.

But he did turn, then very slowly raised his hat and bowed to her. When she looked again, he was gone.

She waited for Ferguson to climb into the carriage, and said, 'Tell Matthew to drive back along the same road.'

Ferguson replied, 'The ship'll stand well out before she changes tack, m'lady. We'll not be able to see anything.'

She sat back in the seat. 'I shall see him.' She looked at the passing cottages. 'And he will know it.'

Captains

As eight bells chimed out from the forecastle belfry,
Captain James Tyacke climbed through the companion
and onto the broad quarterdeck. The air, like everything
else, was wet, clinging, and cold, and the ship seemed
hemmed in by an unmoving curtain of fog. He gripped
his hands tightly behind his back and listened to the
staccato beat of hammers, and the occasional squeak of
blocks as some item of rigging was hauled aloft to the
upper yards. When he looked up, it was uncanny: the top-
masts and topgallant spars were completely cut off by
the fog, as if the frigate *Indomitable* had been dismasted
in some phantom engagement.

He shivered, hating the climate, too used perhaps to
the African sun and the south's clear blue horizons.

He stopped by the empty hammock nettings and
peered down at the water alongside. Lighters were
moored there, and other boats were pulling this way
and that like water-beetles, vanishing and reappearing
suddenly in the mist.

This was Halifax, Nova Scotia. A busy and vital sea-
port, and a pleasant-looking town, from the little he had
seen of it. He touched the nettings, like cold metal on
this dismal day. But not for long, he told himself. Very
soon this work would be completed, which, considering
the winter's bitter weather and the needs of all the other

men-of-war sheltering here, was a record of which to be proud. Six months had passed since they had entered harbour after the savage battle with the two American frigates. The largest prize, *Unity*, had already left for England, and would be receiving all the attention she required. She had been so badly mauled that he doubted she would have survived the long Atlantic crossing if her pumps had not been kept going throughout every watch.

He gritted his teeth to prevent them from chattering. Some captains would have donned a thick boatcloak to keep out the cold. James Tyacke did not entertain the idea. *Indomitable*'s company had to work as best they could in their usual clothing, and he did not believe that he should take advantage of his rank. It was not some facile act to impress the men. It was merely Tyacke's way.

Like the empty nettings. Ordinarily, when the hands were piped to show a leg and make ready for another working day in harbour, the hammocks were neatly stowed there, and kept in the nettings during the day: when the ship was called to battle they offered the only protection from flying splinters for the helmsmen and officers on the quarterdeck. But life was hard enough in a King's ship, Tyacke thought, and here, when the only heating throughout *Indomitable*'s impressive one hundred and eighty feet was the galley stove, wet hammocks at the end of the day would have made things even more uncomfortable.

Figures loomed and faded in the mist, officers waiting to ask him questions, others wanting final instructions before they were pulled ashore to collect the quantities of stores and supplies required by this ship of war. *My ship*. But the satisfaction would not come, and the pride he occasionally allowed himself to feel kept its distance.

It was March, 1813. He stared along the deck. It was impossible to believe that next month he would have been in command of *Indomitable* for two whole years.

What next? Where bound, and to what end? *Indomitable* was more powerful than most of her class. Built as a third-rate, a ship of the line, she had been cut down to perform the role of a heavily-armed frigate, and as she had proved in September when she had stood alongside the U.S.S. *Unity*, she was more than a match for the superior American firepower with her forty twenty-four pounders and four eighteen-pounders, as well as the other weapons she carried.

Surrounded by busy seamen whom he could barely see, Tyacke continued his walk, his forenoon solitude respected. He smiled briefly. It had not been easy, but he had welded them into one company. They had cursed him, feared him, hated him, but that was in the past.

The lessons had been learned. He looked down at the wet deck planking. They had paid for it, too. When the mist cleared as Isaac York, the sailing-master, had claimed it would, the repairs and replaced planks and timbers would be visible despite the caulking and the tar, the fresh paint and the varnish. Men had died aplenty that day in September. Matthew Scarlett, the first lieutenant, impaled on a boarding-pike, his last scream lost in the yells and the fury, the clash of steel and the crash of gunfire. Ships fighting, men dying, many of whom had probably already been forgotten by those who had once known them. And just there ... he glanced at a newly painted shot-garland, Midshipman Deane, hardly more than a child, had been pulped into nothing by one of *Unity*'s massive balls. And all the while the admiral and his tall flag lieutenant had walked the scarred deck, allowing themselves to be seen by the men who, because of press gang or patriotism, were fighting for their lives, for the ship. He smiled again. And, of course, for their captain, although he would never regard it in that light.

Tyacke had always hated the thought of serving in a major war vessel, let alone one that wore an admiral's flag. Bolitho had changed that. And strangely, in his absence, without the admiral's flag at the mainmast truck, Tyacke felt no sense of independence or freedom. Being forced to remain in harbour undergoing repairs while they awaited orders had merely increased his feeling of confinement. Tyacke loved the open sea: more than most, he needed it. He touched the right side of his face and saw it in his mind as he did when he shaved every morning. Scored away, burned, like something inhuman. How his eye had survived was a mystery.

He thought again of those who had fallen here, not least the one-legged cook named Troughton. He could recall the moment when he had assumed command of *Indomitable*, his stomach knotted with nerves as he had prepared to read himself in to the assembled company. He had forced himself to accept the stares and the pity in his previous command, the brig *Larne*. Small, intimate, with every hand dependent on the others, she had been his life. Bolitho himself had once referred to her as the loneliest command imaginable. He had understood that solitude was what Tyacke needed more than anything.

He had known that first day aboard *Indomitable* that those who had waited in the silence for him were undoubtedly more worried about their new captain's character than his disfigurement: he was, after all, the lord and master who could make or break any one of them as he chose. It had not made his ordeal easier, starting again under the eyes of strangers, in what had seemed a vast ship after *Larne*. A company of two hundred and seventy officers, seamen and Royal Marines: a world of difference.

One man had made it possible for him: Troughton. *Indomitable*'s company had watched in disbelief as their new and hideously scarred captain had embraced the man, who had been crippled by the same broadside that had burst in on Tyacke's yelling, sweating gun crews, at what they now called the Battle of the Nile. Troughton had been a young seaman then. Tyacke had always believed him dead, as most of those around him had died when his world had exploded, and left him as he was now.

Now even Troughton was gone. Tyacke had not known until two days after the fight with the Americans. He did not even know where he had come from, or if there was anyone to mourn him.

He felt a slight movement against his cheek, the wind returning. York might be proved right yet again. He was fortunate to have such a sailing-master: York had served as master's mate in this ship, and had won promotion in the only way Tyacke truly respected, through skill and experience.

So the fog would clear, and they would see the harbour once more, the ships and the town, and the well-sited central battery that would repulse any attempt, even by the most foolhardy commander, to cut out an anchored merchantman or some of the American prizes which had been brought here.

Forlorn, and in much the same condition as she had been after the battle, the American frigate *Baltimore* was beyond recovery. Perhaps she would be used as a hulk or stores vessel. But isolated and partly aground as she was now, she was a constant reminder of the day when America's superior frigates had been challenged and beaten.

Sir Richard Bolitho would be back soon. Tyacke hesitated in his regular pacing. Suppose he was directed elsewhere? The Admiralty was never averse to changing its collective mind. In dispatches brought by the last courier brig Tyacke had been warned of Valentine Keen's impending arrival in Halifax: he would hoist his flag in *Valkyrie*, another converted two-decker like *Indomitable*, with Adam Bolitho as his flag captain. It was still hard to fathom why *he* would want to come back to these waters. Tyacke was acquainted with Keen, and had attended his wedding, but he did not consider that he knew him as a man. This would be his first command as a flag-officer: he might be out for glory. And he had recently lost both wife and child. Tyacke touched his burned face again. It could scar a man more deeply than others might realize.

He saw a guardboat pulling abeam, the armed marines straightening their backs in the sternsheets as *Indomitable* took shape above them through the thinning fog.

He returned his mind to *Valkyrie*, still invisible in the misty harbour. Peter Dawes was her present captain, and acting-commodore until Keen's arrival: he was a post-captain, young, approachable, competent. But there were limits. Dawes was an admiral's son, and it was rumoured that he would be raised to flag rank as soon as he was replaced here. Tyacke had always nursed doubts about him, and had told Bolitho openly that Dawes might prove reluctant to risk his reputation and the prospect of promotion when they most needed his support. It was all written in the log now: history. They had fought and won on that terrible day. Tyacke could recall his own fury and despair: he had picked up a discarded boarding axe and had smashed it into one of *Unity*'s ladders. His own words still came in the night to mock him. *And for what?*

He knew Bolitho had warned others about the difference. This was not a foreign enemy, no matter what the flags proclaimed. Not French, or Dutchman, or Spaniard, the old and familiar adversaries. You heard the same voices as your own from these settlers in the new world, who were fighting for what they considered their freedom. Accents from the West Country and the Downs, from Norfolk and Scotland: it was like fighting your own flesh and blood. That was the vital difference in this war.

On one of his visits to *Valkyrie* Tyacke had aired his

views on Bolitho's recall to London. He had not minced his words. Senseless, he had called it. Bolitho was needed here, to lead, and to exploit their hard-won victory.

He had paced the big cabin while Dawes had sat at his table, an expensive glass held in one hand. Amused? Indifferent?

Tyacke had added, 'The weather will ease soon. The Yankees will need to move. If they can't win by sea, they'll press on by land. They'll be able to bring artillery right up to the Canadian frontier.'

Dawes had shaken his head. 'I think not. Some kind of settlement will be negotiated. You really should give their lordships more credit, both for what they are and what they know.'

Tyacke had barely heard him. 'Our soldiers captured Detroit with the whole Yankee army defending it. Do you really think they'll not use every means to retake it, and give our soldiers a bloody nose for their trouble?'

Dawes had been suddenly impatient. 'There are great lakes to cross, rivers to navigate, forts to breach before they can do that. Do you imagine that our American cousins, the "Yankees" as you so colourfully call them, will not measure the cost of such foolhardy action?'

Apart from discussing an invitation to the local army commander-in-chief's Christmas reception, which Tyacke had declined to attend, they had scarcely spoken since.

Becoming an admiral was more important to Dawes than anything, and it was beginning to look as if doing nothing and keeping the main part of the squadron tied up in Halifax was far more attractive than behaving with any initiative that might rebound on him personally, and be seen as folly or worse.

Tyacke began to pace again. Out there, like it or not, there were enemy ships, and they were a constant threat. Dawes had only permitted local patrols, and then had detached nothing larger than a brig, claiming that Adam

Bolitho's escape and vengeful attack in *Zest*, and Bolitho's personal victory would have made the Americans think again before attempting once more to harass convoys between Halifax and the West Indies. Napoleon was on the retreat: the dispatches were full of it. Tyacke swore angrily. He had been hearing that same story for so many years, from the time when Napoleon had landed his army in Egypt, and French fire had burned his face away.

It was all the more reason for the Americans to act now, and without further delay, while British forces and a whole fleet that could otherwise be released for these waters were concentrated on the old enemy, France.

And when peace came, that impossible dream, what would he do? There was nothing in England for him. He had felt like a stranger on his last visit, when he had been given *Indomitable*. Africa, then? He had been happy there. Or was that only another delusion?

He saw the first lieutenant, John Daubeny, waiting to catch his eye. Tyacke had toyed with the idea of accepting a more senior officer to replace Scarlett. Daubeny, like most of the wardroom, was young, perhaps too young for the post of senior lieutenant. Dawes had suggested that one of his own lieutenants be appointed. Tyacke grinned fiercely. That must have decided it. In any case, Daubeny had matured on that September day, like most of them. It was the navy's way. A man died or was transferred: another took his place. Like dead men's shoes after a hanging. Even the pompous Midshipman Blythe, who had been confirmed lieutenant and was now the most junior officer aboard, had proved both efficient and attentive to detail, to Tyacke's surprise, and his own division of seamen, who had known his arrogance as a midshipman, had shown him a grudging respect. They would never like him, but it was a beginning, and Tyacke was satisfied.

'Yes, Mr Daubeny?'

Daubeny touched his hat. 'We shall complete stowage today, sir.'

Tyacke grunted, picturing his ship at a distance, her trim in the water, gauging the feel of her.

He said, 'Tell my cox'n to prepare the gig when it's time. I'll go around her once more. We might still have to move some of that extra powder and shot further aft.' He was not aware of the pride that had crept into his voice. 'This lady will want to fly when she finds open water again!'

Daubeny had noticed. He knew he would never be close to the captain: Tyacke kept his emotional distance, as if he were afraid to reveal his true feelings. Only with Sir Richard Bolitho had Daubeny ever seen him change, had sensed the warmth, the unspoken understanding and obvious respect of each for the other. He recalled them together, here, on this same untroubled deck. It was hard to believe that it had happened, that such chilling sights were possible. His inner voice spoke for him. *That I survived.*

He said, 'I shall be glad to see Sir Richard's flag hoisted again, sir.'

He did not even flinch when Tyacke faced him, as he had once done. How much worse it must be for him, he thought. The stares, the revulsion, and yes, the disapproval.

Surprisingly, Tyacke smiled. 'You speak for us both, Mr Daubeny!'

Tyacke turned away as York, the sailing-master, emerged from the companion, without a glance at the receding fog.

'You were right, Mr York! You have brought better weather for us!' Then he held up his hand and said sharply, 'Listen!' The hammering and the muted thuds between decks had stopped. Only six months since that last ball had smashed into the carnage of broken men. They had done well.

York studied him gravely. So many times in the last two years he had watched the captain's moods, his anguish and his defiance. He had once heard Tyacke say of Sir Richard Bolitho, 'I would serve no other.' He could have said the same himself, of this brave, lonely man.

He said, 'Then we're ready, sir!'

Daubeny was listening, sharing it. At first he had thought he would be unable to fill Lieutenant Scarlett's shoes after he had fallen. He had even been afraid. That was yesterday. Now Scarlett was just another ghost, without substance or threat.

He stared up at the furled sails, moisture pouring from them like tropical rain. Like the ship, *the Old Indom* as the sailors called her, he was ready.

Three weeks outward bound from Portsmouth, Hampshire to Halifax, Nova Scotia, His Britannic Majesty's Ship *Wakeful* was within days of her landfall. Even Adam Bolitho, with all his hard-won experience as a frigate captain, could not recall a more violent passage. February into March, with the Atlantic using every mood and trick against them.

Although it was *Wakeful*'s young captain's first command, he had held it for two years, and two years in a frigate used almost exclusively for carrying vital dispatches to flag-officers and far-flung squadrons was equal to a lifetime in a lesser vessel. South-west and into the teeth of the Atlantic gales, with men knocked senseless by incoming seas, or in danger of being hurled from the upper yards while they kicked and fisted half-frozen canvas that could tear out a man's fingernails like pips from a lemon. Watchkeeping became a nightmare of noise and cruel discomfort; estimating their daily progress, unable even to stream the log, was based on dead reckoning, or, as the sailing-master put it, by guess and by God.

For the passengers down aft, it was uncomfortable but strangely detached from the rest of the ship and her weary company, piped again and again to the braces or aloft to reef the sails when they had only just been given a moment's rest in their messes. Simply trying to carry hot food from the swaying, pitching galley was a test of skill.

Sealed off from the life of the ship, and her daily fight against the common enemy, Adam and his new flag officer remained curiously apart. Keen spent most of his time reading his lengthy instructions from the Admiralty, or making notes as he studied various charts beneath the wildly spiralling lanterns. They burned day and night: little light penetrated the stern windows, which were either streaming with spume from a following gale, or so smeared with salt that even the rearing waves were distorted into wild and threatening creatures.

Adam could appreciate all of it. Had *Wakeful* been an ordinary fleet frigate she would likely have been shorthanded, or at best manned by unskilled newcomers, snatched up by the press or offered for duty by the local assize court. This required trained seamen, who had worked together long enough to know the strength of their ship and the value of their captain. He had thought often enough, *as Anemone had been*.

Whenever he could be spared from his duties Captain Hyde had made it his business to visit them. No wonder he had not hesitated to offer his own quarters for their use: Hyde spent as many, if not more, hours on deck than any of his men.

Whenever possible Adam had sat with Keen in the cabin, and had washed down the wardroom fare with a plentiful supply of wine. To expect anything hot to drink was out of the question. The wine, however, had added no intimacy to their conversations.

Hyde must have noticed that Keen had made no impossible demands, and had not once complained of discomfort, nor had he requested a change of tack to seek out calmer waters even at the expense of losing time. It was obviously something which had surprised Hyde, in spite of Adam's first description of the admiral.

On one rare occasion when Hyde had given up the fight, and *Wakeful* had lain hove-to under storm canvas waiting for the weather to ease, Keen had seemed willing to share his confidences. Afterwards, Adam thought it might have been easier for both of them if they had been total strangers.

Keen had said, 'I cannot tell you how pleased I was to have your letter of agreement to this appointment. We have known one another for a long time, and we have shared and lost many good friends.' He had hesitated, perhaps thinking of *Hyperion*; he had been Bolitho's flag captain when the old ship had gone down, with her flag still flying. 'We have seen fine ships destroyed.' They had listened to the wind, and the sea hissing against the stern windows like a cave of serpents. 'The sea is no less a tyrant than war, I sometimes think.'

He had seemed to want to talk, and Adam had found himself studying his companion with new eyes. When Keen had been piped aboard at Portsmouth with full honours, and the port admiral to welcome him in person, Adam had felt the old hurt and resentment. Keen had worn no mark of mourning, either then or since. Nor had he mentioned Zenoria, other than to acknowledge the port admiral's meaningless murmurs of condolence.

Keen had said, 'When I was your uncle's flag captain, even though I had known him since I was a lowly midshipman, I was uncertain of the measure of confidence between us. Perhaps I did not understand the true difference between the position of flag captain, and a captain like our youthful Martin Hyde. Sir Richard showed me the way, without favour, and without overriding my own opinions merely to exercise the privileges of rank. It meant a great deal to me, and I hope I did not disappoint his trust.' He had smiled, rather sadly. 'Or his friendship, which means so much to me, and which helped to save my mind.'

He could not think of them together. Keen, always so outwardly assured, attractive to women, his hair so fair that it looked almost white against his tanned features. But . . . as lovers. . . . He was repulsed by it.

The boy John Whitmarsh, legs braced against the movement of the deck and lower lip pouting with concentration, had carried more wine to the table.

Keen had watched him, and after he had departed had said absently, 'A pleasant youth. What shall you do with him?' He had not waited for, or perhaps expected, an answer. 'I used to plan things for my boy, Perran. I wish I had had more time to know him.'

The table had been cleared by Whitmarsh and one of the captain's messmen. He had said quietly, 'I want you to feel you can always speak your mind to me, Adam. Admiral and captain, but most of all friends. As I was, and am, with your uncle.' He had seemed uneasy, disturbed then by some thought. 'And Lady Catherine – that goes without saying.'

And then, eventually, *Wakeful* had changed course, northwest-by-north to take full advantage of the obliging Westerlies as, close-hauled, they started on the last leg of their journey.

Of Halifax Keen had remarked, 'My father has friends there.' Again a note of bitterness had crept into his voice. 'In the way of trade, I believe.' Then, 'I just want to be doing something. Peter Dawes might have fresh information by the time we arrive.'

On another occasion, when they had been free to walk the quarterdeck, and there had even been a suggestion of sunlight on the dark, rearing crests, Keen had mentioned Adam's escape, and John Allday's son, who had risked everything to help him, only to fall in the battle with *Unity*. Keen had paused to watch some gulls skimming within inches of the sea's face, screaming a welcome. He had said, 'I remember when we were together in the boat after that damned *Golden Plover* went down.' He had spoken with such vehemence that Adam had felt him reliving it. 'Some birds flew over the boat. We were nearly finished. But for Lady Catherine I don't know what we would have done. I heard your uncle say to her, *tonight those birds will nest in Africa*.' He had looked at Adam without seeing him. 'It made all the difference. Land, I thought. We are no longer alone, without hope.'

As the miles rolled away in *Wakeful*'s lively wake, Adam had shared few other confidences with his new rear-admiral. Others might look at him and say, there is a favoured one, who has everything. In fact, his rank was all he had.

And then, on that last full day when they had both been on deck, the air like knives in their faces.

'Have you ever thought of getting married, Adam? You should. This life is hard on the women, but I sometimes think. . . .'

Mercifully, the masthead had yelled, 'Deck there! Land on th' weather bow!'

Hyde had joined them, beaming and rubbing his raw hands. Glad it was over, more so that he was ridding himself of his extra responsibilities.

'With good fortune we shall anchor in the forenoon tomorrow, sir.' He had been looking at the rear-admiral, but his words had been for Adam. The satisfaction of making a landfall. Even the ocean had seemed calmer, until the next challenge.

Keen had walked to the quarterdeck rail, oblivious to the idlers off-watch who were chattering, some even laughing, sharing the same elation at what they had achieved. Men against the sea.

He had said, without turning his head, 'You may hoist my flag at the mizzen at first light, Captain Hyde.' Then he did turn and face them. 'And, thank you.' But he had been looking past them, through them, as if he had been speaking to someone else.

Hyde had asked, 'May I invite you and Captain Bolitho to sup with my officers and me, sir? It is quite an occasion for us.'

Adam had seen Keen's face. Empty, like a stranger's.

'I think not, Captain Hyde. I have some papers to study before we anchor.' He made another attempt. 'My flag captain will do the honours.'

Perhaps it had been then, and only then, that the impact of his loss had really struck him.

It would have to be a new beginning, for them both.

Richard Bolitho walked across the cabin deck, and paused by the table where Yovell was melting wax to seal one of the many written orders he had copied.

'I think that will be an end to it for today.' The deck was rising again, the rudder-head thudding noisily as the transport *Royal Enterprise* lifted and then ploughed into another criss-cross of deep troughs. He knew Avery was watching him from the security of a chair which was lashed firmly between two ringbolts. A rough passage, even for a ship well used to such violence. It would soon be over, and still he had not reconciled himself, or confronted his doubts at the prospect of returning to a war which could never be won, but must never be lost. He was holding on, refusing to surrender, even when they were separated by an ocean.

He said, 'Well, George, we will dine directly. I am glad

I have a flag lieutenant whose appetite is unimpaired by the Atlantic in ill temper!'

Avery smiled. He should be used to it, to the man, by now. But he could still be surprised by the way Bolitho seemed able to put his personal preoccupations behind him, or at least conceal them from others. *From me.* Avery had guessed what the return to duty had cost him, but when he had stepped aboard the transport at Plymouth there had been nothing to reveal the pain of parting from his mistress after so brief a reunion.

Bolitho was watching the last of the wax dripping onto the envelope like blood before Yovell set his seal upon it. He had not spared himself, but he knew very well that by the time they reached Halifax and rejoined the squadron everything might have changed, rendering their latest intelligence useless. Time and distance were the elements that determined the war at sea. Instinct, fate, experience, it was all and none of them, and ignorance was often fatal.

Avery watched the sea dashing across the thick stern windows. The ship had been more comfortable than he had expected, with a tough and disciplined company used to fast passages and taking avoiding action against suspicious sails instead of standing to fight. The Admiralty orders made that very clear to every such vessel and her master: they were to deliver their passengers or small, important cargoes at any cost. They were usually underarmed; the *Royal Enterprise* mounted only some nine-pounders and a few swivels. Speed, not glory, was her purpose.

They had had only one mishap. The ship had been struck by a violent squall as she was about to change tack. Her fore topgallant mast and yard had carried away, and one of her boats had been torn from its tier and flung over the side like a piece of flotsam. The ship's company had got down to work immediately; they were used to such hazards, but her master, a great lump of a man named Samuel Tregullon, was outraged by the incident. A Cornishman from Penzance, Tregullon was intensely proud of his ship's record, and her ability to carry out to the letter the instructions of the men at Admiralty who, in his view, had likely never set foot on a deck in their lives. To be delayed with such an important passenger in his care, and a fellow Cornishman at that, was bad enough. But as he had confided over a tankard of rum during a visit to the cabin, another transport, almost a sister ship of his own, the *Royal Herald*, had left Plymouth a few days after them, and would now reach Halifax before them.

Bolitho had commented afterwards to Avery, 'Another old Cornish rivalry. I'll lay odds that neither of them can remember how it all began.'

Bolitho had asked him about London, but he had not pressed the point, for which Avery was grateful. During the long night watches when he had lain awake, listening to the roar of the sea and the protesting groan of timbers, he had thought of little else.

He had felt no sense of triumph or revenge, as he had once believed he would. Had she been amusing herself with him? Playing with him, as she had once done? Or had he imagined that, too? A woman like her, so poised, so confident amongst people who lived in an entirely different world from his own. . . . Why would she risk everything if she had no deeper feeling for him?

None of the repeated questions had been answered.

He should have left her. Should never have gone to the house in the first place. He looked across at Bolitho, who was speaking warmly with Yovell, more like old friends than admiral and servant. What would he think if he knew that his wife Belinda had been there that day, obviously just as at home in that elegant and superficial world as all the others?

Yovell stood up, and grimaced as the deck swayed over again. 'Ah, they were right about me, Sir Richard. I must be mad to share the life of a sailor!'

He gathered his papers and prepared to leave, perhaps to join Allday and Ozzard before the evening meal. Allday would be feeling the separation badly, and there would be a long wait for that first letter, which Avery knew he would bring for him to read aloud. Another precious link in the little crew: Allday was a proud man, and Avery had been touched by the simplicity and dignity of his request that Avery read to him the letters from Unis that he could not read for himself.

Would Susanna ever write to him? He wanted to laugh at his own pathetic hopes. Of course she would not. Within weeks she would have forgotten him. She had money, she had beauty, and she was free. But he would think of her again tonight....

He had tried to compare his position with that of Bolitho and his mistress, although he knew it was ridiculous. There was no comparison. Apart from that one memory, what had happened was a closed door, the finish of something which had always been hopeless.

He looked up, startled, afraid that he had missed something or that Bolitho had spoken to him. But they were as before, framed against the grey stern windows, the sea already losing its menace as the fading light obscured it.

Bolitho turned and looked at him. 'Did you hear?'

Yovell steadied himself against the table. 'Another storm, Sir Richard.'

'The glass says otherwise.' He tensed. 'There. Again.'

Yovell said, 'Thunder?'

Avery was on his feet. So unlike a ship of war; too long at sea with nothing but the sea to challenge you. Day after day, week in, week out. And then the boredom and the noisy routine were forgotten.

He said, 'Gunfire, sir.'

78

There was a rap on the door and Allday stepped into the cabin. He moved so lightly when he wanted to, for such a big man, and one who was in more pain from his old wound than he would ever admit.

Bolitho said, 'You heard, old friend?'

Allday looked at them. 'I wasn't sure, an' then.' He shook his shaggy head. 'Not a thing to lie easy on your mind, Sir Richard.'

Avery asked, 'Shall I go and speak with the master, sir?'

Bolitho glanced at the screen door. 'No. It is not our place.' He smiled at Ozzard, who had also appeared, a tray of glasses balanced in his hands. 'Not yet, in any case.'

Eventually Samuel Tregullon made his way aft, his battered hat clutched in one beefy hand like a scrap of felt.

'Beggin' yer pardon, Zur Richard, but ye'll be knowing about the guns.' He shook his head as Ozzard offered him a glass, not because he was involved with his ship but because he usually drank only neat rum. A sailor, from his clear eyes to his thick wrists and the hands that were like pieces of meat. Collier brig, Falmouth packet, one-time smuggler and now a King's man: what Bolitho's father would have described as *all spunyarn and marline spikes*.

Tregullon nodded briefly as Ozzard replaced the glass with a tankard. 'Never fear, Zur Richard. I'll get you to Halifax as I was ordered, an' take you there I will. I can outsail any felon, theirs or ours!' He grinned, his uneven teeth like a broken fence. 'I'm too old a hand to be caught aback!'

After he had gone, the distant gunfire continued for half an hour and then stopped, as if quenched by the sea itself.

The master returned, grim-faced, to say that he was resuming course and tack. It was over.

Bolitho said suddenly, 'Yours is an experienced company, Captain Tregullon. None better at this work, I think you said?'

Tregullon eyed him suspiciously. 'I did, Zur Richard. That I did.'

'I think we should make every effort to investigate what we have heard. At first light the sea may ease. I feel it.'

Tregullon was not convinced. 'I have my orders, zur. They comes from the lords of Admiralty. No matter how I feels about it, I am not able or willing to change those orders.' He tried to smile, but it evaded him. 'Not even for you, zur.'

Bolitho walked to the stern windows and leaned against the glass. 'The lords of Admiralty, you say?' He turned, his face in shadow, the white lock of hair above his eye like a brushstroke. 'We're all sailors here. We all know there is someone far higher who controls our lives, and listens to our despair when it pleases Him.'

Tregullon licked his lips. 'I knows that, zur. But what can I do?'

Bolitho said quietly, 'There are men out there, Captain Tregullon. In need, and likely in fear. It may already be too late, and I am well aware of the risk to your ship. To you and your company.'

'Not least to you, zur!' But there was no fight in his voice. He sighed. 'Very well. I'll do it.' He looked up angrily. 'Not for you, with all respect, zur, an' not for His Majesty, bless his soul.' He stared at his crumpled hat. 'For *me*. It has to be so.'

Bolitho and Avery ate their meal in silence: the whole ship seemed to be holding her breath. Only the creak of the rudder and the occasional thud of feet overhead gave any hint that everything had changed.

At first light, as Bolitho had expected, the wind and sea eased; and with every available telescope and lookout searching for the presence of danger Tregullon shortened sail, and, arms folded, watched the darkness falling away and the sea eventually tinge with silver to mark each trough and roller.

Avery joined Bolitho on the broad quarterdeck, where he was standing in silence by the weather side, his black hair blowing unheeded in the bitter air. Once or twice Avery saw him touch his injured eye, impatient, even resentful that his concentration was interrupted.

Captain Tregullon joined him, and said gruffly, 'We tried, Zur Richard. If there was anything, we were too late.' He watched Bolitho's profile, seeking something. 'I'd best lay her on a new tack.'

He was about to shamble away when the cry came down, sharp and crisp, like the call of a hawk.

'Wreckage in th' water, sir! Lee bow!'

There was a lot of it. Planks and timber, drifting cordage and broken or upended boats, most of it charred and splintered by the fierceness of the bombardment.

Bolitho waited while the ship came into the wind, and a boat was lowered with one of the master's mates in charge.

There were a few dead, lolling as if asleep as the waves carried them by. The boat moved slowly amongst them, the bowman pulling each sodden corpse alongside with his hook and then quickly discarding it, unwilling, it seemed, to interrupt such a final journey.

Except for one. The master's mate took some time with it, and even without a glass Avery could see the dead face, the gaping wounds, all that was left of a man.

The boat returned and was hoisted inboard with a minimum of fuss. Avery heard the master pass his orders for getting under way again. Heavy, unhurried: the ship, as always, coming first.

Then he came aft and waited for Bolitho to face him. 'My mate knew that dead sailor, Zur Richard. I expect we knew most of 'em.'

Bolitho said, 'She was the *Royal Herald*, was she not?'

'She was, zur. Because of our losing the t'gallant mast she overreached us. They was waiting. They knew we was coming.' Then he said in a hoarse whisper, 'It was you they was after, Zur Richard. They wanted you dead.'

Bolitho touched his thick arm. 'So it would seem. Instead, many good men died.'

Then he turned and looked at Avery, and beyond him, Allday. 'We thought we had left the war behind, my friends. Now it has come to meet us.'

There was no anger or bitterness, only sorrow. The respite was over.

5

A Face in the Crowd

Bolitho put down the empty cup and walked slowly to the tall stern window. Around and above him, *Indomitable*'s hull seemed to tremble with constant movement and purpose, so unlike the transport *Royal Enterprise*, which he had left the previous afternoon. He peered through the thick glass and saw her lying at anchor, his practised eye taking in the movement of seamen on her yards and in her upper rigging, while others hoisted fresh stores from a lighter alongside. *Royal Enterprise* would soon be off again on her next mission, with her master still brooding over the brutal destruction of the other transport which had been so well known to him and his people, and less confident now that speed was all that was required to protect them from a determined enemy.

It was halfway through the forenoon, and Bolitho had been working since first light. He had been surprised and touched by the warmth of his reception. Tyacke had come in person to collect him from *Royal Enterprise*, his eyes full of questions when Tregullon had mentioned the attack.

He glanced now around the cabin, which was so familiar in spite of his absence in England. Tyacke had done some fine work to get his ship repaired and ready for sea, for even in harbour the weather did not encourage such activities. But now there was a little weak sunlight to give an illusion of warmth. He touched the glass. It *was* an illusion.

He should be used to it. Even so, the transformation was a tribute to *Indomitable*'s captain. Even here in his cabin, these guns had roared defiance: now each one was lashed snugly behind sealed ports, trucks painted, barrels unmarked by fire and smoke.

He looked at the empty cup. The coffee was excellent, and he wondered how long his stock would last. He could imagine her going to that shop in St James's Street, Number Three, part of the new world she had opened to him. Coffee, wine, so many small luxuries, which she had known he would not have bothered to obtain for himself, nor would any one else.

Keen would be coming aboard in an hour or so: he had sent word that he would be detained by a visit from some local military commander who wanted to discuss the improved defences and shore batteries. A casual glance at any map or chart would show the sense of that. Halifax was the only real naval base left to them on the Atlantic coast. The Americans had their pick, Boston, New York, Philadelphia, as well as scores of bays and estuaries where they could conceal an armada if they so desired.

He wondered how Adam was finding his appointment as flag captain. After the freedom of a solitary command, it might be just what he needed. Conversely, it might remain only a cruel reminder of what might have been.

He closed the canvas folder he had been studying, and considered Keen's report. A convoy of five merchantmen had been ordered to await a stronger escort off the Bermudas for their final passage to the West Indies. Until then, two brigs had been the only vessels Dawes had spared to defend them.

The convoy had never reached the Bermudas. Every ship must have been taken, or sunk.

When he met Keen, he would discover his real thoughts on the matter. The disaster had happened a few days after he had hoisted his flag in *Valkyrie*; there was nothing he could have done. But what of Dawes, acting commodore until Keen's arrival? Perhaps he had had his own reasons for allowing merchantmen to venture unprotected into an area which had become a hunting ground for enemy men-of-war and privateers alike.

He had consulted Tyacke, and Tyacke had not hesitated. 'Thinking too much of keeping his house in good order. I'm told that promotion can sometimes do that to a man.' Hard and blunt, like himself. Tyacke had even been scornful about his two new epaulettes. He had been promoted to post-captain, for rank only, the usual requirement of three years' service as captain having been waived as a mark of favour. 'I'm still the same man, Sir Richard. I think their lordships have a different set of values!' He had relented slightly. 'But I know your hand was in it, and that I do respect.'

Yes, it had surprised Bolitho that his return had, after all, been like a homecoming. And, despite what he hoped for, it was here that he belonged.

He had described the attack on *Royal Herald* and had watched Tyacke's scarred face, thoughtful, assessing each small piece of information and relating it to what he knew.

A prolonged bombardment, to catch and destroy the transport before she could find refuge in darkness. No one had heard the sound of a single shot fired in reply, not even a gesture or a final show of defiance. Nothing. It had been calculated murder. Had it been a trap set for *Royal Enterprise*? For him? Was it possible that a single mind had planned it so carefully, only to see it misfire through a fluke in the weather and an accident?

He had searched through every report Keen had gathered for him, knowing that they would be the first thing his admiral would want to see. Unless another man like Nathan Beer was abroad and at sea, unknown and undetected by the local patrols, which had been ordered to watch for any sudden ship movements, his theory seemed unlikely. But, so too was coincidence.

They wanted you dead.

Not another Nathan Beer, then. Perhaps there was no such officer with his wealth of experience and sense of honour. Beer had been a sailor first and foremost: to kill defenceless men, unable to resist, had never been his way. He wondered if his widow in Newburyport had received Beer's sword, which Bolitho himself had sent to her. Would she care? He found himself staring at the old family sword lying on its rack, where it received Allday's regular attention. Would that help Catherine, if the worst happened? He thought of the portrait she had commissioned for him. The real Catherine, she had called it. The painter had caught her exactly as she had wanted to be remembered, in the rough seaman's clothing she had worn in the open boat. Perhaps she would cherish the old sword. . . .

The door opened slightly, shaking him from his unwelcome thoughts, and Avery peered into the cabin. The brief stay in England had affected him deeply, Bolitho thought. He had always been withdrawn: now he had become remote, troubled and introspective. Bolitho had too much respect for George Avery to pry into it, and they had shared danger too often not to know that this unspoken understanding of one another was an anchor for them both.

Avery said, 'Signal from *Valkyrie*, Sir Richard. Rear-Admiral Keen is about to come over to us.'

'Tell Captain Tyacke, will you?'

Avery said gently, 'He knows.'

Bolitho reached for his heavy uniform coat. Irrationally, he disliked wearing it when he was working in his quarters, perhaps because he sometimes believed that it influenced his decisions, and made him think more like an admiral than a man.

It was true: Tyacke did seem to know everything that was happening in his ship. Maybe that was how he had overcome his resentment, fear, even, of taking command or becoming flag captain after the private world of *Larne*. The purser, James Viney, had been discharged as sick and unfit for further service at sea, and Bolitho suspected that Tyacke had guessed from the outset that Viney had been falsifying his accounts in connivance with equally dishonest chandlers. It was a common enough failing, but some captains were content to let it rest. Not James Tyacke.

He allowed his mind to stray again to the attack. Suppose it had been solely to kill him? He found that he could accept it, but the motive was something else. No single man could make so much difference. Nelson had been the only one to win an overwhelming victory by inspiration alone after he himself had fallen, mortally wounded.

Avery said abruptly, 'I meant to tell you, Sir Richard.' He glanced round, caught off-guard by the tramp of boots as the Royal Marines prepared to receive their visitor with full honours. 'It can wait.'

Bolitho sat on the corner of the table. 'I think it will not. It has been tearing you to pieces. Good or bad, a confidence often helps to share the load.'

Avery shrugged. 'I was at a reception in London.' He tried to smile. 'I was like a fish out of water.' The smile would not come. 'Your. . . . Lady Bolitho was there. We did not speak, of course. She would not know me.'

So that was it. Unwilling to mention it because it might disturb me. He found himself speculating on the reason for Avery's attendance.

'I would not be too certain of that, but thank you for

telling me. It took courage, I think.' He picked up his hat as he heard hurrying footsteps beyond the screen door. 'Especially as your admiral's mood has been far from pleasant of late!'

It was the first lieutenant, still very stiff and uneasy in his new role.

'The captain's respects, Sir Richard.' His eyes moved swiftly around the spacious cabin, seeing it quite differently from either of them, Avery imagined.

Bolitho smiled. 'Speak, Mr Daubeny. We are all agog.'

The lieutenant grinned nervously. 'Rear-Admiral Keen's barge has cast off, sir.'

'We will come up directly.'

As the door closed Bolitho asked, 'Then there was no attempt to involve you in scandal?'

'I would not have stood for it, Sir Richard.'

In spite of the deep lines on his face and the streaks of grey in his dark hair, he looked and sounded very vulnerable, like a much younger man.

Ozzard opened the door and they walked past him.

At the foot of the companion ladder, Bolitho paused and glanced at his flag lieutenant again with sudden intuition. *Or a man who was suddenly in love, and did not know what to do about it.*

When he crossed the damp quarterdeck he saw Tyacke waiting for him.

'A very smart turn-out, Captain Tyacke.'

The harsh, scarred face did not smile.

'I shall pass the word to the side-party, Sir Richard.'

Avery listened, missing nothing, thinking of the reception, the daring gowns, the arrogance. What did they know of men like these? Tyacke, with his melted face, and the courage to endure the stares, the pity and the revulsion. Or Sir Richard, who had knelt on this bloodied deck to hold the dying hand of an American captain.

How *could* they know?

88

The boatswain's mates moistened their silver calls on their lips, side-boys waited to fend off the smart green barge, the twin lines of scarlet marines swayed slightly on the harbour current.

It is my life. There is nothing more I want.

'Royal Marines! *Present....!*' The rest was lost in the din.

Again, they were of one company.

After the long day, and the comings and goings of officers and local officials paying their respects to the admiral, and the degrees of ceremony and respect that applied to each one of them, *Indomitable* seemed quiet, and at peace. All hands had been piped down for the night, and only the watchkeepers and the scarlet-coated sentries moved on the upper decks.

Right aft in his cabin, Bolitho watched the stars, which seemed to reflect and mingle with the glittering lights of the town. Here and there a small lantern moved on the dark water: a guardboat or some messenger, or even a fisherman.

The day had been tiring. Adam and Valentine Keen had arrived together, and he had been aware of the momentary uneasiness when they had been reunited with Tyacke and Avery. Keen had brought his new flag lieutenant as well, the Honourable Lawford de Courcey, a slim young man with hair almost as fair as his admiral's. Highly recommended, Keen had said, and intelligent and eager. Ambitious, too, from the little he had said; the scion of an influential family, but not a naval one. Keen had seemed pleased about it, but Bolitho had wondered if the appointment had been arranged by one of the many friends of Keen's father.

Adam had greeted him warmly, although reserved in front of the others, and Bolitho had sensed the depression he was trying to conceal. Keen, on the other hand, had been very concerned with the war, and what they might expect when the weather moderated. For the destruction of the *Royal Herald* he could offer no explanation. Most of the active American ships were in harbour, their presence carefully monitored by a chain of brigs and other, smaller commandeered vessels. Each of the latter might offer a fine chance of promotion to any young lieutenant if fortune smiled on him: such a chance had once come to Bolitho. He touched his eye, and frowned. It seemed an eternity ago.

He had walked around *Indomitable* with Tyacke, as much to be seen as to inspect the full extent of the overhaul. In her struggle with *Unity*, Tyacke's command had lost seventy officers, seamen and marines killed or wounded, a quarter of her company. Replacements had been found, taken from homeward-bound ships, and a surprising number of volunteers, Nova Scotians who had earned their living from the sea before marauding warships and privateers had denied them even that.

They would settle into *Indomitable*'s ways; but not until they were at sea, as close-knit as her original company used to be, would they know their true value.

Bolitho had seen the startled, curious eyes, those who had never met the man whose flag flew above all of them at the mainmast truck. And some of the older hands who had knuckled their foreheads, or raised a tarred fist in greeting to show that they knew the admiral, had shared the battle and its cost with him, until the enemy's flag had been dragged down through the smoke.

His total command had been christened the Leeward Squadron by Bethune, and their lordships had been more generous than he had dared to hope, giving him eight frigates and as many brigs. That did not include the heavily-armed *Valkyrie*, and *Indomitable*. In addition there were schooners, some brigantines, and two bomb vessels, the request for which the Admiralty had not even questioned. A strong, fast-moving squadron, and it would be joined by the old seventy-four gun ship of the line *Redoubtable*, which had been ordered to Antigua. With suitable intelligence gathered by the smaller patrol vessels on their endless stop-and-search missions, they should be a match for any new enemy tactics. The larger and better-armed American frigates had already proved their superiority, until *Unity* had met up with this ship. And even then. . . . But there was still something missing. He paced back and forth across the black and white squares of the canvas deck covering, his hair almost touching the massive beams. *Royal Herald* had been destroyed, so a ship or ships had avoided the patrols, and perhaps slipped out of harbour, taking advantage of the foul weather. It was pointless to brush it aside, or regard it as a coincidence. And if it had been a deliberate ambush gone wrong, what steps must he take? Very soon now, the Americans would have to launch a new attack. Tyacke had been convinced that it would be a military operation, straight into Canada. Once again, all the reports suggested that any such attack could be contained. The British soldiers were from seasoned regiments, but Bolitho knew from bitter experience in that other American war that often too much reliance was placed upon local militia and volunteers, or on Indian scouts unused to the ways of the hard-line infantryman.

Speed was essential to the Americans. Napoleon was in retreat, and each day of the campaign he was being deserted by friends and erstwhile allies. Surely his defeat was inevitable, perhaps even sooner than strategists in London dared to hope. And when that happened. . . . Bolitho heard again the confidence in Bethune's voice as he had explained how a French defeat would release many more ships to join the American conflict. But until that time. . . . He stopped pacing and strode to the quarter gallery, and stared down at the black, swirling current.

It must have been right there in Bethune's gracious rooms at the Admiralty, and yet neither of them had seen or considered it. He looked at the reflected lights until his eye watered. The carefully worded dispatches, the lists of ships and squadrons that daily protected the vital lifelines to Wellington's armies. Ships that fed his victorious regiments, and made even the smallest advance possible. Even Sillitoe had missed it, perhaps because it had not fitted into his intricate plans and the estimates with which he advised the Prince Regent. Arrogance, over-confidence: it would not be the first time that careful strategy had been undone by those in power who had seen only what they had wanted to see.

The flaw in the pattern of things, like a face in a crowd, there, but invisible.

All they had been able to see was Napoleon's eventual defeat. After twenty years of war it had, at last, seemed like the impossible landfall. He knew that Tyacke had made no attempt to conceal his disgust at Peter Dawes' handling of the squadron in his admiral's absence. Maybe Dawes was another one, blind to everything but his own advancement: promotion, which might vanish like mist if the war should suddenly end.

Bolitho considered his visitors. Keen, contained but enthusiastic at his new appointment, desperately eager to leave the past behind, to overcome his loss. Only Adam seemed unable or unwilling to forget it.

He heard something rattle behind the pantry hatch, a subtle signal from Ozzard that he was still about, in case he was required.

And what of me? So bitter at being parted from the woman he loved that he had failed to heed the instinct gained all those years ago as a frigate captain.

Maybe it was destined to end like this. He had opened the screen door without realizing that he had moved, and the marine sentry was staring at him, transfixed.

Their admiral, coatless despite the damp air between decks, who had only to raise a finger to have every man running to do his bidding. What was the matter with him?

Bolitho heard a murmur of voices from the wardroom. Perhaps Avery was there. Or James Tyacke, although he was probably working alone in his cabin. He never slept for more than an hour or two at a time. Surely there was some one he could talk to?

'Something wrong, Sir Richard?'

Bolitho let his arms fall to his sides. Allday was here, watching him, his shadow moving slowly back and forth across the new paintwork, his face devoid of surprise. As if he had known.

'I want to talk, old friend. It's nothing. . . . I'm not sure.' He turned to the ramrod sentry who was still staring at him, eyes popping, as if his collar was choking him. 'At ease, Wilson. There is nothing to fear.'

The marine swallowed. 'Yessir!' As he heard the door close he wiped his face with his sleeve. His sergeant would have given him hell just for doing that. But he had been with his squad in the maintop with the other marksmen when they had thundered alongside the enemy. Only for the moment, it meant nothing. He said aloud, 'Knew me name! He knew me name!'

Ozzard had poured a tankard of rum and placed it on the table, not too close, in case Allday should take the liberty of thinking that he was his servant as well.

Allday sat on the bench seat and watched Bolitho moving restlessly about the cabin as if it were a cage.

'You remember the Saintes, old friend?'

Allday nodded. Bryan Ferguson had asked him the same thing, while they had been waiting for Bolitho and his lady to return from London.

'Aye, Sir Richard. I recalls it well.'

Bolitho ran his hand down the curved timbers as if to feel the life, the heartbeat of the ship.

'This old lady was there, although I don't remember her, nor could I imagine what she might one day mean to me. Five years old, she was then.'

Allday saw him smile. Like some one speaking of an old comrade.

'So many miles, so many people, eh?' He turned, his face composed, even sad. 'But, of course, we had another ship then. *Phalarope*.'

Allday sipped his rum, although he did not remember reaching for it. There had been many moments like this, before the proud admiral's flags, the fame, and the bloody scandal. So many times. He watched him now, sharing it, very aware that he was one of the few that this man, this hero, could speak with so freely.

He would not be able to tell Unis about it, not until he was with her again. It would be out of the question to ask Lieutenant Avery to pen it for him. It would have to be later, at the right time, like the moment he had told her about his son's death. He glanced up at the closed skylight. *Just a few yards away.*

Bolitho said, 'Admiral Rodney broke the French line that day because the enemy's frigates failed to discover his intentions. Our frigates did *not* fail.'

His eyes were distant, remembering not so much the battle between the two great fleets as the slowness of their embrace, and the slaughter which had followed. He had seen too many such encounters, and he had felt like some physical assault the hostility of those at the Admiralty when he had said that the line of battle was dead. It must have sounded like blasphemy. *We'll not see another Trafalgar, I am certain of it.*

'It is every frigate captain's main concern – his duty – to discover, to observe, and to act.'

Ozzard frowned as the door opened slightly, and Avery hesitated, uncertain why he had come.

'I'm sorry, Sir Richard. I heard . . . somebody said. . . .'

Bolitho gestured to a chair. 'This time you did not have too far to come. Not like riding from Portsmouth to London!'

Avery took a goblet from Ozzard. He looked dishevelled, as if he had been trying to sleep when some instinct had roused him.

Allday, in the shadows, nodded. That was better. More like it.

Bolitho glanced around at them, his grey eyes keen. 'Captain Dawes did not see it, because there was nothing to see. He conserved the squadron's strength, as I so ordered, and repaired the vessels that most needed it. It was like a well-ordered plan, beyond doubt or question.'

Avery said, 'Do you believe that the outcome of the war is still undecided, sir?'

Bolitho smiled. 'We have been fighting one enemy or another for years, for some a lifetime. But always, the French were in the vanguard. Always the French.'

Allday frowned. To him one mounseer was much like another. The old Jacks could sing and brag about it when they'd had a skinful of rum, but when it came down to it, it had always been 'us' or 'them'.

'I ain't sure I follows, Sir Richard.'

'We are intent on defeating the French without further delay, so that we may bring naval reinforcements to these waters to contain the Americans. In turn, the Americans must break our line before that happens. I believe that the *Royal Herald* was destroyed by an unknown force of ships, American or French, maybe both, but under one leader, who will settle for nothing less than the destruction of our patrols and, if need be, our entire squadron.'

Captain James Tyacke was here now, his scarred face in shadow, his blue eyes fixed on Bolitho.

'In all the reports there is no mention of any American resentment at a new French presence, and yet we have missed or overlooked the most obvious fact, that war makes strange bedfellows. I believe that an American of great skill and determination is the single mind behind this venture. He has shown his hand. It is up to us to find and defeat him.' He looked at each of them in turn, conscious of the strength they had given him, and of their trust.

'The face in the crowd, my friends. It was there all the time, and no one saw it.'

Captain Adam Bolitho walked to the quarterdeck rail and watched the afternoon working parties, each separated by craft and skill, gathered around a portion of the main deck like stall holders: no wonder it was often called the market-place. *Valkyrie* was big for a frigate, and like *Indomitable* had begun life as a small third-rate, a ship of the line.

He had met all his officers both individually and as a wardroom at a first, informal meeting. Some, like John Urquhart, the first lieutenant, were of the original company, when *Valkyrie* had been commissioned and had hoisted his uncle's flag, then a vice-admiral's, at the foremast truck. To all accounts she had been an unhappy ship, plagued with discontent and its inevitable companion of flogging at the gangway, until her last, famous battle, and the destruction of the notorious French squadron under Baratte. Her captain, Trevenen, had been proved a coward, so often the true nature of a tyrant, and had vanished overboard under mysterious circumstances.

Adam glanced up at Keen's flag, whipping out stiffly from the mizzen. Here and here, men had died. His uncle had been injured, momentarily blinded in the undamaged eye, the battle lost until Rear-Admiral Herrick, who had been recovering from the amputation of his right arm, had burst on deck. Adam stared at the companion and the unmanned wheel. He could picture it as if he himself had been here. Lieutenant Urquhart had taken charge, and had proved what he could do. A quiet, serious officer, he would soon be given his own command if they were called to action.

He watched the working parties, knowing that every man jack was well aware of his presence. *The new captain*. Already known, because of his achievements in *Anemone* and because of the family name, and the admiral who was rarely out of the news. But to these men, he was simply their new superior. Nothing which had preceded him mattered, until they had learned what he was like.

The sailmaker and his mates were here, cross-legged, busy with palms and bright needles. Nothing was ever wasted, be it a sail ripped apart in a gale or the scrap that would eventually clothe a corpse for its final journey to the sea-bed. The carpenter and his crew; the boatswain making a last inspection of the new blocks and tackles above the boat tier. He saw the surgeon, George Minchin, walking alone on the larboard gangway, his face brick-red in the hard afternoon light. Another man whose story was unknown. He had been in the old *Hyperion* when she had gone down, with Keen as her captain. The navy was like a family, but there were so many missing faces now.

Adam had been on deck at first light when *Indomitable* had weighed, and sailed in company with two other frigates and a brig. She had made a fine sight, towering above the other ships with her pyramids of sails straining and hardening like armoured breastplates in a sharp north-westerly. He had lifted his hat, and had known that his uncle, although unseen, would have returned their private salute. In one way, he envied Tyacke his role as Bolitho's flag captain, even as he knew it would have been the worst thing he could have attempted. This was his ship. He had to think of her as his sole responsibility, and Keen's flag made it an important one. But it would go no further. Even if he tried, he knew he would never love this ship as he had loved *Anemone*.

He thought of Keen, and the sudden energy which had surprised all those accustomed to a more leisurely chain of command. Keen had been ashore often, not merely to meet the army commanders but also to be entertained by the senior government and commercial representatives of Halifax.

Adam had accompanied him on several occasions, as a duty more than out of curiosity. One of the most important people had been Keen's father's friend, a bluff, outspoken man who could have been any age between fifty and seventy, and who had achieved his present prominence by sweat rather than influence. He laughed a good deal, but Adam had noticed that his eyes always remained completely cold, like blue German steel. His name was Benjamin Massie, and Keen had told Adam that he was well known in London for his radical ideas on the expansion of trade in America, and, equally, for his impatience at anything that might prolong the hostilities.

He was not the only person here known to Keen. Another of his father's friends had arrived earlier, with an open-handed commission from the Admiralty to examine the possibilities of increased investment in shipbuilding, not only for the navy, but with the immediate future in mind and with an eye to improving trade with the southern ports. *The enemy* was a term that did not find favour with Massie and his associates.

So what would happen next? Keen had arranged local patrols in a huge box-shaped zone that stretched from Boston to the south-west, and Sable Island and the Grand Banks six hundred miles in the opposite direction. A large area, yes, but not so vast that each patrol might lose contact with the other if the enemy chose to break out of port, or that Halifax-bound convoys or individual ships could be ambushed before they reached safety. Like the *Royal Herald*. A deliberate, well-planned attack with the sole intention of killing his uncle. He was not certain if Keen accepted that explanation. He had remarked, 'We will assess each sighting or conflict at its face value. We must not be dragooned into scattering and so weakening our flotillas.'

A master's mate touched his hat to him, and Adam tried to fix his name in his mind. He smiled. Next time, perhaps.

He heard a light step on the quarterdeck, and wondered why he disliked the new flag lieutenant so much when they had barely spoken. Perhaps it was because the Honourable Lawford de Courcey seemed so much at home with the sort of people they had met ashore. He knew who was important and why, who could be trusted, and who might rouse disapproval as far away as London if he were crossed or overruled. He would be perfectly at home at Court, but in the teeth of an enemy broadside? That remained to be seen.

He steeled himself. It did not matter. They would put to sea in two days' time. It was probably what they all needed. *What I need*.

The flag lieutenant crossed the deck and waited to be acknowledged.

'The admiral's compliments, sir, and would you have his barge lowered.'

Adam waited. When de Courcey said nothing more, he asked, 'Why?'

De Courcey smiled. 'Rear-Admiral Keen is going ashore. Mr Massie wishes to discuss some matters. There will be a social reception also, I believe.'

'I see. *I* wish to discuss an additional patrol with the

99

admiral.' He was angry, more with himself for rising to de Courcey's bait. 'It is what we are here for, remember?'

'If I may suggest, sir. . . .'

Adam looked past him at the town. 'You are the admiral's aide, Mr de Courcey. Not mine.'

'The admiral would like you to accompany him, sir.'

Adam saw the officer of the watch studying the land with his telescope, and doubtless listening to the terse exchange as well.

'Mr Finlay, pipe away the admiral's barge, if you please.' He heard the shrill calls, the immediate stampede of bare feet and the bark of orders: so much a part of him, and yet he felt entirely detached from it. It was not de Courcey's fault. Adam had been a flag lieutenant himself: it had never been an easy role, even when you served a man you loved.

He turned, with some vague intention of clearing the air between them, but the fair-haired lieutenant had vanished.

Later, when he made his way aft to report that the barge was alongside, Adam found Keen dressed and ready to leave the ship.

He studied Adam thoughtfully, and said, 'I have not forgotten about the extra patrol, you know. We should have more news when the schooner *Reynard* returns. She was sent up to the Bay of Fundy, although I think it an unlikely place for the enemy to loiter.'

'De Courcey told you, did he, sir?'

Keen smiled. 'His duty, Adam.' He became serious again. 'Be patient with him. He will prove his worth.' He paused. 'Given the chance.'

There were thumps from the adjoining cabin, and two seamen padded past carrying what was obviously an empty chest to be stowed away.

Keen said, 'I am settling in, you see. Not a ship of the line, but she will suffice for the present. . . . It was sug-

100

gested that I should take quarters ashore, but I think not. Speed is everything.'

Adam waited. Who had suggested it? He saw his youthful servant John Whitmarsh helping a couple of the messmen to unpack another chest.

Why cannot I be like him? Lose myself in what I do best?

There was a small, velvet-covered book on the table. He felt a sudden chill, as though awakening from a cruel dream.

Keen saw his eyes, and said, 'Poetry. My late.... It was packed in error. My sister is unused to the requirements of war.'

My late.... Keen had been unable even to speak Zenoria's name. He had seen the book that day when he had visited her in Hampshire on some pretext. When she had rejected him.

Keen said, 'Are you interested?'

He was surprised at his own calmness, the complete emptiness he felt. Like watching some one else in a mirror.

'It is my intention that young Whitmarsh should learn to read. It might help, sir.'

He picked up the book, hardly daring to look at it.

Keen shrugged. 'Well, then. Some use after all.' Then, 'You will accompany me, Adam?'

He could even smile. 'Yes, sir.' He felt the soft velvet in his fingers, like skin. Like her. 'I shall fetch my sword directly.'

In his cabin, he pressed his back to the door and very slowly raised the book to his lips, amazed that his hands were so steady.

How could it be? He closed his eyes as if in prayer, and opened them again, knowing that it was the same book.

He held it with great care, all the ship noises and

movements suddenly stilled, as though he were in another world.

The rose petals, pressed tightly in these pages for so long, were almost transparent, like lace or some delicate web. The wild roses he had cut for her that day in June, when they had ridden together on his birthday. When she had kissed him.

He closed the book and held it to his face for several seconds. There was no escape after all. He put the book into his chest and locked it: it was an unbelievable relief to discover that he had never wanted to escape from her memory. He straightened his back, and reached for his sword. *From Zenoria.*

6

Bad Blood

Standing like a perfect model above her own reflection, His Britannic Majesty's Ship *Reaper* would have held the eye of any casual onlooker, no less than a professional seaman. A twenty-six gun frigate, very typical of the breed which had entered the revolutionary war with France some twenty years earlier, *Reaper* retained the sleek lines and grace of those ships which, then as now, were always in short supply. To command such a ship was every young officer's dream: to be free of the fleet's apron strings and the whim of every admiral, his real chance to prove his ability, if necessary against impossible odds.

By today's standards *Reaper* would appear small, not much bigger than a sloop of war, and certainly no match for the newer American frigates which had already proved their superiority in armament and endurance.

On this dazzling April day *Reaper* lay almost becalmed, her sails hanging with scarcely any movement, her masthead pendant lifeless. Ahead of her, on either bow, two of her longboats, their oars rising and falling like tired wings, attempted to hold her under command, to retain steerage way until the wind returned.

She was almost at the end of her passage, twelve hundred miles from Kingston, Jamaica, which had already taken her nearly two weeks. At dusk the previous day they had crossed the thirtieth parallel, and tomorrow at first light, if the wind found them again, they would sight the colourful humps of the Bermudas.

Theirs was escort duty, the curse of every fast-moving man-of-war, necessary but tedious, retrimming sails and trying to keep station on their ponderous charges: a test of any captain's forbearance. There was only one large merchantman to deliver to the Bermudas; the rest had been safely escorted to other ports in the Leeward Islands. The heavily-laden vessel, named *Killarney*, would eventually join a strongly defended convoy whose destination was England. Many a seaman had glanced at her motionless sails and felt envy and homesickness like a fever, merely by thinking about it.

Reaper's only consort was a small, sturdy brig, *Alfriston*. Like so many of her hard-worked class, she had started life in the merchant service, until the demands of war had changed her role and her purpose. With the aid of a telescope she could just be seen, well astern of the merchantman, completely becalmed and stern-on, like a helpless moth landed on the water.

But once rid of their slow-moving charge *Reaper* would be free, so why was she different from other frigates which had risen above all the setbacks and disasters of war to become legends?

Perhaps it was her silence. Despite the fact that she carried some one hundred and fifty officers, seamen and marines within her graceful hull, she seemed without life. Only the flap of empty canvas against her spars and shrouds, and the occasional creak of the rudder broke the unnatural stillness. Her decks were clean and, like her hull, freshly painted and well-maintained. Like the other ships which had fought on that September day in 1812, there was barely a mark to reveal the damage she had suffered. Her real damage went far deeper, like guilt. Like shame.

Aft by the quarterdeck rail *Reaper*'s captain stood with his arms folded, a stance he often took when he was thinking deeply. He was twenty-seven years old and already a post-captain, with a fair skin which seemed to defy the heat of the Caribbean or the sudden fury of the Atlantic. A serious face: he could have been described as handsome but for the thinness of his mouth. He was a man whom many would call fortunate, and well placed for the next phase of advancement. This had been *Reaper*'s first operational cruise after completing her repairs in Halifax, and it was his first time in command of her. A necessary step, but he knew full well why he had been appointed. *Reaper*'s previous captain, who had been old for his rank, a man of great experience who had left the more ordered world of the Honourable East India Company to return to service in the fleet, had fallen victim to the ruthlessness of war. *Reaper* had been raked at long range by the American's massive guns, in what was believed to have been a single broadside, although few who were there could clearly remember what had happened. *Reaper* had been almost totally dismasted, her decks buried under fallen spars and rigging, her company torn apart. Most of her officers, including her gallant captain, had died instantly; where there had been order, there had been only chaos and terror. Amongst the upended guns and splintered decks somebody, whose identity was still unclear, had hauled down the colours. Nearby, the battle had continued until the American frigate *Baltimore* had drifted out of command, with many of her people either killed or wounded. Commodore Beer's flagship *Unity* had been boarded and taken by Bolitho's seamen and marines. A very close thing, but in a sea fight there is only one victor.

Reaper could probably have done nothing more; she had already been passed by and left a drifting wreck. But to those who had fought and survived that day, she was remembered only as the ship which had surrendered while the fight had still raged around her. Their lordships knew the value of even a small frigate at this decisive stage of the war, and a ship was only as strong as the man who commanded her. Haste, expediency, the need to forget, each had played a part, but even on this bright spring morning, with the sun burning down between the loosely flapping sails, the feeling was still here. Less than half of *Reaper*'s people were from her original company. Many had died in the battle; others had been too badly wounded to be of any further use. Even so, to the rest of the tightly-knit squadron, *Reaper* was like an outcast, and her shame was borne by all of them.

The captain came out of his thoughts and saw the first lieutenant making his way aft, pausing here and there to speak with the working parties. They had grown up in the same town, and had entered the navy as midshipmen at almost the same time. The first lieutenant was an experienced and intelligent officer, despite his youth. If he had one failing, it was his readiness to talk with the hands, even the new, untrained landmen, as if they were on equal terms, or as equal as any one could be in a King's ship. That would have to change. *Reaper* needed to be brought to her proper state of readiness and respect, no matter what it cost. His mouth twitched. There was another link. He had asked for, and obtained, the hand of the first lieutenant's sister in marriage. His next command would be decided. . . . He broke off as the cry came from aloft. 'Signal from *Alfriston*, sir!'

The captain snapped to one of the attentive midshipmen, 'Take a glass up yourself and see what that fool is babbling about!'

The first lieutenant had joined him. 'The lookout has no skill with flags, I'm afraid, sir.'

'He'd better mend his ways, damn him, or I'll see his backbone at the gratings! It's probably nothing, anyway.'

Somebody called a command and a few seamen ran smartly to the boat tier to execute it. The first lieutenant had grown accustomed to it. The silence, the instant obedience, everything carried out at the double. Try as he might, he could not accept it.

The captain said, 'As soon as we receive orders and rid ourselves of *Killarney*, I shall want sail and gun drill every day, until we can cut the time it takes them to do every little thing. I'll not stand for slackness. Not from any man!'

The first lieutenant watched his profile, but said nothing. Did it so change an officer who had already held a successful command? *Might it change me?*

This afternoon there would be the ritual of punishment. Two more floggings at the gangway, both severe, but one of which could have been avoided or reduced to some lesser penalty. The staccato roll of drums, the crack of the lash on a man's naked back. Again and again, until it looked as if his body had been torn open by some crazed beast. . . .

When he had voiced his opinion about extreme punishment, often at the instigation of some junior officer or midshipman, the captain had turned on him. 'Popularity is a myth, a deceit! Obedience and discipline are all that count, to me and to my ship!'

Perhaps when they returned to Halifax, things might improve.

Almost without thinking, he said, 'It seems likely that Sir Richard Bolitho will have hoisted his flag in Halifax again, sir.'

'Perhaps.' The captain seemed to consider it, sift it for some hidden meaning. 'A flag-officer of reputation. But it has to be said that any admiral is only as strong as his captains – and how they perform.'

The first lieutenant had never served with or under Sir

Richard Bolitho, and yet, like the many he had spoken to, he felt as if he knew him personally.

The captain was smiling. 'We shall see, sir. We shall see.'

The midshipman's voice came shrilly from the mast-head. 'Signal from *Alfriston*, sir! *Sail in sight to the nor' west!*' A small pause, as if the midshipman was frightened of the noise. 'Brigantine, sir.'

The captain rubbed his hands briskly, one of his rare displays of emotion. 'Not one of ours, unless the dispatches are wrong.'

He swung round as the halliards and canvas came alive, the masthead pendant lifting as if suddenly awakened.

The first lieutenant exclaimed, 'The master was right, sir! The wind is coming back!'

The captain nodded. 'Recall the boats and have them hoisted. We are well upwind of friends and stranger alike. We'll add another prize to our list, eh?' He shaded his eyes to watch the two boats casting off the tow lines and pulling back toward their ship. 'Something for your sister's dowry!'

The first lieutenant was surprised at the swift change of mood. It would certainly break the monotony of this snail's pace.

He looked away as the captain added thoughtfully, 'Bring forward the punishment by an hour. It will keep them occupied, and remind them of their duty.'

Calls trilled and men ran to hoist the two dripping boats up and over the gangway while others dashed up the ratlines in readiness to make more sail, even as the slack canvas flapped and then boomed out harder to the wind. The lieutenant watched the sea's face, the black shadows of *Reaper*'s masts and sails blurring like ruffled fur while the hull heeled slightly, and then more firmly to the demands of wind and rudder.

The moment every frigate officer waits for. But the elation would not come.

Captain James Tyacke tucked his hat beneath his arm and waited for the marine sentry to admit him. For an instant, he saw a shadow through the screen door, and was amused. The ever-vigilant Ozzard, keeping a watchful eye out for visitors to these quarters.

He found Bolitho seated at the table, some charts with written notes on them held down by two books bound in green leather, with heavily gilded spines. Tyacke recognized them as some of the collection Lady Catherine Somervell had sent aboard for the admiral. Even here, thousands of miles from England, she was never far away from this restless, sensitive man.

'Ah, James!' He looked up and smiled warmly. 'I was hoping that you would sup with me tonight, and leave your troubles to your lieutenants for a change.'

Tyacke looked past him at the unbroken panorama of the ocean, blue and grey, disturbed here and there by long, glassy swells. In his mind's eye he saw them all, *Indomitable* in the centre, with the two frigates *Virtue* and *Attacker* some eight miles off either beam. At dusk they would draw closer to one another, but in this formation they could scan an imposing range from horizon to horizon. Tyacke could also visualize each captain, just as he knew Bolitho would feel the strength of every ship under his flag. Keeping well up to windward like a loyal terrier, the brig *Marvel* completed this small but effective flotilla.

Bolitho said, 'I can see from your expression, James, that you had forgotten the significance of this day.'

'For the moment, Sir Richard.' There was a brief silence. 'Two years ago, I took command of this ship.' He added quietly, as if it were something private, 'The Old Indom.'

Bolitho waited for him to seat himself. It was like a signal: Ozzard was moving out of his pantry. The flag captain would be staying a while.

Tyacke said, 'We've done a lot in that time.'

Bolitho looked at the leather-bound books, remembering her at Plymouth, in the coach when they had parted. 'I sometimes wonder where it will end. Or even if we are achieving anything by waiting, always waiting, for the enemy to show his teeth.'

'It will come. I feel it. When I was in *Larne*,' for a moment he hesitated as if it was still too painful a memory to discuss, 'the slavers had the whole ocean to pick and choose from. Every cargo of poor devils waiting to be shipped to the Indies and the Americas could be collected . . . or dropped overboard, if they were sighted by us or another patrol. But every so often . . .' He leaned forward in his chair, his scarred face suddenly clear and terrible in the reflected sunlight, 'I *knew*, like you knew about *Unity*. That sixth sense, instinct, call it what you will.'

Bolitho could feel the strength of the man, his deep pride in what he could do. Not something to be taken for granted, not a form of conceit, but true and real, like the old sword on its rack. As he had known in September, when they had walked the deck together, splinters bursting from the planking as sharp-shooters tried to mark them down, two men pacing up and down, making no attempt to conceal their ranks or their importance to those who depended upon them.

Avery, too, had walked with them that day. If he had any friend in this ship other than Bolitho himself, that friend was Tyacke. He wondered if he had confided his present preoccupation to him, and then knew he had not. Two men so different, and yet not dissimilar, each deeply reserved, driven in on himself. No, Avery would not have

110

discussed it with Tyacke, particularly if it concerned a woman.

Unconsciously he had touched the volume of Shakespearean sonnets; she had chosen this edition with care because the print was clear, easy to read. *So far away.* Spring in the West Country. Wagtails on the beach where they had walked; swifts and jackdaws; the return of beauty and vitality to the countryside.

Tyacke watched him, not without affection. Maybe it was better to be alone, with no one to draw your heart, or break it. To know no pain. Then he recalled Bolitho's woman boarding this ship, climbing the side like a sailor to the cheers of the men. It was not true. Just to have somebody, to know that she was there. . . . He pushed the thoughts aside: for him, they were impossible.

'I'd best go up and see the afternoon gun drill, sir.' He stood, his head brushing the deck beams. He did not appear to notice, and Bolitho knew that after *Larne*, *Indomitable* must seem like a palace.

He said, 'Until tonight, then.'

But Tyacke was staring at the screen door, one hand raised as if he was listening to something. They both heard measured steps, then the tap of the sentry's musket as he called, 'First lieutenant, *sir*!'

Lieutenant John Daubeny stepped into the cabin, his cheeks flushed from the salt air.

Tyacke said, 'I heard a call from the masthead. What is it?'

Bolitho felt the sudden tension. He had not heard the call himself. Tyacke had become part of the ship: he *was* the ship. In spite of his personal misgivings when he had been asked to command the flagship, they had become one.

Daubeny squinted his eyes, a habit of his when he was asked a direct or difficult question.

'Signal from *Attacker*, sir. Sail sighted to the nor' west.

111

A brig, one of ours.' He faltered under Tyacke's intense gaze. 'They are certain of it.'

Tyacke said curtly, 'Keep me informed. Muster a good signals party, and tell Mr Carleton to be ready.'

'I have attended to it, sir.'

The door closed, and Bolitho said, 'You have them well drilled, James. This newcomer – what d' you make of her?'

'We're not expecting a courier, sir. Not here. Not yet.' He was pondering aloud. 'At the Bermudas, now, that would be different. A convoy is assembling there, or should be.'

Bolitho shared it, remembering how it felt. Wanting to be up there on deck, and yet aware that it might be regarded as a lack of confidence in his officers, or that they might take his presence for anxiety. He vividly recalled his own time in command, and today was no different. When the watches changed, or the hands were piped to shorten sail, his whole being protested that he should remain aloof, a man apart from the ship that served him.

The sentry called, 'First lieutenant, *sir!*'

Daubeny came back in, more flushed than ever. 'She's the *Alfriston*, sir, fourteen guns. Commander Borradaile . . .'

Bolitho said quickly, 'I don't know him, do I?'

Tyacke shook his head. '*Alfriston* joined the squadron while you were in England, sir.' Then, as an afterthought, 'Borradaile's a good hand. Came up the hard way.'

Bolitho was on his feet. 'Signal *Attacker*, repeat *Alfriston, close on Flag*.' He glanced out through the thick glass. 'I want him here before nightfall. I can't waste another day.'

Daubeny's face was quite untroubled now that he had shifted the responsibility to his superiors. He offered, 'She should be with the Leeward escort, sir.' His confidence wilted under their combined attention. He added, almost humbly, 'It was in orders, sir.'

Tyacke said, 'So it was, Mr Daubeny. Now tell Mr Carleton to make the signal.'

Ozzard closed the door. 'Concerning supper, Sir Richard—'

'It might be delayed.' He looked at Tyacke. 'But we will take a glass now, I think.'

Tyacke sat again, his head still cocked to catch the muffled sounds from the world outside. The squeak of halliards, the voice of the signals midshipman penetratingly clear as he spelled out the signal to his men.

He said, 'You think it's bad, sir.' It was not a question.

Bolitho watched Ozzard approaching with his tray, his small figure angled against the movement of the deck without effort. The man without a past, or one so terrible that it clung to him like a graveyard spirit. So much a part of the little crew.

'I believe it may be our next move, James, albeit a foul one.'

They drank in silence.

Jacob Borradaile, the *Alfriston*'s commander, was not in the least what Bolitho had been expecting. He had been on deck to observe the brig's smart performance as she had tacked this way and that, her bulging sails salmon-pink in the failing light as she had wasted no time in taking position under *Indomitable*'s lee and sending a boat over the heavy swell.

Tyacke had remarked of Borradaile, *a good hand. Came up the hard way.* From him, there could be no higher praise.

As Tyacke escorted him aft into the cabin, Bolitho thought he had never seen such an untidy, awkward-looking figure. Although he must have been about the same age as Avery or Tyacke, he was like some gaunt caricature, with sprouting, badly-cut hair and deep, hollow eyes; only the ill-fitting uniform revealed him to be a King's officer. However, Bolitho, who had met every imaginable kind of man both junior and senior, was immediately impressed. He entered the cabin and took his outstretched hand without hesitation or any trace of awe. A firm grip, hard, like a true sailor's.

Bolitho said, 'You have urgent news.' He saw the man's quick assessment of him, as he might examine a new recruit. 'But first, will you take a glass with me?'

Borradaile sat in the chair Ozzard had carefully prepared in advance. 'Thank 'ee, Sir Richard. Whatever you're taking yourself will suit famously.'

Bolitho nodded to Ozzard. Borradaile had a faint Kentish accent, like his old friend Thomas Herrick.

He sat on the stern bench and studied his visitor. In his fist, the fine goblet looked like a thimble.

He said, 'In your own words. I will see that you are returned to your ship before too long.'

Borradaile stared at a sealed gunport as if he expected to see the brig across the uneasy strip of water. *Alfriston* had been handled well, as if one man and not an entire trained company had been in charge. Tyacke would be thinking much the same, remembering his previous command.

Borradaile said, 'It was *Reaper*, Sir Richard. A day out from Bermuda and she broke away to chase a stranger, a small vessel – brigantine, most likely. *Alfriston* was becalmed, sea like a mill pond, an' our one remaining charge, a company ship called *Killarney*, was no better than we. But *Reaper* had the wind under her skirts and gave chase.'

Bolitho asked quietly, 'Did that surprise you, so close to your destination?'

'I don't think so.'

Bolitho said, 'Man to man. This is important. To me, maybe to all of us.'

The hollow eyes settled on him. Bolitho could almost hear his mind working, weighing the rights and wrongs of something that might end in a court-martial. Then he seemed almost visibly to make a decision.

'*Reaper*'s captain was new to the ship, his first proper patrol away from the squadron.'

'Did you know him?' Unfair maybe, but also perhaps vital.

'Of him, sir.' He paused. '*Reaper* had a reputation. Maybe he was eager to give her back something he thought she'd lost.'

The shipboard noises seemed to fade away as Borradaile related the hours that had decided *Reaper*'s fate.

'There were two frigates, sir. French-built, if I'm any judge, but wearing Yankee colours. They must have sent the brigantine as bait, an' once *Reaper* changed tack to go after it, they showed themselves.' He ticked off the points on his bony fingers. '*Reaper* had run too far down to lee'ard to be able to claw back to her station. They must have been laughin', it was so damned easy for them.'

Bolitho glanced at Tyacke; he was resting his chin on his hand, and his face was like stone.

Borradaile added, 'I could do nothin', sir. We'd barely picked up the wind again. All I could do was watch.'

Bolitho waited, afraid of breaking the picture in the man's thoughts. It was not uncommon. A young captain eager for a prize, no matter how small, and eager too to prove something to his ship's company. He knew of *Reaper*'s bitterness after the battle, when her brave captain, James Hamilton, had been killed in the first broadside. It was so easy to be distracted for the few seconds needed by a skilful and dangerous enemy. *It nearly happened to me when I was so young. . . .*

Borradaile gave a great sigh. '*Reaper* came about as soon as her captain knew what had happened. I watched it all with a big signals glass – I felt I had to. It was madness, I thought. *Reaper* stood no chance, a little sixth-rate against two big 'uns, forty guns apiece was my guess. But what could he do? What would any of us do, I asked myself.'

'Did they engage immediately?'

Borradaile shook his head, his gaunt features suddenly saddened. 'There were no shots fired. Not one. *Reaper* had run out some of her guns by then, but not all of 'em. It was then that the leading Yankee hoisted a white flag for parley and dropped a boat to go across to *Reaper*.'

Bolitho saw it all. Three ships, the others merely spectators.

'An hour, maybe more, maybe less, an' the *Reaper* lowered her flag.' He spat it out angrily. 'Without so much as a whimper!'

'Surrendered?' Tyacke leaned forward into the light. 'Not even a fight?'

Alfriston's commander seemed to truly see him for the first time, and there was compassion in the hollow eyes as they noted the full extent of his injury. 'It was mutiny,' he said.

The word hung in the damp air like something obscene, devastating.

'The next thing I knew was, a boat was sent from *Reaper* with some of the "loyal men".' He turned to Bolitho again. 'And her captain.'

Bolitho waited. It was bad, worse than he had believed possible.

Borradaile spoke very slowly. 'Just before *Reaper* left her station to give chase there were men being flogged at the gangway. I could hardly believe it.' There was disgust and revulsion in his voice, from this, a man who had come up the hardest way of all, through the ranks, to achieve his own command. A man who must have seen every kind of suffering at sea, and brutality, too, in that demanding life below decks.

'Was he dead?'

'Not then, he weren't, sir. The Yankee officers who had gone over to parley had invited *Reaper*'s people to join them. I heard from some of the men who were allowed away in the boat that it was the old cry of "dollars for shillings" – the chance of a new life, better paid and well treated under the Stars and Stripes.'

Bolitho thought of Adam's *Anemone*. Some of her people had changed sides when the flag had come down. But this was different. It was not desertion, which was bad enough: it was mutiny.

'When they agreed, the Yankee told them they could punish their captain in the way they had suffered under his command. That's what they were doing all that time. First a few of the hard men, an' then it was like a madness. They seized him up and flogged him until he was in ribbons. Two hundred, three, who could say? *Alfriston* don't rate a surgeon, but we did what we could for him, an' his senior lieutenant who was stabbed when he tried to defend him. He'll probably live, the poor devil. I'd not be in his shoes for a sack of gold!'

'And then?'

'They boarded the *Killarney* an' stood away. I waited a while and then relaid my course for the Bermudas. I landed the survivors at Hamilton and made my report to the guardship. I was ordered to find an' report to you, sir.' He glanced around the spacious cabin as if he had not noticed it before. 'They could have taken *Alfriston*, too, if they'd a mind.'

Bolitho stood up and walked to the quarter gallery. He could just see the little brig's dark silhouette, her topgallant yards still faintly pink in the dying light.

'No, Commander Borradaile. You had to be the witness, the proof that a mutiny broke out. Perhaps it was provoked, but it can never be condoned. We who com-

117

mand must always be aware of the dangers. And you are here. That is the other reason.'

Borradaile said, 'To bring word to you, sir? That was my thought, also.'

Bolitho asked, 'And the captain?'

'He died, sir, finally. Cursin' and ravin' to the end. His last words were, *they'll hang for it!*'

'And so they will, if they are taken.' He crossed to the untidy figure and took his hand. 'You have done well. I shall see that it is mentioned in my dispatches.' He glanced at Tyacke. 'I'd offer you promotion, but I think you'd damn me for it first! Keep your *Alfriston.*' In his heart, he knew that Borradaile was glad to be rid of the men sent from the surrendered frigate. The shame was still there, deeper now than ever. Like a rotten apple in a barrel, it was better to be free of them.

'See Commander Borradaile over the side, James.' He watched them leave, then returned to the quarter gallery and thrust open a window. The air was surprisingly cold, and helped to steady him.

Avery, who had been present and mute throughout the discussion, observed quietly. 'A well-planned trap, a flag of truce, and mutiny provoked, if provocation were needed. And now, one of our ships under their flag.'

Bolitho faced him, his cheek wet with spray, like tears, cold tears.

'Speak out, man. Say what I know you are thinking!'

Avery lifted his shoulders in a very slight shrug. 'Justice, revenge, call it what we will, but I think I understand now what you said about the face in the crowd. To lure you into a trap, to provoke you into some reckless retaliation. It *is* you he wants.'

Bolitho listened to the trill of calls, as one captain paid his respects to another.

Avery, like Tyacke, probably shared the private conviction of the gaunt commander who had just departed: that

Reaper's captain had paid the just price of tyranny. He was not the first. Pray God he was the last.

He thought of the flag curling far above the deck and seemed to hear her voice. *My admiral of England.*

There was no doubt in his mind where the real responsibility would lie. Or the blame.

7

The Oldest Trick

Adam Bolitho hesitated outside the broad, imposing house and wondered impatiently why he had come. Another reception. Merchants, senior officers from the garrison, people who always seemed to know some one important and with influence. He could have made some excuse to stay aboard *Valkyrie*, but at the same time he knew he was too restless to remain in his cabin or pass an hour or so away with his lieutenants.

How Keen managed to appear unruffled by all these receptions and discussions surprised him. Adam had noticed that despite his good-natured manner and his apparent ease with this imposing people, he rarely lost his way, or allowed himself to be talked out of decisions he considered were in the best interests of his command.

Adam turned his back on the house and stared out across the great natural harbour; *chebucto*, the Indians had once called it. It impressed him as few others had done. From the glittering span of the Bedford Basin to the narrows at the far end, the harbour was teeming with ships, a forest of masts as visible proof of Halifax's growing strategic value. He had heard a general describe it as part of the British defensive square, which included England, Gibraltar and Bermuda. Cornwallis must have been as farseeing as he was shrewd when he had put his roots down here less than seventy years ago and built the first fortifications. Now, commanded by the hilltop citadel, it was further protected by Martello towers more commonly seen in Britanny or southern England, with smaller batteries to deter any enemy foolish enough to attempt a landing.

He looked towards the naval anchorage, but the house hid it from view. He had never believed that his duties as flag captain could be so frustrating. *Valkyrie* had barely ventured out of harbour, and then only to meet an incoming convoy with more soldiers: if they landed many more this peninsula must surely sink under the weight. There was little news of the war. Roads on the mainland were bad, some still impassable. He glanced at the fading light across the harbour, the tiny boat lanterns moving like insects. Here, conditions were already much better. He had even felt the sun's warmth on his face on his walk from the landing stage.

He turned reluctantly away from the sea. The big double doors had opened discreetly, as if they had been waiting for his decision.

A fine old house: not 'old' by English standards, but well proportioned and vaguely foreign, the architecture perhaps influenced by the French. He handed his hat to a bobbing servant and walked towards the main reception hall. There were uniforms aplenty, mostly red, with a few green coats of the local light infantry force. The house had probably been built by some prosperous merchant, but now it was used almost exclusively by people of a world he did not know, or want to. Where men like Benjamin Massie walked a challenging path between politics and the rewards of trade. He had made no secret of his impatience with the state of war between Britain and America, calling it 'unpopular', more as if it were a personal inconvenience than a bitter conflict between nations.

Adam spoke to a footman, his eyes taking in the

121

assembled throng, and noticing Keen's fair hair at the far end. He was with Massie. There were women present, too. That had been rare on previous occasions. Yes, he should have offered some excuse and remained on board.

'Captain Adam Bolitho!'

There was a momentary hush, more out of surprise at his lateness than from interest, he thought. At least the footman had pronounced his name correctly.

He walked down the side of the hall. There were heavy velvet curtains, and two great log fires: these houses were built with a Nova Scotia winter in mind.

'So here you are at last, Captain!' Benjamin Massie snapped his thick fingers and a tray of red wine appeared like magic. 'Thought you'd forgotten us!' He gave his loud, barking laugh, and once again Adam noticed the coldness of his eyes.

He said, 'The squadron's business, sir.'

Massie chuckled. 'That's the trouble with this place, more soldiers than labourers, more men-o'-war than cargoes! I'm told that a few years back there was five times as many brothels as banks!' He became serious instantly, as though a mask had fallen over his face. 'But it's changing. Just get this war over and we'll see some real expansion, whole new markets. And for that we'll need *ships*, and men willing to serve in them without the fear of violent death under an enemy broadside.' He winked. 'Or under the lash of some over-zealous officer, eh?'

Keen had approached them, and was listening. 'And what of my father's other friend? I thought he might meet me here.'

Adam looked at him. Keen had deliberately interrupted, to dampen down any open disagreement before it began. *Am I so obvious?*

'Oh, David St Clair?' He shook his head. 'He'll not be

back for some while yet. Impetuous, that's David. You know what he's like.'

Keen shrugged. 'I have seen little of him. I liked what I knew. Shipbuilding, with backing from the Admiralty – it sounded important.'

'Well, since his wife died. . . .' He touched Keen's sleeve. 'I forgot, Val. I'm sorry. . . .'

Keen said, 'I had heard. So he is travelling alone?'

Massie grinned, his clumsy remark dismissed from his mind. 'No. He's got his daughter with him, can you imagine that? I'll lay odds he's regretting having to mark time for a woman, even if she is family!'

Adam raised his glass, but paused as he saw Keen's expression. Surprise? It was deeper than that.

'I thought she was married.'

Massie took another glass from the tray. 'Nothing came of it. The intended husband was a soldier.'

Keen nodded. 'Yes. So I heard.'

'Well, he decided to follow the drum rather than a pretty ankle!' He gave a heavy sigh. 'Then, with her mother dying so suddenly, she decided to keep David company.'

Keen looked into the nearest fire. 'That's a risk, in my view.'

Massie brushed some droplets of wine from his coat. 'There, you see? You naval and military people regard everything as a hidden danger, part of some sinister strategy!' He glanced at the clock. 'Time to eat soon. Better go and pump the bilges before I give the word.' He walked away, nodding to an occasional guest, deliberately ignoring others.

Keen said, 'You don't care much for him, do you?'

Adam watched a tall woman with bare shoulders bending to listen to her smaller companion, then she laughed and nudged him. She could not have been more blatant if she had been stark naked.

He answered, 'Or those like him, sir.' He saw a footman drawing the vast curtains, hiding the dark water of the harbour from sight. 'Men are dying every hour of the day. It has to be for something more than profit, surely?' He broke off.

'Continue, Adam. Remember your uncle, and what he would say. There are no officers here. Just men.'

Adam put down his glass and said, 'Supplies, and escorts for the ships that carry them, keeping the sea-lanes open – all essential, but they will *never win a war*. We need to get to grips with them as we do with the French, and all the others we have had to fight, not just stand gloating over the prospects of trade and expansion when the bloody work is comfortably past!'

Keen said quietly, 'I wonder if you know how much like Sir Richard you are. If only. . . .' He looked away. 'Damnation!'

But it was not Massie: it was the flag lieutenant, de Courcey.

Adam wondered what Keen had been about to say, and why the lieutenant's arrival had disturbed his customary composure.

De Courcey exclaimed, 'I do apologize, sir, but someone came here, to this house, without any prior arrangement or excuse, and demanded to see you.' He sounded outraged. 'I sent him away with a flea in his ear, you may be sure!' His eyes moved to the footman who had taken his place on the stairs, a staff raised, ready to announce dinner. 'Most inconsiderate!'

Massie was thrusting through the throng like a plough. Keen said, 'Will you deal with it, Adam? I am the principal guest tonight, as you know.'

Adam nodded. He had not known. As he walked with de Courcey to the adjoining room, he asked sharply, 'Who is this intruder?'

'A damned ragged fellow, a scarecrow in the King's coat!'

'His *name*, man.' He controlled his anger with difficulty: everything seemed able to penetrate his defences. He had seen his lieutenants watching him, obviously wondering what was troubling him.

De Courcey said offhandedly, 'Borradaile, sir. Most uncouth. I cannot imagine how he ever. . . .'

He winced as Adam seized his arm. '*Alfriston*'s commander?' He tightened his grip so that de Courcey gasped aloud, and two passing soldiers paused with interest. 'Answer me, damn you!'

De Courcey recovered himself slightly. 'Well, yes, as a matter of fact. I thought that under the circumstances. . . .'

Adam released him and said, 'You are a fool.' He was amazed at how calm he sounded. 'How big a fool, we shall yet discover.'

De Courcey blinked as the footman's staff tapped the stairs three times.

Adam said, 'Wait here. I may want to send word to the ship.'

From another world came the cry, 'Pray be seated, ladies and gentlemen!'

'But, sir! We are expected!'

Adam said sharply, 'Are you deaf as well?' He turned, and walked toward the main entrance.

Meanwhile, Massie and his guests were arranging themselves around the two long tables, each place setting marked with a card, each place denoting the status of each guest or the magnitude of the favour being done.

Massie said significantly, 'I've delayed grace until your young captain can spare himself from his duties.'

Keen sat on Massie's right hand. Facing him was a woman whom he guessed was Massie's special guest. She was beautiful, self-assured, and amused by his scrutiny.

Massie said abruptly, 'Mrs Lovelace. She has a house near Bedford Basin.'

She said, 'I regret that we were not introduced earlier, Admiral Keen.' She smiled. 'It is a bad sign when even our admirals are so young!'

Adam strode between the tables and paused behind Keen's chair. An utter silence had fallen in the room.

Keen felt Adam's breath against his cheek, quick, angry. '*Alfriston*'s brought word from Sir Richard. *Reaper*'s been taken, surrendered.' All the while he was watching Keen's fine profile. 'The admiral intends to remain with the Bermuda squadron until the convoy is safely at sea.'

Keen dabbed his mouth with a napkin. 'Surrendered?' One word.

Adam nodded, seeing the woman sitting opposite for the first time. She smiled at him, and indicated the empty chair beside her.

He said, 'It was mutiny, sir.'

'I see.' Then he looked directly at Adam, his eyes very calm, and, Adam thought afterwards, very well concealing his emotions. 'I trust you have informed the ship?'

He thought of the enraged de Courcey. 'Yes, sir. They will be ready.'

Keen dropped the napkin on to his lap. 'Then *Reaper* is heading this way.' He saw the doubt in Adam's eyes. 'Trick for trick, see?' He stood up, and every face turned towards him. 'I am sorry for the interruption, ladies and gentlemen. I am certain that our host will understand.' He waited for Adam to walk around the table, where a footman had drawn out the empty chair. The sound of his shoes was very loud on the polished floor, reminding him unpleasantly of that snowy day in Portsmouth, at his court-martial.

Massie cleared his throat noisily. 'We'll have grace now, Reverend!'

Adam felt the woman's slippered foot touching his, even as the prayer was being intoned. He was surprised that he could even smile about it.

Trick for trick. Keen was speaking calmly with Massie. *We Happy Few.* It was as if somebody had spoken aloud. He thought of his uncle: the mark he had left on all of them.

His companion said softly, 'You say little, Captain. Should I feel insulted?'

He turned slightly to look at her. Fine, brown eyes, a mouth that was used to smiling. He glanced at her hand, which lay so near to his own at this crowded table. Married, but not to anybody here. Mistress, then?

He said, 'My apologies, ma'am. I am unused to such brilliance, even from the sea.' *Trick for trick.*

A footman loomed over them and her slipper moved away.

But she looked at him again, and said, 'We shall have to see about that, *Captain.*'

Adam glanced at their host. A slip of the tongue; was Keen remembering it even now, when outwardly he was so composed, so in control? Massie had spoken as if he had known of the mutiny. It was not a word to be used lightly. A rumour, a piece of gossip: Massie would have fingers in a lot of pies. It would mean only one thing. *Reaper* was already here.

'Are you married, Captain?'

'No.' It came out too abruptly, and he tried to soften it. 'It has not been my good fortune.'

She studied him thoughtfully, with delicately raised brows. 'I am surprised.'

'And you, ma'am?'

She laughed, and Adam saw Massie glance up at her. At them. She replied, 'Like a cloak, Captain. I wear it when it suits!'

Trick for trick.

*

The *Valkyrie's* chart room was small and functional, the table barely leaving space for more than three men. Adam leaned over the chart, the brass dividers moving unhurriedly across the bearings, soundings and scribbled calculations which, to a landsman, would be meaningless.

The door was wedged open, and he could see the bright sunlight moving like a beacon, back and forth, to the frigate's easy rise and fall. They had left Halifax in company with a smaller frigate, *Taciturn*, and the brig *Doon*. They had left with mixed feelings, the prospect of hunting down *Reaper*, the only possible way of settling the score, set against the very real likelihood of directing fire on one of their own. The Americans would have had no time to replace the surrendered frigate's company, so many of them, except for the officers and professional warrant ranks, would be mutineers.

But that had been five days ago, and he had sensed Keen's uncertainty, his growing anxiety about the next decision.

One point of the dividers rested on Cape North, the tip of Nova Scotia that guarded the southernmost side of the entrance to the Gulf of St Lawrence. Across the strait lay Newfoundland, some fifty miles distant. A narrow passage, but easy enough for a determined captain who wanted to avoid capture and slip through the net. Keen would be thinking the same thing. Adam leaned closer to the chart. Two tiny islands, St Pierre and Miquelon, to the south of Newfoundland's rugged coastline, were in fact French, but at the outbreak of war had been occupied by troops from the British garrison at St John's. Keen had made no secret of his conviction that *Reaper* would be heading for these same islands. *Reaper's* capture by the Americans would still be unknown to any of the local patrols; it would have been an obvious strategy if the enemy had intended to attack the garrison, or prey on shipping in these waters. But the brig *Doon* had investigated the area and had rejoined her two consorts with nothing to report. Beyond lay the Gulf of St Lawrence, the vital gateway to its great river, to Montreal and the lakes, to the naval base at Kingston and further still to York, the administrative, if small, capital of Upper Canada.

But the Gulf was vast, with islets and bays where any ship could shelter, and bide her time until the hunt had passed her by.

He heard shouted commands and the trill of calls. The afternoon watch was mustering aft, the air heavy with greasy smells from the galley funnel. A good measure of rum to wash it down.

He glanced at the sailing-master's log book. May third, 1813. He thought of the small velvet-covered volume in his chest, the carefully pressed fragments of the wild roses. May in England. It was like remembering a foreign country.

A shadow fell across the table: Urquhart, the first lieutenant. Adam had found him a good and competent officer, firm and fair with the hands, even with the hard men, who tested every officer for any sign of weakness. It was never easy to be both as a first lieutenant. When *Valkyrie*'s captain, Trevenen, had broken down with terror at the height of action, it had been Urquhart who had taken over and restored discipline and order. Neither Trevenen, who had vanished mysteriously on his way to face a court-martial, nor his successor, the acting-commodore Peter Dawes, had recommended Urquhart for advancement. Urquhart had never mentioned it, nor had he shown any resentment, but Adam guessed it was only because he did not yet know his new captain well enough. Adam blamed himself for that. He was unable to encourage intimacy in *Valkyrie*: even when he passed a command, he still found himself half-expecting to see other faces respond. Dead faces.

129

Urquhart waited patiently for his attention, and then said, 'I would like to exercise the eighteen-pounders during the afternoon watch, sir.'

Adam tossed down the dividers. 'It is about all we will be doing, it seems!'

He thought of that last night in Halifax, the lavish dinner, with their host, Massie, becoming more slurred by the minute. He thought, also, of the enticing and sensual Mrs Lovelace, laughing at Massie's crude remarks, but keeping her foot against Adam's under the table.

I should not have agreed to this post. Had he accepted it to avoid being marooned in *Zest*?

In his own heart, he knew he had acted out of a sense of obligation, perhaps some need to make reparation. Guilt. . . .

Urquhart looked at the chart: he had a strong, thoughtful profile. Adam could well imagine him with a command of his own.

Urquhart said, 'It's like picking at threads, sir. She could be anywhere.'

'I know that, damn it!' He touched the lieutenant's sleeve. 'I am sorry, John. That was uncalled for.'

Urquhart eyed him warily. It was the first time the captain had called him by his first name. It had been like seeing a different person suddenly, not so much the severe stranger.

He said, 'If we run deeper into the Gulf we shall be hard put to keep together. If we had more ships, then. . . .'

A master's mate whispered around the door, 'Admiral's coming up, sir.'

Adam knew that he was speaking to Urquhart, careful to avoid his captain's eye.

He straightened his back. 'Yes. Well, we shall see.'

Keen was standing by the weather nettings when they

came out of the chart room, and Adam noticed immediately that he looked strained, troubled.

Keen said, 'What time will we alter course, Captain Bolitho?'

Adam replied with equal formality, 'In two hours, sir. We shall steer nor' west.' He waited, seeing Keen's doubt, the unspoken arguments.

'Are *Taciturn* and *Doon* in sight?'

'Aye, sir. The masthead reported both of them at the change of watch. Good visibility. We should see another sail soon. Information maybe, some evidence that she was seen by some passing trader or fisherman.' He looked at Urquhart. 'It is our best hope.'

Keen said, 'We are abeam of Cape North. By nightfall we shall be stretched too far to offer support to one another.'

Adam looked away. He felt a stab of resentment without knowing why. He had been up before first light, and on deck several times during the night. There were plenty of navigational hazards in these waters and the local charts were unreliable, to say the least. It was only right that *Valkyrie*'s watchkeepers should know that their captain was with them.

'From the information brought by *Alfriston*, this would seem the most likely area for independent action. Perhaps tomorrow we could decide whether or not to continue this form of search.'

Keen watched two seamen dragging new halliards along the deck. '*I* will decide. While the light is still good I shall want signals sent to *Taciturn* and *Doon*. The brig can close with us and carry my report to Halifax.' He faced Adam and added shortly, 'We will discontinue the search before dusk.'

'Halifax, sir?'

Keen studied him grimly. 'Halifax.'

He walked toward the companion way, and Adam saw the flag lieutenant waiting there to intercept him.

'Orders, sir?' Urquhart was clearly uncomfortable at having been present during the exchange, and at having sensed a barrier which he had not seen before fall so obviously between admiral and flag captain.

Adam glanced up at the streaming masthead pendant. The wind was holding steady from the south-west. It had not shifted for days; another day would make no difference. And even when they returned to Halifax, it was unlikely that there would be fresh news from Sir Richard.

He realized what Urquhart had asked. 'Carry on as before.'

He was the captain, and yet his was never the final decision. He had always known that, but Keen's curt remark had merely served to emphasize the fact. Perhaps it was because Keen had been used to ships of the line, and had served in frigates as a very junior officer. He tried to smile, to sweep it away. *With the best of teachers.* But Keen had never commanded one. It should not make any difference. But, unreasonably, it did.

As the afternoon watch drew to a close, Keen came on deck again.

'I think it is time to make the signal.' He watched the small figure of John Whitmarsh walking aft, some clean shirts folded over one arm, and smiled unexpectedly. 'To be his age again, eh, Adam?'

The sudden informality, *just men*, was disconcerting. 'Aye, sir. But I think I could manage without some of the past.'

Keen made up his mind. 'You probably think I am giving up too easily. You think we should waste days, weeks even, pursuing what may be a lost cause.'

Adam said, 'I still believe we should continue, sir.'

Keen shrugged. The bridge between them was gone. 'It is my decision. Make the signal!'

Adam saw de Courcey hurrying toward Midshipman Rickman and the prepared hoists of bunting. Back to Halifax, then. Receptions and balls: a ship going stale at her anchorage.

'Deck there! *Taciturn*'s hoisted a signal!'

Adam saw another midshipman reaching for a telescope.

'Aloft, Mr Warren! Lively there!'

He knew Urquhart was watching him. He would never offer his own opinion, or mention what he had seen and heard. Adam shaded his eyes and stared at the sun, like red gold now. But there was still time. If only. . . .

The midshipman's young voice echoed down from the maintop. 'From *Taciturn*, sir! *Enemy in sight to the nor' east!*' Even at that distance and above the drumming chorus of canvas and rigging, Adam could hear his excitement.

Heading for the strait they had just left. Another hour, and they would have missed them. What sort of enemy, that *Taciturn* was so certain?

Warren shouted down again. 'She's *Reaper*, sir!'

Urquhart forgot himself. 'Hell's teeth! You were right, sir!'

Keen had reappeared. 'What is it? Are they sure?'

Adam said, 'Certain, sir.'

'They'll run for it.' He sounded unconvinced. 'Try and lose us in the Gulf.'

Adam beckoned to Urquhart. 'Get the t' gallants on her!' He glanced up at the flag whipping out from the mizzen truck. 'This ship could outpace *Reaper*, no matter what she tried!' He was surprised at his own voice. Pride, where there had been only acceptance; triumph, when he had so recently felt bitterness at Keen's dismissal of his proposals.

Calls squealed and the deck shook to the rush of bare feet as men ran to obey them. He was aware of their excitement, the relief that something was happening, and awe, when some of the new hands looked aloft to see the topgallant sails bursting from their yards, their canvas already hard to the steady wind.

Adam took a glass and rested it on Midshipman Rickman's shoulder. First *Taciturn*; the brig *Doon* was still not in sight from the deck. And then. . . . He tensed, his back chilled despite the lingering warmth of the sun. A thin plume of pale canvas: *Reaper*. Not running, and yet they must have sighted them. Three ships on a converging tack. *Reaper*'s men might fight to the death; they would face it in any case after the brief formality of a court-martial. They would have known the penalty for mutiny from the instant they had hauled down the flag. He licked his dry lips. *And murdered their captain*. . . .

Keen spoke for him. 'They dare not fight!'

Adam turned to Urquhart. 'Beat to quarters, if you please. Then clear for action.' He walked to the taffrail and then back again, his mind grappling with the sudden change of fortune. A show of defiance? A bloody gesture? It would be all of that. *Taciturn* alone outgunned the smaller *Reaper*: *Valkyrie* could blow her out of the water without even getting to close quarters.

Keen said, 'She's holding her course.' He held out his arms as his servant appeared beside him to clip on his sword.

'Cleared for action, sir!'

Adam stared at the first lieutenant. He had barely heard the rattle of drums, the stampede of seamen and marines to their stations, and now all was still again, each long gun fully crewed, the decks sanded, the scarlet coats of the marines visible at the hammock nettings and high in the fighting tops. They had learned well under Peter Dawes, or perhaps it was all due to the impassive Urquhart.

Keen said, 'Make to *Taciturn, close on Flag.*' He turned

away as de Courcey urged the signals party to greater efforts. The flags soared aloft.

'Acknowledged, sir!'

Of the brig *Doon* there was no sign, but her masthead lookouts would be watching, probably glad they were well clear of it.

'*Reaper*'s showing her teeth!'

Without a glass there was no apparent change, but when Adam propped his on the midshipman's shoulder he could see the line of protruding guns along the other vessel's side.

Keen said, 'When you are ready, Captain Bolitho.' They looked at each other like strangers.

Adam shouted, 'Just like the drill, Mr Urquhart!' He saw some of the nearest men turn to grin at him. 'Load and run out!'

'*Open the ports!*' A whistle shrilled from Monteith, the fourth lieutenant, and with a chorus of yells the seamen threw themselves on their tackles and hauled their guns up and through the open ports. With the wind across the quarter, their task was easier. If they changed tack, or lost the wind-gage, it would be different: uphill all the way, as the old gun captains warned.

Adam turned as young Whitmarsh walked unhurriedly between the crouching gun crews and watchful marines, Adam's new hanger held in his hands like a talisman. Adam looked around at the others on the quarterdeck. George Starr, his old coxswain, should be here, Hudson, who had also died, and other faces, so painfully clear that he was caught off-guard.

He waited for the boy to clip on his hanger and said, 'Below with you, my lad! No heroics today!' He saw the dismay on his face and added gently, 'You need no reminding either, do you?'

Keen was beside him. 'What can they hope to achieve?'

Adam saw the telescopes being trained on the distant

Taciturn, heard de Courcey's smooth voice reading out a signal. Then he lowered his glass, his mind suddenly blank. 'They have hostages, sir.'

'So that is what they intend. To sail directly past us, knowing we will not fire!' He seemed to consider it, with disbelief. 'Would they do that?'

'It may be a bluff, sir.' But he knew it was not. It was all the enemy had left. With this wind they would be within range in less than half an hour.

Keen said, 'It would be murder!'

Adam watched him, feeling his anger and revulsion. *His decision*, just as he had insisted earlier.

When Adam remained silent, Keen exclaimed, 'For God's sake, what should I do?'

Adam touched the hilt of his new hanger, the one he had chosen with such care in the old sword cutler's shop in the Strand.

'Men will die in any case if we fight, sir. But to lose *Reaper* now would be an even greater tragedy.'

Keen seemed to sigh. 'Signal *Taciturn* to take station astern of Flag.'

The signal was acknowledged, and Adam watched the leading frigate's sails in momentary confusion as she began to come about as ordered. He could feel both pity and admiration for Keen. He was not going to leave the first encounter to one of his captains. As Richard Bolitho had so often said, here was where the responsibility began and ended, like the flag at the mizzen-truck. *Final*.

He had forgotten about Midshipman Warren, who was still in the maintop.

'Deck, there!' Then shock, disbelief. 'There are prisoners on *Reaper*'s deck, sir!' There was a pause. 'Women, too!'

Keen said sharply, 'D' you still think they're bluffing?'

It was like a nightmare, Adam thought. *Reaper* would suffer the same fate yet again; she would be raked as she had been by the Americans, before she could even get within range.

Urquhart had gone to his station by the mainmast, his sword laid across one shoulder as if he were about to perform a ceremony.

Adam gripped the quarterdeck rail. He did not need to be told what would happen when these long eighteen-pounders, double-shotted as ordered, thundered out at the oncoming ship.

He knew that some of the gun crews were peering aft at him, and wanted to shout at them. *There is no decision to be made. They must not escape.*

He heard de Courcey say, 'Two women, sir. The rest look like sailors.' Even he sounded dazed, unable to accept what he saw.

Adam raised his voice. 'On the uproll, Mr Urquhart! As you bear!' Urquhart knew what to do: they all did. But they had to be held together, and commanded, no matter what they believed.

'Take in the t' gallants!' High overhead, men moved like monkeys, detached from the tension and apprehension on the deck below.

Adam turned to the sailing-master. 'Stand by to bring her up two points, Mr Ritchie. Then we will fire.'

Keen was in the shrouds, oblivious to the spray and risk; he was holding the midshipman's big telescope, his fair hair whipping in the wind.

Like that day at the church in Zennor.... Val and Zenoria.... He closed his eyes as Keen said harshly, 'One of the hostages is David St Clair! His daughter must be with him!'

He thrust the memories aside; this was no place for them. He heard Keen say, 'No bluff, then.' He climbed down to the deck and faced him.

Adam said, 'Stand by!' He forced himself to look at the oncoming frigate, leaning over to expose her bright

137

copper, her gilded figurehead with the upraised scythe suddenly clear and terrible.

Each gun captain would be staring aft at the solitary figure by the rail, looking to a captain whom they knew only by reputation. But every man knew what he would see when *Valkyrie* altered course, and the target filled each port. Here, a man cleared his throat; another turned to wipe the sweat from his eyes.

Suppose they refused to fire on men like themselves?

Adam felt the anger pound through him. They were not like them. *I must not think of it!*

He drew his hanger and raised it shoulder-high.

Dear God, what are we doing?

'Alter course, Mr Ritchie!'

He swung round as the uneven roar of cannon fire rolled and echoed across the short, white-tipped waves.

With disbelief he saw *Reaper's* guns recoiling in a broken broadside, in pairs or singly, until at last only one fired from the bow.

There were leaping patches of foam now; the taller waterspouts of the heavier guns churned up the sea's face and faded almost as suddenly. A full broadside, fired into oblivion.

Keen said, 'They would not fire on us!' He looked at those nearest him. 'Because they knew we would destroy them!'

Adam said, 'The bluff failed.' He saw some of the gun crews staring at each other; two seamen even reached across their eighteen-pounder to shake hands. It was no victory, but at least it was not bloody murder, either.

'Signal her to heave to! Stand by, boarding parties!'

Adam called, 'Be ready to fire. We will take nothing for granted!'

He touched his hat to Keen. 'I'd like to go across myself, sir.'

138

Keen gazed past him as something like a great sigh came from the watching seamen and marines.

'She's struck her colours, thank God.'

Richie, the old sailing-master, wiped his lips with the back of his hand. 'Poor old girl. She's taken all she can, I reckon!'

Adam looked at him. A toughened, unsentimental professional, but in his simple way he had said it all.

Keen said, 'Take good care of St Clair and his daughter. The ordeal must have been dreadful for them.'

Adam saw the boats being swayed up and over the larboard gangway: Urquhart had taught them well. The guns would still be able to fire if necessary, without being hampered by their presence.

'I will, sir.' He stared across at the other ship, her sails flapping as she came into the wind. Another minute and it would have ended differently. As it was. . . . He recalled the sailing-master's words, like an epitaph. For a ship, not for those who had betrayed her.

Keeping in line abreast, *Valkyrie*'s boats pulled steadily toward the other frigate. Tension remained high. If *Reaper*'s captors decided to resist, they might still be able to make sail and escape, or attempt it.

Adam looked over at the other boats. His captain of marines, Loftus, was very conspicuous in his scarlet tunic, an easy target for any marksman, nor would his own own epaulettes have gone unnoticed. He found himself smiling slightly. Gulliver, the sixth lieutenant, glanced quickly at him, perhaps taking comfort in what he saw.

He said, 'This will even the score, sir!'

He spoke like a veteran. He was about twenty years old.

'*Reaper*, ahoy! We are coming aboard! Throw down your weapons!'

Adam touched the pistol beneath his coat. This was

the moment. Some hothead, a man with nothing to lose, might use it as a last chance. Boat by boat they went alongside, and he was conscious of a strange sense of loneliness with *Valkyrie* hidden by this pitching hull. *No chances*. But would Keen order his flagship to open fire with so many of his own men on board?

It was uncanny. Like a dead ship. They scrambled up and over the gangway, weapons held ready, while from the opposite end of the vessel some of the marines were already swarming onto the forecastle. They had even swung round a swivel, and had trained it on the silent figures lining the gun deck.

His men parted to let their captain through, seeing the ship through different eyes now that she had struck. The guns which had fired blindly into the open water moved restlessly, unloaded and abandoned, rammers and sponges lying where they had been dropped. Adam walked aft to the big double wheel, where two of his men had taken control. The hostages, released and apparently unharmed, were grouped around the mizzen mast, while along the gundeck the seamen seemed to have separated into two distinct groups, the mutineers and the American prize crew.

There were two American lieutenants waiting for him.

'Are there any more officers aboard?'

The senior of the two shook his head. 'The ship is yours, Captain Bolitho.'

Adam concealed his surprise. 'Mr Gulliver, take your party and search the ship.' He added sharply as the lieutenant hurried away, 'If any one resists, kill him!'

So they knew who he was. He said, 'What were you hoping to do, Lieutenant?'

The tall officer shrugged. 'My name is Robert Neill, Captain. *Reaper* is a prize of war. They surrendered.'

'And *you* are a prisoner of war. Your men, also.' He paused. 'Captain Loftus, take charge of the others. You

140

know what to do.' To Neill he said, 'You offered British seamen a chance to mutiny. In fact, you and your captain incited it.'

The man named Neill sighed. 'I have nothing to add.'

He watched the two officers hand their swords to a marine. 'You will be well treated.' He hesitated, hating the silence, the smell of fear. 'As I was.'

Then, with a nod to Loftus, he turned and walked toward the waiting hostages.

One, a silver-haired man with an alert, youthful face, stepped forward, ignoring the raised bayonet of a marine.

'My name is David St Clair.' He reached out his hand. 'This is my daughter, Gilia. Your arrival was a miracle, sir. A miracle!'

Adam glanced at the young woman. She was warmly dressed for travel, her eyes steady and defiant, as if this were the ordeal rather than its relief.

He said, 'I have little time, Mr St Clair. I am to transfer you to my ship, *Valkyrie*, before it becomes too dark.'

St Clair stared at him. 'I know that name!' He held his daughter's arm. 'Valentine Keen's ship, you recall it!' But she was observing *Valkyrie*'s seamen and marines, as if sensing the friction between them and their prisoners.

Adam said, 'His flagship. I am his flag captain.'

St Clair said smoothly, 'Of course. He is promoted now.'

Adam said, 'How were you taken, sir?'

'We were on passage in the schooner *Crystal*, out of Halifax, bound for the St Lawrence. Admiralty business.' He seemed to become aware of Adam's impatience and continued, 'These others are her crew. The woman is the master's wife, who was aboard with him.'

'I was told of your business here, sir. I thought it dangerous, at the time.' He glanced at the girl again. 'I was proved right, it seems.'

141

A boatswain's mate was waiting, trying to catch his eye.

'What is it, Laker?'

The man seemed surprised that his new captain should know his name. 'The two Yankee officers, sir. . . .'

'Send them over to the ship. Their own men, too. Lively now!'

His eyes moved to the gangway where one of the guns was still abandoned on its tackles. There was a great stain on the planking, like black tar. It must be blood. Perhaps it marked the place where they had flogged their captain without mercy.

He called, 'And run up our colours!' It was a small enough gesture, amid so much shame.

One of the American lieutenants paused with his escort. 'Tell me one thing, Captain. *Would* you have fired, hostages or not?'

Adam swung away. 'Take them across.'

St Clair's daughter said quietly, 'I wondered that myself, Captain.' She was shivering now, despite her warm clothing, the shock and realization of what had happened cutting away her reserve.

St Clair put his arm around her, and said, 'The guns were loaded and ready. At the last minute some of the men, her original people, I believe, fired them to show their intentions.'

Adam said, 'The American lieutenant, Neill, is probably asking himself the same question that he put to me.' He looked the girl directly in the eyes. 'In war, there are few easy choices.'

'Boat's ready, sir!'

'Have you any baggage to be taken across?'

St Clair guided his daughter to the side, where a boatswain's chair had been rigged for her.

'None. There was no time. Afterwards, they destroyed the *Crystal*. There was an explosion of some kind.'

142

Adam looked around the deserted deck, at his own men, who were waiting to get *Reaper* under way again. They would probably have preferred to send her to the bottom. *And so would I.*

He walked to the side, and ensured that the girl was securely seated.

'You will be more comfortable in the flagship, ma'am. We shall be returning to Halifax.'

Some of *Reaper*'s original company, urged ungently by Loftus's marines, were already being taken below, to be secured for the remainder of the passage.

She murmured, 'What will become of them?'

Adam said curtly, 'They will hang.'

She studied him, as if searching his face for something. 'Had they fired on your ship we would all be dead, is that not so?' When Adam remained silent, she persisted, 'Surely that must be taken into consideration.'

Adam turned suddenly. 'That man! Come here!'

The seaman, still wearing a crumpled, red-checkered shirt, came over immediately and knuckled his forehead. 'Sir?'

'I know you!'

'Aye, Cap'n Bolitho. I was a maintopman in *Anemone* two years back. You put me ashore when I was took sick o' fever.'

Memory came, and with it the names of the past. 'Ramsay, what in *hell's* name happened, man?' He had forgotten the girl, who was listening intently, her father, the others, everything but this one, familiar face. There was no fear in it, but it was the face of a man already condemned, a man who had known the nearness of death in the past, and had accepted it.

'It ain't my place, Cap'n Bolitho. Not with you. That's all over, done with.' He came to a decision, and very deliberately dragged his shirt over his head. Then he said, 'No disrespect to you, miss. But for you, I think we would

143

have fired.' Then he turned his back, allowing the fading sunlight to fall across his skin.

Adam said, *'Why?'* He heard the girl give a strangled sob. It must seem far worse to her.

The seaman named Ramsay had been so cruelly flogged that his body was barely human. Some of the torn flesh had not yet healed.

He pulled his shirt on again. 'Because he enjoyed it.'

'I am sorry, Ramsay.' He touched his arm impulsively, knowing that Lieutenant Gulliver was watching him with disbelief. 'I will do what I can for you.'

When he looked again, the man was gone. There was no hope, and he would know it. And yet those few words had meant so much, to both of them.

Gulliver said uneasily, 'Ready, sir.'

But before the boatswain's chair was swung out to be lowered into the waiting boat, Adam said to St Clair's daughter, 'Sometimes, there are no choices whatsoever.'

'Lower away! Easy, lads!'

Then he straightened his back and turned to face the others. He was the captain again.

8

Too Much to Lose

Richard Bolitho leaned away from the bright sunshine
that lanced through *Indomitable*'s cabin windows to rest
his head against the chair's high back. It was deep and
comfortable, a *bergère*, which Catherine had sent on
board when this ship had first hoisted his flag. Yovell, his
secretary, sat at the table, while Lieutenant Avery stood
by the stern bench watching two of the ship's boats pulling back from the brig *Alfriston*, which had met up with
them at dawn.

Tyacke had made it his business to send across some
fresh fruit. Having commanded a small brig himself, he
would have appreciated its value to her hard-worked
company.

There had been a burst of cheering when *Alfriston* had
hove-to to pass across her dispatches, which was quickly
quelled by officers on watch who had been very aware
of their admiral's open skylight, and perhaps the importance of the news *Alfriston* might have brought to him.

Tyacke had come aft, bringing the heavy canvas satchel
himself.

When Bolitho asked about the cheering, he had replied
impassively, '*Reaper*'s been retaken, Sir Richard.'

He glanced now at the heavy pile of dispatches on the
table. The entire report of the search for, and capture of,
Reaper was there, written in Keen's own hand rather than

that of a secretary. Did he lack confidence in his own actions, or in those who supported him, he wondered. It remained a private document, and yet, despite the seals and the secrecy, *Indomitable*'s people had known its contents, or had guessed what had happened. Such intuition was uncanny, but not unusual.

He listened to the creak of tackles and the twitter of a bosun's call as the next net full of stores was hoisted outboard before being lowered into a boat for *Alfriston*. It was difficult to look at the vast blue expanse of ocean beyond the windows. His eye was painful, and he had wanted to rub it, even though he had been warned against disturbing it. He must accept that it was getting worse.

He tried to concentrate on Keen's careful appraisal of *Reaper*'s discovery and capture. He had missed out nothing, even his own despair when he had seen the hostages paraded on her deck, a human barricade against *Valkyrie*'s guns. He had generously praised Adam's part in it, and his handling of the captured sailors, American and mutineers alike.

But his mind rebelled against the intrusion of duty. In the bag sent over with Keen's dispatch had been some letters, one from Catherine, the first since they had parted in Plymouth some three months ago. He had held it to his face, had seen Yovell's discreet glance, had caught the faint reminder of her perfume.

Avery said, 'The last boat's casting off, Sir Richard.' He sounded tense, on edge. Perhaps he, too, had been hoping for a letter, although Bolitho had never known him to receive one. Like Tyacke, his only world seemed to be here.

Bolitho turned once more to Keen's lengthy report, rereading the information concerning David St Clair and his daughter, who had been prisoners aboard *Reaper*. Taken from a schooner, but surely no accidental encounter? St Clair was under Admiralty contract, and Keen had mentioned that he had been intending to visit the naval dockyard at Kingston and also a ship-building site at York, where a thirty-gun man-of-war was close to completion. The final work on the vessel had apparently been delayed by a dispute with the Provincial Marine, under whose control she would eventually be. St Clair, well used to dealing with bureaucracy, had been hoping to speed things to a satisfactory conclusion. Captains in the fleet might find it difficult to regard such a relatively small vessel as a matter of great importance, but as Keen had learned from St Clair, when in commission the new vessel would be the biggest and most powerful on the lakes. No American craft would be able to stand against her: the lakes would be held under the White Ensign. But should the Americans attack and seize her, completed or not, the effect would be disastrous. It would mean the end of Upper Canada as a British province. Just one ship; and the Americans would have known of her existence from the moment her keel had been laid. In the light of this, St Clair's capture appeared even less of a casual misfortune. His mission had also been known: he had had to be removed. Bolitho thought of the savage gunfire, the pathetic wreckage of the *Royal Herald*. Or killed.

He said to Yovell, 'Have our bag sent over to *Alfriston*. She'll be impatient to get under way again.' He thought of the brig's gaunt commander, and wondered what his feelings had been when he had heard of *Reaper*'s capture, and that her only defiance had been fired deliberately into open water.

Ozzard peered through the other door. 'Captain's coming, sir.'

Tyacke entered and glanced at the littered papers on Bolitho's table. Bolitho thought he was probably like *Alfriston*'s commander, eager to move.

Without effort he could picture his ships on this great, empty ocean: two hundred miles south-west of the

Bermudas, the other frigates *Virtue* and *Attacker* mere slivers of light on opposite horizons. Perhaps if they had not waited, the Americans would have attacked the assembled convoy, their powerful frigates destroying it or beating it into submission, no matter what the escorting men-of-war might have attempted.

A mistake, a waste of time? Or had the Americans outguessed them yet again? The enemy's intelligence sources were without parallel. To know about St Clair and to see his involvement as a direct threat to some greater plan matched the impudent way they had seized *Reaper* and turned the advantage into a shame, news of which would ring throughout the fleet in spite of, or even because of, the punishments which would be meted out to the men who had mutinied against their captain, and against the Crown.

The convoy was well away, and would be standing out into the Atlantic. Their speed would be that of the slowest merchantman, a misery for the escorting frigates and brigs. But safe, in a few days' time.

Before they had left Bermuda, Avery had gone ashore to visit *Reaper*'s first lieutenant at a military hospital in Hamilton. Bolitho himself would have liked to have spoken to the *Reaper*'s only surviving officer, who had been with his captain until the incident's macabre and brutal conclusion, but *Reaper* had been one of his own squadron. He could not become personally involved with men whose warrants he might be called upon to sign.

Reaper's captain had been a tyrant and a sadist, terms which Bolitho would never use without great consideration. He had been moved from another command to make *Reaper* into an efficient and reliable fighting ship once more, and to restore her reputation. But early in his tenure another side of his nature had revealed itself. Perhaps he had, in fact, been moved from that other command because of his own brutality. Any captain sailing alone had to keep the balance between discipline and tyranny firmly in his mind. Only the afterguard, with its thin ranks of Royal Marines, stood between him and open rebellion. And even if provoked, it could never be condoned.

Tyacke said, 'Orders, Sir Richard?'

Bolitho turned away from the glare and saw that Yovell and Avery had left the cabin. It seemed a mutual awareness of his desire to confer privately with his flag captain: a loyalty which never failed to move him.

'I want your views, James. Return to Halifax and discover what is happening? Or remain here, and so weaken our squadron?'

Tyacke rubbed the scarred side of his face. He had seen the letter handed to Bolitho and been surprised by his own envy. *If only.*... He thought of the wine which Catherine Somervell had sent him, like the deep green leather chair in which Bolitho was sitting, her gifts, and her abiding presence in this cabin. With a woman like that....

Bolitho asked, 'What is it, James? You know me well enough to speak out.'

Tyacke dismissed the thoughts, glad that they could not be known.

'I believe the Yankees –' he smiled awkwardly, recalling Dawes, 'the Americans will need to move very soon. Maybe they've already made a beginning. Rear-Admiral Keen's information about the shipbuilder, this man St Clair, points to it. Once we have more ships, as their lordships say we will when Bonaparte is finally beaten, they'll face a blockade of their entire coastline. Trade, supplies, ships, unable to move.' He paused, and seemed to come to a decision. 'I've spoken to Isaac York, and he insists that this weather will hold.' Again he offered a small, attractive smile, which even his disfigurement could not diminish. 'And my new purser *assures* me that we are well supplied for another month. The pips might squeak a bit, but we can manage.'

'Remain on this patrol? Is that what you are telling me?'

'Look, sir, if you were some high an' mighty Yankee with good ships, albeit Frogs, at your disposal, what would you do?'

Bolitho nodded, considering it. He could even see the unknown ships in his mind, as clearly as the hollow-eyed Commander Borradaile had seen them through his telescope. Big, well-armed, free of all authority but their own.

'I'd take advantage of this south-westerly and go for the convoy, even at this stage. A long way, and a risk if you are facing the unknown. But I don't think it is unknown to our man.'

There were muffled cheers on deck, and he left the chair to walk to the stern windows. 'There goes *Alfriston*, James.'

Tyacke watched him, with affection and concern. Every time he thought he knew this man he found there was something more to learn. He noticed that Bolitho was shading his left eye, and saw the sadness and introspection in the profile against the light. Thinking of his letter in that same little brig, and the endless miles and transfers from ship to ship before Catherine Somervell would open and read it. Perhaps thinking, too, of his own independence as a very young commander, when each day was a challenge, but not a burden. A proud man, and a sensitive one, a man Tyacke had seen holding the hand of a dying enemy in *Indomitable*'s last and greatest battle. Who had tried to comfort his coxswain when Allday's son had been killed in that same fight. He cared, and those who knew him loved him for it. The others were content with the legend. And yet his would be the responsibility for sending *Reaper*'s seamen to choke from a yardarm. Tyacke had only known *Reaper*'s captain by reputation. It had been enough.

Bolitho turned from the sea. 'I agree with you, James. We will remain on station.' He walked back to the table and spread his hands on the open dispatches. 'Another day or so. After that, time and distance can become a handicap.' He smiled. 'Even to our enemy.'

Tyacke picked up his hat. 'I'll make the necessary signals to our consorts when we alter course at two bells, sir.'

Bolitho sat down again and rested his head against the warm green leather. He thought of May in Cornwall, the tide of pure colour, thousands of bluebells, the sea sparkling. . . . It would soon be June. He felt his fingers tighten on the arms of the chair she had had made for him. So long. So long. . . .

The familiar sounds faded; the sunlight no longer tormented him as wind and rudder guided this great ship like a bridle.

Then, and only then, did he take the letter from his coat. He held it to his face again, to his mouth, as she would have done.

Then he opened it with great care, always with the same uncertainty, even fear.

My dearest Beloved Richard. . . .

She was with him. Nothing had changed. The fear was gone.

Lieutenant George Avery wedged his feet against his seachest and stared up at the deckhead in his tiny, screened cabin. Feet moved occasionally on the wet planking as men hastened to take in the slack of some running rigging.

Outside it was pitch black, with plenty of stars but no moon. He toyed with the idea of going on deck but knew

151

he would be in the way, or worse, those on watch might think that he had been sent to report on their progress. He glanced at his gently swaying cot and rejected it. Where was the point? He would not be able to sleep, or at least, not for long. Then his doubts would come to torment him. He considered the wardroom, but knew there would be somebody there, like himself unable to sleep, or looking for a partner for a game of cards. Like the dead Scarlett, *Indomitable*'s first lieutenant when she had ceased to be a private ship and had first worn Bolitho's flag. He had wanted so much to have a command of his own, and outwardly had been a good officer, but he was being driven quietly mad by his mounting debts, his inability to stop gambling, and his desperate need to win. Avery had seen David Merrick, the acting captain of marines, sitting in the wardroom earlier, a book open on his lap to deter conversation, but his eyes unmoving. His superior, du Cann, had died that day with Scarlett and many others, but promotion seemed to have brought him no pleasure.

He thought of *Alfriston*, and the letter he had seen resting between the leaves of a book on Bolitho's table. Envy? It went deeper than that. He had even been denied the odd pleasure it gave him to read one of Allday's letters aloud: there had been none for him from Unis, and Avery knew he was troubled, confused by a separation he had been unable to accept. Avery had seen him, too, that afternoon, motionless on the deck, alone despite the bustling hands around him. He was standing at the place where his son had died, maybe trying to see the sense of it all.

He glanced at his small cupboard, thinking of the good cognac he kept there. If he had a drink now, he would not stop.

More feet rushed overhead. The ship was altering course very slightly, the shrouds drumming in a muffled tattoo. And tomorrow – what then? It had been late afternoon when the brig *Marvel* had closed with the flagship. She had sighted two ships to the north, steering east, as far as her commander could tell. He had turned away rather than run up a hoist of signals, and he had acted wisely. Any small vessel would have run for it, if the two ships were the enemy.

But overnight all could change. It could be a waste of time: the ships might have changed tack completely, or *Marvel*'s lookouts might have been mistaken, seeing only what they expected to see, as was often the case in these hit-and-run tactics.

He recalled Bolitho when they had last met, strengthened or troubled by his letter from Catherine, it was not possible to say. He had spoken unexpectedly of his childhood at Falmouth, and his awe of his father, Captain James Bolitho. He had said that he had never doubted or questioned his vocation as a sea-officer, although Avery thought privately that he was more uncertain now than at any other time.

Of the two reported ships he had said, 'If they *are* the enemy, it is unlikely that they will know of *Reaper*'s recapture. Yet. If they are truly after the convoy from Bermuda, then I think they will come at us. They are becoming too used to success. This may be one gamble too many.'

He could have been speaking of somebody else, or some report he had read in his dispatches or in the *Gazette*. Avery had looked around the spacious cabin, the tethered guns on either side, the books, and the fine wine cooler with the Bolitho motto on the top. The same place which had been blasted and blackened in that action, where men had fought and died, and survival had seemed like an accident or a miracle. If he returned to it now, he thought he would probably find Bolitho still sitting in the leather chair, reading one of his books, his fingers occasionally brushing against the letter which he would open again before he turned in.

He ran his fingers through his hair and allowed the thought and the memory to intrude. As if she had suddenly appeared in this tiny hutch, the only place he could truly be alone.

Suppose they had not met? He shook his head as if to deny it. That had only been partly the cause. *I am thirty-five years old. A lieutenant without prospects, beyond serving this man for whom I care more than I would have believed humanly possible.* The same Lieutenant Scarlett, during one of their many heated exchanges, had suggested that he was waiting only for the reward of promotion, for a command of his own, no matter how small. And once, that might have been true. There had seemed no other course, no hope for someone of his station; even the lingering stain of his court-martial would not have been forgotten in the high offices of admiralty.

I am not a round-eyed midshipman, or a young lieutenant with the world still for the asking. I should have stopped there. Stopped, and forgotten her. . . . She was probably laughing about it at this very moment. Just as he knew it would break his heart, if he really believed that she was.

I should have known. A sea-officer who had proved his courage in battle, and in his bitter struggle to live after being wounded. But when it came to women he was a child, an innocent.

But it would not disperse. He was still there, and it was like a dream, something so vivid and unplanned. Something inevitable.

The house had been almost empty; the full staff were only expected to arrive after Rear-Admiral Sir Robert Mildmay's residence in Bath was finally closed and sold.

She had been so calm, amused, he thought, by his concern for her reputation, assuring him that the formidable housekeeper was completely loyal and discreet, and the cook, the only other person residing in the house, was all but deaf. He had often recalled that description, *loyal* and *discreet*. Did it have a double meaning? That her affairs were numerous? He rubbed his forehead. That she might be entertaining some other man even at this moment?

He heard footsteps outside, the click of Captain Merrick's boots. He would be going around his sentries, inspecting places deep in the lightless hull where guards were mounted day and night. Another man with a private torment: unable to sleep, afraid of what dreams might bring. Avery smiled grimly. As well he might.

He opened the shutter of his solitary lantern very slightly, but instead of the small flame he saw the great fire, half red, and half white ash. She had led him by the hand across the room. 'It will be cold tonight.'

He had attempted to touch her, to take her arm, but she had moved away, her eyes in shadow while she had watched him. 'There is some wine on the table. It would be pleasant, don't you think?' She had reached for the tongs beside a basket of logs.

'Let me.' They had knelt together, watching the sparks going up the chimney like fireflies.

She had said, 'I must go. I have things to do.' She had not looked at him. Later, he had realized that she had been unable to.

The house had been like a tomb, the room facing away from the street and the occasional noise of carriage wheels.

Avery had had no experience with women, except for one brief incident with a French lady who had visited sick and wounded prisoners of war. There had been no affection, only need, an urgency which had left him feeling used and vaguely degraded.

155

He was still unable to believe what had happened in London.

She had appeared on the edge of the shadows, her body all in white, her feet bare on the carpet, the feet alone touched by the flickering firelight.

'Here I am, *Mister* Avery!' She had laughed softly, and when he had got up from the fire, 'You spoke to me of your love.' She had held out her arms. 'Show me.'

He had held her, gently at first, then more firmly as he had felt the curve of her spine under his hand, and had realized that beneath the flimsy gown she was naked.

Then, for the first time, he had felt her shivering, although her body was warm, even hot. He had tried to kiss her, but she had pressed her face into his shoulder, and repeated, *'Show me.'*

He had seized the gown, and in seconds had her in his arms again, unable to stop himself, even if his senses had permitted it. He had carried her to the great bed and had knelt over her, touching her, exploring her, kissing her from her throat to her thigh. He had seen her raise her head to watch him as he threw off his clothes, her hair like living gold in the light. Then she had laid back again, her arms spread out as if crucified.

'Show me!' She had resisted when he had gripped her wrists, and had twisted from side to side, her body arched as he had forced her down, and down, finding her, unable to wait, unwilling to restrain his desire.

She had been ready, and had drawn him to her, passionate, tender, experienced, enclosing him deeply in her body until they were both spent.

She had murmured, 'That was love, Mister Avery.'

'I must leave, Susanna.' It was the first time he had called her by name.

'First, some wine.' She had lifted up on one elbow, making no attempt to cover herself. Nor did she resist when he touched her again; she reached out to provoke

156

and arouse him once more, and he had known then that he could not leave her. At dawn's first intrusion they had finally tasted the wine, and had crouched again by the fire, now all but dead in the faint grey light.

The rest had become blurred, unreal. Fumbling into his clothes again while she had stood watching him, quite naked but for his cocked hat. Then he had embraced her once more, unable to find the words, his mind and body still reeling from the impossible dream, which had become reality.

She had whispered, 'I promised you a carriage.'

He had pressed her hair against his chin. 'I shall be all right. I could possibly fly to Chelsea!'

The moment of parting had been painful, almost embarrassing.

'I am sorry if I hurt you, Susanna. . . . I am . . . clumsy.'

She had smiled. 'You are a man. A real man.'

He might have said. 'Please write to me.' But he could not honestly say that he had. The door had closed, and he had made his way down the stairs to the street doors, where someone had placed and lighted a fresh stand of candles for his departure. *Loyal* and *discreet*.

There was a tap at the screen door, startling him, and he found Ozzard standing outside, a small tray beneath his arm. For a moment Avery though he must have been reliving it all aloud, and that Ozzard had heard him.

Ozzard said only, 'Sir Richard's compliments, sir, and he'd like to see you aft.'

'Of course.' Avery closed the door and groped for a comb. Did Ozzard never sleep either?

He sat down again and grinned ruefully. She would be laughing, maybe, but remembering too.

Perhaps he had been a worse fool than he knew. But he would never forget.

He smiled. *Mister Avery.*

*

Captain James Tyacke stepped into the stern cabin and looked around at the familiar faces, his eyes accepting the light with surprising ease after the blackness of the quarterdeck, where little more than a tiny compass lamp pierced the night.

Bolitho was standing at the table, with his hands spread on a chart, Avery by his elbow, while the plump and scholarly Yovell sat at a smaller table, his pen poised over some papers. Ozzard moved only occasionally to refill their cups with coffee but remained, as usual, silent, merely shifting from one foot to the other to betray any agitation he might feel.

And framed against the great span of thick glass windows was Allday, a drawn sword in one hand, while he moved a cloth slowly up and down the blade as Tyacke had seen him do so often. Bolitho's oak: only death would separate them.

Tyacke shut it from his mind. 'All the hands have been fed, Sir Richard. I've been around the ship to have a quiet word with my people.'

He could not have slept much, Bolitho thought, but he was ready now, even if his admiral were to be proved wrong. He had even considered that possibility. The ship's company had been roused early, but they had not yet cleared for action. There was nothing worse for morale than the anti-climax of discovering that the enemy had outguessed or outmanoeuvred them, and the sea was empty.

My people. That was also typical of Tyacke. He was referring to the ship's backbone of professionals, his warrant officers, all skilled and experienced men like Isaac York, the sailing-master, Harry Duff, the gunner, and Sam Hockenhull, the squat boatswain. Men who had come up the hard way, like *Alfriston*'s untidy commander.

Set against them, the lieutenants were amateurs. Even Daubeny, the first lieutenant, was still young for his position, which would not have come his way so soon but for the death of his predecessor. But that one fierce battle eight months ago had given him a maturity that seemed to surprise him more than anybody. As for the others, the most junior was Blythe, only just promoted from the midshipmen's berth. He was big-headed and very sure of himself, but even Tyacke had overcome his dislike of him to say that he was improving. Slightly.

And Laroche, the piggy-faced third lieutenant, who had once received the rough edge of Tyacke's tongue when he had been in charge of a press gang, also lacked experience except for their encounter with *Unity*.

Tyacke was saying, 'The new hands have settled down quite well, sir. As for the Nova Scotians who volunteered, I'm glad they're with us and not the enemy!'

Bolitho stared down at the chart, the soundings and calculations between his hands. Ships meeting, the mind of an enemy, all meaningless if there was nothing when daylight came.

York had been right about the wind. It was even and steady from the south-west, and the ship, under reduced canvas, was lying well to it; when he had been on deck he had watched the spray bursting like phantoms along the lee side and up through the beakhead with its snarling lion.

Avery asked, 'Will they fight or run, Sir Richard?' He saw the alertness in the grey eyes that lifted to him; there was no hint of fatigue or doubt. Bolitho had shaved, and Avery wondered what he and Allday had discussed while the big coxswain had used his razor as easily as if it were broad daylight.

His shirt was loosely fastened, and Avery had seen the glint of silver when he had stooped over the chart. The locket he always wore.

Bolitho shrugged. 'Fight. If they have not already gone about and headed for port somewhere, they will have little choice, I think.' He looked up at the deckhead beams. 'The wind is an ally today.'

Avery watched, at peace now in this company, the consequences of what daylight might bring somehow secondary. He heard the drumming vibration of rigging, the occasional squeal of blocks, and imagined the ship leaning over to the wind, knowing that Bolitho was seeing it also, even as they spoke.

Tyacke would consider the situation rather differently, perhaps, but with the same end in mind. How many times had this ship lived through moments like this? She was thirty-six years old, and her battle honours read like history itself: the Chesapeake, The Saintes, the Nile, and Copenhagen. So many men, so much pain. He thought of Tyacke's fiercely contained pride for the ship he had not wanted. *And she had never been beaten.*

Bolitho said suddenly, 'Your assistant, George – Mr Midshipman Carleton. Doing well, isn't he?'

Avery glanced quickly at Tyacke, who gave the merest hint of a smile, but no more.

'Yes, sir, he is very good with his signals crew. He hopes to be offered promotion. He is seventeen.' The question had disconcerted him: he never really knew what Bolitho might toss his way, or why.

Tyacke said, 'He's a damned sight quieter than Mr Blythe ever was.'

Bolitho felt them relaxing, except Ozzard. He was waiting to hear, to *know.* He would go below, as deep as possible into the hull, when the first shots were fired. He should be ashore, Bolitho thought, away from this life. And yet, he knew that he had nowhere to go, no one who waited for him. Even when they were in Cornwall, and Ozzard lived in his cottage on the estate, he remained profoundly alone.

Bolitho said, 'I want young Carleton aloft.' He tugged out his watch and flicked open the guard.

Tyacke read his thoughts. 'Less than an hour, sir.'

Bolitho glanced at his empty cup, and heard Ozzard say tentatively, 'I could make another pot, Sir Richard.'

'I think it may have to wait.' He turned his head as somewhere, almost drowned out by the muffled hiss of the sea, he heard a man laugh. Such a small thing, but he thought of the wretched *Reaper*: there had been no laughter there. He remembered as if it were yesterday the evening when Tyacke had taken the lordly Midshipman Blythe below deck to visit the crowded seamen's and marines' messes, to show him what he had called 'the strength of a ship'. That had been before the battle. The same strength had prevailed then. He thought of Allday's grief. At a cost. . . .

He said, 'If we fight, we will give of our best.' For a moment it was like hearing someone else's voice. 'But we must never forget those who depend on us, because they have no other choice.'

Tyacke reached for his hat. 'I'll have the galley fire doused in good time, Sir Richard.'

But Bolitho was looking at Avery. 'Go and speak with your Mr Carleton.' He closed his watch, but was still holding it. 'You may pass the word now, James. It will be warm enough today.'

As Ozzard gathered up the cups and the others left the cabin, Bolitho looked over at Allday.

'Well, old friend. Why here, you must be thinking, a tiny mark on this great ocean. Are we destined to fight?'

Allday held out the old sword and ran his eye along the edge.

'Like all them other times, Sir Richard. It was meant to be. That's it an' all about it.' Then he grinned, almost his old self again. 'We'll win, no matter what.' He paused, and the defiant humour was gone. 'Y' see, Sir Richard, we've both got too much to lose.' He slid the blade back into its scabbard. 'God help them that tries to take it away!'

Bolitho walked to the quarterdeck rail and gripped it while he peered up at the towering mainmast with its iron-hard canvas. He was shivering, not because of the cold morning air, but with the instinctive awareness of danger that could still surprise him after a lifetime at sea. The sails were paler now, but there was no horizon, and the only movement he recognized through the thick criss-cross of rigging and flapping canvas seemed to float above the ship, keeping pace with her like a solitary sea bird. It was his flag, the Cross of St George, which flew day and night while he was in command. He thought of her letter in the pocket of his coat, and imagined he could hear her voice. *My admiral of England.*

He could still taste the bitterness of coffee on his tongue, and wondered why he had not forced himself to eat. Tension, uncertainty perhaps. But fear? He smiled. Perhaps he could no longer recognize that emotion.

Figures moved all around him, each one careful not to intrude upon his solitude. He could see Isaac York, a head taller than his mates, his slate-coloured hair blowing in the wind: a good man and a strong one. Bolitho knew that he had even tried to help Scarlett when the extent of his debts had become known. The white breeches of the lieutenants and midshipmen stood out in the lingering darkness, and he guessed that they were preparing themselves for what might happen today, each in his own fashion.

He moved to the compass box and glanced at the tilting card. North-east by north, with the wind still firm across the larboard quarter. Men were working high overhead, feeling for frayed cordage or jammed blocks with the sureness of true seamen.

Tyacke was down on the lee side, his lean figure framed

162

against the pale water creaming back from the bows. One long arm moved to emphasize a point, and he could imagine Daubeny concentrating on every word. They were chalk and cheese, but the mixture seemed to work: Tyacke had a peculiar gift of being able to communicate his requirements to his subordinates without unnecessary anger or sarcasm. At first they had been afraid of him, and repulsed by the hideous scars: eventually they had all overcome such things, and had become a company of which to be proud.

He heard a midshipman whisper to his friend and saw them look up, and he shaded his eyes and stared with them at his flag, the red cross suddenly hard and bright, touched by the first light of dawn.

'*Deck there!*' Carleton's voice was clear and very loud: he was using a speaking-trumpet. 'Sail on the larboard bow!' A pause, and Bolitho could picture the young midshipman asking the masthead lookout his opinion. Tyacke was always careful with his choice of 'eyes': they were invariably experienced sailors, many of whom had grown older with the ships they were serving, or fighting.

Carleton called again, 'She's *Attacker*, sir!' He sounded almost disappointed that it was not a first sighting of the enemy. The other frigate was one of the smaller sixth-rates, and mounted only twenty-six guns. Bolitho frowned. The same as *Reaper*. But she was not like *Reaper*. In his mind's eye he could see *Attacker*'s captain, George Morrison, a tough northerner from Tyneside. But no sadist: his punishment book was one of the cleanest in the squadron.

Avery said quietly, 'He must sight *Virtue* soon, sir.'

Bolitho looked at him, and saw the new light driving the shadows from his face.

'Perhaps. We may have become separated in the night. Not for long.'

163

He knew Allday was close by: he must be standing almost where his son had fallen that day.

He pushed the thought away. This was now. *Attacker* was on her proper station, or soon would be, once she had sighted the flagship. The other frigate, *Virtue*, carried thirty-six guns. Her captain was Roger M' Cullom, in character a little like Dampier, who had been *Zest*'s captain before Adam had taken command. Devil-may-care and popular, but inclined to be reckless. Whether to impress his men or for his own benefit, it was still a dangerous and, as Dampier had discovered, sometimes a fatal flaw.

Sam Hockenhull the boatswain had come aft to speak with the first lieutenant. Bolitho noticed that he was careful to avoid contact with Allday, who still blamed him for sending his son to join the afterguard on the day he had died. The quarterdeck and poop were always ripe targets for enemy sharp-shooters and the deadly swivel guns in close combat: command and authority began and were easily ended here. It was nobody's fault, and Hockenhull probably felt badly about it, although nothing had been said.

Bolitho sensed the restlessness among the waiting seamen. The leading edge of tension and apprehension had passed. They might be relieved later, when there was time to think on it. Now they would feel cheated that the sea was empty. As though they had been misled.

And here was the sun at last, giving a bronze edge to the horizon. Bolitho saw *Attacker*'s topsails for the first time, the faint touch of colour from her streaming mast-head pendant.

Someone gasped with alarm as a muffled bang echoed across the sea's jagged whitecaps. One shot, the sound going on and on for seconds, as if in a mine or a long tunnel.

Tyacke was beside him immediately. 'Signal, Sir Richard. It's *Virtue*. She's sighted 'em!'

Bolitho said, 'Make more sail. Then as soon as. . . .'

Carleton's voice came down from the masthead again. 'Deck there! Two sail in sight to the nor' east!'

There were more far-off shots, in earnest this time.

Tyacke's strong voice controlled the sudden uncertainty around him. 'Hands aloft, Mr Daubeny! Get the royals on her!' To York he called, 'Weather-helm, let her fall off two points!' He rubbed his hands. 'Now we'll see her fly, lads!'

More shots, sporadic but determined. Two ships, perhaps more. Tyacke was looking toward him again.

Bolitho said, 'When you are ready, Captain Tyacke.' Then he looked up as the royals thundered from their yards, adding their power to the straining masts and rigging.

'Beat to quarters, Mr Daubeny! Then clear for action, if you please!'

Daubeny was staring at him. Reliving the past, trying to face the future.

The marine drummers were already below the poop, and at a signal from their sergeant they began to beat out the familiar rattle, the sounds soon lost in the answering rush of feet as idlers and off-watch hands divided into teams, each of which knew precisely what was expected of them. Bolitho stood quite still, aware of the order and purpose around him, gained by months of drills and exercises, and Tyacke's own forceful example.

The cabin beneath his feet would be stripped bare like the rest of the ship, screens torn down, all privacy gone, until the vessel was open from bow to stern. A ship of war.

'Cleared for action, sir!' Daubeny turned back to his captain.

Tyacke nodded. 'That was well done.' Then, formally,

he touched his hat to his admiral. '*Virtue* is engaging without support, Sir Richard.'

Bolitho said nothing. M' Cullom was not the kind to wait. It would be ship to ship, evening old scores, a seizing of the initiative like any frigate captain. Carleton's voice came down like an intrusion.

'Third sail in sight, sir! There's smoke!'

Bolitho said, 'Go aloft, George. Discover what you can.'

Avery glanced at him even as he hurried to the shrouds. Afterwards, he was to recall the pain in his eyes, as if he already knew.

More gunfire, and Bolitho saw the smoke for the first time, like a stain on the shark-blue water. He could feel the deck lifting and then shuddering down as *Indomitable* thrust her fourteen hundred tons into each oncoming roller. Even the yards appeared to be bending like giant bows, every sail full, each shroud and stay bar-taut under her great pyramid of sails.

'Load, sir?' Tyacke's eyes were everywhere, even aloft, where a man had almost lost his hold as he was securing one of the nets which had been spread to protect the gun crews from falling spars.

Bolitho glanced at the masthead pendant. Like an arrow. The enemy could not outpace this ship, nor did they have the time to beat back into the wind. M' Cullom must have seen all this, and set it against the risk. The odds.

'Yes. Load, but do not run out. *Virtue* has given us time. Let us use it!'

Avery called down suddenly, '*Virtue* has lost a topmast, sir! There are two frigates engaging her!' The rest was lost in an angry growl from the gun crews as they paused to peer up at the mainmast, their legs braced on the freshly sanded deck, their expressions shocked, but free of fear. This was different. *Virtue* was one of their own.

Bolitho looked away. *My men.*

More explosions, and then Avery returned to the quarterdeck.

'She can't hope to last much longer, sir.'

'I know.' He spoke sharply, angry with himself at the cost, which was already too high. 'Make to *Attacker*, *Close on the Flag*.' As Avery shouted for the signal party, he added, 'Then hoist *Close Action!*'

So easily said. He felt for the locket under his shirt.

May Fate always guide you.

A tiny mark on this great ocean, he had said to Allday.

He turned and stared along the full length of the ship, past each unmoving gun crew, the lieutenants at the foot of each mast, then beyond the lion, with its upraised paws ready to strike.

The sea was cleaner, and a darker blue now, the sky empty of cloud in the first frail sunlight.

He gripped the sword at his side and tried to feel something, some emotion. No place now for any *perhaps* or *maybe*. Like all those other times, this was the moment. *Now.*

And there lay the enemy.

9

A Flag Captain

Bolitho waited for the bows to rear across another broken roller, then raised the telescope to his eye. The sea was glinting in a million mirrors, the horizon hard and sharp like something solid.

He moved the glass very slowly until he had found the embattled ships, changing shape in a swirling pall of gunsmoke.

Avery said, '*Attacker*'s on station, sir.' He sounded unwilling to disturb Bolitho's concentration.

On station. It seemed only minutes since the signal had been acknowledged; perhaps everything had been frozen in time, with only the three distant ships a reality.

Virtue was still fighting hard, engaging the enemy on either beam, her broadsides regular and well timed despite the ripped and ragged sails, and the gaps in her rigging and spars which revealed the true measure of her damage.

Two big frigates. He could see the Stars and Stripes curling from the leader's gaff, the stabbing tongues of orange flame along her side as her battery fired, and fired again.

The nearest enemy ship was breaking off the action, her smoke rolling down across her adversary as if to swamp her, her sails flapping in disorder but without confusion, as she began to alter course. She was coming fully about. Bolitho searched his feelings: there was neither satisfaction nor even anxiety. To fight, not to run, to grasp what wind she could and use it.

Had she tried to break free and stand away, *Indomitable* would have outsailed her, and raked her at least twice before the other captain had been made to face an inevitable defeat.

What Adam would have done. He smiled faintly, bleakly. *What I would do.*

He called to one of the midshipmen. 'Over here, Mr Blisset!' He waited for the youth to join him, and then rested the telescope on his shoulder. He saw the midshipman grin and wink to one of his friends. *See me? I am helping the admiral!*

Bolitho forgot him and all those around him as he watched a tiny cluster of coloured flags break from the other frigate. She was still engaging the defiant *Virtue*, and the pockmarks in her own sails showed that it was not all going in the enemy's favour.

He rubbed his left eye with his sleeve, angry at the interruption. The signal was being acknowledged, so the engaging vessel was the senior of the two. Almost certainly the same captain who had bluffed *Reaper* into surrender and worse. Who had intended to go after the convoy as he had probably done with others. Had they been his guns, too, which had smashed the transport *Royal Herald* into oblivion? *The face in the crowd.*

Someone shouted, '*Virtue*'s mizzen is going!'

And Isaac York's angry retort. 'We can see that, Mr Essex!'

Bolitho trained the glass still further. He could feel the youth's shoulder quivering: excitement, fear, it could be both.

The frigate was almost bows-on, leaning over as her yards were hauled round to hold her on the opposite tack. So close now, five miles or thereabouts. She would

169

soon be on a converging course. Tyacke must have antici-
pated it, had put himself in the other captain's place
when he had ordered York to let *Indomitable* fall off two
points. Either way, they would hold the wind-gage. It
would be a swift, and possibly decisive, embrace.

The enemy frigate was trying to head further into the
wind, but her flapping canvas filled again while she held
her present course.

Bolitho heard Tyacke say, almost to himself, *'Got you!'*

'Royal Marines, stand to!' That was Merrick. A good
officer, but one who had always been dominated by du
Cann, who had been torn to bloody shreds by a swivel
even as he had led his marines onto the American's deck.
Was Merrick hearing his voice even now, as he ordered
his men to their stations?

He moved the glass again, his lips dry as he saw *Virtue's*
blurred shape falling downwind, obviously out of command, her steering gone, her remaining sails whipping in
the wind like ragged banners.

Tyacke again. 'Starboard battery, Mr Daubeny! Open
the ports!'

A whistle shrilled, and Bolitho imagined the portlids
lifting like baleful eyes along their spray-dappled side.

'Run out!'

Bolitho lowered the glass and murmured a word of
thanks to the midshipman. He saw Avery watching him,
and said, 'The senior captain is holding off for the
present.'

Tyacke joined him and exclaimed angrily, 'To let
another do his work for him, the bastard!'

There was a puff of smoke from the approaching frigate, and seconds later a ball slapped down beyond
Indomitable's thrusting jib-boom. Bolitho said, 'You may
shorten sail, Captain Tyacke.' He could have been speaking to a stranger.

Tyacke was shouting to his lieutenants, while high

above the tilting deck the topmen were already kicking
and fisting the wild canvas under control, yelling to one
another as they had done so often during their endless
drills and contests, mast against mast. Bolitho straightened his back. It was always the same: the big maincourse
brailed up to lessen the risk of fire, but leaving the
crouching gun crews and the barebacked seamen at
the braces and halliards feeling exposed and vulnerable.

He stared at the drifting *Virtue*. If she survived this
day, it would take months to repair and refit her. Many
of her people would not see that, or any other day.

But her flag still flew, hoisted with pathetic jauntiness
to an undamaged yard, and through the smoke he could
see some of her seamen climbing on to the shattered
gangways to cheer and gesture as *Indomitable* surged
towards them.

Avery tore his eyes away from the other ship and
looked toward Bolitho as he said, 'See? They can still
cheer!' He pressed one hand to his eye, but Avery had
seen the emotion and the pain.

Tyacke leaned on the rail as if to control his ship single-
handed.

'On the uproll, Mr Daubeny!' He drew his sword and
lifted it, until the first lieutenant had turned towards him.

'When you are ready, Mr York!'

York raised a hand in acknowledgment. 'Helm a-lee!
Hold her steady there!'

Responding to the quarter-wind, *Indomitable* turned
slightly and without effort, her long jib-boom slicing
above the other ships like a giant's lance.

'Steady she is, sir! Nor' by east!'

'*Fire!*'

Controlled, gun by gun, the broadside thundered out
from bow to quarter, the sound so loud after the distant
sea-fight that some of the seamen almost lost their grip
on the braces as they hauled with all their strength to

drag the yards round, to harness the wind. The oncoming frigate had been waiting, to draw closer, or to anticipate Tyacke's first move. By a second or an hour, it was already too late, even before it had begun.

Bolitho watched *Indomitable*'s double-shotted broadside smashing into the other ship, and imagined that he saw her stagger as if she had run aground. He saw great holes in the sails, the wind already exploring them and tearing them apart. Severed rigging and shrouds dangled over her side, and more than one gunport had been left empty, blinded, its cannon running free to cause more havoc inboard.

'Stop your vents! Sponge out! Load! Run out!'

Even as the enemy fired, the gun crews threw themselves into their work in a barely controlled frenzy.

Gun captains peered aft where Tyacke stood watching the other frigate. Perhaps he could exclude all else but the moment and his duty; he certainly did not seem to notice as one of the packed hammocks was torn apart by a jagged splinter a few yards from his body.

Bolitho felt the hull jerk as some of the other frigate's iron found its mark. The range was closing fast; he could even see men running to retrim the yards, and an officer waving his sword, before Tyacke's arm came down and the guns hurled themselves inboard on their tackles once more. Through the black shrouds and stays the American frigate looked as if she would run headlong into *Indomitable*'s side, but it was an illusion of battle, and the sea churned between the two ships was as bright as before.

Bolitho snatched up a glass and walked to the opposite side, expecting to see the senior American frigate running into the fight, with only the smaller *Attacker* standing in her way. He stared with disbelief as he realized that she had already gone about, and was making more sail even as he watched.

Avery said hoarsely, 'Not bluffing this time, sir!'

There was a wild cheer as the frigate's foremast began to fall. He imagined he could hear the terrible sounds of splintering wood and tearing rigging, although his ears were still deaf from the last broadside. So slow, so very slow. He even thought he could see the final hesitation before shrouds and stays snapped under the weight, and the whole mast, complete with yards, top and sails, thundered down alongside, dragging the vessel round like some giant sea-anchor.

He watched the range closing fast, the American frigate turning clumsily while some of her men ran to cut the mast adrift, their axes like bright stars in the smoky sunshine.

Daubeny called, 'All loaded, sir!'

Tyacke did not seem to hear. He was watching the other ship as she drifted helplessly to the thrust of wind and current.

The American officer was still waving his sword, and the huge Stars and Stripes streamed as proudly as before.

'*Strike, damn you!*' But Tyacke's voice held no anger or hatred; it was more a plea, one captain to another.

Two of the enemy's guns recoiled in their ports and Bolitho saw more packed hammocks blasted from their nettings, and seamen reeling from their weapons while one of their number was cut in half by a ball, his legs kneeling in grotesque independence.

Tyacke stared at Bolitho. Nothing was said. The sudden silence was almost more painful than the explosions.

Bolitho glanced at the enemy ship, and saw that some of her seamen who had been running seconds earlier to hack away the dragging wreckage had stopped as if stricken, unable to move. But here and there a musket flashed, and he knew that her invisible marksmen could not be cheated for much longer.

He nodded. 'As you bear!'

The sword fell, and in one shattering roar the starboard battery fired into the drifting smoke.

Daubeny yelled, *'Reload!'*

Stooping like old men, the gun crews sponged out the hot guns and rammed home the fresh charges and shining black balls from the garlands. At one of the ports the men hauled their gun back, oblivious even to the sliced corpse and the blood that soaked their trousers like paint. A fight they could understand; even the pain and fear that kept it close company were part of it, something expected. But a drifting ship, unable to steer and with most of her guns either unmanned or out of action, was something different.

A lone voice shouted, 'Strike, you bloody bastard! Strike, for Jesus' sake!' Above the wind in the rigging, it sounded like a scream.

Tyacke said, 'So be it.' He dropped his sword and the guns exploded, the vivid tongues of flame appearing to reach and touch the target.

The smoke funnelled downwind, and men stood away from their guns, their eyes red-rimmed in smoke-grimed faces, sweat cutting stripes across their bodies.

Bolitho watched coldly. A ship which could not win, and which would not surrender. Where the working party had been gathered there was only splintered timber and a few corpses, tossed aside with brutal indifference. Men and pieces of men, and from her scuppers there were tiny threads of scarlet, as if the ship herself was bleeding to death. Daubeny had removed his hat, probably without knowing what he had done. But he stared aft again, his face like stone as he called, 'All loaded, sir!'

Tyacke turned toward the three figures by the weather rail: Bolitho, Avery close beside him, and Allday a few paces away, his naked cutlass resting on the deck.

One more broadside would finish her completely, with so much damage below deck that she might even burst into flames, deadly to any vessel that came near her. Fire was the greatest fear of every sailor, in both war and peace.

Bolitho felt the numbness. The ache. They were waiting. Justice; revenge; the completeness of defeat.

His was the final responsibility. When he looked for the other American ship, he could barely find her beyond the smoke. But waiting, watching to see what he would do. *Testing me again.*

'Very well, Captain Tyacke!' He knew that some of the seamen and marines were staring at him, with disbelief, perhaps even disgust. But the gun captains were responding, answering the only discipline they understood. The trigger-lines were pulled taut, each man staring across his muzzle, the helpless target filling every open port.

Tyacke raised his sword. Remembering that moment at the Nile when hell had burst into his life and had left its mark as a permanent reminder? Or seeing just another enemy, a fragment of a war which had outlived so many, friends and foes alike?

There was a sudden burst of shouting and Bolitho shaded his eyes to watch the solitary figure on the enemy's torn and bloodied quarterdeck. No sword this time, and one arm hanging broken, or even missing in the dangling sleeve.

Very deliberately and without even turning towards *Indomitable*, he tugged at the halliards, and almost fell as the big Stars and Stripes spiralled down into the smoke.

Avery said in a tight voice, 'He had no choice.'

Bolitho glanced at him. Like Tyacke, another memory? Of his own little schooner surrendering to the enemy, while he lay wounded and helpless?

He said, 'He had every choice. Men died for no good purpose. Remember what I told you. *They* have no choice at all.'

He looked in Allday's direction. 'Bravely, old friend?'

Allday lifted the cutlass and balanced the blade on one hand.

'It gets harder, Sir Richard.' Then he grinned, and Bolitho thought that even the sunshine was dim by comparison. 'Aye, set bravely!'

Tyacke was watching the other vessel, the brief savagery of action already being crowded aside by the immediate needs of command.

'Boarding parties, Mr Daubeny! The marines will go across when the ship is secured! Pass the word for the surgeon and let me know the bill – we'll see the cost of this morning's show of courage!'

Indomitable was responding, the carpenter and his crew already below, hammers and squeaking tackles marking their progress through the lower hull.

Then Tyacke sheathed his sword, and saw the youngest midshipman observing him closely, although his eyes were still blurred with shock. Tyacke looked steadily back at him, giving himself time to consider what had so nearly happened.

He barely knew the midshipman, who had been sent out from England as a replacement for young Deane. His eyes moved unwillingly to one of the quarterdeck guns. Right there, as others had just fallen.

'Well, Mr Campbell, what did you learn from all this?'

The boy, who was only twelve years old, hesitated under Tyacke's gaze, unused as yet to the scars, and the man who bore them.

In a small voice he answered, 'We *won*, sir.'

Tyacke walked past him and touched his shoulder, something he did not often do. He was more surprised than the midshipman at the contact.

'*They lost*, Mr Campbell. It is not always the same thing!'

Bolitho was waiting for him. 'She's not much of a prize, James. But her loss will be felt elsewhere!'

Tyacke smiled. Bolitho did not wish to speak of it, either.

He said, 'No chance of a chase now, Sir Richard. We have others to care for.'

Bolitho stared at the dark blue water, and the other American frigate, which was already several miles clear. 'I can wait.' He tensed. Someone was crying out in agony as others attempted to move him. 'They did well.'

He saw Ozzard's small figure picking his way through the discarded tackles and rammers by the guns. So much a part of it, and yet able to distance himself from all the sights and sounds around him. He was carrying a bottle, wrapped in a surprisingly clean cloth.

Tyacke was still beside him, although aware of those on every hand who were demanding his attention.

'They're lucky, Sir Richard.'

Bolitho watched Ozzard preparing a clean goblet, oblivious to everything but the job in hand.

'Some may not agree, James.'

Tyacke said abruptly, '*Trust*, sir.' One word, but it seemed to hang there even as he walked away for the final act with a vanquished enemy.

Bolitho raised the goblet to his lips as the shadow of the enemy's topmast laid its patterns on the deck beside him. He saw some of the bloodied seamen pause to watch him; a few grinned when they caught his eye, others merely stared, needing to recognize something. To remember, perhaps, or to tell somebody later, who might want to know about it. He found himself touching the locket beneath his shirt. She would understand what it meant to him. Just that one word, so simply put.

While the sun climbed higher in the clear sky to raise a misty haze on either horizon, *Indomitable*'s company worked with scarcely a pause to cleanse their ship of the scars and stains of battle. The air was heady with rum, and it was hoped that a meal would be ready by noon. To the ordinary sailor, strong drink and a full belly were considered a cure for almost everything.

Below the sounds of repair and the disciplined activity, on *Indomitable*'s orlop deck the contrast was stark. Beneath the ship's waterline, it was a hushed place that never saw daylight, nor would it until she was broken up. Through the ship's length it was a place for stores and spare timber, rigging and fresh water, and in the carefully guarded magazines, powder and shot. Here was the purser's store, with slop clothing and tobacco, food, and wine for the wardroom, and in the same darkness, broken here and there by clusters of lanterns, some of *Indomitable*'s company, midshipmen and other junior warrant officers, lived, slept, and by the light of flickering glims studied and dreamed of promotion.

It was also a place where men were brought to survive or to die, as their wounds and injuries dictated.

Bolitho ducked low between each massive deck beam and waited for his eyes to accept the harsh change from sunlight to this gloom, from the relief and high spirits of the victors, to the men down here who might not live to see the sun again.

Because of their opening broadsides and Tyacke's superior ship-handling at close quarters, *Indomitable*'s casualties, her bill, had been mercifully light. He knew from long experience that that was no consolation to the unlucky ones down on the orlop. Some were lying, or propped against the great curved timbers of the hull, bandaged, or staring at the little group around the make-shift table where the surgeon and his assistants, the loblolly boys, worked on their patients: their victims, the old Jacks called them.

Bolitho could hear Allday's painful breathing, and did not know why he had chosen to accompany him. He must be grateful that his son had been spared this final indignity and despair.

They were holding a man down on the table, his nakedness still revealing the powder stains of battle, his face and neck sweating as he almost choked on the rum which was being poured down his throat before the leather strap was put between his teeth. The surgeon's apron was dark with blood. No wonder they called them butchers.

But Philip Beauclerk was not typical of the uncaring, hardened surgeons who were usually found throughout the fleet. He was young and highly skilled, and had volunteered with a group of other surgeons to serve in ships of war, where it was known that conditions and the crude treatment of wounds often killed more men than the enemy. After his present commission Beauclerk would return to the College of Surgeons in London, where, with his colleagues, he would contribute his knowledge to a practical guide, which might help to ease the suffering of men like these.

Beauclerk had done well during the fight with the U.S.S. *Unity*, and had offered great support to Adam Bolitho when he had been brought aboard after his escape from prison. He had a composed and serious face, and the palest and steadiest eyes Bolitho had ever seen. He recalled the moment when Beauclerk had mentioned his finest tutor, Sir Piers Blachford, who had been researching the same conditions himself aboard *Hyperion*. Bolitho saw him even now, his tall, heron-like figure striding between decks, asking questions, talking to anyone he chose, a severe man, but possessing great qualities of courage and compassion, which had made even the hardest seamen respect him. Blachford had been in *Hyperion* to her last day, when she had finally given up the fight and gone down, with Bolitho's flag still flying. Many had gone down with her: they could be in no better company. And they still sang about his old ship, *How*

Hyperion Cleared the Way. It always brought a cheer in the taverns and the pleasure gardens, even though those who cheered her name rarely had any idea what it was like. What *this* was like.

For a few seconds Beauclerk looked up, his eyes like chips of glass in the light of the swinging lanterns. He was a very private man, no easy thing to achieve in a crowded warship. He had known for some time of Bolitho's damaged eye, and that it had been Blachford who had told him that there was no hope for it. But he had said nothing.

The wounded seaman was quieter now, whimpering to himself, not seeing the knife in Beauclerk's hand, the saw held ready by an assistant.

'You are welcome here, Sir Richard.' He watched him, assessing him. 'We are nearly done.' Then, as the seaman twisted his face toward the admiral, he gave a brief shake of his head.

Bolitho was deeply moved, and wondered if this was why he had come. This man might die: at best, he would be one more cripple thrown on the beach. His leg had been crushed, no doubt by a recoiling gun.

Tyacke's words still haunted him, from that September day when so many others had fallen. *And for what?* An enemy frigate taken, but so badly damaged that it was unlikely she would survive a sudden squall, let alone fight in the line. *Virtue* had also been severely mauled, and had lost twenty of her men. Surprisingly, her captain, the devil-may-care M' Cullom, had survived without a scratch. This time.

Indomitable had lost only four men killed, and some fifteen wounded. Bolitho moved to the table and took the man's wrist, the surgeon's mate stepping aside, staring at Beauclerk as if for an explanation.

Bolitho closed his fingers around the man's thick wrist, and said gently, 'Easy, now.' He glanced at Beauclerk and saw his lips form the name. 'You did well, Parker.' He raised his voice very slightly and looked beyond, into the shadows, knowing that others were listening to his empty words. 'And that applies to you all!'

He felt the wrist start to shake. It was not a movement, but a mere sensation, like something running through him, out of control. It was terror.

Beauclerk nodded to his assistants and they seized the leg, their eyes averted as the knife came down and cut deeply. Beauclerk showed no hesitation, no outward emotion, as his patient arched his back and tried to scream through the strap. Then the saw. It seemed endless, but Bolitho knew only a matter of seconds had passed. It was followed by a sickening thud as they dropped the leg into the 'wings and limbs' tub. Now the needle, the fingers bright and bloody in the swaying lantern light. Beauclerk glanced at Bolitho's hand on the man's wrist, the admiral's gold lace against the smoke-grimed skin.

Somebody murmured, 'No good, sir. Lost him.'

Beauclerk stood back. 'Take him.' He turned to watch as the dead seaman was dragged from the table. 'It's never easy.'

Bolitho heard Allday clearing his throat. Seeing it all again, as if it were his own son, floating away, eventually sinking into the depths. *And for what?*

He stared at the table, the pools of blood, the urine, the evidence of pain. There was no dignity here in death, no answer to the question.

He walked back toward the ladder and heard Beauclerk ask, 'Why did he come?' and did not linger to hear the reply. Beauclerk saw the instant guard in Allday's eyes and added, quite gently, 'You know him better than any man. I should like to understand.'

''Cause he blames himself.' He recalled his own words when the American flag had come down. 'It gets harder, see?'

181

'Yes. I think I do.' He wiped his bloody hands. 'Thank you.' He frowned as two of the injured men raised a hoarse cheer. 'That will not help him, either.' But Allday had gone.

When he returned to London it would all be so different. His experience might help others one day: it would certainly assist him in his chosen career. He looked around, recalling the admiral's austere face after that other battle, as it must have been after all those which had preceded it. And the day his nephew had been brought aboard. More like two brothers, he thought. Like love.

He smiled, knowing that if they saw it, his assistants might think him callous. London or not, nothing would ever be the same.

The captain's quarters in *Indomitable* were no longer as spacious as they had been during her life as a two-decker, but after his previous command of the brig *Larne* James Tyacke still found them palatial. Although cleared for action like the rest of the ship, they had remained undamaged by the swift bombardment, as they were on the larboard and disengaged side.

Bolitho sat in the proffered chair and listened to the muffled thuds and dragging sounds from his own stern cabin, as screens were replaced and the smoke stains were washed away, until the next time.

Tyacke said, 'We got off very lightly, Sir Richard.'

Bolitho took a glass of cognac from Tyacke's coxswain, Fairbrother. He looked after his captain without fuss or fancy, and seemed a man pleased with his role, and the fact that his captain called him by his first name, Eli.

He gazed around the cabin; it was neat but spartan, with nothing to reveal any hint of the character of the man who lived and slept here. Only the big sea-chest was familiar, and he knew it was the one in which Tyacke used to carry the silk gown he had bought for the girl he intended to marry. She had refused him after his terrible injury at the Nile. How long he had carried the gown was unknown, but he had given it to Catherine to wear when he had found them after their ordeal in *Golden Plover*'s longboat. Bolitho knew she had sent it back to Tyacke when they had reached England, beautifully cleaned and pressed, in case there should be another woman in the future. It was probably in the chest at this moment, a reminder of the rejection he had suffered.

Tyacke said, 'I've made a full report. The prize is nothing much.' He paused. 'Not after we'd finished with her. She had over fifty killed, and twice as many wounded. She was carrying a lot of extra hands, for prize crews, no doubt. If they'd managed to board us. . . .' He shrugged. 'A different story, maybe.'

He studied Bolitho curiously, having heard about his visit to the orlop and that he had restrained one of the badly wounded as the surgeon had taken off his leg. He thought with a mental shudder of Beauclerk's pale eyes. A cold fish, like the rest of his breed.

Bolitho said, 'She was the U.S.S. *Success*, formerly the French *Dryade*.' He looked up at Tyacke, and felt his scrutiny like something physical. 'Her captain was killed.'

'Aye. It was like a slaughterhouse. Our gun captains have learned well.' There was the pride again, which even the horror he had described could not diminish.

He held his goblet to the light and said, 'When I became your flag captain, it was an even greater challenge than I had expected.' He gave his faint, attractive smile. 'And I knew I was going into deep water from the start. It wasn't just the size of the ship, and my responsibility to all her people, but also my role within the squadron. I had been so used to a small command – a seclusion which, looking back, I know I myself created.

And then, under your flag, there were the other ships, and the whims and weaknesses of their captains.'

Bolitho said nothing. It was one of those rare moments of confidence, something he did not wish to interrupt, a mutual trust which had made itself felt between them from the very beginning, when they had first met in Tyacke's schooner *Miranda*.

Tyacke said abruptly, 'I started keeping my own log book. I discovered that a flag captain should never rely on memory alone. And when your nephew was brought aboard wounded, after his escape from that Yankee prison, I made notes on everything he told me.' He glanced at a sealed gunport as if he could see the American prize riding under *Indomitable*'s lee. Victors and vanquished were working together aboard her to fit a jury rig, which, with luck and fair sailing, might take her to Halifax.

'There was a lieutenant aboard the *Success*. A young man, so badly hurt by splinters that I wondered what was keeping him alive.' He cleared his throat, as if embarrassed by the emotion his voice revealed. 'I talked with him for a while. He was in great pain. There was nothing anyone could do.'

Bolitho saw it with a poignant clarity, as if he had been there with them. This strong, remote man sitting with an enemy, perhaps the only one truly able to share his suffering.

'In some ways he reminded me of your nephew, sir. I thought it was the battle, being beaten, knowing he was paying with his life. But it wasn't that. He simply could not believe that their other ship had cut and run – had left them to fight alone.'

There were whispering voices outside the door, officers needing advice or instructions. Tyacke would know of their presence, but nothing would move him until he was ready.

He said, 'The lieutenant's name was Brice, Mark Brice. He had prepared a letter to be dispatched should the worst happen.' He was momentarily bitter. 'I've warned others about that kind of maudlin sentiment. It's . . . it's asking for death.'

'Brice?' Bolitho felt a chill of recognition run through him, as though he were hearing Adam's own voice as he had described it to him. 'It was a Captain Joseph Brice who invited Adam to change sides when he was captured.'

Tyacke said, 'Yes. He was that captain's son. An address in Salem.'

'And the letter?'

'The usual, sir. Duty and love of country, not a lot of value when you're dead.' He picked up a small book from the table. 'Still, I'm glad I wrote it down.'

'And the other ship, James? Is that what's troubling you?'

Tyacke shrugged heavily. 'Well, I learned quite a bit from them. She's the U.S.S. *Retribution*, another ex-Frenchman, *Le Gladiateur*. Forty guns, maybe more.' Then he said, 'There's no doubt in my mind that these were the ships that took *Reaper*.' He glared at the door. 'I shall have to go, sir. Please make use of these quarters until yours are ready.'

He hesitated by the door, as though grappling with something. 'You were once a flag captain yourself, sir?'

Bolitho smiled. 'Yes. A very long time ago, in a three-decker. *Euryalus*, one hundred guns. I learned a great deal in her.' He waited, knowing there was more.

Tyacke said, 'The American lieutenant had heard about it. Your time in *Euryalus*, I mean.'

'But that was all of seventeen years ago, James. This lieutenant, Brice, would hardly have been old enough. . . .'

Tyacke said bluntly, '*Retribution*'s captain told him.

About you, about *Euryalus*. But he died before he could tell me anything more.'

He opened the door a few inches. 'Wait!' There were a few murmurings from beyond, and then he added sharply, 'Well, do it, or I'll find somebody else better suited.' He turned toward Bolitho again. '*Retribution*'s captain is named Aherne.' He hesitated. 'That's all I know.'

Bolitho was on his feet, without realizing that he had left the chair. The big three-decker *Euryalus* had seemed the final step to flag rank, and he had carried even more responsibility than was usual for a flag captain. His admiral, Rear-Admiral Sir Charles Thelwall, had been old for his rank; he was dying, and he knew it. But England was facing heavy odds, with France and Spain confident of an early invasion. It had been in *Euryalus* that he had first met Catherine. . . .

Tyacke's coxswain held out the bottle. 'Another, Sir Richard?'

Bolitho saw Tyacke's unconcealed surprise when he accepted. He said slowly, 'Dangerous times, James.' He was thinking aloud. 'We were ordered to Ireland. A French squadron was reported ready to support an uprising. Had it come about, the balance might have shifted against England there and then. There was even worse to follow . . . the great mutinies in the fleet at the Nore and Spithead. Dangerous times, indeed.'

'And Ireland, sir?'

'There were a few battles. I think the strain of the responsibility finally killed Sir Charles Thelwall. A fine man, a gentle man. I much admired him.' He faced Tyacke, his eyes suddenly hard. 'And of course there was the inevitable aftermath of recrimination and punishment meted out to those who had conspired against the King. It proved nothing, it solved nothing. One of those hanged for treason was a patriot called Daniel Aherne, the scapegoat who became a martyr.' He picked up his glass, and found that it was empty. 'So, James, we have found the missing face: Rory Aherne. I knew he had gone to America, but that is all I know. Seventeen years. A long time to nurture hatred.'

Tyacke said, 'How can we be sure?'

'I am certain, James. Coincidence, fate, who knows?' He smiled briefly. '*Retribution*, eh? A good choice.'

He thought suddenly of Catherine's words to him, when they had first been thrown together. *Men are made for war, and you are no exception.*

That was then, but can we ever change?

Aloud he said, 'Call me when we get under way, James. And thank you.'

Tyacke paused. 'Sir?'

'For being a flag captain, James. That, and so much more.'

10

Time and Distance

Sir Wilfred Lafargue put down the empty cup and walked to one of the tall windows of his spacious office. For such a heavily-built man he moved with remarkable agility, as if the young, eager lawyer was still there, a prisoner of his own success. Lafargue had once been described as handsome, but now, in his late fifties, he was showing signs of good living and other excesses which even his expensively cut coat and breeches could not disguise.

The coffee was good: eventually, he might send for more. But he was content for the moment to stand looking out of this window, one of his favourites, across the City of London, where, despite more buildings than ever before, there were still many restful parks and ornamental gardens. This was Lincoln's Inn, one of the centres of English law, and the prestigious address of many legal practices which served a world of both power and money.

This particular house, for instance, had once been the London residence of a famous general, who had met an ignominious death by fever in the West Indies. Now it held the offices of the legal firm which bore his family name, and of which Lafargue was the senior partner.

He idly watched some carriages as they rattled past on their way to Fleet Street. It was a fine day, with clear blue sky above the spires and impressive buildings. From the far window he would be able to see St Paul's, or at least the dome of the cathedral; it was a sight that always pleased him. Like the centre of things, in his world.

He considered the visitor who was waiting to see him. His staff had been busy on her behalf, but this would be his first meeting with the lady in question, Lady Catherine Somervell. When he had mentioned the appointment to his wife she had been sharp, even angry, as if it offended her personally in some way.

He smiled. But then, how could she understand?

Now he would see for himself what the notorious viscountess was really like. She was certainly one of the most discussed women of the day: if only a tenth of it was true, he would soon discover her strength and her weakness. She had risen above it all, the scandal and the secret slander. The fact that her last husband had died mysteriously in a duel had been conveniently forgotten. He smiled more broadly. *Not by me.*

He turned with irritation as a door opened slightly, and his senior clerk peered in at him.

'What is it, Spicer?' The offices revolved around the senior clerk, a dedicated man who missed no detail in all the legal papers and documents that passed through his hands. He was also very dull.

Spicer said, 'Lady Somervell is about to leave, Sir Wilfred.' He spoke without expression. When the Prime Minister, Spencer Perceval, had been assassinated by some lunatic at the House of Commons the previous year, he had announced it in much the same fashion, as if it was a comment on the weather.

Lafargue snapped, 'What do you mean, leaving? That lady has an appointment with me!'

Spicer was unmoved. 'That was nearly half an hour ago, Sir Wilfred.'

Lafargue contained himself with an effort. It was his practice to keep clients waiting, no matter how high or low they stood on the social scale.

It was a bad beginning. He said curtly, 'Bring her in.'

He sat at his vast desk and watched the other door. Everything was in its place, a chair directly opposite him, an impressive background of leather volumes from floor to ceiling behind. Sound, reliable, like the City itself. Like a bank.

He rose slowly as the doors were opened and Lady Catherine Somervell entered the room. It was far too large for an office but Lafargue liked it for that reason: it often intimidated visitors who had to walk almost its full length to reach the chair by the desk.

For the first time in his experience, the effect was completely reversed.

She was taller than he had expected, and walked without hesitation or uncertainty, her dark eyes never leaving his face. She was dressed all in green, and carrying a broad-brimmed straw hat with a matching ribbon. Lafargue was intelligent enough to appreciate that his clumsy ploy of allowing her to wait could never impress a woman like this.

'Please be seated, Lady Somervell.' He watched the easy way she sat in the straight-backed chair, confident, but wary. Defiant, perhaps. 'I regret the delay. Some difficulty arose at the last minute.'

Her dark eyes moved only briefly to the empty coffee cup.

'Of course.'

Lafargue sat down again and touched some papers on his desk. It was hard not to stare at her. She was beautiful: there was no other possible description. Her hair, so dark that it might have been black, was piled above her ears, so that her throat and neck seemed strangely unprotected. Provocative. High cheekbones, and now the merest hint of a smile as she said, 'So what news may I expect?'

Catherine had seen the assessing glance. She had seen

190

many such before. This illustrious lawyer, recommended by Sillitoe when she had asked for his advice, was no different, in spite of the grand setting and the air of showmanship. Sillitoe had remarked, 'Like most lawyers, his worth and his honesty will be measured by the weight of his bill!'

Lafargue said, 'You have seen all the details of your late husband's affairs.' He coughed politely. 'Your pardon. Your previous husband, I mean. His business ventures prospered even during the war between Great Britain and Spain. It was his surviving son's wish that you receive that which was always intended for your own use.' His eyes flicked down to the papers. 'Claudio Luis Pareja was his son by his first marriage.'

She said, 'Yes.' She ignored the unspoken question: he would know, in any case. When Luis had asked her to marry him he had been more than twice her age, and even his son, Claudio, had been older than she. She had been afraid, desperate, lost, when the small, amiable Luis had taken her as his bride. It had not been love as she now knew it to be, but the man's kindness, his need of her, had been like a door opening for her to step through. She had been a mere girl, and he had given her vision and opportunity, and she had learned the manners and graces of the people he knew or did business with.

He had died when Richard Bolitho's ship had taken control of the vessel in which they had been passengers, on their way to Luis's estate in Minorca. She had known afterwards that she loved Richard, but she had lost him. Until Antigua, when he had sailed into English Harbour with his flag flying above the old *Hyperion*.

She could feel the lawyer's eyes exploring her, although when she looked at him directly he was examining his papers again.

She said, 'So I am a very rich woman?'

'At the stroke of a pen, my lady.' He was intrigued

that she had shown neither surprise nor triumph, not since they had first exchanged letters. A beautiful widow, envied, wealthy: the temptation would be a great one for many men. He thought of Sir Richard Bolitho, the hero, whom even common sailors seemed to admire. He glanced at her again. Her skin was brown like a country woman's, like her hands and wrists. He speculated on their life together when they were not separated by the ocean, and the war.

The thought made him remark, 'I have heard that things are moving at last in North America.'

'What is that?' She stared at him, one hand moving to her breast. How quickly it could happen. Like a shadow, a threat.

He said, 'We received word that the Americans attacked York, crossed the lake in force and burned the government buildings there.'

'When?' One word, like a stone falling into a still pond.

'Oh, some six weeks ago, apparently. News is very slow to reach us.'

She stared at the window, at the fresh leaves visible beyond it. Six weeks. The end of April. Richard might have been there: he would be involved, in any case. She asked quietly, 'Anything else?'

He cleared his throat. Her unexpected anxiety had encouraged him: perhaps she was vulnerable after all.

'Some story of a mutiny in one of our ships. Poor devils, one can hardly blame them.' He paused. 'But there are limits, and we *are* at war.'

'What ship?' She knew he was enjoying her concern in some way. It did not matter. Nothing else did. Not the money, unexpected gift though it was from poor Luis, dead these many years. She asked more sharply, 'Can you remember?'

He pursed his lips. '*Reaper*. Yes, that was it. Do you know her?'

'One of Sir Richard's squadron. Her captain was killed last year. I do not know her, beyond that.' How could he understand? Mutiny.... She had watched Richard's face when he had described it, and what it cost the guilty and the innocent alike. He had been involved in the great naval mutinies, which had stunned the entire country at a time when the enemy was expected to invade. Some had believed it was the first fire of the same revolution which had brought the Terror to France.

How Richard would hate and loathe such an outbreak in his own command. Would blame himself for not having been there when the seeds were sown.

A total responsibility. And a punishment to him, also.

Lafargue said, 'Now, the other matter we discussed. The lease of the property has become available.' He watched her hand at her breast, the glittering pendant moving to betray the heightened pulse. 'The owner of the lease, an earl impoverished by bad luck or over-confidence at the tables, was more than willing to exchange deeds. Expensive property, madam. And occupied.'

He knew; of course he knew. She said, 'By Lady Bolitho.' She glanced down at the ruby ring on her hand, which he had given her in the church at Zennor on the day Valentine Keen had married Zenoria. It wrenched at her heart. They would all be waiting for her in Falmouth: the admiral's lady, or whore, as the mood dictated. 'It was my decision. I intend to lower the cost of the lease.' She looked up suddenly, and Lafargue saw the other woman in her eyes, the woman who had braved the sea in an open boat after shipwreck, who had captured the hearts of all who knew her. Now, in her face, he could see that everything he had heard of her was true.

She added, 'And I intend that she shall know it!'

Lafargue rang a small bell, and his senior clerk, with one other, appeared as if by magic.

He stood up and watched Spicer preparing the documents, a fresh pen already placed by her hand. He looked at the ring, assessing the cost: it was of rubies and diamonds, like the pendant she wore, which was in the shape of a fan. He thought of his wife and wondered how, or even if, he would describe his day to her.

Spicer said, 'Here and here, my lady.'

She signed her name quickly, recalling the small, untidy lawyer's office in Truro, which had handled the Bolitho affairs for generations. Chairs filled with files and dog-eared documents, far too dusty to ever have been used. Not surprisingly, it had been the portly Yovell who had guided her there when she had told him what she had heard from Seville. From Spain, where she had left childhood behind.

Untidy, yes, but she had been received there as if she had always belonged. As John Allday would have described it, *one of the family.*

Lafargue said, 'We are accustomed to such transactions, my lady. A head so beautiful should never be troubled by affairs of business.'

She looked up at him, and smiled. 'Thank you, Sir Wilfred. I value your skills as a lawyer. Flattery I can have at any time from a Billingsgate porter!'

She stood, and waited while Lafargue took her hand, and after a small hesitation held it to his lips.

'It has been an honour, my lady.'

She nodded to the two clerks, and saw the smile on the impassive features of the one named Spicer. It was a day he would remember, for whatever reasons of his own.

Lafargue made a last attempt. 'I noticed that you arrived in Lord Sillitoe's carriage, my lady. . . .' He almost flinched as the dark eyes turned toward him.

'How observant of you, Sir Wilfred.'

He walked beside her to the double doors. 'An influential man.'

She regarded herself in a tall mirror in passing. Her next visit was to the Admiralty, and she wondered if Bethune would eventually tell her about the attack on York and the mutiny.

'With respect, my lady, I think that even Lord Sillitoe would regard you as a challenge.'

She faced the lawyer again, her heart suddenly heavy. Wanting not to be alone: wanting Bolitho, needing him.

'I have found that a challenge can so easily become an obstacle, Sir Wilfred. One which may need to be removed. Wouldn't you agree?'

Back at his favourite window, Sir Wilfred Lafargue saw the liveried coachman hurry to open the carriage door for her. One of Sillitoe's hard men, he thought, more like a prize-fighter than a servant. He saw her pause to watch a clutter of sparrows drinking from a horse-trough's overflow. Distance hid her expression, but he knew she did not see or care for the passers-by who glanced at her.

He tried to arrange his impressions rationally, as he might marshal facts and arguments in a law suit, or with an opposing brief. But all he could find was envy.

The Old Hyperion inn at Fallowfield was crowded on this warm June evening, mostly with workers from the surrounding farms, enjoying the companionship of their friends after a long day in the fields. Some sat outside at the scrubbed trestle tables, and the air was so still that the smoke from their long pipes hung in an unmoving canopy. Even the banks of tall foxgloves barely quivered, and beyond the darkening trees the Helford River gleamed in the fading light like polished pewter.

Inside the inn every door and window stood open, but the older customers, as was their habit year round, gathered by the great fireplace, although it was empty but for a tub of flowers.

Unis Allday glanced from her parlour door and was satisfied with what she saw. Familiar faces, thatchers from Fallowfield, and the carpenter and his mate who were still working on the local church, where she and John Allday had been married. She repressed a sigh, and turned to the cot where their child, little Kate, lay sleeping. She touched the cot: another reminder of the big, shambling sailor who was so far away. He had even made the cot with his own hands.

She heard her brother, another John, laughing at something as he drew and carried tankards of ale. A one-legged former soldier of the 31st Foot, he lived in a tiny cottage nearby. Without his company and support, she did not know how she would have managed.

She had had no letter from Allday. Over four months had passed since he had walked through that door to take passage to Canada, with the admiral he served and loved like no other. Lady Catherine would be feeling much the same loneliness, she thought, with her own man on the other side of the ocean, even though she had travelled far and wide herself. Unis smiled. She had never been further than her native Devon before coming to live in Cornwall, and although she had settled in well, she knew that to the local people she would always be a foreigner. She had been attacked on the coast road on her way here, by men who had attempted to rob and assault her. John Allday had saved her that day. She could even talk about it now, but not to many. She touched some flowers on the table. The stillness, the warm, unmoving air was making her restless. If only he was back. She tested the idea. For good and always. . . .

She looked once more at the sleeping child, and then walked out to join her brother.

He said, 'Good business today, love. Picking up.' He

watched an unwavering candleflame. 'There'll be a few ships' masters cursing and swearing if they have to lie becalmed all night in Falmouth Bay. It'll mean they'll have to pay another day's wages!'

She said, 'What about the war, John? Out there, I mean.'

He said, 'Soon be over, I expect. Once the Iron Duke forces the French to surrender, the Yankees'll lose the stomach for a war on their own.'

'You do think that?' She remembered John Allday's face when he had finally told her about his son, and how he had died in the fight with the Americans. Was it only last year? When he had come home and had taken their child, so tiny in his big hands, and she had told him she would not be able to carry another, would never give him another son.

His reply was still stark in her mind. *She'll do me fine. A son can break your heart.* She had guessed then, but had said nothing until he was ready to tell her.

'Someone's on the road.' He looked toward the window, and was not aware of the sudden fear in her eyes.

She heard the sound of a single horse, and saw the men around the empty grate pause in their conversation to stare at the open door. A horse usually meant authority out this way, so close to Rosemullion Head. The coastguard, or revenue men, or some of the dragoons from Truro, searching for deserters or hunting down footpads.

The horse clattered across the cobbles and they heard someone hurrying to assist the rider. Her brother said, 'That's Lady Catherine. I'd know her big mare anywhere.'

He smiled as his sister straightened her apron and her hair, as she always did.

'I'd heard she was back from London. Luke said he saw her.'

She came through the door, her dark hair almost touching the low beam. She seemed startled that there were so many customers, as if she were hardly aware of the time of day.

Some of the men stood up, or shuffled as though they would make the effort, and one or two voices called, "Evenin' to 'ee, m'lady.'

She held out her hand. 'Please sit down. I am sorry. . . .'

Unis reached her, and guided her to the small parlour. 'You shouldn't be out alone on this road, m' lady. 'Twill be dark soon. 'Tisn't safe these days.'

Catherine sat and pulled off her gloves. 'Tamara knows the way. I am always safe.' She took Unis's hand impulsively. 'I needed to come. To be with a friend. And you are that, Unis.'

Unis nodded, shocked by the quiet desperation in her voice. It did not seem possible. The admiral's lady, a woman of courage as well as beauty, accepted even here where scandal, like sin, could be condemned openly every Sunday in church and chapel. . . .

'None stronger, m' lady.'

Catherine stood, and crossed to the cot. 'Young Kate,' she said, and reached down to adjust the covering. Unis watched, and was oddly moved.

'Shall I make some tea, or maybe coffee? An' I'll see that someone rides with you when you go back to Falmouth. Five miles can be a long way on your own.'

Catherine barely heard her. She had rested very little since her return from London. There had been no letter waiting from Richard: anything might be happening. She had ridden to the adjoining estate to visit his sister, Nancy, and found Lewis Roxby very ill. Despite the stroke he had suffered, he had taken little heed of his doctors' warnings. Without his hunting and his entertaining, and his hectic life as landowner, magistrate and squire, he could neither see nor accept any future as an invalid. Nancy had known: she had seen it in her eyes. Lewis was not merely ill this time; he was dying.

Catherine had sat with him, holding his hand while he had lain propped up in his bed, his head high enough for him to see the trees, and his stone folly, which was almost completed. His face had been grey, his grip without strength. But from time to time he had turned his head to look at her, as if to reassure her that the old Lewis Roxby was still there.

She had told him about London, but had not mentioned the unexpected settlement with which Luis's estate had endowed her. Nor had she told him about her visit to Richard's town house. The lawyer, Lafargue, had sent word to Belinda of her intended arrival, but her visiting card had been returned at the door, torn in two halves. But Belinda knew now that the house where she lavishly entertained, and lived in a style to which she had been unaccustomed before her marriage, was the property of the woman she hated. It would change nothing between them, but it might prevent her asking for more money. She would never admit to her circle of friends that she was living in a house owned by the one she had openly called a prostitute.

She heard herself say, 'Something a little stronger, Unis. Some brandy, if you have any.'

Unis hurried to a cupboard. Was it possible, that there was no one else she could turn to now that Sir Richard was away? Perhaps Bryan Ferguson and his wife at the big grey house were too close, painful reminders of those others who were absent: Bolitho's 'little crew', as she had heard John call them.

Catherine took the glass, wondering where the brandy had come from. Truro, or run ashore along this rocky and treacherous coast by freetraders in the dark of the moon?

Beyond the door, the conversation and laughter had

resumed. It was something to relate to their wives when they finally reached their own homes.

Unis said gently, 'When ... I mean ... if Sir Lewis gives up the fight ... what will become of all that he's worked for? Just the son of a local farmer, they tells me, and now look at him. A friend of the Prince himself, owner of all that land – will his son not take over?'

Now look at him. A grey, tired face. Every breath an effort.

'I believe that his son is making a name for himself in the City of London. Lewis wanted it. He was so proud of him, and of his daughter. There will be many changes, no matter what happens.'

She sat for some time in silence, thinking of the visit to the Admiralty, which had been her final task in London. Bethune had greeted her warmly, professing surprise at her arrival, and had offered to take her to a reception somewhere, and introduce her to some of his particular friends. She had declined. Even as she had sat in that familiar office, watching him, listening to him, she had sensed his genuine interest in her, the undeniable charm which might lead him into serious trouble if he became careless or over-confident in his affairs. He had been unable to give her any information about the war in North America, although she had suspected that he knew more than he was saying. On her last night in Chelsea she had lain awake on the bed, almost naked in the bright moonlight across the Thames, and had considered what might have happened if she had pleaded with Bethune to use all his influence, and his obvious affection and admiration for Richard, to enable him to be brought back to England. She had had little doubt what the price would have been. She had felt the sudden tears scalding her eyes. Could she have gone through with it? Given herself to another, whom instinct told her would have been kindness itself? She knew she could not have done it. There were no secrets between herself and Richard, so how could she have pretended with the man she loved?

To think that she could even consider such a bargain disgusted her. They called her a whore. Perhaps they were right.

Nor had she been able to tell Lewis what had happened after she had left Belinda's house. In the square, she had seen the child walking with her governess. If the place had been crowded with a hundred children, she would still have known it was Elizabeth, Richard's daughter. The same chestnut hair as her mother, the poise and confidence, so assured for one so young. She was eleven years old, and yet a woman.

'May I speak with you?' She had immediately sensed the governess's hostility, but she had been totally unprepared when Elizabeth had turned to look up at her. That had been the greatest shock of all. Her eyes were Richard's.

She had said calmly, 'I am sorry. I do not know you, ma'am.' She had turned away, and walked on ahead of her companion.

What could I have expected? Hoped for? But all she could think of was the child's eyes. Her contempt.

She stood up, listening. 'I must leave. My horse. . . .'

Unis saw her brother in the doorway. 'What is it, John?'

But he was looking at the beautiful woman, her long riding habit torn in places where she had ridden carelessly, too close to the hedgerows.

'The church. The bell's tolling.' Then, as though making a decision, 'I can't allow you to ride at this hour, m' lady.'

She appeared not to hear him. 'I must go. I promised Nancy.' She walked to the open window, and listened. The bell. An end of something. The beginning of what?

John had returned. 'One of the keepers is here, m' lady. He'll ride with you.' He hesitated, and looked at his sister as if appealing to her. 'Please. Sir Richard would insist, if he were here.'

She held out her hands to them. '*I know.*'

Some envied her, others hated her, and one at least feared her after her visit to the lawyer. She must not give way now. *But without him I am nothing, have nothing.*

She said, 'I needed to be with friends, you see. *Needed to be.*'

Tamara was already outside the door, eager to leave.

Sir Lewis Roxby, Knight of the Hanoverian Guelphic Order and friend of the Prince Regent, was dead. She remembered his many bluff kindnesses, and particularly the day when, together, they had found Zenoria Keen's body.

The King of Cornwall. So would he always remain.

11

A Warning

Richard Bolitho and Rear-Admiral Valentine Keen stood side by side and stared out across the crowded anchorage of Halifax harbour.

The sun was strong, the air warmer than for a long time, and after the restricted confines of a frigate, even one as large as *Indomitable*, Bolitho was very conscious of the land, and the peculiar feeling that he did not belong here. The house was the headquarters of the general officer commanding the garrisons and defence of Nova Scotia, and below the wooden verandah soldiers were marching back and forth, drilling in platoons, front ranks kneeling to take aim at an imaginary enemy while the second ranks prepared to march through them and repeat the process: manoeuvres the army had perfected over the years, which had eventually turned the tables on Napoleon.

But Bolitho was looking at the anchored frigate directly opposite. Even without a telescope, he could see the damage and the piles of broken timber and rigging on her decks. She still flew the Stars and Stripes, but the White Ensign was hoisted above it as a symbol of victory. She was the U.S.S. *Chesapeake*, which had been brought to action by His Britannic Majesty's ship *Shannon*. The fight had been brief but decisive, and both captains had been wounded, the American mortally.

Keen said, 'A welcome victory. *Shannon* towed her prize into Halifax on the sixth. Couldn't have happened at a better time, with all our other setbacks.'

Bolitho had already heard something of the engagement. *Shannon*'s captain, Philip Bowes Vere Broke, was both experienced and successful, and had been cruising up and down outside Boston, where *Chesapeake* lay at anchor. It was rumoured that he had been grieving over the loss of so many of his contemporaries to the superior American frigates. He had sent a challenge into Boston in the best tradition of chivalry, requesting that Captain Lawrence of the *Chesapeake* should come out and 'try the fortunes of their respective flags'. If Broke had had one advantage over his American adversary, it was his dedication to and insistence upon gunnery and teamwork. He had even invented and fitted sights to all his main armament. It had won the day, but nobody had shown more distress than Broke himself when Lawrence had succumbed to his wounds.

Now, lying just beyond her like a guilty shadow, was the smaller frigate *Reaper*. A guardboat was moored alongside, and her upper deck was marked with tiny scarlet figures where Royal Marine sentries kept watch over the imprisoned mutineers.

Keen glanced at him, seeing the strain on his profile as he lifted his face to the sun.

'It is good to be of one company again.'

Bolitho smiled. 'Only for the moment, Val. We shall have to be on the move again shortly.' He shaded his eyes to look across at *Indomitable*, where Tyacke was taking on fresh water and supplies while final repairs were carried out. It was Tyacke's reason, or rather his excuse, for not accompanying him to this meeting.

He heard Avery talking quietly with Keen's flag lieutenant, the Honourable Lawford de Courcey. They would have little or nothing in common, he thought, and he had gathered that Adam did not care much for him, either. It was just as well. There was no room for complacency here, even amongst friends. They needed an edge, a purpose, like the old sword at his side.

There had been letters awaiting his return to Halifax, both from Catherine: he could feel them now in his coat. He would read them as soon as he could, then again later, and more slowly. But there was always the first anxiety, like a fear, that she would have changed towards him. She would be lonely beyond measure.

He turned away from the sun as he heard de Courcey greeting someone, and then another voice, a woman's.

Keen touched his arm. 'I should like you to meet Miss Gilia St Clair. I sent you word of her presence aboard *Reaper*.'

So easily said, but Bolitho had already gone through Keen's carefully worded report on *Reaper*'s surrender, and the discharge of her guns into empty sea. He felt that Keen and Adam had disagreed about something at the time. It might reveal itself later.

His shoe caught on something as he turned, and he saw Avery's vague outline move towards him. Troubled; but protective of him, as always.

It was so dark after the brilliant sunlight and the dazzling reflections from the harbour that the room could have been curtained off.

Keen was saying, 'I wish to present Sir Richard Bolitho. He commands our squadron.'

It was not to impress: it was genuine pride. Val, as he had always been, before Zenoria's death, before Zenoria. Perhaps Catherine was correct in her belief that he would easily recover from his loss.

The woman was younger than he had expected, in her late twenties, he thought. He had an impression of a pleasant, oval face and light brown hair; the eyes were level and serious.

205

Bolitho took her hand. It was very firm; he could easily imagine her with her father aboard the stricken *Reaper*, watching *Valkyrie* running out her powerful broadside.

She said, 'I am sorry to intrude, but my father is here. I had hoped I could discover. . . .'

Keen said, 'He is with the general. I'm sure it is quite all right for you to stay.' He gave his youthful grin. 'I will take full responsibility!'

She said, 'I wanted to know about York. My father was going there to assist with the completion of a ship.'

Bolitho listened in silence. Her father's plans were not the source of her concern.

Keen said, 'I expect you will be returning to England sooner rather than later, Miss St Clair?'

She shook her head. 'I would like to remain here, with my father.'

The door opened, and an urbane lieutenant almost bowed himself into the room.

'The General's apologies, Sir Richard. The delay was unintentional.' He seemed to see the girl for the first time. 'I am not certain. . . .'

Bolitho said, 'She is with us.'

The adjoining room was large and crammed with heavy furniture, a soldier's room, with two vast paintings of battles on the walls. Bolitho did not recognize the uniforms. A different war, a forgotten army.

The general seized his hand. 'Delighted, Sir Richard. Knew your father. Fine man. In India. He'd be damned proud of you!' He spoke in short, loud bursts, like mountain artillery, Bolitho thought.

Other faces. David St Clair: good handshake, firm and hard. And there was another soldier present, tall, very assured, with the unemotional bearing of a professional.

He bowed slightly. 'Captain Charles Pierton, of the Eighth Regiment of Foot.' He paused, and said with a certain pride, 'The King's Regiment.'

Bolitho saw the girl's hands gripped together in her lap. Waiting with a curious defiance which succeeded only in making her appear suddenly vulnerable.

David St Clair said quickly, 'Are you feeling well, my dear?'

She did not answer him. 'May I ask you something, Captain Pierton?'

Pierton glanced quizzically at the general, who gave a brief nod. 'Of course, Miss St Clair.'

'You were at York when the Americans attacked. My father and I would have been there too, had circumstances not dictated otherwise.'

Her father leaned forward in his chair. 'The thirty-gun ship *Sir Isaac Brock* was burned on the slipway before the Americans could take her. I would have been too late in any case.'

Bolitho knew that she did not even hear him.

'Do you know Captain Anthony Loring, of your regiment, sir?'

The soldier looked back at her steadily. 'Yes, of course. He commanded the second company.' He turned to Bolitho and the other naval officers. 'Ours was the only professional force at York. We had the militia and the York Volunteers, and a company of the Royal Newfoundland Regiment.' He glanced at the girl again. 'And about one hundred Mississauga and Chippewa Indians.'

Bolitho noted how easily the names rolled off his tongue: he was a seasoned campaigner, although this vast, untamed country was a far cry from Spain or France. But the others would know all these facts. It was merely an explanation for the girl's benefit, as if he thought it was owed to her.

He continued in the same grave, precise manner. 'The defences at Fort York were poor. My commanding officer believed that eventually the navy would be able to send more vessels to the lakes, to hold off the Americans until larger men-of-war were constructed. There were some seventeen hundred American soldiers that day, almost all of them regulars and well-trained. We had to gain time, to evacuate the fort and finally to burn the *Sir Isaac Brock*.'

She stood, and walked to the window. 'Please continue.'

Pierton said quietly, 'Captain Loring took his men to the lower shore where the Americans were landing. He gallantly led a bayonet charge and dispersed them. For a time. He was wounded, and died shortly afterwards. I am sorry. A good number of our men fell that day.'

Keen said, 'I think you might be more comfortable in another room, Miss St Clair.'

Bolitho saw her shake her head, heedless of her hair, which had fallen loosely across her shoulder.

She asked, 'Did he speak of me, Captain Pierton?'

Pierton looked at the general, and hesitated. 'We were hard pressed, Miss St Clair.'

She persisted. *'Ever?'*

Pierton replied, 'He was a very private person. A different company, you understand.'

She left the window and crossed over to him, then she put her hand on his arm. 'That was a kind thing to say. I should not have asked.' She gripped the scarlet sleeve, unaware of everyone else. 'I am so glad that you are safe.'

The general coughed noisily. 'Sending him to England on the first packet. God knows if they'll learn anything from what happened.'

The door closed quietly. She had gone.

Captain Pierton exclaimed, *'Damn!'* He looked at the general. 'My apologies, sir, but I forgot to give her something. Perhaps it would be better to send it with his other effects to Ridge . . . our regimental agent in Charing Cross.'

Bolitho watched as he took a miniature painting from

his tunic and laid it on the table. Charing Cross: like the casual mention of the Indians fighting with the army, it seemed so alien here. Another world.

Keen said, 'May I?'

He held the miniature to the sunlight and studied it. 'A good likeness. Very good.'

A small tragedy of war, Bolitho thought. She had sent or given him the miniature, even though the unknown Loring had decided not to encourage a more intimate relationship. She must have been hoping to see him again when her father visited York, perhaps fearing what she might discover. Now it was too late. Her father probably knew more than he would ever disclose.

Keen said, 'Well, sir, I think it should be returned to her. If it were me . . .' He did not go on.

Thinking of Zenoria? Sharing the same sense of loss?

The general frowned. 'Perhaps you're right.' He glanced at the clock. 'Time to stop now, gentlemen. I have a very acceptable claret, and I believe we should sample it. After that. . . .'

Bolitho stood near the window, studying the captured American, *Chesapeake*, and the *Reaper* beyond.

He asked, 'And what of York, Captain Pierton? Is it secure?'

'Unfortunately, no, Sir Richard. My regiment withdrew in good order to Kingston, which is now doubly important if we are to withstand another attack. If the Americans had gone for Kingston in the first place. . . .'

'Well?'

The general answered for him. 'We would have lost Upper Canada.'

Two servants had appeared with trays of glasses. Keen murmured, 'I shall not be a moment, Sir Richard.'

Bolitho turned as Avery joined him by the window. 'We shall not wait longer than necessary.' He was concerned at the expression in the tawny eyes: they were deeply introspective, and yet, in some strange way, at peace. 'What is it? Another secret, George?'

Avery faced him, making up his mind. Perhaps he had been struggling with it all the way from the ship to this place of stamping boots and shouted orders.

He said, 'I received a letter, sir. A letter.'

Bolitho twisted round and grasped his wrist. 'A letter? Do you mean....'

Avery smiled, rather shyly, and his face was that of a much younger man.

'Yes, sir. From a lady.'

Outside, in the sun-dappled passageway, Keen sat beside the girl on one of the heavy leather couches.

He watched her as she turned the miniature over in her hands, recalling the calm acceptance in her face when he had given it to her. Resignation? Or something far deeper?

'It was good of you. I did not know....'

He saw her mouth quiver, and said, 'While I command here at Halifax, if there is anything I can do to serve you, anything you require....'

She looked up into his face. 'I will be with my father, at the Massie residence. They are ... old friends.' She lowered her eyes. 'Of a sort.' She looked at the miniature again. 'I was younger then.'

Keen said, 'It is....' He faltered. 'You are very brave, and very beautiful.' He tried to smile, to break the tension within himself. 'Please do not be offended. That is the very last thing I intend.'

She was watching him, her eyes steady once more. 'You must have thought me a fool, an innocent in a world I know not. The sort of thing to bring a few laughs in the mess when you are all together as men.' She thrust out her hand, impetuous, but sharing his uncertainty. 'Keep this, if you like. It is of no further use to me.' But the careless mood would not remain. She watched him

210

take the miniature, his lashes pale against his sunburned skin as he gazed down at it. 'And . . . take care. I shall think of you.'

She walked away along the passage, the sun greeting her at every window. She did not look back.

He said, 'I shall depend on it.'

He walked slowly back toward the general's room. Of course, it could not happen. It could not, not again. But it had.

Adam Bolitho paused with one foot on the high step and looked up at the shop. With the sun hot across his shoulders and the sky intensely blue above the rooftops, it was hard to remember the same street obscured by great banks of snow.

He pushed open the door and smiled to himself as a bell jingled to announce his entrance. It was a small but elegant place which he thought would fit well into London or Exeter.

As if to some signal, a dozen or so clocks began to chime the hour, tall clocks and small, ornate timepieces for mantel or drawing room, clocks with moving figures, phases of the moon, and one with a fine square-rigger which actually dipped and lifted to each stroke of the pendulum. Each one pleased and intrigued him, and he was walking from one to another examining them when a short man in a dark coat came through a doorway by the counter. His eyes instantly and professionally examined the uniform, the bright gold epaulettes and short, curved hanger.

'And how may I be of service, Captain?'

'I require a watch. I was told. . . .'

The man pulled out a long tray. 'Each of those is tested and reliable. Not new and untried, but of excellent repute. Old friends.'

Adam thought of the ship he had just left at anchor:

ready for sea. It was impossible not to be aware of the captured American frigate *Chesapeake* in the harbour, which he had seen from *Valkyrie*'s gig. A truly beautiful ship: he could even accept that at one time he would have wanted no finer command. But the emotion would not return: the loss of *Anemone* had been like having part of himself die. She had been escorted into Halifax by her victorious opponent *Shannon* on the sixth of June. *My birthday*. The day he had been kissed by Zenoria on the cliff track; when he had cut the wild roses with his knife for her. So young. And yet so aware.

He glanced at the array of watches. It was not vanity: he needed one now that his own had disappeared, lost or stolen when he had been wounded and transferred to the U.S.S. *Unity*. They might as well have left him to die.

The shopkeeper took his silence as lack of interest. 'This is a very good piece, sir. Open-faced with duplex escapement, one of James McCabe's famous breed. Made in 1806, but still quite perfect.'

Adam picked it up. Who had carried it before, he wondered. Most of the watches here had probably belonged to army or sea officers. Or their widows. . . .

He found himself thinking with increasing bitterness of Keen's interest in David St Clair's daughter Gilia. At first he had thought it was merely pity for the girl; Keen might even have been making comparisons with Zenoria, whom he had rescued from a convict transport. She had carried the mark of a whip across her back as a constant and cruel reminder, the mark of Satan, she had called it. He was being unfair to Keen, more so perhaps because of his own guilt, which never left him. That, willing or otherwise, Zenoria had been his lover.

He asked suddenly, 'What about that one?'

The man gave him an approving smile. 'You are an excellent judge as well as a brave frigate captain, sir!'

Adam had become accustomed to it. Here in Halifax,

despite the heavy military presence and the comparative nearness of the enemy, security was a myth. Everyone knew who you were, what ship, where bound, and probably a whole lot more. He had mentioned it with some concern to Keen, who had said only, 'I think we give them too much credit, Adam.'

An indefinable coolness had come between them. Because of Adam's threat to fire on the *Reaper*, hostages or not, or was it something of his own making or imagination, born of that abiding sense of guilt?

He took the watch, and it rested in his palm. It was heavy, the case rubbed smooth by handling over the years.

The man said, 'A rare piece, Captain. Note the cylinder escapement, the fine, clear face.' He sighed. 'Mudge and Dutton, 1770. A good deal older than yourself, I daresay.'

Adam was studying the guard, the engraving well worn but still clear and vital in the dusty sunlight. A mermaid.

The shopkeeper added, 'Not the kind of workmanship one finds very often these days, I fear.'

Adam held it to his ear. Recalling her face that day in Plymouth, when he had picked up her fallen glove and returned it to her. Her hand on his arm when they had walked together in the port admiral's garden. The last time he had seen her.

'What is the story of this watch?'

The little man polished his glasses. 'It came into the shop a long while ago. It belonged to a seafaring gentleman like yourself, sir... I believe he needed the money. I could find out, perhaps.'

'No.' Adam closed the guard very carefully. 'I will take it.'

'It is a mite expensive, but ...' He smiled, pleased that the watch had gone to a suitable owner. 'I know you are a very successful frigate captain, sir. It is right and proper that you should have it!' He waited, but the responding

213

smile was not forthcoming. 'I should clean it before you take it. I can send it by hand to *Valkyrie* if you would prefer. I understand that you are not sailing until the day after tomorrow?'

Adam looked away. He had only just been told himself by Keen before he had come ashore.

'Thank you, but I shall take it now.' He slipped it into his pocket, haunted by her face once more. The local people of Zennor still insisted that the church where she and Keen had been married had been visited by a mermaid.

The bell jingled again and the shopkeeper glanced around, irritated by the intrusion. He met all kinds of people here: Halifax was becoming the most important sea port, and certainly the safest, set as it was at the crossroads of war. With the army to defend it and the navy to protect and supply it, there were many who regarded it as the new gateway to a continent. But this young, dark-haired captain was very different from the others. Alone, completely alone, alive to something which he would allow no one else to share.

He said, 'I am sorry, Mrs Lovelace, but your clock is still misbehaving. A few days more, perhaps.'

But she was looking at Adam. 'Well, Captain Bolitho, this is a pleasant surprise. I trust you are well? And how is your handsome young admiral?'

Adam bowed to her. She was dressed in dark red silk, with a matching bonnet to shade her eyes from the sun. The same direct way of looking at him, the slightly mocking smile, as if she were used to teasing people. Men.

He said, 'Rear-Admiral Keen is well, ma'am.'

She was quick to notice the slight edge to his reply.

'You have been shopping, I see.' She held out her hand. 'Will you show me?'

He knew that the shopkeeper was observing them with interest. No doubt he knew her well, and her reputation would make a fine piece of gossip. He was surprised to find that he had actually taken out his watch to show her.

'I needed one, Mrs Lovelace. I like it.' He saw her studying the engraved mermaid.

'I would have bought something younger for you, Captain Bolitho. But if it's what you want, and it takes your fancy. . . .' She glanced out at the street. 'I must go. I have friends to entertain later.' She looked at him directly again, her eyes suddenly very still and serious. 'You know where I live, I think.'

He answered, 'On the Bedford Basin. I remember.'

For a second or two her composure and her humour were gone. She gripped his arm, and said, 'Be careful. Promise me that. I know of your reputation, and a little of your background. I think perhaps you do not care for your own life any more.' When he would have spoken she silenced him, as effectively as if she had laid a finger on his lips. 'Say nothing. Only do as I ask, and be very careful. Promise me.' Then she looked at him again: the invitation was very plain. 'When you come back, please call on me.'

He said coolly, 'What about your husband, ma'am? I think he may well object.'

She laughed, but the first vivid confidence did not return. 'He is never here. Trade is his life, his whole world!' She played with the ribbon of her bonnet. 'But he is no trouble.'

He recalled their host, Benjamin Massie, that night when the brig *Alfriston* had brought the news of *Reaper*'s mutiny and capture. Massie's mistress then, and perhaps the mistress of others as well.

'I wish you well, ma'am.' He recovered his hat from a chair, and said to the shopkeeper, 'When I check my ship's affairs against my watch, I shall remember you and this shop.'

She was waiting on the steps. 'Remember what I have said to you.' She studied his face, as if seeking something in it. 'You have lost that which you can never rediscover. You must accept that.' She touched the gold lace on his lapel. 'Life must still be lived.'

She turned away, and as Adam stepped aside to avoid a mounted trooper, she vanished.

He walked back toward the boat jetty. *Be very careful.* He quickened his pace as he caught sight of the water and the great array of masts and spars, like a forest. Whatever action they took, it would be Keen's decision: he had made that more than clear. But why did it hurt so much?

He thought suddenly of his uncle, and wished he could be with him. They could always talk; he would always listen. He had even confessed his affair with Zenoria to him.

He saw the stairs and *Valkyrie*'s gig moored alongside. Midshipman Rickman, a lively fifteen-year-old, was speaking with two young women who were doing little to hide their profession from the grinning boat's crew.

Rickman straightened his hat and the gig's crew came to attention when they saw their captain approaching. The two girls moved away, but not very far.

Adam said, 'Back to the ship, if you please, Mr Rickman. I see that you were not wasting your time?'

Two blotches of scarlet appeared on the youth's unshaven cheeks, and Adam climbed quickly into the boat. *If only you knew.*

He glanced toward the captured American frigate and the other, *Success*, which *Indomitable*'s broadsides had overwhelmed in minutes, recalling the young lieutenant who had died of his wounds, son of the Captain Joseph Brice who had interviewed him during his captivity. A sick but dignified officer, who had treated him with a courtesy reminiscent of Nathan Beer. He wondered if

Brice knew, and would blame himself for guiding his son into the navy.

Face to face, blade to blade with men who spoke the same language but who had freely chosen another country. . . . Perhaps it was better to have an enemy you could hate. In war, it was necessary to hate without questioning why.

'Oars *up*!'

He stood and reached for the hand rope. He had barely noticed the return journey to *Valkyrie*.

He saw the flag lieutenant hovering by the entry port, waiting to catch his eye. He raised his hat to the quarter-deck, and smiled.

It was, of course, easier to hate some more than others.

Rear-Admiral Valentine Keen turned away from *Valkyrie*'s stern windows as Adam, followed by the flag lieutenant, entered the great cabin.

'I came as soon as I could, sir. I was ashore.'

Keen said gently, 'It is no great matter. You should have more leisure.' He glanced at the flag lieutenant. 'Thank you, Lawford. You may carry on with the signals we discussed.'

The door closed, reluctantly, Adam thought. 'More news, sir?'

Keen seemed unsettled. 'Not exactly. But the plans have changed. *Success* is to leave for Antigua. I have spoken with the Dock Master, and I can see we have no choice in the matter. Halifax is crammed with vessels needing overhaul and repair, and *Success* was in a very poor condition after her clash with *Indomitable* – as much due to severe rot as to Captain Tyacke's gunnery, I suspect.'

Adam waited. Keen was trying to make light of it. *Success* was badly damaged, yes, but would sail well enough after work was completed on her rigging. But

Antigua, two thousand miles away, and in the hurricane season. . . . It was taking a chance.

'There is another big convoy due within a week or so, supplies and equipment for the army, nothing unusual in that. Sir Richard intends to take *Indomitable* and two others of the squadron to escort them on the final approach. There is a possibility that the Americans might attack and attempt to scatter or sink some of them.' He regarded him calmly. '*Success* must have a strong consort.' He glanced around the cabin. 'This ship is large enough to fight off any foolhardy privateer who might want to take her.' He smiled thinly. 'And fast enough to get back to Halifax, in case of more trouble.'

Adam walked to the table, and hesitated as he saw the miniature lying beside Keen's open log book. It took him completely by surprise, and he scarcely heard Keen say, 'I am required to remain here. I command in Halifax. The rest of our ships may be needed elsewhere.'

He could not take his eyes from the miniature, recognizing the subject at once. The smile, which had been painted for some one else to cherish, to keep.

Keen said abruptly, 'It will be nothing to you, Adam. Certain other commanders, I would have to consider more carefully. *Success* will be safer in English Harbour. At best, she can be used as a guardship, and at worst, her spars and weapons will be put to good use there. What do you say?'

Adam faced him, angry that he could not accept it, that he himself had no right to refuse.

'I think it's too risky, sir.'

Keen seemed surprised. '*You*, Adam? You talk of risk? To the world at large it will merely be the departure of two big frigates, and even if enemy intelligence discovers their destination, what then? It will be too late to act upon it, surely.'

Adam touched the heavy watch in his pocket, remembering the small shop, the peaceful chorus of clocks, the owner's matter-of-fact mention of *Valkyrie*, almost to the time of her departure.

He said bluntly, 'There is no security here, sir. I shall be away for a month. Anything could happen in that time.'

Keen smiled, perhaps relieved. 'The war will keep, Adam. I trust you with this mission because I want you to carry orders to the captain in charge at Antigua. A difficult man in many ways. He needs to be reminded of the fleet's requirements there.'

He saw Adam's eyes move to the miniature once more. 'An endearing young lady. Courageous, too.' He paused. 'I know what you are thinking. My loss is hard to believe, harder still to accept.'

Adam clenched his fists so tightly that the bones ached. *You don't understand. How can you forget her? Betray her?*

He said, 'I will make all the arrangements, sir. I'll pick a prize crew from spare hands at the base.'

'Who will you put in charge of *Success*?'

Adam contained his anger with an almost physical effort. 'John Urquhart, sir. A good first lieutenant – I'm surprised he hasn't been chosen for promotion, or even a command.'

The door opened an inch, and de Courcey coughed politely.

Keen said sharply, 'What is it?'

'Your barge is ready, sir.'

'Thank you.' Keen picked up the miniature, and after a moment's hesitation placed it in a drawer and turned the key. 'I shall be aboard later. I'll send word.' He looked at him steadily. 'The day after tomorrow, then.'

Adam thrust his hat beneath his arm. 'I'll see you over the side, sir.'

Keen nodded to two midshipmen who sprang out of

his way by the companion ladder. 'I'd be obliged if you would take my flag lieutenant with you when you sail. Good experience. See how the professionals do things.' He seemed about to say something else, but changed his mind.

As the barge pulled away from *Valkyrie*'s shadow, Adam saw the first lieutenant walking across the quarterdeck in deep conversation with Ritchie, the sailing-master.

They eyed him as he approached, and Adam was again reminded that he did not truly know these men, just as he accepted that it was his own fault.

'Come forrard with me, Mr Urquhart.' To the master he added, 'You've been told, I take it.'

'Aye, sir. The Leeward Islands again. Bad time o' year.' But Adam was already out of earshot, striding along the starboard gangway with Urquhart in step beside him. Below, men working at the gun tackles or flaking down unwanted cordage paused only briefly to glance up at them.

Adam halted on the forecastle deck and rested one foot on a crouching carronade, the 'smasher', as the Jacks called them. Opposite them lay the captured *Success*, and although her side and upperworks still bore the scars of *Indomitable*'s iron, her masts were set up, with men working on the yards to secure each new sail. They had done well to achieve so much in so short a time. And beyond her, the beautiful *Chesapeake*, and *Reaper* swinging, untroubled, to her cable. Did ships know or care who handled, or betrayed, or loved them?

Urquhart said, 'If the weather stays friendly, we'll not have much trouble, sir.'

Adam leaned over the rail, past one great catted anchor to the imposing gilded figurehead: one of Odin's faithful servants, a stern-faced maiden in breastplate and horned helmet, one hand raised as if to welcome her dead hero to Valhalla. It was not beautiful. He tried to thrust the thought aside. Not like *Anemone*. But through the smoke and the din of war, it would certainly impress an enemy.

'I want you to take charge of *Success*. You will have a prize crew, but only enough hands to work the ship. Her fighting ability has not yet been determined.'

He watched the lieutenant's face, strong, intelligent, but still wary of his captain. Not afraid, but unsure.

'Now hear me, Mr Urquhart, and keep what I ask of you to yourself. If I hear one word from elsewhere it will lie at your door, understood?'

Urquhart nodded, his eyes very calm. 'You can rely on that.'

Adam touched his arm. 'I rely on *you*.'

He thought suddenly of the miniature of Gilia St Clair. Her smile, which Keen had appropriated as his own.

'Now, this is what you must do.'

But even as he spoke, his mind still clung to it. Perhaps Keen was right. After the battle, losing his ship and the agony of imprisonment, there was always a chance of becoming crippled by caution.

When he had finished explaining what he required, Urquhart said, 'May I ask you, sir, have you never feared being killed?'

Adam smiled a little, and turned his back on the figurehead.

'No.' He saw John Whitmarsh walking along the deck beside one of the new midshipmen, who was about his own age. They both seemed to sense his eyes upon them and paused to peer up into the sun at the shadows on the forecastle. The midshipman touched his hat; Whitmarsh raised one hand in a gesture which was not quite a wave.

Urquhart remarked, 'You certainly have a way with youngsters, sir.'

Adam looked at him, the smile gone. 'Your question,

221

John. It is true to say that I have . . . died . . . many times. Does that suit?'

It was probably the closest they had ever been.

12

Code of Conduct

Lieutenant George Avery leaned back in his chair and put one foot on his sea-chest as if to test the ship's movement. In the opposite corner of the small, screened cabin Allday sat on another chest, his big hands clasped together, frowning, as he tried to remember exactly what Avery had read to him.

Avery could see it as if he had left England only yesterday, and not the five months ago it was in fact. The inn at Fallowfield by the Helford River, the long walks in the countryside, untroubled by conversation with people who only spoke because they were cooped up with you in a man-of-war. Good food, time to think. To remember. . . .

He thought now of his own letter, and wondered why he had told the admiral about her. More surprising still, that Bolitho had seemed genuinely pleased about it, although doubtless he thought his flag lieutenant was hoping for too much. *A kiss and a promise.* He could not imagine what Bolitho might have said if he had told him all that had happened on that single night in London. The mystery, the wildness, and the peace, when they had lain together, exhausted. For his own part, stunned that it could have been real.

His thoughts came back to Allday, and he said, 'So there you are. Your little Kate is doing well. I must buy her something before we leave Halifax.'

Allday did not look up. 'So small, she was. No bigger than a rabbit. Now she's walking, you say?'

'Unis says.' He smiled. 'And I'll lay odds that she fell over a few times before she got her proper sea-legs.'

Allday shook his head. 'I would have liked to see it, them first steps. I never seen anything like that afore.' He seemed troubled, rather than happy. 'I should've been there.'

Avery was moved by what he saw. Perhaps it would be useless to point out that Bolitho had offered to leave him ashore, secure in his own home, after years of honourable service. It would be an insult. He recalled Catherine's obvious relief that Allday was staying with her man. Maybe she sensed that his 'oak' had never been more needed.

Avery listened to the regular groan of timbers as *Indomitable* thrust through a criss-cross of Atlantic rollers. They should have made contact with the Halifax-bound convoy yesterday, but even the friendly Trades could not always be relied upon. This was a war of supply and demand, and it was always the navy who supplied. No wonder men were driven to despair by separation and hardships which few landsmen could ever appreciate.

He heard the clatter of dishes from the wardroom, somebody laughing too loudly at some bawdy joke already heard too often. He glanced at the white screen. And beyond there, right aft, the admiral would be thinking and planning, no doubt with the scholarly Yovell waiting to record and copy instructions and orders for each of the captains, from flagship to brig, from schooner to bomb ketch. Faces he had come to know, men he had come to understand. All except the one who would be uppermost in his mind, the dead captain of *Reaper*. Bolitho would regard the mutiny as something personal, and the captain's tyranny a flaw that should have been removed before it was too late.

Justice, discipline, revenge. It could not be ignored.

And what of Keen, perhaps the last of the original Happy Few? Was his new interest in Gilia St Clair merely a passing thing? Avery thought of the woman in his arms, his need of her. He was no one to judge Keen.

He looked up as familiar footsteps moved across the quarterdeck. Tyacke, visiting the watchkeepers before darkness closed around them and their two consorts. If the convoy failed to appear at first light, what then? They were some five hundred miles from the nearest land. A decision would have to be made. *But not by me.* Nor even by Tyacke. It would fall, as always, to that same man in his cabin aft. The admiral.

He had not mentioned the letter to Tyacke: Tyacke would probably know. But Avery respected his privacy, and had come to like him greatly, more than he would believed possible after their first stormy confrontation at Plymouth more than two years ago. Tyacke had never received a letter from anyone. Did he ever look for one, ever dare to hope for such a precious link with home?

He handed Unis's letter to Allday, and hoped that he had read it in the manner he had intended. Allday, a man who could recognize any hoist of signals by their colours or their timing, whom he had watched patiently instructing some hapless landman or baffled midshipman in the art of splicing and ropework, who could carve a ship model so fine that even the most critical Jack would nod admiringly, could not read. Nor could he write. It seemed cruel, unfair.

There was a tap on the door and Ozzard looked in. 'Sir Richard's compliments, sir. Would you care to lay aft for a glass?' He purposefully ignored Allday.

Avery nodded. He had been expecting the invitation, and hoping that it would come.

Ozzard added sharply, 'You too, of course. If you're not too busy.'

Avery watched. Another precious fragment: Ozzard's rudeness matched only by Allday's awakening grin. He could have killed the little man with his elbow. They knew each other's strength, weakness too, in all likelihood. Maybe they even knew his.

His thoughts dwelled again on the letter in his pocket. Perhaps she had written it out of pity, or embarrassment at what had happened. She could never realize in ten thousand years what that one letter had meant to him. Just a few sentences, simple sentiments, and wishes for his future. She had ended, *Your affectionate friend, Susanna.*

That was all. He straightened his coat and opened the door for Allday. It was everything.

But Avery was a practical man. Susanna, Lady Mildmay, an admiral's widow, would not remain alone for long. Perhaps could not. She had rich friends, and he had seen for himself the confidence, born of experience, she had displayed at the reception attended by Bolitho's wife and by Vice-Admiral Bethune. He could recall her laughter when he had mistaken Bethune's mistress for his wife. *Is that all I could hope for?*

Susanna was available now. She would soon forget that night in London with her lowly lieutenant. At the same time, he was already composing the letter he would write to her, the first he had written to anyone but his sister. There was no one else now.

He walked aft towards the spiralling lantern, the rigid Royal Marine sentry outside the screen doors.

Allday murmured, 'I wonder what Sir Richard wants.'

Avery paused, hearing the ship, and the ocean all around them.

He answered simply, 'He needs us. I know very well what that means.'

It was cold on the quarterdeck, with only the smallest

226

hint of the daylight which would soon show itself and open up the sea.

Bolitho gripped the quarterdeck rail, feeling the wind on his face and in his hair, his boatcloak giving him anonymity for a while longer.

It was a time of day he had always found fascinating as a captain in his own ship. A vessel coming alive beneath his feet, dark figures moving like ghosts, most of them so used to their duties that they performed them without conscious thought even in complete darkness. The morning watch went about their affairs, while the watch below cleaned the messdecks and stowed away the hammocks in the nettings, with barely an order being passed. Bolitho could smell the stench of the galley funnel; the cook must surely use axle-grease for his wares. But sailors had strong stomachs. They needed them.

He heard the officer-of-the-watch speaking with his midshipman in brusque, clipped tones. Laroche was a keen gambler who had felt the rough edge of Lieutenant Scarlett's tongue the very day Scarlett had been killed in the fight with the U.S.S. *Unity*.

It would be six in the morning soon, and Tyacke would come on deck. It was his custom, although he had impressed on all his officers that they were to call him at any time, day or night, if they were disturbed by any situation. Bolitho had heard him say to one lieutenant, 'Better for me to lose my temper than to lose my ship!'

If you doubt, speak out. His father had said it many times.

He found he was walking along the weather side, his shoes avoiding ring-bolts and tackles without effort. Catherine was troubled; it was made more apparent by her determination to hide it from him in her letters. Roxby was very ill, although Bolitho had seen that for himself before he had left England, and he thought it a good thing that his sister felt able to share her worries and hopes with Catherine, when their lives had been so different from one another.

Catherine had told him about the Spanish inheritance from her late husband, Luis Pareja. All those years ago, another world, a different ship; they had both been younger then. How could either of them have known what would happen? He could recall her exactly as she had been at their first meeting, the same fiery courage he had seen after the *Golden Plover* had gone down.

She was concerned about the money. He had mentioned it to Yovell, who seemed to understand all the complications, and had accompanied Catherine to the old firm of lawyers in Truro, to ensure that 'she was not snared by legal roguery', as he had put it.

Yovell had been frank, but discreet. 'Lady Catherine will become rich, sir. Perhaps very rich.' He had gauged Bolitho's expression, a little surprised that the prospect of wealth should disquiet him, but also proud that Bolitho had confided in him and no other.

But suppose.... Bolitho paused in his pacing to watch the first glow of light, almost timid as it painted a small seam between sky and ocean. He heard a voice whisper, 'Cap'n's comin' up, sir!' and a few seconds later Laroche's pompous acknowledgement of Tyacke's presence. 'Good morning, sir. Course east by north. Wind's veered a little.'

Tyacke said nothing. Bolitho saw it all as if it were indeed broad daylight. Tyacke would examine the compass and study the small wind-vane that aided the helmsmen until they could see the sails and the masthead pendant: he would already have scanned the log book on his way here. A new day. How would it be? An empty sea, a friend, an enemy?

He crossed to the weather side and touched his hat. 'You're about early, Sir Richard.' To any one else, it would have seemed a question.

Bolitho said, 'Like you, James, I need to feel the day, and try to sense what it might bring.'

Tyacke saw that his shirt was touched with pink, as the light found and explored the ship.

'We should sight the others directly, sir. *Taciturn* will be well up to wind'rd, and the brig *Doon* closing astern. As soon as we can see them I'll make a signal.' He was thinking of the convoy they were expecting to meet: there would be hell to pay if they did not. Any escort duty was tedious and an enormous strain, especially for frigates like *Indomitable* and her consort *Taciturn*. They were built for speed, not for the sickening motion under the reefed topsails necessary to hold station on their ponderous charges. He sniffed the air. 'That damned galley – it stinks! I must have a word with the purser.'

Bolitho stared aloft, shading his eye. The topgallant yards were pale now, the sails taut and hard-braced to hold the unco-operative wind.

More figures had appeared: Daubney the first lieutenant, already pointing out tasks for the forenoon watch to Hockenhull the boatswain. Tyacke touched his hat again and strode away to speak with his senior lieutenant, as though he were eager to get started.

Bolitho remained where he was while men hurried past him. Some might glance toward his cloaked figure, but when they realized that it was the admiral they would stay clear. He sighed faintly. At least they were not afraid of him. But to be a captain again. . . . *Your own ship.* Like Adam. . . .

He thought of him now, still at Halifax, or with Keen making a sweep along the American coast where a hundred ships like *Unity* or *Chesapeake* could be concealed. Boston, New Bedford, New York, Philadelphia. They could be anywhere.

It had to be stopped, finished before it became another draining, endless war. America had no allies as such, but would soon find them if Britain was perceived to be failing. If only. . . .

He looked up, caught off guard as the lookout's voice penetrated the noises of sea and canvas.

'Deck there! Sail on larboard bow!' The barest pause. "Tis *Taciturn*, on station!'

Tyacke said, 'She's seen us and hoisted a light. They have their wits about them.' He looked abeam as a fish leaped from the glassy rollers to avoid an early predator.

Laroche said in his newly affected drawl, 'We should sight *Doon* next, then.'

Tyacke jabbed his hand forward. 'Well, I hope the lookout's eyesight is better than yours. That fore staysail is flapping about like a washerwoman's apron!'

Laroche called to a boatswain's mate, suitably crushed.

And quite suddenly, there they were, their upper sails and rigging holding the first sunshine, their flags and pendants like pieces of painted metal.

Tyacke said nothing. The convoy was safe.

Bolitho took a telescope, but clung to the sight before he raised it. Big and ponderous they might be, yet in this pure, keen light they had a kind of majesty. He thought back to The Saintes, as he often did at times like this, recalling the first sight of the French fleet. A young officer had written to his mother afterwards, comparing them with the armoured knights at Agincourt.

He asked, 'How many?'

Tyacke again. 'Seven, sir. Or so it said in the instruction.' He repeated, 'Seven,' and Bolitho thought he was wondering if their cargoes were worthwhile or necessary.

Carleton, the signals midshipman, had arrived with his men. He looked fresh and alert, and had probably eaten a huge breakfast, no matter what the galley smelled like. Bolitho nodded to him, remembering when a ship's rat fed on breadcrumbs from the galley had been a midshipman's delicacy. They had said it tasted like rabbit. They had lied.

Tyacke checked the compass again, impatient to make contact with the senior ship of the escort and then lay his own ship on a new tack for their return to Halifax.

Carleton called, 'There is a frigate closing, sir, larboard bow.' He was peering at the bright hoist of flags, but Tyacke said, 'I know her. She's *Wakeful*....' Like an echo, Carleton called dutifully, '*Wakeful*, thirty-eight, Captain Martin Hyde.'

Bolitho turned. The ship which had brought Keen and Adam out from England, after which the *Royal Herald* had been pounded into a coffin for her company. Mistaken identity. Or a brutal extension of an old hatred?

Carleton cleared his throat. 'She has a passenger for *Indomitable*, sir.'

'*What?*' Tyacke sounded outraged. 'By whose order?'

Carleton tried again, spelling out the hoist of flags with extra care.

'Senior officer for duties in Halifax, sir.'

Tyacke said doubtfully, 'That must have been a potful to spell out.' Then, surprisingly, he smiled at the tall midshipman. 'That was well done. Now acknowledge.' He glanced at Bolitho, who had discarded his cloak and was facing into the frail sunlight.

Bolitho shook his head. 'No, James, I do not know who.' He turned and looked at him, his eyes bleak. 'But I think I know why.'

Wakeful was coming about, and a boat was already being swayed up and over the gangway in readiness for lowering. A smart, well-handled ship. The unknown senior officer would have been making comparisons. Bolitho raised the glass again and saw the way falling off the other ship, the scars of wind and sea on her lithe hull. A solitary command, the only kind to have. He said, 'Have

231

the side manned, James. A boatswain's chair too, although I doubt if it will be needed.'

Allday was here, Ozzard, too, with his dress coat, clucking irritably over the admiral's casual appearance.

Allday clipped on the old sword, and murmured, 'Squalls, Sir Richard?'

Bolitho looked at him gravely. He of all people would remember, and understand. 'I fear so, old friend. There are still enemies within our own ranks, it seems.'

He saw the marines stamping to the entry port, picking up their dressing, their bayonets gleaming like silver. Showing a mark of respect, a salute to yet another important visitor. Equally, they would not question an order to place him in front of a firing-squad.

Avery hurried from the companion hatch, but hesitated as Tyacke looked over at him and shook his head very slightly in warning.

Indomitable was hove-to, her seamen obviously glad of something to break the monotony of work and drill.

Wakeful's gig came alongside, rolling steeply in the undertow. Bolitho walked to the rail and stared down, saw the passenger rise from the sternsheets and reach for the guide-rope, disdaining the assistance of a lieutenant, and ignoring the dangling chair as Bolitho had known he would.

Coming to judge the *Reaper*'s mutineers. How could it be that they should meet like this, on a small pencilled cross on Isaac York's chart? And whose hand would have made this choice, unless it were guided by malice, and perhaps personal envy?

He made himself watch as the figure climbing the side missed a stair and almost fell. But he was climbing again, each movement an effort. As it would be for any man with only one arm.

The colour-sergeant growled, 'Royal Marines. . . . *Ready!*' more to cover his own surprise at the time it was taking the visitor to appear at the entry port than out of necessity.

The cocked hat and then the rear-admiral's epaulettes appeared finally in the port, and Bolitho strode forward to meet him.

'Guard of honour! *Present arms!*'

The din of the drill, the squeal of calls and the strident rattle of drums drowned out his spoken welcome.

They faced one another, the visitor with his hat raised in his left hand, his hair quite grey against the deep blue of the ocean behind him. But his eyes were the same, a more intense blue even than Tyacke's.

The noise faded, and Bolitho exclaimed, 'Thomas! You, of all people!'

Rear-Admiral Thomas Herrick replaced his hat and took the proffered hand. 'Sir Richard.' Then he smiled, and for those few seconds Bolitho saw the face of his oldest friend.

Tyacke stood nearby, watching impassively; he knew most of the story, and the rest he could fathom for himself.

He waited to be presented. But he saw only an executioner.

Herrick hesitated inside the great cabin as if, for a moment, he was uncertain why he had come. He glanced around, acknowledging Ozzard with his tray, remembering him. As usual on such occasions, Ozzard revealed neither surprise nor curiosity, no matter what he might be thinking.

Bolitho said, 'Here, Thomas. Try this chair.'

Herrick lowered himself with a grunt into the high-backed *bergère* and thrust out his legs. He said, 'This is more like it.'

Bolitho said, 'Did you find *Wakeful* a mite small?'

Herrick smiled slightly. 'No, not at all. But her captain,

Hyde – a bright young fellow with an even brighter future, I shouldn't wonder – he wanted to *entertain* me. Humour me. I don't need it. Never did.'

Bolitho studied him. Herrick was a year or so younger than himself, but he looked old, tired, and not only because of his grey hair and the deep lines of strain around his mouth. They would be the result of his amputated arm. It had been a close thing.

Ozzard padded nearer and waited.

Bolitho said, 'A drink, perhaps.' There was a thud on deck. 'Your gear is being brought aboard.'

Herrick looked at his legs, stained and wet from his climb up the ship's tumblehome. 'I can't order you to take me to Halifax.'

'It is a pleasure, Thomas. There is so much I need to hear.'

Herrick looked across at Ozzard. 'Some ginger beer, if you have any?'

Ozzard did not blink. 'Of course, sir.'

Herrick sighed. 'I saw that rascal Allday when I came aboard. He doesn't change much.'

'He's a proud father now, Thomas. A little girl. In truth, he shouldn't be here.'

Herrick took the tall glass. 'None of us should.' He examined Bolitho as he sat in another chair. 'You look well. I'm glad.' Then, almost angrily, 'You know why I'm here? The whole damned fleet seems to!'

'The mutiny. *Reaper* was retaken. It was all in my report.'

'I can't discuss it. Not until I've carried out my own investigation.'

'And then?'

Herrick shrugged, and winced. His pain was very evident. The steep climb up *Indomitable*'s side would have done him no good.

'Court of inquiry. The rest you know. We've seen enough mutinies in our time, eh?'

'I know. Adam captured *Reaper*, by the way.'

'So I hear.' He nodded. 'He'd need no urging.'

Calls shrilled overhead and feet thudded across the planking. Tyacke was under sail, changing tack now that the way was clear.

Bolitho said, 'I must read my dispatches. I'll not be long.'

'I can tell you some of it. We heard just before we weighed anchor. Wellington has won a great victory over the French at Vitoria, their last main stronghold in Spain, I understand. They are in retreat.' His face was closed, distant. 'All these years we've prayed and waited for this, clung to it when all else seemed lost.' He held out the empty glass. 'And now it's happened, I can't feel anything, anything at all.'

Bolitho watched him with an indefinable sadness. They had seen and done so much together: blazing sun and screaming gales, blockade and patrols off countless shores, ships lost, good men killed, and more still would die before the last trumpet sounded.

'And you, Thomas? What have you been doing?'

He nodded to Ozzard and took the refilled glass. 'The *scraps*. Visiting dockyards, inspecting coastal defences, anything no one else wanted to do. I was even offered a two-year contract as governor of the new sailors' hospital. *Two years*. It was all they could find.'

'And what of this investigation, Thomas?'

'Do you remember John Cotgrave? He was the Judge Advocate at *my* court-martial. He sits at the top of the legal tree where the Admiralty's concerned. It was his idea.'

Bolitho waited, only the taste of cognac on his tongue to remind him that he had taken a drink. There was no bitterness in Herrick's tone, not even resignation. It was as if he had lost everything, and believed in nothing, least of all the life he had once loved so dearly.

'They want no long drawn-out drama, no fuss. All they want is a verdict to show that justice is upheld.' He gave the thin smile again. 'Has a familiar tune, don't you think?'

He looked towards the stern windows, and the sea beyond. 'As for me, I sold the house in Kent. It was too big, anyway. It was so empty, so desolate without . . .' He hesitated. 'Without Dulcie.'

'What will you do, Thomas?'

'After this? I shall quit the navy. I don't want to be another relic, an old salt-horse who doesn't want to hear when he is surplus to *their lordships'* requirements!'

There was a tap at the door, and as the sentry had remained silent Bolitho knew that it was Tyacke.

He entered the cabin and said, 'On our new course, Sir Richard. *Taciturn* and *Doon* will remain with the convoy as you ordered. The wind's freshening, but it'll suit me.'

Herrick said, 'You sound pleased with her, Captain Tyacke.'

Tyacke stood beneath one of the lanterns.

'She's the fastest sailer I've ever known, sir.' He turned the scarred side of his face towards him, perhaps deliberately. 'I hope you will be comfortable on board, sir.'

Bolitho said, 'Will you sup with us this evening, James?'

Tyacke looked at him, and his eyes spoke for him.

'I must ask your forgiveness, sir, but I have some extra duties to attend to. At some other time, I would be honoured.'

The door closed, and Herrick said, 'When I've left the ship, he means.' Bolitho began to protest. 'I do understand. A ship, a King's ship no less, has mutinied against rightful authority. At any time in war it is a crime beyond comparison, and now when we face a new enemy, with the additional temptation of better pay and more humane treatment, it is all the more dangerous. I will doubtless hear that the uprising was caused by a captain's brutality ... sadism ... I have seen it all before, in my early days as a lieutenant.'

He was speaking of *Phalarope*, without mentioning her name, although it was as if he had shouted it aloud.

'Some will say that the choice of captain was faulty, that it was favouritism, or the need to remove him from his previous appointment – that too is not uncommon. So what do we say? That because of these "mistakes" it was a just solution to dip the colours to an enemy, to mutiny, and to cause the death of that captain, be he saint or damned sinner? There can be no excuse. There never was.' He leaned forward and glanced around the shadowed cabin, but Ozzard had vanished. They were alone. 'I am your friend, although at times I have not shown it. But I know you of old, Richard, and could guess what you might do, even if you have not yet considered it. You would risk everything, throw it all away on a point of honour and, may I say it, decency. You would speak up for those mutineers, no matter what it cost. I tell you now, Richard, it would cost you everything. They would destroy you. They would not merely be victims of their own folly – they would be martyrs. Bloody saints, if some had their way!'

He paused: he seemed wearied suddenly. 'But you do have many friends. What you have done and have tried to do will not be forgotten. Even that damned upstart Bethune confided that he feared for your reputation. So much envy, so much deceit.'

Bolitho walked past the big chair and laid his hand for a moment on the stooped shoulder.

'Thank you for telling me, Thomas. I want a victory, I crave it, and I know what this has cost you.' He saw his reflection in the salt-smeared glass as the ship fell off another point or so. 'I know how you feel.' He sensed the wariness. 'How I would feel if anything happened to separate me from Catherine. But duty is one thing, Thomas ... it has guided my feet since I first went to sea at the age of twelve ... and justice is something else.' He walked around, and saw the same stubborn, closed face, the determination which had first brought them together in *Phalarope*. 'In battle I hate to see men die for no purpose, when they have no say and no choice at all in the matter. And I'll not turn my back on other men who have been wronged, driven to despair, and already condemned by others who are equally guilty, but not charged.'

Horrick remained very calm. 'I am not surprised.' He made to rise. 'Do we still sup this evening?'

Bolitho smiled: it came without effort this time. They were not enemies; the past could not die. 'I had hoped for that, Thomas. Make full use of these quarters.' He picked up the dispatches, and added, 'I promise you that nobody will attempt to entertain you!'

Outside the cabin he found Allday loitering by an open gunport. He had simply happened to be there, in case.

He asked, 'How was it, Sir Richard? Bad?'

Bolitho smiled. 'He has not changed much, old friend.'

Allday said, 'Then it *is* bad.'

Bolitho knew that Tyacke and Avery would be waiting, united even more strongly because of something which was beyond their control.

Allday said harshly, 'They'll hang for it. I'll shed no tears for 'em. I hates their kind. *Vermin*.'

Bolitho looked at him, moved by his anger. Allday had been a pressed man, taken the same day as Bryan Ferguson. So what had instilled in them both such an abiding sense of loyalty, and such courage?

It was no help to understand that Herrick knew the answer. So did Tyacke. *Trust*.

13

'Let Them Never Forget'

John Urquhart, *Valkyrie*'s first lieutenant, paused in the entry port to recover his breath while he stared across at the captured American frigate *Success*. The wind was rising very slightly, but enough to make her plunge and stagger while the small prize crew fought to keep her under command.

He regarded the orderly, almost placid scene on the quarterdeck of this ship, in which he had served for four years, noting the curious but respectful eyes of the midshipmen, reminding him, if it were necessary, of his own crumpled and untidy appearance; then he glanced up at the sky, pale blue, washed-out and, like the ocean, almost misty in the unwavering sunshine.

He saw Adam Bolitho speaking with Ritchie, the sailing-master. Ritchie had been badly wounded in the first clash with the U.S.S. *Unity*, when the admiral had been almost blinded by flying splinters, and the previous captain's nerve had broken. A day he would never forget. Neither would Ritchie, cut down by metal fragments: it was a wonder he had lived. Always a strong, tireless sailing-master of the old school, he was still trying not to show his pain and refusing to recognize his terrible limp, as if in the end it would somehow cure itself.

Urquhart touched his hat to the quarterdeck. There

were countless men like Ritchie on the streets of any sea port in England.

Adam Bolitho smiled. 'Hard pull, was it?'

Urquhart nodded. Three days since they had quit Halifax, with only about five hundred miles to log for it. With the perverse winds and the prospect of storms, it was not the time of year for any one to be complacent, least of all the captain. But while Urquhart had been away from *Valkyrie* aboard the battered prize, the captain seemed to have changed in some way, and was quite cheerful.

Urquhart said, 'I've had the pumps going watch by watch, sir. She's built well enough, like most French ships, but the rot is something else. The old *Indom* gave her more than her share, I'd say!'

Adam said, 'We'll let *Success* fall off a point or so. That should ease the strain.' He stared abeam at the sea's face, set in a moving pattern of blue and pale green; it had an almost milky appearance, broken now and then by a lingering blast of wind, a north-easterly, which could make every sail strain and thunder like a roll of drums. The sea here looked almost shallow, and the drifting gulf weed intensified the effect. He smiled. But there were three thousand fathoms beneath the keel hereabouts, or so they said, although no one could know.

He watched the other frigate's sails lifting and puffing in the same passing squall. 'We'll take her in tow tomorrow, Mr Urquhart. It may slow us even more, but at least we'll stay in company.' He saw Urquhart's eyes move beyond his shoulder and heard the flag lieutenant's brisk footsteps on the deck. De Courcey had kept out of his way, and had in fact probably been instructed to do so by Keen. But would he learn anything on this passage? His future seemed already assured.

De Courcey touched his hat, with a cool glance at Urquhart's dishevelled appearance. 'Is all well?' He looked at Adam. 'Isn't it taking longer than expected, sir?'

Adam gestured across the nettings. 'Yonder lies the enemy, Mr de Courcey. America. In fact, Mr Ritchie insists that we are due east of Chesapeake Bay itself. I have to believe him, of course.'

Urquhart saw the sailing-master's quick, conspiratorial grin. It was more than that. It was pleasure that the captain could now joke with him. They had all known that Captain Adam Bolitho was one of the most successful frigate captains in the fleet, and the nephew of England's most respected, and loved, sailor, but it had been impossible to know him as a man. Urquhart also saw and was amused by the flag lieutenant's sudden alarm as he peered abeam, as if he expected to actually see the coastline.

Adam said, 'Two hundred miles, Mr de Courcey.' He glanced up as the masthead pendant cracked out like a long whip.

Urquhart wondered if he missed the sight of a rear-admiral's flag at the mizzen truck, or was he savouring this independence, limited though it would be?

The previous day, the lookouts had sighted two small sail to the south-west. They had been unable to leave the damaged *Success* to give chase, so the strangers might have been anything, coasters willing to risk the British patrols if only to earn their keep, or enemy scouts. If the captain was troubled by it, he was disguising it well.

De Courcey said suddenly, 'Only two hundred miles, sir? I thought we were heading closer to the Bermudas.'

Adam smiled and touched his arm lightly, something else Urquhart had not seen him do before.

'The nor' easterlies are friendly, Mr de Courcey, but to whom, I wonder?' He turned to Urquhart, excluding the others, his face calm, assured. 'We'll pass a tow at first light. After that. . . .' He did not continue.

Urquhart watched him walk away to speak with the sailing-master again. So certain. But how could he be? Why should he be? He considered the previous two captains, the intolerant and sarcastic Trevenen, who had broken in the face of real danger, and had vanished overboard without trace, and Captain Peter Dawes, the acting-commodore, who had been unable to think beyond promotion. Any fault would reflect badly on a first lieutenant, and Urquhart had intended never to fully trust a captain again, for his own sake. No one else would care what became of him.

De Courcey remarked, 'I wonder what he truly thinks?' When Urquhart remained silent, he went on, 'Works all of us like a man possessed, and then when he has a spare minute, he sits down aft, teaching that boy servant of his to write!' He laughed shortly. 'If that is what he is really doing!'

Urquhart said quietly, 'It is rumoured that Captain Bolitho is very skilled with both blade and pistol, Mr de Courcey. I suggest you do nothing to foster or encourage scandal. It could be the end of you, in more ways than one.'

Adam came back, his face in a small frown. 'May I ask you to take a meal with me, John? I doubt if *Success*'s fare is any sounder than her timbers!'

Urquhart smiled without reservation. 'I would be grateful, sir. But are you certain?' He looked up at the pendant, then at the real strength the two helmsmen were using against the kick of the wheel.

'Yes, I am sure of it. They need the wind, the advantage of it. For us to fight with only the land at our backs, first light will be soon enough.' He looked at him keenly. 'If I'm wrong, we shall be no worse off.'

For only a second, Urquhart saw the face he had just evoked for de Courcey. He could well imagine those same eyes, calm and unblinking along the barrel of a

242

pistol in some quiet clearing at dawn, or testing the edge of his favourite sword. And quite suddenly, he was glad of it.

Adam said, almost casually, 'When this is over and we are back about our rightful affairs, I intend to put you forward for promotion.'

Urquhart was taken aback. 'But, sir – I don't think – I am satisfied to serve you. . . .' He got no further.

Adam said, 'That's enough,' and shook his arm a little for emphasis. 'Never say that, John. Never even think it.' He looked up at the sky and the quivering belly of the main topsail. 'My uncle once described his first command as *the greatest gift*. But it is much more than that.' His eyes hardened. 'Which is why I mistrust those who betray such a privilege.' Then he seemed to shake off the mood. 'At noon, then. Today is Friday, is it not?' He smiled, and Urquhart wondered why there was no woman in his life. 'Tonight the toast will be, *a willing foe and enough sea room*. A perfect sentiment!'

That evening the wind rose again, and backed to north-east-by-north. Urquhart was pulled once more to the *Success*, and was drenched in spray before he was halfway across.

Somehow, he did not care. The stage was set. And he was ready.

Captain Adam Bolitho walked across the black and white checkered deck covering and stared through the tall stern windows. The wind had eased a good deal overnight, but still made its presence felt in short, fierce gusts, dashing the spray high over the ship until it pattered from the dripping sails like rain.

He saw the murky outline of the other frigate, her shape distorted by the caked salt on the glass, her bearing so extreme that she appeared out of control, adrift.

It had been hard work to pass the tow across at first

light, requiring tough, experienced seamanship, or as Evan Jones, the boatswain, had been heard to remark, 'All brute force and bloody ignorance!' But they had done it. Now, yawing drunkenly to each gust of wind, the *Success* fought her tow like a beast being led to slaughter.

He heard eight bells chime from the forecastle and made himself leave the windows. He glanced around the big cabin. Keen's quarters: he had almost expected to see him here at the table where he had placed his own chart within easy reach, so that Ritchie or the lieutenants should not be able to watch his concern as one more hour passed. He leaned on the table, the American coast-line under one palm. He had seen his uncle do this, holding the sea in his hands, translating ideas into action. *In so many ways we are very alike. But in others. . . .*

He straightened his back and looked up at the skylight as somebody laughed. Urquhart had kept his word. Others might suspect his intentions, but nobody knew. And they could still laugh. It was said that when Trevenen had been in command, any sound had been offensive to him. Laughter would be like insubordination or worse.

He thought of the book of poems which Keen had given him, here in this very cabin, with, he believed, few memories of the girl who had owned it, and not knowing the pain it had aroused. And here, he had seen the miniature that Gilia St Clair had intended another to keep and cherish.

More voices came down from the quarterdeck and for a moment he thought he heard a lookout. But it was only another working party, splicing, stitching, repairing: a sailor's lot.

The door opened and the boy John Whitmarsh stood looking in at him.

Adam asked, 'What is it?'

The boy said, 'You've not touched your breakfast, Cap'n. Coffee's cold, too.'

Adam sat in one of Keen's chairs and said, 'No matter.'

'I can fetch some fresh coffee, sir.' He looked at the chart and said gravely, 'Cape Breton to. . . .' He hesitated, his lips moving as he studied the heavy print at the top of the chart. 'To Delaware Bay.' He turned and stared at him, his eyes shining. 'I *read* it, sir! Just like you said I would!'

Adam walked into the other cabin, unable to watch the boy's excitement and pleasure. 'Come here, John Whitmarsh.' He opened his chest and withdrew a parcel. 'D' you know the date of today?'

The boy shook his head. 'It be Saturday, sir.'

Adam held out the parcel. 'July twenty-first. I could not very well forget it. It was the day I was posted.' He tried to smile. 'It was also listed in *Anemone*'s log as the date when you were volunteered. Your birthday.' The boy was still staring at him, and he said roughly, 'Here, take it. It's yours.'

The boy opened the parcel as if it were dangerous to touch, then gasped as he saw the finely made dirk and polished scabbard. 'For me, sir?'

'Yes. Wear it. You are thirteen years old. Not an easy passage, eh?'

John Whitmarsh was still staring at it. 'Mine.' It was all he said, or could say.

Adam swung round and saw the second lieutenant, William Dyer, staring in from the passageway.

Dyer seemed to be a reliable officer and Urquhart had spoken well of him, but it was too good a piece of gossip to miss. What he had just witnessed would soon be all over the wardroom. The captain giving gifts to a cabin boy. Losing his grip.

Adam quietly said, 'Well, Mr Dyer?' They could think what they damned well pleased. He had known few acts of kindness when he himself had been that age. He could scarcely remember his mother, except for her constant

245

love, and even now he did not understand how she could have given herself like a common whore in order to support her son, whose father had not known of his existence.

Dyer said, 'The master sends his respects, sir, and he is anxious about our present course. We will have to change tack shortly for the next leg – a hard enough task, even without that great drag on the tow-line.'

Adam said, 'The master thinks that, does he? And what do you think?'

Dyer flushed. 'I thought it better coming from me, sir. In Mr Urquhart's place, I felt it was my duty to bring his unease to your notice myself.'

Adam walked back to the chart. 'You did well.' Had Urquhart seen the folly of his idea? For folly was what it would be. 'You deserve an answer. So does Mr Ritchie.'

Dyer gaped as Adam swung round and shouted, 'The skylight, John Whitmarsh! Open the skylight!'

The boy climbed on a chair to reach it, his new dirk still clutched in one hand.

Adam heard the wind gusting against the hull and imagined it ruffling the sea's face, like a breeze on a field of standing corn. The cry came again. *'Two sail to th' nor' east!'*

Adam said sharply, 'That is the answer, Mr Dyer. The enemy was not asleep, it seems.' To the boy he said, 'Fetch my sword, if you please. We shall both be properly presented today.'

Then he laughed aloud, as if it were some secret joke. 'July twenty-first, 1813! It will be another day to remember!'

Dyer exclaimed, 'The enemy, sir? How can it be certain?'

'You doubt me?'

'But, but . . . if they intend to attack us they will hold the wind-gage. All the advantages will be theirs!' He did not seem able to stop. 'Without the tow we might stand a chance. . . .'

Adam saw the boy returning with his captain's hanger. 'All in good time, Mr Dyer. Tell Mr Warren to hoist Flag Seven for *Success* to recognize. Then pipe all hands aft. I wish to address them.'

Dyer asked in a small voice, 'Will we fight, sir?'

Adam looked around the cabin, perhaps for the last time. He forced himself to wait, to feel doubt, or worse, a fear he had not known before *Anemone* had been lost.

He said, 'Be assured, Mr Dyer, we shall win this day.' But Dyer had already hurried away.

He raised his arms so that the boy could clip on his sword, as his coxswain, George Starr, had used to do: Starr, who had been hanged for what he had done aboard *Anemone* after her flag had come down. Without knowing that he spoke aloud, he repeated, 'We shall *win* this day.'

He glanced once more at the open skylight, and smiled. A very close thing. Then he walked out of the cabin, the boy following his shadow without hesitation.

Midshipman Francis Lovie lowered his telescope and wiped his streaming face with the back of his hand.

'*Flag Seven*, sir!'

Urquhart eyed him grimly. It had come as he expected, but it was still a shock. The captain's private signal.

He took the telescope from Lovie's hands and trained it towards the other ship. His ship. Where he had been trusted, even liked by some when he had stood between *Valkyrie*'s company and a tyrant of a captain. As it must have been in *Reaper*, and in too many other ships. Adam Bolitho's words seemed to intrude through all his doubts and uncertainties. *I mistrust those who betray such a privilege.* He watched the familiar figures leap into the lens, men he knew so well: Lieutenant Dyer, and beside him the most junior lieutenant, Charles Gulliver, not long ago

a midshipman like the one who was sharing this dangerous task with him. Lovie was seventeen, and Urquhart
liked to believe that he himself had played his part in
making him what he was. Lovie was ready to sit his
examination for lieutenant.

He moved the glass slightly, feeling the warm spray on
his mouth and hair. Ritchie was there, listening intently
with his master's mates close by, Barlow, the new lieutenant of marines, his face as scarlet as his tunic in the misty
sunlight. Beyond them the mass of sailors, some of whom
he knew and trusted, and others whom he accepted
would never change, the hard men who saw all authority
as a deadly enemy. But fight? Yes, they would do that
well enough.

And there was the captain, his back towards him, his
shoulders shining and wet as if he did not care, did not
feel anything beyond his instinct, which had not failed
him.

Lovie asked, 'What will the captain tell them, sir?'

Urquhart did not look at him. 'What I will tell *you*,
Mr Lovie. We will stand by the tow, and break it when
we are so ordered.'

Lovie watched his profile. Urquhart was the only first
lieutenant he had ever known, and secretly he hoped that
he himself would be as good, if he ever got the chance.

He said, 'The fuse you laid, sir. You've known all this
time.'

Urquhart watched the image in the glass. Men cheering: but for the wind they would have heard the sound
from here.

'Guessed would be closer to the truth. I thought it was
a last resort to prevent the prize being retaken.' He
lowered the glass and regarded him intently. 'And then,
suddenly I understood. Captain Bolitho *knew*, and had
already decided what he must do.'

Lovie frowned. 'But there's two of them, sir. Suppose. . . .'

Urquhart smiled. 'Aye, suppose – that one word, which never appears in dispatches.' He recalled Adam Bolitho's face when he had first come aboard and had read himself in: a sensitive, guarded face, which betrayed little of what it must have cost him to lose a ship, be a prisoner of war, and endure the ritual of a court-martial. When, very rarely, he allowed himself to relax, as he had yesterday when they had shared a meal, Urquhart had glimpsed the man behind the mask. In some ways, still a prisoner. Of something, or someone.

Urquhart said, 'You stand fast and watch the tow. Call me immediately if anything happens.' He was about to add something humourous, but changed his mind abruptly and headed for the companion way. Knowledge came like a blow in the face, something he could not forget or ignore. Lovie was standing where he had left him, perhaps dreaming of the day when he, too, would wear a lieutenant's rank.

Urquhart clattered down the ladder and stood for a few minutes in the shadows to compose himself. It was not the first time this had happened, and he had heard others, more experienced, speak of it. But in his heart he knew that Midshipman Lovie would not be alive by the end of the day.

A gunner's mate was watching him, a slow match moving in his fist like a solitary evil eye.

'All ready, Jago?' It was something to say. The gunner's mate was a true seaman, which was why he had picked him in the first place. Trevenen had had him flogged for some trivial offence and Urquhart had clashed with the captain about it. The rift had cost him dearly; he knew that now. Even Dawes had never mentioned the possibility of promotion to him. But his efforts had earned him Jago's trust, and something far stronger, although he would carry the scars of that unjustified flogging to the grave.

Jago grinned. 'Just give the word, sir!'

No question, no doubts. Perhaps it was better to be like that.

He looked up the ladder, to a patch of pale blue sky. 'The boats will be warped alongside. The rest is up to us.'

He walked on through the ship, where many men had once worked and lived, hoped too. Men who spoke the same language, but whose common heritage had become like an unbroken reef between nations at war.

Urquhart listened to the creak of the tiller, and the lonely clank of a single pump.

It was almost done. The ship was already dead.

Ritchie called, 'Course is south south-east, sir. Steady as she goes.'

Adam walked a few paces to the rail and back again. It seemed strangely still and quiet after the tapping drums had beaten *Valkyrie*'s seamen and marines to quarters. He had felt the sudden unnerving excitement, and after that, the cheering. It had been unexpected, and over-whelming. These men were still strangers for the most part, because he had kept them so, but their huzzas had been infectious, and he had seen Ritchie forgetting himself so far as to shake hands with George Minchin, the surgeon, who had made a rare appearance on deck to listen to the captain speaking. Minchin was a butcher of the old orlop tradition, but in spite of his brutal trade and his dependence on rum, he had saved more lives than he had lost, and had won the praise of the great surgeon, Sir Piers Blachford, when he had been aboard *Hyperion*.

Lieutenant Dyer said, 'The enemy are on the same bearing, sir.'

Adam had seen them briefly, two frigates, the same ones or others unknown to him. Perhaps it did not matter. But he knew that it did.

He glanced astern and pictured the two ships as he had last seen them. Their captains would have marked *Valkyrie*'s every change of course, no matter how small. They would expect them to cast off the tow: any captain would, unless he wanted to sacrifice his ship without a fight.

Suppose they did not swallow the ruse? He might lose Urquhart and his prize crew, or be forced to leave them, if only to save his own command.

Run? He beckoned to the signals midshipman. 'Mr Warren! Get aloft with your glass and tell me what you see.' He turned, and watched de Courcey walking stiffly to the lee side as if to study some marines, who were climbing to the maintop with more ammunition for the swivel there. He had removed his epaulette and the twist of gold lace that proclaimed him to be admiral's flag lieutenant, perhaps in the hope of offering a less tempting target if the enemy drew close enough.

Adam heard the midshipman yell, 'The rear ship wears a broad-pendant, sir!'

He breathed out slowly. A commodore then, like Nathan Beer. . . . He dismissed the thought. No, not at all like the impressive Beer. He must forget him. It was not merely foolish to show admiration for an enemy, it was also dangerous. If this was the man his uncle suspected, there could be no admiration. Out of personal hatred, he had already tried to avenge himself on Sir Richard Bolitho by any means he could invent, and Adam was almost convinced that it was the same mind which had planned to use him as bait to tempt his uncle into a rescue attempt. He often thought of that bare but strangely beautiful room, where he had been interrogated by the American captain, Brice. Perhaps Brice would recall that meeting when he received news of his son's death.

Hatred was the key, if it was in fact Rory Aherne, whose father had been hanged for treason in Ireland. An incident long forgotten in the confusion and pain of many years of war, but he had not forgotten: nor would he forgive. Perhaps it had given this unknown Aherne a purpose, and allowed him to achieve a measure of fame which might otherwise have escaped him. A renegade, a privateer, who had found a place in America's young but aggressive navy. Some might sing his praises for a while, but renegades were never fully trusted. Like John Paul Jones, the Scot who had found glory and respect in battles against England. Nevertheless, he had never been offered another command, famous or not.

He frowned. *Like my father....*

There was a dull bang, which echoed around the ship as if the sound were trapped in a cave. The solitary ball ripped abeam of the *Success* before splashing down in a cloud of spray.

Somebody said, 'Bow-chaser.'

Dyer remarked, 'First shot.'

Adam took out his watch and opened the guard, remembering the dim shop, the ticking clocks, the silvery chorus of chimes. He did not glance at the mermaid, trying not to think of her or hear her voice. *Not now.* She would understand, and forgive him.

He said, 'Note it in the log, Mr Ritchie. The date and the time. I fear that only *you* will know the place!'

Ritchie grinned, as Adam had known he would. Was it so easy to make men smile, even in the face of death?

He closed the watch with a snap and returned it to his pocket.

'Leading ship is changing tack, sir. I think she intends to close with the prize!'

The lieutenant sounded surprised. Baffled. Adam had

tried to explain, when the lower deck had been cleared and the hands piped aft. All night long the two American frigates had beaten and clawed their way into the teeth of the wind. *All night long*: determined, confident that they would take and hold the wind-gage, so that *Valkyrie* could either stand and fight against the odds, or become the quarry in a stern-chase, to be pounded into submission at long range or finally driven aground.

They had not cheered out of any sense of duty: they had seen and done too much already to need to prove themselves. Perhaps they had cheered simply because he had told them, and they knew, just this once, what they were doing, and why.

He strode to the shrouds and climbed into the ratlines, his legs soaked with spray as he levelled his telescope at a point beyond Urquhart's temporary command.

There she was. A big frigate, thirty-eight guns at least, French-built like *Success*. Before the glass misted over, he saw hurrying figures massing along the enemy's gangway. *Success* was under tow, her guns still secured and unmanned. The whole of Halifax had probably heard about it, and there were many other ears only too ready to listen.

He returned to the deck. 'Make the signal, Mr Warren. *Cast off!*'

He could see the upper yards of the enemy frigate criss-crossing with those of *Success*, but knew that they were not yet close, let alone alongside. There were a few shots: marksmen in the tops testing the range, seeking a kill like hounds after a wounded stag.

Success seemed to suddenly grow in size and length as the tow broke free and she yawed around, her few sails in wild disorder to the wind.

Adam clenched his fists against his thighs. *Come on. Come on.* It was taking too long. They would be up to her in minutes, but still might sheer away if they suspected anything.

Warren said hoarsely, 'One boat pulling away, sir!'

Adam nodded, his eyes stinging but unable to blink. Urquhart's boat would be next, and soon. Or not at all.

More shots, and he saw the gleam of sunlight on steel as the boarders prepared to hack their way aboard the drifting prize. He tried to shut it from his thoughts. He shouted, 'Stand by to come about, Mr Ritchie! Mr Monteith, more hands on the weather braces there!' He saw the gun captains crouched low and ready, while they waited for the next order.

He felt rather than saw de Courcey by the quarterdeck rail, speaking rapidly to himself, as though he were praying. The enemy's yards were being hauled round, to lessen the impact when the two hulls ground together.

Adam saw the boat pulling away from both ships, fear giving them the strength and the purpose.

Somebody said quietly, 'The first lieutenant's left it too late.'

He snapped, 'Hold your bloody noise, damn you!' and barely recognized his own voice.

Ritchie saw it first: all the years at sea in many different conditions, matching his eye against sun and star, wind and current. A man who, even without a sextant, could probably find his way back to Plymouth.

'Smoke, sir!' He glared round at his mates. 'By Jesus, *he done it!'*

The explosion was like a fiery wind, so great that despite the thousands of fathoms of sea beneath them, it felt as if they had run aground on solid rock.

Then the flames, leaping from hatches and through fiery holes that opened in the decks like craters, the wind exploring and driving them until her sails became blackened rags and her rigging was spitting sparks. The fires spread rapidly to the American grappled alongside, where jubilant figures had been cheering and waving their weapons only seconds before.

Adam raised his fist.

'For *you*, George Starr, and *you*, John Bankart. *Let them never forget!*'

'There's the other boat now, sir!' Dyer sounded shocked by what he was seeing, the very savagery of it.

Ritchie called, 'Standing by, sir!'

Adam raised the telescope, and then said, 'Belay that, Mr Ritchie.'

He had seen the first lieutenant at the tiller, the remaining seamen lying back on their looms, no doubt staring at the exploding flames which had almost consumed them. Beside Urquhart lay the midshipman, Lovie, staring at the smoke and the sky, and seeing neither.

To those around him Adam said, 'We'll pick them up first – we have the time we need. I'll not lose John Urquhart now.'

The two frigates were completely ablaze, and appeared to be leaning toward one another in a final embrace. *Success*'s bilge had been blown out in the first explosion, and, grappled to her attacker, she was taking the American with her to the bottom.

A few men were splashing about in the water; others floated away, already dead or dying from their burns. From a corner of his eye Adam saw Urquhart's small boat drifting clear of *Valkyrie*'s side. It was empty: only the midshipman's coat with its white patches lay in the sternsheets to mark the price of courage.

He hardened himself to it, and tried to exclude the sounds of ships breaking up, guns tearing adrift and thundering through the flames and choking smoke, where even now a few demented souls would be stumbling and falling, calling for help when there was none to respond.

Midshipman Warren called, 'The other ship's standing away, sir!' Adam looked at him and saw the tears on his cheeks. All this horror, but he was able to think only of his friend, Lovie.

Ritchie cleared his throat. 'Give chase, sir?'

Adam looked at the upturned faces. 'I think not, Mr Ritchie. Back the mizzen tops'l while we recover the other boat.' He could not see the American ship with the commodore's broad-pendant: it was lost in the smoke, or the painful obscurity of his own vision.

'Two down, one to go. I think we can rest on a promise.'

He saw Urquhart coming slowly toward him. Two members of a gun's crew stood to touch his arm as he passed. He paused only to say something to Adam's servant, Whitmarsh, who, despite orders, had been on deck throughout. He would be remembering, too. Perhaps this was also vengeance for him.

Adam stretched out his hand. 'I am relieved that you did not leave it too late.'

Urquhart looked at him gravely. 'Almost.' His handshake was firm, thankful. 'I'm afraid I lost Mr Lovie. I liked him. Very much.'

Adam thought of one of his own midshipmen, who had died on that other day. It was pointless, destructive to have friends, to encourage others to form friendships which would only end in death.

When he looked again, *Success* and the American were gone. There was only a great haze of smoke, like steam from a volcano, as if the ocean itself were burning in the deep, and wreckage, men and pieces of men.

He walked to the opposite side and wondered why he had not known. To hate was not enough.

14

Verdict

Rear-Admiral Thomas Herrick stood squarely by the quarterdeck rail, his chin sunk in his neckcloth, and only his eyes moving while *Indomitable*, under reduced sail, glided slowly toward her anchorage.

'So this is Halifax.' His eyes followed the running figures of the extra hands who were answering the boatswain's hoarse shout. Only then did he turn his head and glance at the captain on the opposite side of the deck. Tyacke was studying the landmarks, the nearest ships, anchored or otherwise, his hands behind him as if he were unconcerned.

Herrick said, 'A good ship's company, Sir Richard. Better than most. Your Captain Tyacke would be hard to replace, I'm thinking.'

Bolitho said, 'Yes,' sorry that they were soon to be parted, and also saddened on behalf of the man he had once known so well. He had offered Herrick the full use of the ship while she was in Halifax, and typically, Herrick had refused. He would take the accommodation he had been offered. It was as if it was painful for him simply to see and feel a ship working around him again.

York, the sailing-master, called, 'Ready when you are, sir!'

Tyacke nodded, without turning. 'Wear ship, if you please!'

'Man the lee braces there! Hands wear ship!' The calls shrilled and more men scampered to add their weight to haul the yards around. 'Tops'l sheets!'

Two fishermen stood in their heavy dory to wave as they passed through *Indomitable*'s shadow.

Bolitho saw one of the midshipmen waving back, then freeze as he found the captain's eyes on him.

'Tops'l clew lines! Roundly there – take that man's name, Mr Craigie!'

Bolitho had already noticed that *Valkyrie* was not at her usual anchorage, nor was the American ship *Success*. He was not surprised that the latter had been moved. The harbour, large though it was, seemed to be bursting with ships, men-of-war, merchantmen and transport vessels of every type and size.

'Helm a' lee!'

Slowly, as though recalling her earlier life as a ship of the line, *Indomitable* turned into the light wind, the panorama of houses and rough hillside gliding past her jib-boom, as if the land and not the ship was moving.

'Let go!'

The great anchor dropped into the water, spray dashing as high as the beakhead and its crouching lion while the ship came obediently to rest.

'I'll have the gig take you ashore, Thomas. I can send my flag lieutenant with you until you are ready. . . .'

The bright blue eyes studied him for a moment. 'I can manage, thank you.' Then he held out his remaining hand, his body visibly adjusting to the movement, as if still unaccustomed to the loss. 'I can see why you have never quit the sea for some high office ashore or in the Admiralty. I would be the same, if they had allowed it.' He spoke with the same curious lack of bitterness. 'I'll wager you'd find no Happy Few in that damned place!'

Bolitho took his hand in both of his own. 'There are not too many left, I'm afraid, Thomas.'

They both looked along the deck, the busy seamen, the marines waiting by the entry port, the first lieutenant leaning out from the forecastle to check the lie of the cable. *Even here*, Bolitho thought. Charles Keverne had been his first lieutenant in the three-decker *Euryalus*, when he had been a flag captain himself. A reliable officer despite a hasty temper, with the dark good looks which had won him a lovely wife. About twelve years ago, as a captain, Keverne had commanded this same ship, when she had been a third-rate. Together they had fought in the Baltic. Once again, *Indomitable* had triumphed, but Keverne had fallen there.

Herrick watched his sea-chest and bags being carried on deck. The gig was already hoisted out: the contact was almost severed.

Herrick paused by the ladder, and Bolitho saw the Royal Marine colour-sergeant give a quick signal to his officer.

Herrick was fighting with something. Stubborn, strong-willed, intransigent, but loyal, always loyal above everything.

'What is it, Thomas?'

Herrick did not look at him. 'I was wrong to regard your feeling for Lady Somervell so ill. I was so full of grief for my Dulcie that I was blind to all else. I tried to tell her in a letter. . . .'

'I know. She was very moved by it. And so was I.'

Herrick shook his head. 'But I can see now, don't you understand? What you've done for the navy, for England, no less – and yet still you drive yourself.' He reached out and seized Bolitho's arm. 'Go while you can, Richard. Take your Catherine and be grateful. Let some one else carry this goddamned burden, this war that nobody wants, except those who intend to profit from it! *It is not our war*, Richard. Just this once, accept it!'

Bolitho could feel the strength of the man in the grip

259

of the solitary hand. No wonder he had forced himself to climb the ship's side, to prove what he could do, and who he was.

'Thank you for saying that, Thomas. I shall tell Catherine when I write to her next.'

Herrick walked beside him to the entry port. His bags and sea-chest had vanished. He saw Allday waiting, and said, 'Take care, you rascal.' He stared past him at the land. 'I was sorry to hear about your son. But your daughter will give you much happiness.'

Allday looked at Bolitho. It was as if he had known what Herrick had just said, had felt the very urgency of the plea.

'He won't listen to me, Mr Herrick. Never does!'

Herrick held out his hand to Tyacke. 'She does you credit, Captain Tyacke. You have suffered for what you have earned, but I envy you, for all that.' He turned toward Bolitho and removed his hat. 'You, Captain, and one other.'

The calls shrilled and the marines' bayonets flashed in the bright sunlight.

When Bolitho looked down once more, the gig was already backing water from the side. He watched until it was lost beyond an anchored brigantine. Then he smiled. Typically, again, Herrick did not look back.

Tyacke fell into step beside him. 'Well, I don't envy him *his* job, Sir Richard. It's *Reaper*'s captain who should be on trial. I've run better slavers up to the mainyard before now!'

Bolitho said, 'He may surprise us, but I agree. His is a thankless task.' But the force of Herrick's words refused to leave him, and he could not imagine what it must have cost him to speak them.

Tyacke said suddenly, 'This victory you mentioned, Sir Richard. Some place in Spain, you said?'

It was said to be Wellington's greatest triumph over

the French so far. The war could not last much longer, surely.

Bolitho replied, 'They speak of months, not years any more, James. I have learned not to hope too much. And yet. . . .' He watched the courier schooner *Reynard* speeding toward the harbour mouth, her ensign dipping in salute as she passed abeam of his flagship. A small, lively command for the young lieutenant who was her lord and master. Like *Miranda*, the schooner which had been Tyacke's first command; he would be thinking of it now, and of their own first wary meeting. What they had now become to one another.

He said abruptly, 'Well, James, the war is still with us here, so I *shall* have to accept it!'

Bolitho stood by a window and watched his flag lieutenant walking along the stone-flagged terrace, carrying his hat in the warm sunshine. In the background, the anchorage was so crowded that it was hardly possible to see *Indomitable*. But for his flag curling in the wind, she might have been any one of them.

Valentine Keen was saying, 'I decided to send *Valkyrie* to Antigua. She was the only ship powerful enough to escort the prize and frighten off any over-eager enemy.'

In the glass Bolitho saw Keen's reflected arm wave across the litter of papers and dispatches which the schooner *Reynard* had delivered to him. Bolitho had sensed a moment's uneasiness when the schooner had sailed smartly abeam as he had been speaking to Tyacke: *Reynard*'s youthful commander had known then that Keen was here, otherwise he would have made his report on board *Indomitable*.

'*Valkyrie* met with two American frigates. It is all here in Adam's report, which he passed to *Reynard* when they happened to meet at sea.'

261

'And one was destroyed, Val. *Valkyrie* suffered no losses but for a midshipman. Remarkable.'

'Yes, they picked up a few survivors, not many, apparently, and discovered that the ship that went down with *Success* was the U.S.S. *Condor*. A Captain Ridley was in command, killed, with most of his people, it seems.'

'And the other frigate was the *Retribution*.'

Keen did not seem to hear him. 'I did not intend that either *Valkyrie* or the prize should be put at unnecessary risk. Had I been aboard, I would have made certain that a more open course was observed. Captain Bolitho was too near to the enemy coast.'

'Two hundred miles, you say?' He turned from the glare, his eye suddenly painful. 'You and I have trailed our coats a good deal nearer than that, in our time!'

'I think it was deliberate.' Keen faced him across the table. 'I know he is your nephew, and I am the first to appreciate that. But I think it was an impetuous and dangerous course of action. We could have lost both ships.'

Bolitho said, 'As it was, Val, we exchanged a broken-down prize which would have taken months or perhaps years to overhaul and refit, for one of a group which has been a thorn in our side since our return to Halifax. Your place was here, while you were waiting to receive the latest convoy. You made the right decision, and it was yours to make. And as the one in command, Adam had no choice but to act as he did. I would expect that of any of my captains. You must know that.'

Keen recovered himself with an effort. 'The survivors also confirmed your belief that Captain, now Commodore Rory Aherne was in command of the group.' He banged his hand down on the papers, and anger put an edge to his voice. 'He might have taken my flagship!'

'And Adam – where is he now?'

Keen plucked his shirt away from his skin. 'He had

orders for the Captain in Charge at Antigua. He will return here when he has carried out my instructions.'

'Remember when you were my flag captain, Val. Trust extends in two directions. It has to be the strongest link in the chain of command.'

Keen stared at him. 'I have never forgotten that. I owe everything to you . . . and Catherine.' He smiled, ruefully, Bolitho thought, and said, 'And to Adam, I know that!' He touched his pocket, and Bolitho wondered if he carried the miniature there. So that was it. This was, after all, Benjamin Massie's house, and the St Clairs would be staying here also. It was not difficult to guess what had come between Keen and his flag captain. *The girl with moonlit eyes.*

In fairness, it might prove to be the best thing that could happen to Keen. As Catherine had predicted. . . . A brave and defiant young woman, one strong enough to help Keen in his future. And able to stand up against his father, he thought grimly.

Adam would not regard it in that light at all.

'And what of the latest intelligence, Val?'

Keen took two goblets from a cupboard. 'The Americans have brought two more frigates to Boston. I ordered *Chivalrous* and the brig *Weazle* to patrol outside the port. If they come out. . . .'

Bolitho said, 'I think they will. And soon.' He looked up, and asked, 'And York – is there any more news?'

Keen shrugged. 'Very little. It takes so long to reach here. But David St Clair told me that weapons and supplies were stored there for our ships on the lakes. They might have seized or destroyed them. Either way, it will make our vessels less able to control Lake Erie, which St Clair insists is the vital key to the whole area.'

'And tell me about *Miss* St Clair.' He saw Keen start, so that some of the claret he was about to pour pattered onto the table. He added gently, 'I shall not pry, Val. I am a friend; remember that, too.'

Keen filled the two goblets. 'I admire her greatly. I have told her as much.' He faced him again. 'Perhaps I delude myself.' He gave his boyish smile, which Bolitho had seen from his youth to this moment, and seemed relieved that he had at last spoken openly about it.

Bolitho thought of Adam's despair, his agony when he had read Catherine's letter, breaking the news of Zenoria's lonely and terrible death. But he said, 'Thank you for sharing it with me. I wish you good fortune, Val. You deserve it.' He returned the smile, touched by Keen's obvious relief. 'I mean it. You cannot be an admiral all of the time!'

Keen said suddenly, 'I am told that Rear-Admiral Herrick is here. Transferred to *Indomitable* when you made your rendezvous with the convoy.' He did not attempt to soften his tone.

'I know there was no love lost between you, Val. He does not relish this mission, let me assure you.'

Keen said shortly, 'The right man for the task, I think. He has known what it is to sit on both sides of the table at a court-martial!'

'That is past, Val. It has to be.'

Keen persisted, 'But what can he do? Ninety men, British sailors. Hang them or flog them? The crime was done, the penalty is already decided. It has always been so.'

Bolitho moved to the window again, and saw Avery speaking with Gilia St Clair.

Without turning he asked, 'When you met up with *Reaper*, and before she struck to you, did you believe that Adam would order the guns to fire on them?' He waited a few seconds. 'Hostages or not?'

'I . . . am not certain.'

Bolitho saw the girl throw back her head and laugh at

something Avery had said. Caught up in a war, and now in something more personal. She had talked with Adam: she would have known, or guessed, how near death might have been that day.

He walked away from the window, turning his back on the light. 'The schooner *Crystal* in which the St Clairs were on passage when *Reaper* captured them – who owned her?'

'I believe it was Benjamin Massie. You have a very good memory for names.'

Bolitho put down the glass, thankful for the sunlight behind him, hiding his face and his thoughts.

'It's getting better all the while, Val!'

Richard Bolitho stepped on to the jetty stairs and waited for Tyacke and his flag lieutenant to follow him. Across the heads of the barge crew Allday was watching him, sharing it all with him, even if he probably saw things differently.

Bolitho said to him, 'I'm not certain how long we shall be.'

Allday squinted into the hard light. 'We'll be here, Sir Richard.'

They walked up to the roadway in silence, and Bolitho noted that the air felt cooler despite the sun. It was September: could the year be passing so quickly?

He thought of the letter he had received from Catherine, telling him of Roxby's final hours, and describing the funeral in detail so that he felt he had been there with her. Quite a grand affair, as was appropriate for a knight of the Hanoverian Guelphic Order: Roxby had been well liked by his own set of people, respected by all those who worked for him, and feared by many others who had crossed his path in his other role as magistrate. He had a been a fair man, but he would have had little patience with today's happenings. Even in the barge Bolitho had sensed the tension, the oarsmen avoiding his eyes, Avery staring abeam at the anchored *Reaper*, and Tyacke quite detached from it all, more withdrawn than he had been for many months.

He raised his hat to a troop of soldiers as they clattered past on perfectly matched horses, their young ensign raising his sabre with a flourish at the sight of an admiral's uniform.

All these soldiers. When would they be called upon to fight, or was the die already cast? Tyacke, like David St Clair, had been right about the Americans and their determination to take and hold the lakes. They had made another raid on York, and had burned supply sheds and military equipment which had been abandoned when the British army had retreated to Kingston three months ago. The need to wrest control of Lake Erie from the Americans was vital, to protect the line of water communications and keep open the army's only supply route, without which they would be forced into further retreat, and perhaps even surrender.

He saw the barracks gates ahead of them, and realized with pleasure that he was not out of breath.

The guard had turned out for them, with bayonets glinting as they walked into the main building. A corporal opened the doors for them, and Bolitho saw his eyes move briefly to Tyacke's disfigured face, and then just as hastily away. He knew that Tyacke had noticed, and wondered if that was why he was so unusually remote. He was intensely aware of the stares, the pity, and the revulsion: he was never allowed to forget, and Bolitho knew that that was why he avoided going ashore whenever possible.

More doors and clicking heels, and then they entered a large, spartan room containing a table and two rows of chairs. Keen and Adam were already present, as was the languid de Courcey. A dusty-looking civilian clerk sat at one end of the table, a major of the Royal Marines at the other. Despite the room's bare austerity, it already had the atmosphere of an official court.

They shook hands, more like strangers than friends. Bolitho had seen very little of Adam since his return from Antigua, but had written to congratulate him on his destruction of the prize and her attacker, with the loss of only one man. It was hard to tell what Adam really thought about it.

The other door was opened and Rear-Admiral Thomas Herrick walked straight to the table and sat down, his eyes moving briefly across their faces, his own impassive, with nothing to reveal the strain under which he had placed himself with his personally conducted enquiry into the loss and recapture of His Britannic Majesty's frigate *Reaper*.

Bolitho knew that Herrick had read all the statements, including that taken by Avery from *Reaper*'s badly injured first lieutenant at Hamilton, and Adam's account of the recapture from the Americans when *Reaper*'s guns had been discharged into the sea. Herrick had also spoken with David St Clair, and very likely with St Clair's daughter. Bolitho recalled the moment at the general's house when the youthful captain of the King's Regiment had handed the girl's miniature over to Keen. This latest attack on York had occasioned no more casualties, as the British army had not returned to the burned-out fort, but she must have thought of it, all the same: the man she had loved, and had believed had cared deeply for her, lying up there somewhere with his dead soldiers. The Americans had quit York after only three days; perhaps the stores and weapons they had hoped to find were already gone, or had been destroyed during the first attack. Compared with many other battles, the action was not one of the most significant, but in proportion it was certainly one of the bloodiest; and the full consequences were still to be measured.

Herrick looked up from his file of papers.

'This is an official court of enquiry into the loss and recapture of His Britannic Majesty's Ship *Reaper*, intelligence of which I am authorized and ordered to summarize for the Lords of Admiralty, for their guidance and final approval.'

He waited for the clerk to pass him another sheet of paper.

'We are all very well aware of the consequences of bad example, and of poor leadership. It is often too simple to be wise after an event which has already done so much wrong and caused so much damage.' For only a moment, his blue eyes rested on Bolitho. 'In all these years of war, against one foe or another, we have won many victories. However, we have never won the freedom to question or challenge what we did, or why we were so ordered.' He almost smiled. 'And I fear we never will, in our lifetimes.'

He looked down again. 'We require no reminding of the absolute need for order and discipline at all times. Without them, we are a shambles, a disgrace to the fleet in which we serve.' His shoulder moved, and the empty sleeve swayed slightly; he did not appear to notice. 'It is a lesson which any captain forgets at his peril.'

Bolitho glanced at his companions. Keen and Adam had both been his midshipmen, and had learned the hazards and the rewards on their way up the ladder of promotion. De Courcey was listening intently, but his expression was devoid of understanding. James Tyacke was leaning back in the shadows as if to conceal his face, but his hands, which rested in his lap, were very tense, locked together as if he, too, were preparing for the inevitable. Like those others who would be waiting: some ninety souls, whose suffering under a sadistic captain would soon be obliterated in the name of justice.

He saw Adam gazing at him with unblinking eyes, his face drawn, as if he were in pain. But Bolitho knew it was a deeper pain even than the body's wounds: he was reliving the loss of his ship, the flag coming down while he lay where he had fallen on that bloody day. Remembering those who had fought and died at his bidding. Men who, as Herrick had rightly said, had never known the freedom to question or challenge what they were ordered to do.

He thought Adam must be remembering their many long conversations, each gaining from the other's experience. He was headstrong and impetuous, but his love had never been in doubt, caring always for the man who would be called upon to sign the warrants for those condemned to be hanged, or at best flogged into something inhuman.

Bolitho touched the locket beneath the fresh shirt he wore, and thought he saw understanding in Adam's face.

Herrick was saying, 'The Americans are, fortunately, a nation of magpies. They are slow to throw away items which may be of historic interest at some later time.' He gestured to the clerk, and waited while he opened a large, canvas-covered volume.

Herrick continued, without expression, '*Reaper*'s punishment book. It tells me more than five hundred written reports and dying declarations. This captain was not long in command and on his first active service as such, and yet this book reads like a chapter from Hell itself.'

Bolitho could almost feel Tyacke's sudden tension. Wanting to speak out. But Herrick knew for himself what quarterdeck tyranny could be: Bolitho had become his captain in *Phalarope* all those years ago only because the previous captain had been removed. Another tyrant.

'To go back to that day, gentlemen. The mutiny, which

we now know was both inspired and encouraged by the Americans who boarded that unhappy ship. There were ringleaders, of course, but without American aid and a ready presence, who could swear to the truth of what would have happened?' He peered at his papers, as he must have done every day since his arrival in Halifax. 'Vengeance is a terrible disease, but in this case it was probably inevitable. We know that *Reaper*'s captain died as a result of the flogging he received that day.' He looked up sharply, his eyes hard. 'I have known common seamen die even under a *legal* flogging. We must not allow the deed to overshadow or dispel the cause.'

Two army officers strode past the closed doors, their noisy laughter dying instantly when they realized what was happening within. Herrick frowned. 'These observations are in my personal report, which will be presented to their lordships.' His eyes shifted to Bolitho. 'When I am gone from here.'

The frigate *Wakeful* had been taking on stores and water as he had been pulled ashore. Her work done on this station, she would be speeding back to England for fresh orders. Herrick would be taking passage in her again. Being 'entertained'.

Herrick glanced at a tumbler of water, but apparently rejected the idea. 'My considered conclusion in this miserable affair is that the two ringleaders, Alick Nisbet, Master-at-Arms, and Harry Ramsay, maintopman and able-bodied seaman, are detained, with a recommendation for the maximum penalty.'

Bolitho saw Adam clenching his fists until the knuckles were drained of blood beneath the tanned skin. He had heard about the man Ramsay, once of *Anemone*, whose mutilated back was living proof of the ship's punishment book. The other man was a surprise: the master-at-arms was the symbol of discipline and, when necessary, punishment aboard any King's ship, and he was usually hated for it.

And now the rest. He wanted to stand up and speak on behalf of the men he did not even know, but it would have damaged whatever frail hope they might still have.

Herrick continued, 'My further instruction is that all the other seamen and landmen involved be returned to their duties forthwith. They have suffered enough, and yet, when called, they would not, could not fire upon ships of this navy, no matter what the refusal would have cost them.'

Tyacke exclaimed, 'Hell's teeth! They'll crucify him when he gets back to London!' He turned and looked at Bolitho, his eyes revealing a rare emotion. 'I would never have believed it!'

Herrick said with no change of expression, 'I will insist that a new captain be appointed to *Reaper* without delay.' He glanced at Bolitho, then at Keen. 'That responsibility must be yours.'

Keen stood. 'My flag captain has already suggested such an officer for promotion, sir. Lieutenant John Urquhart.' He paused. 'I will support it, sir.'

Herrick said, 'Can you manage without him?'

Keen looked at Adam, who made a gesture of agreement, and said, 'We will, sir.'

Herrick beckoned to the clerk and the major of marines.

'Sign after my signature.' He straightened his back, and winced. 'It is done.' Then he said shortly, 'I wish to speak to Sir Richard Bolitho. Alone.'

It seemed an age before the others had filed out, and the room was silent.

Bolitho said, 'You did that for me, Thomas.'

Herrick said, 'I would relish a glass – a wet, as that rascal Allday calls it.' Then he looked up at him, searching for something, and finding it. 'I have nothing to lose,

Richard. My flag will never fly again after this last passage. Maybe we shall meet again, but I think not. The navy is a family – you have often said as much. Once released from it, you become ordinary, like a ship laid up.'

A horse clattered noisily across the yard by the gates, reminding Bolitho poignantly of Catherine and her Tamara. How would he tell her, describe to her all that Herrick had said, and had thrown away....

Herrick walked to the doors, his shoulder angled stiffly, his face clearly showing the pain of his wound. He said, '*You* have everything to lose, as would all those godforsaken souls who depend on you, and those like you.' He added bitterly, 'Though I've yet to meet one!'

An invisible hand opened the doors, and Bolitho saw Avery waiting for him, his tawny eyes moving between them, trying to understand.

'We have had a messenger from the lookout, Sir Richard. The brig *Weazle* is entering harbour. She has signalled that the American vessels have left Boston with others from New York. They are steering north-east.'

Bolitho said quietly, 'So they're coming out. Pass the word to Captain Tyacke, George. I shall be aboard as soon as I can.' Avery hurried away, but stopped uncertainly and stared back at them.

Herrick said, 'Listen! Cheering! How could they know already?'

They walked down the steps together, while the cheering rolled across the harbour like one great voice.

Bolitho said, 'They always know, Thomas. The family, remember?'

Herrick looked back toward the barracks, his eyes suddenly, deeply fatigued.

'Take good care, Richard.' He touched his sleeve. 'I shall raise a glass to you when that young puppy hauls anchor for England!'

At the jetty they found Allday standing at the tiller of the admiral's barge with the crew grouped on the stairs, grinning hugely. Their places had been taken by officers, three of them captains, including Adam.

Herrick held out his hand to Tyacke. 'Your work, I presume, sir?'

Tyacke did not smile. 'All we could do at such short notice.'

Bolitho followed him down the stairs, recalling Tyacke's words. *They'll crucify him.* But Herrick would have his way. Perhaps the 'damned little upstart' Bethune had used his influence. He would know the man he had served as a midshipman better than many, and perhaps had attempted to help by subtle means.

Allday had seen Herrick's face and said awkwardly, 'I don't get too many chances to tell the officers what to do, an' that's no error!' Then he said, 'Good luck, Mr Herrick.' Just for those seconds they were back on board *Phalarope*, young lieutenant and pressed man.

The barge pulled away, the stroke surprisingly smart and regular. As they wended between the anchored men-of-war the cheering escorted them, some of it from *Reaper* herself. And this time Herrick did look back, although it was doubtful if he could see anything.

Bolitho turned away, and saw that Keen was speaking quietly with Gilia St Clair. And suddenly, he was glad for them.

'Call a boat, James. Sailing orders.'

Tyacke was gazing impassively after the barge. 'Aye, Sir Richard. But first. . . .'

Bolitho smiled, but shared the unspoken sadness. 'A wet. So be it.'

15

No Din of War

Richard Bolitho flattened the chart very carefully on his table and opened a pair of brass dividers. He could feel the others watching him, Avery standing by the stern windows, Yovell seated comfortably in a chair, paper and pens within easy reach as always.

Bolitho said, 'Two days, and we've sighted nothing.' He studied the chart again, imagining his ships as they might appear to a cruising sea bird: five frigates sailing in line abreast, with *Indomitable*, the flagship, in the centre. The extended line of frigates, half of his entire force, could scan a great expanse of ocean in this formation. The sky was clear, with only a few streaks of pale cloud, the sea a darker blue in the cool sunlight.

He thought of the solitary patrolling frigate, *Chivalrous*, which had sent the brig *Weazle* to Halifax with the news that the Americans were on the move again. In his mind's eye he could see *Chivalrous*'s captain, Isaac Lloyd, an experienced officer, twenty-eight years old. He would be trying to keep the enemy in view, but would have sense enough not to be trapped into engaging them.

Two days, so where were they? In the approaches to Halifax, or out further still towards St John's in Newfoundland? He had discussed various possibilities with Tyacke and York. When he had suggested the Bay of Fundy to the north-west of Nova Scotia, York had been adamant.

'Unlikely, sir. The bay has the world's highest tides, twice a day for good measure. If I was the Yankee commander I wouldn't want to get trapped in the middle of that!'

Bolitho had been warned of the situation in the Bay of Fundy. His Admiralty Instructions had already stated that the tides could rise and fall as much as fifty feet and more, with the added risk to smaller vessels of fierce tidal bores. No place to risk a frigate, even the large Americans. Or *Indomitable*.

He thought of Herrick, on his way now across the Atlantic to throw his findings in someone's face at the Admiralty. Had he been glad to leave, after all? Or deep inside, was the old, tenacious Herrick still hating what amounted to a dismissal from the only life he knew?

It had obviously had a great effect on Tyacke. He had been more withdrawn than ever after Herrick had been taken out to the frigate which was to carry him back to England.

He tossed the dividers onto the chart. Perhaps this was all a waste of time, or worse, another ruse to draw them away from something more important.

He walked to the stern windows, and felt the ship lifting and leaning beneath him. That, too, he could see in his mind, *Indomitable* close-hauled on the larboard tack, the wind holding from the south-east as it had for most of the time since they had weighed anchor. Adam was openly fretting at having been left at Halifax, but *Valkyrie* was their second most powerful frigate: Keen might need her.

Adam had not hesitated in recommending his first lieutenant for promotion to the questionable command of *Reaper*. A challenge for any man, but Adam had said bluntly, 'I'd have taken her myself, had I been free to do so.' Were things between him and Val so strained?

Avery said gently, 'We could have missed them overnight, Sir Richard.'

'If they were looking for us, I think not.' Bolitho dismissed the thoughts, and recalled himself to the matter at hand. 'Ask Mr York to let me see his notes again, will you?'

The cabin was tilting over once more, and the brass dividers clattered onto the deck. Yovell tried to lean down to recover them, but the angle was so extreme that he sank back in his chair and mopped his face with a bright red handkerchief. But lively or not, the *Old Indom* was riding it well. As York had remarked with his usual cheerful confidence, 'Like a bald-headed barque she is, Sir Richard. Stiff in any wind and stiff when she's not!'

Yovell said suddenly, 'You could describe me as a civilian, could you not, Sir Richard? Despite the warlike surroundings, and our way of life, I am not truly bound to the niceties and traditions of sea-officers?'

Bolitho smiled at him. He never changed. Not even in that wretched longboat, when his hands had been raw and bleeding from pulling on an oar with the others. With Catherine.

'I hope you remain so.'

Yovell frowned, then polished his small gold-rimmed spectacles, something he often did when he was pondering a problem.

'Mr Avery is your flag lieutenant – he stands between you and the captain and serves both.' He breathed on his spectacles again. 'He is loyal to both. He would never speak behind the captain's back, because you are friends. It would seem like a betrayal of trust, and the association which has grown between them.' He smiled gently. 'Between all of us, if I may say so, Sir Richard.'

There was complete silence from the pantry. Ozzard would be there, listening.

'If it troubles you, then tell me. I felt something was

amiss myself.' He turned towards the sea again. Yovell's remark had touched him more than he cared to accept, reminding him uncomfortably of Herrick's comments on the Happy Few. In truth, there were not many left now. Keverne, who had once commanded this ship; Charles Farquhar, once a midshipman like Bethune, who had been killed aboard his own command at Corfu. And dear Francis Inch, eager, horse-faced, married to such a pretty woman at Weymouth. Her name was Hannah. . . . He recalled it with effort. And so many others. John Neale. Browne, with an 'e', and Avery's predecessor, Stephen Jenour. So many. *Too many.* And all dead.

He turned from the light as Yovell said quietly, 'Captain Tyacke received a letter in Halifax. It was in the bag delivered by the schooner *Reynard*.'

'Bad news?'

Yovell replaced his spectacles with care. 'I am told that it had travelled far. As is often the way with the fleet's mail.'

Bolitho stared at him. Of course. Tyacke never received letters. Like Avery, until he had been sent one by his lady in London. It was so typical of Avery to remain silent, even if he knew the cause of Tyacke's withdrawal. He would understand. Just as he had understood Adam's anguish at having been a prisoner of war.

'Is it all over the ship?'

'Only the flag lieutenant knows, sir.'

Bolitho touched his eyelid, and recalled the gown Catherine had been given when *Larne* finally found them. When she had returned it to Tyacke, she had expressed the wish that it might be worn by someone worthy of him. . . .

He clenched his fist. Surely not the same woman? It could not be; why, after so long, and after the cruel way she had rejected him, and his disfigured face? But in his heart, he knew that it was.

He saw Catherine, as clearly as if he had looked at her locket. They had no secrets. He knew of her visits to London, and that she occasionally consulted Sillitoe for his advice on investing the money from Spain; he trusted her completely, as she trusted him. But what if. . . . He thought of Tyacke's silence and reticence, the reawakened pain that must be hidden. What if. . . . Catherine needed to be loved, just as she needed to return love.

'If I spoke out of turn, Sir Richard. . . .'

Bolitho said, 'You did not. It is good to be reminded sometimes of things that truly matter, and those who are out of reach.'

Yovell was reassured, and glad that he had spoken out. As a civilian.

The other door opened and Ozzard padded into the cabin, a coffee pot in his hands.

'Is that the last of it, Ozzard?'

Ozzard glanced severely at the pot. 'No, Sir Richard. Two weeks more, at most. After that. . . .'

Avery returned to the cabin, and Bolitho saw him waiting while he took a cup from the tray, gauging the moment when the ship staggered through a confusion of broken crests. Ozzard had poured a cup for the flag lieutenant, almost grudgingly. What did he think about; what occupied his mind in all the months and years he had been at sea? A man who had obliterated his past, but, like Yovell, an educated one, who could read classical works, and had the handwriting of a scholar. It seemed as if he wanted no future, either.

Bolitho took the notes Avery had brought, and said, 'One more day. We might fall in with a courier from Halifax. Rear-Admiral Keen may have more news.'

Avery asked, 'These American ships, sir – will they wish to challenge us?'

'Whatever they intend, George, I shall need every trick

we can muster. Just as I will need all of my officers to be at their best, if fight we must.'

Avery glanced at Yovell, and lowered his voice. 'You know about the captain's letter, sir?'

'Yes. Now I do, and I appreciate and respect your feelings, and your reluctance to discuss it.' He paused. 'However, James Tyacke is not only the captain of my flagship, he *is* the ship, no matter how he might dispute that!'

'Yes. I am sorry, Sir Richard. I thought – '

'Don't be sorry. Loyalty comes in many guises.'

They looked at the door as the sentry called, 'First lieutenant, *sir*!'

Lieutenant John Daubeny stepped into the cabin, his slim figure angled in the entrance like that of a drunken sailor.

'The captain's respects, Sir Richard. *Taciturn* has signalled. Sail in sight to the nor' west.'

Avery remarked quietly, 'She'll have a hard beat to reach us, sir.'

'One of ours, you believe?'

Avery nodded. '*Chivalrous*. Must be her. She'd soon turn and run with the wind otherwise.'

Bolitho smiled unconsciously at his judgment. 'I agree. My compliments to the captain, Mr Daubeny. Make a signal. *General*. To be repeated to all our ships. *Close on Flag*.'

He could see them, tiny dabs of colour as the flags broke from their yards, to be repeated to the next vessel even though she might barely be in sight. The chain of command, the overall responsibility. Daubeny waited, noting everything, to go in the next letter to his mother.

Bolitho glanced up at the skylight. Tyacke with his ship. A man alone, perhaps now more than ever.

'I shall come up at seven bells, Mr Daubeny.'

But the first lieutenant had gone, the signal already hoisted.

He touched the locket beneath his shirt.

Stay close, dear Kate. Don't leave me.

They met with the thirty-gun frigate *Chivalrous* in late afternoon, *Indomitable* and her consorts having made more sail to hasten the rendezvous. It would also ensure that Captain Isaac Lloyd could board the flagship with time to return to his own command before nightfall, or in case the wind freshened enough to prevent the use of a boat.

Lloyd was only twenty-eight but had the face of an older, more seasoned officer, with dark, steady eyes and pointed features that gave him the demeanour of a watchful fox. He used the chart in Bolitho's cabin, his finger jabbing at the various positions which York had already estimated.

'Six of them all told. I could scarce believe my eyes, Sir Richard. Probably all frigates, including a couple of large ones.' He jabbed the chart again. 'I signalled *Weazle* to make all haste to Halifax, but I fully expected the Yankees to try and put a stop to it.' He gave a short, barking laugh: a fox indeed, Bolitho thought. 'It was as if we did not exist. They continued to the nor' east, cool as you please. I decided to harry the rearmost one, so I set me royals and t' gallants and chased them. That changed things. A few signals were exchanged, and then the rearmost frigate opened fire with her chasers. I had to admit, Sir Richard, it was damn' good shootin'.'

Bolitho sensed Tyacke beside him, listening, perhaps considering how he might have reacted in Lloyd's shoes. Yovell was writing busily and did not raise his head. Avery was holding some of York's notes, although he was not reading, and his face was set in a frown.

Lloyd said, 'It got a bit too warm, and I reduced sail.

Not before that damn Yankee had brought down a spar and punched my forecourse full of holes. I thought that maybe he'd been ordered to fall back and engage *Chivalrous*. I would have accepted that, I think. But I says to meself, no, he don't intend to fight, not now, anyways.'

Bolitho said, 'Why?'

'Well, Sir Richard, he had all the time he needed, and he could see I had no other ship to support me. I knew he would have put his boats in the water, had he meant to show his mettle.' He grinned. 'He may have carried more guns than my ship, but with all those boats stowed on deck we could have cut down half his men with their splinters in the first broadside!'

Tyacke roused himself from his silent contemplation and said abruptly, 'Boats? How many?'

Lloyd shrugged, and glanced through the smeared windows as if to reassure himself that his ship was still riding under *Indomitable*'s lee.

'Double the usual amount, I'd say. My first lieutenant insisted that the next ship in the American's line was likewise equipped.'

Avery said, 'Moving to a new base?'

Tyacke said bluntly, 'There is no other base, unless they take one of ours.' When Lloyd would have said something, Tyacke held up one hand. 'I was thinking. Remembering, while you were speaking just now. When it was decided that the slave-trade was not quite respectable, unbefitting civilized powers, their lordships thought fit to send frigates to stamp it out. Faster, better-armed, trained companies, and yet. . . .' He turned and looked directly at Bolitho. 'They could never catch them. The slavers used small vessels, cruel, stinking hulls where men and women lived and died in their own filth, or were pitched to the sharks if a King's ship happened to stumble on them.'

Bolitho remained silent, feeling it, sharing it. Tyacke

was reliving his time in *Larne*. The slavers had come to fear him: *the devil with half a face*.

Tyacke continued in the same unemotional tone, 'All along that damnable coast, where the rivers came out to the Atlantic, the Congo, the Niger and the Gaboon, the slavers would lie close inshore, where no man-of-war of any consequence would dare to venture. Which was why they evaded capture and their just deserts for so long.' He glanced at the young captain, who did not avoid his eyes. 'I think you fell in with something you were not supposed to see.' He moved to the chart and laid his hand on it. 'For once, I think our Mr York was wrong. Mistaken. They didn't give chase, Captain Lloyd, because they could not. They *dared* not.' He looked at Bolitho. 'Those boats, sir. So many of them. Not for picking up slaves like those cruel scum used to do, but to put an invading army ashore.'

Bolitho felt the shock and the truth of his words like a cup of icy water in his face.

'They're carrying soldiers, as they did on the lakes, except that these are larger vessels, with something bigger in prospect at the end of it!'

He thought of the army captain who had survived the first attack on York, and of the reports which had filtered through with information of a second attack three months later. Perhaps Lake Erie had already fallen to the Americans? If so, the British army would be cut off, even from retreat. The young captain had described the Americans at York as being well-trained regulars.

Bolitho said, 'If these ships entered the Bay of Fundy but turned north, and not towards Nova Scotia, they could disembark soldiers who could force their way inland, knowing that supplies and reinforcements would be waiting for them once they reached the St Lawrence. It would seal off all the frontier districts of Upper Canada, like ferrets in a sack!'

He gripped Lloyd's hand warmly in farewell. 'You did not fight the American, Captain Lloyd, but the news you have carried to me may yet bring us a victory. I shall ensure that you receive proper recognition. Our Nel would have put it better. He always insisted that the Fighting Instructions were not a substitute for a captain's initiative.'

Tyacke said roughly, 'I'll see you over the side, Captain Lloyd.'

As the door closed, Avery said, 'Is it possible, sir?'

Bolitho half-smiled. 'Do you really mean, is it likely? I think it is too important to ignore, or to wait for a miracle.' He listened to the trill of calls as the fox-like captain went down to his gig.

Tyacke returned, and waited in silence while Bolitho instructed his secretary to send a brief dispatch to Halifax.

'We shall alter course before nightfall, James, and steer due north. Make the necessary signals.' He saw the concern in the clear eyes that watched him, from the burned remains of the face. 'I know the risks, James. We all do. It was there for all of us to see, but only you recognized it. Your loneliest command was not wasted. Nor will it be.' He wondered if Tyacke had been going over it all again. The letter, the girl he might scarcely remember, or not wish to remember. One day he might share it; at the same time, Bolitho knew that he would not.

'D' you think your man Aherne is with them?'

'I am not certain, but I think it possible that he may have fallen out of favour with his superiors, like John Paul Jones.' *Like my own brother.*

Tyacke was about to leave, but turned when Bolitho said with sudden bitterness, 'Neither side can win this war, just as neither can afford to lose it. So let us play our part as best we can. . . . And then, in God's mercy, let us go home!'

*

They stood crowded together around York's chart-table, their shadows joining in a slow dance while the lanterns swung above them.

More like conspirators than King's men, Bolitho thought. It was pitch black outside the hull, early dark as he had known it would be, the ship unusually noisy as she rolled in a steep swell. There was no land closer than seventy miles, Nova Scotia's Cape Sable to the northeast, but after the great depths to which they had become accustomed they sensed its presence. Felt it.

Bolitho glanced at their faces in the swaying light. Tyacke, his profile very calm, the burns hidden in shadow. It was possible to see him as the woman had once done: the unscarred side of his face was strongly boned and handsome. On his other side the master was measuring his bearings with some dividers, his expression one of doubt.

Avery was crammed into the small space too, with Daubeny the first lieutenant bobbing his head beneath the heavy beams as he tried to see over their shoulders.

York said, 'In broad daylight it's bad enough, sir. The entrance to the bay, allowing for shallows and sandbars, is about twenty-five miles, less, mebbee. We'd not be able to hold our formation, and if they are ready and waiting....' He did not go on.

Tyacke was still grappling with his original idea. 'They can't go in and attack anything in the dark, Isaac. They'd need to take soundings for most of the bay. The boats could be separated, swamped even, if the worst happened.'

York persisted, 'The whole of that coastline is used by small vessels, fishermen mostly. A lot of the folk who made their homes in New Brunswick after the American rebellion were loyalists. They've no love for the Yankees, but....' He glanced at Bolitho. 'Against trained soldiers, what could they do?'

284

Bolitho said, 'And if they have already carried out a landing, those ships might be waiting for us to appear like ducks in a waterfowler's sights. But it takes time – it always does. Lowering boats, packing men and weapons into them, more than likely in the dark, and with some of the soldiers half sick from the passage.... Marines, now, that would be different.' He rubbed his chin, aware of its roughness: one of Allday's shaves then, if there was time. He said, 'Our captains know how to perform. We have exercised working together, although not with Mr York's unwelcoming bay in mind!' He saw them smile, as he had known they would. It was like being driven, or perhaps led. Hearing somebody else speak, somehow finding the faith and confidence to inspire others. 'And we must admit, the plan, if that is what they have in mind, is a brilliant one. Seasoned soldiers could march and fight their way northwards and meet with their other regiments on the St Lawrence. What is that, three hundred miles? I can remember as a boy when the 46th Regiment of Foot marched all the way from Devon to Scotland. And doubtless back again.'

York asked uneasily, 'Was there more trouble up north then, sir?'

Bolitho smiled. 'No, it was the King's birthday. It was his wish!'

York grinned. 'Oh, well, that's different, sir!'

Bolitho picked up the dividers from the chart. 'The enemy know the risks as well as we do. We shall remain in company as best we can. Each captain will have his best lookouts aloft, but they cannot work miracles. By dawn we shall be in position, *here*.' The points of the dividers came down like a harpoon. 'We may become scattered overnight, but we must take that chance.'

Tyacke studied him in silence. *You will take it*, his expression said. Bolitho said, 'If I were the enemy commander I would send in my landing parties, and perhaps

285

release one of my smaller ships as close inshore as possible to offer covering fire if need be. That would even the odds.' He put down the dividers very carefully. 'A little.'

Tyacke said, 'If we're wrong, sir. . . .'

'If *I* am wrong, then we will return to Halifax. At least they will be prepared there for any sudden attack.' He thought of Keen when he had spoken of St Clair's daughter: he might become a vice-admiral sooner than his highest hopes, if the enemy had outwitted this makeshift plan.

He saw Avery bending over the table to scribble some notes in his little book, and for a second their eyes met. Did Avery know that his admiral was barely able to see the markings on the chart without covering his damaged eye? He felt the sudden despair lift from his spirit, like a dawn mist rising from the water. Of course they knew, but it had become a bond, a strength, which they willingly shared with him. Again he seemed to hear Herrick's words. *We Happy Few. Dear God, don't let me fail them now.*

Then he said quietly, 'Thank you, gentlemen. Please carry on with your duties. Captain Tyacke?'

Tyacke was touching his scars; perhaps he no longer noticed that he was doing it.

'I would like to have the people fed before the morning watch, sir. Then, if you agree, we will clear for action.' He might have been smiling, but his face was in shadow again. 'No drums, no din of war.'

Bolitho said lightly, 'No *Portsmouth Lass*, either?' The same thought returned. Like conspirators. Or assassins.

Tyacke twisted round. 'Mr Daubeny, do not strain your ears any further! I want all officers and senior warrant officers in the wardroom as soon as is convenient.' He added, almost as an afterthought, 'We had better assemble our young gentlemen as well on this occasion. They may learn something from it.'

York left with Daubeny, probably to confer with his master's mates. It would keep them busy, and a lack of sleep was nothing new to sailors.

Avery had also departed, understanding better than most that Tyacke wished to be alone with Bolitho. Not as the officer, but as a friend. Bolitho had almost guessed what his flag captain was going to say, but it still came as a shock.

'If we meet with the enemy, and now that I have weighed the odds for and against, I think we shall, I would ask a favour.'

'What is it, James?'

'If I should fall.' He shook his head. 'Please, hear me. I have written two letters. I would rest easy and with a free mind to fight this ship if I knew. . . .' He was silent for a moment. 'One is for your lady, sir, and the other for somebody I once knew . . . thought I knew . . . some fifteen years back, when I was a young luff like Mr Know-it-all Blythe.'

Bolitho touched his arm, with great affection. It was the closest to the man he had ever been.

He said, 'We shall both take care tomorrow, James. I am depending on you.'

Tyacke studied the well-used chart. 'Tomorrow, then.'

Later, as he made his way aft to his quarters, Bolitho heard the buzz of voices from the wardroom, rarely so crowded even in harbour. Two of the messmen were crouching down, listening at the door as closely as they dared. There was laughter too, as there must have been before greater events in history: Quiberon Bay, The Saintes, or the Nile.

Allday was with Ozzard in the pantry, as he had known he would be. He followed Bolitho past the sentry and into the dimly lit cabin, with the sea like black glass beyond the windows. Apart from the ship's own noises, it was already quiet. Tyacke would be speaking to his officers, just as he would eventually go around the messdecks and show himself to the men who depended on him. Not to tell them why it was so, but how it must be done. But the ship already knew. Like *Sparrow* and *Phalarope*, and *Hyperion* most of all.

Allday asked, 'Will Mr Avery be coming aft, Sir Richard?'

Bolitho waved him to a chair. 'Rest easy, old friend. He'll find a minute to pen a letter for you.'

Allday grinned, the concern and the pain falling away. 'I'd take it kindly, Sir Richard. I've never been much for book-learnin' an' the like.'

Bolitho heard Ozzard's quiet step. 'Just as well for the rest of us, I daresay. So let us drink to those we care about, while we can. But we'll wait for the flag lieutenant.' He looked away. Avery had probably already written a letter of his own, to the unknown woman in London. Perhaps it was only a dream, a lost hope. But it was an anchor, one which was needed by them all.

He walked to the gun barometer and tapped it automatically, recalling Tyacke's acceptance of what must be done, his confidence in his ship. And of his words. 'If I should fall. . . .' The same words, the same voice which had spoken for all of them.

Avery entered the cabin even as the sentry shouted his arrival.

Bolitho said, 'Did it go well, George?'

Avery looked at Ozzard and his tray of glasses.

'Something I heard my father say, a long time ago. That the gods never concern themselves with the protection of the innocent, only with the punishment of the guilty.' He took a glass from the unsmiling Ozzard. 'I never thought I would hear it again under these circumstances.'

288

Bolitho waited while Allday lurched to his feet to join them. *Tomorrow, then.*

Thinking of Herrick, perhaps. Of all of them.

He raised his glass. 'We Happy Few!'

They would like that.

16

Lee Shore

Lieutenant George Avery gripped the weather shrouds and then paused to stare up at the foremast. Like most of the ship's company, he had been on deck for over an hour, and yet his eyes were still not accustomed to the enfolding darkness. He could see the pale outline of the hard-braced topsail, but beyond it nothing save an occasional star as it flitted through long banners of cloud. He shivered; it was cold, and his clothing felt damp and clinging, and there was something else also, a king of light-headedness, a sense of elation, which he thought had gone forever. Those days when he had been in the small schooner *Jolie*, cutting out equally small prizes from the French coast, sometimes under the noses of a shore battery. . . . Wild, reckless times. He almost laughed into the damp air. It was madness, as it had been madness then.

He swung himself out and wedged his foot onto the first ratline, then, slowly and carefully, he began to climb the big signals telescope hanging across his shoulder like a poacher's gun. Up and up, the shrouds vibrating beneath his grip, the tarred cordage as sharp and cold as ice. He was not afraid of heights, but he respected them: it was one of the first things he could remember when he had been appointed midshipman under his uncle's sponsorship. The seamen, who had been rough and independent although they had shown him kindness, would rush up the ratlines barefooted, the skin so calloused and hardened that they scorned the wearing of shoes, which they would keep for special occasions.

He stopped to regain his breath, and felt his body being pressed against the quivering rigging while the invisible ship beneath him leaned over to a sudden gust of wind. Like cold hands, holding him.

Even though he could see nothing below him but the unchanging outline of the upper deck, sharpened occasionally when a burst of spray cascaded over the gangways or through the beakhead, he could imagine the others standing as he had left them. So different from the usual nerve-wrenching thrill when the drums rattled and beat the hands to quarters, the orderly chaos when a ship was cleared for action from bow to stern: screens torn down, tiny hutches of cabins where the officers found their only privacy transformed into just another part of a gundeck, furniture, personal items and sea-chests dragged or winched into the lower hull, below the waterline, where the surgeon and his assistants would be preparing, remaining separate from the noise before battle: their work would come to them. On this occasion clearing for action had been an almost leisurely affair, men moving amongst familiar tackle and rigging as if it were broad daylight.

As ordered, the hands had been given a hot meal in separate watches, and only then was the galley fire doused, the last measure of rum drained.

Tyacke had remained by the quarterdeck rail, while officers and messengers had flowed around him, like extensions of the man himself. York with his master's mates, Daubeny, the first lieutenant, with a junior midshipman always trotting at his heels like a pet dog. And right aft by the companion way where he had walked with Sir Richard, Avery could see that in his mind also.

291

Where the command of any ship or squadron began or ended. He smiled as he recalled what Allday had said of it. 'Aft, the most honour, Forward, the better man!' Bolitho had been holding his watch closely against the compass light, and had said, 'Go aloft, George. Take a good glass with you. I need to know instantly. You will be my eyes today.'

It still saddened him. Did those words, too, have a hidden meaning?

And Allday again, taking his hat and sword from him. 'They'll be here when you needs 'em, Mr Avery. Don't want our flag lieutenant gettin' all tangled up in the futtock shrouds, now, do we?'

He had written the letter Allday had requested. Like the man, it had been warmly affectionate, and yet, after all he had seen and suffered, so simple and unworldly. Avery had almost been able to see Unis opening and reading it, calling her ex-soldier brother to tell him about it. Holding it up to the child.

He shook his head, thrusting the thoughts aside, and started to climb again. Long before any of their letters reached England, they might all be dead.

The foremast's fighting top loomed above him, reminding him of Allday's joke about the futtock shrouds. Nimble-footed topmen could scramble out and around the top without interruption, those on the leeward side hanging out, suspended, with nothing but the sea beneath them. The fighting top was a square platform protected by a low barricade, behind which marksmen could take aim at targets on an enemy's deck. It matched the tops on the other masts, above which the shrouds and stays reached up to the next of the upper yards, and beyond.

The foremast was perhaps the most important and complicated in the ship. It carried not only the bigger course and topsails, but was connected and rigged to the bowsprit, and the smaller, vital jib and staysails. Each time a ship attempted to come about and turn across the eye of the wind, the small jib sails would act like a spur or brake to prevent her floundering to a standstill, taken all aback with her sails flattened uselessly against the masts, unable to pay off in either direction. At the height of close action, the inability to manoeuvre could mean the death of a ship.

He thought of Tyacke and York and men like them, the true professionals. How many people ashore would ever understand the strength and prowess of such fine sailors, when they saw a King's ship beating down-channel under a full press of sail?

He dragged himself between the shrouds and took the easier way into the foretop by way of a small opening, the 'lubber's hole', as the old Jacks derisively termed it.

There were four Royal Marines here, their white crossbelts and the corporal's chevrons on one man's sleeve visible against the outer darkness.

'Mornin', sir! Fine day for a stroll!'

Avery unslung the telescope and smiled. That was another thing about being a flag lieutenant, neither fish nor fowl, like an outsider who had come amongst them: he was not an officer in charge of a mast or a division of guns, nor a symbol of discipline or punishment. So he was accepted. Tolerated.

He said, 'Do you think it will be light soon?'

The corporal leaned against a mounted swivel gun. It was already depressed, and covered with a piece of canvas to protect the priming from the damp air. Ready for instant use.

He replied, ''Alf hour, sir. Near as a priest's promise!'

They all laughed, as if this were only another, normal day.

Avery stared at the flapping jib and imagined the crouching lion beneath it. What if the sea was empty

293

when daylight came? He searched his feelings. Would he be relieved, grateful?

He thought of the intensity in Bolitho's voice, the way he and Tyacke had conferred and planned. He shivered suddenly. No, the sea would not be empty of ships. *How can I be certain?* Then he thought, *Because of what we are, what he has made us.*

He tried to focus his thoughts on England. London, that busy street with its bright carriages and haughty footmen, and one carriage in particular.... She was lovely. She would not wait, and waste her life.

And yet, they had shared something deeper, however briefly. Surely there was a chance, a hope beyond this cold dawn?

The corporal said carefully, 'I sometimes wonders what he's like, sir. The admiral, I mean.' He faltered, thinking he had gone too far. 'It's just that we sees him an' you walkin' the deck sometimes, and then there was the day when 'is lady come aboard at Falmouth.' He put his hand on his companion's shoulder. 'Me an' Ted was there. I'd never 'ave believed it, see?'

Avery did see. Replacing Catherine's shoes and remarking on the tar on her stocking after her climb up this ship's side. The flag breaking out, and then the cheers. Work them, drive them, break them; but these same men had seen, and remembered.

He said, 'He *is* that man, Corporal. Just as she is that lady.' He could almost hear Tyacke's words. *I would serve no other.*

One of the other marines, encouraged by his corporal, asked, 'What will us do when th' war's over an' done with?'

Avery stared up at the great rectangle of sail, and felt the raw salt on his mouth.

'I pray to God that I shall be able to choose something for myself.'

The corporal grunted. 'I'll get me other stripe an' stay in the Royals. Good victuals an' plenty of rum, an' a hard fight when you're needed! It'll do me!'

A voice echoed down from the crosstrees. 'First light a-comin', sir!'

The corporal grinned. 'Old Jacob up there, he's a wild one, sir!'

Avery thought of Tyacke's description of the seaman named Jacob, the best lookout in the squadron. Once a saddle-maker, a highly skilled trade, he had found his wife in the arms of another man, and had killed both of them. The Assizes had offered him the choice of the gibbet or the navy. He had outlived many others with no such notoriety.

Avery withdrew the big telescope from its case, while the marines made a space for him and even found him something to kneel on.

One of them put his hand on the swivel gun and chuckled. 'Don't you go bumpin' into old Betsy 'ere, sir. You might set 'er off by accident, an' blow the 'ead off our poor sergeant. That'd be a true shame, wouldn't it, lads?' They all laughed. Four marines on a windswept perch in the middle of nowhere. They had probably no idea where they were, or where bound tomorrow.

Avery knelt, and felt the low barricade shivering under the great weight of spars and canvas, and all the miles of rigging that ruled the lives of such men as these. *Of one company.*

He held his breath and trained the glass with great care, but saw only cloud and darkness. Old Jacob on his lofty lookout would see it first.

He was shivering again, unable to stop.

''Ere, sir.' A hand reached out from somewhere. 'Nelson's blood!'

Avery took it gratefully. It was against all regulations: they knew it, and so did he.

The corporal murmured, 'To wish us luck, eh, lads?'

Avery swallowed, and felt the rum driving out the cold. The fear. He stared out again. *You will be my eyes today.* As if he were right beside him.

And suddenly, there they were. The enemy.

Captain James Tyacke watched the shadowy figures of Hockenhull, the boatswain, and a party of seamen as they hauled on lines and secured them to bollards. Every one of *Indomitable*'s boats was in the water, towing astern like a single unyieldy sea anchor, and although he could scarcely see them, he knew that the nets were already spread across the gundeck. The scene was set.

Tyacke searched his feelings for doubt. Had there been any? But if so, they were gone as soon as the old lookout's doleful voice had called down from the foremast crosstrees. Avery would be peering through his glass, searching for details, numbers, the strength of the enemy.

York remarked, 'Wind's falling away, sir. Steady enough, though.'

Tyacke glanced over at Bolitho's tall figure framed against the pale barrier of packed hammocks, and saw him nod. It was time: it had to be. But the wind was everything.

He said sharply, 'Shake out the second reef, Mr Daubeny! Set fores'l and driver!' To himself he added, *where are our damned ships?* They might have become scattered during the breezy night; better that than risk a collision, now of all times. He heard the first lieutenant's tame midshipman repeating his instructions in a shrill voice, edged with uncertainty at the prospect of something unknown to him.

He considered his other lieutenants, and frowned. Boys in the King's uniform. Even Daubeny was young for his responsibilities. The words repeated themselves in his mind. *If I fall. . . .* It would be Daubeny's skill, or lack of it, that would determine their success or failure.

He heard Allday murmur something and Bolitho's quick laugh, and was surprised that it could still move him. Steady him, like the iron hoops around each great mast, holding them together.

The marines had laid down their weapons, and had manned the mizzen braces as the driver filled and cracked to the wind.

He knew that Isaac York was hovering nearby, wanting to speak to him, to pass the time as friends usually did before an action. Just in case. But he could not waste time in conversation now. He needed to be alive and alert to everything, from the men at the big double wheel to the ship's youngest midshipman, who was about to turn the half-hour glass beside the compass box.

He saw his own coxswain, Fairbrother, peering down at the boats under tow.

'Worried, Eli?' He saw him grin. He was no Allday, but he was doing his best.

'They'll all need a lick o' paint when we picks 'em up, sir.'

But Tyacke had turned away, his eyes assessing the nearest guns, the crews, some bare-backed despite the cold wind, standing around them, waiting for the first orders. Decks sanded to prevent men slipping, in spray or perhaps in blood. Rammers, sponges, and worms, the tools of their trade, close to hand.

Lieutenant Laroche drawled, 'Here comes the flag lieutenant.'

Avery climbed the ladder to the quarterdeck, and Allday handed him his hat and sword.

He said, 'Six sail right enough, Sir Richard. I think the tide's on the ebb.'

York muttered, 'It would be.'

'I think one of the frigates is towing *all* the boats, sir. It's too far and too dark to be sure.'

Tyacke said, 'Makes sense. It would hold them all together. Keep 'em fresh and ready for landing.'

Bolitho said, 'We can't wait. Alter course now.' He looked at Tyacke, and afterwards he imagined he had seen him smile, even though his features were in shadow. 'As soon as we sight our ships, signal them to *attack at will.* This is no time for a line of battle!'

Avery recalled the consternation at the Admiralty when Bolitho had voiced his opinions on the fleet's future.

Tyacke called, 'Alter course two points. Steer north-east by north!' He knew what Bolitho had seen in his mind, how they had discussed it, even with nothing more to go on than Captain Lloyd's sighting report and his own interpretation of the extra boats carried by the enemy. Tyacke gave a crooked grin. *Slavers, indeed.*

Men were already hauling at the braces, their bodies angled almost to the deck while they heaved the great yards round, muscle and bone striving against wind and rudder.

Tyacke saw Daubeny urging a few spare hands to add their weight to the braces. But even with the Nova Scotian volunteers, they were still short-handed, a legacy of *Indomitable*'s savage fight against Beer's *Unity.* Tyacke straightened his hat. It was unnerving when he considered that that was a year ago.

Bolitho joined him by the rail. 'The enemy have the numbers and the superior artillery, and will readily use both.' He folded his arms, and could have been discussing the weather. 'But he is on a lee shore and knows it. Being a sailor, I am sure he was never consulted about the choice of landing places!' He laughed, and added, 'So *we* must be sharp about it.'

Tyacke leaned over to consult the compass as the helmsman called, 'Nor' east by north, sir! Full an' bye!'

Tyacke peered up at each sail, watchful and critical as his ship leaned over comfortably on the starboard tack. Then he cupped his hands and shouted, 'Check the forebrace, Mr Protheroe! Now belay!' He said almost to himself, 'He's only a boy, dammit!'

But Bolitho had heard him. 'We were all that, James. Young lions!'

'*Chivalrous* is in sight, sir! Larboard quarter!'

Just an array of pale canvas riding high into the dull clouds. How did he know? But Tyacke did not question the lookout: he knew, and that was all there was to it. The others would be in sight soon. He saw the first feeble light exploring the shrouds and shaking topsails. So would the enemy.

The wind was still fresh, strong enough, for the moment anyway. There would be no land in sight until the sun came out, and even then. . . . But you could feel it all the same. Like a presence, a barrier reaching out to rid the approaches of all ships, no matter what flag they paraded.

Tyacke touched his face, and did not notice Bolitho turn his head towards him. So different now, out in the open, to see and to be seen. Not like the choking confines of the lower gundeck on that day at the Nile, when he had almost died, and afterwards had wanted to die.

He thought of the letter in his strongbox, and the one he had written in reply. Why had he done it? After all the pain and the despair, the brutal realization that the one being he had ever cared for had rejected him, *why?* Against that, it was still hard to believe that she had written to him. He remembered the hospital at Haslar in Hampshire, full of officers, survivors from one battle or another. Everyone else who had worked there had pretended to be so normal, so calm, so unmoved by the pervasive suffering. It had almost driven him crazy. That had been the last time he had seen her. She had visited the hospital, and he now realized that she must have been sickened by some of the sights she had seen. Hopeful, anxious faces, the disfigured, the burned, the limbless, and others who had been blinded. It must have been a nightmare for her, although all he had felt at the time had been pity. For himself.

She had been his only hope, all he had clung to after the battle, when he had been so savagely wounded in the old *Majestic*. Old, he thought bitterly: she had been almost new. He touched the worn rail, laid his hand on it, and again was unaware of Bolitho's concern. *Not like this old lady.* Her captain had died there at the Nile, and *Majestic*'s first lieutenant had taken over the ship, and the fight. A young man. He touched his face again. *Like Daubeny.*

She had been so young. . . . He almost spoke her name aloud. *Marion.* Eventually she had married a man much older than herself, a safe, kindly auctioneer who had given her a nice house by Portsdown Hill, from where you could sometimes see the Solent, and the sails on the horizon. He had tortured himself with it many times. The house was not very far from Portsmouth, and the hospital where he had wanted to die.

They had had two children, a boy and a girl. *They should have been mine.* And now her husband was dead, and she had written to him after reading something about the squadron in the newsheet, and the fact that he was now Sir Richard Bolitho's flag captain.

It had been a letter written with great care, and without excuse or compromise: a mature letter. She had asked for his understanding, not for his forgiveness. She would value a letter from him, very much. *Marion.* He thought, as he had thought so often, of the gown he had bought for her before Nelson had led them to the Nile, and the way that Sir Richard's lovely Catherine had given the same gown grace and meaning after they had lifted her from that sun-blistered boat. Had she perhaps given him back the hope that had been crushed by hatred and bitterness?

'Deck there! Sail in sight to the nor' east!'

Tyacke snatched a glass from the rack and strode up to the weather side, training it across the deck and through the taut rigging. A glimpse of sunshine, without warmth. Waters blue and grey.... He held his breath, able to ignore the marines and seamen who were watching him. One, two, three ships, sails filling and then flapping in an attempt to contain the wind. The other ships were not yet visible.

We have the advantage this time. But with the wind as it was, their roles could quite easily change.

He lowered the glass and looked at Bolitho. 'I think we should hold our course, Sir Richard.'

Just a nod. Like a handshake. 'I agree. Signal *Chivalrous* to *close on Flag.*' He smiled unexpectedly, his teeth white in his tanned face. 'Then hoist the one for *Close Action.*' The smile seemed to evade him. 'And keep it flying!'

Tyacke saw his quick glance at Allday. Something else they shared. A lifeline.

'*Chivalrous* has acknowledged, sir.'

'Very good.'

Bolitho joined him again. 'We will engage the towing vessel first.' He looked past Tyacke at the other frigate's misty sails, so clean in the first frail light. 'Load when you are ready, James.' The grey eyes rested on his face. 'Those soldiers must not be allowed to land.'

'I'll pass the word. Double-shotted, and grape for good measure.' He spoke without emotion. 'But when we come about we shall have to face the others, unless our ships give us support.'

301

Bolitho touched his arm and said, '*They will come*, James. I am certain of it.'

He turned as Ozzard, half-crouching as if he had expected to find an enemy engaged alongside, stepped from the companion way. He was carrying the admiral's gold-laced hat, holding it out as if it were something precious.

Tyacke said urgently, 'Is this wise, Sir Richard? Those Yankee sharp-shooters will be all about today!'

Bolitho handed his plain sea-going hat to Ozzard, and after the slightest hesitation pulled the new one onto his spray-damp hair.

'Go below, Ozzard. And thank you.' He saw the little man bob gratefully, with no words to make his true feelings known. Then Bolitho said calmly, 'It is probably madness, but that is the way of it. Sane endeavour is not for us today, James.' He touched his eye and stared at the reflected glare. 'But a victory it must be!'

The rest was drowned out by the shrill of whistles and the squeak of blocks, as the great guns were cast off from their breechings and their crews prepared to load.

He knew that some of the afterguard had seen him put on his new hat, the one he and Catherine had bought together in St James's Street: he had forgotten to tell her of his promotion, and she had loved him for it. A few of the seamen raised a cheer, and he touched his hat to them. But Tyacke had seen the anguish on Allday's rugged face, and knew what the gesture had cost him.

Tyacke walked away, watching the familiar preparations without truly seeing them. Aloud he said, 'And a victory you shall have, no matter what!'

Bolitho walked to the taffrail where Allday was shading his eyes to peer astern.

Like feathers on the shimmering horizon, two more ships of the squadron had appeared, their captains no doubt relieved that the dawn had brought them together again. The smaller of the two frigates would be *Wildfire*, of twenty-eight guns. Bolitho imagined her captain, a dark-featured man, bellowing orders to his topmen to make more sail, as much as she could carry. Morgan Price, as craggy and as Welsh as his name, had never needed a speaking trumpet, even in the middle of a gale.

Allday said, 'That's more like it, Sir Richard.'

Bolitho glanced at him. Allday had not been concerned about the other ships. Like some of the others on the quarterdeck, he had been watching the cluster of boats falling further and further astern, drifting to a canvas sea anchor, to be recovered after the action. It was a necessary precaution before fighting, to avoid the risk of additional wounds being caused by splinters. But to Allday, like all sailors, the boats represented a final chance of survival if the worst happened. Just as their presence on deck would tempt terrified men to forget both loyalty and discipline, and use them as an escape.

Bolitho said, 'Fetch me a glass, will you?'

When Allday had gone to select a suitable telescope, he stared at the distant frigate. Then he covered his undamaged eye, and waited for the pale topsails to mist over or fade away altogether. They did not. The drops the surgeon had provided were doing some good, even if they had a sting like a nettle when first applied. Brightness, colour; even the sea's face had displayed its individual crests and troughs.

Allday was waiting with the telescope. 'Set bravely, Sir Richard?'

Bolitho said gently, 'You worry too much.'

Allday laughed, relieved, satisfied.

'Over here, Mr Essex!'

Bolitho waited for the midshipman to reach him, and said, 'Now we shall see!'

He rested the heavy glass on the youth's shoulder and

carefully trained it across the starboard bow. A fine clear morning had emerged from the cloud and chilling wind: winter would come early here. He felt the young midshipman's shoulder shiver slightly. Cold; excitement; it was certainly not fear. Not yet. He was a lively, intelligent youth, and even he would be thinking of the day when he would be ready for examination and promotion. Another boy in an officer's uniform.

Three ships at least, the rest not yet in sight. Almost bows-on, their sails angled over as they tacked steeply across the wind. Far beyond them was a purple blur, like a fallen cloud. He pictured York's chart, his round handwriting in the log. Grand Manan Island, the guardian at the entrance to the Bay. The American would be doubly aware of the dangers here: being on a lee shore, with shallows as an extra menace once the tide was on the turn.

He stiffened and waited for the midshipman's breathing to steady; or perhaps he was holding his breath, very aware of his special responsibility.

A fourth ship, a shaft of new sunlight separating her from the others, bringing her starkly to life in the powerful lens.

He knew Tyacke and York were watching him, weighing the odds.

Bolitho said, 'The fourth ship has the boats under tow. The flag lieutenant was not mistaken.' He heard Avery laugh as Tyacke remarked, 'That makes a fair change, sir!'

Bolitho closed the glass with a snap and looked down at the midshipman. He had freckles, as Bethune had once had. He thought of Herrick's assessment. *The upstart.*

'Thank you, Mr Essex.' He walked to the rail again. 'Bring her up closer to the wind, James. I intend to attack the towing ship before she can slip the boats. Filled or

304

empty, it makes no difference now. We can stop them landing, and within the hour it will be too late.'

Tyacke beckoned to the first lieutenant. 'Stand by to alter course.' A questioning glance at the sailing-master. 'What say *you*, Isaac?'

York squinted his eyes to stare up at the driver and the mizzen topsail beyond it. 'Nor' east by east.' He shook his head as the driver's peak with the great White Ensign streaming from it almost abeam flapped noisily. 'No, sir. Nor' east is all she'll hold, I'm thinking.'

Bolitho listened, touched by the intimacy between these men. Tyacke's command of small ships had left its mark, or maybe it had always been there.

He shaded his eyes with his hand to observe the ship's slow response, the long jib-boom moving like a pointer until the enemy ships appeared to slide slightly from bow to bow.

'Steady she goes, sir! Course nor' east!'

Bolitho watched the sails buck and shiver, uncomfortable this close to the wind. It was the only way. Only *Indomitable* had the firepower to do it in one attack. *Chivalrous* was too small, the rest too far away. Their chances would come soon enough.

Avery folded his arms close to his body, trying not to shiver. The air was still keen, making a lie of the strengthening sunlight that painted the broken wavelets a dirty gold.

He saw Allday staring around, his eyes searching: a man who had seen it many times before. He was studying the open quarterdeck, the scarlet-coated marines with their officer, David Merrick. The gun crews and the helmsmen, four of the latter now, with a master's mate close beside them. Tyacke standing apart from the rest, his hands beneath his coattails, and the admiral, who was explaining something to the midshipman, Essex. Something he would remember, if he lived.

Avery swallowed hard, knowing what he had seen. Allday, probably more experienced than any other man aboard, was seeking out the weaknesses and the danger points. Past the tightly-packed hammock nettings and up to the maintop, where more scarlet coats showed above the barricade. Where an enemy's fighting top might be if they were close enough. Thinking of the sharp-shooters, said to be backwoodsmen for the most part, who lived by their skills with a musket. Avery was chilled by the thought. Except that these marksmen would be armed with the new and more accurate rifles.

Was that the source of Allday's worry, then? Because of Bolitho's gesture, the hat with the bright gold lace, and all that it meant, and could mean, at the moment of truth. It was said that Nelson had refused to remove his decorations before his last battle, and had ordered that they should be covered before he was carried below, his backbone shot through, his life already slipping away. Another brave, sad gesture. So that his men should not know their admiral had fallen, had left them before the fight had been decided.

It was plain on Allday's homely features, and when their eyes met across the spray-patterned deck, no words were needed by either man.

'Deck there! The boats is bein' warped alongside!'

Bolitho clenched his fists, his face suddenly unable to conceal his anxiety.

Avery knew, had guessed even from the moment Bolitho had mentioned the primary importance of the boats. Despite the risks and the stark possibility of failure, he had been thinking of the alternative, that *Indomitable* would be forced to fire on boats packed with helpless men, unable to raise a finger to defend themselves. Was this part of the difference in this war? Or was it only one man's humanity?

Tyacke shouted, 'Something's wrong, sir!'

York had a telescope. 'The Yankee's run aground, sir!' He sounded astonished, as if he were over there, sharing the disaster.

Bolitho watched the sunlight catch the reflected glare from falling sails and a complete section of the vessel's mainmast. In the silence and intimacy of the strong lens, he almost imagined he could hear it. A big frigate, gun for gun a match for *Indomitable*, but helpless against the sea and this relentless destruction above and below. The boats were already filled or half-filled with blue uniforms, their weapons and equipment in total disarray as the truth became known to them.

Bolitho said, 'Prepare to engage to starboard, Captain Tyacke.' He barely recognized his own voice. Flat, hard, and unemotional. Somebody else.

Daubeny shouted, 'Starboard battery! *Run out!*'

The long twenty-four pounders rumbled up to and through their ports, their captains making hand signals only to avoid confusion. Like a drill, one of so many. A handspike here, or men straining on tackles to train a muzzle a few more inches.

The other ship had slewed around slightly, wreckage trailing alongside as the tide continued to drop, to beach her like a wounded whale.

The wheel went over again, while York turned to watch the land, the set of the current, feeling if not seeing the danger to this ship.

'Course nor' by east, sir!'

Bolitho said, 'One chance, Captain Tyacke. Two broadsides, three if you can manage it.' Their eyes met. *Time and distance.*

Midshipman Essex jerked round as if he had been hit, and then shouted, 'Our ships are here, sir!' He waved his hat as distant gunfire rolled across the sea like muffled thunder. Then he realized that he had just shouted at his admiral, and dropped his eyes and flushed.

'On the uproll!'

Bolitho looked along the starboard side, the gun captains with their taut trigger-lines, the emergency slow-matches streaming to the wind like incense in a temple.

Daubeny by the mainmast, his sword across one shoulder, Philip Protheroe, the fourth lieutenant, up forward with the first division of guns. And here on the quarterdeck, the newest lieutenant, Blythe, staring at each crouching seaman as if he was expecting a mutiny. The stranded ship was drawing slowly abeam, the floundering boats suddenly stilled as the reluctant sunlight threw *Indomitable*'s sails across the water in patches of living shadow.

Daubeny raised his sword. 'As you bear!'

Lieutenant Protheroe glanced aft and then yelled, *'Fire!'*

Division by division, the guns roared out across the water, each twenty-four pounder hurling itself inboard to be seized and manhandled like a wild beast.

Bolitho thought he saw the shockwave of the broadside rip across the water, carving a passage like some scythe from hell. Even as the first double-shotted charges and their extra packing of grape smashed into the boats and exploded into the helpless ship, Protheroe's men were already sponging out their guns, probing for burning remnants with their worms before ramming home fresh charges and balls.

The quarterdeck guns were the last to fire, and Blythe's voice almost broke in a scream as he yelled. 'A guinea for the first gun, I say! A guinea!'

Bolitho watched it all with a strange numbness. Even his heart seemed to have stopped. Tyacke had trained them well; three rounds every two minutes. There would be time for the third broadside before they came about, to avoid running aground like the stricken American.

Tyacke was also watching, remembering. *Point! Ready!*

Fire! The drill, always the drill. Slaves to the guns which were now repaying his hard work.

A whistle shrilled. 'Ready, sir!'

'Fire!'

Boats and fragments of boats, uniformed soldiers thrashing in the water, their screams engulfed as their weapons and packs carried them down into bitter cold. Others who had been able to reach the ship's side were dragging themselves back to a security they could recognize, only to be torn down by the next controlled broadside. The American was burned and scarred by the weight of iron, but mostly it was the blood that was remarkable. On the hull, and down the side, where even the water shone pink in the sunlight.

In a brief lull, Bolitho heard Allday say, 'If they'd been first, sir, they'd have given no quarter to us.' He was speaking to Avery, but any reply was lost in the next roar of cannon fire.

Outside this pitiless arena of death, another struggle was taking place. Ship to ship, or two to one, if the odds were overwhelming. No line of battle, only ship to ship. Man to man.

York said hoarsely, 'White flag, sir! They're finished!'

True or not, they would never know, for at that moment the third and last broadside smashed into the other ship, shattering forever the scattered remnants of a plan that might have been successful.

As men staggered from *Indomitable*'s guns and ran to the braces and halliards in response to shouted commands to bring the ship about and into the wind, Bolitho took a final glance at the enemy. But even the white flag had vanished into the smoke.

Daubeny sheathed his sword, his eyes red-rimmed and bright.

'*Chivalrous* has signalled, sir. The enemy has broken

off the action.' He looked at his hand, as if to see if it were shaking. 'They did what they came to do.'

Tyacke tore his eyes from the flapping sails as his ship turned sedately across the wind, the masthead pendant rivalling Bolitho's Cross of St George as they streamed across the opposite side.

He said harshly, 'And so, Mr Daubeny, did *we!*'

Bolitho handed the telescope to Essex. 'Thank you.' Then to Tyacke, 'General signal, if you please. *Discontinue the action. Report losses and damage.*' He looked across at the tall signals midshipman. 'And, Mr Carleton, mark this well and spell it out in full. *Yours is the gift of courage.*'

Avery hurried across to assist the signals party, but once with them he paused, afraid to miss anything, his head still reeling from the roar of the guns and the immediate silence which had followed.

Bolitho was saying to Tyacke, '*Taciturn* will take command and lead our ships to Halifax. I fear we have lost some good men today.'

He heard Tyacke reply quietly, 'We could have lost far more, Sir Richard.' He tried to lighten his tone. 'At least that damned renegade in his *Retribution* failed to appear.'

Bolitho said nothing. He was staring across the quarter to the distant smoke, like a stain on a painting.

Avery turned away. The gift of courage. Our Nel would have appreciated that. He took the slate and pencil from Carleton's unsteady hands.

'Let me.'

Tyacke said, 'May I change tack and recover the boats, Sir Richard?'

'Not yet, James.' His eyes were bleak. Cold, as that dawn sky had been. He gazed up at the signal for Close Action. 'We are not yet done, I fear.'

17

The Greatest Reward

Captain Adam Bolitho removed his boatcloak and handed it to an army orderly, who was careful to shake it before carrying it away. It had begun to rain with the abruptness of a squall at sea, and the drops were hard and cold, almost ice.

Adam crossed to a window and wiped away the dampness with his hand. Halifax harbour was full of shipping, but he had scarcely glanced at the anchored vessels while he had been pulled ashore in the gig. He could not become accustomed to it, accept that he had to go to the land in order to see his admiral.

Keen had sent word that he needed to speak with him as soon as possible, when, under normal circumstances, they could have met aft in *Valkyrie*'s great cabin.

He thought of John Urquhart, now acting-captain of the ill-fated *Reaper*. Perhaps Keen's summons had come at the right moment. Urquhart had been with him in the cabin, about to take his leave to assume command of *Reaper*, and their farewell and the significance of the moment had moved Adam more than he had believed possible. He knew that he had been seeing himself, although he had been much younger when he had been offered his first ship. But the feelings, gratitude, elation, nervousness, regret, were the same. Urquhart had said, 'I'll not forget what you have done for me, sir. I shall endeavour to make use of my experience to the best of my ability.'

Adam had answered, 'Remember one thing, John. You are the captain, and they will know it. When you go across to her presently to read yourself in, think of the ship, *your* ship, not what she has been or might have become, but what she can be for you. All your officers are new, but most of the warrant ranks are from the original company. They are bound to make comparisons, as is the way with old Jacks.'

Urquhart had looked up at the deckhead, had heard the tramp of boots as the marines took up their positions to see him over the side. It had all been in his face. Wanting to go, to begin: needing to stay where all things were familiar.

Adam had said quietly, 'Don't concern yourself now with *Valkyrie*, John. It will be up to Lieutenant Dyer to fill your shoes. It is his chance, too.' He had gone to the table and opened a drawer. 'Take these.' He had seen the surprise and uncertainty on Urquhart's face, and added abruptly, 'A bit weathered and salt-stained, I fear, but until you find a tailor. . . .'

Urquhart had held the epaulettes to the light, all else forgotten. Adam had said, 'My first. I hope they bring you luck.'

They had gone on deck. Handshakes, quick grins, a few cheers from some of the watching seamen. The twitter of calls, and it was done. Moments later they might hear the calls from *Reaper* across the harbour.

Just before they had parted Urquhart had said, 'I hope we meet again soon, sir.'

'You will be too busy for social events.' He had hesitated. 'In truth, I envy you!'

A door opened, and de Courcey stood waiting for him to turn from the window.

'Rear-Admiral Keen will see you now, sir.'

Adam walked past him without speaking. De Courcey was different in some way, oddly subdued. Because he had shown fear when the two American frigates had hove into view? *Did he really imagine I would run carrying tales to his admiral, as he would have done about me?*

It was the general's room which he had visited with Keen and Bolitho on another occasion, with the same large paintings of battles and dark, heavy furniture, and he realized that this had probably been Keen's idea, rather than ask him to join him at the Massie residence.

He saw that Keen was not alone, and the other man, who was about to leave, was David St Clair.

St Clair shook his hand. 'I am sorry you were kept waiting, Captain Bolitho. It seems I may be needed here in Halifax after all.'

Keen waved him to a chair as the door closed behind his other visitor. Adam studied him with interest. Keen looked strained, and unusually tense.

He said, 'I have received fresh dispatches from the Admiralty, but first I have to tell you that Sir Richard was correct in his belief that control of the lakes was vital.' He glanced around the room, thinking of that day in the summer when the army captain had described the first attack on York. When Gilia had asked about the officer who had been killed. 'The army could not hold the vital line of water communications, and at Lake Erie they were beaten. A retreat was ordered, but it was already too late.' He slapped his hand on the table and said bitterly, 'The army was cut to pieces!'

'What will it mean, sir?' Adam could not recall ever seeing Keen so distressed. So lost.

Keen made an effort to compose himself. 'Mean? It means we will not be able to drive the Americans out of the western frontier districts, especially not now, with winter fast approaching. It will be another stalemate. We, in the fleet, will blockade every American port. They'll feel that as deeply as any bayonet!'

Adam tried to think without emotion. His uncle was at sea, and the brig *Weazle* had brought word that he was investigating the whereabouts of some enemy frigates reported heading north-east. They could be anywhere by now. He thought of Keen's words, *winter fast approaching.* The fierce, bitter rain, the fogs, the damp between decks. Where had the time gone? It was October, by only a day or two, and yet you could feel it.

He roused himself from his thoughts and found that Keen was watching him gravely. 'Sir Richard, your uncle and my dear friend, is to be withdrawn. That was the main point of the dispatches. I shall remain in charge here.'

Adam was on his feet. 'Why, sir?'

'Why, indeed? I am informed that Sir Alexander Cochrane will be taking over the whole station, which will include the Leeward Squadron. A far bigger fleet will be at his disposal, both for blockade duties and for land operations with the army. In Europe, Napoleon's armies are in retreat on every front. It is a land war now. Our blockade has served its purpose.' He turned away, and said with the same soft bitterness, 'And at what a price.'

Adam said, 'I think Sir Richard should be told without delay.'

'I need all available frigates here, Adam. I have scarcely a brig available to retain contact with our patrols, let alone watch over enemy movements.'

'Sir Richard may have been called to action, sir.'

'D'you imagine I've not thought as much? I couldn't sleep because of it. But I cannot spare any more ships.'

Adam said coolly, 'I understand, sir. As your flag captain, I am required to advise, and to present conclusions. My uncle would be the very first to steer away from favouritism, or from encouraging action taken purely out of personal involvement.'

'I hoped you would say that, Adam. If I were free to act. . . .'

Adam turned away as the same orderly entered with a tray and glasses. 'With the General's compliments, sir.'

He said, 'But you are not free, sir, not so long as your flag is flying above this command.'

Keen watched the soldier's steady hand as he poured two large measures of cognac. The general lived well, it seemed.

Adam held the glass to the light from the window. Already it was as grey as winter, like a symbol of time's relentless passage.

Keen swallowed deeply, and coughed to regain his breath. Then he said, 'You may go, thank you.' When they were alone again, he said, 'The warrants for the two mutineers were presented this morning. Have no fear – I signed them. Sir Richard will be spared that, at least.' It seemed to spark off another memory. 'John Urquhart took command today, did he not?'

Adam said, 'Yes. The custom will prevail, sir. Both prisoners will be hanged, run up to the main yard by their own ship's company. *Reaper*'s.'

Keen nodded almost absently, as if he had been listening to a stranger.

'I will order *Reaper* to sea immediately. Captain Urquhart can find Sir Richard and carry my dispatches to him. I'll not begin that ship's new life with a damned execution!'

There were voices outside: de Courcey with the next visitors.

Keen glanced irritably at the door. 'There is another matter, Adam. If you would prefer to take another appointment, I would understand. It has not been easy.'

315

He looked at him directly, his eyes very still. 'For either of us.'

Adam was surprised that he did not even hesitate. 'I would like to remain with you, sir.' He put down the empty glass. 'I shall return to *Valkyrie* in case I am needed.'

For the first time, Keen smiled. 'You will always be that, Adam. Believe me.'

The same orderly was waiting for him with his cloak. 'Stopped rainin', sir.'

He thought of Urquhart, how he would feel when he was ordered to proceed to sea with all possible despatch. Relieved, probably. And of the mutineer, Harry Ramsay, whom he had tried to help, although he had suspected that he was guilty. At least he would be spared the final degradation of being hanged by his own shipmates.

'A moment, Captain Bolitho!'

He turned, and as if to a secret signal the front doors swung shut again.

She was warmly dressed, her cheeks flushed from the cold air. He waited, seeing her as she had been that day when *Valkyrie*'s powerful broadside had been ready to fire. None of them would have survived, and she would know it.

He removed his hat, and said, 'I trust you are well, Miss St Clair?'

She did not seem to hear. 'Are you remaining as flag captain to Rear-Admiral Keen?'

So Keen had confided in her. He was again surprised, that he did not care.

'I am.'

He glanced down as she laid one hand on his sleeve. 'I am so glad. He needs you.' Her eyes did not falter. 'And, for his sake, so do I.'

Adam studied her. He supposed that she would also

know about the battle for Lake Erie, and the regiments involved.

He said, 'You have my good wishes.' He allowed himself to smile, to soften it. 'Both of you.'

She walked with him to the door. Then she said, 'You knew Rear-Admiral Keen's wife, I believe?'

He faced her again. 'I was in love with her.' It was madness; she would tell Keen. Then, he was quite certain that she would not.

She nodded: he did not know whether she was satisfied or relieved. 'Thank you, Captain. . . . I can understand now why you love your uncle. You are both the same man, in many ways.'

She tugged off her glove, and it dropped to the floor. Adam stooped to recover it, and she did not see the sudden distress in his eyes.

He took her hand, and kissed it. 'You do me too much honour, Miss St Clair.'

She waited until the door had been pulled shut behind him. Her father would be impatient to see her, wanting to tell her about his new appointment here in Halifax. It would be good to see him happy, occupied with his work again.

But all she could think of was the man who had just left her, whose austere face had seemed very young and vulnerable for those few seconds, when he had picked up her glove. Something which even he had been unable to hide. And she was both moved and gladdened by it.

At four bells of the afternoon watch His Majesty's Ship *Reaper* weighed anchor, and under topsails and jib wended her way towards the entrance and the open sea. Many eyes followed her, but no one cheered or wished her well. Captain Adam Bolitho followed her progress until she was lost from view. She was free.

'Deck there! Boats in the water, dead ahead!'

317

Tyacke walked to the compass box and then stopped as eight bells chimed out from the forecastle.

'I *was* beginning to wonder, Mr York.'

The sailing-master rubbed his hands. 'By guess and by God, sir. It usually works!'

Tyacke peered along the length of his ship, the guns lashed firmly behind shuttered ports, men working, not certain what to expect. *Indomitable* was steering due west, the wind sweeping over the larboard quarter, the spray as heavy and cold as rain.

He looked aft again and saw Bolitho by the taffrail, not walking but standing, oblivious to the men around him and the marines at the nettings, where they had remained since the attack on the American boats.

York moved closer and murmured, 'What ails the admiral? We prevented the landings, more than most of us dared to hope.'

Tyacke stared at the horizon, hard, hard blue in the noon light. A sun without warmth, a steady wind to fill the topsails, but without life.

Even the casualties amongst the squadron had been less than would have been suffered in a straightforward fight. But the Americans had been eager to stand away, unwilling to risk a running battle for no good purpose. If they had rallied and reformed, it would have been a different story. As it was, the frigate *Attacker* had been dismasted, and the smaller *Wildfire* had been so badly holed by long-range and well-sighted shots that she had been down by the head when she had finally been taken in tow. Most of the casualties had been in those two ships: thirty killed and many others wounded. It had been time to discontinue the action and Bolitho had known it. Tyacke had watched his face when the signals had been read out, giving details of damage and casualties. Some might think that the admiral was relieved because *Indomitable* had not been in the thick of it, and was unmarked. If they believed that they were bloody fools, Tyacke thought.

He swung round. *'What?'*

Lieutenant Daubeny flinched. 'I was wondering, sir, about relighting the galley fire. . . .'

Tyacke controlled his anger with an effort. 'Well, *wonder away*, Mr Daubeny!' He glanced aft again, unable to forget the quiet voice, as if Bolitho had just spoken to him. When he had reported that there were no more boats in the water by the stranded and smoke-shrouded American ship, Bolitho had said, 'It was murder, James. Justified in war, but murder for all that. If that was the price of victory, I don't wish to share a part of it!'

Tyacke said abruptly, 'That was unfair. Pass the word for the purser and arrange an extra tot of rum for all hands. Food too, if there is any, but the galley fire *stays out* until I know what's happening.'

Daubeny said, 'I see, sir.'

Tyacke turned away. 'You do not, Mr Daubeny, but no matter.' To York he said, 'Sir Richard feels it, Isaac. Cares too much. I've not seen him like this before, though.'

York tucked some dishevelled grey hair beneath his hat. 'He's fair troubled, right enough.'

Tyacke walked to the compass box and back again. 'Let me know when you can see the boats from the deck. It will give the hands something to do when we hoist 'em inboard.' He clapped the master on the shoulder. 'A good piece of navigation, Mr York.' He turned as Allday walked aft from the companion. 'You know him best, Allday. What do you think?'

Allday regarded him warily. 'It's not for me to say, sir.' He followed Tyacke's eyes to the figure by the taffrail, the hero others never saw. So completely alone.

He made up his mind. The captain was a friend; it was not merely idle curiosity.

'He knows, sir.' He glanced at the hard, glittering horizon; unlike the admiral, he did not have to shade his eyes. 'It's today, y' see?'

Tyacke said sharply, 'The Yankees are gone, man. They'll not be back, not till they're ready and prepared again. Our ships will reach Halifax and the dock-master will foam at the mouth when he sees all the repairs that need doing!'

But Allday did not respond, nor did he smile.

He said, 'There's always the. . . .' He frowned, searching for the word. 'The scavenger. My wife's brother was a line-soldier – he told me. After a battle, men lying wounded, calling out for help, with only the dead to hear them. And then the scavengers would come. To rob them, to answer a cry for help with a cut-throat blade. *Scum!*'

Tyacke studied his lined face, aware of the strength of the man. The admiral's oak. He heard York's steady breathing beside him. He could feel it too: knew it, the way he read the wind's direction and the set of the current in the painted sea. Tyacke was not superstitious. At least, he believed he was not.

Allday was carrying the old sword, which was part of the legend.

He said quietly, 'We'll fight this day, sir. That's it an' all about it!'

He walked aft, and they saw Bolitho turn toward him, as if they had just met on a street or in some country lane.

York said uneasily, 'How can that be, sir?'

Allday was saying, 'The hands are going to draw a wet, Sir Richard. Can I fetch you something?'

Bolitho glanced down as he clipped the old sword onto his belt.

'Not now, old friend.' He smiled with an effort, understanding that Allday needed reassurance. 'Afterwards, that would be better.'

He reached out to touch his arm, and then halted.

'Deck there! Sail on th' larboard bow!'

They were all staring round, some at the empty sea, and others aft towards their officers. Avery was here, a telescope in his hands, his eyes darting between them. To miss nothing, to forget nothing.

Bolitho said, 'Aloft with you, George. In my own mind, I can already see her.' He held up one hand. 'Take your time. The people will be watching you.'

Allday took a deep breath, feeling the old pain in his chest. *Scavenger.*

Bolitho knew that Tyacke had turned toward him, and called to him, 'Alter course. Steer west by south. That should suffice for the present.'

He turned away from them, and watched a solitary gull swooping around the quarter gallery. The spirit of some old Jack, Allday thought.

'Deck there!' Avery was a fast climber, and had a good carrying voice: he had told him that he had been in a church choir in his youth. In that other world. 'She's a frigate, sir! I – I think she's *Retribution!*'

Bolitho murmured, 'I know she is, my friend.' He frowned, as Allday's hand went to his chest. 'I'll not have *you* suffer for it!'

He raised his voice. 'You may beat to quarters again, Captain Tyacke. We have some old scores to settle today!' He laid his hand on the sword's hilt at his hip, and it was cold to the touch. 'So let us pay them in full!'

Lieutenant George Avery waited for the motion to ease, and knew that more helm had been applied. He raised his telescope, as he had on the first sight of enemy ships only hours ago. It felt like a lifetime. The same marines were still in the foretop, staring at the oncoming American as her sails emptied and filled violently, while she leaned over to the pressure. She was a heavy-looking frigate under a full press of canvas, the spary bursting beneath her beakhead and as high as the gilded figurehead. The gladiator, a short stabbing-sword glinting in the hard glare.

The corporal said, 'The Yankee's crossin' our bows, lads.' But his comment was really intended for the flag lieutenant.

Avery studied the other ship, forcing himself to take his time, not to see only what he expected to see. The corporal was right. The *Retribution* would eventually cross from bow to bow; more importantly, she would find herself to leeward of *Indomitable*'s broadside once they were at close quarters. He estimated it carefully. Three miles at the most. Tyacke had reduced sail to topsails and jib, driver and reefed forecourse, and *Indomitable*'s progress was steady and unhurried, a floating platform for her twenty-four pounders.

He lowered the glass and looked around at his companions. Somehow, they managed to appear very jaunty and smart in their glazed leather hats with the cockade and plume over the left ear. He noticed also that they had all shaved. They were fastidious about such details in the Corps.

'Won't be long, lads.' He saw the corporal glance at the swivel gun, 'Betsy'. He would know what to expect. They all did.

He nodded to them, and lowered himself quickly onto the ratlines. On deck once more, he strode aft, catching the hurried glances from the gun crews, a half-wave from young Protheroe. On this deck, the gun was god. Nothing else mattered but to fire and keep firing, to shut out the sights and the sounds, even when a friend cried out in agony.

He found Bolitho with Tyacke and the first lieutenant, observing from the quarterdeck. Here, too, the marines had come to life, like scarlet soldiers taken from a box, lining the packed hammock nettings while elsewhere sentries stood guard at hatches or ladders, in case a man's nerve cracked and terror tore discipline apart.

Avery touched his hat. 'She's *Retribution* right enough, Sir Richard. She wears a commodore's broad-pendant. Fifty guns, at a guess. She changed tack.' He thought of the corporal again, the doubt in his voice. 'She'll lose the wind-gage if she remains on that tack.'

York said, 'She steers nor' east, sir.' Unruffled. Patient. Bolitho saw him tap the youngest midshipman's arm as the child reached for the half-hour glass beside the compass box. 'Easy, Mr Campbell, don't warm the glass! *I* have to write the log, not you!'

The twelve-year-old midshipman looked embarrassed, and momentarily forgot the growing menace of the American's tall sails.

Bolitho took a telescope and trained it beyond the bows. *Retribution* had no intention of altering course, not yet. He studied the other frigate: well-built, like so many French vessels, designed to one standard for the convenience of repair and replacement, not at the whim of an individual ship-builder like most British men-of-war. When *Taciturn* and the other damaged ships reached Halifax, they would be hard put to find a mast or a spar that would match any one of them.

He said, 'He is deliberately dropping downwind, James.' He sensed that Daubeny was leaning forward to listen, squinting in concentration.

Tyacke agreed. 'Then he intends to use the extra elevation the wind gives him to fire at full range.' He glanced up at the braced yards, the flag and pendant streaming towards the enemy, and said grimly, 'He'll try for our spars and rigging.'

Avery turned away. The corporal had seen it, but had not fully understood. Both Bolitho and Tyacke must accept it.

Bolitho said, 'Chain-shot, James?'

Tyacke shook his head. 'I did hear they were using langridge, that damnable case-shot. If so. . . .' He swung away as though to consult the compass again.

Bolitho said to Avery, 'It can cripple a ship before she can fight back.' He saw the concern in Avery's tawny eyes, but he did not fully comprehend. *Damnable*, Tyacke had termed it. It was far worse than that. Packed into a thin case, each shot contained bars of jagged iron, loosely linked together so that when they burst into a ship's complex web of rigging they could tear it to pieces in one screaming broadside.

He saw Tyacke gesturing to the gun crews and making some point urgently to Daubeny with each jab of his finger.

That was the advantage of langridge; but against that, it took far longer to sponge and worm out each gun afterwards to avoid a fresh charge exploding in the muzzle as it was rammed home. It took time, and Tyacke would know it.

Bolitho rubbed his damaged eye and felt it ache in response. *If I were James, what would I do?* He was astonished that he could even smile, recalling that almost forgotten admiral who had met his pleading for a command with the withering retort, *Were* a frigate captain, Bolitho. . . .

I would hold my fire and pray that the regular drills hold firm, if all else fails.

Lieutenant Blythe called, 'The enemy's running out, sir!'

Tyacke said, 'Aye, and he'll likely check each gun himself.'

Bolitho saw Allday watching him. Even Tyacke had accepted Aherne, had given him body and personality. A man with so much hatred. Retribution. *And yet if he crossed this very deck, I would not know him.* Perhaps it was the best kind of enemy. Faceless.

Once again, he looked at the sky and the searing reflections beneath it. Two ships with an entire ocean to witness their efforts to kill one another.

He covered his undamaged eye and tested the other. His vision was blurred; he had come to accept that. But the colours remained true, and the enemy was close enough now to show her flag, and the commodore's broad-pendant standing out in the wind like a great banner.

Tyacke said, 'Ready, Sir Richard.'

'Very well, James.' So close, so private, as if they shared the deck only with ghosts. 'For what we are about to receive. . . .'

Tyacke waved his fist, and the order echoed along the upper deck.

'*Open the ports! Run out!*' And from the waist of the ship where the gunner's mates were already passing out cutlasses and axes from the arms chest, Lieutenant Daubeny's voice, very clear and determined.

'*Lay for the foremast, gun captains! And fire on the uproll!*'

The older hands were already crouching down, as yet unable to see their target.

Tyacke yelled, 'Put your helm down! Off heads'l sheets!'

Indomitable began to turn, using the wind across her quarter to her best advantage. Round and further still, so that the other frigate appeared to be ensnared in the shrouds as *Indomitable*'s bowsprit passed over her, to hold her on the larboard side.

The distance was falling away more quickly, and Bolitho saw the topmen darting amongst the thrashing sails like tiny puppets on invisible strings.

The air quivered and then erupted in a drawn-out explosion, smoke billowing from the American's guns which was then driven inboard and away across the water.

It seemed to take an age, an eternity. When the broadside ploughed into *Indomitable*'s masts and rigging, it was as if the whole ship was bellowing in agony. Tiny vignettes stood out amidst the smoke and falling wreckage. A seaman torn apart by the jagged iron as it ripped through the piled hammocks, and hurled more men, screaming and kicking, to the opposite side. Midshipman Essex, stockstill, staring with horror at his white breeches, which were splashed with blood and pieces of human skin cut so finely that they could have been the work of a surgeon. Essex opened and closed his mouth but no sound came, until a running seaman punched his arm and yelled something, and ran on to help others who were hacking away fallen cordage.

Avery stared up, ice-cold as the fore topgallant mast splintered apart, stays and halliards flying like severed snakes, before thundering down and over the side. He wiped his eyes and looked again. It was suddenly important, personal. He saw the four scarlet figures in the top, peering up at the broken mast, but otherwise untouched.

'A hand here!'

Avery ran to help as York caught one of his master's mates, who had been impaled on a splinter as big as his wrist.

York stepped into his place, and muttered hoarsely, 'Hold on, Nat!'

Avery lowered the man to the deck. He would hear nothing ever again. When he was able to look up once more, Avery saw the American's topgallant sails standing almost alongside. He knew it was impossible; she was still half a cable away.

He heard Daubeny shout, 'As you bear! *Fire!*'

Down the ship's side from the crouching lion to this place here on the quarterdeck, each gun belched fire and smoke while its crew threw themselves on tackles and handspikes to hasten the reloading. But not double-shot-ted this time. It would take too many precious minutes.

A marine fell from the nettings without a word; there was not even a telltale scar on the deck planking to mark the shot.

Bolitho said, 'Walk with me, George. Those riflemen are too eager today.'

'Run out! Ready! Fire!'

There was a cracked cheer as the *Retribution*'s mizzen mast swayed and toppled in its stays and shrouds, before falling with a crash that could be heard even above the merciless roar of cannon fire. York was holding a rag against his bloody cheek, although he had not felt the splinter which had opened it like a knife.

He called, 'Her steering's adrift, sir!'

Bolitho said sharply, 'Helm down, James! Our only chance!'

And then the enemy was here, no longer a distant picture of grace and cruel beauty. She was angled toward them, the water surging and spitting between the two hulls even as *Indomitable*'s long jib-boom and then her bowsprit rammed into the enemy's shrouds like some giant tusk.

The force of the impact splintered *Indomitable*'s main yard, broken spars, torn rigging and wounded topmen falling on Hockenhull's spread nets like so much rubbish.

Tyacke shouted at his gun crews, 'One more, lads! *Hit 'em!'*

Then he staggered and clapped one hand to his thigh, his teeth bared against the pain. Midshipman Carleton ran to help him, but Tyacke gasped, 'Pike! Give me a pike, damn you!'

The midshipman thrust one towards him and stared at him, unable to move as Tyacke drove the pike into the deck and held himself upright, using it as a prop.

Bolitho felt Allday move closer, Avery too, with a

327

pistol suddenly in one hand. Across the debris and the wounded he saw Tyacke raise a hand to him, a gesture towards the fallen masts. A bridge, joining them with the enemy.

The guns roared out and recoiled again, the crews leaping aside to pick up their cutlasses, staggering as though with a deadly fatigue while they clambered across to the other ship which had been forced alongside, *Indomitable*'s splintered jib-boom dangling beside the enemy's figurehead.

There was a bang from the swivel gun in the foretop, and a hail of canister raked a group of American seamen even as they ran to repel boarders. The marines were gasping and cheering as they fired, reloaded, and then threw themselves on the hammocks to take aim again. And again. Above it all, Bolitho could hear Tyacke shouting orders and encouragement to his men. He would not give in to anything, not even the wound in his thigh. After what he had already suffered, it was an insult to think that he might.

Lieutenant Protheroe was the first on *Retribution*'s gangway, and the first to fall to a musket which was fired into his body from only a few inches away. He fell, and was trapped between the two grinding hulls. Bolitho saw him drop, and remembered him as the youngster who had welcomed him aboard.

He shouted, 'To me, Indoms! *To me*, lads!'

He was dragging himself across, above the choppy water, aware of flashing pistol fire and heavier calibre shot, and of Allday close behind, croaking, 'Hold back, Sir Richard! We can't fight the whole bloody ship!'

Bolitho was finding it difficult to breathe, his lungs filled with smoke and the stench of death. Then he was aboard the other ship, saw Hockenhull, the squat boatswain, kill a man with his boarding axe and manage to grin afterwards at Allday. He must have saved him from being struck down. In the terrible blood-red rage of battle, the consuming madness, Bolitho could still remember Allday's son, and that Allday had blamed Hockenhull for posting him to the vulnerable quarterdeck, where he had died. Perhaps this would end that festering grievance.

Avery dragged at his arm, and fired point-blank into a crouching figure that had appeared at their feet. Then he, too, staggered, and Bolitho imagined he had been hit.

But Avery was shouting, trying to be heard above the shouts and cries and the clash of steel, blade to blade.

Then Bolitho heard it also. He lurched against a wild-eyed marine, his bloodied bayonet already levelled for a second thrust, his mind still refusing to understand. Faint but certain. Someone was cheering, and for a chilling moment he imagined that the Americans had had more men than he had believed, that they had managed to board *Indomitable* in strength. Then Tyacke must be dead. They would not otherwise get past him.

Avery gripped his arm. 'D' you *hear*, sir?' He was trembling, and almost incoherent. 'It's *Reaper*! She's joined the squadron!'

The explosion was sudden, and so close that Bolitho found himself flung bodily to the deck, his sword dangling from the knot around his wrist. It had felt like a searing wind, the dust and fragments from the blast like hot sand. Hands were pulling him to his feet; Allday, with his back turned, exposed to the enemy as he steadied him amongst the press of dazed and breathless men.

Bolitho gasped, unable to speak, to reassure him, but the agony in his eye was making it impossible.

He said, '*Help me.*'

Allday seemed to understand, and tore his neckerchief from his throat and in two turns had tied it around Bolitho's head, covering his injured eye.

It was like being deaf, with men crawling or kneeling

in utter silence beside the wounded, and peering into the faces of the dead.

Retribution's seamen were staring at them, bewildered, shocked, beaten. Their flag had fallen with the broken mizzen mast, but they had not surrendered. They had simply ceased to fight.

The explosion had been confined to the ship's quarter-deck. A bursting cannon, carelessly loaded for a final desperate show of defiance, or perhaps a burning wad from one of Tyacke's guns when they had fired that last broadside with muzzles almost overlapping those of the enemy. A small group of American officers were waiting near the shattered wheel, where helmsmen and others lay in the ugly attitudes of violent death.

One lieutenant held out his sword, and instantly Allday's cutlass and Avery's pistol rose in unison.

Bolitho touched the bandage across his eye, and was grateful for it. He said, 'Where is your commodore?' He stared at the fallen mast, where men were still trapped in the tangled rigging like fish in a net. *Reaper* was closer, and the cheering was still going on; and he wished that he could see her.

The lieutenant stooped, and uncovered the head and shoulders of his commodore.

He handed his sword, hilt first, to Avery, and said, 'Commodore Aherne, sir. He sometimes spoke of you.'

Bolitho stared down at the face, angry and contorted, frozen at the instant of death. But a stranger.

He looked beyond them, toward the open sea. Had Aherne heard the cheers, and recognized *Reaper* too?

He turned inboard again. It was right, it was justice, that it should be *Reaper*. Now a witness to victory, and to folly.

He looked around at the breathless, gasping men, the madness gone from them as they dragged the wounded and the dying away from the blood-stained chaos on deck, talking to one another, some without realizing that those who answered were the enemy.

Through the clinging smoke he could see Tyacke facing him across the narrow strip of trapped water, still propped on his pike, with the surgeon on his knees applying a dressing. Tyacke raised one bloodied hand in salute. Perhaps to his ship. To the victor.

Bolitho said, 'Help me back to *Indomitable*.' It was impossible to smile. Had he really cried, *To me, Indoms*, only minutes ago?

Allday took his arm and guided him, watching out for anything that might take him unaware. He had guessed what had happened, and now he was certain of it. He had seen too much to be shocked or awed by the sights on every hand: in his own way, despite the brutal ugliness of death everywhere, he was satisfied.

Once again they had come through, and they were still together. It was more than enough.

Bolitho hesitated, and looked around at the two embattled ships. Men had leaned over to touch his coat as he had passed; some had grinned and spoken his name; a few had openly wept, ashamed, perhaps, that they had survived when so many had fallen.

Now they all fell silent to listen as he looked beyond them and saw *Reaper*'s topsails suddenly bright in the hard sunlight. He touched the locket beneath his stained shirt, and knew she was close to him.

'It is a high price to pay, and we have paid it many times before. But we must not forget, for if we do, it will be at our peril!' He raised his head and stared up at his flag at the mainmast truck, so clean, and removed from the suffering and the hate.

'Loyalty is like trust, and must surely reach in both directions.' He looked at the slow-moving topsails again. 'But it is the greatest reward of all.'

It was over.

Epilogue

The carriage with the Bolitho crest on its doors, freshly washed that morning, came to a halt by the church. It was cold even for March, but Catherine Somervell did not notice it.

Bryan Ferguson opened the door and lowered the step for her.

'Why not wait in there, my lady? 'Tis warmer, to be sure.' He seemed concerned, anxious that something might go wrong even now. She took his hand and stepped down onto the cobbles, and glanced toward the waterfront.

It was like any other day, and yet it was entirely different. Even the people seemed to be waiting, drawn together as was so often the way in seaports. A rumour, a message, a signal-gun, or a ship in distress. The people of Falmouth had seen it all before.

She adjusted her long green cloak, and the fastening at the throat. She had dressed carefully, taken her time, even though every fibre of her body had screamed at her to leave the house without delay. It still did not seem possible that Richard was coming, that he was probably within a mile of Falmouth at this moment.

She could recall the exact time when the letter had been brought by fast courier from Bethune at the Admiralty. She had already received one from Richard; it had touched on the battle, but he had avoided mentioning the many who had died. Bethune had told her that *Indomitable* was ordered to Plymouth, to be handed over to the care of carpenters and riggers there, eventually. But she was to be paid off upon arrival. A battered ship with her own memories and wounds, and like many of her company, she would wait now, and see if she was needed again.

The church clock at King Charles the Martyr chimed very slowly. Noon. She had been deeply suspicious of Bethune's written suggestion that she await Richard's return in Falmouth, and briefly she had conjured up old or unknown enemies who, even at this last precious opportunity, would attempt to reunite Richard with his wife under some pretext or other.

When she had composed herself and considered it, dismissing her fears, she knew the real reason. *Indomitable* was to be paid off in Plymouth, and Richard would be saying farewell to so many familiar faces. Others had already left, like shadows, carrying memories she could only imagine. He did not want her to see the ship now, but to remember her as she had been when she had climbed aboard, and they had cheered her for it, and Richard's flag had broken out above all of them.

He was alive; he was coming home. It was all that mattered. She had sensed that there were other matters, which Bethune had left unwritten. *I am ready.*

To Ferguson she said, 'I shall be all right. I shall know you are here.' She brushed a strand of dark hair from her eyes, and looked up at Young Matthew on his box, framed against the cold, pale sky. 'Both of you.'

There would be others here today. Unis, waiting for John Allday, although she had not yet seen her: this was a private moment for all who shared it. Perhaps it symbolized, more than anything, the elusive dream of peace, after so many years of sacrifice and separation.

Bethune had said that the war was almost over. The allies had scored another crushing victory over Napoleon at Laon, and Wellington had captured Bordeaux: there was even talk of disbanding the local militia, the sea fencibles too. She thought with regret and affection of Lewis Roxby; how proud he would have been on this day. Nancy had visited her often: a sailor's daughter as well as Richard's sister, she was a great comfort to Catherine. And without Roxby's presence filling every room at that great, empty house, it had helped her also. But she would stay away today. She understood, better than most.

She walked on, towards the moored vessels in the harbour, the swaying masts and spars which were now so familiar to her. The smells, too, were a far cry from the slums of her childhood, or the elegant London she had shared with Richard. Fresh bread and fish, tar and oakum, and the salt of the ever-present sea.

She saw people glance at her, some with curiosity, some familiarity, but without hostility. She would always be a stranger here, but never an intruder, and she was grateful for that.

She saw one of the coastguards with his companion, the same pair who had been on the beach as the tide had receded, and she had taken Zenoria's slight, broken body in her arms.

He nodded and removed his hat to her. 'Fine day, m'lady.'

'I hope so, Tom.'

She walked on, until she stood on the very edge of the jetty. And the war in North America? It took second place to most of these people, for whom France had been the enemy for so long. Too long.

Samuel Whitbread, the wealthy and influential brewer, had thundered out in the House of Commons that the war with America should be ended without delay. He had reminded the honourable members of that other occasion when peace had been grudgingly signed after the War of Independence, and Pitt had then remarked, *A defensive war can only end in inevitable defeat.* She lifted her chin. So be it, then.

She heard laughter and noisy voices, and turned to see a group of discharged sailors loitering, watching the harbour. The ones she had heard Allday scornfully denounce as old Jacks who refought their battles every day in the inns and ale-houses, until the parlour lanterns were swinging like those of a ship in Biscay.

But they belonged here today: they were members of what Richard would call the family. One or two of them waved in acknowledgement, privileged to be part of his homecoming. She turned away. There was not one whole man amongst them.

Someone exclaimed, 'There she be, lads!'

Catherine looked across the water, her face like ice in the wind off Falmouth Bay and here in Carrick Roads.

Tom the coastguard said, ''Tis the *Pickle*. Quite right an' proper.'

For my benefit?

She watched the little schooner moving between some moored lighters, distinguished from her merchant sisters only by a large, new White Ensign streaming from her peak.

H.M. Schooner *Pickle. Right and proper.* Her eyes pricked with sudden emotion, but she was determined to miss nothing. *Pickle* was a fairly regular visitor here, as she was at every port and naval station between Plymouth and Spithead. Carrying dispatches and mail, and sometimes passengers, to the port admirals, or to the ships resting from their arduous blockade duties, sheltering in Torbay and protected from the gales by Berry Head.

But here, *Pickle* would always be remembered for her part in a single, greater event. She had run into Falmouth,

335

and from here her commander, Lieutenant John Lapeno-
tiere, had taken a post-chaise non-stop to the Admiralty,
a journey of some thirty-seven hours. And all the way
the cry had gone with him, of England's greatest victory
at Trafalgar, to raise the heart of the nation. And to
numb it just as quickly, with the news that Nelson, the
people's hero, was dead.

She wondered if Richard had made any comparison,
but knew he would not. His memories would be with
James Tyacke and the others.

She touched her throat. *And his hopes with me.*

She saw the sails being brought under control, heaving
lines snaking ashore to seamen and onlookers alike.
Pickle had come alongside, her ensign very clear against
the grey stones. Lieutenant Avery and Yovell would come
by road with Richard's possessions. . . . She was filling her
mind with irrelevant thoughts to control her emotion.

The chair, the wine cooler which she had had made
when the other had been lost with his ship. *If it had
survived the last action.* . . . She walked to the end of the
jetty, unfastening her cloak so that he should see her,
and his fan-shaped pendant resting at her breast.

She saw the blue and white of uniforms, heard people
on the jetty raising a cheer, not merely for the hero, but
for Falmouth's own son.

The baker's wife was here with her small daughter, the
child looking pleased but rather puzzled by the bunch of
wild daffodils which she had been given to present as
their own welcome.

Then she saw him, straight-backed and tall in his fine
gold-laced coat, the old family sword at his side. And
close on his heels, turning only to wave to the men on
the schooner, was Allday, as she had known he would
be.

She stood and watched him, oblivious to the cold. It
was so important, too important to ruin in the presence

of all these smiling, cheering faces. There were tears, too: there would be many who were not so lucky today. But the tears would not be hers.

The baker's wife gave her little girl a gentle push, and she trotted forward with her daffodils.

Catherine clenched one fist until she felt her nails break the skin, as Richard brushed against the child with his knee.

Allday was there in an instant: she had heard that he was good with children. The puckered face which had been about to burst into tears was all smiles again. The moment was past.

Catherine held out her arms. Richard had not seen the child. *He could not.*

Afterwards, she did not recall speaking, although she must have said something. Allday had grinned, and had made light of it.

Only in the carriage did she hold him, take his hands and press them against her to disperse his uncertainty, and his despair.

It was not a dream, and the ache would be gone until the next time, if it had to be.

Once he kissed her neck, and she heard him say, 'Don't leave me.'

She had answered strongly, for both of them, *'Never.'*

Beyond the harbour, the sea was quieter now. Waiting.